I0762241

JOHNNY APPLESEED

AND THE TUSCORAURA ELVES

BY

G. K. R. LINDENBERG

This novel is entirely a work of alternative history. The names, characters and incidents, and even the author himself, belong to an alternate timeline. Any resemblance to persons, living or dead, or events or localities in other dimensions is entirely coincidental.

Xaris Living LLC
Hardcover Second Edition 2021
Illustrated and Unabridged
ISBN 978-1-7348346-7-3

Cover Design by oliviaprodesign @ fiverr.com

Cover Art by pavellog @ fiverr.com
in collaboration with
sabartstudio @ fiverr.com

Title Page Art by Anna Taubel
in collaboration with
doantran @ fiverr.com
renflowergrapx @ fiverr.com

Praise for Johnny Appleseed and the Tuscoraura Elves

"This epic tale of the Tuscoraura Elves manages to pull off a hilarious and insightful parody on our quirks and foibles as Americans while retaining a profound reverence for those values that make us most truly who we are."

~ Sir George Warshington

"...a one-of-a-kind spoof of fantasy tropes mixed with clever plotting, fun characters, and a profound message."

~ Kit Marlowe

"Never could I have imagined that funny and epic could be such perfect neighbors until I met them among the Tuscoraura Elves."

~ Sir Benjamin Franklyn

"A masterclass in American culture."

~ Charles de Tocqueville

". . . the first time fantasy has gone so far as to get so close to home."

~ Sarah Wentworth Mourten

"Lindenberg relies on his extensive experience in real-life medieval combat zones to recreate for the reader a fantasy experience like none other."

~ Dame Frances Marian

Being the Prelude to the

Vinlander Chronicles

of the Clayborn

BY

G. K. R. LINDENBERG

XARIS LIVING LLC

TABLE OF CONTENTS

*Please note this book is the unabridged version of
Florenz Nightingale and the Sword of Layban.
Acts and scenes not found in that book are listed as "Bonus" here.

Dedication

To David and Louis Mallozzi, who guided and encouraged the shaping of this text with their brilliant ideas and enthusiasm over many years.

25th of March, 2021
Feast of the Annunciation

Please visit our website for more information on *Johnny Appleseed and the Tuscoraura Elves*
gkrlindenberg.com

If you have feedback for the author, catch any typos, or simply have questions about the clayborn world of Vinland please contact gkrlindenberg@outlook.com

We invite you to consider supporting the author on www.patreon.com/gkrlindenberg

Acknowledgments

First and foremost, I would like to thank my wife for the many sacrifices of time and attention that she made to enable me to write this book.

Thanks also goes to my dear friend Mathieu, who made this project possible on a practical level.

Finally, my gratitude extends to my editor and proofreader, Lee Ann at FirstEditing, who worked with incredible industry and creativity to keep this work innovative without getting too wonky.

Special Thanks to these Talented Artists

Page 1 – ***King of the Hill*** by sabartstudio @ fiverr.com
Page 33 – ***Amhirst at Ithica*** by pavellog @ fiverr.com
Page 78-79 – ***Ambush*** by sabartstudio @ fiverr.com
Page 156 – ***The Bough Breaks*** by pavellog @ fiverr.com
Page 239 – ***Sacagawea*** by Anna Taubel
in collaboration with abhay1029 @ fiverr.com
Page 381 – ***Johnny Appleseed*** by pavellog @ fiverr.com
Author's Portrait by abhay1029 @ fiverr.com
Shentalpee City by Anna Taubel
in collaboration with doantran @ fiverr.com
and with renflowergrapx @ fiverr.com

A Note from the Author [G. K. R. Lindenberg]

to one kind enough to pick up this book and read

As the esteemed Professor J. R. R. Tolkien pointed out in the commentaries to his chronicle on the War of the Rings, the proper plural for dwarf is *dwarrow* but his publisher changed the word to *dwarfs*.

This distressed the professor deeply because he feared his readers might mistake the dwarvish peoples in his story for some kind of "maggot-folk bred in stone" (*Letters*, 156). In the end, they compromised at *dwarves*, and that is the standard to this day.

Studious scholars (and meteorologists) will tell you that a female of elvish ethnicity is an elve, not an elf, so you will find her thus correctly spelled in these pages.

This and many other orthographic enhancements are standardized in the glossary at the end of this work. Now, with the Bard we pray:

Oh God! That one might read this book of fates
    and see the revolutions of time,
the cloud-capped towers, the gorgeous estates,
    the solemn temples, the great globe sublime.
May this poet's pen turn them into lofty shapes,
    and give to airy nothings a local shine
with names that spur new seeds to germinate
    from fallen logs to holy life in full prime.
A flock of blessings light upon these, my book-kin.
    Bluster images with edifying insight within.
Mend the mottled fabric of these lines
    with that flawless warp and woof of thine,
and in the sacred sanctuaries of their minds
    leave only a graceful skein behind.

ACT I

KING OF THE HILL

Scene 1: A Long-Expected Party

Shentalpee City on Tuscoraura Mountain
Frige's Day Nones. Afternoon, 24th of March, 1283
Eve of the Feast of the Annunciation (New Year's Eve)

A middle-aged gnomid stewardess knocks at the office of the dungaree of Foreign Trade. Madame Jeanne Ranglursdottir calls through the door, "Bartlebee, come in! Any news?"

"Yes, Madame Dungaree," answers the gnomid squeaking the hinges while opening the solid oak door. "The League of Licornes has sent a courier to inform you that your human guest has arrived in the marchlands. They will accompany him until the wood elf villages leading off Thor's Base. From there, they presume that you shall provide your own escort."

Madame Jeanne Ranglursdottir, the dungaree of Foreign Trade for Shentalpee City, looks up cheerfully and says, "Fantastic, Bartlebee! Fetch the largest Thor's Hammer pendant in my collection for Reverend Appleseed and then inform Captain Manzone that he shall accompany me with two bravos dressed in their finest uniforms. I want everyone to know that the Council of Perfects is endorsing this talk. Understood?"

Bartlebee curtsies as a formality. "Understood, Madame Dungaree . . . but I'd prefer not to."

The dungaree of Foreign Trade closes her eyes and rests her forehead in the palm of her hand. Thinking through her response to the rebellious stewardess, she forces a calm smile on her face and says, "Never mind, Bartlebee. I will see to it myself."

Captain Manzone, a dashing high elf with a ruddy complexion, handsome features, and striking a fine appearance in an outfit that would make the three musketeers jealous, shoves open the door and proclaims, "Madame Dungaree! You should not allow such insolence! Only say the word and I shall school this impertinent gnomid in manners once and for all."

An ultralight leaf-bladed sword hangs from his left hip and a long main-gauche dagger sticks out from behind his back. He reaches for both.

"Calm down, Captain Manzone. I will deal with it. For now, I'll need your bravos to help me with some chores. Once we're all done, be a dear and fetch me a big Thor's Hammer pendant for our guest, please."

"Yes, Madame Dungaree." With his dashing plan dashed to pieces, Captain Manzone resigns himself to picking up the slack for the lazy stewardess and straps on an apron. As he goes about the mansion for some housekeeping chores his only consolation is that he gets to slap his bravo underlings on the head with a feather duster when they accidentally spill some cinders on the umbrella stand. Once all the nooks and crannies are tidy, he fetches a jewel-encrusted golden necklace.

Taking the Thor's Hammer pendant from him, she pats him on the shoulder with pride and approval in her eyes. Captain Manzone was a wild elfling back in the day and his knack for swordplay got him in serious trouble. Ever since she hired him as her security chief, he has shown more loyalty and diligence than all her other employees put together.

Eager to find her guest, Dungaree Jean walks out the front door with Captain Manzone and two hired bravos. Across the suspension bridge from her treetop platform on Red Giant's Base is Thor's Base. It's the treelofted uptown city center for shopping and hanging out among the high elves. It's also the only place in Shentalpee City where you can catch a dwarf-operated pulley elevator down to the forest floor.

Even before the elevator gets halfway down, Dungaree Jeanne spots Johnny Appleseed caught in the press of wood elves. Each one is dressed to the nines with so much gold jewelry for the New Year's Eve party that Appleseed's shiny tin pot hat sticks out head and shoulders above the crowd like Don Quixote's helmet of Mambrino among King Midas' children.

He waits patiently, admiring the scenic beauty of the wood elf village green. Trimmed shrubs, weeded wildflowers, butterfly bushes, and artistically arranged rocks give the wood elves pride—they uphold the tradition of manicured nature at its best.

As soon as the operator dwarf opens the elevator's gate, Dungaree Jeanne runs over to give Johnny Appleseed a warm hug. He has to go down on one knee to hug her back, since even with her vigorous posture, she stands only a few inches above four feet.

Reaching up to put the Thor's Hammer pendant around his neck, Dungaree Jeanne says in near-perfect Aenglish, a language she learned for business, "It's so good to see you again, Reverend Appleseed! As a mark of honor, the fire elves of Tuscoraura Mountain wish to offer you this pendant and to escort you with an honor guard while you are here among us."

On their way back to the elevator, the frolicking of the elves gets so loud and rambunctious that Johnny Appleseed can barely hear what she is trying to tell him over the squeals and excited conversations of the lucky wood elves holding an invitation to the New Year's Eve party. Wafting through the press of slender bodies is a tidal wave of scents from the very best elven perfumes and colognes.

Johnny Appleseed shouts back, "What's that? With all this ruckus, I can't hear a lick of what you're saying; and all that elven perfume makes my nose runny and my ears stuffy!"

"Come with me!" Dungaree Jeanne slides through the crowd of wood elves and presents the elevator dwarf in charge of operations with a roughhewn piece of carton sealed in wax with the Council of Perfect's triangular eye emblem—that would be the equivalent of a VIP ticket for her guest in modern times. He reads it with lifted eyebrows and then tacks his way up the press of bodies, breaking open a path for the VIP guest to cut straight to the front of the line and loads them onto the elevator.

The tin pot on Johnny Appleseed's head is by now so famous that even the pagan elves recognize this Christian missionary. It does not escape Dungaree Jeanne's notice, as a master artisan in the Fashion and Couture Guild of Shentalpee City, that the same old, faded blue overalls he was wearing last year still hang over his bony shoulders and down his legs now. His white, collared shirt is new since the last time she saw him but no less ragged and frayed, being woven of a more fragile linen fabric.

She, on the other hand, always dresses in a fresh outfit for each occasion. Right now she sports the very best in springtime business casual wear—a white cashmere scarf and cropped blue denim jacket over a sunshine-yellow satin dress. She plans to change into something a little more . . . flashy before making her public appearance in her official role in the ceremony as his translator.

As they ride up the VIP elevator flanked by the elf bravos, Fire Elf City comes into view. Johnny Appleseed needs a deep breath to take it all in. Thor's Base, the awe-inspiring central plaza of the high elves on Tuscoraura Mountain, strikes his eye with its unearthly splendor. Wooden planks of flooring hang one hundred fifty feet above him as the swaying elevator cranks upward under the might of some burly dwarfin arms and some clever dwarven mechanisms. Seeing the heights, Reverend Appleseed's stomach queases and his head dizzies around for a moment.

"Are you all right?" worries Dungaree Jeanne.

"Oh, I'm fine; happy to see you, and just plain old giddified that your elfy Council of Perfects wants to hear the Good Spell of the Lord Jesus."

The cheer in her eyes drains away as she broods on his words. The Council of Perfects does not want to hear about Jesus—that much is for sure. If only she had a guess at their real goal, she might massage her hesitations away or form a plan to kick them off balance. For a savvy business elve used to gaining the edge over her competitors and taking charge of large-scale operations, being clueless about the whole deal spoils her peace of mind and drains some of the joy out of this happy reunion. As the elevator rises up, she gets that sinking feeling as if she just might be leading her good friend like a lamb to the slaughterhouse.

Once up top on the interwoven wooden planks holding the city up, a series of magnificently wrought wooden buildings protrudes higher still. Each one stretches up into the sky like Valhalla, hall of the gods. Dungaree Jeanne smiles seeing the awe on Johnny Appleseed's face and comments, "The old folk of Tuscoraura Mountain swear that the ancient architects who designed these imposing elven skyscrapers had seen Asgard with their own eyes. Just look at those harmonious arches and façades!"

"Ham and cheese or fillet of scrod? I'm not hungry, thank you."

Dungaree Jeanne says, "Oh dear, all that perfume really has stuffed up your ears. Never mind all that; do you have your speech ready?"

Johnny Appleseed smiles, "The Lord said to the Prophet Isaiah, 'I will give you the words I want you to say. I will cover you with my hands and protect you.'"

Dungaree Jeanne voices her uneasiness one more time. "Are you sure you want to go through with this? You are going to be preaching to a tough audience of skeptical elves. They always have a trick or two up their sleeves and you may not see it coming."

"If I can't see it coming then just lead me to the pillars like the blind Samson and with God's strength, I will bring the house down."

As the sun warms the afternoon high in the sequoia treetops, the sweet scent of pine begins to fill the spring air. Red-breasted robins and blue jays flutter in closer to squawk out the tingling tones of their thrill. On this festive day, throngs of well-dressed elves gather in the amphitheater to listen to an odd Christian preacher.

The wood elves are curious but the high elves of Shentalpee City just want to get the New Year's party started. They sit down restlessly and shush anyone who sounds too happy about being here.

The gray-haired umpire-in-chief of the Tuscoraura fire elves, Kibbler Earnestson, walks up onto the stage. Robed in silky green with a red tweed vest and yellow velvet sash, he speaks in Runic, the official language of the high elves. "Mesdames, mesdemoiselles, messieurs, ladies, and gentelves. Four score and seven years ago, our ancestors brought forth upon this Tuscoraura Mountain a new fire elf colony, conceived in hard work and dedicated to the proposition that of all the clayborn in Vinland we fire elves are created better.

"Since then, Shentalpee City's fire elves have become the leader in nearly every industry, from cookie baking to fashion design, and we have made of this sequoia grove a treetop paradise and a worthy home to the Alfheim gods our ancestors brought to the New World from their citadel deep within Mount Ragnarök.

"Up here, high above the forest floor, we touch the friendly skies at the break of each new day and our fingertips tremble with wonder as we reach for something special in the skies."

The high elves, who dwell high up in Shentalpee City, nod with approval at his eloquent flattery. The wood elves, who live on the forest floor below, shuffle in their seats. Few wood elves have the leisure to study Runic well enough to grasp his high-flown speech.

Umpire Kibbler switches to Eldric, their native language, so they can all understand. "Neither the high elves nor the wood elves among us are afraid to ask the deeper questions about life, religion, politics, and philosophy, and so despite the ridiculous tin hat and unfashionable overalls, please welcome the renowned human missionary Reverend Johnny Appleseed."

The high elves applaud coldly and the wood elves are too intimidated to make any more noise.

Johnny Appleseed stands up to shake his hand.

Yikes!

"You're not supposed to stand up next to an umpire in public if you are taller than he is. Look at how short you made him look! Where are your manners?" His translator, Dungaree Jeanne, hisses between clenched teeth. She yanks his hand so hard that Reverend Appleseed flips back over his chair. His tattered pant hems and dirty bare feet stick straight up over his head.

You see, the truth is that elves were always rather short, despite their schemes to appear otherwise.

Contrary to what Professor Tolkien and other prominent historians of elves would have you believe, elves were never taller than humans, even in their so-called Golden Age. Elf skeletons discovered from archeology sites dating back to the thirteen century reveal that most full-grown elves, like gnomes and dwarves, averaged around four and a half feet in height back then, as they do today.

To avoid the humiliation of appearing short, Umpire Kibbler dashes to his chair, but even with Johnny Appleseed sprawled out backwards on the wooden stage, the missionary's long toes, bony ankles, and hairy legs whirling around high in the air nearby have a way of making the proud elf appear small and insignificant. Kibbler is not just another umpire among the fire elves, he is *the* umpire-in-chief over all of Shentalpee City. And yet, for all his posturing and anxiety, he cannot add an inch to his stature.

In the back row, the umpire's daughter, Florenz, buries her face in her hands. Florenz inherited her mother's dark elve features. As you can guess, in a society where image is everything, standing out from the crowd is not highly esteemed and Umpire Kibbler has already spent a lot of his political clout keeping bullies away from his daughter.

The umpire-in-chief has many rivals, but not one has ever dared criticize his love and care for Florenz. He has always been one of the most devoted fathers an elve could wish for. He attends all Florenz's archery tournaments and helps her with her alchemy projects. Every morning he combs through her thick curls—dyed blonde, as is expected of a proper high elve—and he cooks dinner with her after work.

For now, poor Florenz can only hope this preacher man has something clever to say or the backlash could spell the demise of her family's political fortunes.

Once Umpire Kibbler is safely back in his seat, Johnny Appleseed calmly rolls around onto his feet, clears his throat, and starts to preach. "It's mighty kind of y'all to invite me here to this New Year's Eve party. For Christians, each calendar year starts with the Feast of the Annunciation. On that day, almost thirteen hundred years ago, an angel appeared to a young girl from Nazareth and started the story of our salvation."

Fire elf society here is segregated—high elves on the right, wood elves on the left. Johnny Appleseed looks them in the eyes one after another. Suddenly, he chokes on some phlegm. The wood elves look ordinary enough, but the uncanny uniformity among the high elves strikes him as odd, almost creepy. Except for Florenz, a dark elve on her mother's side, the high elves all have light skin, blond hair, high cheeks, wide foreheads, sculpted chins, pointy ears, celestial noses, and blue, green, or violet eyes.

Not a single scruffy or laid-back high elf in sight: all he sees are overdone hairdos, elegant ball gowns, silk shirt collars, and dapper waistbands. The view is picture-perfect—disturbingly too perfect.

Johnny Appleseed hocks up a wad of cud from the back of his throat and attempts to spit it out discreetly behind the polished hardwood stage so no one notices. They do. The elves all gasp and groan.

Florenz nearly faints. This bumpkin's act is spiraling out of control. She's already lagging in the polls. Her father would take it hard if she loses in the upcoming elections for the next umpire-in-chief. She's got to get him off the stage by hook or by crook.

Gizzard and mind cleared, Reverend Appleseed resumes his sermon in Aenglish, which Dungaree Jeanne translates into Eldric with a loud, assertive, and confident voice. It goes something like this: "Oooooh, the Lord is good to me, and so I thank the Lord for giving me the things I need; the sun and the rain and the apple seed. The Lord is good to me. Amen! Amen! Amen! Amen! Amen!"

Johnny Appleseed sings this prayer with amazing enthusiasm. He slaps his knees and stomps his feet in perfect harmony while his hips do a little jig.

Apparently, the prayer's rhyme scheme gets lost in translation, or something like that, because the elves in the audience just sort of wince. For Johnny Appleseed, that good, old-time rhythm lifts his soul toward spiritual realms above. For the high elves . . . not so much. They purse their lips and roll their eyes, keeping their souls bound to the material world below.

Florenz bites her nails and rocks back and forth. She looks at her best friend, Zena, sitting next to her and gasps. "How can you be giggling like that? He's making my father look ridiculous. Your mother's the one who invited that preacher man. You're supposed to be my best friend. Can't you make him stop?"

Zena shrugs as if she doesn't care. "That's how it goes in the game of politics. As the wood elves say, 'If you want to look good, just smile.'"

Florenz glares. "Is that what this is all about? Do you really think that pulling a stunt like this'll make you the first umpire-in-chief of wood elve heritage?"

"I'm gorgeous, smart, and athletic. I can pull it off."

"Oh really? When my father told me I had to run in the elections, I only wanted to find a way to bow out gracefully. But on second thought, I think it's time for Shentalpee City to elect its first umpire-in-chief of dark elve heritage."

Zena's carefree giggle turns into a sly grin. "All right, then. Game on."

Scene 2: The Lake Woebegone Effect

Port of Cayuga. Northern tip of Lake Cayuga
in the Confederacy of the Seven Nations
Frige's Day Terce. Morning, 24th of March, 1283
Eve of the Feast of the Annunciation (New Year's Eve)

A-CHOO!

"A kerchief for your nose, my lord?" asks Brother Curtal Tuck. The cleric with smart eyes and hard-earned wrinkles digs into his waist pouch for a clean rag. "You should tend to that sneeze before it gets serious. It's been bugging you for weeks."

"Bah humbug," replies the baron of Amhirst as he blows his nose on the friar's kerchief. Though surrounded by a cleric, two sorcerers, a physician, and three heralds, the baron does not stop straining his voice and shouting out orders. "I want those horses and wagons loaded onto the boats immediately!"

The baron's chief herald, Sir Sean Madigan, objects. "My lord, the camp is rife with disease. Several horses have already gone blind."

The baron of Amhirst rages. "Don't worry about the horses being blind; just load the wagons!"

Two prison guards drag the defeated Frankish viceroy of Vinland, Samuel de Champlane, in chains down the paved path along the lakeshore. A few Frankish merchants peek out from their moored vessels to see for themselves the sad fate of their beloved "Uncle Sam." His haggard face, bushy, white eyebrows and scraggly, white beard remind them they should have joined the army when they had the chance.

New Frankland has recently suffered a total defeat in a war against the Aenglish Crown, and now it's too late for good intentions, especially where the former viceroy is going.

An Aenglish knight gives the command to load up the wagons and board the boats, but the bleak looks on the faces of his men spur him to relay their complaints to the baron of Amhirst. "My lord, the men are beginning to grumble. They keep asking why they have been forced to rush all the way to this dismal Irokian port on a lake no one has ever even heard of, after we have endured so many woes for you at Montroyal."

The baron of Amhirst forces a smile on his face. "Tell the men that this is Lake Woe-be-gone! Our hardships will end somewhere over this lake."

Uncle Sam mutters, "More like somewhere over the rainbow."

The Aenglish knight slaps the defeated Frankish viceroy for his cheeky comment. Weak and maltreated, Uncle Sam stumbles and falls into the lake. The knight seems ready to let him drown but the water is barely waist-deep, and the handcuffed prisoner manages to stand up on his own. The knight complains, "Zounds! Am I supposed to fish you out of Lake Woebegone?"

Uncle Sam replies, "Do not ask what you can do for me. Ask what you can do for my country."

"New Frankland is gone. This is all New Aengland now. You have to stop living in the past and start thinking about getting out of the deep waters."

"Let every Aenglishman know, whether he wishes me well or ill, that I shall pay any price, bear any burden, meet any hardship, support any friend, oppose any foe, to assure the revival of New Frankland."

Annoyed at his lazy knight and the prattling prisoner, the baron points at the knight and says, "I want you to pull him out of the water." Then he points to Uncle Sam and says, "I want you—"

HA-TISH-OO!!!

His violent sneeze sends snot everywhere.

"Bless you!" his entourage calls out politely, pretending not to notice how gross the baron looks.

The baron resumes his thought and points at Uncle Sam. "I want you to keep your mouth shut."

Amhirst's personal physician, Doctor Estrange, analyzes his illness with the best explanation medieval medicine has to offer. "Clearly, my lord, those pestilential Kaybec marches, along with significant sleep deprivation, have trapped a bitter rheum in your spleen, ascending into your nostrils. A few leeches in the right place will clear that up for you."

The baron of Amhirst waves his hand vigorously, but the snot still dangles from it as he speaks. "Nonsense! It's just a cold. Hand me another kerchief!"

Amhirst blows his nose, wipes his fingers, and hands the slimy kerchief to his herald, Sir Sean, who reminds him, "My lord, you were about to inform these troops, who fought so valiantly for you beneath the walls of Montroyal, what we're doing in this backwater village. Not even those of us on your privy council know why we're here."

The baron perks up as he speaks. "Ah, yes! Start spreading the news; we're leaving today!"

Sir Sean's shoulders sag at what he is hearing; he just does not see the sense in it. "But we just arrived last night!" he exclaims. "We are in no shape to leave this morning! Please give the troops a rest."

Doctor Estrange adds his objections. "The troops and horses are exhausted. You are seriously straining their humors. We must rest or else disease will defeat this valiant army, which the Frankish could not!"

The baron of Amhirst raises his palm to stop them. "I haven't slept more than two hours a night for the last month. My eyes burn, my throat is sore, and phlegm fills my nostrils from dawn to dusk. I'm not demanding any more of my troops than I'm demanding of myself. We'll rest once we reach New Amsturldam. It's ripe for the plucking now. We must seize the day!"

Doctor Estrange cannot believe his ears. "Rest in New Amsturldam!?! You're going to wake up in a city that doesn't sleep!"

KER-TI-SCHOO!

"Bless you!" his advisors say in unison.

"My career has languished so far. It's time to make a brand-new start of it in old New Amsturldam."

"But it's a mess over there! Ever since Count Richard Nicolas conquered Thane Petur Styvesant's Vikings, many lords have been battling to be king of the hill, top of the list—number one!"

The baron of Amhirst smiles despite his bleary eyes and reddened nose. "Exactly! I want to be a part of it."

"What claim do you have? The king has only appointed you governor of Fort Pitt and Montroyal. You missed the conquest of New Amsturldam."

"We'll be backing the claim of a trusted friend, Sir Samuel Maverick."

Sir Sean racks his memory. "As I recall, that Maverick is a man who acts with an independent mind. What makes you so sure that as duke of New Amsturldam he'll just hand the title over to you?"

The baron of Amhirst stops his horse suddenly and dismounts. An uncanny silence creeps through the wind as the baron wheels around to gloat over the prisoner. All eyes fall upon Uncle Sam, the bloodied Frankish viceroy of Vinland, sprawled across the gangplank.

With a low voice as if talking to himself, Lord Geoffrey Amhirst announces, "My dear Sir Sean, I have no mind to ask Sir Samuel Maverick to hand over his paltry title as duke. New Amsturldam means more to me than just another city—it is the start of an empire. In return for my support, he will join those who shall proclaim me the first Aenglish viceroy of Vinland."

"Viceroy of Vinland!?!" They all gasp at the notion.

HAT-SCHIII!

"Bless you!" they mumble one after the other, still trying to fathom the baron's ambitions.

The baron of Amhirst continues monologuing away his scheme. "I wrote to the duke of Yourke back in February, informing him that Sir Samuel Maverick had taken New Amsturldam from Thane Petur Styvesant and his Vikings. In the same letter, I explained that those of us who planned the conquest had always intended to rename it New Yourke in his honor, but that we uncovered a plot by the duke of Lancaster to use his toady, Count Richard Nicolas, to usurp his claim and rename it New Lancaster, despite arriving too late to aid in the conquest."

Sir Sean Madigan wrinkles his brow in dismay. "But, uh, my lord . . . Count Richard Nicolas conquered New Amsturldam two weeks ago. Sir Samuel Maverick is the one who arrived too late for the conquest."

"Ah-ha!" exclaims the baron. "That's the beauty of it. Since I correctly anticipated the events, the king will read my version first and he will read Count Nicolas's version several weeks later. When it comes to credibility, Sir Sean, it's first come, first deserve."

"That's a dangerous play, my lord. King Eddard Longshanks is very shrewd. What if he discovers your falsehood?"

"When we were boys, we used to steal apples from a farmer. To catch us thieves, he would smear the apples with red tarberry juice, since the stain is hard to remove. I noticed this and took a bite from the biggest apple I could find using only a leaf to help guide it to my mouth, but I left the apple on the tree. When the other boys tried to steal apples, the farmer made them turn up their palms and caught them red-handed. He looked at me, but I had no red on my palms. I innocently asked him for the big apple off his tree that was already bitten into. As far as he was concerned I hadn't stolen it and it was worthless to him, so he gave it to me."

"So what's the moral of that story?"

"New Yourke is my big apple. I bit into it before Lord Nicolas conquered it. Good timing, combined with tact, gets you far in the game of politics."

The baron's cleric, Brother Curtal Tuck, scratches his tonsured pate. "I don't get it."

A-TCHOUM!

"Bless you!" they say with a little more confidence this time around.

"Listen carefully. King Eddard cares nothing about truth or falsehood. His preoccupation is with finding lords who know how to win. The king feels that his advisor, Earl William Pitt, is a winner. So, when Fort Duquesne surrendered to the Crusade, I offered to rename it Fort Pitt in his honor. That was enough to convince the king to name me governor. As governor of Fort Pitt, I had the right to lead an army, so we set out and conquered Montroyal. The point is, I'm winning. The duke of Yourke is a winner. King Eddard will play along, as long as we keep winning."

Sir Sean Madigan thinks about it for a short while and then squirms. "A very good strategy, my lord; but there *is* one flaw to your plan."

"Oh really? Enlighten me if you would, Sir Sean."

"Although you have conquered several key cities in Vinland, you are only a baron. There are several higher-ranking Aenglish nobles on this continent who have been equally victorious in battle. Count Richard Nicolas won many battles for King Eddard in Welchland before conquering New Amsturldam, and Earl James Wolf has recently taken Kaybec. Viscount Sean Pridow is now master of Fort Niagara. They are all stronger candidates for viceroy than you are."

The baron of Amhirst rubs his chin and says, "All good points, Sir Sean, except that there *is* one item on their résumé that makes them weaker candidates for viceroy than I am."

"What's that?"

"They're all dead."

Sir Sean Madigan scoffs at the suggestion. "They were all in perfect health last I heard. What makes you so sure they're dead?"

HAI-KU!

"With vict'ry at hand,
"they died fighting in battle.
"Trust me. I made sure."

No one says, "Bless you."

Scene 3: The Producer

Amphitheater at Thor's Base, Shentalpee City
Frige's Day Nones. Afternoon, 24th of March, 1283
Eve of the Feast of the Annunciation (New Year's Eve)

Ignoring the elves' flustered grimaces and looks of disdain, Reverend Appleseed preaches on. "Being able to ascend into the trees and visit with the companions to the eagles, friends of the squirrels, and delegates to the clouds, is an honor I would've never imagined available to me in all of God's glorious creation."

Upon hearing Dungaree Jeanne's translation of his flattering and poetic comment, the elves soften their harsh expressions. Florenz breathes a sigh of relief.

"And so I've come here today to offer you a few more marvels of creation so as you can share in his goodness and his providence even better.

"My pappy always told me, 'It's not polite to ask a friend to worship the Lord on an empty stomach.' From that time onward, I decided to make sure everybody in Vinland's got a full belly so as we could sing together songs of praise to our God. Why the apple? Adam and Eve ate apples before getting kicked out of paradise. Since we can't get back in until the Lord comes again, we'd might as well stock up on a few apples out here to munch on while we're waiting."

He reaches behind the chest flap of his overalls and pulls out an apple. He bites into it. Taking his time to chew and swallow that first chunk, he then goes for another bite . . . and another. *Crunch!*

The elves look at him, mesmerized.

He winks back at them and says, "It's healthy for you too. An apple a day keeps the doctor away."

With that, he grabs another apple from his overalls, shines it on his shirt, and says, "Here, Chief! Sink your teeth into one of these and tell me what you think."

He tosses the apple at Umpire Kibbler but Dungaree Jeanne, with quick reflexes, intercepts his pass and says in Aenglish, "Of course we'd all love to sample the fruit of your labors, Reverend Appleseed, but food will be served after your talk. Don't want to spoil anyone's appetite by snacking in between meals, do we?"

Johnny Appleseed shrugs and says, "Suit yourself." He then pulls out a thin sheet of lead and two separate pouches of white powders from deep inside his overalls and dumps them all in a wooden bowl. Immediately, blackflame billows up from the bowl.

"In my travels, I found that oftentimes, people've got plenty of food, but it goes bad before they can eat it. This blackflame chills vegetables, meats, and fruit juices to keep them from spoiling quickly. Stick a little brazier of this blackflame in your cupboard and your food'll stay fresh for weeks.

"It's perfectly safe. It takes metals as kindling, so it won't set trees or living creatures on fire. It burns clean; no smoke. You don't even need to blow on it or stoke it up. Leave a lead plate in here and instead of ashes or soot, you'll find a beautiful piece of stained glass."

Reverend Johnny Appleseed wraps the end of his ragged linen shirt around his hand, using the hem as a mitt, and reaches into the brazier. With a quick snatch, he pulls out a nice slab of crystalline yellow glass.

He draws a few oohs and aahs from the audience.

Umpire Kibbler stands up, clapping deliberately, and calls out, "Cottage humans clap their hands to show appreciation. Let us thank Reverend Appleseed in gestures that his own culture understands."

Warmer applause erupts.

After Johnny Appleseed sits back down, Umpire Kibbler peers over to make sure the tall human is firmly settled into his chair before daring to walk over next to him again. On his way back onto the stage, the high elf leader pauses to unruffle his green robes and straighten his yellow sash, emphasizing his renewed sense of self-worth.

The umpire-in-chief of Shentalpee City concludes the New Year's Thor's Enlightenment Discourse (TED) with a short speech in Eldric. "This blackflame is an intriguing new fire technology. The smith gods, Weyland, Vulcan, and Hephaestus, have hidden the blackflame from the other gods cautiously, and Prometheus seems to have altogether forgotten to distribute it among mortals.

"But this is to our advantage! We get the first crack at it. Not long ago, we felt invincible for having deciphered the code of Athabask fire. After learning about it from the canoe humans, we combined it with Graec fire and perfected it into our own unquenchable elf fire.

"The clayborn of Vinland are forgetting our prowess with fire weaponry. Goblins encroach in our lands, humans rob fire elf merchants, and dwarves cook up new fire recipes in an attempt to vie with us. We must study and unlock the secrets of this blackflame if we are to reassert our military dominance in Vinland.

"Before me, I see row after row of stunningly good-looking, stylishly dressed geniuses. If anyone can master this blackflame it's you, o fire elves of Tuscoraura Mountain!"

The elves rap their knuckles on the wooden benches and clink their silver and gold rings and bracelets for applause, as is their custom. Cheers whistle through the assembly like a howling wind.

Dungaree Jeanne blurs her translation of the umpire-in-chief's words. She's guessing Johnny Appleseed has no intention of becoming an arms dealer.

Meanwhile, Umpire Kibbler carries the wooden bowl of blackflame back to the colossal statue of Thor behind them and puts it inside a brazier. "I hereby dedicate this blackflame in honor of Thor, the chief protector of this treetop colony. Let us all take upon ourselves the sacred duty to analyze its alchemical composition, to unlock its artistic and industrial potential . . . and most of all, to weaponize it!"

The high elves stand up with great enthusiasm and extend their right hands straight up into the air, chanting, "Kibbler, hail! Kibbler, hail!"

Dungaree Jeanne chooses not to translate that last bit of information for Reverend Appleseed either.

Florenz leaps up cheering and joins her father on stage. Meanwhile, Zena stews in her seat, grumpy and resentful. Knowing a good deal of Aenglish herself, Zena mulls over her mother's reluctance to translate accurately for the missionary.

In a flash of inspiration, she hatches a plan to cool the rising enthusiasm for Umpire Kibbler and sap the political momentum he is winning for Florenz.

Grinning wildly, Zena steps over to Johnny Appleseed and drops a pouch of gold coins in his lap. He looks up at her, a bit confused. "What's this?"

Zena answers in her heavily accented Aenglish, "Tuscoraura double eagles—pure gold coins worth twenty dollars each."

Reverend Appleseed is so shocked he barely manages to speak. "Okay, but what's it for? I'm offering you these gifts freely."

Zena gives him a wink. "We call it earnest money. Umpire Kibbler Earnestson has family tradition of holding onto good deal. He not want you to give the dark fire to anyone else. This money to be followed by much more if you keep it our little secret."

Appleseed scratches his ear and tilts his head back. "Tell him that I serve the Lord and not Mammon!"

"You should be afraid to stand up to him and tell him yourself. He is too powerful!"

Without another moment's hesitation, he stands to his full height and hands the money bag over to Umpire Kibbler. "I don't want your hush money!"

Despite his high heels, Umpire Kibbler's head barely reaches up to Appleseed's bushy, gray beard. His shortness is painfully obvious to all the high elves there. The entire audience gasps at a second—and this time, intentional—act of effrontery against their umpire-in-chief's short stature.

Umpire Kibbler shoots an angry look in Dungaree Jeanne's direction. "Madame Dungaree, tell your Christian preacher here that the base ledges tend to be rather low for exceedingly tall men such as himself, and newcomers get vertigo real easy when they see for themselves how high up we really are."

Scene 4: Petals on a Wet, Black Brow

Port of Ithica. Southern tip of Lake Cayuga
in the Aenglish Lordship of Vinland
Frige's Day Compline. Night, 24th of March, 1283
Eve of the Feast of the Annunciation (New Year's Eve)

It is a dark and stormy night. Frigid rain slices through the roiling sky. The haggard and sorely pressed soldiers under the command of the baron of Amhirst disembark onto the slippery docks at the Port of Ithica. Spurred by hopes for warm fires and featherbeds within Ithica's walls, they slosh their way up the cold, muddy roads.

Along the quay, black rain clouds dump sheets of chilled fury across Amhirst's brow like petals of divine wrath. Along the wearisome road, the raindrops slow to a gentle trickle, only to pick up again moments later. The alternation jangles the nerves of the soldiers and horses alike. Both bray like wild beasts as the storm proves itself a more relentless, ruthless, and intractable foe than the Frankish ever were.

Clanging raindrops on the soldiers' metal helmets add a noisy torture to the bitter cold. For the knights and mounted sergeants in mail, the precipitation stiffens the rusting chain links until their arms grow too rigid to even wipe the snot from their faces and soaks the rusty chill deep into their bones.

The baron of Amhirst, past his sneezing fit but still suffering from a runny nose and starting to go feverish, yells out with authority: "Why have we stopped?" **Sniff** "Ithica is right there!"

Sir Sean is quick to answer. "The vanguard is standing before the gates of Ithica now, my lord, but a messenger just arrived saying that the town has barred its gates to our soldiers!"

"What on middle earth are you talking about, Sir Sean? Why are they refusing us entry? This is an army of Aenglishmen. Are the Ithicans not loyal subjects of the Aenglish Crown?" The baron fumes.

"Perhaps if you reason with the captain of the gatehouse, you might rekindle his patriotic fervor . . ."

Amhirst shouts hoarsely, "Patriotic fervor?" **Sniff** "I'll strike the fear of God into that knave's heart!" He spurs his horse to a brisk trot and rides to the front of his halted column of soldiers.

Despite the raindrops splashing in his eyes, he catches a glimpse of Ithica's town guards and identifies which one is the gate tower's captain merely by the way he carries himself. The baron of Amhirst has a knack for sifting out men and women with power. As he yells, he realizes his voice is getting hoarse. "What is the meaning of this?! I am Lord Geoffrey, baron of Amhirst, and commander-general of His Highness King Eddard's expeditionary forces to Montroyal. The king's soldiers have a right to be quartered in any Aenglish town." **Sniff** "In the name of the king, I order you to open these gates!"

Although far away and watery-eyed, the baron imagines he can detect a sardonic curl in the captain's lip. "Begging your pardon, my lord, but them joints on the gate took a hit from, you know, a catapulted boulder during the last siege by those cheese-eating Franks. Now the dang portcullis is all wrecked and our engineers can't fix it until next week!"

With cold rain seeping down his back, Amhirst loses patience. "What sort of tomfoolery are you playing at, man?" **Sniff** "You shall open these gates to my troops at once or suffer the king's wrath!"

"Tut, tut, Lord Jiffy; it ain't gentlemanly to go making threats like that. They're liable to stick to the roof of your mouth!" The captain of the gate tower guard struts around with a show of bravado.

The baron of Amhirst clenches his fists. "Do you realize that there are over five thousand soldiers at my command?! They are soaked to the bone and in no mood to sit here all night. One word from my mouth and they'll unleash a torrent of" **Sniff** "blood!"

"You lot of bed-wetters can unleash a torrent of wee-wee for all I care." The captain of the gate tower guard wags his steel-mailed fanny and saunters away from the wall. In his place, a scholarly looking elder wearing carnelian red and dark-gray academic robes and holding a large, metallic staff with a comfortable, red velvet grip in the middle approaches the wall.

The scholar calls down to him: "Lord Amhirst, you would do better allowing your herald to speak for you. You are losing your voice, and you are about to lose your army as well. You dare threaten to attack Ithica?

"Ithica is home to the Silvermorn College of Sorcerers and I am its grand sage, Ezra Cornwell. We have over three hundred brilliant young apprentice sorcerers eager to demonstrate the military applications of their proficiency with source stones. They could sweep away your iron-clad army with their staves quicker than they could sweep up my study with three hundred bewitched brooms!" Cornwell deftly twirls his staff to demonstrate his skill and awaits a reply.

Amhirst confers with Sir Sean Madigan and then lets his herald do the speaking for him. "The baron of Amhirst has no wish to start any conflicts with loyal subjects of the Aenglish Crown, only to remind you that since we are a royal army with a commission directly from King Eddard himself, we have the right to quarter our troops in Aenglish towns. We are here to exercise our royal prerogative."

"Royal prerogative, eh? We'll see about that." Master Cornwell beckons a large, mail-armored man wearing a tabard with the Aenglish Crown's heraldic coat of arms: three gold lions passant guardant on a gules field along with King Eddard's personal badge consisting of the Queen Mother's Provençal golden rose with a green stalk and his late father's Plantagenet sprig of broom.

The man shouts out authoritatively, "His Royal Highness, Eddard, king of Aengland, prince of Welchland, lord of Erinland, duke of Baskony, duke of Aquatania, and count of Picardy, commands you to hold your peace. The mayor of Ithica reminds you about the atrocities committed by unruly Aenglish soldiers against those loyal to the Aenglish Crown at Fort Bedford. In light of those excesses, he insists that you send your troops in unarmed and one at a time."

Sir Sean Madigan fumes. "We have six thousand soldiers who need food and housing immediately! Of that number, nearly four hundred are sick or wounded! We can't queue up for days waiting to get inside one at a time! The king's commission accords us the right to quarter troops in Aenglish towns!"

The man replies, "The King's charter to Ithica grants the mayor the right to decide how and where

Aenglish troops will be quartered. On the king's authority, I order you to back your troops away from these walls."

The baron trots his shivering horse forward a few more paces and wipes the cold rain from his face. "On the king's authority?" **Sniff** "Who in the wild blue blazes do you think you are?"

"I am Sir Walter Rally, the royal coroner for Ithica," the man replies with a bold air, despite the wet rains lashing against his face and armor.

"Royal coroner? I've never heard of such an office."

"The wise King Eddard has heard too many cases where both sides make claims in the name of the Aenglish Crown, so he has appointed coroners who alone have authority to speak for the Crown."

"Balderdash!" the baron barks out, quickly losing any semblance of patience. "We'll show them who has the Aenglish Crown's authority! Sir Sean, tell the offensive coordinators to ready the battering rams."

Grand Sage Ezra Cornwell calls forth hundreds of apprentice sorcerers to take up defensive positions along the wall. Cornwell holds out his large rod of lodestone. In the hands of this master sorcerer, it becomes one of the most powerful weapons in medieval warfare.

The grand sage pulls down his hood (to protect against the rain—contrary to popular misconceptions, real historical sorcerers only wore hoods outdoors during inclement weather, to keep the rain out of their eyes, and never wore them inside just to appear creepy and mysterious). With his face hooded from the rain, he meditates for a moment. Gradually, he begins to regulate his breathing and pulse until the polarization of his lodestone grows stronger and switches from attracting metal to repelling it. Then, with a flick of the grand sage's wrist, Amhirst and his armored bodyguards go flying backwards off their horses.

Amhirst's tall frame, on top of such a tall horse, makes for a harder fall than the rest of the knights. Afraid his master might have broken his neck, Amhirst's diligent squire rushes to help him to his feet.

Alive but with the wind knocked out of him from the fall, Amhirst still manages to wheeze out his defiance. "Sorcerers, eh? We'll show him what we can do with sorcery! Slingers! Clear the walls! Engineers! Bring forth for the battering ram!"

His squire repeats the baron's command to the heralds. Like opera singers, they use voices to amplify and project sound as far as megaphones.

Sir Isaac Davies, captain of the baron's slinger company, readies his troops in under a minute and lines them up to strafe the walls. Incidentally, this same Davies would organize the first company of patriotic minutemen from the town of Akten in the duchy of Masswachoosut Bay and would give his life heroically for the cause of freedom during the Battle of Lexton and Concord a few years later.

At his command, the Aenglish slingers whirl smooth, round stone pellets over their heads, then launch them at the young sorcerers on the battlements. From five hundred yards accuracy is impossible, but a constant peppering of weighty stones is usually enough to keep a wall's defensive squads hunkered down long enough to bring up scaling ladders and a battering ram.

Usually.

Against Cornwell's apprentice sorcerers, it is another matter entirely. Since lodestones, the source stones for elemental earth, are only effective against metal, sling stones or bone-tipped arrows normally keep battlesages at bay. But the apprentice sorcerers at Silvermorn let their imaginations run wild.

Wind sorcerers blow into pipes of nacre, the source stone for elemental air, also known as mother of pearl, and buzz into pitch-bored conch shell trumpets to whip up gusts of wind at hurricane velocities, shooting the sling stones and bone-tipped arrows back over Amhirst's battle lines with terrifying force.

Water sorcerers with glass-encased salt crystals at the tips of their ivory rods drive the blustery rain out in concentrated streams, power-washing the slingers and archers off their feet. Fire sorcerers with their pyrite-studded canes send whirling vortices of fire blazing through the night and steaming the rain to create a thick, blinding fog.

The baron of Amhirst watches all these developments with grim determination from the sidelines. Sir Sean Madigan comes galloping back to report to him. Amhirst shouts, although his failing voice barely scratches out more than a whisper, "What are the reports from the unit captains, Sir Sean?"

"Not good, my lord. You might not want to hear it."

"Generals have to watch what they don't want to see and listen to what they don't want to hear."

"Right. Here it goes then. The truth is that our center is crumbling from the onslaught of the elements brought on by all those sorcerers, and the reserve teams are refusing to get into the field. The wounded are literally piling up on top of each other from the violence of the wind and the rain."

Lord Amhirst slaps him on the back. "Don't lose courage, man!" **Sniff** "Tell the troops there is pork roasting on a spit and a side of beef waiting for them inside Ithica and I have a plan to get it.

"First, we are going to divide our battlesages into three groups and send them forward there, there, and there," he says, pointing to clusters of apprentices using the less common source stones—wind, fire, water.

Lodestones, the source stones for earth sorcery, have traditionally been the main tool for training battlesages, who specialize in making life difficult for warriors who rely on steel for their weapons and armor. The apprentices equipped with lodestones are wielding them like the savvy soldiers they aspire to become. The wind, fire, and water apprentice sorcerers, on the other hand, prance around with rowdy zeal. Their battle stances are sloppy.

Amhirst observes, "See how they lean over the walls. Our marksmen should be able to pick off a few."

Sir Sean disagrees. "With wet bowstrings and soggy slings, we won't take down enough to turn the tide."

Lord Amhirst does not lose resolve. "Through this dismal rain, the one thing I can see clearly is that those apprentices are having fun. This is a big game for them. We just need a quick kill or two from our sharpshooters to bring home the deadly realities of war. As soon as Cornwell sees a few of his students getting killed in action, he will withdraw them all. Mark my words!"

Sir Sean sends out the marching orders. Soon Amhirst's crossbowmen and slingers move into position behind the battlemages and battlesages. On their mark, the first volley of crossbow bolts and sling stones flies up against the walls.

The Silvermorn apprentices deflect the sorcery, magic, quarrels, and stones aimed at them, displaying true teamwork and skill. Volley after volley, Amhirst's troops fail to hit anyone on the town's ramparts.

Amhirst's own battlemages and battlesages ply their tricks, spells, and cantrips, but the ensorcelled winds and rains from the Silvermorn apprentices lash back at them with overwhelming gale-storm force.

A conjured hurricane sweeps Amhirst's best and brightest off their feet. The plan is not going well.

"Battlesages, rally!" Sir Sean's voice booms.

Wearing armor of horn scales or bone plating, the baron's remaining battlesages slosh through the cold mud to gather up any of the storm-battered marksmen willing to stay in the fight.

Having realized that they are reckoning with a truly powerful foe, one gnome battlesage tries a forgotten tactic using some old kite shields from the reserve wagon. Although kite shields were a valuable mainstay for the Frankish knights who vanquished the armies of Aengland in 1066, by 1283 they have become outdated tech, lacking the stopping power of the new heater shields. Still, by constructing a small kite shield fort she could position her crossbow troops to score a few hits.

With most of the army swept away, and facing overwhelming odds, the brave battlesage straps a kite shield to her back but then gets caught in a tremendous updraft of wind. It lifts her off her feet high into the air. That battlesage, well-known among Vinlanders of all races in later generations as Merry Pippins, happens to be one of my ancestors.

Carried from one current of drafts to the next, she eventually drops face-first in the mud right in the middle of eleven down-hearted crossbowmen. She smears the mud off her face and says, "You see! Flying on a kite can be quite fun."

The crossbowmen laugh. Her pluck and good humor lift their spirits.

With a simple wave of her hand she calls out, "Let's give them a spoonful of their own medicine and make them go fly a kite of their own!"

Something sparks to life inside these eleven muddy crossbowmen and they crawl through the muck and mire on their hands and knees behind her while cowardly soldiers scramble away from the battlefield. Merry Pippins leads them to the supply wagon with the old kite shields. She then pushes on closer to the walls and orders them to set up a shield fort. Once in position, they crank up their crossbows for a volley.

After they have cocked their bowstrings and loaded their bolts, the crossbowmen look to Merry Pippins and await her orders. Merry Pippins explains her plan. "On three, we are going to pull a supercalifacted expialidox on source stones one, nine, six, and four."

One of the crossbowmen, named Bert, interrupts with his terrible cockney accent: "I amn't got um idear whater yikie just said."

A crossbow-dwarf crouched next to him named Ernie, who happens to be his loyal friend, despite his odd sense of humor and an even odder laugh, tells him, "Don't worry, no one ever understands whatever you say either. Just take your shot on three and don't miss."

"Rawtee ho!"

Merry Pippins meditates and focuses her lodestone staff at specific Silvermorn apprentices. Her staff starts to vibrate with a humming noise. She counts out, "One . . . two . . . three!"

From the kite shield fort, crossbow bolts cut through the rain and the night with terrifying speed and strike several hooded young sorcerers with such force that they are carried off the wall back down into the streets of Ithica behind them.

Sir Sean sees it and whoops in triumph, "Whoo-ee! They managed to strike down a few apprentices!"

The baron of Amhirst strains to see. "Where?"

"Over there, behind those kite shields, my lord! You'll see a dozen soldiers all dirty in the mud."

The baron of Amhirst sniffs. "That dirty dozen over there, eh? Let's see what Cornwell thinks about that!"

No mistake about it—Cornwell is devastated. A wrenching knot twists the grand sage's gut at seeing the violence escalate to lethal proportions. He will be delivering eulogies instead of diplomas this year. Not wishing to endanger any more young lives, Cornwell calls them off. "Sorcerers' apprentices! Withdraw!"

Seeing this, the baron of Amhirst exults and shouts with what is left of his voice, "Call up the siege ladders! It looks like meat is back on the menu, boys!" He spurs his horse forward to lead his demoralized troops in a daring charge from the front while Sir Sean Madigan uses his thunderous voice to echo the war cry.

Eeesh!

The baron's optimism is a bit hasty. The death of the apprentices only spurs their mentors to finish this fight with unnecessary roughness.

The instructors at Silvermorn College gather at the top of the gate tower to combine their powers. They wave their staves, rods, and canes with all the focus their disciplined minds can dedicate to the task. Pillars of fire and windy tornadoes descend upon the attacking hosts and spray raindrops, shields, helmets, swords, and spears into the clutter before the walls. A speckled tidal wave of rainwater and discarded equipment crashes down upon the infantry companies surging forward and demolishes their siege ladders.

Together with two highly skilled colleagues, Master Cornwell points his lodestone staff directly at the baron of Amhirst. With a twist of their wrists and a grunt from their guts, the three powerful sages hoist the feisty baron up into the air. The magnetic force of the lodestone staves acting upon his steel mail armor zips him up toward the top of the gate tower.

The captain of the gatehouse guard reaches out to grab him mid-flight with a gloating smile. "Well now, Lord Jiffy, the mayor's puttin' out a cordial invitation for you to sort out this little difference of opinion you been havin' with the coroner. We'll see who really represents the king's authority around these parts."

"Never!" shouts the dangling baron.

"Oh well. The coroner says that if you ain't got a likin' for the king's authority, we could always drop you off the walls and let ya go hash it out face-to-face with God's authority."

The baron of Amhirst retains his composure as he hangs over the tower's edge. "I am God's good servant, but the king's first."

Scene 5: Florenz's Nightingale

Shade Gap.
Five Miles Northwest of Tuscoraura Mountain
Frige's Day Matins. Midnight, 24th of March, 1283
(The medieval new day did not start until sunrise.)
Eve of the Feast of the Annunciation (New Year's Eve)

Two reindeer fly fearless and fleet through the gloom of the moonlit forests around Tuscoraura Mountain. The rush of wind startles a pair of turtledoves from their roost. Having no mind for their cooing, the two dark figures cling to their swift steeds.

As the damp of the river fog drifts over them silently, only the sparks of their steel-shod hooves against pebbles signal their approach to the goblin ritual mounds overlooking the Shade Gap.

The midnight hour is close at hand and goblins lurk. Their demon gods haunt the barren rockface in search of blood. A foul stench wafts through the air and slides down the stony, cold hills at the unwelcome visitors.

A savage place! Unholy and disenchanted as ever the waning moon has spied upon. An evil sanctuary covered in scratched boulders and spilled blood. Here the two panting reindeer come to a stop.

Chilled but unafraid, Florenz dismounts and pulls from her saddlebag a small, cloth-wrapped crate. Tucking it under her arm, she crawls through the underbrush, closing in on the goblins dancing to the sound of their drums. Her dress has ribbons and filigree that the brambles and thorns shred as she moves.

Though the night assails her comeliness, Enganyon follows after her like a sailor after the siren's song.

He takes one peek ahead and tugs at her hem. "Oh, look at that. They're human! It's not a problem for elves to meddle with. Let's go home."

Amid the tattooed and roughhousing goblins, a half-dozen humans wallow in captivity. Stripped down to their undergarments, they are cuffed with rough vines to a line of wooden stakes. Gruff goblins prod and poke at them with stone-tipped spears. Glib goblinesses chatter and chant over them in preparation for sacrifice to the goblin god of death and conquest.

Florenz doesn't back down. "There's a choice we're making by being here and I'm saving those lives."

Enganyon starts to whimper, "What about all those goblins? What can the two of us do against so many?"

Florenz will hear none of it. She scolds him, "We can't just let the other races in our land keep dying a pointless death at the hands of those goblins!"

"Not pointless at all! That goblin chieftain's got a sacrificial dagger with a phoenix talon blade. I'd say their deaths will be very pointy."

"Coward."

Enganyon's voice squeaks despite all his efforts to keep it low. "What is it with you, Mademoiselle Florenz? Isn't being a fairy-tale princess good enough? You're rich, gorgeous, and powerful! You don't have to pretend you're some kind of hero as well."

"So you're saying I'm not really a hero?"

"Yes, no! What I'm saying is . . . to me, you're more than a hero. You're a . . . a . . . a superhero. But we can't just ask all those goblins to stop sacrificing their captives to their god, Poopoo, so why risk our lives?"

"It's Poodoo. They worship Poodoo. And you're right—we can't tell them to stop the bloodshed; but Poodoo can. If a singing nightingale flies over their ritual, they believe Poodoo has sent them a sign to release their captives alive. Here's the nightingale."

She pulls the cloth covering off her crate and reveals it to be a small cage with a nightingale inside.

"How do you know it's going to fly in the right direction and sing on cue?"

"I don't." Florenz looks at the nightingale. "But I have to believe that there's a Higher Power out there guiding nature and protecting the lives of the innocent."

She opens the cage door. The nightingale flies out and swerves off in the wrong direction without a peep.

Enganyon raises his eyebrows. "Well, that was certainly anticlimactic. It's really been a treat playing the good guy with you, Mademoiselle Florenz, but I don't need to be an augur to tell you it's time for us to head home. I'll saddle up Prancer and Donner."

"So you're saying you're not really a good guy?"

"Nope, not with all those bloodthirsty goblins around us and nothing but a few human lives at stake over there. I'll pass on the whole good guy thing, thank you. In general, my personal philosophy is to stay neutral between good and evil. In all of life's straits, I look to steer the middle course. When facing the perils of the high seas, I'm a buccaneer of mediocrity. 'Armed and harmless' is the motto when my flags unfurl. A middling champion for moderation—that's me. I uphold all high ideals but fanatically adhere to none."

"Oh, Monsieur Enganyon, you are ridiculous. If you're going to leave me here alone, do me a favor and cause a big distraction on your way out. Maybe I could sneak up close enough to cut their bonds."

"Impossible, Mademoiselle Florenz! I could never abandon you. Instead, I urge you to join me in the comfortable median and together we'll live a long, happy life. Maybe we'll even rule over the fire elves as husband and wife—with your father's help."

"Don't be ridiculous! Are you going to cause that distraction or not?"

"Sorry, my love, but I can't oblige you on this one. It goes against my principles."

"What principles!?! You sound so indifferent to the sufferings of others that I'd believe you've already filled out an application to become an evil villain."

"You'll find most evil villains are really sensitive, caring people deep down inside. They've just got a lot of angst to deal with."

"What does angst mean?"

"Whether you realize it or not, you know the meaning of angst. Umpire Drayton exiled your mother, and your father only gathered up enough political clout to fight back seven years too late. You grew up unfairly deprived of a mother and spoiled by your overworked father with privileges you haven't earned. You're moonlighting as a do-gooder to make up the difference. I'd say that same angst could push you to commit some evil villainy, given the right conditions."

"Monsieur Enganyon, leave. I'll do this by myself."

Enganyon grabs her hand and kisses it. "No! Not without you! You know I just can't stop loving you."

She pulls her hand away. "Hey! No ring, no touchie. Besides, how do I know you'd still love me if my father lost all his wealth and political connections?"

"See that? That's the angst talking now. You're well on your way to becoming an evil villain after all."

"Never."

"Never say never."

"You just said it, twice."

Enganyon sighs with a playful smile. "I'm just not going to win with you, am I?"

Turning away from him, Florenz starts sneaking in closer to the captives and whispers, "No, nay, never."

"Ahhhhh!" Enganyon screams.

She looks back to shush him quiet, but he's gone.

"Monsieur Enganyon? Are you all right?" Florenz scans the forest anxiously. All the while, she doesn't hear the footsteps creeping up behind her.

She takes three paces forward. Under the moonlight, she sees a sight that almost stops her heart. She tries to scream but terror takes the sound before she makes it.

A goblin lurker grabs her neck and drags her up the rocky mound until they reach the ululating goblinesses around the human captives. They pipe to the foul spirits ditties of no tone and dance with daffodils in their hair.

The goblin lurker hands Florenz over to the green-skinned ladies who snatch her up and start picking off her jewelry, pouches, belts, boots, and knives. After they've rough-handled her in every way possible, they tie her to a stake near the human prisoners.

She is both relieved and disappointed that Enganyon is not with them. Perhaps he's safe, or maybe he's dead. *Oh, Enganyon, where art thou?*

Forgetting her own discomfort at the tight bindings, her mind goes to work coming up with an escape plan for herself and the humans. Suddenly, she sees him. Enganyon's plight ties a knot in all the threads she's been working out.

Across the stony sacrificial mound, just behind the giant slate altar, goblins are crowding around a black cauldron filled with a steaming, white pigment. They are dipping Enganyon's right foot into the white pigment and placing it on their foreheads.

Florenz shrieks, "What are they doing to him?"

To her surprise, one of the human captives answers her in Elvish Runic, "Do not fear, Mademoiselle elve. They do him little harm. They take unto themselves the Mark of the Feet. Goblins like to collect a white footprint on their right hand or forehead from as many light elves as they are able to capture. It is a token of piety and allegiance to their god, Poodoo."

Though she'd said her words in Eldric, the dialect exclusively spoken by fire elves, she switches to Runic, the language common to all high educated light elves.

"How comes it about that thou speakest Runic?"

The human replies, "I am a master silversmith. Whilst I was still a journeyman, I trained with the sea elves of Martha's Vineyard. Any silversmith in Vinland of worth speaks some Elvish Runic, just as any ironsmith of worth speaks at least some Dwarvish Runic."

Florenz is so amazed at how well this human speaks Runic that she forgets about Enganyon momentarily and asks the human, "Who art thou, and how hast thou fallen into the clutches of these goblins?"

"Master Paul Riviere of Baston. Whilst I was stationed at Fort William Henry, we were besieged by the Heron clan and some Frankish insurgents. We surrendered under terms that we should be allowed our weapons. Certain Heron warriors, however, broke the treaty and demanded our weapons. Those who resisted perished. We all ran for our lives, but soon after reaching the forests, I was captured by goblins and brought here.

"May I, in turn, ask thy name and how comes it that thou hast fallen captive, Mademoiselle Elve?"

"I came here with a nightingale to rescue thee and thy companions. Goblins release their captives if a passing nightingale sings. Our bird flew awry."

"My deepest regrets, fair lady, that thy plan miscarried and that now thou sharest our fate."

Florenz leans her head back on the stake in deep frustration and says, "If only I knew some witchcraft to recall that wayward nightingale."

"The best witchcraft is a mind tuned to nature," replies Paul Riviere, and he starts to whistle. Florenz marvels at how perfectly his whistling imitates the intricate songs of a nightingale.

The goblins hush each other and cock their necks, peeking anxiously at the night sky. Miracle of miracles, Florenz's nightingale flies in and lands on top of Paul Riviere's stake, chirps out a quick ditty, then flies off.

A long pause follows but then a larger goblin, whose sun-dried, dark-green skin has enough tattoos, body piercings, and war trophies to leave no doubt that he is a renowned war chieftain, bellows in triumph.

All the goblins on the sacrificial mound overlooking Shade Gap break into a new flurry of chanting, hopping, and chest-beating. The party breaks up soon enough and the yawning goblins pack up their goodies, including all of Florenz's jewelry, and wander off.

All the captives remain tied hand and foot to their stakes except Enganyon. The white pigment on his foot was hot enough to scald all the skin from his knee down. He writhes with pain in such grandiose gestures as not to notice that he is free.

Florenz calls out to him, "Monsieur Enganyon! Are you all right? Speak to me!"

He courteously replies, "Ouch!"

"Can you find a sharp object to free us with?"

He stops groaning and pulls out her silver dagger with a smirk. "You mean like this? A gobliness was toting it around and I figured you'd want it back."

Florenz can't hide her joy at his craftiness. "Yes! Monsieur Enganyon, your sleight of hand has saved the day! You're my hero! Quickly, free us before those goblins change their minds."

"I can't walk, but I can toss it to you."

"So I can free the humans like a hero? How sweet!"

He tosses it within reach of her bare feet. Handling it deftly with her toes, Florenz slices away the vines tying her to the stake. She then frees Paul Riviere and the other humans, but Enganyon continues to sulk on the ground. She offers him a hand. "You big sissy, I'll fetch Donner and you can just ride him home."

Enganyon stays put and starts to tear up. His lips pucker like a child whose candy just got stolen. "No! We can't go back! Not like this! Our jewelry is gone, our clothes are raggedy and . . . and look! My foot is all glopped up and ugly!"

Paul Riviere walks up and hands her the silver dagger. He thanks her in Elvish Runic. "Thou hast our eternal thanks, Mademoiselle Elve, for saving our lives! If there is anything we can do to repay—"

Enganyon butts in. "Actually, thou couldst get us new clothes and some subtle but elegant jewelry—"

Florenz stuffs a rag in Enganyon's mouth and talks over him. "What my companion means to say is that it is highly shameful for elves to be so disheveled. To walk among our fellow elves in tattered garments and lacking jewelry is no less shameful to us than if thou had to walk among thy peers with no clothes at all."

Paul Riviere nods thoughtfully. "Yes, indeed. I have learned as much about ye elves. Never fear! Whilst at Fort William Henry, many of the soldiers had sticky fingers, so I buried three stashes of silver wire and smithing tools. We shall find one and I shall smith thee simple but elegant jewelry to get thee home without disgrace."

Delirious with gratitude, Florenz bows so deeply she nearly kisses the ground at his feet.

Enganyon objects in Eldric. "Hey, you don't have to worship him like that. He's just paying us back for saving his life."

Florenz gives him a sharp look. "Monsieur Enganyon, he is the one who saved our lives by whistling to my lost nightingale. Now he is showing greater concern for our well-being than his own. In my mind, that makes him the truest hero of us all."

Enganyon shrugs. "Yeah, he's a nice guy, but it's not like the fate of Vinland is riding on his shoulders."

"Perhaps," replies Florenz. "Now, Master Riviere, how shall we reach these three stashes of thine?"

"One is by land, and two are by sea."

Florenz replies, "Let us go by sea. My mother was a pirate queen and I yearn for the open waves. Though I love reindeer, I have no more taste for midnight rides."

Scene 6: The Scarlet and the White

Town Hall of Ithica
Frige's Day Compline. Night, 24th of March, 1283
Eve of the Feast of the Annunciation (New Year's Eve)

Standing on the top step of the town hall, Mayor Hiram Ulysses sees the baron of Amhirst, wrapped in chains, approach. He bows. With a gentle motion of his hand, he issues his invitation. "Please, step right up, Lord Amhirst. The coroner believes you might enjoy meeting some of my guests."

Soaking wet, wheezing, and with snot dripping from his nose like a leaky faucet, Lord Geoffrey, baron of Amhirst, commander-general of the Aenglish Crown's expeditionary forces in Montroyal, stands before Mayor Hiram Ulysses with the bearing of a conquered conqueror, no less than Vercingetorix before Caesar after the Battle of Alesia. The captain of the tower guard removes the fetters from the baron's wrists but two Ithican guards stand by close enough that their body odor becomes oppressive.

A detachment of town militia, in soaking-wet padded armor and armed to the hilt with spears, swords, crossbows, and long axes, stand inside guarding Sir Sean Madigan. Lord Amhirst notices his herald sitting on the bench with a dejected face.

"Get up!" Amhirst snaps. "This is no time to be warming a bench, Sir Sean. I need you to get your head in the game. Get up, I say!"

Sir Sean pulls himself together and follows his leader. After Amhirst and his herald walk into the room, Mayor Hiram Ulysses speaks up. "Allow me to commend you, Sir Sean, for your loyalty in turning yourself in as our prisoner. Have a seat and allow me to introduce you to some men whose opinions I trust. Ithica's coroner, the Honorable Sir Walter Rally, and Master Ezra Cornwell, chancellor of the Silvermorn College of Sorcerers. At the end of the table is a very holy Dominican friar, Father Peter Sheen. Father Sheen was recently appointed special inquisitor for the Blackflame Heresy in Vinland."

The baron of Amhirst gathers his pride and nods his head before speaking. "What an august gathering! Now, Lord Mayor, can you please explain to me how you dare refuse to quarter the king's troops in your town as is our right by Aenglish Law?"

The coroner steps right up to field that question. "The king's authority has been abused too often throughout his realms. Law-abiding subjects of the Aenglish Crown cannot be forced to quarter troops without their consent. If we let several thousand armed men run loose in this city, they will begin breaking into homes, roasting chickens and pigs for a midnight snack, taking advantage of the womenfolk, and roughing up anyone who stands in their way.

"Before you attacked this Aenglish city, we offered to ask for volunteers and assign your troops quarters, one by one, in an orderly manner."

"Poppycock! You know full well that we'd never be able to house all my troops if we ask for volunteers."

"Aenglish Law is clear. Maybe you were hoping to find a lawyer's excuse to add Ithica to your conquests?"

"Bah! I don't give a goose quill for lawyers. I act in the king's interest. My troops have had a long march.

Many are sick. If they are forced to spend the night in the cold and rain, we won't make it to New Yourke—I mean, New Amsturldam—with sufficient forces."

"New Amsturldam has already been conquered and as far as I know, Count Richard Nicolas intends to rename it New Lancaster. Your little slip of the tongue piques my curiosity. You say you're hoping to bring sufficient forces to . . . overthrow Count Nicolas, perhaps, and rename the city New Yourke instead?"

Without batting an eyelash, Amhirst deflects the mayor's accurate accusations in a masterful way. "Regrettably, Count Nicolas had a very unfortunate and untimely accident at sea. Sufficient troops will be necessary to restore order in the absence of his leadership since the Viking population is restive and on the edge of rebellion. Only a firm and steady hand will avert more bloodshed.

"From what I hear, the acting governor, Sir Samuel Maverick, has some . . . shall we say, 'unorthodox' methods for dealing with dissent. The situation is grave, and I need to get to the scene quickly and with my troops healthy enough to deal with it."

"Dire situation indeed. Please show us the king's orders appointing you mayor of New Amsturldam."

"The crisis is too new, but I assure you—"

The coroner cuts him off mid-sentence with a raised hand. "Yes, yes, I've heard it all. What we have here is a clear case of yet another power-hungry noble abusing the Crown's authority to trample the rights of the king's loyal subjects. Attacking a town loyal to the king is either an act of treason or rebellion. The punishment for both is death. Do you deny the charges?"

The coroner stares straight into the eyes of the baron of Amhirst, clearly hoping to provoke him to act rashly. The baron of Amhirst does not flinch, but calmly takes stock of the situation. He realizes every man at this table hopes for his death except one—the inquisitor.

"You know, politics is never a good conversation topic at the dinner table." With a show of respect, Amhirst turns toward Inquisitor Sheen. "What we should be discussing is the soundness of our religion in Vinland. Can you tell me now, Reverend Inquisitor Sheen, about this Blackflame Heresy and how I, as a loyal son of Holy Mother the Church, can help extirpate this threat to the faith in Vinland?"

Inquisitor Sheen is happy to oblige. He explains, "Fire promotes warmth, light, and life—all symbols of God's goodness. Heretics go around sputtering on about this new discovery they call blackflame, but it is contrary to nature—it chills, hides, and kills. The Cathars in Europa preached a religion where the soul is good and the body is bad."

"Oh, do tell. I know so little about these Cathars."

"The Cathars take their name from the Graec word for pure, *katharos,* but the Graecs are too orthodox to call them pure so they call them *vrykolakas* instead."

The baron of Amhirst, not much of a theologian, puts on a serious face and nods as if he agrees. "*Piña coladas* . . . *daiquiris* . . . it's all Graec to me. But I can tell that this is all so very serious. We must do something!"

"Indeed," replies the inquisitor. "They finally developed a spiritual technology whereby they are able to purify their own souls from their bodies in this life. They use the blackflame to accomplish this."

Amhirst's eyes widen with comprehension. "So basically, you are telling me that they want to be dead."

Inquisitor Sheen lifts a finger in the air. "Oh no! Not dead . . . undead!"

The baron of Amhirst rubs his chin pensively as he speaks. "You know, dear Father Inquisitor, that my sword has always been at the service of Holy Mother the Church, but these worldly men around us seem bent upon my destruction. If only the Holy Office of the Inquisition could assert its influence in this matter, you would find in me a worthy champion to combat this Blackflame Heresy."

The coroner and the mayor seethe at Amhirst's attempt to undermine their authority through the Church. Seeing the consternation on the faces of the powerful men around the table, Inquisitor Sheen proceeds cautiously and wisely. "As an inquisitor of the Holy Church of Roma, I have no jurisdiction over secular matters here . . ."

The captain of the gate tower guard snickers with glee at that last comment and makes a gesture as if tightening a noose around his neck, then points to Amhirst. They all look at him with irritation over his indiscretion. The captain fakes a burp, puts a fist over his mouth, and mutters, "Excuse me."

The inquisitor continues. "If you should confess your sins, as a priest, I have Christ's authority to absolve you of them. That would not interfere with any punishment the civil authorities might impose."

Amhirst knows there is a way out. "But . . ."

"But," continues the inquisitor. "If you take up the cross against the Blackflame Heresy as a Crusader, it would grant you a plenary indulgence from all temporal and spiritual punishments due to those sins—including the death penalty."

Trying to repress a smile, the baron of Amhirst lifts his eyebrows in a show of theatrical piety and hopes on his life that the inquisitor will go with it. "Yes, a plenary indulgence is just what my soul needs about now. I confess that I have greatly sinned and I sincerely repent of it all. Before you all, I take up the cross and the Crusader's vow to never return home until the Blackflame Heresy is wiped from the face of Vinland."

The inquisitor holds up his hand to restrain the baron's enthusiasm. "The efforts of valiant Crusaders over the past two centuries have been stifled by insincere oath-takers and weak-willed Christians. Before agreeing to bestow upon you the Crusader's cross, I must put your resolve to the test.

"An informant has tipped me off that a heretic is currently visiting the fire elf community at Tuscoraura Mountain. He goes by the name of Johnny Appleseed."

All the notables in the room gasp. Mayor Ulysses exclaims, "But he's such a kindly old man!"

The inquisitor raises his hand to silence the objectors. "We have many undeniable reports of crazed, undead wendigos infesting the forests around Tuscoraura Mountain. Wendigos arise from blackflame rituals, and Johnny Appleseed is handing out blackflame wherever he goes. He must be stopped!"

Inquisitor Sheen gives out harsh looks. "Not a single one of you gentlemen sitting around this table feels he has the time, money, or manpower to escort me safely through the goblin king's territories between here and Tuscoraura Mountain to investigate. I declare by the authority that Holy Mother the Church has invested in me that if the baron of Amhirst can provide suitable soldiers to escort me safely to Tuscoraura Mountain with haste, I will grant him the Crusader's cross and a plenary indulgence, exempting him from any of the punishments you may have had in mind for him. We must reach Tuscoraura Mountain before Appleseed eludes our grasp once again."

A cunning grin returns to the gate tower captain and he says, "That goblin king, Gog the Destroyer, ain't much of a king, but boy, he's got the 'destroyer' part down all right. Waren't a single goblin who took a liking to Gog in them Magog forests but they's all scared witless of him. Them goblins ain't happy until they got some sicko as king who whips the snot out of 'em day and night.

"Mark my words, you go traipsin' through them irreverent lands with a man of God and you's invitin' a right ugly death. Ain't no army going to save you. I betcha, they ain't enough miracles in the Bible to get y'all there and back again alive."

The inquisitor is unfazed. "Miracles, my dear captain, are God's calling cards. As a man of God, I deal in them every day."

The tough captain chokes out a cynical laugh. "Like I says, sorry I's got to be the one to break the bad news to ya, but miracles ain't good enough—not when it comes to Gog and his Magog goblins."

A loud bang at the door startles the gathering. The captain of the guards races to the door to check out the disturbance. No sooner does he touch the door than it breaks off its hinges and crashes into the captain's face. Sir John Henry, a heavily muscled ranger of Aphrican origins, slams the door clear off its jambs with his massive wooden mallet. He steps inside the room, and more leather-armored rangers flood in behind him.

Master Cornwell quickly lifts a lodestone rod from under his robes to ward off the invaders but his sorcery only sends the steel blades and mail on the Ithica town guards flying backward. The rangers have no steel on them—being clad in leather armor and brandishing wooden mallets, clubs, quarterstaves, and bows with bone or silver-tipped arrows. Having experienced the mayhem caused by three hundred budding sorcerers at the walls, Sir Robert Roger and his rangers are a little worse for wear, but all the wiser.

The brawny ranger Sir Jim Bowey holds a large silver knife, whose sleek design would later become the pattern for his famous line of Bowey knives. Neither source stones nor magica wands have any effect on silver but somehow, silver has a devastating effect upon the undead. Sir Jim Bowey was not the first to discover this, but the silver war knives he would go on to craft after his retirement from adventuring have since become extremely popular with young adventurers.

Capitalizing on the element of surprise and taking full advantage of the agility their light armor affords them, the rangers quickly surround and knock out of the fight any remaining town guards. The Erinish bard among the rangers, Sir Gilbert Sullivan, skilled in *bataireacht,* and hefting a huge blackthorn shillelagh, pounces on Chancellor Cornwell and his battlesage bodyguards, knocking the lodestone rod from the chancellor's hand and kicking the other two over. "Now don't be makin' a fuss, gentlemen. Methinks it wouldn't sit well with the missus to hear that I knocked about such noble bollixes as yourselves."

The mayor and the coroner hardly get a chance to stand up and spin their heads around the room before they find their hands tied behind their backs. Sir Robert Roger shoves them back into their seats and hovers over them menacingly. "Thank you for the warm welcome, Mister Mayor and Honorable Sir Coroner, but I know you have other guests coming. The baron and my boys are sick and tired of crashing parties."

The mayor cries out, "How did you manage to get in here? The only way in is through Easy Street, and I've posted more guards there than along all the other roads in Ithica combined!"

Sir Robert Roger points out the back window. "The road to Easy Street goes through the sewer."

Amhirst twirls his fingers gracefully in the air. "But wait, my valiant ranger captain! The mayor and I have just come to an agreement. You and your company of rangers are about to become the secular arm of the Holy Inquisition to root out the Blackflame Heresy from Vinland."

"Why would setting a different color fire make someone a heretic?" Sir Robert Roger asks, still trying to process why the baron is trying to call off this overwhelmingly successful rescue mission.

"Permit me to explain," interrupts Inquisitor Sheen. "The Tuscoraura elves were using blackflame to dabble in necromancy. Their goal was to raise up an army of obedient thralls. Instead, they reanimated crazed, blood-thirsty undead wights called wendigos who hate life in every form. They kill trees, animals, and innocent travelers. The Holy Office of the Inquisition took all sources of blackflame from the elves to stop them but Johnny Appleseed seems to be offering them a new source of it. He must be arrested and questioned before the elves return to necromancy and stir up any more unnatural troubles in the heart of Vinland."

Sir Robert Roger still cannot believe it. "Why would such a nice old man have so sinister intentions?"

"Under the guise of seeking reform, he has shaken the Church in Vinland to its foundations, claiming to build a New Church. What arrogance and pride! We suspect that he has already seduced the famous archbishop of Fort Detroit to his ways, and he must be stopped before any more important ecclesiastical figures are led astray."

The baron of Amhirst puts on a piteous frown. "This is a grave threat indeed! I put my troops at your disposition, Holy Inquisitor. But alas! A great many of them lie out in the roads and fields around Ithica, exposed to the rain and chill. They are cold, tired, sick, and wounded. If only we could find suitable housing from the elements! Surely then I could spare these dauntless rangers to do God's work."

Inquisitor Sheen announces to the edgy men around him, "David entered the house of God, and he and his companions ate the consecrated bread, which was not lawful for them to do, but only for the priests.

"Vow to send these rangers of yours to Tuscoraura Mountain and I will have the respective rectors open Holy Savior Benedictine Monastery and the Church of the Annunciation to house your troops—after we repose the Blessed Sacrament to a secure location, of course. Your troops will receive protection from the elements, warm soup, and fresh blankets. The monks and clerics will tend to the sick and wounded."

With almost child-like glee, the baron of Amhirst says, "God has answered our prayer for deliverance! Sir Robert Roger, take your rangers to protect Inquisitor Sheen all the way to Tuscoraura Mountain and back."

The coroner interrupts the jubilation of the moment, saying, "One month, Lord Amhirst! If your rangers fail to show up here in one month, we will have the right to nullify your crusading vow—and send your head to the chopping block."

Inquisitor Sheen stomps his foot impatiently. "Enough bickering! The heretic Johnny Appleseed has slipped through our fingers too many times. We will leave at first light in the morning. Rangers, are you ready to take up the cross?"

Sir William McIntosh swipes an apple off the table and tells the baron, "You know, no one could stop us if we decided to just uptail with the wind and blow out of here scot-free."

The baron of Amhirst is having none of it. "I gladly submit to imprisonment at the hands of these men. The delays I face in reaching New Yourke—um, New Amsturldam—are trifling compared to the blessing of having the Holy Inquisition as an ally."

Scene 7: Mere Magiculture

Reflecting Pool at Thor's Base, Shentalpee City
Frige's Day Evening, 24th of March, 1283
Eve of the Feast of the Annunciation (New Year's Eve)

A harmonious female voice in concert with her harp resonates high on Tuscoraura Mountain with a purity and range that would make the best practitioners of Celtic music tear up with awe at its beauty. Sighing elves listen and watch as Zena treads lightly across the aromatic pine boards in her flowing, white evening gown toward the colony's only magica tree.

Sprouting from a large, ornate ceramic pot, the magica tree sits in the middle of a reflecting pool wide enough that no one can approach within ten feet of the tree without climbing into the pool. Its stem is dark blue and the innermost leaves are a lush green. As the branches unfurl farther from the stem, the leaves yellow out a little until they start blending into a Halloween orange. The outermost leaves are bright red with violet tips, like fireworks. Hanging beneath the most mature branches are tiny golden fruit buds.

Five feet above the magica tree, an aqueduct curves past the colossal statue of Thor that overlooks the outdoor theater. Cool, clear mineral water springs from the heart of Tuscoraura Mountain and cascades down the aqueduct into the reflecting pool. A rainbow weaves in and out of the mist as it showers the pool with its glowing crystal droplets.

With a gentle, graceful motion, Zena steps up onto the ledge of the pool, singing and playing the harp.

Her music finds the melody that stirs a long-lost dream in Johnny Appleseed's heart. Maybe it was his first love, his awkward eloquence in chasing her with a frog, and her rambunctious innocence in making him kiss it that left such a fond but forgotten memory. Or perhaps it was the day God the Father first lifted his soul up to the seventh heaven and locked inside it the sure faith that good will overcome evil in the end.

Whatever it is that holds him, Dungaree Jeanne's words bring him out of the nostalgic trance. "My dear Zena's teenage years have been bumpy, but she has a good heart and it comes through in her voice. The songs she sings are ancient elf lullabies preserved in our tradition from mother to child, but she breathes a minty freshness into them by her heartfelt passion to cherish the gifts of nature and to use them for the good of all."

Johnny Appleseed feels some culture shock when he sees Zena descend into the reflecting pool, wading her way toward the magica tree. He agrees, saying, "As we say in Kentikie, her voice could soften a hardened criminal's liver like a wad of butter on a hot griddle. Still, that's the first time I have seen a girl in her right mind go sloshing around in a public fountain pool without any sergeants trying to arrest her."

"She has a license to tame the magica tree. Any gruff move or threatening stance toward it makes the tree vanish. A gentle gait, calm demeanor, and soothing presence can get a person close enough to cull one of the branches before it disappears. Mage Nittany, the dean of Pinne Mage University, has witnessed Mademoiselle Zena touch this same magica tree before. She will come back in a few weeks to observe her.

"If Mademoiselle Zena successfully cuts off a magica branch, then Mage Nittany will help her turn it into a magica wand and allow her to start her apprenticeship as a freshman magicultor at Pinne Mage University."

"Good for her. My, my, look how that aqueduct spits out its waters so high above the pool! Every time the wind blows, it drizzles all over the platform."

An immensely proud mother, Dungaree Jeanne cannot help telling him everything she knows about magiculture, even though she has an inkling that Johnny Appleseed might know more about magica trees than he's letting on. "Magica trees only grow beneath waterfalls because they need the rainbow light refracted through the spray. That's why you see all those glass prisms dangling from the sides of the aquifer. Taste and see how refreshing this water is."

Dungaree Jeanne picks up a cup off a small stand with twenty or so white ceramic cups on black iron ring holders around the center staff, making it look like a little black-and-white Christmas tree. She scoops some spring water up to the brim and hands it to Appleseed.

The good reverend takes a sip and smiles with a gleam in his eyes. "Mmmm. 'Whosoever shall give you a cup of water to drink in my name,' Christ says, 'she shall not lose her reward.' I am deeply honored that you invited me and most grateful for your kindness to me. May the Lord bless you and your family."

Out of the corner of her eye, she spots a group of rowdy teenagers gathered around the umpire-in-chief. "I fear our Council of Perfects was more open to your gift of blackflame than to hearing you preach God's word. They're very hostile towards Christianity."

"Saint Paul built tents so he could work and live among those who were not open to hearing God's word. I give out apples and blackflame so every corner of Vinland can hear the good news."

Staring absently at them for a brief moment, Dungaree Jeanne sees Enganyon wearing crutches with a big cast around his foot. He nods to Umpire Kibbler and then starts moving toward them with a purpose, followed by a dozen or more other high elf teenagers.

Dungaree Jeanne instantly snaps out of her trance. "Reverend Appleseed! Permit me to take you on a walking tour of our beautiful city before dinner. It will help you work up an appetite and will leave you with some fond memories to cherish. We get a lot of honeymooners visiting here. They call Tuscoraura's treetop colony the Venice of the Skies."

Reverend Johnny Appleseed thinks about that last statement for a moment. "Venison pies? None for me, thank you. Sounds delicious, but I don't eat deer."

Dungaree Jeanne stops and thinks for a moment. "Oh! Not at all! We don't eat deer either. Deer are sacred in our culture since we ride them."

Johnny Appleseed asks, "Are there many vegetarians in Shentalpee City?"

As Enganyon's teens get closer, her danger instincts set off alarms ringing out loud in every corner of her skull. She drags Reverend Appleseed off in the opposite direction and comments, "Some high elves do refrain from eating meat entirely, but most are out for blood."

Hiding from the teens in the crowd would be useless given the shiny tin pot rising about a foot and a half above the sea of shoppers, but the tight spacing breaks up the teenagers' little clique. Having no one nearby to impress, the isolated teens lose their mischievous grins and get distracted by the vendors dangling shiny silver wires, red sealing wax, and other fancy baubles before their eyes.

The tall wooden basilica is saliently visible from every angle of the colony. The roof is a marvel of engineering, with tens of thousands of little twigs tightly bound together to waterproof the edifice. Giant tin rings clasp the flying buttresses, bracing them like mystical dragons frolicking about the main columns. They are elegantly carved to lean back as if taking in a breath to puff a stream of fire against the trellised walls, but they are cleverly positioned so they are actually propping up the basilica with their painted wings.

Reverend Appleseed looks up at the huge wooden building in awe. "Is this a church?"

"Not unless money is your god. The huge building is what we call a *vasilika* in Eldric, our native fire elf language, meaning that it is designed like an old Roman tribunal chamber. When you say *basilica* in Aenglish, you mean a church. There are some similarities. For example, we observe a respectful silence inside, almost like a church. To keep trade civilized, the merchants inside the basilica are not allowed to talk to customers unless the customer goes into their booth and asks about an item.

"A few of us single moms used to call this basilica 'the outlet' because we could bring our elflings here to run around and let out all their energy before settling them for bed and the merchants couldn't say anything to stop us.

"Inside, the merchants have so many restrictions and pay so many rents and taxes that you will only find high-end, top-quality handcrafts and wares there. If you want a bargain, you have to cruise through these makeshift tents over here or visit one of those dinky stalls over there. They've got food stands everywhere in between. There are no restrictions on how the merchants approach customers so over the years, Malarkey Plaza has become an aggressive open-air market. We just call it 'the mall' for short.

"We can go in to get an ear full of malarkey, just to get a genuine Tuscoraura elf experience if you'd like."

"Thank you kindly, ma'am, but all that caterwauling and hullabaloo gives me a headache. I think I'll need a rest." He starts to sit down on a long wooden structure that looks like a bench.

"Wait! Don't sit there. We call that the perimeter. These balustraded railings mark the edge of Thor's Base. Each baluster is masterfully carved with a scene from our *eldralfar* folklore, so it's sacred. You're not supposed to touch them. We can sit in the amphitheater if you'd like a break from the noise."

Like a wooden Colosseum, the amphitheater's tall wooden walls wrap about three-quarters of the way around the central stage, to leave open a view of the colossal copper statue of Thor's Hammer. All around lacquered wooden carvings depict elven folkloric scenes in low relief.

Appleseed asks, "What does el-dandruffer mean?"

"*Eldur* is our word for fire so we call our dialect of the light elvish languages *Eldric*. The word *alfar* means elves. We call ourselves fire elves, *eldralfar*. All the different tribes of light elves have their own dialect—the cliff elves speak *Klipsk,* the murk elves speak *Dusternish,* the sea elves speak *Nissic,* and so on. The educated high elves among them all speak Runic."

"So why was Umpire Kibbler giving his speech in Runic if everyone speaks Eldric?"

"It's more universal. All light elves—cliff elves, murk elves, sea elves, forest elves, and so forth—learn it. Runic, in fact, is not a language in itself, but rather a class of languages that rely on the Futhark alphabet with elvish, dwarvish, and human varieties. Among humans, Latin has overtaken Runic in the north of Europa as the language of education, but light elves and whaler dwarves still use Runic. The Runic word for fire is *shenta,* and *alpee* is the word for elves. We call our home *Shentalpee Vorsche* in Runic or Fire Elf City.

Johnny Appleseed fingers through his voluminous gray beard, taking it all in. "Fascinating! What does this one here mean? Looks like a big rabbit got his tail caught on fire."

"This one tells the story about where fire elves came from. That big rabbit you are pointing to is actually the fire giant god Halogi. Many centuries ago, the fire elves inhabited a hollow mountain named Mount Ragnarök, in Alfheim. Molten rocks at the bottom kept it warm all year round and the cliffs were so sheer and steep inside that no one could attack us.

"The fire elves hired dwarves to carve tunnels and chambers inside those cliffs and living there was quite luxurious—for over five hundred years, the fire elves did not suffer a single raid from an outside invader.

"Our ancestors knew Mount Ragnarök was a volcano but assumed it was dormant. You know what they say about making assumptions. Anyway, it began spewing toxins and miasma into their city and brought about the end of the world as they knew it.

"Many of the survivors formed the first major wave of emigration from Nordland to Vinland. Even though many fire elf colonies have scattered across Vinland over the past two and a half centuries, they all see themselves as here only temporarily. When Mount Ragnarök is deemed safe once again, they believe they will return."

Although it is only the end of March, the evening is quite warm and the tin pot on his head doesn't help. Johnny Appleseed, though seated on a bench, wipes the sweat from his forehead.

Dungaree Jeanne, a considerate host, takes notice and says, "You must be so thirsty. Let me treat you to some elderberry juice at the garden patio. We have a restaurant there called the Gazebo. Everything is fresh squeezed and mixed with pure ingredients. I know you'd love it."

"Oh, thank you kindly. Don't mind if I do."

In the garden patio restaurant, the elven architecture strikes the eye with the same grandeur as the forbidden city of the Chinese Son of Heaven. Their wooden pavilions curve with the grace of an imperial pagoda and are decorated with luminescent silk banners like flying red, white, and blue lanterns.

Dungaree Jeanne shows him to an empty round table in the garden and invites him to sit under the ornate wooden awning. A gnome waiter approaches and she orders a round of elderberry juice fruit cups. "The gardens have covered pavilions next to the aquifer that we call *gyosebo* in Eldric, from the word 'gyose,' which is like your Aenglish word *gush*. We call this garden Falling Water. The aquifer is the lifeblood of our colony and each time we drink, we drink to the prosperity and good health that it brings.

"The pavilions are owned by the state, but a very wealthy Jewish wood elf leases the entire garden for his Gazebo restaurant. We can eat at these open air tables or go under the pavilions if it rains."

Johnny Appleseed gives her a cheeky grin and comments, "So these gazebos are actually restaurants offering refuge against both inclement weather and the midmorning munchies."

"And against loneliness. We often come here with friends to enjoy each other's company and the scenery."

Johnny Appleseed sits back and says, "My, my, this is a lovely place to soak in the view of the beautiful forests and mountains you have here."

The drinks arrive. The gnome waiter puts both cups in front of her and awaits payment. Dungaree Jeanne gives him a coin and slides one of the drinks over to Johnny Appleseed and points behind him. "Yes, and the single ladies enjoy the view over that way."

Johnny Appleseed turns around and blushes. Behind him, in a large military drilling square, dozens of muscular elves are training intensely with their shirts off. Their arms have that wiry strength of acrobats, and the constant exercise keeps their abs and pecs sharp and chiseled, like marble statues. Some are sparring with wooden swords, quarterstaves, and bare fists, but most of them are getting in a sweaty workout with intense calisthenics led by an instructor who seems to enjoy showing off his extreme physical fitness.

Hatchoo!

"Gezondhide!" Dungaree winks and downs her elderberry juice.

Johnny Appleseed takes a deep breath of clean mountain breeze. Together they sit there sipping and commenting and looking around for quite some time. Thor's Base is a work of art in itself. One tree is much stouter than the others. At its crest emerges a colossal statue of Thor himself, stretching out his mighty hammer as if to call down lightning from the sky and assume its power.

He points to the statue and asks, "Is that why you call it Thor's Base?"

Dungaree Jeanne looks behind her and replies, "Yes. The fire elves honor seven patron gods, one for each giant sequoia—Sun—Moon—Tiw—Woden—Thor—Frige—and Saturn. But the greatest of these is Thor, and the tree dedicated to the god of thunder towers over the rest. The statue is green from tarnished copper, carried by boat from mines in Nordland.

"In fact, every tree line elf colony has a copper statue dedicated to Thor's hammer at its highest point. They say that the gods are jealous of high elves who live too close to the sky and will strike them down with lightning. Thor's Hammer supposedly protects us from lightning, but that's all superstition. It's just the Council of Perfects using religion to maintain symbolic control over society."

Reverend Appleseed covers his mouth as if apologetic for contradicting her. "It seems there is some wisdom in it. Lightning tends to strike the highest tree in the forest or the tallest mountain peak in the range. While it is true that some ambitious or greedy people use the face of religion to mask their evil deeds, more often religion just lays out clearly the laws of nature that are too dangerous to be ignored."

Dungaree Jeanne says, "Perhaps that is true. High elves are rather hostile toward religion, so we rarely discuss such issues. Ah! Here comes Mademoiselle Zena now."

Having touched her magica tree, Zena emerges from the pool with her long, flowing, white robe dripping wet but carrying a huge, cheerful smile. She comes over to the Gazebo and says in her less polished Aenglish, "You see me, Reverend Appleseed? I touch magica tree long time. Soon I am made apprentice for magica school at Pinne Mage University."

Johnny Appleseed gives her an encouraging clap and says, "Congratulations! I heard Mage Nittany is very excited to have you as her pupil."

"You know Mage Nittany?"

"I have spent my entire life in these forests. Each tree is like family to me. Mage Nittany jokingly calls me a tree hugger. She comes to me with questions about magica trees growing in the wild."

"Where are the wild magica trees?"

"Oh that's a secret I've got to keep for your own safety. Some bad folk out there wouldn't think twice about hurting a lovely young lady such as yourself to get their hands on a magica grove. They'd just chop it down like lumber and sell it off for a handful of beans."

"Beans?"

"Figure of speech. They don't understand the value of those trees. By the way, you can't keep the blackflame under Thor's statue like that."

Dungaree Jeanne explains, "Excuse me, Reverend Appleseed, but once the umpire-in-chief dedicates a gift to Thor, it is considered sacrilege to remove it. The punishment for sacrilege is death."

Zena adds, "Thor is not your god, but you must respect that he is our god."

"Yeah, yeah, I get it but listen to me. Blackflame absorbs light. If you keep the blackflame brazier so close to the magica tree, you'll starve that rainbow right out of the waterfall. Without rainbow light your dreams for becoming a magicultor at Pinne Mage University will all black out."

Zena covers her mouth and gasps, "Oh no! Maybe Monsieur Enganyon will know what to do!" She runs off in a panic.

Johnny Appleseed asks, "Who is Enganyon?"

Dungaree Jeanne rolls her eyes, then looks down with a sad face. "A cocky teenager from an old and powerful high elf family. She thinks that making him her boyfriend will add both excitement to her life and prestige to her campaign for umpire-in-chief. Zena doesn't know what she is getting into."

"What exactly *is* she getting into, if you don't mind my asking?"

"For one thing, she's repeating history. I wanted to marry the Monsieur Enganyon's father and in the end, despite all his promises, he left me for an elve of higher standing. She was the daughter of the umpire-in-chief at the time so I guess I can't blame him for wanting to attach himself to a powerful family but at the time it hurt me deeply."

"I'm sorry. It sounds like a bitter experience."

"Bitter? Me? Not at all! The elf I ended up marrying was quite a catch. My marriage to her father was a happy one. I tell Zena that I felt like a sun-burnt elve who wasted days and weeks fishing for a tiny catfish from a small boat before suddenly realizing I had caught a whopper of a trout. He loved me all along."

"That's good to hear."

"Or rather, when you struggle so hard to reel in a scrawny, scum-sucking low-life, the whole ordeal becomes rewarding when you see him salted and roasted alive on an open spit. The umpire-in-chief's daughter was a termagant and she made him suffer her obnoxious personality day in and day out until he finally came to me in tears sorry that he left me."

"Nope. Not bitter at all."

"It ended bitterly. My husband saw the Monsieur Enganyon's father crying on my knees and suspected foul play so he challenged him to a duel. My husband was a brilliant swordself so Engany cheated in the duel. He poisoned my husband before the duel began. The Council of Perfects declared my husband the winner after his death but for a young widow with a baby girl who was never going to see her father, it wasn't much of a consolation."

Johnny Appleseed gives her a compassionate nudge. "Believe me when I tell you from personal experience that God makes himself the best Father a child could ever need when we invite him into our hearts with child-like trust and simplicity of heart."

"Yes, I believe it. But Zena never invited God into her life so her heart is very empty right now. She is trying to fill it with a powerful boyfriend and an even more powerful position in our government. Our current umpire-in-chief here at Shentalpee City will have his term expire by midsummer and he is campaigning to have his daughter, the Mademoiselle Florenz, elected in his place. Normally, my dear Zena would have no chance at going up against such a powerful family, but the Mademoiselle Florenz has a darker complexion."

"What does that have to do with anything?"

Dungaree Jeanne waves her hand slowly as she speaks. "You know high elves judge people by their looks, and among elves, the fashion gurus insist that fairer skin allows you to wear more striking colors. It is all a smokescreen for a deep-seated insecurity.

"In any event, my daughter thinks she has a chance of getting elected umpire-in-chief at seventeen years old because Florenz's mother was from the *dökkálfar*—dark elves—and many fire elves are too stubborn to vote for an elve with dark ancestry.

"Delusions of grandeur. The way politics work here, Zena has no chance of defeating Florenz in an election for Dancing Queen at her high school prom much less for chief of state over Shentalpee City."

"What is a high school prom?"

"Oh, just another silly elf tradition. Elves are always looking for an excuse to throw a party."

As they talk, Enganyon's teenagers start to gather behind them with mischief written all over their faces. Dungaree Jeanne hides her alarm but she knows they are up to no good. She yanks Johnny Appleseed by the collar, adding, "And elves seem to find ways to crash a party too. Come on! Let me show you a special place to watch the sunset like you've never seen it before—away from prying eyes."

They walk quickly and take frequent turns until they lose sight of Enganyon's gang of teens.

Glittering in her misty-moon blue, diamond-studded evening gown, Dungaree Jeanne strides out across a suspension bridge away from Thor's Base. Even as the suspension bridge wobbles under her brisk steps, her gait and upright posture never waver.

Neither rushed nor hesitating, her hips sway on high heels that tread lightly and decisively on the wood planks beneath her. Lesser men would have easily been enchanted by the influence of her unrelenting femininity and fallen on one knee by now to profess their ardent love, but Johnny Appleseed walks behind her with a cheerful innocence.

She glides up a set of stairs with the stamina of a professional athlete, but Johnny Appleseed does not allow her to outpace him. His highly ambulant lifestyle keeps him firm and fit, even in graying old age.

Johnny Appleseed asks, "Who was the boy on crutches following us?"

Although she's been trying to downplay their evasive maneuvers, Dungaree Jeanne is not entirely surprised that he knows exactly why they've been rushing around in their tour of Shentalpee City.

She sighs. "That was the monsieur Enganyon. He's the son of one of the most powerful high elves in Shentalpee City. My dear Zena and Mademoiselle Florenz have been best of friends for most of their childhood, but between the election and the monsieur Enganyon's charms, they've been at odds lately.

"It's really a shame because my husband died before my dear Zena was born and Umpire Kibbler has been the only father figure she's ever known. He's really encouraged her to follow her dreams."

Johnny Appleseed gives her a compassionate nudge. "Believe me when I tell you from personal experience that God makes himself the best Father a child could ever need when we invite him into our hearts with child-like trust and simplicity."

"Yes, I believe it. But my dear Zena never invited God into her heart so it's very empty right now. She's trying to fill it with a powerful boyfriend and an even more powerful position in our government. She wants whatever she can't have and because of it, I'm afraid she'll lose all the happiness I've worked so hard to provide for her."

"It sounds like you've got a lot weighing on your mind. Hope my visit won't make it any harder on you."

"Do you know what I do when I feel the weight of the world on my shoulders? Come, I will show you."

Dungaree Jeanne walks even faster up a long flight of wooden stairs. When they reach the top, she waltzes across a garden patio and sweeps her right arm across the cityscape below. "Perfect peace abides up here. The sky can never belong to despots. People grovel to the powerful and carry out all manner of atrocities, but one hundred fifty feet above the ground their power ceases, their influence fades, their authority disappears.

"Ah, Reverend, to live in the heart of the sky! Let your imagination soar! Set your fantasies free up here where no one can take you down!"

Johnny Appleseed approaches the ledge and looks at the skyline that sets Dungaree Jeanne's fantasy free.

The glowing, red horizon behind the setting sun lends fascinating hues of pastel yellow, deep blue, and purple majesty to the scene. The evergreen sequoias sprout girders and trestles across one base after another like a skyward paradise floating on clouds. The forest floor is so far down he can't even see it in the dim shadows of the rising moonlight.

As he leans on the elf-sized railing gazing out into the picturesque scenery all around him, the high elf teenagers reconvene behind him. This time they have a large dog with them. They giggle and snicker and set the dog loose on him. The dog's body mass and velocity hold enough momentum to carry Johnny Appleseed over the ledge but the good reverend seems oblivious to the peril.

Dungaree Jeanne hears the heavy thumps of the snarling dog's paws as it barrels toward her guest. She sees the dog about to make Umpire Kibbler's prophecy about tall men falling over low railings come true.

She screams.

Johnny Appleseed's eyes flick over to his screaming friend and follow her panicked gaze to the ferocious dog racing at him. He raises his hands up to the heavens in prayer and the next moment, the dog turns docile, padding up to him at a gentle trot. It starts sniffing his pant legs. Reverend Appleseed pets the friendly animal and it begins to rub its tush up against his knees. The teenagers disappear into the evening twilight.

Dungaree Jeanne stops screaming and swallows hard. Still panting, she asks, "What just happened?"

"Oh, this poor little fellow is just hungry."

"That's not what I saw. I know that dog and he's become quite wild of late. He was about to attack you. With a wave of your hands you calmed him down. Do you have some kind of power over wild beasts?"

"It was just a little miracle. Not to us, O Lord, not to us but to your name give the glory. You could say I'm a Christian druid. I spend a lot of time in the wilderness and often pray the prayer of Daniel in the lions' den. Miracles happen all the time if you have faith enough to notice.

"By the way, you mentioned that you know this dog. What's his name?"

"His name's Fido. He's Old Mother Hubbard's dog. The Hubbard clan was once the wealthiest and most powerful of the high elves at Tuscoraura; now she can't even afford a bone for her dog, so he started going around begging. The high elves don't like stray dogs and treated him roughly. Ever since then the dog has had a mean streak."

Johnny Appleseed rubs the dog's shoulders and chin, asking, "Are there some scraps around here that we can offer our sweet little Fido?"

Dungaree Jeanne finally calms down her breathing and suggests, "Let's head back to the garden party. The Council of Perfects is sponsoring a boar roast on the council chamber's front steps out of the public funds. We could throw him a bone."

Johnny Appleseed shakes his finger at the dog. "Sit here, Fido, and we'll bring you a little treat if you're a good doggie."

Fido sits and wags his tail, licking his lips as if he knows he's won a treat from the tall visitor.

The public festivities to celebrate Appleseed's visit are quite an extravaganza, although the good reverend himself was not specifically invited to the party. To honor their guest's gift of apple seeds, they have placed an apple in the boar's mouth and baked several apple pies. Umpire Kibbler has provided a large number of soft-baked cocoa chunk cookies and spiced chokecherry cider out of his own personal funds. To make the occasion memorable, he has declared the reception dinner open to wood elves as well.

Well-paid, armored dwarves act as elevator operators, courtesy staff, bodyguards, and bouncers all in one, making sure the right people—and only the right people—make it onto Thor's Base without a hitch.

Posh, black-robed halflings with slicked-back, dark, wavy hair and white sashes carry trays with hors d'oeuvres and amuse-gueules, pickled fish eggs, goat hoof paste, and other elven delicacies.

While Dungaree Jeanne asks the caterers to provide her with a spare bone for the dog and a tasty treat for her guest, Johnny Appleseed leans over the edge and takes a deep breath. *Quite a long way down!*

She brings him a spinach quiche pie and he nibbles it gratefully. "Thank you, ma'am. As we say in Kentikie, praise the Lord and pass the gravy."

Dungaree Jeanne tugs his arm. "Come! There's one other place you must see. It's called Worship Base."

After delivering the bone to an effusively grateful Fido, they cross a few more suspension bridges and reach Worship Base. Dungaree Jeanne tells him, "The other twelve bases have only one sacred space each, but Worship Base has several large temples. Over there is the Temple of Saturn, which serves as a hub for trading with passing vendors and traveling merchants. My appointment as Dungaree of Foreign Trade entitles me to a corner office on the second floor.

"That rounded building is the Temple of Bragi, which we call the radial city music hall because of its round shape and the supporting arches that radiate from it. We hold most of our concerts there. Elves are brilliant musicians and my dear daughter, Zena, has perfect pitch, so she is much sought after even at her young age.

"And down there is the Temple of Astrea, which is an observatory for the stars. Oh, look! The first star is starting to twinkle. Make a wish!" she suggests politely.

"I don't see it." Appleseed points up to the heavens, hoping to locate it. "Is it over yonder somewhere?"

Dungaree Jeanne grimaces. "You're not supposed to point at stars. It's bad luck. Just look.

"See! It's that little star twinkling over there, so high up above the world, like a diamond in the firmament. Astrologers say that starlight is the fifth element—

aether—but Christians say that the stars are angels singing God's praises, isn't that right?"

Johnny Appleseed says, "It's true that when Christ was born in Bethlehem, the angels filled the heavens with light and sang, 'Glory to God in the highest, and on Earth, peace to people of goodwill.' As to what the stars are made of, I can only wonder."

"So did you make a wish?"

"Oh, a guy like me does not get wishes from stars,"

"They say it makes no difference who you are. When you wish upon a star, your dreams come true! What are your dreams?" Dungaree Jeanne prods as if to remind him of an important lesson from his childhood.

"Well, I have a dream that one day every valley shall be exalted, every hill and mountain shall be made low, the rough places will be made plain, and the crooked places will be made straight, and the glory of the Lord shall be revealed, and all flesh shall see it together—humans, elves, dwarves, halflings, goblins, and trolls. We are all sons and daughters of Adam and Eve, and Jesus died for us all, light and dark-skinned, green-skinned and pink."

"Wow! What a noble wish!"

"But come, it's getting late. You're invited to stay at Betzy Rose Mansion, my home, for as long as you wish. It's not far from here."

"Thank you for your hospitality. As a rule, I only stay in one place as long as I'm needed, then I have to move on. My hope is to end hunger and spread the good word to all of Vinland. I'll have to leave bright and early in the morning."

Dungaree Jeanne peers out into the forest one last time. "Then please, take a moment to soak it all in. There's so much beauty around us for just two eyes to see. Oh, if I were a painter I don't know which I'd paint—the calling of the ancient aethereal stars or the assembling of the angels above Bethlehem.

"And see there! The mountains are drifting off to sleep with the innocence of children. What a gorgeous evening!"

Johnny Appleseed looks over the ledge with her. "Boy, we're mighty high up. It makes my head dizzy."

"We call that vertigo," Dungaree Jeanne explains. "Live here long enough and you'll hardly feel it."

Just then, the rowdy group of teenage elves reappears. Though hobbling on crutches Enganyon manages to strut forward, showing off his fancy white tunic and blue denim pants with black boots. His slicked-back, half-braided, platinum-blond hair sparks envy and awe within the gang of teens.

Dungaree Jeanne greets him in Runic to keep it all very formal. "Good evening, Monsieur Enganyon, so nice to see that thou art wearing the blue variety of my denim pantaloons. What brings thee here?"

Balancing on one foot, Enganyon slaps his hip and replies in the common tongue, Eldric, "Yeah, I'm wearing my blue dungaree's for you, Jeanne. Blue is your favorite color, right?"

Dungaree Jeanne maintains her speech in Runic. "Thou shalt address me as Madame Dungaree, young elf. Now, if thou hast no further business with us, please step aside."

Enganyon snickers and says in Eldric, "Me and my buddies here just wanted to personally extend a few words of welcome to your Christian guest. It's very nice of him to give us all that blackflame for free."

She sighs and says with one-half exasperation and the other half sarcasm in Runic, "How courteous of thee! But unfortunately, thou hast never bothered to learn Aenglish."

Enganyon just smirks and hops over to Johnny Appleseed anyway. "No worries, Madame Dungaree," he retorts. "There's always the universal language of friendly gestures." With that, he lurches off his crutches and swings around delivering what is supposed to look like a heartfelt pat on the back but ends up being a hand-whipping whack.

The less-than-gentle blow propels the good reverend forward over the ledge, giving him a truly breathtaking view of the one-hundred-fifty-foot drop as he plummets downward.

Enganyon leans over the railing and mumbles out loud, "Oops, that's gonna hurt—if he survives . . ."

ACT II

WEE WEE WEE
ALL THE WAY HOME

Bonus Scene A: Great Expectations

Betzy Rose Mansion, Red Giant's Base, Shentalpee City
Saturn's Lauds. Dawn, the 25th of March, 1284
Feast of the Annunciation (New Year's Day)

When the morning sun rises amid the cheerful chirping of the chickadees, Zena wakes up in an overly cheerful mood, reliving the memories of Umpire Kibbler's humiliation with relish and replaying in her mind all of Enganyon's bold promises to help her save the magica tree from the blackflame, flagrantly misinterpreting them as professions of love.

Throwing off the covers, she wraps herself in her morning robe and picks her favorite pigeon up out of his loft. She calls him Post. Out of all the carrier pigeons, Post is the only one that seems to like being petted. She gently strokes him as she enters the kitchen, only to ruffle his feathers when she sees that the breakfast table is not set. "Bartlebee!" she calls out. "Where's my breakfast?"

No response.

"Bartlebee! Breakfast!"

Nothing but silence.

"Where'd she go this early in the morning?"

With a huff, Zena takes out the flakes of corn they use for feeding the pigeons, gives some to Post, and then enjoys a bite herself. *Not bad,* she muses. While rummaging through the pantry, she finds some maple syrup to sweeten the bland aftertaste. The halflings of the garden gnome tribe below produce delicious elk milk and fortunately the milk gnome, Granger, delivered it on time this morning.

She shakes a few corn flakes into her pigeon's feeding bowl and then takes out a bowl for herself. Then she pours some maple syrup and elk milk on top of her own corn flakes and tastes them with a spoon. *Hmm . . .* It puts a smile on her face. *Pretty good . . . more than just good, they're . . .*

"Great morning to you, Zena dear!" Her mother interrupts her train of thought.

Zena looks up and says with a wide smile, "Wonderful morning to you too, Jeanne! How's the apple guy doing?"

"Mademoiselle Zena! You may call me Mother or Madame Dungaree, but you will not address me by my given name."

"Oh my knobby knees, Mom, lighten up! Don't you realize that your first name is making your denim products stylish? The high elves are still calling them Dungaree's, but—get this—the wood elves are calling them Jeanne's! You are famous! Monsieur Enganyon and I are congratulating you, not insulting you."

"Mademoiselle Zena, you fancy yourself Monsieur Enganyon's soul mate but you have nothing in common with him except a profound lack of respect for your elders. One of the greatest hardships I have had to endure in life is that, as a single mother, I was so busy with building my business that I have not always been there for you the way I wanted to be. I'm sorry for that. I wish it could have been different. But as for your attitude, there's no excuse. I can't imagine what's gotten into you lately."

"What's gotten into *me* lately? Let's talk about what's gotten into Bartlebee. She's been getting lazier and lazier. Can you believe it? There was no breakfast ready when I got up! So I've been forced to eat Post's cereal for breakfast."

"Who is Post?"

"My favorite messenger pigeon, Mom. Anyway, I tried sweetening them with maple syrup and mixed them right into my elk's milk."

Dungaree Jeanne frowns at the thought of an elf eating animal feed. "Ugh, pigeon corn flakes for breakfast! How do they taste?"

"They're grrreat! Right now, I am actually thinking that manufacturing a quick and tasty breakfast option would be a better business venture with the Monsieur Kellock than using Madame Besom's idea of hazel wood sticks and birch twigs to make brooms. I still think she is a witch and only uses them for flying around. She never actually sweeps up the dust off her front porch anyway."

Dungaree Jeanne rubs her eyes. "Zena dear, please don't waste your meeting with Monsieur Kellock on flaky ideas like that. I worked really hard to find a creative and energetic investor who could help you get your own business on its feet."

"Yeah, and this has been going on for how long? Why can't you just train me into your denim business? I've got fashion ideas that could change the attire outlook for all of Vinland. Think about it—high-rise Jeanne's for urban living, bootcut Jeanne's for pioneers who get their pants ripped on the frontier, relaxed, faded Jeanne's for household comfort. Enganyon is going around telling everyone that he only wears blue Jeanne's. He's a trendsetter, you know. Give it three months and everyone is going to forget that brown or green Jeanne's were ever a thing."

"That's enough out of you, young lady! You're extremely talented, but sometimes I think it's getting to your head. Elbowing your way into my business is reckless and foolish. Dynasties don't work. Period."

Zena cuts in as if they've been agreeing all along. "Case in point: I love the Mademoiselle Florenz, but she'll make a terrible umpire-in-chief. She has no political instincts. Our glorious umpire-in-chief is deluded to foist his dynastic ambitions on her."

Dungaree Jeanne resumes where she left off. "And I'm not going to make the same mistake with you. You are simply not going to waltz in on my denim business with all these ridiculous fashion notions and turn a profit. You have to start from the ground up, like everyone else in the business world, and learn through your own hard-won experience on the job."

Zena puts her corn flakes bowl down and rubs her chin thoughtfully. "Fair point, Mom; but you could always hire me on as a consultant."

Exasperated, Dungaree Jeanne sighs, saying, "Look, Mademoiselle Zena, let's drop it. Right now, I need you to prepare breakfast for the Reverend Appleseed. He's in the guest room and the doctor said his leg is broken. I'm going to go down to the garden gnome shire to hire someone to replace Bartlebee."

"What's the matter with Bartlebee? Did she quit?"

The pounding sound of the huge brass knocker at the front door stops Dungaree Jeanne before she can answer the question. She sighs and heads over to the door to open it. "Who could it possibly be at this hour of the morning?"

Of all the elves in the colony, it's Enganyon. He's standing slick-haired and cocky as ever on the front steps of her mansion at the head of a small crowd of elf teens who seem to have nothing better to do with their lives than follow him around. As soon as she realizes he's there, Zena drops her corn flakes bowl and pigeon and runs upstairs to change out of her morning robe.

A cloth wrap holds together a bundle of wooden splints around Enganyon's left leg and he holds a pair of crutches tucked below his armpits. He says with a smile, "Good morning, Madame Dungaree! I was expecting your stewardess, Bartlebee, to answer the door. No big deal! Someone said the apple guy miraculously survived the fall. I'd like to pay him my respects . . . I mean, a visit."

When Dungaree Jeanne sees the cocky teenager, she snarls, "Oh, my quivering eyelashes, Monsieur Enganyon! What on middle earth did you think you were doing? You could have killed him!"

"It was just a friendly greeting. How's I supposed to know he had vertigo and would topple so easily? Anyway, when I heard the old man's still alive, I hobbled on over here to extend to him a few words of welcome." His toadies laugh as if he were a stand-up comedian.

"Umpire Kibbler already extended to him the customary words of welcome."

"Well then, this would not be the first time that Umpire Kibbler wishes he could trade places with me."

"What on middle earth do you mean by that, young elf?" Dungaree Jeanne asks with suspicion and dread.

Enganyon looks around and snaps his fingers. "You know . . . like have me extending a welcome and have him be the one shoving the old man over the ledge."

His lackeys laugh out loud, pretending they are trying to hide it, but really doing their best to make sure Enganyon notices them.

Dungaree Jeanne is horrified at the treasonous implications of his words, although she knows full well that the umpire threatened to do exactly that. An old hand at politics, Dungaree Jeanne suspects a trap. "How dare you even imply such an accusation, Monsieur Enganyon! Guests are sacred among fire elves! Umpire Kibbler had no intention of harming him and would never wish to trade spots with you."

The teenage arrogance in Enganyon's eyes only redoubles, as if he's had great practice getting mouthy with his elders. "Oh, you should have seen the look in his eye when I took Mademoiselle Zena to the Leif Erikson Ball . . . he was wishing he were me all night long! He-he-he!"

Again, his cronies elbow each other, giggling and snickering out their supposed rebellion. Dungaree Jeanne knows them all quite well and is sure that once they set off for their respective universities, this pretense of being rebellious will drop away to focus on their studies and making their parents proud. Enganyon's rebelliousness, on the other hand, seems much deeper, and his influence on Zena causes her genuine alarm.

Dungaree Jeanne strategically places her hands on her hips akimbo style for full motherly outrage effect. "Remind me to make sure my daughter never makes a mistake like that again."

"Hello, Mother!" interrupts Zena, appearing at the doorway with a playful smile and a wink at Enganyon. She has thrown on some fancier clothes, done her hair up and applied makeup with a speed and precision that would make a pit crew of horse racing squires jealous. "You know, after deep meditation I have come to the conclusion that I've learned so much wisdom from my past mistakes that I ought to make a few more. So please, Monsieur Enganyon, come and be our guest. After all, guests are sacred among fire elves."

Dungaree Jeanne growls at Zena, "Here is some free wisdom for you—a fish would never get hooked if it learned when to keep its mouth shut."

Enganyon is suddenly wearing the face of a lost puppy begging for a place in his new master's heart. "Now that I am your sacred guest, may I see the Reverend Appleseed, Madame Dungaree?"

Seething with anger but unwilling to violate elf hospitality customs, Dungaree Jeanne leads the rebellious teenager, hopping along on his crutches, to the Johnny Appleseed's guestroom.

A part of her sincerely hopes that Enganyon is here to apologize but the rest of her fears that he's more likely here to finish the job. Captain Manzone, as sharp as a cookie that has razor blades baked right into it, sees his boss nod and follows them all in with hands on his sword and dagger.

The creaking door wakes him as it opens and the sleepy missionary greets his visitors with the only elvish words he knows in a big Kentikie-Aenglish accent, "Hale ant sail!"

Dungaree Jeanne reintroduces the young elf in Aenglish. "May you be happy and healthy, Reverend Appleseed. This is Monsieur Enganyon Gandorfson."

Reverend Appleseed gives him a cheerful smile. "Happy to see you! Thank you for your kind visit."

"Maybe you remember that this is the young elf who accidentally knocked you over the platform ledge. He has come to apologize." Dungaree Jeanne then turns to Enganyon and says in Eldric, "What would you like to say to the reverend, Monsieur Enganyon?"

Enganyon smirks and says in Eldric. "Wow! I'm very impressed to hear that you didn't die."

Dungaree Jeanne hems at Enganyon without translating his words to Johnny Appleseed. "That didn't sound like an apology."

Reverend Appleseed sits up in his cramped bed, wincing in pain, and asks, "What did he say?"

With a sigh, Dungaree Jeanne tells the reverend that Enganyon has not apologized quite yet, more just marveling at the miracle that he is still alive.

Johnny Appleseed replies, "Tell him that it says in the Good Book that the Lord shall give his angels charge over you to keep you in all your ways. They shall bear you up in their hands lest you dash your foot against a stone."

"Impressive. Is that from one of your Aenglish poets?" asks Dungaree Jeanne.

Captain Manzone has half a mind to just grab the teenager and twist his arm behind his back until he says something respectful for a change. The only objection from the other half of his mind is that Enganyon is in crutches and would go around Shentalpee City telling everyone it wasn't a fair fight.

"It is from sacred Scripture," Reverend Appleseed replies. He tries to put on a pleasant face but feels the tension in the air and the pain in his leg all too well.

An awkward silence ensues, and Dungaree Jeanne casts Enganyon a withering scowl.

Enganyon finally relents. "Okay, okay, I'm getting to it. Tell him I am sorry and that I am asking his forgiveness for my excessive friendliness." Dungaree Jeanne grits her teeth and delivers a more heartfelt rendition of Enganyon's words in Aenglish.

When he hears the translation, he chuckles merrily with a good Kentikie wheeze. "Tell him the Lord says to forgive your brother not until seven times, but until seventy times seven. That gives him four hundred eighty-nine more attempts to send me flying before I give him a shove of my own, hardy-har-har!"

Hearing the translation, Enganyon grins, then says with a modicum of sincerity, "Your God is mighty to save you. Perhaps you will tell me about more such Christian teachings next time I visit. Right now, I too am suffering from a leg injury and need to rest up a bit before the big tournament coming up soon."

Appleseed concludes with a short sermon. "We serve a God who so loved the world that he gave his only begotten Son to carry our sin and our shame to the cross and grave, so that whosoever believes in him should not perish but have everlasting life. Think about it, and come back tomorrow if the Holy Spirit moves you." Dungaree Jeanne repeats his words to Enganyon.

"I will," the slightly less cocky teenage elf promises with a bow. He then rotates around on his good leg and swings down the corridor nimbly on his crutches without touching the bandaged leg to the floor.

Zena makes as if to follow Enganyon out the door but Dungaree Jeanne snatches her arm with a weary sort of tenderness and says in Aenglish, "Mademoiselle Zena would like to visit with you for a short while since you are our honoured guest. I taught her to speak Aenglish and Gnorrachi, the language of the garden gnomes, as a little girl. She can also read Dwarvish Runic, Nabotean, Avrith, and Latin—surprisingly well, I might add, for one who studies so little . . ."

Johnny Appleseed puts on an air of optimistic cheer for her as well. "Very impressive! On top of all that, your daughter has a mighty fine sense of humor."

Dungaree Jeanne shakes her head. "Humor? My Zena? Are you sure you are not confusing her with another elve girl? They say that to you humans, we elves all look alike."

"No, that's her. She was the one giggling through my whole sermon and handing out earnest money."

Dungaree Jeanne shoots Zena an angry look.

"No harm done—she has a very pretty smile."

Dungaree Jeanne harbors a faint hope that Reverend Appleseed's words might touch her daughter's heart or at least soften her teenage attitude. "My daughter's pretty smile has become a problem of late. Two young elves have grown especially flirtatious with he recently. The first is Monsieur Enganyon Gandorfson of Clan Rashbold, whom you just met. The other is a brilliant and talented wood elf named Mister Lynx Cougarson of Clan Highrune. Perhaps you have some wisdom in matters of love to share."

Reverend Johnny Appleseed humbly replies, "I have no wisdom of my own when it comes to matters of romance. But the word of God says that love is patient. Love is kind. Love is not envious or boastful or arrogant or rude. It does not insist on its own way. It is not irritable or resentful. It does not rejoice in wrongdoing but rejoices in the truth. It bears all things, believes all things, hopes all things, endures all things. True love never ends."

Always eager to talk about her love life, Zena lights up and says in broken Aenglish, "Hmmm. Monsieur Enganyon is more patient, but Mister Lynx is more kind—yes, he is too nice. Perhaps Monsieur Enganyon is arrogant and rude but Mister Lynx can be boastful. So who is having true love?"

Dungaree Jeanne sees her chance. "The good reverend has not yet had the chance to meet Mister Lynx, dear." Turning to Johnny Appleseed she says, "If you please, Reverend Appleseed, I would like to invite him to meet you. To my knowledge, he is the only wood elf on Tuscoraura Mountain who speaks Aenglish as well as Mademoiselle Zena. Though as a wood elf he is of a lower social class, he is very smart, talented, and respectful. He is also a Christian. Would you like Mademoiselle Zena to fetch him for you?"

Zena wheels on her mother and says in Eldric, "But, Mom! I have to meet with my campaign advisors! Many high elves are unhappy that you even invited a Christian missionary but they approve Umpire Kibbler's plan to weaponize the blackflame. This is going to be a crucial time for swinging public opinion back in our favor. They want to roll Umpire Kibbler's shortness into an advertisement about Mademoiselle Florenz's short-sighted policies."

Dungaree Jeanne cannot believe she is hearing this from her daughter. "How shallow can they possibly be? Why would you pick campaign advisors who sound like they barely graduated from middle school?"

"Because middle schoolers have the best feel for the pulse of the colony. That's why they call it middle school—they're right in the middle of everything."

Sensing the conflict, Reverend Appleseed raises his hands and says in Aenglish, "Oh, please, I don't want to inconvenience anybody . . ."

Dungaree Jeanne presses the issue. "No inconvenience at all. Mademoiselle Zena has a political debate with Mademoiselle Florenz coming up and she is just too nervous about it. Running a few errands will help take her mind off it for a while."

Zena folds her arms but Dungaree Jeanne threatens to cut funding and the fight is over before it began. Zena needs the money for her campaign and storms out of the room like a spoiled child pouting.

Reverend Appleseed admits to himself silently that he would not mind the company. The prospect of sitting in a bed with that throbbing pain in his leg all alone for weeks on end makes the thought of an Aenglish-speaking visitor quite a relief. "Thank you for your kindness and consideration. It sounds like Lynx—I mean, Mister Lynx—would be a wiser choice for Zena's future husband than this Monsieur Enganyon."

"Oh, definitely, but I am afraid Mademoiselle Zena is not overly prone to heeding good advice."

"You know, teenage girls almost always feel attracted to the bad boy at first. Their emotions are so passionate, but I know a simple trick to turn it around."

Dungaree Jeanne has been Zena's mom too long to get her hopes up. "If we could bottle it, we'd be rich."

"Someone already did. I am more interested in storing up treasures in heaven. But I'll make sure Zena gets a little sip of wisdom despite herself."

Dungaree Jeanne starts to back out of the room. "You will have to excuse me for now, Reverend Appleseed. I must now go scold Zena for running out of the room without properly taking leave of you."

It turns out that Zena actually went upstairs to her room instead of going out to invite Lynx to visit with Johnny Appleseed. After some heated words that he can hear from downstairs, Zena comes back in and says in Aenglish, "I apologize, Reverend Appleseed, that I did not say excuse me well. Election is soon and I am—how do you say it in Aenglish?—stressed . . . anxious."

"Which election is that, may I ask?"

"Umpire-in-chief of the Tuscoraura Elves."

"You're mighty young for so much responsibility."

"Tuscoraura umpire-in-chief stands first in Council of Perfects and must be most perfect. I am talented, good-looking, and intelligent. It is not me that I want to be umpire-in-chief. Tuscoraura fire elves know that Umpire Kibbler wants his daughter to be umpire-in-chief after him but she is not perfect. Many elves say that I must become umpire-in-chief to save Tuscoraura elves. You say in Latin, *vox populi vox Dei.*"

"No, I'm sorry. What does it mean?"

Zena is surprised that a human cleric would not know Latin . . . unless he is not a real cleric after all. She keeps her doubts to herself and finishes up the conversation with the proper courtesies. "We are democracy. Voters decide their leaders. It is not for Umpire Kibbler to say who is next leader. Thank you for your time. I must beg your pardon and say adieu."

Dungaree Jeanne interrupts, "Oh, my rumbling stomach! We forgot to bring breakfast! Reverend Appleseed must be starving. Mademoiselle Zena, be a good girl and fetch our sacred guest some of that breakfast Bartlebee was supposed to prepare, please."

If it were not for the fact that her campaign needs every penny it can get, Zena would have stormed out of the room again. She swallows her pride and heads down to the kitchen.

While rummaging through the pantry, Zena sees their lazy halfling stewardess moseying around the larder, assembling a splendid meal. Zena quickly calls out in Eldric, "Bartlebee, there you are! So glad to see you are finally preparing breakfast! Mother is in a funk . . . you know how she gets when she hasn't had her wheat ties. I'll take that tray to our guest and you can make another one for me when I get back."

Without any emotion, the gnomid stewardess replies, "This is for myself, mademoiselle."

A little flustered, Zena pretends that the comment was not as rude as it sounded. "Well then, make a bigger one for our guest, quickly. He is so tall; I suppose he eats a lot."

Bartlebee bows curtly. "I would prefer not to." With that, Bartlebee carries her silver tray of food into the stewardess's chambers and closes the door.

Putting her hands on her hips, Zena huffs, "Well, I never! What on middle earth has gotten into her?"

Zena goes charging after Bartlebee and tears open the door to her chambers, but before any more words are exchanged, Dungaree Jeanne intercepts her and points at the clepsydra on the wall. "Oh my pointy ears, look at the time! I'm late for a very important date! Come along now, Mademoiselle Zena! Would you excuse us, dear Bartlebee?"

Bartlebee slouches back into her armchair sipping tea, splattering a few scalding-hot drops onto an expensively bound and newly arrived Nabotean copy of *Le Roman de la Rose*. Zena chokes with horror at the sacrilegious treatment of the book but Dungaree Jeanne whisks her away.

Zena looks at her mother wide-eyed and gasping. Her demeanor and stance say it all. "Are you just going to let her get away with that? Servants need to be put in their place—"

Dungaree Jeanne pulls her daughter by the hand and mutters forcefully in Aenglish so that Bartlebee cannot understand, "Walk with me and tread lightly. Bartlebee knows your little secret, Mademoiselle Zena. If she talks, we'll be ruined!"

Scene 1: Woolly Monastics

Juniata River Bend
Twelve Miles Northwest of Tuscoraura Mountain
Spy Woden's Day Prime
Early Morning, 5th of April, 1284

"Ite missa est," Inquisitor Sheen intones in Latin. His eyes convey sincere piety but also carry a war-weary pluck of worldly pragmatism. Having celebrated Mass on a tree stump, he reads out the psalms from his breviary to three odd-looking friars.

Several rangers who attended the inquisitor's Mass stand up and ready their gear for another day's march. Sir Kip Karlson, the only halfling ranger in the company, remarks to his companions, "First time in my life I get to hear the Bible every day."

"Yeah, almost heaven," replies Dame Frances Marian, the only female ranger in the company. She surveys the area with one hand on her brow. "We'll need all the prayers we can get. See the blue streaks on those mountain ridges across the Juniata River? Those are goblin territorial markings, older than the trees. They'll be lurking behind us soon enough . . ."

Sir Robert Roger did not attend the Mass but comes striding over quickly and barks, "Get ready, Priest; we have a long march ahead of us today."

"Thank you, Sir Ranger. My companions and I will finish reciting the psalms shortly," replies the inquisitor.

Oddly for this epoch, his three companion friars are mismatched in color, but they are all even more oddly mismatched in their backstories. The inquisitor himself is a somewhat tallish dwarf, a hair above five feet tall, conventionally handsome by any standard with a plain but dignified gray beard. His white robes signify membership in the Dominican order of preachers.

His first companion, Brother Umbert, is an unusually short halfling Franciscan friar, a gnome of mixed Lutin and Folletto ancestry, standing barely three and a half feet tall. He wears reddish-brown robes. The halfling serves as the inquisitor's scribe, traveling magicultor, and scholar of ancient lore.

The inquisitor's second companion, Brother Indigo, is a giant from the Mohawk Nation, standing two inches over seven feet high. Missing his right arm and wearing a patch over his right eye, he is dressed in the purplish-gray robes of the Tironensian order. His role as porter technically makes him the spokesman for the group, but his actual job is more eloquently summed up in the bulging muscles on his left arm and the huge club tucked just beneath it.

The inquisitor's third companion, Brother Crowe, is an average-height Aenglish human monk wearing the black robes of the Benedictine order. He serves as the group's cook and bursar. At one time a thief himself, he guards the group's purse from his former colleagues. Brother Crowe's transition from the streets into the monastery was not a smooth one but thanks to patient mentorship, this man's talents now serve the Lord well.

The four clerics of the Inquisition, though different in so many ways, stand together firmly.

Sir Robert Roger fumes. "We don't have time to wait around for you to babble on with your prayers. Goblin wildhunters are lurking in these forests."

Brother Umbert interrupts them. "Excuse me, Sir Robert Roger, but you always seem to rush us when it's time to pray, saying we have to avoid goblins. But I don't think you even know where the goblins are."

Brother Umbert's balding head retains only a thin wisp of bright-red hair that dangles in the middle of his forehead, but it's enough to call him a fiery redhead. Gnomes average about four and a half feet in height but a Folletto, a gnome from the island of Sycilie, normally only reaches about four feet when full-grown. At three and a half feet, one might say that being extra-short among a tribe of extra-short people has added an extra layer of spunk to Brother Umbert's temper.

"Of course I do! Just follow those country roads and they'll be all over you lickety-split." Sir Robert Roger waves his hand off to the south.

Brother Umbert rubs his chin. "Hmm, all my memories tell me we've been heading down those same country roads for the past two days. If I didn't know better, I'd say you're leading us right to them."

Inquisitor Sheen raises his voice. "That's quite enough, Brother Umbert! I am sure the rangers have an adequate defensive plan in place. How many more days before we reach the elf settlement, Sir Ranger?"

"Don't worry, Priest. I'll get you to the place you belong," Sir Robert Roger mutters.

Brother Umbert pipes up again, his face turning red. "You know what I think? I think you have no idea where Tuscoraura Mountain really is!"

Sir Robert Roger shoots back, "The whole point of a hidden elf colony is that it's *hidden*. You don't just walk in the front door over the welcome mat. They know how to keep outsiders out."

"So you keep interrupting our prayers just so you can blow around like a breeze, hoping to stumble upon a hidden elf colony?"

"Brother Umbert, silence!" Inquisitor Sheen cuts him off. Turning to Sir Robert Roger he says calmly, "Sir Ranger, Johnny Appleseed has eluded us time and time again. We are eager to reach Tuscoraura Mountain before he leaves, but prayer is essential to our mission. Please just tell us how you plan to get us to the elf colony without being attacked by goblins?"

Sir Robert Roger shrugs his shoulders. "We'll send out scouts to pinpoint exactly where to head next. It's typical military strategy."

Brother Umbert starts getting personal. "Your knowledge of military strategy is quite shabby if you plan to send your troops out to get hacked apart by goblin lurkers piecemeal."

Sir Robert Roger walks over to him and invades the halfling's personal space with his tall and muscular physique. "For your information, imp, I wrote the book on military strategy for rangers."

Brother Umbert snarls, "Yeah, I know. I read it, and I wasn't impressed."

"You think you're so smart, don't you?"

"Let me put it this way. Have you ever heard of Plato, Aristotle, Socrates?"

Sir Robert Roger narrows his eyes. "You're a moron if you think you're smarter than those guys."

Brother Umbert pushes the tall ranger back. "Well, this moron has read them all in the original Graec. I even reconstructed Aristotle's second book of the *Poetics* from the fragments at a cemetery in Praga."

Inquisitor Sheen steps in sternly. "Whoa! That's quite enough out of you, Brother Umbert. How many times must I echo that warning from the book of Proverbs: pride comes before the fall? Instead of arguing about how smart you are, you should keep a humble silence. We're going to pray for guidance by the Holy Spirit to show us the way."

Sir Robert Roger throws his hands up into the air with outrage. "Oh, come on! This is ridiculous! We don't have time to waste with saying prayers! I am the military professional here and I give the orders."

Inquisitor Sheen shakes his head and calmly replies, "We are not military professionals, so we cannot risk a confrontation with goblins. When your scouts find a safe route to Tuscoraura Mountain, we'll follow your lead. In the meantime, we'll plan on staying here and praying for God to send us guidance."

Sir Robert Roger says, "You go ahead and wait for a miracle. But as for me, I'm going to put my faith in a keen eye and sound military tactics. We'll see who gets us there first."

The inquisitor resumes reading the psalms to his companions while Sir Robert Roger organizes teams of scouts to search for the elf colony.

About an hour after the ranger scouting parties have departed, Inquisitor Sheen sends Brother Indigo, the Mohawk giant in purplish-gray robes, to refill their waterskins at the Juniata River. Once a famous warrior, Brother Indigo lost his right arm and right eye in battle. Lacking depth perception and having to relearn to handle a weapon with his left hand sent him into a deep depression until he turned to prayer. He realized the glory won by following warlords into battle in this life is of little worth compared to the glory of following Christ along the way of the cross into the next.

That spiritual revelation pulled him out of his depression and led him to join the Abbey of Tiron near his home village of Ossernenon. Years later, the abbot received orders from one of the Lord High Papal Inquisitors in Vinland, Maderno Cardinal Orsini, to release Brother Indigo from the abbey to serve as porter for Inquisitor Sheen. Nobody had to guess why the Mohawk monk had been singled out for service.

When he reaches the river, he puts the waterskins down and dips them one by one under the water.

A gray-haired elf strolls up next to him and says, "You don't want to be drinking out of the Juniata River. It's dark and dusty. I can show you some real potable water, blue as if it were painted on the sky."

Without looking up, Brother Indigo says, "I am a stranger to blue water."

The elf kneels down to scoop a handful of water from the river and tastes the water with a big slurp. "Hmmm, told you so. It's got that misty taste of moonshine, so bitter that it puts a teardrop in the eye. How about you give me a few biscuits from your pouch and I'll show you where the sweet water is?"

Ignoring him, Brother Indigo stands up and starts to tie the waterskins together. The hungry old elf tugs on the sleeve of his only arm, begging silently. Brother Indigo asks him, "Can you take us home?"

"And where might home be?"

Brother Indigo says simply, "Home is the place where you belong. We have plenty of food to share."

The gray-haired elf snaps his fingers. "Come to think of it, these mountains remind me that I should have been home yesterday. All I need are a few loaves of bread, a slab or two of meat and some cheese . . . oh, it's been quite a while since I've had any cheese."

Instead of negotiating, Brother Indigo just picks up all four waterskins and walks back to the camp.

The elf takes fright seeing the armed rangers and runs off to climb a tree. Brother Crowe hears the rustling in the trees and spots him immediately. With the excitement of an answered prayer, he points up with his finger and shouts out, "An elf!"

The inquisitor's party follows his finger with their eyes up to the gray-haired elf sitting on the branch of a large elm tree above the rangers' campsite, like a wise old owl ready to offer advice on taking licks at life.

"So you want me to take you to my home?" the elf says in fluent Aenglish with a distinct Elvish accent.

Inquisitor Sheen smiles at him. "Ah, welcome, sir elf! Yes, we are hoping to visit Tuscoraura Mountain."

The elf returns the smile like a merchant used to charming customers. "Tuscoraura Mountain, is it? Your purple-robed giant of a monk asked me about taking him to my home but he never asked me where my home is. As a matter of fact, it is quite a chore to get him to say anything at all."

"The friars on my staff have taken a vow of silence. Brother Indigo is our porter, so he is allowed to offer introductions and extend words of greeting to guests." Giving Brother Umbert a dirty look, the inquisitor adds, "Unfortunately, he is the only one in our brotherhood with a penchant for silence."

The elf snickers. "So he's a one-eyed, one-armed, giant purple people greeter who doesn't like to talk?"

Dame Frances Marian peers over her lunch and sees Inquisitor Sheen talking up into the trees. She spots the elf that managed to sneak past the rangers' lookouts. Alarmed at the security breach, she yells. "To arms!"

Hearing the call, the startled rangers drop their stew and scramble for their weapons. They lick the grease off the tips of their fingers, string their bows, and notch their arrows, pointing them at the elf. Sir Robert Roger is outraged and shouts, "Who let him in?"

Seeing all the fuss and the arrows pointed at him, the elf swings down from the elm tree and hits the ground with amazing agility for his age. He swiftly rolls behind Brother Indigo and begs, "Please, Mister purple people greeter, don't let them shoot me!"

Inquisitor Sheen is quick to respond. "Sir Robert Roger, order your rangers to stand down."

Sir Robert Roger snorts. "It's just a short, pigeon-toed, undergrown elf. He's no threat to us."

The gray-haired elf swaggers and struts over to Sir Robert Roger as if he just won a bout of armed combat. "You're not so tough!"

Seeing trouble brewing, Brother Crowe hurriedly whisks the elf away from the ranger captain and offers him some stew. The elf takes the stew and gobbles it down as if he has not eaten in a week. "Mmm ummm. This sure is some fine eating. But that's not the reason I came down to land in your camp. I can guide this ragtag band of yours to the Tuscoraura elf colony—for a price. Can you pay?"

"Well, bless the Lord my soul!" Inquisitor Sheen proclaims. "You are the answer to our prayers. May I ask your name, kind sir?"

"Master Shoemaker Gulliber Swiffson of Clan Adidazar, at your service. I can guide you to the Tuscoraura elves if you bag up some of this delicious stew for me and my party of adventurers over yonder."

Inquisitor Sheen is more than happy to oblige. "Indeed, this is our bursar and our cook, Brother Crowe. He will pack some up to bring to your friends."

"Much obliged; but what's a bursar?"

An unremarkable man of average build, most people find Brother Crowe's long, jet-black hair greased back and thin goatee more creepy than charming. Even the way he wears his Benedictine robe with its large, black cowl gives off the impression of a shadowy hood rather than a prayer shawl. Some habits die hard.

Inquisitor Sheen explains, "Our vow of poverty requires us to share all our wealth. As our bursar, Brother Crowe carries the communal purse. He handles the money and provisions for our brotherhood."

Master Gulliber squints at the slick-haired bursar with the curly handlebar mustache and the pointy chin puff. "He sure looks strange to me . . ."

Inquisitor Sheen adds, "All the same, he is one of us. You and your party can share our food and we will pay you a fair wage for acting as our guide. Now, can you take us to Tuscoraura Mountain?"

"Well, the Tuscoraura elves are a private people," says Master Gulliber as he gobbles down a second bowl of stew. "Technically, it's against the law to lead an outsider in without a formal invitation from the Council of Perfects. But I think we can work something out. As my wife always says—actually, I hear her voice now, she's calling me. Gentlemen, begging your pardon, but I must take my leave. I'll talk it over with her and let you know our answer in the morning."

Brother Crowe hands him a medieval doggie bag to carry out the stew. Master Gulliber bows and says, "Much obliged, Frater."

To celebrate the miraculous appearance of the elf, Inquisitor Sheen pulls out his rosary beads and invites the company to pray together in thanksgiving to the Lord for hearing their prayers.

Sir Robert Roger interrupts the celebration abruptly. "Okay, Priest, your friar just unwittingly led an elf straight into our camp. We need to tighten up security and implement some new procedures if we are going to make it to Tuscoraura Mountain alive."

Brother Umbert, his face reddening with anger, speaks up instantly. "You just saw how our prayers were answered. Instead of apologizing, you become even more insufferable."

Sir Robert Roger puffs out his chest. "So what about this vow of silence I keep hearing about? How's that working out for you, Brother Umbert?"

Straightening his back, Brother Umbert squeaks out in his nasally, lisping tone, trying to sound assertive, "You are a bully, and I have always made a point of standing up to bullies."

"No wonder it worked! At your height, they must have thought you were kneeling to them."

Inquisitor Sheen intervenes. "Brother Umbert!"

Brother Umbert looks back and forth from Inquisitor Sheen and Sir Robert Roger as if struggling to control his temper when suddenly, his eyes bulge wide open. "Uh, Father Sheen . . ."

"Brother Umbert, I order you to keep silence!"

"But this is an emergency."

"What? You mean you have to relieve yourself in the woods?"

He stutters. "No, too late for that!" As the midsection of his brown robe trickles with a growing dark spot and yellow liquid drips down his legs, his lips quiver and he whimpers, "Goblins! Everywhere!"

Scene 2: The Great Raspberry

Wood Elf Village Leading off Fennel Base
Spy Woden's Day Terce. Morning, 5th of April, 1284

Along the forest floor, tucked close to the trunks of the sequoia trees beneath Thor's Base, a happy-go-lucky young elf dressed in a green shirt and light-brown Dungaree trousers strolls up to a fruit and vegetable stand waving his hand and greeting the pretty young vendor. "Health and happiness to you, Miss Buttercup."

A bright, cheery smile greets him in return. "Welcome, Mister Lynx; you bring sunshine to this place. Can I interest you in some apples? Reverend Johnny Appleseed's visit has really sparked interest in planting apple trees. You can eat these delicious apples and there are free seeds inside to plant your own apple trees if you wish."

Even at ground level, it is a prestige item to own real estate attached to a sequoia tree. Slate shingles testify to the success of Buttercup's family fruit and vegetable business. Her charm and feminine wiles have played a part in their recent upturn in sales. Lynx chuckles to himself awkwardly. "Actually, I'm here to talk about a bad apple."

Buttercup instantly erases any friendliness from her face and switches mode to a blank expression of bureaucratic impartiality. "I'm sorry, but we don't offer refunds on bad apples. We cannot put them back, since even one rotten apple spoils the bunch."

"Yes, so I've heard . . ." Lynx picks up one of her apples and polishes it on his shirt. "Actually, I was speaking about one of your customers metaphorically."

"I don't seem to recall a customer named Metafor Ickly or anything like that. Do you have a civil dispute with him or is this a criminal case?" she asks in a standoffish manner.

"Neither, it's just a personal matter. What can you tell me about Monsieur Enganyon Gandorfson?"

The expression on Miss Buttercup's face darkens to a mien of cruel calculation that would pluck the feathers off an angel's wings. Nervous and intimidated by her sudden rush of anger, Lynx accidentally stumbles back into the apple cart and tips it over. "Sorry," he says with a troubled grin. "I didn't mean to upset the apple cart. I'll pick those up for you."

As he gathers the apples that fell on the ground Buttercup comes over with a bag and puts the dirty apples in it. "You are going to have to pay for those. That'll be two farthings for the apples and the sack."

Lynx takes out two silver quarters and tucks them in her palm. She snatches them away and parades back behind her stand like a bully who just shoved over a little kid. Resentment at her treatment builds inside his chest until Lynx decides to press on so as to get his money's worth out of this confrontation. "So now, you were going to tell me about Monsieur Enganyon."

"Was I? I don't recall promising you anything. But since we are in a democracy, you have the right to hear my political opinions. Monsieur Enganyon is the best choice for umpire-in-chief and he would be on the ballot if it weren't for that brat, Mademoiselle Florenz. Her father is rotten to the core."

Lynx is suddenly confused. "Wait, Mademoiselle Florenz is a nice girl. She's nothing like her father."

"The apple rarely falls far from the tree."

Lynx cannot believe how confused this pretty fruit seller has become. "Yeah, maybe for green apples; but look at this orange apple here. You don't let something like this just fall on the ground. You pick it off the tree and put it in a basket. It's the same with Mademoiselle Florenz. She's handpicked, kind, and respectful. She would make a great umpire-in-chief. But Monsieur Enganyon just causes trouble for no reason, like a rebel without a cause. I don't get why all the girls dig him."

Buttercup huffs. "You are comparing apples and oranges. Monsieur Enganyon has the appearance of being cool and rebellious but he is a good elf deep down inside. But Mademoiselle Florenz puts on this act of being oh-so-sweet and charming but she is a snake born from a brood of vipers."

Confrontation is not Lynx's specialty, out of sheer nervousness he picks up a small bucket of beans and starts fidgeting with it. "You sound so sure of yourself but I think I know a little something about Monsieur Enganyon that might change your mind."

"What would you know of Monsieur Enganyon? Look, are you going to spill the beans or buy them?"

"You might be surprised to know that he meets up with Mademoiselle Florenz at the Shade Gap often."

Buttercup just shrugs. "So what? That's where the goblins do their ritual sacrifices. Maybe they're trying to get the drop on the goblins there."

"Oh come on! You can't seriously believe that!"

"I have no doubt they're going to hit pay dirt."

Lynx cannot fathom why Buttercup is changing her tune so suddenly. "You seriously think Mademoiselle Florenz and Monsieur Enganyon are going to figure out a way to eradicate the goblins from the hinterlands?"

"No, the beans!" shouts Buttercup. "The way you're holding them like that they'll all fall out onto the dirt and you're going to have to pay for those as well."

Frustrated at her stubbornness, Lynx gets even more truculent. "You should be happy about that. It seems to be your favorite way to make a sale."

"I don't need your money. What were you doing spying on them at the Shade Gap anyway? What legitimate business could an elf like you have over at that goblin sacrificial altar?"

Lynx takes up the challenge to justify himself. "Well, you know Dasher and Dancer and Prancer and Vixen, Comet and Cupid?"

"Yes, they are some of the most famous war reindeer in our colony. So what?"

"But do you recall the most famous reindeer of all?"

"Maybe Donner or Blitzen, I guess—why?"

"It ought to be Rudolph! He has a shiny, red nose; it's very sensitive. Last Saturn's Day, the League of Licornes was holding a recruiting tournament. Thanks to Rudolph I won the race, but they didn't award me a free commission as a junior cavalry officer."

"No one has ever heard of a red-nosed reindeer named Rudolph. I can assure you of that much."

"That's because until last Saturn's Day, they never let poor Rudolph participate in any of the reindeer war games. On that foggy tournament morning, the sandman said to me in a dream, 'Rudolph's nose is so bright, he'll guide your way, Lynx.'

"When I woke up I harnessed him, and all of the other reindeer riders laughed and called us foul names when we lined up at the starting gate. Then we were off, and the fog was so thick that even the adjudicators got lost. Rudolph seemed to smell every tree and branch and shrub that I could not see. He galloped onward at full tilt, even though we were all blinded by the mist. He carried me across the finish line a full half-hour ahead of the first adjudicator. After no one showed up for a while I started to doubt, so I scouted ahead until I found myself at the Shade Gap.

"When the fog cleared, guess whom I saw running around out there with Mademoiselle Florenz?"

Buttercup waves him away. "Oh, Mister Lynx, don't even go there. Everybody knows you are jealous because Mademoiselle Zena likes him instead of you."

Lynx gets so upset at the accusation that his hand knocks some beans all over his shirt. "For your information, it was Monsieur Enganyon running around with no splints on his leg, getting all lovey-dovey with Mademoiselle Florenz! He's faking his injuries and playing two ladies at the same time. You need to help me warn both elves about his character before he breaks their hearts."

"Look, Mister Lynx, you are full of beans."

"Fine, don't believe me, but I need you to explain to Mademoiselle Zena what kind of elf Monsieur Enganyon really is so that she won't have the same terrible experience with him that you had."

"How obnoxious of you! I had a wonderful experience with him. Monsieur Enganyon was nothing but a gentleman to me while we dated."

He takes a bite from one of his newly purchased apples that fell on the ground. "If you keep quiet, he is just going to hurt other maiden elves. I hope you can live with yourself." Lynx scrunches his face and realizes that the apple is riddled with worms. He spits out his mouthful and wipes off the rest.

Buttercup gives Lynx a spiteful glance and sneers. "How do you like them apples?"

Lynx looks down and sees the figs in front of him. "Can I have a fig to get the awful taste of the worms out of my mouth? That was gross!"

"I don't give a fig. Look, Monsieur Enganyon and I found true love together but we realized that we just couldn't be together for reasons beyond our control, okay? It's complicated."

"That kind of love is only true in fairy tales."

"You can go now, Monsieur Lynx. I guess true love is meant for someone else, but not for you."

Lynx stomps off toward his home with his bag of dirty apples, not even bothering to pay for the beans he spilled on his tunic. He finds a secluded spot behind some shrubbery and falls to his knees. On the forest floor one hundred fifty feet beneath the grandiose network of platforms supporting the high elf colony among the giant sequoias, the young wood elf weeps.

Grief surges through him in waves and he prays, "O Lord, show me what to do. Love is out to get me. Disappointment haunts all my dreams."

Then he sees her face.

"Ahh! You scared me!"

"Mister Lynx, are you all right?" Zena bends down and puts a hand on his shoulder. "It looks like you were crying."

"Oh, me? I'm not crying. No, I was just snacking on some apples and it turns out one of them was actually an onion. It's fine; I was hoping to make a garden salad later on. What can I do for you, Mademoiselle Zena?"

"Okay, whatever. My mother asked me to fetch you because you are the only wood elf on Tuscoraura Mountain we know who speaks Aenglish. My mother got the council's permission to invite a Christian missionary named Reverend Johnny Appleseed to deliver the Thor's Enlightenment Discourse for New Year's Eve and he accidentally fell over the edge of Worship Base."

Lynx's red eyes glaze over in total bewilderment. "Wait, what?"

"Well, Monsieur Enganyon sort of slapped him on the back too hard and Reverend Appleseed is so tall that the railing didn't do its job."

"So Monsieur Enganyon killed him?"

Zena starts pulling Lynx up onto his feet. "No, no, no! Monsieur Enganyon would never intentionally hurt anyone. One of the lower branches caught the missionary, but he hurt his leg pretty bad. Now he is lying in our guest room all by himself. My mother is very busy organizing her next trade convoy and she was hoping you would pay him a courtesy visit so he will not have to be alone all the time."

Lynx gets annoyed at all the excuses she makes for Enganyon and says, "Do you realize that the Major Leagues are all holding tournaments this month? I should have won the League of Licornes tournament, but I finished the race before even the adjudicators got to the finish line. So they used that as an excuse to deny me a commission. Now I have to try out for the Justiciar League right after lunch, and my main competitor is none other than your slap-happy friend, Monsieur Enganyon. Maybe he should be babysitting your missionary instead of me since he's the one who almost killed him and all."

Zena pushes Lynx a few feet forward, not taking his attitude. "Monsieur Enganyon already went over to apologize but he doesn't speak any Aenglish! Besides, his leg is in terrible pain. He can only stay out of bed for so long before the pain becomes unbearable."

Lynx doubles back and folds his arms, ready for a confrontation. "On that subject, I was just telling Miss Buttercup over there that after the League of Licornes refused to award me the commission I won at their tournament—"

Zena grows furious and interrupts him. "Mister Lynx Cougarson, excuse me if I interrupt your rant, but you can't feel sorry for yourself just because the League of Licornes treated you unfairly. Self-pity is toxic, and the more you indulge in it, the easier it will be for every little setback to tear you down.

"Now get up off your behind and go compete in the Justiciar League Tournament! You are a better shot than Monsieur Enganyon. I've seen you both shoot myself. You'll win; I'm sure."

The expression of shock on Lynx's face slowly drifts into a warm smile. "Thank you for that vote of confidence, Mademoiselle Zena. I . . . I don't know what to say—"

"You never do, Mister Lynx," says Zena. "Just smile and keep on the sunny side. See you after the tournament!" She places her Thor's Hammer pendant around his neck and kisses him on the cheek.

She walks off and he just stands there in stunned silence until after she is out of sight. And that's when he finally lets the words drip off his tongue like a glob of honey, "I love you, Zena . . ."

She pops her head back around the corner and with a snide grin calls back to him, "I know!"

Back up on Thor's Base, you would have thought you were at a fashion show, so chic and dapper are all the high elves in the outdoor amphitheater. On the stage sit Florenz Kibblersdottir and Zena Jeannesdottir, extravagantly dressed as if their lives depended on it. Makeup, jewelry, lace, frills, and glass slippers are not good enough for them today—both candidates have calculated every detail to look like the kind of leader the Tuscoraura elves want for their future.

Although she has Drowish (dark elf) lineage on her mother's side, Florenz has dyed her curly hair extravagantly blonde, full of body and volume. Her dress is an amethyst satin with lavender highlights. All her jewelry is platinum or silver, in a bold statement about the temperature of her skin. Deep-blue gems, black pearls, red and violet precious stones are inlaid sparingly but impart a grandiose look in both size and luminosity. The centerpiece is the famous Star of Corundum, fashioned after the one worn by Helen of Troy when she first met Paris.

Zena walks over to the front stage and bows to the audience in a showy gesture of respect. Although her black dress and vest have the same high-quality satin glow as Florenz's and a lusciously glamorous design, her jewelry lacks the zing and surprise that Florenz's arrangement delivers, especially since Zena is without a centerpiece. Her budget simply could not tolerate the kind of extreme makeover Florenz's team has put together. Still, Zena's poise, confidence, and studied movements capture their attention.

Zena hopes to make up for Florenz's budgetary head start with a stirring and bold speech. "This election year, I would like to change an unfortunate trend in our democratic system. Instead of bashing and criticizing each other, I propose that we simply share our views on how we see ourselves fulfilling the role of umpire-in-chief. I am sure Mademoiselle Florenz has the same mindset as I do on this one and that we can keep this debate polite and positive.

"In the Magnificent Charter that they left for our guidance to preserve the prosperity and the racial purity they brought with them from Alfheim, our Founding Mothers and Fathers state emphatically that true excellence is as rare as a pearl in an oyster shell.

"Prodigious parents do not necessarily produce prodigious children. Here I quote our Magnificent Charter: 'Nepotism and primogeniture always bring about decay in political, social, and economic structures when institutionalized by law or unofficially condoned by the customs of a people.'

"Mademoiselle Florenz Kibblersdottir indeed has the advantage of growing up in one of the most illustrious high elf families in Shentalpee City. Her ancestors have managed the same businesses, have led the same social clubs, and have controlled the same governmental posts for generations.

"My mother's pedigree, in contrast, was hard-won through her resourcefulness, talents, and dedication. Many of you still remember her as the young wood elve who earned her status as a high elve by taming a unicorn. Shentalpee City has always counted its unicorn honor guard as the emblem of its vitality and the resourcefulness of its citizens.

"My mother's ingenuity restored our pride in our traditions, revived our enthusiasm for the Magnificent Charter, and set her up for success in the business world. Creativity has been her hallmark and innovation her calling card. When you care enough to wear the very best, you wear a Dungaree.

"But I do not stand here before you today asking you, o brilliant and gorgeous elves of Tuscoraura, to vote for me because of who my mother is but because of who I am, thanks to her. The Magnificent Charter of Tuscoraura Colony forbids us from instituting any form of dynasty in our selection of leadership but instructs us to elect the umpire-in-chief who is the fittest to rule.

"My mind is fit. My memory holds word for word the poetry of all the Runic sagas and wisdom sayings of elf lore that define our cultural heritage. In school, I worked out all the propositions in the geometry of Euclid and Apollonius on my own with only the five postulates. Not only do I speak Aenglish and Gnorrachi but my literacy in Dwarvish Runic, Latin, Avrith, and Nabotean has enabled me to read the works of more philosophers, historians, and orators than most garden gnomes even own in all their impressive libraries.

"My body is fit. I have won every competition in archery, running, reindeer riding, and wrestling that my high school ever set up. My title as Miss Tuscoraura has held for the last two years and my first entry in the Saturnalia fashion contest this year met with rave reviews both as a model and as a designer.

"My spirit is fit. The muses inspire me in every art. I love to draw, compose poetry, dance, and gaze at the stars. When I sing or play flute, I have perfect pitch. My love of music has been the entryway to taming this magica tree you see behind me. It is with great pride that I can announce in three weeks' time, Mage Nittany will observe me cull my first magica branch as an apprentice magicultor at Pinne Mage University.

"Looking out before me at this crowd of smart, athletic, and artsy elves, I know that our Founding Mothers and Fathers would consider you fit in mind, body, and spirit to carry on the ideals they described in the Magnificent Charter. Only by returning to those ideals can we make this colony great once again and bring about a new Golden Age for Shentalpee City.

"This is my vision for the chief umpirage, with your vote. May the gods bless you all with prosperity, insight, and good health for many years to come."

Fervent applause erupts as Zena sits down and smiles. By their reactions, she has no doubt she'll be able to keep her lead over Florenz in the polls.

Now the pressure is on for Florenz. Though innately shy, Florenz is no stranger to public appearances and approaches the stage with an arsenal of smiles and poses. "As you all know, Mademoiselle Zena and I have been best of friends since childhood. In the electoral debates, we hoped to focus our discussions on policy and avoid personal attacks or mudslinging—but I cannot. This latest scandal runs too deep."

Flabbergasted, the high elves stare at Florenz in disbelief. Political discourse in Tuscoraura has always been in the gutter but to hear the sweet, mild-mannered Florenz jump straight into the slime hits them all from left field. They would have assumed that the overweening ambitions of the misfit, Zena, might drive her to aim below the belt, but not Florenz.

Still, Florenz is presenting them with a chance to hear some dirt on Zena, and none of them has any intention of passing up on the offer. They tune their pointy ears in.

Florenz looks at them wide-eyed, almost as if horrified to hear the words coming out of her own mouth, but she has their attention and does not waste a moment of it. "It has recently come to the attention of the Council of Perfects that Madame Jeanne, the dungaree of Foreign Trade, has a halfling stewardess named Bartlebee who has sold the alchemical plans to our top-secret weapon, elf fire, to the renowned dwarf mercenary Master Chief Engineer Tom Thumb.

"The investigation is likely to drag on for months, but I believe you all have the right to know this before the elections. My father has worked day and night over the past twelve years to rebuild Shentalpee City's military infrastructure. If Zena's umpirage squanders our military edge in fire technologies, a disaster worse than the eruption of Mount Ragnarök could befall us right here on Tuscoraura Mountian.

"The Justiciar League is currently conducting a full investigation of Bartlebee's betrayal and will ascertain whether or not our monopoly over the colony's top-secret elemental weapon remains intact. Any evidence of collaboration—or even negligence—on the part of Madame Jeanne Ranglursdottir in allowing this elf fire leak could brand her a traitor. My sincerest hope is that this is all one, big misunderstanding and that we can clear our dungaree of Foreign Trade from guilt and seal up the leak.

"If not, may the gods help us."

Florenz steps down from the stage. The crowd sits in stunned silence at what they just heard.

Zena's face drains white like spilled milk.

Conviction for treason will result in the confiscation of all her family's goods and property by the Council of Perfects, permanent exile for herself, and execution for her mother.

Worst of all, Zena could never marry Enganyon with a scandal of those proportions weighing on her dowry. Zena's mind stews. *This is not over, Mademoiselle Florenz! If you think I won't fight back, you are mistaken—gravely mistaken!*

Scene 3: Genesis

Shade Gap.
Five Miles Northwest of Tuscoraura Mountain
Spy Woden's Day Terce. Morning, 5th of April, 1284

A muscular, five-and-a-half-foot-tall, green-skinned goblin with a stone-tipped spear charges at Sir Robert Roger from behind. Brother Umbert pulls a magic wand from up his sleeve. "Alakazam!" He shouts his magic word out, loud enough to give away their exact location to every goblin within a hundred yards.

Suddenly, the charging goblin loses his spear—in fact, it magically disappears into thin air. The baffled and unarmed goblin keeps running and crashes awkwardly into Sir Robert Roger without doing any real harm. Sprawled in the dirt, they grapple for only a few seconds before the goblin's vastly superior physical strength overpowers the ranger captain. The goblin hoists him over his head, spins him around, and tosses him into a group of nearby rangers aiming their arrows at him. In a trice, the goblin dashes back into the forest.

The rest of the rangers, already on high alert, shoot their arrows and fling their hatchets, but the goblins prove elusive foes.

Barrel-chested, big-fisted, and massively muscular, the goblins have no armor and fight with fire-hardened wood or chipped stone weapons. They compensate for the lack of metalworking in their warcraft with higher degrees of cunning in battle.

Although goblins only tend to reach somewhere between five and five-and-a-half feet tall for adult males and about four-and-a-half to five feet tall for adult females, both goblins and goblinesses are much stronger than the tallest and heaviest humans. By age twelve, a healthy goblin whelp could arm wrestle two muscle-bound humans at the same time and easily win.

In caves deprived of the light of day, their skin turns a pale-gray hue. But when continuously exposed to the sun, their skin tans to a dark green. This adaptation acts as a natural camouflage and helps them blend easily into forests and grasslands.

Their most astounding adaptation to the wild is their regenerative capabilities; healing broken bones, and recovering from serious infections in half the time as other races. Their foreheads are narrow and slope back steeply with thick, bushy brows, long chins, and wide cheekbones. All goblins have a pronounced overbite, which distinguishes them from trolls, whose jaws carry a tusked underbite.

After the initial goblin attack, Inquisitor Sheen remains in prayer but Brother Crowe has drawn two long knives and Brother Indigo holds in his left and only hand the large, knotty club that has been dangling from his rope belt all the while. Brother Umbert skulks around the underbrush with his magic wand, pointing it outward like a viper ready to strike.

After taking a nasty tumble, Sir Robert Roger sets himself back on his feet and readies himself for action, shouting out orders to the rangers. "Form a perimeter!"

Then he turns to Brother Umbert and states, "I owe you thanks for saving my life with that little magic trick, but now you've got to tell the inquisitor and your holy buddies to huddle behind those rocks inside our defensive circle. We can't risk your lives in combat."

Brother Umbert does not retreat. "The inquisitor is praying. God will keep him safe."

Sir Robert Roger yells, "Get the inquisitor behind those rocks or I'll carry him there myself!"

The standoff ends when a skull-sized boulder flies into the ranger camp. Poorly aimed, it does not hit anyone. Sir Jon Stark, the first lieutenant for the rangers, shouts, "Keep your eyes open and shoot at anything that moves!"

When the next boulder arrives, Sir Ethen Allan calls out, "I saw a goblin toss it about fifty yards to the northeast, but he ducked behind a tree before I had a chance to shoot at him!"

"Incoming!" Sir Daniel Boone screams in a terrified then suddenly hushed voice. From the opposite direction of the flying boulders, goblin lurkers rush in at the rangers. The boulders were just a distraction and the goblins are wickedly fast on their feet.

The first ambushing goblin swings a gnarly oaken club at Sir Richard, the ranger posted in the rear. The blow puts the dazed ranger out of the fight and three goblins charge directly into the gap. They quickly reach the middle of the rangers' defensive circle and start swiping at the other rangers from behind.

The rangers a few paces back shoot their arrows at the ambushing goblins. Although the rangers' arrows bite against their flesh, the goblins have an amazing instinct for spinning just before being struck with the rangers' well-aimed arrows. Their spinning motion takes all the penetration out of the arrowheads.

Despite getting all slashed up by the sharp arrowheads from the rangers' longbows, the goblins press their attack. Dame Frances Marian pulls out a long knife but a fat goblin with a scrimshaw ox bone club knocks the knife aside, numbing her hand. Another shorter goblin dashes at her from her blind spot and tries to clobber her with a backhand swing from his heavy ashen spear shaft, but her sixth sense tells her to dive out of the way in the nick of time. She retreats.

Seeing that the tactical situation is lost, Sir Robert Roger blows his horn to withdraw to the river.

With all the rangers' attention on the goblins in their midst, they fail to notice the goblins emerging from behind bushes, trees, and ditches lobbing smooth stones at the distracted rangers. Several rangers get hit from behind and fall to the ground, stunned.

Sir Robert Roger picks up his hatchet and tries to rescue the situation with a daring countercharge, but a short goblin trips him with a whack of his spear behind the knees and the fight is back to square one. Looking around, Sir Robert Roger notices his rangers are badly bruised, but none have received mortal wounds so far. Hoping to keep the bloodshed to a minimum, he shouts, "Don't go for the kill! They are trying to spook us. Keep moving back toward the river and stay alert!"

Meanwhile, Inquisitor Sheen continues praying. Brother Indigo smacks down a goblin with his huge, gnarly club before the goblin can get to the inquisitor.

The Mohawk brother then twirls his club around to deflect a stone ax from a different goblin on his right. Brother Umbert makes the stone ax disappear with his magic wand and Brother Crowe slashes at that same goblin just above the eyebrows. A few heartbeats later, the blood trickles down into his eyes copiously and the blinded, unarmed goblin stumbles off into the forest.

They do not pursue because Inquisitor Sheen has ordered them to avoid loss of life at all times.

Although the three monks are holding their own fairly well, the groaning and stunned rangers lose ground. Three larger goblins decked out with tattoos, body piercings, and war trophies to signal that they are chieftains walk into the combat zone. The first looks older, mostly bald, and with a salt-and-pepper goatee. Dry, dark-green, weathered skin wraps tightly around his bulging muscles. His perfect six-pack abs and the veins crawling all over his arms, neck, and legs bespeak a goblin driven by a life-long obsession for destruction.

To his left walks a tall but less muscular goblin. This one has all the tattoos and body piercings of the other two, but far fewer war trophies hang about his neck or on his belt. Unusual for a goblin, he has a full head of hair. Long and black, his braids dangle down past his shoulders. His fine nose, narrow forehead, and sharp chin give him a ladylike charm.

On the right side of the elder chieftain marches a hulking goblin, just over six feet tall, with a loose-hanging gut and arms so thick he could take down a bull with one hand. His neck is stooped and his back hunches over slightly. The flapping jowls on his cheeks and his pig-like nostrils are both ugly and intimidating.

Apparently, the hulking goblin is looking for a challenge and points to Brother Indigo, saying, "Boom shakalaka do wa ditty diddy dum ditty do!"

Inquisitor Sheen calls out in response, "Gaggle aowl yahoo terwitter whoop!"

Sir Robert Roger grimaces and moans, "Seriously? What is he doing? Calling the birds to help us?"

Brother Umbert responds, "He has the mystical gift of tongues. He's speaking Gobbledygook, the language of the Magog goblins."

The salt-and-pepper-haired old war chief grunts in surprise, then says, "Wiki yootoob amuson paipaal!"

Inquisitor Sheen replies, "Inztagrahm reddet blogsbot lynktyn ne'flicks?"

The pretty boy chieftain asserts himself as a negotiator. "Bing taobao sohu yip baidu alixpriss!"

The older goblin chieftain nods, "Ebaie."

The inquisitor tells Sir Robert Roger, "The Mighty Gog, exalted king over all the goblins in the forests of Magog, has agreed in his benevolence to spare you your lives if you put your weapons down and allow them to bind you."

"How do we know he won't just kill us?"

"The exalted goblin king says he will allow his son, Skaar, to be your personal hostage, Sir Robert Roger, until all your followers are safely returned to you."

"If he's so benevolent, why doesn't he just let us go now? We're not trying to pick a fight with anybody."

"It seems we have trespassed upon their sacred territory. They need to perform a ritual with our blood to cleanse the pollution we have brought. If we give our blood willingly, it only needs to be one drop. If they have to take it from us unwillingly, then they have to pour out all of it."

"Okay, Priest, I'm taking your word for it. Tell him to send us his son first as a ransom and then we will atone for our trespasses."

Inquisitor Sheen tells the goblin king they are willing to give up their freedom for the promise of safety. "Boosh klin'in boosh opama drumb."

The goblin king gives the command to bind them up. "Alecksa!"

The goblins tie up the rangers and inquisitors, then lead them to the top of the northernmost mountain, overlooking the Shade Gap. The site looks like a pile of randomly scattered stones but as Inquisitor Sheen's trained eye surveys the patterns, the ritualistic arrangement of the stones pops out at him like a 3D message suddenly becoming visible in the swirling patterns of an optical illusion design. For all its naturalistic calm and peacefulness, this area is actually an outdoor temple for ritual murder!

Several curved boulders mark off this mountaintop clearing and form a circle of arches around the main altar. The altar itself is just a huge, stone slab that has been tossed on top of the central pile of stones. Its surface is uneven and slightly tilted, but from the layers of dark stains, it seems to be used often. Blood and restless spirits abound here.

A pang of doubt pinches the inquisitor's soul. An unsettling feeling that the goblin king may have lied about sparing their lives tightens his throat.

Their goblin captors arrange them in a semicircle with their right hands on their chests. From the other corner, some goblins carry a wicker basket cage into the semicircle. It holds a teenaged boy dressed as a monk with a strange, hempen halter around his neck.

Sir Robert Roger presses his knife tightly against the throat of his hostage, the goblin king's son. "Tell him no sudden moves. We want the monk boy to go free as well."

Inquisitor Sheen gets worried and asks the goblin king, "Gobble makdoe arbee panda supway dunkin pitsada hut?"

The goblin chief laughs with a deep growl and says, "Chicaboom noon-egg solo manga wookey bantha Poodoo!"

The inquisitor translates. "The mighty Gog says that you were lucky to escape with your lives, but the monk boy will be a human sacrifice to their god, Poodoo."

Bonus Scene B: Fletcher in the Rye

Wood Elf Village Green Leading off Blue Hen's Base,
Spy Woden's Day Sext.
Noontide, 5th of April, 1284

Tense, the bright-yellow-fletched arrow trembles on the young elf's bowstring sinew. Sweat and skin oil lubricate Lynx's red fingertips, threatening to slip too early. Lynx pleads with his fingers to hold on tight and steady while they pull back just a little farther. His first shot in the Justiciar League Tournament has to reach a straw, bull-shaped target one hundred fifty yards away. He can barely make out the details on it other than two bright-red dots on its face for the eyes and the green dot on its side representing the heart.

Lynx knows that the big, bull-shaped hay bale has a long wooden stake running through the middle with a small roll of parchment attached to the top. The winner of this tournament will walk away with nothing more than a few lines of Runic scribbling on that parchment. For a young wood elf, that parchment is the ticket to a new life more fantastic than living in Charlie's chocolate factory: a free commission as a junior officer in the prestigious Justiciar League.

Among the Tuscoraura elves, military service is divided into leagues, much like arts and crafts are divided into guilds: the Alcornseatic League for unicorn heavy cavalry (now only an honorary league for lack of unicorns, though a small club of hardcore fire elves train wild boar as heavy cavalry instead), the League of Licornes for unicorn and reindeer light cavalry that carry out patrols or hit and run raids, (again, now nearly all reindeer for lack of unicorns), the Ivy League for tree climbing scouts and rangers, and the Justiciar League for police work on Shentalpee City. The Justiciar League prides itself in its sharpshooters skilled in the traditional elf recurve bow. Membership in the Justiciar League carries all the responsibilities and prestige of a peace officer and wartime soldier in one badge.

Today, Lynx's wildest dreams, hopes, and ambitions are at stake on the parchment on the back of that straw bull.

He feels his fingertips start to go numb. A distant tingling sensation warns him that the bowstring is about to slip. Still, Lynx heaves back on the bowstring just a little harder—he simply does not trust his musty old bow to carry his yellow-fletched arrow out all the way down to the end zone. He aligns his sights, exhales gently, and launches a Hail Mary.

TWANG!

His arrow whistles swiftly across the field and sails right over the bull's head. A clean miss.

Twelve other colored arrows smack into the straw bull's side. All the other contestants are high elves who have been enrolled in archery classes since infancy—nursed with crafted rattles and baubles to strengthen their grip, steady their hand, and widen their draw span. Lynx, lucky number thirteen in this contest, is the only wood elf competing and the only one to miss.

"He's wasting our time even coming out here," mutters a contestant loudly enough for all to hear.

"That wood elf bow is junk," says another.

"He's out of his league!" sneers a third.

Lynx recognizes his mistake immediately. Not trusting his meager wood elf bow to cover that kind of distance, he drew back on the string too hard, but the tournament arrows are tipless flight arrows, not the heavily weighted hunting arrows he has been practicing with every morning since last year. This time, Lynx pulls back gently but firmly on the bow and stops when the bowstring tells him it has stretched itself to the limits of its comfort zone. He will not underestimate his bow again.

He exhales and his fingertips slip off the bowstring.

THUNK!

Bull's-eye! Even from one hundred yards away, his keen elf eyes can see his yellow-fletched arrow sticking out of the straw bull's red eye.

Enganyon's purple-and-green-fletched arrow lands just outside the heart in the blue zone for five points.

Taking aim for the bull's other eye, Lynx leans slightly to the left, takes a breath in and out. Release.

FLUMP!

One of the competitors comes over, asking, "Who's the rogue hitting both bull's eyes from way out here?"

Appreciating the attempt at congratulations, Lynx walks up to the elf and reaches out for a handshake. "Mister Lynx Cougarson of Clan Highrune, at your service. Nice to meet you, monsieur!"

The high elf just looks at him and leaves his hand hanging. "Oh, you're the wood elf . . . Gandorfson is going to be mad to hear about this." He walks away.

Lynx feels lonelier than ever. As the contestants walk forward to the middle of the field, Lynx tallies up Enganyon Gandorfson's score: one arrow on the green heart for seven points and the other two just outside it at five points each for a total of seventeen points. Even though Enganyon has his foot in a splint, he shoots better than all the other elves—all except Lynx, who earned nine points for each bull's eye for a total of eighteen. Lynx is leading the competition by one point!

One hundred yards away the target is a straw bear. Feeling too blessed to be stressed, Lynx hits both red eye dots and then the green heart dot for a perfect twenty-five points. (No points are awarded for hitting the same eye twice.)

Enganyon's score for this round is as good as most elves could hope for: five points for landing an arrow just below the green heart dot, seven for correcting his aim, and nine for nailing his arrow into the bear's red eye for a total of twenty-one points.

A quick mental calculation tells Lynx that he is now five points ahead of Enganyon. A rush of pride swells in his heart and it goes to his head as he mutters to himself, "Yeah that's right—I'm out of your league, but it's only because I'm in a league of my own."

For the last round, the target is a large, straw troll. Bringing the thirteen contestants up to the fifty-yard line, the Justiciar League adjudicator, Captain Hawkeye, announces, "This last round represents close range shooting but don't think it's the easiest. You have a time limit to loose all your arrows. I will start off in the end zone and make a fifty-yard dash back here. By the time I cross the line, any arrow that has not yet left the plane of the bow will be disqualified. Understood?"

The high elves all nod and take three arrows out of their quivers, plant two on the fifty-yard line and notch the third. Lynx has no clue what is going on, so he just follows their lead and copies their setup.

Captain Hawkeye gets in position and shouts, "Ready, aim, loose!"

As the captain starts his fifty-yard dash, Lynx aims for the right eye dot.

SWOOP!

Too high! At this range, the flight arrows have no arc! Lynx hits just above the troll's eye! Oh no!

The high elf contestants dip their bows forward to reload their arrows directly from ground. Lynx reloads his bow, and decides to play it safe. He shoots for the troll's heart instead of the troll's other eye. He has no time to aim and just shoots, relying on pure instinct.

SHLACK!

His arrow hits the troll's heart. Captain Hawkeye is almost here. Quickly but calmly Lynx dips down, notches his arrow, and looses it.

SWOOSH! Troll's-eye!

Captain Hawkeye steps over the fifty-yard line.

Quickly tallying the score, Lynx reckons that his yellow-notched arrows have earned him seven points for the heart, nine for the eye, and only three points for the one that went a little too high, for a total of nineteen. Two of Enganyon's purple-and-green notched arrows are clustered inside the troll's heart (seven points each) and one hit the troll's eye (nine points), for a total of twenty-three points. Good shooting, but not enough to overcome the five-point lead Lynx gained from the first two rounds.

That's it! Lynx wins by one point!

A smile breaks forth on his face like the morning sunrise and a fist pump in the air celebrates his triumphant entry into the ranks of high elf society as a junior commissioned officer in the Justiciar League.

All of the high elves who lost wear long, dejected faces, but Enganyon's sour expression carries a higher level of disgust and outrage than the rest. Using his bow as a walking cane, he limps over to his gnome valet, who brings him his reindeer. Lynx overhears Enganyon say, "Send a message to Vandsee Estates that I will meet her at the Gap this evening."

Double win! Thanks to Rudolph's keen red nose and his unfair disqualification from the League of Legends Tournament, Lynx knows exactly which Gap he is referring to. All he needs to do is convince Zena to accompany him to the Shade Gap and all her fantasies about Enganyon will crash and burn in the fire pit of harsh reality.

The gnome valet helps Enganyon lift his splinted leg up into the reindeer's stirrup and he gallops off without further ado.

Eager to collect his prize and get over to Dungaree Jeanne's mansion to visit Johnny Appleseed and announce to Zena his triumph, Lynx taps Captain Hawkeye on the shoulder as he consults with the other representatives of the Justiciar League. "Would you mind if I just go grab that commission and head off? I have some urgent business to take care of."

Captain Hawkeye's confident and calm demeanor flickers in a split second of weakness as he wrestles with his high elf's sense of honor and truth. The next moment he recovers and says, "I am sorry, son, but your last arrow was loosed after I crossed the fifty-yard line. The Justiciar League is awarding the commission to Monsieur Enganyon Gandorfson."

"Wait! You saw it. You were still a good pace and a half in front of me when I loosed my last arrow."

"The Justiciar League has only keen-eyed professionals here and they are all saying that your last arrow did not break the plane of your bow before I stepped across it. Minus the disqualified arrow, your performance totals fifty-three points to Monsieur Enganyon's sixty-one points."

A bomb explodes in Lynx's chest. He stammers, "But . . . but . . . he just rode off without waiting for the official tally. Doesn't that mean he forfeits?"

"He has a serious leg injury that he is still recovering from. My colleagues feel the rule does not apply in this circumstance."

Lynx stands there stunned like a deer in headlights—um, I mean torch lights. Anyhow, his mind desperately scrambles for something intelligent to say but all that comes out of his mouth is sort of a guttural, stomach-cramp-toned, "Oh . . ."

Captain Hawkeye quickly walks away. Guilt and the fear of confrontation over this issue are written all over his face. It does not take an oracle to know that the case is closed and the decision already made—a wood elf simply will not be allowed into the ranks of the Justiciar League today.

Lynx broods over his injury. Once upon a time, wood elves had the right to earn a place in the order of high elves. Now even the Justiciar League will sink to any level of injustice to prevent it.

Then a voice reminds him that he cannot appear weak. Okay, don't just stand there looking stupid. You can't let them see you cry. What next? Oh yeah! Go get Zena to come with you to Shade Gap this evening. Once she sees with her own two eyes that Enganyon is faking his leg injury to spend more time on these secret trysts with Florenz it'll break her heart, but just maybe the crack will be wide enough for you to find a way in.

Satisfied with his plan of action, Lynx steels his upper lip and calls out to the Justiciar League officers who just unfairly deprived him of his victory, "Messieurs Officers! Injustice anywhere is a threat to justice everywhere. I tremble for this colony when I reflect that God is just; that his justice cannot sleep forever."

Scene 4: Poor Richard's Comeback

Town Hall of Ithica
Spy Woden's Day Sext. Noontide, 5th of April, 1284

"Ah, welcome, Grand Sage Cornwell!" The baron of Amhirst puts on his most charming smile. "It is most gracious of you to allow me this opportunity to clear up the misunderstanding between us when we first arrived. Please have a seat by the fire. May I offer you some wine?"

The grand sage wears his academic robe without the hood. His face is stern, and his attitude is skeptical. "The Silvermorn College of Sorcerers deeply mourns the students who lost their lives in defense of Ithica, a town they had called home while studying with us."

"Regrettable," says the baron as his chief herald, Sir Sean, comes over to pour out two cups of wine for the baron and his guest. Cornwell refuses so Sir Sean places both cups on a little table beside the fireplace.

The baron is wearing red slippers and a smooth, red robe that is the closest medieval garb to a roaring twenties smoking jacket. "A tragedy, really. Such bright promise for the future cut short because their leaders failed them. You and I need to put our heads together to make this right. A simple apology, no matter how sincere, just won't be enough."

Grand Sage Cornwell stares Amhirst straight in the eye. "You took the words right out of my mouth."

"It's because we both have the same vision for leadership in Aenglish society." Amhirst stalls, waiting for the grand sage to relax and let down his guard.

"Quite frankly, my lord, your vision of leadership resembles that of a bully on a child's playground."

"That's exactly why I asked you to come. Such misperceptions can only lead to more unnecessary bloodshed. We must come to an understanding before it costs us any more Aenglish lives."

"What more do I need to understand? You attacked the walls of Ithica and my students rallied to its defense. Some of them died."

The baron looks at him with pleading eyes. "Please have a seat, Master Grand Sage. We discuss such weighty issues, and it would only be proper to observe the suitable decorum in our conversation."

Grand Sage Cornwell stiffly takes a seat on the couch and says, "Only because of the grave responsibility on my shoulders of informing the families of those deceased students do I force myself to sit down and hear you out."

The baron of Amhirst sits across from him and stares into the fire as if in deep thought. He says, "Yes, these parents are making great sacrifices to send their sons and daughters to Silvermorn in hopes of ensuring a successful niche for their future. They are immensely proud of their child's talents and accomplishments."

Amhirst looks at Cornwell thoughtfully, but Cornwell keeps quiet.

"I've just heard too many cases of brilliant young sorcerers returning home only to find out that the Sorcerers' Guild demands that they travel farther afield because all the local jobs are taken. Unemployed sorcerers have a bad reputation for causing mischief."

Still no response from Cornwell, but Amhirst can tell he is touching on a raw nerve.

"As a way of putting the past in the past and opening up a brighter future, I'll offer to hire any and all unemployed graduates of Silvermorn."

Cornwell perks up and asks, "At full wages?"

"Absolutely, at full wages."

"Fourpence a day?"

"Thruppence a day starting wages until they prove their worth. I usually pay at least double for competent ones. Several sorcerers at my court are making a dollar and sixpence a day after accomplishing legendary quests in my service. They could retire before forty, but they enjoy the position so much, they stay on."

"And you will put this in writing?"

"Yes, we have prepared a document extending the patronage of my court to Silvermorn College."

"But you have no authority here in Ithica."

"That might change, and soon enough. Believe me—this contract benefits you as much as it benefits me. If my authority were to extend to this region, it would entail a revision of nearly all charters granted by local authorities. Signing this would ensure your educational mission continues uninterrupted."

"May I read this contract you are proposing?"

The baron of Amhirst nods his head gravely, using all the body language of a person speaking to a peer of equal social status. Grand Sage Cornwell is under no illusion that the baron's deference is anything more than a veil for his threats and bullying.

Amhirst beckons Sir Sean, who is sitting quietly in a corner, and he brings the baron's proposal forward with much gravitas.

"Be a good man and wait in the hallway while the chancellor considers this deal, would you, Sir Sean?"

Sir Sean bows and exits the room. The grand sage reads the scroll carefully while the baron waits, sipping his wine.

After a long pause, Cornwell says, "I need you to indemnify the families of the fallen students."

"Agreed."

"And refund them the tuition they paid so far."

"How about we split the refund so we each pay half? After all, the tuition went into your coffers."

"Unacceptable." The grand sage stands up. "You are putting a lot of faith in the Inquisition's ability to bail you out of a very ugly situation. If Inquisitor Sheen fails to return to Ithica from Tuscoraura Mountain, your rangers would find it considerably more difficult to mount another rescue operation before your beheading. We will be prepared the next time around."

Amhirst starts dropping some bigger names. "Not necessary. It's a done deal. Reports are coming in that my rangers have already succeeded in bringing the good inquisitor to Tuscoraura Mountain, and the Cardinals Orsini have already invited me to a meeting in Salim. You no longer have any legal grounds to carry out your proposed execution.

"King Eddard has agreed to expand the role of the Inquisition in Vinland significantly over the next few years and, seeing my devotion and piety, the Cardinals Orsini are offering to put my name forward as Aenglish viceroy of Vinland to oversee the whole process. My policy is that it is better to have more friends than enemies. Surely you see the wisdom in that."

"I have seen little wisdom in your policies thus far. Good evening to you." The grand sage walks toward the door.

Amhirst stands up and calls after him, "There is one other issue I could help you with—Richard Chandler."

Grand Sage Cornwell freezes with his hand on the doorknob. He turns around slowly. "Are you the one that tipped his former master off to his presence here? Leverage, I suppose."

Amhirst puts his hand over his heart. "Never would I dream of such skullduggery!"

"But if someone else should dream it up, you would be game to capitalize on it, I am sure. All right then, tell me how you know about Richard Chandler."

"The crumbs I like to toss for the little birdies outside my window seem to have attracted a few magpies. Across their chatter, I learn a lot."

"Sounds like a bird-brained form of skullduggery to me. What do you intend to do with this leverage you have on him?"

"You have seen how I confront my enemies. I want to show you how well I treat my friends. Call him in, will you, Grand Sage?"

"It's late in the evening, and all the apprentices have gone to bed."

Amhirst calls out, "Sir Sean!"

The baron's herald opens the door immediately. "You called, my lord?"

"Fetch young Richard Chandler, will you?"

"He's right here, my lord. Also, a messenger from the Pony Express has arrived."

"Have Brother Tuck handle it for me."

"Begging your pardon, my lord, but the halfling working for the Pony Express insists the letter is for your eyes only."

"Tell him I will receive him as soon as I have concluded an agreement with the grand sage. Now, please send Apprentice Chandler in."

"Very well, my lord."

Amhirst cannot restrain a little smirk at Cornwell's surprise seeing the jovial young man walk in. His nose is round as a ball and his face plump and smooth. His wavy, brown hair falls back from his high forehead, giving him an air of intelligence and confidence. Richard Chandler shakes Cornwell's hand and says, "Thank you so much for arranging this meeting, Grand Sage Cornwell!"

The baron of Amhirst ushers the young man to the fireplace. "Welcome! Come in, Apprentice Chandler. Have a seat and let me pour you some wine."

Richard Chandler sits right down and makes himself comfortable. "You are too kind, my lord. Your generosity to your friends is legendary, but to treat a runaway slave in the employ of your bitterest enemy with such cordiality defies all comprehension."

"Happy to oblige, Richard," answers Amhirst. "Or should I call you, Benjamin?"

The young man laughs. "Ah! You figured me out. My father always used to tell me, 'Love your enemies, for they tell you the truth about yourself.'"

Amhirst echoes Benjamin's laugh theatrically. "That is precisely why I invited you here—to show you what kind of friend I could be if only we can work out a way to dispel this enmity between your college and my regime. Tell me, Benjamin, about your troubles."

The grand sage gives the young man a look of warning to keep quiet. Benjamin Chandler nods to him as if submitting to his request and then immediately pours his heart out to Amhirst. "My father, Josiah, is a candlemaker from Ecton, a little community of humans within the shire of the Hampton Hobs.

"Life was hard for the family back in Aengland so he came to Baston as an indentured servant. When I was ten years old, he paid for two years of my education at a monastery near Cambridge in hopes of having a son gain prominence in the Church. But when funds ran out, he apprenticed me to my older brother, James, who had set up his own tallow candlemaker's workshop.

"James was jealous of my ability to read and of my natural aptitude for sorcery. He strictly forbade me from reading any more books and promised to hunt me down whenever I tried to sneak off to a monastery library. One after another, I visited every library in Baston, thirsty for knowledge. He became so familiar with all those libraries that the hide-and-seek we were playing ceased to have any sporting fun left in it.

"A friend of mine tipped me off that the law granting serfs freedom after living one hundred and one days in a chartered Aenglish town also applies to contracted apprentices who enlist in a chartered military, academic, or religious institution within Aenglish domains.

"So, I stole away to Ithica in pursuit of a career in sorcery, with the hopes that it would take my brother more than one hundred and one days to find me. Unfortunately, he seems to have gone all the way around the world in eighty days.

"Now that he's here, he'll drag me back to Baston and lock me in a dark, dank room. The boredom of candle making will be the mildest of my punishments.

My brother will think up ways to get back at me—and trust me, he has an active imagination when it comes to inflicting misery on others."

The baron of Amhirst listens to the story intently. "How old are you now, young Benjamin?"

"Nineteen, sir."

"How would you like to fulfill your father's dream to make a cleric of you in Brother Tuck's monastery?"

Benjamin puts his fist to his mouth and coughs slightly. "My lord, a very credible astrologer has told me that the stars forbid me to take on monastic vows. I was born precisely between two conjunctions that would really bring disaster upon me and Holy Mother the Church if I did take the vow of . . . ehem—"

"Your astrologer has perhaps seen a weakness for pretty ladies in your eye?" suggests Amhirst.

"The astrologer was a very pretty lady herself, but she told me I was the sort of rebel destined to transform colonial Vinland. Perhaps we could talk about the dreams I have for my own life, instead of my father's dreams for me."

Amhirst snaps his fingers and sits up excitedly. "She has seen the fire in your eyes, Mister Benjamin Chandler, and I have seen it too! On that desk there I have a document declaring you a frankelyn in my court. The moment you sign it, you will be free from your apprenticeship to your brother by your oath of civic service to the barony of Amhirst.

"Naturally, you'd be able to pursue your studies here at Silvermorn. Your aethereal experiments in harnessing the power of lightning with a kite and a key have already gained notoriety among your peers. All I ask is that you go on a quest or two, if needed."

Ebullient and optimistic, Benjamin Chandler turns to the grand sage and asks, "What do you say, Grand Sage? This seems to me like the opportunity of a lifetime—the answer to all our problems."

"It's your life, Richard. No doubt we would be thrilled for you to continue your studies as a sorcerer's apprentice with us here at Silvermorn. However, I have a feeling your debt of gratitude to the baron of Amhirst will get more and more encumbered with obligations until studies will become impossible."

Amhirst jumps in before Benjamin Chandler has a chance to think it over too much. "The contract stipulates that as my frankelyn, you would be obliged to leave Silvermorn in my service no more than one semester every other year. You would graduate with your Master's degree in Sorcery in five years tops, potentially earlier. We'll even throw in paid summers, whether or not we call you up for service."

"Done," says the apprentice chandler, standing up to shake Amhirst's hand.

The baron of Amhirst turns a triumphant smile to the grand sage. "We can agree on one thing, dear Chancellor—we both recognize talent when we see it.

"Shall we agree to a mutually beneficial contract then? Guaranteed employment for all Silvermorn graduates who seek it in my court. Indemnities and half-tuition refunds for the families of the students who fell at the walls. An official elevation of Benjamin Chandler to the rank of frankelyn in my baronial court. Let's move on with the future, shall we?"

Cornwell looks long and hard at his star pupil. "Throw in Chandler's full tuition and you have a deal."

With a coy smile Amhirst concludes, "You drive a hard bargain, Chancellor, but I'm in no mood to drag this out any further.

"Sir Sean, the document, please."

Sir Sean pops back in with the scroll on a tray, followed by Brother Tuck, armed with a quill pen, inkwell, lit candle, and some sealing wax. Amhirst picks up the scroll and unfurls it in front of the grand sage, then dictates the negotiated conditions for his cleric to write down. Cornwell leans over Brother Tuck's shoulder reading and rereading every word as it goes down on the parchment.

Brother Tuck's penmanship, spelling, and grammar are impeccable and, despite his better judgment, Cornwell can find no technicality for backing out of this deal. A deep sinking feeling warns him that he is heading down a direful path, but he waves it off for the sake of his students and their loved ones. "Mind you, Lord Amhirst, a contract signals a political alliance, not an act of abject submission to your whims."

Amhirst's mind is already elsewhere and he blankly agrees, "Yes, yes, yes. Of course."

Cornwell begrudgingly signs and seals the scroll.

Benjamin Chandler gets up and puts an arm around the grand sage's shoulders as if sharing a family hug. The grand sage is nonplussed by the excessive show of familiarity, but he holds his tongue.

Chandler tries to lighten the dour mood. "What the noble grand sage means to say is that without freedom of thought, there can be no such thing as wisdom. We will always tell you the truth as best as we can discern it. Whether you take that as a token of friendship or enmity depends on the greatness of your spirit."

Amhirst admires the young man's quick wit and feels reassured that the tuition scholarship Cornwell muscled into the deal will be money well spent. "Brilliantly stated, young man. Now if you will excuse me, it seems an urgent message through the Pony Express is waiting for me. Make no mistake about it—in the upcoming days, we will plan a celebration of our newfound accord for all Ithicans: feasts, tournaments, dramas, and entertainers."

Benjamin jumps right into his new role. "As your new frankelyn, I would be honored to serve on the planning committee for this celebration, my lord."

Ushering them out, the baron concludes with a grandiose swirl of his arm, "As my frankelyn, you shall be the head of that committee. Good evening, Grand Sage! Adieu!"

With an almost polite shove, the baron steers Cornwell out of the room and waves his herald and the halfling messenger waiting at the door to come inside.

The messenger hands him a sealed letter but Amhirst does not touch it. He waves to his herald. "Whose seal is it, Sir Sean?"

The halfling courier in long riding boots—about as long as his short legs can fit into—steps past Sir Sean Madigan briskly. "Begging your pardon, my lord, but even the seal is for your eyes only."

"All right, set it on the table," says the baron of Amhirst. "Sir Sean is my most trusted advisor, but your discretion is commendable. Here, let me pour you some wine while you warm yourself by the fire."

"Sorry, my lord, but we have an oath that prevents us from ungodly language and strong drink."

The baron of Amhirst nods. "Yes, that was my understanding. I wanted to make sure you actually are with the Pony Express. Few people know about your special work requirements.

"Several of my enemies have plotted my demise with false letters and poisoned packets. Your insistence that I be the only one to see this delivery came across as suspicious, but you passed the test. Here's a newly minted groat for your troubles."

The halfling postal worker looks at the coin quizzically. "How much is a groat worth, my lord?"

Benjamin Chandler loves math and explains, "Four pennies. He that spends a groat a day idly, spends idly above six pounds a year."

Sir Sean adds, "It'll more than cover a hearty meal and a good night's rest at the Dancing Pony."

Amhirst concludes, "You are dismissed for now. What did you say your name was again?"

"Underhill, my lord."

"Oh, that's a splendid name for a halfling. Mister Underhill, please check back at my door first thing in the morning before you depart, in case I have an immediate response for the sender."

"Yes, my lord." The halfling bows respectfully. His frizzy sideburns sway with every motion of his head. Though his eyes are young, his sun-dried brow and rugged cheeks speak of a rough life in the saddle with few creature comforts.

After the Pony Express rider exits the room, Sir Sean Madigan picks the letter up off the table. "It's the seal of Cardinal Orsini."

Amhirst asks, "Which one? Each of the three Orsini brothers keeps wanting to make his importance felt over the other two."

Sir Sean inspects it closely but looks up and says, "Can't tell. The imprint on the wax is all smudged and fuzzy. My guess is they want you to know it's really from them while still retaining a measure of deniability. One swipe of the thumb would efface it entirely."

Benjamin asks politely, "May I have a look?"

Amhirst raises his eyebrows. "By all means! You are in my court now, Mister Frankelyn—a trusted advisor."

The flattery takes its effect on the new frankelyn. He looks at it carefully and reports, "I'd say this is coming from the office of Maderno Cardinal Orsini, my lord. He has made quite a reputation for himself as being the brains behind their witch trials. Paterno Cardinal Orsini is the ferocious one—the reason the people of Baston have started calling them the Three Bears.

"Actually, if my paltry Italian serves me right, *orsino* is the diminutive form of *orso*. We should be calling the Orsini brothers the Three Little Bears. It's the little one among them, Piccolo Cardinal Orsini, who adds the whimsical unpredictability to the whole operation that makes the very sound of the word *Inquisition* drive terror into the hearts of the general populace."

"Terror hardly begins to describe it, Mister Frankelyn," comments Sir Sean dryly. "It's one thing to be condemned to torture and death for a crime you never committed. It's another thing entirely to be condemned to Hell for a sin you never committed."

Amhirst waves his fingers to shoo away the whole conversation and says, "Putting a little fear of God into the hearts and minds of the Bastonians can be useful. Anyhow, what does the letter say?"

Sir Sean breaks open the seal and unfurls the scroll. "It's in Latin, my lord."

"Let's have Brother Tuck read it carefully. I want to know anything you can deduce from the letter, not just its contents. Was it written with an agitated hand? Is he trying to impress me with the cost of the parchment? Is the tone subtly threatening or is he trying to hide desperation or some less obvious vulnerability?"

Brother Tuck motions toward a seat near the hearth fire and the baron nods. He sits and examines the letter, front to back, turning it over and reading it twice.

The baron's patience eventually begins to wear thin. He asks, "What can you tell us?"

"Without a little more context, it will be hard for me to surmise exactly the implications. But Cardinal Maderno writes to ask for help investigating a very delicate matter."

Benjamin snaps his fingers and calls out, "I was right! It *is* Maderno after all!"

Amhirst commends him patiently. "Very good, Benjamin. Now, let's hear what it says."

Brother Tuck clears his throat. "Uh, yes. After the formalities it says, and I quote, '. . . now that you have been appointed by King Eddard the secular strong arm of the Holy Inquisition in Vinland.' I'm not sure what he means by that."

The baron of Amhirst sips his wine by the fireside. "Yes, yes, in my letter describing our relationship with Inquisitor Sheen, I implied that our patronage might expand by royal decree, without getting into specifics. My contacts at King Eddard's court in Lunden should hammer out something official in a few months. For now, time is of the essence, so until I get a response from the king, I'm improvising as I go along."

"Very well, my lord," says Brother Tuck.

"So what does the Inquisition want of me?"

"It says they had an intruder break into their residence in Salim. Um . . . let's see here . . . yes, so I'll do my best to translate these few paragraphs here:

> Your stay in Ithica has made you the closest friend we have to a very delicate and confidential matter. Upon successful completion of this quest, we will guarantee your appointment as viceroy of Vinland by His Holiness Pope Martin and support any accusation of heresy you make against your enemies.

Last night, a document of inestimable value was stolen from our residence. The Roman Curia has charged Raymond Bertrand de Goethe, the archdeacon of Auch, a powerful and well-connected cleric from Frankland, with the task of extirpating all Cathar heretics from the lands of Oxitania and Longbardia. The archdeacon sent to us a certain Parisian doctor by the name of Georges Faust, asking us to aid and abet him in every possible manner.

As it turns out, his quest was to locate and obtain the lost Sword of Layban. After much diligence, Doctor Faust discovered this ancient artifact in the possession of the Hill Dwarves of Cumorah. The dwarves demanded of him the exorbitant fee of 8,000 gold florins or 2,400 silver marks for this ancient artifact. Reluctantly, he obtained the funds in the form of a banknote from the Knights Templar preceptory in Rofchester. According to the agreement, the Hill Dwarves of Cumorah were to exchange the sword for the banknote after the Templar loremasters had verified its authenticity.

The verification process took several months but on the feast of Saint Mary the Egyptian, documents finally arrived from the Templar loremasters certifying the authenticity of the Sword of Layban. The Templar bankers duly forwarded the payment to the Hill Dwarves of Cumorah and sent Doctor Faust a receipt of the transaction along with a safe deposit slip so that he could come claim the sword from their vaults in the Templar Preceptory of Rofchester.

Upon receiving these documents, Doctor Faust handed them to us for safekeeping in our residence before he went into Baston to purchase equipment and hire adventurers to escort him safely and secretly to Rofchester and back.

That morning before leaving to hear cases, my brother Piccolo put the Templar safe deposit slip to claim the Sword of Layban in a secret compartment in his parlor chair. Under his bed, he devised a trapdoor to conceal the Templar certification of authenticity and the purchase receipt for the sword.

By the grace of divine Providence, all three of us returned home early that day and saw that all our parlor chairs had been tampered with, but that Piccolo's had been completely disassembled. No doubt, someone tipped the thief off.

Fearing the worst, we rushed upstairs and surprised a young girl with curly, blonde hair rummaging through Piccolo's bed. Before we could get a good look at her face, she escaped with great dexterity out the second-floor window and eluded the Swiss guards we sent after her. Fortunately, she did not find the receipt and certificate hidden under the trapdoor beneath Piccolo's bed.

Asking ourselves how it would be possible for an intruder to know precisely where and when to look for these documents, we could only conclude that we had been betrayed by one of our household servants. Normally, we dismiss all our servants while we are away and lock up the residence carefully.

It was Piccolo who noticed that a bowl of porridge had been eaten in our absence. The porridge in the pot was too cold for the cook to have accidentally left it on the fire while away and too hot for him to have extinguished the flame before leaving. Therefore, the cook must have been in the house while we were away and warmed up the porridge for Goldilocks after letting her into the house.

Before he expired, we learned from the cook that although Goldilocks has the safe deposit slip, she does not yet know which Templar bank holds the

> Sword of Layban in its vaults. That is why she needed the receipt as well.
>
> Your quest, Lord Amhirst, should you choose to accept it, is to recover the Sword of Layban and deliver it to us in Salim before Goldilocks and her coconspirators can find it. Without the safe deposit slip, you may need to break into the vault and steal it yourself.
>
> If you or any of your agents are caught or killed, the Holy Office of the Inquisition will disavow any knowledge of your actions. This letter is to be burnt immediately after reading it, upon pain of excommunication.

Brother Tuck tosses it into the fire. Quickly, Amhirst grabs a fire poker and tries to rescue the letter but the flames consume it with such a burst of light and smoke as to leave little doubt that it had been brushed with linseed oil before sending.

The baron of Amhirst huffs as he sits back down. "Brother Tuck, your obedience in following instructions is commendable, but if backed in a corner, that letter could have been useful."

Brother Tuck stands up to the baron. "With all due respect, my lord, if you pulled out a letter like that when backed in a corner, you would be dead before you could think of a proper use for it."

"Oh, all right," concedes the baron. "What is so important about this sword, anyway?"

Brother Tuck sits back down and clears his throat. "If my memory serves, the Sword of Layban is used as part of a blackflame ritual in the art of necromancy."

Benjamin Chandler adds, "Some of the students were talking about that the other day. I think it can transform a living person into an undead state. They were calling it a type of evil transubstantiation."

Brother Tuck corrects him. "There is no evil form of transubstantiation. The proper term in theology for that would be *transmogrification*."

Amhirst rubs his chin. "Confusing, isn't it? When I pledged myself to support Inquisitor Sheen, did I not take the Crusader's vow to fight the blackflame heresy in Vinland? Now the Holy Office of the Inquisition is asking me to fetch an artifact that would allow them to engage in blackflame necromancy. Doesn't that violate my own Crusader's vow?"

Brother Tuck tugs at the collar of his monk's cowl and says, "Theologically speaking, we can make a distinction. You only swore to fight the blackflame heresy in *Vinland*. This Sword of Layban will be shipped off to *Frankland*. By removing it from Vinland, you will be keeping it out of the hands of blackflame heretics here and thus fulfilling your vow."

Amhirst pauses, then says, "It disturbs me how easily you are able to convince me that black is white and white is black."

"Both are liturgical colors, my lord."

Amhirst shrugs and turns to his herald, saying, "Sir Sean, what's your opinion? Is it possible to take on this quest without risking war with the Knights Templar?"

"One way immediately comes to mind, if it pleases your lordship."

"Go on."

"Remember that party of adventurers you hired to hunt down the heir of the late Marquis Ducaine? I'm quite sure they don't know they're working for you—at least they've asked no questions."

Amhirst thinks for a moment and replies, "Yes, you sent them out years ago, if I recall correctly. I thought they had abandoned that quest."

Holding up a bone amulet with scrimshaw letters he says, "Apparently not. They brought me this amulet as proof that they succeeded."

"Why didn't you tell me this before?"

"They just arrived yesterday to inform me that their quest has been accomplished. They're waiting for their reward at the Dancing Pony."

"How did they find us here?" asks the baron.

"If they could track down a boy that nearly every Frank in Vinland is trying to hide, how hard could it have been for them to track down your army?"

"Supposedly, they don't know I hired them."

"Don't worry, my lord. They're all hush-hush."

The worry on the baron's forehead visibly heightens. "Their silence doesn't prove their ignorance of my involvement in the plot to assassinate young Laurence Ducaine. They could use it against me."

"Their silence proves they understand the risk of double-crossing us, my lord."

"We'll discuss it later. Right now, we have to decide whether or not to seek out this Sword of Layban for the cardinals of the Inquisition and, if so, whom to send.

"A war with the Templars would ruin us, and I'm not so sure we'll be able to count on your adventurers' discretion or thoroughness on this one. This quest is time-sensitive, and they took years to accomplish the last quest. Besides, this amulet proves nothing. The boy might still be alive for all we know."

"Think of it from the other direction, my lord. Our treasury is full from our recent conquest of Montroyal, my lord. Why risk stiffing these adventurers out of the reward they earned for fulfilling this quest right at the moment when they are our only option to cement our alliance with the Holy Office of the Inquisition?"

"Only option? A whole army is at my disposal."

"You can't send the whole army. Only a small party of adventurers with no formal links to you can complete a quest like this. We don't have time to putz around weighing options and conducting job interviews for qualified but obscure candidates.

"Let's not underestimate Goldilocks. She's got a three-day head start on us. We must assume that she has friends in every town and village from Baston to Oregan. She probably speaks a dozen languages and knows every local custom. She'll blend in, disappear. Unless we send out a crack team of elite adventurers right away, she will have the Sword of Layban before our people even reach Rofchester."

Amhirst shakes his head, gets up, and starts pacing around the room. After a short while he announces, "Sir Sean, I don't like it. I simply don't trust these adventurers. They're sloppy, slow, and inconsistent. A quest of this importance requires someone quick, efficient, and loyal."

"That presents a paradox, my lord. You expect us to entrust this quest to someone who has no association with you but is perfectly loyal and competent."

Amhirst snaps his fingers and stops pacing. "Wait! I have an idea! These adventurers could prove useful if only we appointed a proper leader to keep them in check. We would need someone whose loyalty I trust not to cheat me, but has no known public association with me that could get me in trouble with the Templars if caught, and is clever enough to tangle with sly adventurers. I do believe we have found our man." He and Sir Sean slowly turn their heads to gaze at the youngest person in the room. "What do you say, Benjamin Frankelyn?"

Scene 5: Winning One for the Gipper

Betzy Rose Mansion, Red Giant's Base, Shentalpee City
Spy Woden's Day Nones. Afternoon, 5th of April, 1284

When Madame Dungaree opens the door, joy suffuses her face. "Health and happiness, Mister Lynx! You bring light to this place. I knew you'd come! Mademoiselle Zena isn't home right now but our guest is eager to meet you. Walk this way, if you please."

Clearly making an effort to put on a brave face, Lynx smiles and says, "Health and happiness to you, Madame Dungaree. Please, don't trouble yourself. Bartlebee can show me the way."

A jolt of pain and embarrassment streaks across her eyes. "Oh, um . . . Bartlebee is away on . . . personal leave. It was an unexpected family matter and I haven't managed to replace her yet. I'd be happy to walk with you myself but before we go in, I can't help but notice you look a little sad."

"Not sad, just frustrated. Just before coming here, I won the Justiciar League tournament by one point over Monsieur Enganyon. He was so angry that he left early but when I went up to claim my commission as a Junior Officer, the adjudicators disqualified my last arrow and awarded the commission to Monsieur Enganyon."

"Oh, that's too bad. I'm so disappointed at how they've been treating you. Wait...did you say Monsieur Enganyon left early? Maybe you could argue that he forfeited the tournament by quitting."

Lynx flings his hands out and flops them back to his sides like an elfling that just missed recess. "I already tried. They said his leg injury exempted him from that rule. It's no use, Madame Dungaree. They're always going to find an excuse to keep a wood elf like me out of the major leagues."

She puts her hand on his back and leads him through the corridor to the guest room saying, "Don't give up, Mister Lynx. They think they're so smart, but you'll outsmart them when the time is right."

Compared to the homes of other high elves of her wealth and status, Dungaree Jeanne's residence, called Betzy Rose Mansion, is like a Spartan war camp. Against any other standard, her treetop mansion is no less spectacular than Cinderella's castle at the Magic Realms theme park in D'Isigny World. Magnificent murals, elegant arches, and fancy furniture line every step of the way from the front door to the guest room.

Up in Shentalpee City, real estate is sold by the square inch, not the square foot, so the hallways are just broad enough to let two people pass by each other cozily while admiring the great art along the way. Tables and chairs are recessed into lofted nooks so as not to take up any precious floor space. Not only are the wooden ceiling tiles richly carved, lacquered, and filigreed, but also the wall panels and floorboards make a serious attempt to hold your attention with their decorative ingenuity.

Still, despite all this elegance, Betzy Rose Mansion's décor is staid, almost a bare-bones concept for avoiding extravagance compared to her high elf neighbors.

The fourth door past the waiting room is the guest room. The parlor and the dining room are downstairs so that visitors to the household do not need to go traipsing through the private quarters of the permanent residents upstairs. Bartlebee's room is just past the kitchen with her own servant's entrance across the way.

You cannot see it easily from the bottom of the glittering staircase but once you get to the second floor, the impressive furnishings and refined decorations mellow out significantly to a posh but sparing nexus of bedrooms, the largest of which is currently used as a library and study. The main staircase—complete with the kind of glamorous steps and railings a fairy-tale princess would need to make a dramatic entrance for her suitors waiting down below—overhangs Johnny Appleseed's guest room.

Gently knocking on the door, Dungaree Jeanne hears a muffled hoot from inside and takes it as an invitation to come in. Nearly all high elf dwellings share a wall or two with their neighbors so soundproofing is one of the top architectural priorities. That makes it nearly impossible to eavesdrop in Shentalpee City—I say nearly impossible because Zena somehow manages to overhear every whisper from one end of the mansion to the other.

Anyway, Dungaree Jeanne opens the door and shows Lynx in. Reverend Appleseed seems to be waking up from a nap and gets reminded in the process of all the pain in his leg. The expression on his face lets them all know he is doing his best to endure it bravely.

Lynx extends a hand and says in Aenglish, "Pleasure to meet you, Reverend Appleseed."

Johnny Appleseed takes Lynx's hand and pretends to smile despite the pain shooting up and down his leg. "Are you the young wood elf who speaks Aenglish?"

"My name is Hare Gipper. You say Mister Lynx in Aenglish, no? I am wood elf, like you say. If I speak

Aenglish, you listen and say yes or no." Lynx laughs and when Reverend Appleseed realizes he is trying to be funny he joins in the laughter, just to be polite.

The reality is Johnny Appleseed barely understands Lynx's thick Elvish accent. He sighs with noble resignation. It's going to be a long couple of months up here as the only human in Shentalpee City.

Madame Dungaree backs out of the room, saying in her crisp, fluent Aenglish, "Well, I'll leave you two to get acquainted. If Mademoiselle Zena does return, I'll make sure to send her up to you as well."

The mention of Zena's name spikes a surge of confusion and fear within Lynx's innermost thoughts. He came here intending to tell Zena about Enganyon's relationship with Florenz at the Shade Gap but what if she reacts to the news as irrationally as Buttercup did?

"Pleasure to meet you, Hare Gipper. Do you know about our Lord and Savior Jesus Christ?"

Totally distracted with his own problems, Lynx answers absent-mindedly, "Yes, I do. He is very nice guy, thank you."

Johnny Appleseed says with a fatherly concern, "Something's bothering you, Hare Gipper. It ain't hard to tell. As we say in Kentikie, you look like a cat on a hot, lead-shingled roof."

Lynx confesses at once, "You know Mademoiselle Zena? I love her too much but she love bad elf. His name is Monsieur Enganyon Gandorfson."

"Yes, I've met this Enganyon fellow. You could say he taught me how to fly. Hardy har-har!"

Now it is Lynx's turn to pretend to smile. It is hard to believe even a Christian missionary would take an assassination attempt so lightly. "Monsieur Enganyon is liar and Mademoiselle Zena believe him always. He pretend he like Mademoiselle Zena but he only want to win elve girl who win election. He think Mademoiselle Florenz is better winner so he go to Shade Gap with her. I think to tell Mademoiselle Zena so she see that he love Mademoiselle Florenz but I think she not listen."

Reverend Appleseed rubs his beard and thinks for a while. "Hmm," he says cautiously. "If she has such poor judgment, maybe you would be better off transferring your affections to another young maiden."

Lynx throws his hands up in the air. "But it is not me that I think that I can love other elve! I not choose elve that I love. Mademoiselle Zena is beautiful, smart, and . . . how you say? . . . magical. She soon have magica wand. Her mother is very rich and she tame unicorn! How many Aenglish girls tame unicorn?"

"Most Aenglish girls don't believe in unicorns . . ."

"Wait . . . not believe? What Aenglish girls say when they see pony with horn on head?"

"People believe what they want to believe and rarely allow what they see or don't see to get in the way of that, once they've made up their minds."

"Yes! That is how Mademoiselle Zena do to me! She always believe Monsieur Enganyon and she is mad to me when I say to her that he is bad elf."

Johnny Appleseed gives him a hard but kind look and says, "Let's take a step back for a moment, Hare Gipper. Would you still love her if she lost her good-looks, her wealth, and her talents?"

"I not so sure what you want to say."

"You said Enganyon wants to marry the winner of the election. How different is your love? What I'm asking is this: do you really love Zena . . . I mean,

Mademoiselle Zena . . . for who she is or are you just impressed with all that she has going for her now?"

"I not so sure."

"My intuition tells me her heart belongs to Monsieur Enganyon, but Madame Dungaree does not like him and she thinks you're a better influence."

"Your intuition is good."

"When it comes to winning the heart of a sassy young woman, nice guys finish last, Mister Gipper. I suggest you find a lady whose heart beats at a speed closer to yours."

"But I not let Mademoiselle Zena marry bad elf."

"You have to let her decide that for herself. The more you insist, the worse she will resent you for forcing her to face a truth she's not yet ready to handle.

"Besides, this Enganyon fellow might not be so bad after all. Jonah got angry when he heard God had forgiven the Ninevites after they repented of their sins. What if Enganyon comes around and does some good with his life? Are you going to be able to accept God's mercy for him? Christ came to call sinners, you know."

Lynx folds his arms. "Yes, I know. I am Christian like prophet Healaman. I know that Christians love enemies but Mademoiselle Zena not want—"

Knock, knock!

Johnny Appleseed calls out, "Who's there?"

They hear a muffled voice say, "Hatch."

Johnny Appleseed asks, "Hatch who?"

Zena peeks her head inside smiling and says, "Gezondhide!" When she sees Lynx speaking with Johnny Appleseed, she raises her eyebrows and greets him in Eldric, "Health and happiness to you, Mister Lynx! You bring light to our house! Can I have a word with you for a minute?"

"Sure, Mademoiselle Zena," replies Lynx in Eldric, suddenly turning weak and submissive. "I was just telling Reverend Appleseed I was hoping to see you."

She giggles apologetically and asks in Aenglish, "Pardon, Reverend Appleseed, please give me permission that I speak with Lynx in Eldric for little bit? We have, um . . . family problem."

Johnny Appleseed asks cheerfully, "Are you pregnant? I've placed plenty of unexpected babies in loving families. No need to hide any embarrassments from me. I'm too old to blush at life."

Zena's jaw hangs open for a few moments before she recovers. "Uh, no . . . that is not it at all. I will say it in Aenglish if it makes you feel more comfortable."

"As you wish, my fair lady. If there's any assistance I can provide to you and your mother, I will. Your kindness to me has been overwhelming."

Zena sits down next to Lynx and puts on a serious face. She tells him in Aenglish, "Mademoiselle Florenz has announced to Tuscoraura high elves that our stewardess, Bartlebee, has stealed alchemy for elf fire from my mother and she is selling to mercenary dwarf, who has name Master Chief Engineer Tom Thumb—very famous and very powerful dwarf. We not do it, but Bartlebee is our stewardess and we take blame."

Johnny Appleseed runs his fingers through his beard. "Why would Mademoiselle Florenz say all this about you, if it's not true?"

Zena takes a deep breath. "She wants to win election! Our early fathers and mothers have invented alchemy for . . . how do you say . . . ooze to make elf fire. You throw it at enemy and they go up in big fire and nothing can put out fire, not even water. Elf fire is very important to fire elves. We feel safe because only we know elf fire. If dwarves know elf fire, fire elves feel very scared. We are not special anymore. No one votes for elve who loses elf fire alchemy."

Again Johnny Appleseed nods and comments, "So you have gallons of unquenchable fire ooze up here in the treetops? Not the safest idea, is it?"

Lynx explains, "Shentalpee City is builded on sequoia. Sequoia is fire tree. Fire not harm sequoia. Fire good for sequoia. It make pine cone open and give new seed. Sequoia tree need fire and fire elf need fire."

Turning back to Zena, Johnny Appleseed asks, "Do you need my help to prove that these accusations are not true?"

A worried look settles on Zena's face. "Yes and no. My mother says that Bartlebee stole alchemy to other fire, we call it Athabask fire. Athabask fire not so strong as elf fire and you put salt on it and it goes out. So alchemy to true elf fire is still safe.

"But even so it is still bad. If all world knows that dwarves have Athabask fire, they think that fire elves not so special, even with elf fire. I already tell you that Umpire Kibbler wants that Tuscoraura elves make more weapons so that we be stronger than our enemies. If our enemies have all same weapons—or if our enemies *think* they have all same weapons—they will attack Shentalpee City. And that is no good. The fire elves say best weapon is one we never use."

Tears well up in the corners of Zena's eyes. Lynx puts a hand on her shoulder to encourage her, just as she did for him earlier on. Zena sniffles and pulls out an embroidered silk handkerchief. Without thinking, she switches to Eldric. "If we arrest Bartlebee right away and make sure that Tom Thumb's dwarves don't get their grubby, overgrown hands on that Athabask recipe, the Council of Perfects is willing to acquit my mother of all charges before the case goes to trial.

"If we fail, my mother will be publicly prosecuted for leaking state secrets. If she is convicted, the council could revoke our status as high elves, confiscate all our property, and even have her executed as a traitor!"

Lynx stands up. Striking his most chivalrous pose, he declares in Eldric, "I will find Bartlebee for you, Mademoiselle Zena! I place my bow at your—"

Guessing from his body language that Lynx is about to make big promises, Johnny Appleseed cuts him off and says in Aenglish with a loud, assertive voice, "What young Mister Lynx means to say is that he is flattered by the trust and confidence you have placed in him and that he will give your dilemma serious consideration.

"In the meantime, he has a matter of similar peril that he has to handle at the Shade Gap this very night. Perhaps if you, little missy, could help him with his quest at the Shade Gap, he could help you with your quest in handling all that elf fire business. Isn't that right, my boy?"

Lynx blinks. Suddenly a light goes on in his eyes and he stutters in Aenglish, "Oh . . . um . . . yes, that is right. You can help me with my . . . um . . . quest at Shade Gap tonight, then I can help you with your quest to get Bartlebee."

Zena looks askance at Johnny Appleseed, then nods to Lynx and says in Eldric, "Yes, I agree to help you if you solemnly promise to see this quest for Bartlebee through to the end. If Bartlebee escapes on a swift pony, we may need to take on Tom Thumb and his dwarf engineers."

Lynx puffs out his chest with pride. "Rudolph could run down a halfling pony any day of the week."

Zena smiles with a sly, satisfied grin, convinced that she has thoroughly manipulated every weakness in Lynx's chivalrous nature, and announces, "Very well then, let's get our gear ready. Hi ho! It's off to Shade Gap we go!"

Scene 6: Blasphemous Rhapsody

Shade Gap
Five Miles Northwest of Tuscoraura Mountain
Spy Woden's Day Compline. Night, 5th of April, 1284

Brother Umbert blurts out to Sir Robert Roger, "We can't let them kill him! Show him you mean business. Cut off the goblin's ear or something!"

Inquisitor Sheen interrupts, "Our Lord healed Malchus's ear. We are not to resort to violence except in self-defense."

Sir Robert Roger, holding the dagger to the throat of the old chieftain's son, says, "Sorry, little monk, I tried but it's just not going to happen that way. The deal was to keep my men safe. If I harm his son, he will kill all my rangers." He turns to Brother Umbert. "It's too bad about the boy, but at this point, there is nothing we can do about it."

Brother Umbert squeaks, "We would be material accomplices to murder if we do nothing!"

"All we can do now is pray, Brother Umbert," says Inquisitor Sheen, resigned. "We put our trust in God."

The goblin captors make the rangers and the monks kneel between two stone arches painted with pictograms. The goblins have set up tents around the pagan temple. The inquisitor's gift of tongues is powerful enough that he can slowly read the words of the goblin prophets written on the archway walls and encampment banners.

Inquisitor Sheen focuses on them prayerfully and as the words form in his mind, it suddenly clicks and the sign flashes out its warning, "Here on these hallowed grounds, you will behold the rites that voices may never share. Thou shalt not talk without speaking. Thou shalt not listen without hearing. Defilers of these stones are doomed."

One goblin wearing a coyote fur draped across his head and shoulders fills a flagon from a barrel and makes the inquisitors and rangers drink it, saying, "Koolaed!"

Brother Umbert refuses. "I will not partake in this heathen ceremony!"

Sir Robert Roger shouts, "Just drink the koolaed, and let's get this over with!"

Brother Crowe takes a swig, then another, and exclaims with a grin, "Hops!"

Among the group of captive rangers is a young apprentice named Nathan Hayle. The coyote goblin passes him by. He asks, "What hops?"

Dame Frances Marian says, "Hops is a bitter seasoning from Bohemia that preserves drinks from spoiling. Whenever available, I add hops and vinegar to my canteen to keep the water from going rancid and ward off scurvy. Actually, I find it tasty. Ahem! Mister Goblin, could I have another swig of your koolaed?"

Nathan Hayle sours his face when he takes a sip. "Tasty? Says the lady who drinks vinegar every day."

Sir Robert Roger looks at one of the goblin acolytes and says, "Over here, let me try some of that."

The goblin acolyte scoops some more out and the ranger captain quaffs the entire flagon. Having all drunk the koolaed, the rangers comply with their part in preparing themselves for the human sacrifice. Brother Umbert, however, folds his arms in protest.

Inquisitor Sheen says, "Brother Umbert, drink the koolaed or they will offer you to their god, Poodoo!"

Brother Umbert wrinkles his face in indignation. "Is this real life or just a fantasy? The inquisitor himself is telling me to take part in a human sacrifice ritual!"

Two goblins drag the wicker basket cage holding the young monk toward the sacrificial altar. He is a tall, lanky human teenager sporting a peach fuzz mustache. His wears a Carmelite brown robe and white cape.

The hulking goblin who seems to be the chieftain's older son pulls the young monk out of the cage with one hand. Towering over the other goblins, this hulking goblin stands an inch or two over six feet tall. He wears little more than a purple loincloth and his bulging muscles make the strongest goblins around him seem scrawny.

He is decked out with white and black tribal paints and carries a ceremonial phoenix claw in his right hand. He shouts, "Malileo gandango scaramanifico!"

All look to Inquisitor Sheen for a translation but the inquisitor says nothing.

Brother Umbert makes the sign of the cross and cries out, "Look, Inquisitor Sheen! That boy is a monk! Spare him his life from this monstrosity!"

The inquisitor remains silent.

The young monk turns his collar to the cold and damp and says, "Don't stir trouble for yourselves over me. I'm just a poor boy. I need no sympathy! If you object too loudly, they will kill you too."

The goblin king approaches the altar wearing a ceremonial headdress with vulture feathers, snake fangs, and coyote skulls. The hulking goblin hands his father the ceremonial phoenix talon. Then the goblin king sprinkles a powder into the altar flame and it explodes with a frightful boom.

The flash of demon light stabs the eyes of the inquisitors and rangers, splitting the night.

The young monk continues to intone the words of the psalm, "Yes, though I walk through the valley of the shadow of death, I will fear no evil. For you are with me, O God. Your rod and staff give me comfort." And in the naked light of that flash Brother Umbert sees ten drowsy people, maybe more, close enough to rescue the boy but no one dares to disturb the sound of the inquisitor's silence.

"Fools," says Brother Umbert. "Don't you know that the silence of good people in the face of evil grows like a cancer? Hear my words. At least we can teach these goblins by our deaths that we do not approve of killing innocent lives."

But his words fall like silent raindrops and run off the stones without soaking in. The only echoes come from the wells in the caverns beneath.

And the goblins bow and pray to the demon gods they made out of stone.

Despite Brother Umbert's protests, the goblin king carries on as if nothing really matters and says, "Basem illa mammia."

They pour koolaed into Brother Umbert's mouth but he spits it out all over the goblin king. Two goblin acolytes grab him and put him on the sacrificial altar. All the courage drains from his face as he blubbers to himself, "Wait! What . . . what are they doing?"

At last, the thought of losing his feisty but dear friend moves Inquisitor Sheen to risk failing his quest of reaching Tuscoraura Mountain for the Holy Office of the Inquisition. Thus, he speaks out to the old war chief in Gobbledygook, "I know that you are powerful, mighty Gog, and that your anger with my friend must be equally powerful. I count on your greatness to bargain for his life. With your wisdom, I'm sure we can work out an arrangement that will be mutually beneficial and avoid any unpleasant confrontation."

The chief grunts, "Heck no, I won't let him go!"

Not understanding the words exchanged between the two but seeing the disappointment on the inquisitor's face at the goblin king's reply, Brother Umbert whimpers, "Too late, my time has come. It sends shivers down my spine. My body aches."

A goblin shaman approaches the altar and throws another handful of powder into the fire. It explodes and seems to put the goblin king into a trance. He begins to prophesy in a sacred goblin tongue that only goblin shamans and Inquisitor Sheen, because of his mystical gift of tongues, can understand. "Hello, darkness, my old friend, I've come to offer you this boy as a human sacrifice as you instructed me in that softly creeping vision. The seeds of long life and a glorious future were planted in my spleen while I was sleeping. May this offering ensure that I always destroy my enemies and may it keep us safe from wendigos."

The goblin king drags the young monk up to the altar and lifts the phoenix talon dagger high over his head, aiming to strike the boy's heart.

Seeing death close in on him, the young Carmelite monk panics. "Mama, ooh, I don't want to die!"

With a sudden smile alighting on his face, Brother Umbert shouts, "Wait! I see a little silhouette of an elf in the trees. We are saved!"

Scene 7: A Long Shot

Shade Gap
Five Miles Northwest of Tuscoraura Mountain
Spy Woden's Day Matins
After Midnight, 5th of April, 1284

The trees do not grow tall on the mountaintops overlooking the Shade Gap, but Lynx perches himself two hundred yards away on an aspen tree with enough foliage to conceal his movements. Zena crouches close behind him still wondering why exactly Lynx invited her out to spy on this goblin ritual. Although the greenish-yellow glow from the tips of the goblin torchbearers' ten-foot poles cast an unnatural hue across the horizon, like a grim dawn, the evening stars are still romantic, so she decides to focus on the starlight and daydream the night away while Lynx figures out what he really wants to do here.

Her thoughts drift to seven wedding plans to match seven different scenarios that she can imagine where Enganyon finally confesses that he loves her. Her reveries halt when she notices the halfling monk—whom we know to be Brother Umbert—pointing straight at them. Most of the goblins turn their heads to look but the goblin king remains entranced, ready to carry out the sacrifice.

Lynx shudders. Two hundred yards away foul spirits gambol and innocent lives are under the knife. The wind blows one way, then the next. He steadies his bow arm, draws the bowstring back, and exhales. Casting fate to the wind, Lynx sends his shot.

The yellow-fletched arrow streaks through the dark toward the heart of the goblin king on a mission of mercy to save the two monks from a diabolical death.

It misses.

The arrow glides high and wide, then unexpectedly buries itself in the goblin king's wrist. Covered with koolaed and spittle, the goblin king drops the ceremonial dagger. Blood drips freely down past his elbow but his trance is undisturbed.

Uncomfortable groans reverberate on the mountaintop and the goblins' faces are covered with worry and discord. For devout goblins, interrupting a human sacrifice is a very ill omen indeed. The goblin king, not realizing he dropped the sacrificial dagger, purses his lips and readies himself to finish it.

Sir Robert Roger's hostage, the goblin with long, dark hair, smiles confidently seeing the confusion well up. With a sudden lurch of his head backwards he breaks Sir Robert Roger's nose. All it takes is a quick flick of his wrist, and he twists the long knife away from his throat. The black-haired goblin gives the ranger a fierce elbow in the chest, knocking the wind out of him, then snatches the steel hatchet from his belt.

The wheezing ranger captain looks on helplessly as the black-haired goblin runs toward the sacrificial altar calling out, "Kwid prow kwow!"

Before we get locked into the narrative of this famous battle, my dear reader, permit me to close the curtain over the stage to project some basic background details up before your eyes so we can make sense of this imbroglio. The goblin king in this scene, Gog the Destroyer was a large and fearsome goblin who became one of the most daring brigands of his time. He preyed on travelers throughout the entire region south of the Confederacy of the Seven Nations.

The notoriety gained from his cruelty in torturing his prisoners to make them reveal stashes of valuables won him a marriage proposal from Okarim Blackhammer, war chief of the Bigtooth goblins. This war chief had a daughter of enormous size and was so proud of her strength and skill in combat that he fretted continuously about not being able to find a suitor worthy of her, until he heard about Gog.

Once married to his large gobliness bride, Gog promptly murdered his new father-in-law right in front of Blackhammer's elite bodyguards. Duly impressed with Gog's boldness, the leaderless Bigtooths hailed him as their new war chief, took the name Magogs, and set off to subjugate other goblin tribes to Gog's rule.

The most formidable of his adversaries was Ctong, king of the Weemaway goblins. The protracted war drained the resources of both groups of goblins. To end the war, a Weemaway prince named Skaar—the handsome, black-haired goblin who just pummeled Sir Robert Roger—sent King Gog a message offering to betray his own father, King Ctong, in return for adoption into Gog's family and a leadership role among the Magog goblins. King Gog did not hesitate to accept the offer because he knew that his hulking first-born son, named Samba, had already established himself as his successor among the Magog goblins. Skaar posed no challenge.

But Skaar also asked that after King Ctong's death, King Gog should take Skaar's mother, Zilla, as his second wife to both add legitimacy to his adoption and prevent her murder, since the slaughter of a defeated chief's family was customary. With all these details ironed out Skaar invited his father, King Ctong, to perform a special ritual called the sacrifice of the eight wonders. He was to slay eight of the largest trolls they could capture on a slate altar by the shores of Lake Attawandaron to appease the goblin god of war, Serkas

Seven of these wonders, as it turns out, were unbound trolls and the eighth wonder was King Gog.

King Ctong quickly saw that he had been led into a trap and suspecting his wife's involvement in the betrayal, he grabbed his queen consort, Zilla, and climbed to the top of the entire slate building with her in his arms. The building was the elaborate entrance to an abandoned dwarf slate mine that the Weemaway goblins used for cave painting, bloody sacrifices, screaming, and other primal rituals.

Gog and the trolls sent fire-hardened, sharpened-tipped wooden sticks and flying rocks up at him but Gog gave the trolls strict instructions not to harm his future wife. (Originally he planned to betray Skaar and his mother along with King Ctong, but seeing Zilla's intense beauty made Gog desire her as a wife, so he stuck to the original plan.) Exasperated, Gog called up to him, "Put Zilla down! She is Gog's Zilla now!"

Irate at her husband's tactic of using her as a meat shield against the sticks and stones flying up at them, Gog's Zilla wrestled with King Ctong and they both fell into Lake Attawandaron. After a prolonged struggle underwater, only Zilla swam ashore. In her hands she held King Ctong's iron crown and placed it on King Gog's head as the new king of the Weemaway goblins.

King Gog took his wife Zilla into his special confidence—all the while his newly adopted stepson, Skaar, plotted to overthrow him. By some strange twist of fate, or conjunction of the stars, or guidance by the hand of Providence, Zena, Lynx, the rangers, and the inquisitors happened to be at the altar the same night that Skaar had planned to betray and murder his stepfather, King Gog.

So Skaar did not initiate his rebellion because Lynx interrupted the human sacrifice. It just happens that Lynx's arrow pushed Skaar's sloppy plan across the finish line. They say that the players who stumble onto the center stage of history often wander there from out of back-alley flukes.

Now, we raise the curtain once again on our unlikely heroes.

On Skaar's cue, several black-haired Weemaway goblins rise up to their feet and start hurling stones at King Gog. The goblin king's champion, Otzi, a grizzly bear of a goblin, deftly snatches the first few stones out of the air before they hit the goblin king and then drags him down behind the shelter of the altar.

The entranced goblin king shows no awareness of danger until the long, black hair of his stepson comes hurtling toward him with the ranger's steel hatchet in hand. Still dodging rocks, Otzi intercepts the hatchet with his bare hands. The deflected axe cuts a gash deep into the base of his thumb. Ignoring the pain, Otzi grabs a copper axe from his own belt and the two wrestle for control of each other's weapon.

The goblin king's eyes bulge with rage and he lets out a bloodcurdling war cry. He picks up the ceremonial dagger with his uninjured left hand and slashes out at his rebellious stepson, Skaar.

Just as suddenly as it began, the terrifying war cry ends with a gurgling hiss. An obsidian spear protrudes through the goblin king's huge chest. Gog's bride, Zilla, lets go of the spear and runs away, escorted by loyal Weemaway warriors. The goblin king's lifeless body spills over onto the altar, smooshing Brother Umbert's head into the stone underneath his armpit. The halfling whines, "Oh no! I'm pinned down and I can't get up!"

King Gog's hulking, green older son, Samba, up to now has been thoroughly taken aback by the upheavals but his stepmother's treacherous deathblow to his father gives him the focus he needs to get his head back into the fight. Seeing Skaar wrestling with Otzi, Samba delivers a solid punch square into Skaar's face. The punch lands so hard that it knocks his stepbrother out of Otzi's grip. Right then the hulking green Samba realizes that he has just painted his stepbrother's face with enough black and blue to provide him with a goblin's excuse for retreating from the fray. (Goblins will not follow a war leader who retreats from a fight without a visible injury.)

Skaar bares his bloodied teeth at Samba in triumph and slips back through the press of Weemaway goblins hooting and howling as if they wanted a fight. None of them would dare confront Samba in single combat but outnumbering him, they feel the courage to put on a good show.

His father's death does not automatically confer the status of warchief upon Samba. He has to earn it. The Magog goblins all flee except for Otzi, a masterless champion. Samba's battle for survival begins.

First, the waterskin bearer hops up onto the altar and tries to squirt koolaed in Otzi's face but his combat instincts are too sharp to fall for that old trick and with a quick kick to the knees, Otzi spills the koolaed and its bearer all over the altar.

Next, sneaking up behind Samba's back, a torchbearer tries to burn him with the greenish-yellow flame but Samba spins around and roars with such ferocity that the torchbearer flees, too scared to touch him with his ten-foot pole.

Then, two reckless goblins leap up onto the altar, stepping all over the tied-up monks. Samba leaps in between them and deflects a spear thrust from the first into the belly of the second goblin behind him. Otzi follows up with his copper hatchet, beheading the first.

Clearly, Samba is not cursed. Several Weemaway goblins vault up onto the altar to challenge him unarmed but Otzi keeps them at bay with wild swings of his own until Samba yanks the spear from his former assailant's belly. Once armed, he joins Otzi's fight.

Down on the altar's face, Brother Umbert strains under the weight of a dead gobliness fallen on top of him. He realizes the struggle is futile. He whirls his eyes around and spots the ceremonial dagger lying right behind the young monk. He whispers as loudly as he can without attracting attention, "What's your name, Frater?"

"I don't know."

"What do you mean you don't know?"

"Brother David was my religious name," he says, unsure of himself. "But I don't think I'm a Carmelite anymore, so I'm supposed to go by my baptismal name. But I was a foundling on the monastery doorstep and no one ever told me my baptismal name."

"Whatever your canonical status with the Carmelites may be, you're still a cleric. I'll call you Brother Clarke."

"Why Clarke?" asks the confused young monk.

Brother Umbert cannot help but throw in some of his knowledge. "Have you ever heard of a cooper?"

"Sure, that's a barrel maker."

"How about a wainwright?"

"Um, I think they're in the wagon business."

"Right. A cooper is trained to make barrels, and a wainwright is trained to fix wagons. Likewise, a clarke is trained as a cleric to heal, counsel, and guide. You're trained. That makes you a clarke, doesn't it, Frater?"

"I suppose it does."

"Good. Now then, Brother Clarke, the ceremonial dagger is right behind you. Just scooch back a bit and cut yourself free."

Brother Clarke rolls over onto the ceremonial dagger and wiggles around so he can slide his fingers around the handle. His blind attempts wind up with him accidentally cutting his ring finger deeply before he finally succeeds in clutching the handle and sliding the blade against the ropes.

The dagger is so sharp that it easily slices through the thick vines used to bind his hands. When he turns to free Brother Umbert, he notices that his right hand is covered with blood.

The dagger itself is nothing more than a four-inch-long phoenix claw fused onto the top of a stick with a glob of melted copper to bind them together. There is no attempt at artistry or even tidiness in the craftsmanship but its sharpness alone explains why it was chosen as a sacred implement in a ritual sacrifice.

Instead of rescuing Brother Umbert, the young monk sways, waving the dagger around recklessly.

Brother Umbert barks, "Hey, watch where you swing that thing! Don't you know that a phoenix talon has powerful soporific effects?"

Brother Clarke yawns and asks, "What does *soporific* mean?"

"That means it will put you to sleep."

Before he finishes his sentence, Brother Clarke collapses back onto the altar, snoring as loud as a lion sleeping in the night.

The goblins hack and slash at each other mercilessly. Not sure if Lynx angered them with his sacrilegious interruption of the ceremony or if they are just too prone to infighting for their own good, Zena snaps into action. She strings her own bow and starts launching poisoned arrows into the wild press of scuffling goblins.

Elves are not particularly fond of goblins, especially these goblins who have been terrorizing travelers in the forests around Tuscoraura Mountain. Being an elve of her times, Zena enjoys the chance to bloody her enemies with too much zeal. Lynx tugs at her sleeve and urges her. "Come on, Mademoiselle Zena! Now we can rescue the halflings and the humans."

Taking great satisfaction in dealing out death and destruction, she brushes him off, "It's still too risky! Let's improve the odds by killing off these goblins."

Back up in the aspen tree overlooking the ritual site, Lynx sees the young human monk tumble over right before freeing the halfling monk. He dreads the worst for them and announces to Zena, who is still sending poisoned arrows into the crowd of goblins, "I'm going to rescue the innocent people down there before the goblins kill them all."

Zena cannot believe Lynx's naïve plan. She whispers back harshly, "No, you can't go! There are still too many goblins. Besides, even if you do free them, the humans would stab you in the back."

"Why would they do that if we're helping them?"

"Humans are the most ungrateful of all the clayborn. If they see your valuables, they wouldn't bat an eyelash at murdering the very same elf who saved them from bondage to steal it all."

Lynx wipes the sweat from his brow. "I'll just free the two halflings and they can free the humans."

"The goblins will hear you and run you down."

"It's my life I'm risking, not yours."

Zena raises her voice, welling up with emotion. "Lynx, I care about you. I really do. You're so precious to me. Please don't risk your life just to save those humans. They're not worth it."

Lynx pauses for a moment, trying to hold back the tears. A black-haired Weemaway goblin appears at the sacrifice site, rifling through the belongings of the rangers and bundling up their spare weapons to take away. One ranger, Sir Thomas, resists, and the goblin stabs him in the ribs with cold disinterest.

Lynx looks Zena in the eye and says, "I know you can't appreciate it, but I can't turn a blind eye while innocent lives are lost, even if they are only humans."

Lynx surveys the scene to find the best path for sneaking over to free the captives. A rocky gully allows him a quick and concealed path to the altar. With his plan decided upon, he quietly slides down the aspen tree and starts to sneak over to rescue the halfling.

Before he gets far, he spots a little nook in a large pile of rocks that would make the perfect hiding spot and slides himself in.

"Hey, watch it!" says an older elf's voice in Eldric from deeper inside the nook.

"Ahhh!" The surprise of getting caught soon fades into wonderment at finding another fire elf in his hiding spot. When his heartbeat settles down, Lynx asks in Eldric, "Who are you?"

"Master Shoemaker Gulliber Swiffson of Clan Adidazar, at your service. Am I safe in guessing you are a fellow wood elf of Tuscoraura?"

"You are, but your name is not familiar to me."

"That's because I disappeared from Tuscoraura Mountain before you were born. Anyway, no time to chitchat. I'm here to rescue these humans."

"Actually, I was just going to rescue the halfling and let him help the humans escape. A good friend warned me not to trust humans. They have a reputation for ingratitude. Besides, my mother always told me that traipsing around with goblins lurking about is not good for my health."

Master Gulliber nods. "All too true. All right then, let's free that garrulous halfling up there on the altar; but be careful! Try to keep in step with me."

Master Gulliber pops his head up to check for goblins. Confident no one has seen him, he waves to Lynx and the two wood elves crawl up on the altar. There is a dead gobliness warrior splayed across Brother Umbert. Her huge frame pins his arms and legs down so that he can't budge an inch.

Master Gulliber moves next to Brother Umbert, lies down on his back, and gets his legs under the dead gobliness. Lynx catches on and positions himself side by side. With a silent heave-ho, they roll her off the altar. The halfling monk seems to be thanking them, but his babbling is in a language they don't understand.

Lynx simply draws his leaf-bladed short sword and cuts through the vines that were tying the halfling monk's hands together. He whispers to Master Gulliber, "Job's done! Let's get out of here."

Suddenly, they both turn their heads and see a goblin running toward them. Master Gulliber lets out a foul word. On foot, goblins are the fastest runners of all the races in Vinland, so both elves duck behind the other side of the altar and try to vanish from sight. Lynx gets down on his hands and bear-walks to a corner of the altar where he can tuck himself inside a small niche.

The sound of the goblin's footsteps moves up onto the altar. Lynx readies his short sword and smears the blade with some poison. He does not have the kind of money to afford an exceptionally fast-acting nerve agent but if he can get in a first prick with a surprise attack and wear the goblin down with a few adroit dodges and parries, he could have a chance at winning the fight.

As usual, nothing goes according to plan. The goblin leaps down from the altar and lands facing Lynx, who is still wedged into his hiding spot. Lynx lunges forward to stab the goblin but a quick swipe from the goblin's war club knocks his short sword out of his hand. Cornered, Lynx tries to slip by him but the goblin snatches Lynx by the scruff of his neck, lifts him into the air, and squeezes slowly to make him suffer.

As Lynx dangles up off his feet above the ground, trying desperately to pry the powerful fingers from around his throat, he kicks and punches to no avail. Just as he feels he is about to pass out, he drops to the ground like a potato sack and bangs his knee on a rock.

Catching his breath, he turns around to see Zena standing triumphantly over the goblin's lifeless body. She does have the money to afford quick and deadly poisons for her sword and arrows. She twirls her sleek blade in the air and asks with a big, friendly smile, "Why do I always have to save your aaaaahhhhh!"

A second lurking goblin, cloaked in a black bear's pelt, crushes Zena's sword arm and right hip with a dreadful swipe of his ashen club. It is a swift and silent blow but the raw power in the goblin's arm crashes into her lithe frame, shattering bones and sending her into shock. The goblin bends down and starts picking the jewelry off her while she moans in delirious agony. Unarmed, Lynx's grief-crazed mind can only come up with one plan—a desperate charge with his bare hands.

The goblin looks up but carelessly swats him aside with a heavy backhand, then gets back to picking the jewelry off Zena's outfit and limbs. Lynx sees stars and can't figure out which way is up, never mind getting back on his feet for another charge.

Master Gulliber whistles at the goblin and calls to him in Eldric, saying, "Yoo-hoo! Over here!" which would have sounded to our modern Aenglish ears more like, "Thou eat trash! Hernia!" had we been there ourselves. Next to him, Lynx sees a vaguely familiar older elve dangle her jewelry like a curbside sales rep.

Having helped himself to the most impressive pieces from Zena's outfit, the goblin swaggers over with the same greedy confidence as an unnoticed five-year-old stealing the prize from an open cereal box down a lonely supermarket aisle. Just as the goblin reaches for the jewelry, the elf lady unfurls a sling, twirls it twice, and hurls the stone at the goblin's masculine parts for an up-close and personal sales pitch.

The goblin keels over. Master Gulliber grabs Zena's poisoned blade and sticks it to him. Their boldness breathes new life into Lynx. He wills himself back into action and hoists Zena's broken body into his arms.

Moving a trauma patient with possible spine, neck, and head injuries is a bad idea but Lynx does not think. He runs on pure emotion—grief, passion, anger, fear, desperation. Holding Zena close to his chest and hoping that somehow getting her back to Tuscoraura Mountain will save her, he runs.

And he runs.

The dark earth haunts his mind. Time takes its toll. His berserker frenzy chills. The thorns scrape his legs. The weight of Zena's body burns the muscles in his arms. His chest heaves. The wind scrapes his lungs. A low-hanging branch smacks his head.

Through an opening in the trees, he sees the garden gnome village on the edges of the marchlands of Tuscoraura Mountain. Garden gnomes have good doctors. With that one grain of blind hope, he collapses.

Zena wavers in and out of consciousness and moans, "The goblins! Watch out, Mister Lynx."

Lynx, sincerely touched by her concern and utterly exhausted, says, "Hush, my darling, don't fear, my darling. The goblins sleep tonight."

She stammers, "B…b…but where are we?"

"Near the village, the peaceful gnome village . . . the goblins sleep tonight."

"When will we go home?"

"When daylight comes, we'll go home."

Zena asks, "Is it okay if I sleep then?"

"Yes, my darling, to sleep . . . perchance to dream."

With that, they both pass out amid the shrubs of the marchlands.

ACT III

SUGAR AND HEISTS
AND EVERYTHING NICE

Bonus Scene A: Louis and Clarke

Elf Colonial Marchlands, Tuscoraura Mountain
Maundy Thor's Day Prime.
Early Morning, 6th of April, 1284

It's a brilliant morning, and the svelte does gyrate and gambol in the waves of grass. All breezy are the hemlock groves that mark the ancient graves.

Leading the group of rescued rangers toward Shentalpee City, Master Gulliber holds up a hand. "Stop! You must camp here until I come back. Humans are not allowed in the marchlands."

Sir Robert Roger points ahead. "I see a clearing. Is the elf colony on the other side?"

"Yes."

Inquisitor Sheen insists, "Then we are coming too. We have no time to waste."

Master Gulliver's wife, Missus Puma, waves her hands excitedly. She speaks some Aenglish . . . some. "No, no, no! There is *landomere* in Eldric. I not know say in Aenglish but Tuscoraura elves have *bergfleet flag*. Very dangerous for *goyar*. You not elf. You not walk in marchlands. You take six foot, seven foot, eight foot, crunch! They hit you. You dead no see *bergfleet flag*."

Master Gulliber concludes, "My wife wants to say that the marchlands you see there are patrolled by our elite Ivy League scouts with poisoned arrows. They shoot to kill when they see any *goyar*—our word for non-elves—trying to cross. Please, please wait here. I must get permission from the Council of Perfects for you to cross safely."

Sir Robert Roger is upset. "Fine, but your wife stays here with us to make sure you don't double-cross us."

Master Gulliber gets angry. "You don't take my wife, human! We saved you from the goblins and this is your thanks? I can snap my fingers and the Ivy League will have you all dead before you can blink twice."

Missus Puma twinkles her fingers to calm him down and says to him in Eldric, "It's okay, Gulliber. I want to find that poor elve and her friend. She was in very bad shape. If they agree to help me find her, I will agree to stay with them. Humans don't trust each other—how would they know to trust us?"

Master Gulliber huffs, "That's exactly my point. I don't trust their leader at all."

Missus Puma replies in a soothing tone, "You trust Louis, don't you? He'll guard me while you're gone."

"Fine." Master Gulliber explains his wife's compromise to Sir Robert Roger, emphasizing that she and Louis, the hefty young shoemaker with a two-handed battleaxe, want to look for the wounded elve and her friend. The ranger captain agrees.

Master Gulliber scampers off quickly and Sir Robert Roger orders the rangers to set up camp and assign lookouts. He himself settles down for a nap.

Louis asks him, "Aren't we going to send out search parties for the wounded elve girl and her friend?"

Sir Robert Roger looks at him, annoyed. "It's not our problem. We were up all night because of Poodoo. Now if you'll excuse me, I need a nap."

Brother Umbert jumps into the conversation. "What an ungrateful cretin you are! Those elves saved our lives. Now they're injured and you take a nap?"

Inquisitor Sheen pulls him by the back of his cowl, saying, "Stop, Brother Umbert! We've come this far through prayer and trusting in God. God has blessed us with the gift of prophecy and we'll use it."

Sir Robert Roger is curious. "What's this 'gift of prophecy' going to do for you?"

Brother Umbert just cannot keep his mouth shut. "Inquisitor Sheen has been blessed with the gift of tongues that allows him to speak in both angelic and clayborn languages. He has the gift of healing that allows him to cure wounds and illnesses and he also has the gift of prophecy, which allows him to detect significant objects or people within sixty feet."

Sir Robert Roger grunts, "What if they are more than sixty feet away?"

"That's why we need a search party."

Sir Kip Karlson, the halfling ranger, thumbs off to the northwest. "By your leave, Captain. I've been keeping an eye on the paths all night. I'm confident I could get within sixty feet of the elves. Hopefully, with the gift of healing that poor elve will have a chance."

"You, sir," replies Sir Robert Roger, "have first watch while the company sleeps."

"I'll take it," comes a deep, Frankish voice. They all turn and see the giant Sir Paul Bunyan. "I'm tired, but I can make it through first watch. Sir Kip Karlson is our best tracker. If anyone can find them it's him."

Missus Puma looks at Louis. "We go?"

Louis nods to her and unslings the battleaxe from his back. "Sir Kip, we are deeply grateful for your guidance. Sir Paul, we appreciate the hardship in losing the extra sleep."

With that, Sir Kip heads out with Missus Puma, Louis, and the four inquisitors back toward the forest. Sir Robert Roger calls after them, "Take the young monk with you. We don't need to babysit him here."

They turn around and see Brother Clarke tagging along behind them. He looks at them like a lost puppy.

With a warm smile Brother Umbert pulls out the goblin king's ceremonial dagger from a bone sheath with primitive etchings. Up close it just looks like a giant, four-inch claw. He hands the dagger to Brother Clarke. "It is the phoenix talon you fetched for me last night. My vow of poverty as a Franciscan prevents me from keeping it but I believe the Carmelite rule allows you to hold onto a gift until your prior says otherwise."

"Yes, I suppose it does," replies Clarke. Brother Umbert's friendly welcome and generous gift endears him deeply to the newest member of the inquisitor's retinue. Clarke reaches out with a scarred and trembling hand for the dagger. Whatever toxins put him to sleep on the goblin altar call out to him more fiercely than booze to a tippler but he resists the urge to intentionally cut himself with it to get another fix.

The inquisitor claps his hands to get the group moving. "Very well, then, Brother Clarke. You're one of us now. Shall we find those poor elves who helped us earlier?"

Led by Sir Kip Karlson, the four inquisitors, Missus Puma, Louis, and Clarke head off through the forest brush. Sir Kip's innate sense of direction and tracker skills guide them in directions they would never have suspected likely to find the two mysterious elves who rescued them but somehow this gnome ranger inspires full trust in them all.

While he walks, Inquisitor Sheen moves his fingers along a string of beads, whispering, but no one hears what he is saying distinctly. Suddenly he veers to the right and picks up the pace. After a short jog, they find the two elves lying unconscious. The noise of their excitement wakes Lynx up. His breathing is fitful and his legs refuse to obey him when he tries to sit up.

Zena's limbs are bent in directions they were never designed to go. The gurgling pant and the blood dripping from her nose and mouth tell those with medical training that her splintered ribs have punctured a lung.

The inquisitor kneels over Zena and continues to pray in his incomprehensible language. After a short while, he opens his eyes and calmly states, "In the name of Jesus, arise and be healed."

Zena opens her eyes and squirms a bit. Her broken bones straighten out and her crushed hip and shattered rib cage knit themselves back together. A little disoriented and unsettled at finding herself surrounded by strangers, she struggles to get to her feet.

Amazed, Louis asks, "How did you do that?"

"Jesus says that anything we ask in his name with faith will be granted."

"But I ask for stuff in his name and it never works."

"You must learn to honor his name in your life, words and thoughts and ask with faith."

"How do I do that?"

"You must stop taking the Lord's name in vain and renew your faith with prayer and fasting."

"Oh well," says Louis. "I'll leave it to you monks."

"A holy life is for everyone," adds Brother Umbert.

Missus Puma takes hold of Zena's hand and says to her in Eldric, "Hale ant sail! Fate heater thou?"

Zena introduces herself with an unbalanced curtsy. "Egg heat Mademoiselle Zena Jeannesdottir fro Otter Manganime, Ant thou?"

Missus Puma puts on a motherly smile. "Egg heat Frown Puma Arminsdottir fro Otter Harrun. Game at keenest thither. Thou oak saga Aenglish?"

Looking around, Zena seems all of a sudden to recognize where she is. She nods and starts to walk away, leaving Lynx behind.

Missus Puma asks in Aenglish, "Where you go?"

Zena nods politely and replies in Aenglish, "Daylight has come. I want to go home."

Inquisitor Sheen comments, "It sounds like she's still in shock." He turns to Zena and says, "Please, Mademoiselle elve, please wait here for a little while and I will pray for your friend."

Zena looks down and sees Lynx lying bruised and half-awake. She asks, "Are you a holy man?"

"A dwarf doing the Lord's work, actually."

Zena babbles, "Come, Mister holy man, rally my companion. Daylight's come and I want to go home."

Ignoring the slight at being called a man, the dwarf inquisitor prays over Lynx in his incomprehensible language, then opens his eyes and says confidently, "In the name of Jesus, arise and be healed."

The big bruise on Lynx's forehead fades away. Louis bends down to help him up onto his feet.

Lynx rubs his head and asks, "Far on egg?"

Missus Puma asks him if he speaks Aenglish. "Saga thou Aenglish?"

"Yes."

Louis immediately asks him, "Do you remember how you got here?"

Lynx looks at Louis with a blank stare and then he starts to remember and says in Aenglish, "I walk all night and then I run."

Now that Lynx is back, Zena seems to be still dazed and speaks absent-mindedly in Aenglish, "Daylight's come and I want to go home."

Holding out a piece of cloth wrapped up in a bag, Missus Puma says in Aenglish, "No, no, Mademoiselle. Please, no forget jewelry. Look, a beautiful bunch right in my bandana!"

Zena opens the bandana and sees the bling. "My jewelry!" she exclaims. "Where did you find it?"

Missus Puma tries to explain in her broken Aenglish so everyone understands. "Many goblins! Hide the deadly black attacker. Louis kill him with axe. Your jewelry we find and we stash in bandana."

Feeling her gold and gems seems to return Zena to her senses a little. She puts some on and tucks the rest in belt pouches under her coat. "Thank you, Frown Puma! Come, Hare Gipper! We go home now."

Lynx is still amazed at the miraculous healing. He says in Aenglish, "Thank you for heal me and my friend, holy dwarf cleric. I am Hare Gipper, but in

Aenglish you say Mister Lynx, no? Beautiful girl, her name is Mademoiselle Zena. It is same in Aenglish. She is great warrior and princess of my heart."

Missus Puma explodes with excitement and throws her arms around Lynx. She says in Eldric, "Mister Lynx Cougarson! Yes, yes, you have your mother's eyes! I am Missus Puma Arminsdottir of Clan Highrune! You were only a little baby when I left Wildcat Base."

Still disoriented, Lynx does not quite know what to say. He stammers in Eldric, "Yes, I belong to Clan Highrune, but I am not a baby anymore."

"No, no! You were a little baby when we left but we're back now and look at the big, strong elf you have become! What a brave young lad you are! Your parents must be so proud."

The awkwardness of the moment overwhelms Lynx. He tells her in Eldric, "My father died a long time ago and my mother remarried a murk elf."

Inquisitor Sheen interrupts the awkward family reunion, speaking with the gift of tongues so they all hear in their own language. "Pleased to meet you, Hare Gipper! I am Inquisitor Sheen, a priest with the Order of Preachers. Our large Mohawk friend in gray is our porter, Brother Indigo. This is our bursar Brother Crowe in the black robe and in brown is our halfling magicultor and scholar, Brother Umbert. This one over here in the white and brown robes is the young Brother Clarke, whom you saved from the goblin king's dagger with that amazing shot to his wrist."

Lynx's already red face deepens a shade.

Zena mutters, "He was aiming for goblin's heart."

Clarke sticks up for him. "Either way, that shot was one big win for the Gipper! It saved my life."

Zena huffs and is about to give her comeback when suddenly Lynx, to defuse the awkward bomb, interrupts her, bows to Inquisitor Sheen and says, "I am Christian. Auntie Nephy Lehies speak to us about Jesus and I listen very much."

Inquisitor Sheen approaches Lynx with a question. "Do you know a preacher named Johnny Appleseed?"

Lynx smiles in agreement. "Naturally! He is good Christian man. You all speak and be friends."

Zena intrudes on Lynx's offer of welcome with angry suspicion. "Reverend Appleseed is guest at my house. Why you want to talk to him?"

Seeing her attitude, Inquisitor Sheen nudges to the truth with circumspection. "The Church authorities want to inquire about matters of faith and morals."

Missus Puma tugs Zena's sleeve and whispers into her ear loud enough for the others to hear, "Mademoiselle Zena. These heilaugur matter as if logger glue ease. Hen moot guest thine hand take."

Zena nods to Missus Puma and then stares hard at the inquisitor. "You arrest Reverend Appleseed?"

Inquisitor Sheen realizes the game is up and says plainly, "He must defend the purity of his faith before a panel of experts. Don't worry—he will get a fair trial."

Zena puts her left hand on her hip and waves her right pointer finger at him. "No, no, no! Reverend Appleseed is our guest. If you arrest our guest, I must kill you. That is *eldralfar* law."

"Then at least give me a chance to speak with him so he can mend his ways. No trial."

"No. I tell him you are here and he comes to you if he want to speak. You not come to my house. Ready, Hare Gipper? Daylight's come and I want to go home."

They turn to walk away but Inquisitor Sheen calls out to Lynx, "Hare Gipper, please hear me out. The Holy Office has warned Johnny Appleseed about blackflame. It is unnatural and dangerous. Why do you think so many wendigos infest these forests? It's the blackflame. There's no other explanation!"

Lynx hesitates but Zena has no qualms. "Blackflame is good for elf city." She then says to Lynx, "Egg fur ham, Hare Gipper. Wilt thou coma mitt mere?"

She walks away but Lynx stands, frozen in deep inner conflict about whether to believe the inquisitor's words. He finally says to the inquisitor, "But he give gifts to feed hungry people—apple seed and blackflame so food not go bad. He dogfennel for help people that drink too much firewater and . . . and book of Bible."

Inquisitor Sheen says in a sad tone of voice, "Even good things can have evil uses. Apple seeds grow apple trees but can be used to make deadly poisons. All you need is about two hundred seeds, about a handful, to kill a full-grown human—less for an elf. Dogfennel will destroy the liver if taken with firewater. The Bible is called the Good Book but no prophecy of Scripture is made for private interpretation. Uninformed opinions give rise to false prophets and divisions. At his last supper, Jesus prayed for his followers, 'May they be one as you and I, Father, are one.' Christianity is about unity. A kingdom divided will not stand."

Clarke volunteers, "I'll go."

Inquisitor Sheen is confused. "Excuse me?"

Clarke says, "I'm a monk with enough training in theology to understand the issues at stake. I am also not an inquisitor. Maybe Reverend Appleseed would be willing to talk with me to clear up any confusions."

Inquisitor Sheen thinks for a moment, "We have been tracking him for months and this is the closest we've ever come to speaking with him. I'd hate to let an opportunity like this slip through our fingers. If that is our only option, I would have to instruct you carefully but we could make it work. I'm not out to trip him up. I just need to make sure he is clear on what he can and cannot do as a Christian preacher.

"Hare Gipper, if Reverend Appleseed is unable to come out here to see me, please ask him if he'd at least be willing to have Clarke go visit him. If he and Clarke could come to an agreement, you have my word that the Inquisition will leave him in peace."

Lynx takes a moment to process the inquisitor's words, then he replies, "I will say to him your words. If he is bad and hurt elves and make Christians argue as you say, then I help you destroy him. If he is good and you want to hurt him, then I will destroy you."

Lynx turns around and jogs off to join Zena. Daylight has come and she wants to go home.

Bonus Scene B: Louis the Amorous

Elf Colonial Marchlands, Tuscoraura Mountain
Maundy Thor's Day Terce. Morning, 6th of April, 1284

After that rattling confrontation, Sir Kip Karlson leads the inquisitors back to the ranger camp. Sir Paul Bunyan greets them and asks, "Did you find the elves?"

Louis impetuously says, "Inquisitor Sheen prayed on beads and mumbled a lot but he led us straight to them. Then he miraculously healed them."

Sir Paul Bunyan lets out a big yawn. "So the girl elve is all better? Where are they now?"

Inquisitor Sheen says, "She is back to full health, praise be to God. Why don't you rest now? My companions and I can guard the camp."

Sir Kip says, "Only rangers can keep a watch. Sir Paul, thank you for covering for me but I'll take over while you get some sleep. I've got a lot on my mind."

"Then at least allow me to keep you company in the course of your vigilance. You have already endured a great hardship for my sake."

Sir Kip replies, "For the sake of the elves who saved us from the goblins. It was a debt of gratitude."

Sir Umbert adds, "A debt humans don't pay."

Using the gift of tongues, Inquisitor Sheen says, "Missus Puma, we are also most grateful to you and your husband for leading us here. Please use my bedroll to get some sleep while we wait for your husband's return. You must be exhausted."

Missus Puma, Louis, and Clarke are feeling quite tired as well. Brother Umbert's sleeping mat is a better fit for Missus Puma and as soon as he unrolls it, she falls asleep before her head hits the pillow. Louis and Clarke want to help but doze off instantly, leaving Inquisitor Sheen alone to help Sir Kip stay awake.

When Sir Robert Roger wakes up, he rouses the rangers and orders them to drill and train, except for the ones posted as lookouts. The commotion stirs Louis from his sleep and he goes over to Sir Robert Roger to ask if he can help with guard duty. Sir Robert Roger admires his pluck and says, "Tell me, young man, you are pretty handy with that battleaxe. I saw you take the head off that black-furred goblin last night with one clean stroke. Sir Gawain and the Green Knight would have both been proud of you. How would you feel about an apprenticeship with the rangers? Young Nathan Hayle over here is our only one so far."

Louis smiles at the compliment but says, "I'm not sure I have the legal right to switch apprenticeships. I have already been apprenticed to a shoemaker."

Sir Robert Roger replies, "This is Vinland and we are under Aenglish Law. If a serf does one hundred and one days apprenticeship in a city, he is freed from his serfdom. If a city apprentice does one hundred and one days military service, he is free of his apprenticeship. And if a soldier hides in a monastery for one hundred and one days, he isn't considered a deserter anymore."

"It might be more complicated than that."

"How so?"

"It's a long story."

"After training, we'll have plenty of time to hear long stories. That old elf didn't look like he was going to hurry getting back. For now, you and Clarke over there should let Sir Jim Bowey show you how to handle a knife. The young monk almost killed himself with his own dagger in the heat of battle."

Sir Jim Bowey swoops right in and ushers the two teens off to their makeshift training field and says, "Gentlemen, pay close attention, do exactly what I tell you, and you'll be top-notch rangers in no time."

Clarke points to himself in surprise and says, "But I'm a monk!"

Sir Jim Bowey hands him a wooden long knife and says, "You *were* a monk. Now you have to survive in the wild. If you don't learn how to use that knife well, you won't be anything but wolf chow."

Clarke has no desire to argue and Louis is eager to learn to fight with a knife so without further ado, Sir Jim Bowey starts drilling them.

After the training, Sir Robert Roger reiterates his offer to take Louis on as an apprentice ranger. When Louis hesitates, Sir Robert Roger insists that Louis sit down and tell them his story. Louis admits that he enjoys the brotherhood among the rangers and that a life of adventure tickles his fancy.

Feeling the vibes of Louis's youthful enthusiasm for their way of life, the off-duty rangers gather around the campfire in a big circle to hear his story.

"There was once an old woman who lived in a shoe shop in Fort Bedford. After her husband, Old Man Rhebuck the shoemaker, passed away, she used to make a living off orphans, sending us out to beg every day. Soon enough, the townsfolk assumed she was running an orphanage, so they would bring her all the lost children who had no home.

"They say my parents came to Fort Bedford from Fort Joliette in the Illenoy Country after our house was destroyed in a hobgoblin raid. We were happy for a short time until my parents died of cholera and I was entrusted to Old Lady Rhebuck.

"She pretended to be happy about having me but she had so many children, she didn't know what to do with us all. She gave us nothing to eat but a slice of bread and some chicken broth once a day and if anyone complained, she would just whip us all soundly and send us to bed hungry.

"She heard about a successful shoemaker from Baston whose shoe business was doing extremely well, so she sold some of us to him as apprentices; but in reality, we were little more than slaves.

"Master Nikephoros was a stingy, cruel man. He made us work from dawn till dusk every day except the Lord's Day and his foreman would not let us take a day off even if we got sick or injured. Life as an apprentice shoemaker was hard, but at least we got two square meals a day and a roof to sleep under. Most of all, we were learning a trade that would someday help us earn our way to freedom.

"Thanks to Missus Puma and Master Gulliber, freedom came to me much sooner than I ever expected. It all began one day when a halfling entered our workshop out of the blue and asked for a pair of shoes that might fit him. I told him that halflings normally don't wear shoes so he would have to order a custom pair; custom orders have to be paid in full up-front.

"He said he did not have enough money on him so he gave me a high-quality churchwarden pipe and some longbotham leaf, telling me to hold it as collateral until he could come up with the money to cover costs. I took his measurements and made the shoes for him.

"A month later, he still had not returned, but a dwarf needed a pair of shoes urgently and it happened that the shoes I'd made for the halfling fit the dwarf perfectly, so he paid me for them and left. Gnomes rarely wear shoes anyway. And so, assuming the halfling would never come back, I handed the dwarf's coins over to Master Nikephoros and secretly kept the churchwarden pipe and the longbotham leaf for myself.

"During my lunch break the next day, I snuck off for a little smoke. It was raining, so I had to find somewhere indoors where no one would notice the sight and smell of smoke."

Sir Robert Roger interjects, "Slim chance of that."

Louis looks at the inquisitors and blushes slightly. "Actually, longbotham leaf has an aroma like incense and so I figured that, since it was a churchwarden pipe, it was meant to be smoked in a church."

Brother Umbert gets all agitated and waves his hands dramatically. "I cannot believe the disrespect! To smoke while at church!"

Inquisitor Sheen responds to that last remark, "Brother Umbert, do not judge! Brother Louis here was not smoking a pipe while praying. He was praying while smoking a pipe."

Brother Umbert will not hear of such excuses. "Wait, wait, wait! Tobacco is not good for the body, neither for the belly, and is not good for those around him who have to breathe it in. He should not be smoking at all."

"It does have some uses as an herb for bruises and sick cattle," replies Inquisitor Sheen. "Besides, longbotham leaf is not tobacco, strictly speaking. As Brother Louis says, it is more like incense. Let us listen to his story without passing any more judgments, please. You don't see him judging you on how well you keep your vow of silence, do you?" Then the inquisitor says, "Please continue, Brother Louis."

"In any event, for better or for worse, I crept through the church hoping no one would see me. Rounding the corner of the narthex toward the altar of St. Blaise, I hid behind a statue covered with a big, red cloth. Reaching up to the candles for blessing throats, I used one to light up my pipe. Almost at once, I started coughing up phlegm spastically; then, I realized that the cloth was really a little red riding hood covering not a statue but a pretty young lass. Right there behind me, little Miss Claire Muffet sat on a hassock eating her curds and whey—"

Clarke interrupts. "Wait! What's a hassock?"

"You're a cleric—you should know. It's a tuffet."

Clarke demurs, "Most people don't know what a hassock *or* a tuffet is."

Louis shrugs. "It's a cushion they use to kneel; sometimes, they call it a kneeler."

"Right, okay," says Clarke. "You could have said that the first time around."

Louis continues his story. "So anyway, I asked her why she was eating in church. She said that her older brother, Humbert, is a great guy but that he loves cheese so much that if she doesn't hide her curds and whey, she never gets more than a bite. The church is the only place her dear 'Humpty' never comes.

"I told her that I had been given a churchwarden pipe so I thought I'd come to church to smoke it. She actually got the joke and we both laughed and chitchatted until the bell tolled for midday Mass.

"I told her I had to get back to work and she asked me where I worked.

"I said, 'Oh I'm just an apprentice to that old Graec shoemaker, Master Nikephoros.' My master was quite wealthy, so I hoped to impress her with my career.

"She was like, 'Wait, you mean you work for that super-rich Bastonian shoemaker?'

"I said, 'Yes, business is good, thanks be to God.'

"She clasped her hands like she had just discovered a buried treasure and said, 'Oh, an astrologer not long ago gave me a very strange horoscope. He said I'd find happiness when I learned how to walk in someone else's shoes. I have always dreamed of wearing those special shoes Master Nikephoros makes with the custom design for the right foot and a converse design for the left. One-size-fits-all just doesn't fit me.'

"I know it was stupid, but I lied and blurted out, 'Why, I just happen to have a pair of shoes that didn't fit a customer right. Do you mind if I measure your feet? If those shoes fit, you can wear them.'

"She blushed and covered her mouth. 'Oh that would make me so happy! Finally, my horoscope will come true! I have been wearing these dirty old things for over six months now. They are so drab, and chafe my feet all the time. My papa just does not understand a lady's needs.'

"She put her foot up on the tuffet next to her and I marked my palm with the charcoal from the candle lighter. Barely had I finished measuring her right foot when she suddenly leapt up and screamed. 'Ahhh! It's a spider!'

"The rain had washed a spider out of the water spout of the drain tile. Along came the spider and sat down beside her. I said. 'Oh, it's just an itsy, bitsy spider. I've got it.' So I smooshed it with my thumb.

"She screamed. 'Eww! That's so gross!' And then she ran away.

"Despite the awkward goodbye, I decided I was in love with her and would make those trendy converse shoes to impress her, despite the fact that the only item I could afford from my budget was a shoestring.

"To complete this project, I would have to find some scraps and cobble them together after everyone else had gone to sleep.

"That night, it rained and it poured so heavily that the noise of the raindrops alone could easily drown out the footsteps of a housebreaker. Gathering up my courage, I tiptoed through the foreman's house. The old man was snoring so loud that I managed to steal the key to the workshop from the cupboard above his head without waking him up.

"Though knowing I'd be soaking wet when I arrived, I ran to the workshop, opened the door and crept inside, careful not to be seen. Assuming I was safe, I strolled downstairs to the workbenches whistling a carefree tune. Lo and behold, there at the workbenches were two elves, Missus Puma and Master Gulliber!

"My whistling died down, but I did not want them to think I was a burglar so I casually said something like, 'Hi . . . um . . . hello, I mean, hale ant sail, sir elf and dame elve!' I was told to address a female elf with a v—elve. 'I'm Louis, one of the apprentice shoemakers here. I'm running behind on a project so I figured I'd work on it tonight.'

Missus Puma jumps into the story. "At that time, we were slaves, you know! We so happy that we see Louis. I say to him, 'We help you. You help us.'"

Louis then continues. "On my shoestring budget, there was no chance I could make little Miss Muffet a decent pair of shoes, so I showed Missus Puma the measurements I had copied from my hand to a dirty old rag and promised I would do anything I could to help her. Master Gulliber told me they could provide the materials and make me shoes according to those measurements if I found their jewelry."

Sir Robert Roger wrinkles his face and looks at Missus Puma. "Jewelry? I thought you said you were slaves. Didn't you want him to help you get home?"

Missus Puma says, "Yes, yes, but elf cannot be free without jewelry. No-jewelry elf is like no-clothes elf. We cannot go home without jewelry. We say to Louis, 'Master Nikephoros has elf jewelry of us! Please, Mister Louis, we say. Get back elf jewelry.' He say yes. So we make shoes for his naughty girl."

Louis takes over the narrative from there. "The rain was still pouring and the old foreman was still snoring but when I tried to replace the keys in the cupboard over his head, I dropped them. He immediately sat upright at the sound and bumped his head on the cupboard so hard that it knocked him out cold. He didn't get up until the next morning. Still, I was not sure if he saw me or not.

"Getting into the master's mansion would be tough. During my lunch break, I went back to the Church of Saint Martin to hear Mass, hoping to see Miss Muffet, but she was not there.

"As I left, a goose was wandering through the churchyard. An answered prayer! I caught it and caged it, then ran to Master Nikephoros's mansion under the pretext of delivering a goose that his wife had ordered.

"He was quite rich and had a big, fancy oak door with a big, fancy brass knocker. I banged it on the door a few times and the downstairs maid opened up. 'What is it, young man?'

"'One goose, ma'am. Delivery for the cook,' I said.

"'Are you sure?'

"I thought she was challenging my story so I tried to look confident. 'But the cook—'

"She interrupted me. 'Let's have a gander. I know the cook thinks that goose meat is more tender but I say the gander's meat is sweeter.'

"She inspected the bird more closely and waved me away. 'Go around back and use the servants' entrance. Don't dally, you hear!'

"The servant's entrance was left unlocked so I hustled up the stairs to look around for the jewelry.

"The goose was not happy about the cage and honked so much that it drew the attention of the household staff. I heard footsteps coming so I let the goose out and pretended it got away. The housekeeper came up. 'What are you doing up here, young man?'

"I told her, 'I was supposed to get a goose for the cook but we realized it was a gander.'

"'What's sauce for the goose is sauce for the gander! Send whatever it is to the kitchen.'

"'It escaped from its cage, ma'am. I'm doing my best to recover it.'

"'How could you be so clumsy?'

"'It's a wild goose . . . um, I mean a wild gander."

"'The parlor maid will help you grab it quickly and make your way out of here as soon as possible. I'll not have you rambling about upstairs on this wild goose chase—or wild gander chase, or whatever.'

"Searching the upstairs and downstairs rooms as quickly as possible, I stumbled into the lady's chamber when I heard the parlor maid calling out, trying to find the goose . . . or rather, the gander. 'Goosey, goosey, gander, whither shall you wander?'

"The gander walked out of the closet wearing a bonnet and honking away nervously. I laughed and said, 'It's a goose after all. See! She's wearing a bonnet like an old mother goose!'

"The parlor maid was a good-humored woman and quipped, 'Silly goose! Parading with a goose step now?'

"I ran over and grabbed it for the friendly parlor maid and handed it to her, saying, 'Let's make sure this goose is cooked, shall we? Would you mind carrying it down for me? I think I lost a shoe in one of the rooms.'

"She replied, 'Happy to oblige!' and hustled down the stairs with the poor creature.

"I ducked into the last room and searched around. Suddenly, I heard a girl giggling, so I rolled under the bed just in time to hear the master's son brag, 'I can show you the most marvelous jewelry you have ever seen in your life. If you are friendly enough, I'll even let you pick out a piece for yourself.'

"The girl stepped inside the room. To the great pain of my heart, from under the bed I recognized the shoes as those of little Miss Muffet!

"The young man gets down on his hands and knees. I thought he was going to check under the bed so I prayed desperately to God, 'Please don't let me get caught. This is for the elves, not for myself!'

"Behold! Miracle of miracles, instead of looking in my direction, he pried open a loose floorboard and took out a chest, saying, 'This is my jewelry collection. There are rare pieces in here—even some exotic elf jewelry.'

"Little Miss Muffet squealed with delight, saying, 'Oh, Nike! It's stunning!'

"It all made sense. What does someone who steals jewelry want? More jewelry!

"Can I see your ring? Take it off," Nike demanded.

"Miss Muffet replied, 'Oh, Nike, not until after we are married. You promised.'

"The words stung me to the core. She was planning on marrying this crook? Still in shock, I realized the movement of the feet and the grunts sounded like the master's son, Nike, was trying to force the ring off Miss Muffet's finger. She cried out, 'No, Nike. Not like this!'

"I was about to crawl out to confront the dastardly fellow when I heard him say, 'Just give me your ring and I'll let you go. You won't leave until I have it!'

"She sobbed, 'Take the ring, you filthy animal!' With that, she ran out of the room weeping hysterically. Young Nike dropped the ring in the chest, hastily tucked it under the floorboards, and left the room.

"Thanks be to God that he was too distracted to spot me hiding only a few feet away under his bed. After the commotion settled down, I pried open the floorboard, took out Miss Muffet's ring and all the elf jewelry I could find, and hurried out the back."

Missus Puma jumps into the conversation. "Louis give us jewelry and we give him shoes for girl. We see ring for girl and he say he give ring to girl too. We say no give ring to girl but he not listen."

Louis grunts. "Yes, I guess I was just too young and too smitten with puppy love to listen to good advice. The next day during my lunch break, I went back to the same tuffet in the church where we met, smoking my churchwarden pipe before Mass. The quiet sanctuary gave my mind rest and I felt a voice inside me saying, 'Listen to the elves. Let go of little Miss Muffet.' But I could not let go. I was convinced I had found true love. The shoes and the ring would prove to her how powerful my love for her was.

"As those thoughts passed through my head, she showed up with a little bowl of curds and whey. She smiled at me warmly and it melted away the last doubt. I showed her the shoes. She blushed a gentle pink. 'They're beautiful, Louis. But why show them to me?'

"I cleared my throat, gathered my courage and said, 'Hi! These are for you. Unlike ordinary shoes, each shoe is specially fitted to each foot. This one goes on your right foot and conversely, this one goes on the left.'

"I helped her get the right one on, then she took the left one. As soon as she was wearing the other shoe, her face flushed red and her hands covered her mouth as she gasped, 'They are so beautiful! They fit perfectly . . . I'll never be able to afford shoes like these!'

"'They're a gift.'

"She looked at me amazed. 'I don't know what to say . . . I just can't take these from you without paying.'

"She started to take them off but I insisted. 'No charge. If the shoe fits, wear it.'

"She whirled around with a little pant. 'Indeed, they fit like a glove . . . I can't believe you want to give them to me for free,' she said in a surprised voice. 'You are the dearest young man I ever met,' she sighed. 'I have to go before my brother, Humpty, notices I am gone, but promise you'll meet me tomorrow at Old MacDonald's farm at dusk.'

"'I promise,' I said, my brain filling with fantasies.

"She leaned into me. 'Let me give you a hug!'

"When she hugged me, it was all over. I lost every last shred of common sense I had ever stitched together in my life. Ignoring Missus Puma's advice I blurted out, 'Here, take this ring. I believe it belongs to you.'

"Faster than a twig snapping beneath a rockslide, her entire countenance splintered into a thousand slivers. Her voice shucked off its kindness and took on a demented growl. Her eyes went from serenity to insanity in a trice. Her whole body mutated from girlish charm to ogre's wrath. 'How dare you!'

She burst out of the church sobbing hysterically.

"I sat down, stung to the heart. My eyes barely blinked, my fingers hardly even twitched. Frozen in stillness, an arctic chill ripped my innards out, winds of doubt and regret howling through my soul. 'I should have listened to the elves. Ahhhh!'

"My churchwarden pipe sat in my hand like a lone chimney on a mountain peak. As I sat there in church, a storm raged in my heart. Should I go to Old MacDonald's farm or not? In my foolish, love-stricken mind, I convinced myself I should go. Master Nikephoros and his son would be seeking revenge, and Old MacDonald's farm was just around the mountain in Cumberland Valley, about three miles west of Fort Bedford. Its forests and hills made it a good place to hide.

"Maybe little Miss Muffet would come to her senses and want to clear up our misunderstanding. After all, a promise is a promise.

"Foolishly, I went."

"Old MacDonald's farm was just through the pass in the Southern Mountains. It was fertile land and a prosperous farm at one point, but he had fallen on hard times. His wife and five sons all died before he reached the age of fifty. His two daughters were married off to men who lived far away in Gettysburgh and Handover.

"As he progressed into his sixties, his mind grew senile and many of his animals died. Old MacDonald could not accept that his farm was empty. He used to talk to his wife and sons as if they were still there, and he would go spread empty feed sacks into the empty pig pens and cow troughs, making with his own mouth the sounds the animals should have been making.

"'With an oink, oink here and a moo, moo there. Here a neigh, there a bray, everywhere a woof, woof.' He would wander through his farm believing he was feeding his animals. Eventually, he got too old to move around on his own and just sat in his cottage making the sounds to himself.

"Because the barns were clean and deserted, they had become a favorite place for young lovers and hobos to get some privacy for free. When word got around, Old MacDonald's sons-in-law built up a big rock wall to fence off his farmstead from unwanted visitors.

"That was years ago, and the wall has been crumbling ever since under the strain of poor craftsmanship and constant usage. When I got there it was still late afternoon and having nothing better to do, I paced around on top of the stone wall.

"At one point, a big chunk of the top layer wobbled under my foot and I slid off. Fortunately, I twisted around fast enough to land on my feet, but the fall was high enough that I hit the ground and banged my tailbone. It hurt like the devil inside my broken heart.

"At sunset it grew chilly, but I kept telling myself, 'She'll be coming around the mountain and when she comes, I'll go out and patch this all up.'

"A cock crowed. I rubbed my cold fingertips together and tucked them under my armpits while a gnawing doubt seized my heart. A rooster crowing at night isn't a good sign. It was pretty bad for Saint Peter.

"Then I saw the old red rooster strutting by, pecking the ground for worms. That eased my fears for some reason. Letting myself get carried away with my fantasies, I started imagining her driving six white horses in an elegant carriage.

"After the pain in my tailbone subsided and feeling returned to my fingers, I decided to divert my crazy thoughts by rebuilding the section of the wall I had knocked over. I did a lousy job balancing the stones on top of each other. It didn't really matter at the time; it was just a distraction to keep my mind occupied.

"At long last, through the dark-blue haze of early evening, the moonlight shone clear through the dewy chill and I spotted a hooded red cloak—the same red riding hood that little Miss Muffet wore the day I'd first met her in church.

"I laughed in a fit of joy and relief. *She is coming after all!* In my mind, the only debate was whether to run out to greet her or to play it cool and wait for her to greet me. She had invited me here, after all. As my eyes adjusted and focused on the little red riding hood, her motions did not seem dainty or delicate or in any way giddy for a chance at true love.

"Her shoulders were big and square. Her feet had shoddy boots caked with mud. Her gait was gruff, determined, angry. My foreboding turned to panic. The frame was too tall, her shoulders too broad to be little Miss Muffet. She looked more like a wolf on two legs. I climbed up the stone wall and called out, 'Little Miss Muffet! What big hands you have!'

"A young man pulled back the hood and replied mockingly, 'The better to beat you with, dearie!'

"The crunch of betrayal, rejection, and confusion shattered my already broken heart like repeated strokes of a sledgehammer on brittle, old pottery shards. Thou unarmed, I gathered up the nerve to confront little Miss Muffet's curd-snatching brother. Bitterness and rage filled my heart and I called out from the top of the stone wall, 'Well, if it isn't Humpty Dumpty!'

"'Louis,' he snarled, holding up the ring. 'You're a wanted man. You burglarized Madame Nikephoros' jewelry, assaulted my sister, and stole her ring.' From beneath the little red riding cloak, Humbert pulled out a bearded battleaxe with a long spike in back—a cruel weapon with cruel intent, to be sure.

"'Wait!' I protested as soon as I realized he got the story all mixed up. 'Let me tell you the truth!'

"'Never mind the truth. I have an axe to grind!' Humbert heaved the battleaxe over his head and charged at me wildly. I simply jumped down the other side of the stone wall. Humbert, a big, oafish churl, had to struggle to get over the high wall. By the time he managed it, I'd leapt back over to the other side.

"He then yelled out his strategy, 'Think you are so smart? I'll just straddle the fence and the next time you jump down, it will be to your grave.'

"Humbert started to lumber his way up the stone wall again. I had to think quick. With that massive battleaxe in his powerful hands, all Humbert would need is one good blow and it would all be over. As I waffled back and forth on the stone wall, the anxiety of indecision rekindled the pain in my tailbone.

"Suddenly, I had an idea. Folding my arms I stared him down, daring him to come at me. He sensed something was up and hesitated. Then he farted. I taunted him, saying, 'Humpty Dumpty shat on a wall!'

"At first he followed me slowly, trying to maintain his balance, but I moved away too quickly. He realized he could never catch me at that pace so he hustled after me even as the both of us struggled to keep our balance on top of the wall.

"In Humbert's blind rage, he did not notice my legs stretch over the crumbling section of the wall. He stomped right on the loose flagstones that I'd sloppily rebuilt earlier that evening. As he was whirling his battleaxe above his head, the stone gave out from under him and he had a great fall. He hit his head on the rocks on his way down and more loose stones fell on top of him where he landed.

"My first reaction was to grab Humbert's battleaxe and run away to Harrisburgh, but I could not leave my new elf friends behind in captivity to that cruel shoemaker. So with the battleaxe I headed back to town to free them.

"Little did I know that Master Gulliber and Missus Puma had already escaped. When the watchmen spotted me from the walls they arrested me at once. I spent the night in jail, and the city magistrate brought me to trial before a jury of notable townsfolk.

"Up until that time, I had heard about how corrupt our legal system was. It never hit home until my innocence did nothing to dissuade the court from handing me a death sentence. If it wasn't for a miracle, I wouldn't be alive to tell this story."

"The next morning, the magistrate slammed his gavel on the sound block and called the court to order. 'Master Nikephoros Spaulding, prominent member of the Shoemaker's Guild, accuses Louis, apprentice shoemaker, of stealing jewelry from his house. Miss Claire Muffet, dairy maiden, accuses Louis, apprentice shoemaker, of stealing her ring and murdering her brother. Your defense, Louis, apprentice shoemaker?'

"I did not know what to say, so I just said, 'Not guilty, Your Honor.'

"Then Master Nikephoros came up to the bench and spoke with malice stuck between his teeth. 'All my servants can testify that they saw Louis enter my house claiming to deliver a goose immediately before the jewelry was stolen, even though I had not ordered any such delivery.'

"'Your defense, Apprentice Louis?'

"'It was a gander, not a goose, and the housekeeper said she wanted it.'

"'Had Master Nikephoros asked you to deliver it?'

"'No,' I said.

"'Did you steal the jewelry from his house?'

Striving to be judicious with my words, I replied, "'No, I did not steal his jewelry.'

"'So you admit that you entered a house unbidden by the master of the house immediately before the jewelry was stolen?'

"'Yes.'

"'Hmm, very suspicious,' he said. 'As for the matter of Miss Muffet's brother, she claims that you stole her ring and that he confronted you about it. Instead of returning the ring, you murdered him. Do you agree with her account?'

"'I did not steal her ring and I did not kill her brother.'

'The watchmen who apprehended you claim that you were apprehended at the southern gates after hours, carrying a battleaxe from the direction of Old MacDonald's farm, where Miss Muffet's brother was murdered. Miss Muffet's father has testified that the battleaxe belonged to his son, Humbert Muffet. Do you deny their testimonies?'

"'No, Your Honor.'

"'Hmm, very suspicious. After hearing the evidence, I turn this matter over to the jury to decide whether or not Louis, apprentice shoemaker, should be hanged for his crimes. But let me say that in all my years as a magistrate, never has a man's guilt been so clearly manifest as in this case. Members of the jury, I leave you to make your own decision.'

"Just then, the newly appointed coroner of Fort Bedford led his cavalcade back into the courtroom. The coroner said, 'It has come to my attention that this young man, Louis the apprentice shoemaker, is unlawfully accused of murder. I declare your verdict invalid on the grounds that you have not even inspected the body of the deceased man in question.'

"The magistrate burped and waved him off. 'You have no jurisdiction in this matter, sir. Please take your filthy animals out of this courtroom or I will have the town watch remove them without your consent.'

"The coroner replied, 'You just stated that Miss Muffet's brother was murdered at Old MacDonald's farm, which lies outside the city limits. As the Fort

Bedford city magistrate, you only have jurisdiction over crimes committed within city limits. This case is entirely within my jurisdiction, not yours.'

"The magistrate backed off a bit. 'Perhaps, in retrospect, I should have called you in. But the jury is ready to pass its judgment. A jury's decision is binding, even for a coroner such as yourself.'

"The coroner dismounted and said, 'Esteemed members of the jury, permit me a few questions.'

"They agreed.

"'First, Miss Muffet,' the coroner said. "You accuse Louis of murdering your brother. How did you know your brother was dead? Have you seen his dead body? Can you describe how he died?'

"Miss Muffet stuttered, 'I . . . I know that he went to Old MacDonald's farm to confront Louis about stealing my ring. When he didn't return and Louis was apprehended with his battleaxe, I assumed the worst.'

"'Miss Muffet,' replied the coroner. 'If you suspected your brother was murdered, you should have raised the hue and cry. If you were there, it was your duty to stop it.'

"'I wasn't there. I didn't know that he was murdered . . . I assumed . . .'

"'So then on the basis of a mere assumption, you just testified under oath that Louis murdered your brother. Did you see him do it?'

"'No,' she mumbled.

"'Miss Muffet, you claim that Louis stole your ring. Is this another assumption?'

"'No, Your Honor. I know for certain that Louis stole my ring and that my dear Humpty went to Old MacDonald's farm to confront him about it.'

"He held up the ring and said, 'Miss Muffet, is this ring in my hand the same ring that Louis allegedly stole from you?'

"'Yes, it is, Your Honor.'

'This morning, two concerned citizens raised the hue and cry, as was their civic duty—a civic duty you neglected—and I gathered all the king's horses and all the king's men to inspect Old MacDonald's farm. We found your dear Humpty beneath a crumbling section of wall with his skull shattered. There was nothing we could do to mend it. His lifeless fist was still clenched, with this ring inside. If Louis had murdered him in order to keep the ring, why did he leave it with your brother's corpse?'

"'I don't know, Your Honor.'

"'Citizens of the town watch, which of you arrested Louis late last night?'

"Two men raised their hands.

"'You there, man. You testify that Louis murdered Humbert Muffet with an axe?'

"'Yes, sir, we saw him coming from Old MacDonald's farm and we took the murder weapon out of his hands."

"'Did either of you, keepers of the peace, trouble yourselves to inspect the body of Humbert Muffet?'

"'No need, sir. His guilt was as clear as day.'

"'Was there anything about his appearance last night when you arrested him that is different from how he appears today? Anything at all?'

"'None, Your Honor. We took him directly to jail.'

"'Was he covered in blood?'

"'No, Your Honor.'

"'Was the axe you took from him covered in blood?'

"'No, Your Honor.'

"'Ladies and gentlemen of the jury, I personally inspected the body of Monsieur Humbert Muffet and found a great quantity of blood from a stone that had crushed his skull. Can anyone explain to me how Louis, the apprentice shoemaker, could have hacked Humbert, a bigger and stronger man, to death without suffering a single wound in retaliation and without spattering even the slightest drop of blood on his own person or smearing any blood on his axe blade?'

"Silence filled the courtroom. Eventually, Master Nikephoros spoke up. 'He threw the rock . . . he must have thrown the rock at Humpty's head.'

"'I will get to you presently, sir, but for now I must ask Louis why he was going to Old MacDonald's farm.'

"'Miss Muffet asked me to meet her there.'

"'Miss Muffet, do you deny that you asked Louis to meet you at Old MacDonald's farm?'

"Little Miss Muffet started to tear up.

"'Miss Muffet, one of the town watch has stated that he stopped your brother for carrying a battleaxe through the city streets. Your brother showed him his axe permit and this ring, claiming that Louis stole it. It struck the town watchman as odd that your brother was going out to recover something he already owned. Now, I ask you under oath before this jury, did you send your brother out to recover the ring or did you send him out to spring a trap that you set up for Louis?'

"She ran out of the courtroom, sobbing hysterically.

"The coroner went on. 'Ladies and gentlemen of the jury, I hope the order of events are as clear to you as they are to me. Humpty Muffet sat on a wall. Humpty Muffet had a great fall. All the king's horses and all the king's men under my command as coroner were not able to put Humpty Muffet back together again.

"Clearly, Miss Muffet set up an ambush. She gave her brother, Humpty Muffet, her ring, and posted him with a battleaxe behind a wall at Old MacDonald's farm where she asked Louis to meet her.'

"Silence filled the courtroom.

"For a second time, Master Nikephoros had the nerve to break the silence with his own bombast. 'That story makes less sense than a child's nursery rhyme. Why would Miss Muffet want to murder a young man if he had done nothing to hurt her?'

"'Aha! Thank you, Master Nikephoros, for providing the answer with your own brazenly stupid question. You have testified that Louis stole jewelry from your house. Can you tell us where you kept it?'

"'In a box under the floor in my son's room.'

"'Perhaps it was this box?'

"'Maybe . . .'

"'If it is not yours, then by law, a treasure chest with no owner belongs to the king.'

"'On closer inspection, I can testify that it's mine.'

"'All right then. It has a great quantity of jewelry still in it. Are you claiming that Louis only stole one piece of jewelry from it and left the rest? What thief would take the trouble to break into a house and leave most of the jewelry box untouched?'

"'He must have . . . uh . . . taken all the pieces he could hide in his purse.'

"'Can you describe the pieces of jewelry that he allegedly took from this chest?'

Master Nikephoros twitched his fingers in the air. "'A few rings, bracelets, pendants . . . you know.'

"'No, I don't know. You claim that Louis stole jewelry from you but no jewelry has been found on his person nor anywhere among his possessions. Furthermore, you cannot describe in detail any of the missing pieces of jewelry.'

"'I'd have to go through it and see what's missing.'

"'You needn't bother.'

"'What?'

"'I can show the court the one piece of jewelry that has gone missing from this box.' The coroner then held up Miss Muffet's ring. 'On the same day that Louis delivered the goose—or gander—to your house, your housekeeper told me that she saw Miss Muffet wearing this ring when she entered the house with your son, but she also noticed that she left the house without it.'

"Master Nikephoros wrung his hands in anger, swearing, 'I'll kill her!'

'That's what she said. In fact, you also murdered her predecessor for reporting previous jewelry thefts to the magistrate now here present. She said that you colluded with the magistrate to cover up several murders in exchange for a share of the stolen jewelry. When Miss Muffet reported the theft of her ring to the magistrate, he threatened to kill her unless she would be willing to blame it on someone else, someone who also happened to be in the house on the same day that her ring was stolen—your apprentice, Louis.'

"The whole room hummed with consternation, surprise, and outrage. The magistrate was stunned hearing all his secret crimes exposed so publicly. He banged the gavel pathetically. 'Contempt of court! Contempt of court! Bailiff, please remove the coroner and his men from the courtroom.'

"The coroner stated with great authority, 'Master Shoemaker Nikephoros Spaulding and Magistrate Philipp Wilhelm Grimm, in the name of King Eddard of Aengland I am placing you both under arrest for the murder of Miss Margaret Bower, former housekeeper to Nikephoros Spaulding, and for conspiracy to murder Louis, apprentice shoemaker, in order to cover up your crimes. Anyone in this courtroom who attempts to aid or abet the suspects in resisting arrest will share the charges with these men.'"

Louis shakes his fists and says, "Oh, it was glorious! The coroner's men-at-arms and sergeants drew their weapons and the bailiff and the captain of the town watch all shivered in their boots and stepped back.

"If Master Gulliber and Missus Puma had not gone to the coroner and solved the case for him, he would not have had time to gather the evidence before my trial. So they saved my life.

"For his part, the coroner was more than happy to use this case to establish his authority over and above the corrupt local magistrates. He kindly returned to me Humbert's battleaxe and offered to escort us all safely to Three Springs. From there, we continued on foot to Tuscoraura Mountain. By the time we met you our food supply had run out and we were very hungry."

Sir Robert Roger claps loudly and says, "Delightful tale, Louis. Even if only half of it is true, you certainly have the mettle to become a ranger's apprentice. Now how about you, Clarke? What wild adventures led you to the point of that savage goblin's knife? Clearly, you were a monk, but with the proper dispensations, perhaps we could make a ranger's apprentice of you as well."

Clarke folds his hands together and says, "Since Louis has shared his story, I suppose it is only fair that I share a little of mine."

Bonus Scene C: A Clarke out of Water

Elf Colonial Marchlands, Tuscoraura Mountain
Maundy Thor's Day Sext. Noontide, 6th of April, 1284

Clarke settles into the lush grass and says, "My own past is a mystery to me. I grew up at Mount Carmel Monastery near Niagara Falls as an oblate."

Louis interrupts, "What is an oblate?"

Clarke replies. "It means my parents left me at the monastery as a child. I was too young to remember them. The only heirloom they left me was a bone amulet. No one even ever told me my own baptismal name. All Carmelite brothers take a new name. David is the name I received as a monk. I must have been young because I can't remember anything from before that time. I once asked the prior about my real name but the prior told me to leave the past behind and forbade me from any further inquiries.

"Honestly, not knowing my real name never really bothered me until I lost the amulet. All I know about it is that my mother left it with me and insisted that the prior allow me to keep it. It was the only token of her love for me I ever had. Somehow I felt close to her whenever I wore it, even though I can't remember what she even looked like.

"In any event, on the day before the Feast of Saint Joseph, I went fishing in a canoe on the Niagara River. According to our rule, monks are not allowed to eat any meat at all, except that we are allowed to eat fish on special feast days. I knew a few excellent spots to find some nice-sized bass and walleye.

"Having set out after matins on the dark, deserted river, I fished with the ardor of Saint Peter himself. By the time I heard the monastery bell tower strike terce, my fingers were already red and blistered from hauling in the twine fishnets, my arms ached and trembled from hours of rowing, my robes were soaked and my feet were pruned and shriveled from the puddles of gunk the bottom of my canoe roiled up by eviscerated yellow perch, angry rainbow trout, flopping paddlefish, and crapping crappie.

"The abbot had asked me to fill a large barrel with fish and I was only halfway there. A cool wind wafted across the surface of the Niagara River. The warm smell of spring thaws rising up in the air brought a wave of drowsiness over me. My head grew heavy and my sight grew dim. The fragile sunlight soothed and burned at the same time so I pulled the hood over my head and let the puffy sleeves scrunched up behind my elbows drop down over my hands for a quick nap.

"Suddenly, my net dragged excitedly in the water and pulled me out of a deep sleep. After a brief and violent struggle, I hauled in a huge trout. Once inside, it slapped the bottom of the canoe with its wriggling, writhing, raw rebellion. It rocked the canoe violently.

"Stabbing at it with my steely knife, I just could not kill the beast. It flopped so vigorously that it flung itself back into the river. Exhausted, I leaned over to see if I could reach it before it swam away but a stubby, red, furry paw grabbed my wrist. I yanked my hand free of its grasp but then it latched onto the prow of my canoe.

"My heart thumped wildly as I imagined some saber-toothed sea monster clawing its way toward me. Then another red paw joined the first. The other end of the canoe lifted so high in the air that I had to scramble backwards to keep from capsizing. The red paws squeezed the canoe edge like a vise grip and hauled up a strange figure in a wooden mask.

"Carved out of painted basswood, the loud, red mask vaguely resembled a gnome head, the way you see it on a totem pole with wide lips, a narrow nose and beady eyes, all with slits for the person behind it to see and breathe. Black and white lines crisscrossed the red mask in geometric patterns that were deep enough to put your finger inside and trace, like a children's puzzle. The lines converged into vague animal shapes like the kind of pictograms you see on the wall of a cave-dweller's hideout.

"With another yank, the masked halfling dragged himself inside my canoe. Dressed in red fox skins heavily laden with water from his swim, the halfling slumped to the bottom of the canoe. On his chest pulsated a bronze amulet holding a reddish-brown stone, rough-hewn, but humming with some kind of esoteric power.

"The exertion of kicking himself out of the water and clambering into my canoe seemed to finish him off. He panted and stared at me absently as if he were about to faint. A strange, spooky shock ran down my spine as I took a good look at this halfling's mask. From behind the eye holes, two intelligent eyes squinted as if straining to recognize me. But strangest of all, the irises were red! A black paste was smeared beneath his eyes but the rest of his skin—as far as I could tell—was completely white.

"The next moment he exhaled as if satisfied at who I was, then closed his tired eyes and passed out. Up ahead in the distance, I saw a shimmering light. Hoping it might be the solution to my problems, I paddled toward it.

"As it turned out, the shine was sunlight twinkling off the wet hair and perfect, smooth skin of a woman. A stream of long, black hair trailed behind two beautiful, feminine arms. With a stroke and a swoosh she slid across the water on her side, her green hip breaking the surface leading down to a giant, green fishtail.

"A mermaid? A siren? I wondered, but tried not to think too hard. As a monk, our rule admonishes us not to stare at women. But I was utterly and helplessly captivated by the beauty of this mermaid. Perhaps mermaids don't count if they are not really women.

"Oh, such a lovely face! The sheer delight of her feminine form struck pangs in my chest. Could this be a heavenly vision, or a temptation from the infernal depths below?

"She smiled at me as if letting me know how much she enjoyed being stared at. Hazel-brown eyes flecked with sea-green sparkles met me just above the water's surface. Her mouth was red, a deep, bruised red, like she had been puckering long and hard in her eagerness to kiss me.

"Nothing in my seven years of monk training in the art of illustrating manuscripts and chanting Latin ever prepared me for the starkly contrasting colors of a mermaid's physique or the musicality in her soothing voice. Her abundant, black hair swirled around her like a cloud of ink just beneath the surface. She had the nose, chin, and forehead of a fairy queen and exuded a special charm of epic proportions with her sly wink and a tilt of her head.

"I was so enthralled, so utterly enchanted with her that I realized only just then that my mouth was hanging wide open. After some urgent pleading from my brain, my right hand finally agreed to wipe away some of the drool leaking out the side. The mermaid circled around the canoe in playful show for a while then she glided up to me, barely more than an arm's length away. 'Toss him in,' she said in a melodic tone.

"'W . . . W . . . What?' I stuttered in utter shock.

"With a coy sidestroke, she batted her eyelashes at me and pointed to where the masked halfling lay panting, unconscious, dripping with river water, sweat, and desperation. Her hips emerged from the water, green and scaly, wrapped in one of my fishnets. My throat tightened. Her voice filled my mind with a hypnotic persuasion, as if her advice was the only conceivable course of action I should follow.

"'Push him into the river,' she repeated, this time with more authority.

"I hesitated. The halfling's red, scary mask, ugly eyes, and baneful silence had already given me half a mind to do just that, and her feminine wiles had a mesmerizing effect on my brain, eclipsing reason. The mermaid did a casual backstroke, displaying the full glory of her feminine . . . fishy . . . figure.

"Once she was sure she had scrambled my reason, her voice trilled, 'Come on! You know I love you!'

"'I know she loves me,' I repeated mindlessly.

"For a fish of a woman, she was quite a catch. A flash fantasy ran through my imagination. I saw myself dressed in a dark-blue samite groom's tabard and cape with a gold belt, calfskin boots with a pair of silver dollar buckles, standing in a huge, marble cathedral with a queen-sized baptismal font where she could swim around in a white-laced bridal gown, then looking lovingly into my eyes she would say, 'I do.'

"Retreating back into reality, my eyes returned to the ugly, red-masked halfling groaning with effort to catch his breath in his troubled sleep. Poverty, chastity, and obedience—that was when my life's training kicked back in. Consecrated to God, I needed to worry about impressing the Heavenly Father with my good deeds rather than impressing girls—or mermaids—with evil deeds.

"My calling is to care for the weak, the vulnerable, and the sick. I felt sorry for the little guy. By coming aboard my canoe, he made himself my guest, protected by the universal laws of hospitality. In welcoming guests, our forefathers in the Bible brought angels under their roofs. The red-masked halfling just didn't look like he was feeling up for a swim at that moment.

"I said no.

"At first the mermaid, as if incapable of understanding the word *no,* straightened herself up in the water like a duck expecting another piece of popcorn. But when she saw the hesitation in my eyes turn into defiance, her sun-sweet smile turned into a stormy scowl. Her alluring lips twisted into a snarl.

"The mermaid dove out of sight and fear trickled into my pores until I hardened my nerve in a firm resolve to resist the mermaid's manipulations. A moment of calm settled over the waters like a baby blanket a mother would toss over a cradle.

"I began to paddle for shore. With a huge splash, the mermaid shot up from beneath the river's surface and jerked the paddle out of my hands. The whole canoe rocked back and forth violently and I was sure it would capsize. She swooshed around the canoe behind me and then threw the paddle like a javelin a long distance downstream.

"Looking at me square in the face with narrowing eyes she said, 'Last chance, darling! You're up no small creek without a paddle.'

"I grew utterly defiant. 'He's my guest. For all your tricks, you won't get between him and me.'

"'You mean "between him and I,"' said the mermaid, correcting my grammar.

"'"Me" is the object of a preposition,' I insisted.

"She laughed. '*You* are the object of only one proposition—dump the halfling in the water or you both go over the falls.'

"In my moment of temptation, I had recourse to Scripture and recited from memory, 'Deep calls out to deep in the roar of God's waterfalls; all his waves and breakers will sweep over me.'

"Leaning back, she heaved her chest out of the water and said, 'We could have had something special between us. Pity you aren't man enough to go for it.' With that, she allowed herself to be completely submerged.

"In utter desperation, I tried to paddle the canoe with my hands toward the shore, but a knife poked up through the bottom of the canoe and we started shipping water.

"The mermaid shot up out of the water one last time. Her wet figure was magnificent and deadly to behold. Spraying an explosion of frothing, white droplets in every direction before leaving, she decided she just had to go out with a splash."

"The knife poke seemed to have nicked the halfling because he finally came to. Sitting up, he took off his mask. His skin was albino-white.

"Clearly, exhaustion and fear must have taken his skin down a shade paler, closer to zombie-white. Pulsing, blue veins bulged out from his temples, complementing the bluish-purple bags under his sleep-deprived eyes. The sun-scorched, bloodshot webbing across the whites of his eyes clashed against the almost fluorescent pinkish-red hue of his irises. Except for the patches of black smear under his eyes, the sun had burned irregular rings of nauseous salmon color around his eyes and along his varicose neck.

"With great presence of mind and extraordinary physical strength, the albino halfling hefted my fish barrel in the air and dumped the water and fish out. He then set it in the water next to my sinking canoe and clambered inside. Just before my canoe disappeared beneath the choppy river water, he grabbed my elbow and hauled me aboard.

"The barrel wobbled constantly until he forced me to squat down on the bottom of the barrel. Now stabilized, he reached under his fox-skin suit and pulled out some soggy leaves. He stuffed some in his mouth and then shoved the rest into mine.

"I peeked over the barrel's edge and saw that we were swiftly heading for Niagara Falls. At that point I figured I might as well chew it even if it turned out to be poisonous, since we were going to die anyway.

"After swallowing his soggy salad, I saw the albino halfling put his red mask back on and start to unravel a rope. He tied one end around the mouth of the barrel and tossed the other end out onto the river. Then he sat down on the bottom of the barrel and relaxed.

"He seemed to have the situation perfectly under control so I sat down and relaxed as well.

"Time went by and we picked up speed toward the falls. The red-masked albino halfling did nothing but pull out a stout, gnarled magica wand that he had kept sheathed in his belt.

"Finally, the rushing sound of the falls got louder and louder. I stood up for another peek and saw a rock breaking through the cascading waves. My first assumption was that the rope was supposed to catch onto the rock somehow but it just trailed behind us.

"I started to tell the halfling, 'If you have a plan, now would be a good time—'

"From behind his mask, he just shushed me.

"I pulled out the amulet that was my only connection to my birth mother and prayed if she were in heaven to either save me or prepare my soul to meet her there.

"The halfling yanked the amulet out of my hands and tossed it out of the barrel.

"That was right when we went over the falls.

"I screamed and shrieked like a man plummeting to his death, but he waved his wand as he said, 'Abracadabra!'

"The next thing I knew, we flopped onto a cave floor like two wet fish sliding out of a net. Water poured over the mouth of the cave with cataclysmic sound and fury but I felt safe, almost cozy, and warm. Through the droplets of water, a rainbow shimmered through and landed right on top of us.

"I looked at my hands and saw red, orange, yellow, green, blue, and violet. The vivid colors on my skin brought a smile of relief, then an uncontrolled chuckle. The albino halfling laughed along and took off his mask again. The rainbow light seemed to feel good on his pale skin as well.

"When we finally recovered from our laughing fit, I eyed the cave of wonders. Right behind us grew a sturdy magica tree and I could see the branch where he had plucked off the leaves for us to eat.

"Suddenly, my eyes bulged when I noticed a pot of gold at the end of the rainbow. Not like a little porridge pot; I am talking about a huge, whopping cauldron full of gold rings, bracelets, earrings and armbands, golden goblets, plates, and big, gold bars. I tried to ask him where we were but he did not seem to understand anything I had to say. He gave me no clue who he was or why that sadistic mermaid was trying to kill him.

"So that's my story."

Louis balks at the abrupt ending. "Hold on now! What was the pot of gold for? You didn't tell us how you got out of the cave! How did you end up a prisoner of the goblins? Finish your story please!"

"Oh all right," moans Clarke, like a boy getting punished for not finishing his homework. "It turns out the albino halfling was very nice. He invited me to sup with him and offered me towels and a blanket while my robe dried off. He changed out of his fox skins and into some more normal clothes—more like a scholar. He read, wrote in notebooks, and had an alchemy workstation set up deeper inside the cave.

"After a few days, a group of halflings showed up early in the morning. One spoke a little Aenglish and identified himself as a river gnome. He said they would take me to their stronghold where I would be safe and have all my questions answered. I didn't even know I had questions to ask, but I had already overstayed my welcome with the albino. He didn't enjoy guests.

"We got onto a river barge at the bottom of the falls and covered many miles quickly because they were all strong rowers and we followed the current. The next day, we ran into a blockade. The goblins had chopped down a large tree by the river's edge and ambushed us.

"The goblins lobbed javelins and hurled large stones at our boat. The river gnomes fought back courageously, shooting their slings and arrows with outrageous good fortune. The goblins withered under our counterattack—well, the gnomes' counterattack, really—I didn't have a weapon, and wouldn't have known what to do with one if I did.

"A bellowing scream filled the air and the goblin war chief charged at us. The other goblins all leaped out of their hiding places into the water, which was only chest-deep at the ford. When the goblins closed in on our barge, the river gnomes took up their polearms against a river full of troubles.

"The first goblin to climb aboard roared loudly and swatted at their swordstaves and war bills with his club but a cunning gnome snuck up behind him and quieted him with a bare bodkin in the back. The goblin let out a grunt and dripped with sweat before dreaded death carried him off to that undiscovered country from whose frontier no traveler returns.

"Their skill with polearms was such that the goblins simply could not climb aboard, but the goblins would not stop harassing us. To end the stalemate, some of the river gnomes tried to row back upstream, but in this regard the currents turned awry and beached the riverboat before they had a chance to steer the boat around. Once beached, the boat fell easy prey to the goblin boarders.

"The river gnomes fought to the death instead of surrendering or attempting to flee but I just knelt down and prayed for God to have mercy on my soul. Since I offered no fight, they took me prisoner.

"And that, honorable sir rangers, is how I ended up on the sacrificial altar. The rest, as they say, is history."

Bonus Scene D: Greater

Elf Colonial Marchlands, Tuscoraura Mountain
Maundy Thor's Day Sext. Noontide, 6th of April, 1284

As the sun reaches its peak over Tuscoraura Mountain, Zena and Lynx come to the fork in the road that branches off on the left to Lynx's wood elf village and on the right to the elevators leading to Betzy Rose Mansion, Zena's home on Red Giant Base.

The walk home has been quite. Both have had much to ponder. Before they part ways, Zena asks, "So now that I helped you on your quest to save your friends, you are going to help me on my quest to track down Bartlebee, right?"

For a moment, Lynx has no idea what she is talking about. His mind is focused on the troubling accusations against Johnny Appleseed. Then he remembers that he dragged Zena out to the Shade Gap to catch Enganyon and Florenz in a dalliance together in exchange for offering his help with the Bartlebee quest. "Right. Right. Thank you for helping me break up that evil goblin ritual. What a miracle it took for the both of us to be walking home safe and sound! And yes, of course I will help you on your quest."

Zena notices Lynx heads off to the left. "Um, where are you going, Mister Lynx?"

"Home."

"No you won't! You are supposed to compete in the Ivy League Tournament this afternoon."

"Mademoiselle Zena, I already won the Justiciar League Tournament and the League of Licornes

Tournament, and both leagues have come up with rather lame excuses to award first place to a high elf because they cannot bear the thought of having a wood elf in their ranks. The Ivy League is the most elitist league of them all. Why even waste my time?"

"Mister Lynx Cougarson of Clan Highrune! Ambition should be made of sterner stuff! Monsieur Enganyon told me he won the Justiciar League Tournament fair and square, and he is an honorable elf. If you want to become a high elf, you will have to learn, like the rest of us, that a high character is built up with the stones of perseverance in adversity."

"Right now, I am headed to the stables to rent a reindeer to go collect Rudolph and Dasher. We left them at the Shade Gap. And right now, you are going to march up there and earn a place among the high elves by winning the Ivy League Tournament."

"Rudolph! Oh, I totally forgot! I'll come with you. There might still be goblins lurking out there."

"No you won't! You go up and compete. If you think you've been treated unfairly, then this is your chance to show the whole colony. Everyone will be there. I can take care of myself and you can stop feeling sorry for yourself! Not another word. Go!"

Ferocity, wisdom, and that old puppy love for Zena boil up in his heart. She's right and he knows it. Lynx takes off at a brisk jog to the elevators leading up to Thor's plaza.

At this point, he no longer cares about earning the status of a high elf. A fighting spirit is welling up in his soul and it's a fight for something greater. He's not sure what that something greater is at the moment but he trusts he'll find out soon enough.

Scene 1: Catch an Elve by the Toe

Elf Colonial Marchlands, Tuscoraura Mountain
Maundy Thor's Day Sext
Afternoon, 6th of April, 1284

Florenz looks around nervously and notices Lynx is missing. She left him there. Trembling guilt drips from the corner of her right eye. She left him when he was surrounded by goblins near the altar. She wanted to help but Enganyon had convinced her to run.

Angst. That's what Enganyon called it: angst.

She went out to Shade Gap hoping to save a few humans from the goblin sacrificial rites but instead she abandoned her compatriot—one of the sweetest wood elves she knows—to their blood-thirsty clutches.

But wait! Here he comes now.

Lynx is alive!

His eyes are heavy, his hands are trembling, and his shoulders are stooped. He plops down on the bench and just closes his eyes. Leaning his head back, he breathes such a woeful sigh you'd think it was his last.

Florenz doesn't dare ask what happened. She cannot let the high elves know she's been moonlighting as a hero to save humans—especially not her father.

With a wink to his daughter, Umpire-in-Chief Kibbler Earnestson steps up on a raised platform and announces, "Mesdames, mesdemoiselles, messieurs, ladies, and gentelves, we all have stakes in today's tournament and I doubly so. First, as umpire-in-chief, I want to see our colony recruit the finest and fittest elves to bolster the ranks of the Ivy League. They are our first line of defense, securing our borders against goblin raiders, human poachers, gnome spies, and dwarf troublemakers of every sort.

"Second, as a father, I want to see my daughter perform well so she can pledge her strong hands and nimble body to the service of our great colony. Some of you, no doubt most of you, are feeling put off by the conflict of interest. In years past, an unofficial tradition has developed whereby the umpire's immediate family has had to sit out these tournaments to prevent their family ties from bringing an unfair advantage.

"Even with this precautionary measure in place, many elves still criticize these recruitment tournaments because they feel the judges lean partially toward those who are politically well-connected rather than those who are the most qualified.

"To rectify this imbalance, I am offering to pay for a scholarship—out of my own personal funds—for a commission as a junior officer in the Ivy League to any elf or elve who comes up as the second-place winner, if my daughter takes first place. This way, she will not be depriving anyone of a well-deserved scholarship."

The news startles the crowd and excited murmurs ripple throughout Thor's Base. The dean of the Ivy League himself, Dean Halvard Prinson of Clan Sandford, replaces Umpire Kibbler on the stage and announces in a loud voice, "The rules for this tournament will be the same as always—the first elf to make it to the highest point of Tiw's Tree shall win a free commission as a junior officer in the Ivy League.

"Earlier today I expressed my concern about the unprecedented participation of Mademoiselle Florenz Kibblersdottir in this tournament, but our assembly of senior officers feels the umpire-in-chief's offer to pay for the commission of his daughter's runner-up is a fair way to compensate.

"Before we begin, a warning—the Ivy League is not for the fainthearted, but it is not for the rash or reckless either. It requires self-control and good judgment. Any elf or elve who directly or indirectly causes a fellow contestant to suffer permanent injury or death will be barred from the Ivy League, with no possibility for appeal, on top of the usual civil and criminal penalties.

"And now . . . contestants, take your places!"

They all circle around Tiw's Tree. It is the only one of the seven sacred trees supporting Thor's Base with low-lying branches that can be reached from the platform. The rules are simple—get to the top first. The sport resembles a special mix between gymnastics and martial arts because the competitors punch, kick, knee, and elbow each other while climbing—a vertically ascending wrestling match with a touch of acrobatics.

"Contestants, ready? Three . . . two . . . one . . . go!"

Florenz, Lynx, and Screech, a small but tenacious high elve from Clan Antmiony, scramble to the west side of the tree where the branches are spaced farthest apart, making the climb more difficult but giving their ascent less chance of getting stymied by a fistfight.

On the east side, where the branches interweave like a tidy set of monkey bars, the main pack of elves clusters up for an easier climb but with more violence in the fray. Only a few yards up from the starting block the pushing, shoving, grabbing, elbowing, and scuffles get desperate and ruthless.

On the west side, Screech takes the lead quickly. She is only an inch over four feet in height, but she has unusually large hands and feet. She climbs quickly and easily. Florenz and Lynx follow close behind.

Despite his fatigue after having saved the humans from the goblin ritual, Lynx seems to be powered by some unearthly rage and strains his way up, neck and neck with Screech. His ferocity draws too much attention as a fist comes slamming across his face. He hears his nose crack and slips down a branch. The elf who punched him is a reject from the east side scuffle and retreats from the tournament altogether to avoid retaliation, but Lynx has no time to waste on revenge. He quickly wipes his nose with his left sleeve—luckily, only snot. *No blood, no foul!*

With Lynx out of the way for the moment, Florenz races past him, hot on the heels of Screech. Umpire Kibbler's generous offer has had the side effect of keeping the most dangerous roughhousing away from her since she poses no threat by winning. When Screech reaches a branch that dead-ends, Florenz realizes she has made a terrible mistake.

Like a flying squirrel, Screech leaps off the branch to another that hangs quite a way off, covering a distance Florenz can't jump across safely. Reluctantly, Florenz backtracks and loses second place.

Although the east side is a much quicker climb, the scuffle has taken a steep toll in attrition among the competitors. In overall first is Dyre. Although both his parents are wood elves, his physique is bulky and dark-haired, suggesting some dwarf ancestry. He is by nature a friendly sort of chap but having grown up constantly picked on, slow with words, and gifted with exceptional physical strength, Dyre has learned to use his fists to settle arguments.

As they climb higher, those on the east side are forced by the arrangement of branches to move west.

When Screech's eyes meet Dyre's, she desperately surges upwards, hoping to outpace him. Unfortunately for her, the easy climb on the east side has given Dyre too much of a lead to be easily outmaneuvered. He knows she is the quicker climber and that his only chance at staying in first place is with brute force.

Seeing him close in on her, Screech leaps away to a far-off branch that will put a safe distance between them but Dyre snatches Screech's ankle in midflight. Had Screech just let him pass, she might have outpaced him on the final sprint upward.

She does not think. Being grabbed at the ankle triggers a vicious defense mechanism in her muscle memory and Screech struggles so hard to break free that she falls. Fearing for her safety, Dyre holds on to her ankle. He lets her dangle upside down until she finally calms down.

Had he just let her free fall, he might have stayed in first place, but his chivalrous act in making sure she stayed safe gives Florenz and Lynx the chance to catch up to him.

Realizing he has lost his chance, Dyre bottlenecks the route up and allows Lynx past. "Go, Lynx! I'll hold them off. At least one of us wood elves has to win!"

In a heartbeat, the race has narrowed down to Florenz and Lynx, with Lynx in the lead thanks to Dyre's cooperation. Now the wild animal in Florenz comes out. If Lynx wins, she loses everything—the race *and* her reputation as a warrior, and no one will vote for an elve who does not know how to put up a good fight. In the heat of the moment, Florenz pulls out her silver dagger, the same one Enganyon recovered from the gobliness, and pins Lynx's left boot to the tree.

Technically an illegal move, the adjudicators below pretend not to notice. Lynx has the clarity of mind to realize there is no point in fighting with her or blaming the adjudicators. He can still win second place. Quickly, he kicks his boot off and veers onto a divergent branch to avoid further conflicts.

With the route ahead of her cleared away, Florenz shimmies up the homestretch branch, the one that is painted red and has a small knife gash notched into it. Every Ivy League champion climber in the past twenty years has considered that marker the top notch. With five feet left before Florenz's victory, Lynx swings his legs out and uses the springiness of the divergent branch to pole-vault himself up to a nearby branch that leads almost as high as Florenz's top-notch branch.

Although he is close enough to leap onto Florenz's branch and wrestle her for first place, Lynx instead wraps his arms around the tip of his branch and twists his whole body until his legs stick straight up into the air like a defiant flagpole. Immediately afterward, Florenz reaches up and taps the top notch.

The victory horn blows.

Lynx swings himself around and looks at Florenz. She looks at him and realizes that by making himself a living elf flagpole, he technically reached the highest point above Tiw's Tree first. To ensure her victory, she wraps her arms around the branch and tries to swing her legs above her head as well.

But the last twenty years have not been gentle on the top-notch branch. Year after year, violent scuffles have weakened its integrity. When Florenz swings her legs out, the bough breaks and sends her sailing in free flight two hundred fifty feet above the forest floor.

Seeing the danger, Lynx reaches out with his right arm and prays for a miracle. Before either of them even start to process the physics of her trajectory, their hands wrap around each other's wrists. Florenz dangles from one arm. The panicking audience gasps and shrieks.

Thrashing about, Florenz finally grabs onto a branch and starts to climb down slowly.

Once Florenz and Lynx reach the platform at Thor's Base, the crowd cheers wildly in relief and celebration. Some even start chanting Lynx's name; but the adjudicators confidently shove through the densely packed bodies and lift Florenz's hand in the air, proclaiming, "The winner! The Ivy League offers Mademoiselle Florenz Kibblersdottir a well-merited commission as a junior officer in the Ivy League!"

Unsure about his fate and feeling pressure in his bowels, Lynx heads towards the privy. Umpire Kibbler calls for silence. "Hear ye! Hear ye! I have an important question. Dean Halvard, do the rules not state that the first person to reach the highest point wins?"

"A feat your daughter accomplished admirably."

Kibbler boldly says, "It seems to me that Mister Lynx Cougarson reached the highest point first."

Barely able to believe his keen ears, Lynx freezes when he realizes he is peeing in his pants.

Dean Halvard is not happy. "You can't be serious! If you allow him to get away with that stunt, then it will set a precedent. Winners will have to stick their feet in the air from now on."

Umpire Kibbler folds his arms smugly as he speaks. "A good skill to have for a tree climber, wouldn't you say, Monsieur Dean? Young Mister Lynx reached the highest point first, performed an incredible acrobatic stunt, and single-handedly saved my daughter's life; yet you did not hesitate to disqualify him."

Florenz is shocked out of her wits upon hearing her father trying to rob her of her victory. He's sapping the political momentum that such a prestigious win would give her campaign! She hears the dean insist, "Young Mister Lynx has abandoned our company and has thus disqualified himself."

"Not at all, he is right over there!"

Several hundred elves turn and stare at Lynx. The front of his pants are all wet. He sheepishly lifts his left hand and wiggles his fingers at them. Anyone who saw him leave with what appeared to be frustration and bitterness written all over his face would have assumed he was a sore loser when, in fact, finding a restroom was his most pressing concern.

Sparing Lynx from the unflattering spotlight, Umpire Kibbler then announces, "True to my word, I shall pay for Mister Lynx Cougarson of Clan Highrune to be commissioned as a junior officer in the Ivy League in hopes that he will bring to the prestigious military unit entrusted with the defense of our borders a new level of excellence."

The wood elves go crazy, recklessly stomping up and down, whistling, squealing, cheering, whooping, and slapping each other on the back. None can remember the last time a wood elf won a commission in a major military league.

At that moment, Florenz realizes that her father just won over all the wood elves to her side. *Zena's wood elf ancestry won't win voters now.*

The one who has fared worst of all from Umpire Kibbler's confrontation is Dean Halvard. Humiliated at having his judgment called into question so publicly, he nearly chokes on the news that the umpire-in-chief is sponsoring a wood elf as a junior officer in his elite Ivy League.

His voice cracks with emotion as he forces himself to speak. "The Ivy League is proud to welcome this year's tournament winner, Mademoiselle Florenz Kibblersdottir of Clan Ithelion. The Ivy League has been the great guardian of our colony along its borders. Never have we been defeated, because the Ivy League only admits the best and the brightest elves. We have detected the echoes of the subtlest burglar-gnomes' footsteps and heard the breath of dwarves from far enough to shoot them in the dark. We have felt the shadows of the Magog goblins fall on—"

The dean's voice trails off as a heavily bound goblin is led into Thor's Base by longhouse humans.

The dean snarls, "Who let that beast up here?"

Umpire Kibbler nudges the dean aside and takes center stage. With more thespian artistry than sincerity of feeling he announces sadly, "It is with deep regret that I announce a report from my security staff only moments ago—a goblin has penetrated Tuscoraura Mountain, lurking past the Ivy League patrols undetected. If it had not been for our allies, the longhouse humans, he might have rampaged through the wood elf villages unchecked."

The longhouse human war chief tugs on a hemp rope tied to the hulking, green goblin's neck, taking him through the dense crowd of elves toward the stage. Although tightly bound from neck to toe, the goblin snaps and bellows at the elves as he passes, clearly taking great delight in how easy it is to scare them. Florenz and Lynx recognize him as the son of the goblin war chief performing those human sacrifices.

Umpire Kibbler continues his speech. "Not only did this hulking goblin sneak past the Ivy League patrols, but so did the entire band of longhouse humans who tracked him down. Even after pricking it with sedatives, it took seven of their strongest to wrestle this monstrous goblin to the ground and not a single Ivy Leaguer showed up to help them. This battle took place inside the marchlands near Weaving Widow's Peak."

Umpire Kibbler waits for full dramatic effect as the elves shiver with fear and outrage. Hearing that a goblin reached the marchlands is like hearing that an armed criminal sat on your front porch and no one noticed. Goblins are not supposed to be able to get so close to their elven settlement.

"We owe these allies our lives and our thanks. Out of my own funds I have already paid a reward of five thousand dollars in Tuscoraura double eagles to these warriors who captured the goblin. I hope the Ivy League will be willing to match my donation to the longhouse humans to make sure our friendship and treaties with them stay strong. If, Thor forbid, another more dangerous enemy should find a way to bypass the Ivy League's defenses, we ought to be able to count on human military support, just as they know they could count on us elves.

"Without further ado, I present Chief Skaruren."

Chief Skaruren holds up a hand and says in a thunderous voice, "Se'g Honyaweh!"

To Florenz's great surprise, Enganyon's father, Gandorf Mithranderson, steps up next to the tall human, completely unafraid of appearing short. Chief Skaruren stands a full-bodied six and a half feet above the stage. Despite the chief's muscular physique and height, the six-footer goblin's chest is so broad and his bulging pecs, shoulders, and biceps are so intimidating that he looks much larger than the chief, despite being a half-foot shorter. Meanwhile, Enganyon's father stands there next to them both, puffing out his chest and waving his skinny arms with not the slightest hint of shame at his puny height a few inches below five feet.

Enganyon's father is skilled in the language of the longhouse humans and translates the chief's words into Runic for the benefit of the high elves in the audience. "The big, blue sky above has wept tears of compassion upon my people for centuries untold. In daylight, the sun rises from the east and moves west.

"Every day a new wave of affliction rises in the east and pushes westward, but every night the stars come out again fixed in the heavens.

"Tuscoraura Mountain is our home. Every inch of its soil is sacred to us. We will not be moved from here. The Magog goblins come like clouds to cover the night sky. The next day, we shine again. The Frankish and Aenglish humans come like lightning and thunder and to dim our eyes and deafen our ears. The next day, we see and hear again.

"These hillsides hide the ashes of our ancestors. The mountain peaks remember their footsteps. The streams and rivers run with their blood.

"When the elves climb up in trees and keep watch above our heads with the squirrels, they honor our ancestors. When the halflings burrow under the soil and pile up food under our feet with the chipmunks, they honor our ancestors. When the dwarves tunnel deep into the mountains finding the waters whose springs give us cool drink, they honor our ancestors. The spirits of the generations past and the Great Spirit, who speaks to us in dreams, protect us all.

"But those who come to walk over our lands that did not welcome them; those who come to take away our food that we did not lay before them; those who come to spoil our water that does not recognize their reflection—against them, the fight is ours. Against them, allies are strong. Against them, united we stand."

The roar of applause is deafening. Even Florenz cannot restrain herself from cheering the noble and ingenious chief who has proven himself such a loyal and effective ally to the elves.

Kibbler laborers, stewards, and household guards file into Thor's Base and adorn the longhouse human warriors with leatherwork headbands, golden bracelets, and jeweled necklaces. They drape gold filigree woven velvet capes around their shoulders and wrap embroidered silk sashes around their waists. They buckle elegant silver blades with gem-encrusted scabbards to their hips.

When Umpire Kibbler finishes decorating the longhouse humans, the crowd eyes Dean Halvard, expecting similar pomp and fanfare. Completely taken unawares, Dean Halvard does his best to improvise a suitable reward. He removes from around his neck the symbol of his office as dean of the Ivy League, the Carcanet of Light and Truth Flourishing.

Exquisite and more valuable than all of Kibbler's gifts combined, the gift of the Carcanet provokes mixed emotions among the elves. On one hand, it certainly exempts the dean from having to come up with any more gifts to balance out Umpire Kibbler's display of generosity. On the other hand, giving away such a masterpiece of the jeweler's art, such a significant icon of their cultural heritage, such a major portion of their patrimony—to a human! It boggles their minds, offends their proprieties, and rakes against their values.

The umpire-in-chief waits for the elves in the audience to vent their outrage before continuing. "Although the praise in subduing the goblin rests so squarely on the shoulders of our human allies, the blame for overlooking it belongs to each and every one of us. We elves are so proud of our individual skills that we forget the value of collaboration.

"To remedy this problem, I have decided to create a new post on the Council of Perfects—an overseer for all the military leagues in our colony. In an emergency session just before this tournament, legislation was approved naming Monsieur Gandorf Mithranderson the first Major Leagues Umpire in fire elf history. His role will be to coordinate and direct homeland security, making sure all three major military leagues, the Justiciar League, the Ivy League, and the League of Licornes work together for the good of the colony."

Fortunately, Lynx has already soiled his pants so there is no new shock when he wets them again. In a single afternoon, not only has Umpire Kibbler suddenly become his patron in purchasing a commission for him in the Ivy League, thereby elevating his social standing in Shentalpee City to that of a high elf, but now Enganyon's father is his new boss!

Scene 2: The Odd Party

Gorsline Mill at High Falls, Town of Rofchester
in the Aenglish Lordship of Vinland
Tiw's Day Lauds. Dawn, 18th of April, 1284
Eve of the Feast of Saint Aelfheah, Bishop and Martyr

A beautiful human rogue folds her arms in a huff. She has long, straight, black hair, leather armor, and plenty of daggers strapped about her hip, arms, and legs. Losing patience, she complains, "So what are we doing here? I think it's about time you started sharing some information with us, Mister Silence Dogood. You've been a little too tight-lipped about this whole operation for my liking."

Benjamin Frankelyn smiles. "You know what they say, 'Well done is better than well said.'"

"Well said, Mister Silence," replies the snarky rogue. She is also the leader of the party.

A half-goblin cleric agrees with the pretty young rogue. "Silence can be a virtue, but the line between virtue and vice is growing thinner. We are starting to get the impression that you're not so much here to help us as to spy on us."

"You are obviously the prophet in this party of adventurers, Brother . . . what's your name?"

The half-goblin cleric makes a loud blowing sound with his wide, greenish-red lips and says, "Brother? I'm a much higher-level cleric than a brother. My name changes with every monastery I get kicked out of, but you may address me as Monsignor Oscar Meyer."

"Well then, Monsignor Meyer. How about lunch?" Benjamin Frankelyn opens up a sack and hands out trenchers of bread, cold meats, and small wheels of cheese to the party of adventurers. The relaxed environment and the scenic view strike up some lively chitter-chatter between a dark elf magicultor and a human fighter. Together with the human rogue and the half-goblin cleric, they make up the party of adventurers that Amhirst sent to assassinate the last surviving heir to the throne of Fort Duquesne.

Amid the din of the waterfalls and grist mills behind them, Benjamin Frankelyn talks over their chitchatting in an assertive but discrete voice. He announces, "My secrecy is for your own safety. Three can keep a secret, as long as two of them are dead. I intend to keep you all alive. It is of utmost importance to your success—and indeed, to your own survival—that curious ears do not hear the details of your quest."

"Hey, it's your quest too," butts in the dark elf magicultor. Dressed like a pirate with a bandana on his head, a bright-red sash, puffy, black pants, and tall leather boots that fold over at the knees, he carries an assortment of knives wide enough to make him look like a wandering cutlery salesman and holsters a magica wand. "Our success is your success. That's what being a party of adventurers is all about."

Benjamin Frankelyn replies, "Not really. I am mostly here to spy on you, as Monsignor Meyer so accurately prophesied. The last time my patron gave you a quest, you took about three years too long and came back with nothing but an amulet; rather unconvincing evidence that you had accomplished the quest successfully. Nevertheless, he paid you for your services in full. If you fooled him once, shame on you, but if you fool him twice, shame on him.

"I am here to make sure you get the job done with no excuses. If I don't return to vouch for you, no reward. Understood?"

All of a sudden, the party of adventurers gets significantly less chatty.

Benjamin Frankelyn appreciates their undivided attention and continues. "It is supposed that you don't know anything about the quest-giver. If you stumble upon any hints about his identity, please practice every diligence in feigning ignorance. The job is extremely dangerous and extremely important. Any foul-ups would cause a fury and a menace like—"

"Yeah, yeah, yeah," interrupts the beautiful rogue. "We know the spiel. Just cut to the chase."

Benjamin Frankelyn straightens himself up and says, "All right. A special sword was deposited in a Templar safe deposit box, but a thief stole the deposit slip. Our patron needs us to recover that sword before the thief does."

The fighter in the party has long, white hair and a well-trimmed, white beard. He is equipped with heavy chain mail, a brimmed chapel-de-fer steel hat, and a steel-rimmed heater shield. A heavy, winged mace, clings to his belt along with his arming sword and war dagger. He says, "You don't have to play those games with us. Our regard for the law is neutral. We don't mind stealing a sword from the Knights Templar vaults before the real owner gets it first."

"Not at all. I meant what I said," counters Benjamin Frankelyn. "The safe deposit slip has been stolen, and your job is to recover the sword for the true owner before the thief can use the stolen safe deposit slip to lawfully steal the sword.

"We have several ways to do this. One, we could counterfeit a fake safe deposit slip, or two, we could break into the vault and take it for ourselves."

"What do we know about the thief?" asks the beautiful rogue.

He points to her and says, "Hey, you, why don't you give me a name so I can address you properly?"

"'Hey, you,' is fine with me. Proper is not my thing these days."

"Did I mention that you get no reward if I don't feel like I can vouch for you at the end of this quest?"

She rolls her eyes. "Let's go with Ariel."

"Okay, Miss Ariel, to answer your question about the thief, we know practically nothing. The owners of the safe deposit slip caught a glimpse of her as she was jumping out of the window. She was the size of a human child and had large, blond curls. They have code-named her Goldilocks."

"Are you sure the thief is even human or are you just assuming?" asks the piratey dark elf. "I mean, dark elves sometimes have blonde, curly hair. Just saying."

"Possible, but extremely unlikely," replies Benjamin Frankelyn. "Now, may I ask your name, sir elf?"

"How about 'Yeehaw'? No, wait, that's too obvious. I've got a better one, 'Whoopee'! My name is Whoopee. I like the sound of that."

Benjamin Frankelyn rubs his brow. "Do you expect anyone to take you seriously with a name like that?"

"No, but if you've got a name like Moneybags or Mountain of Gold, people take you too seriously. So I'm sticking with Whoopee, thank you."

"All right, then, Whoopee. My guess is that Goldilocks is just some poor, innocent, helpless girl that the real crooks pressured into doing their dirty work for them. Speaking of which, Miss Ariel, we'll use your good looks to avoid suspicion. Can you put on an innocent, helpless girl act?"

She snarls, "That's me—innocent and sweet."

"Okay, great. Like I said, you just need to pretend, Miss Ariel. I don't mean to presume there is anything innocent or sweet about you. Your role will be to create an account with the Templars and store an item in one of their safe deposit boxes.

"First off, an authentic deposit slip will serve as a template for counterfeiting one of our own, and second, creating the chance to walk through the vaults will allow us to map it out so we can figure out which safe deposit box we need to crack, if need be. You could tell them you inherited a few gold bars and will need to put them somewhere for safekeeping."

The white-haired fighter asks in a loud voice, "And when do we come back to get the gold bars?"

"Never," replies Benjamin Frankelyn. "I purchased a few pyrite-coated lead bars on the way. They should be the right color and weight to pass off as gold."

The white-haired fighter objects, "Mister Dogood, pyrite is fool's gold. Templar bankers are no fools."

Benjamin Frankelyn is not the least bothered by the objection. He replies to the old fighter with a confident tone, "Then just leave the bars in the sack. Bankers don't ask questions. It's their job. So what's your name anyway, old man?"

"Willis."

The dark elf whines, "Willis, we're supposed to be using code names. Now he knows your real name!"

"He didn't know that until you told him. He would have thought Willis *wasn't* my real name."

Benjamin Frankelyn interrupts their little side spat and says, "All right, whatever. Sir Willis, you and I are going to—"

"Please, please, please!" Willis halts him in mid-sentence. "I'm not a knight, just a champion. You can call me Willis the Champion, or just plain old Willis, but none of this *Sir* stuff."

"Okay, Willis the Champion, as I was saying, you and I—"

"On second thought, let's keep it to Willis. The whole champion thing is for special occasions only."

"Fine, fine. Willis it is. So you and I—"

"And don't call me Miss Ariel. It's just Ariel. I'm not fond of getting confined in ladylike society."

Benjamin Frankelyn pauses for a deep breath and asks, "Anyone else have comments about names or characters before we proceed?" He looks around; all project innocence at the disruptions. "Okay, if that's all settled, then let's continue with the heist. Willis, you and I will pose as Knights Paladin passing by on a holy quest. We recently lost track of a necromancer who claims to have purchased his sword from a thief who stole it from a Templar vault."

Willis asks, "Why would a necromancer need a sword? They usually stick to rune-inlaid staves and enchanted daggers."

"It's a flaming sword."

Willis objects again, "Sorry, buddy, but I've been in this business a lot longer than you have. Flaming swords are for guys like me to fight the undead, not for necromancers who want to reanimate them."

"This sword does blackflame."

The dark elf looks at him suspiciously. "Are you making this up? If this story gets too far-fetched, they won't believe us."

"Getting them to believe the story is my job. Your job will be to follow the Templar vault-keeper back into the vaults and stay hidden."

The dark elf notes, "Hey, you! I've got news—they don't let nobody back there. It's called security."

Benjamin Frankelyn looks at the dark elf, then points to the half-goblin cleric. (The other half of his family is dwarf.) His shoulders are massive but his gut is trim. "A goblin-dwarf that wide should have a paunch belly. You will go in as the cleric's belly."

Willis jumps in. "Wait! That's brilliant—use their own security measures against them! Templars believe outhouses are a security threat so they dig cesspits for their privies indoors. Monsignor Meyer can just say he needs to use the privy and Whoopee can jump out and hide in the cesspit all day."

"Wha'choo talkin' 'bout, Willis?" snaps Whoopee.

Benjamin Frankelyn works up emotion as he thrills about the genius of the plan. "Yes, that's it! After you jump off, Whoopee, we'll inflate a leather wineskin to replace the paunch belly."

The dark elf says, "No way! Your plan stinks."

Monsignor Meyer adds, "It won't work. The privy's in the dungeon. He'll be trapped behind prison bars."

Benjamin Frankelyn hands Whoopee a wire with a wooden handle at each end. "Unwind the wooden handle like this, slip the wire around any bolts or bars, and then just keep working it back and forth. This wire will cut through just about anything, eventually."

Ariel says, "If the Templars find their dungeon cut open, they'll lock down the fort until they find him."

Benjamin Frankelyn looks at her with penetrating eyes. "They won't find him. It's our good fortune that the Thieves' Guild has already constructed a tunnel most of the way into the fort and were willing to sell us access to it. Once we've located the safe deposit box, all we have to do is pick the lock and break out through the tunnel. Ariel, you up for picking Templar locks?"

Ariel purses her lips. "Yeah, with the right tools."

Whoopee says, "I object to my role in this."

Willis replies, "Welcome to the party, pal."

"Sorry, team, but the water clock is dripping. We start tomorrow at first light."

"Tomorrow? I need to know what kind of lock it is and get the right tools to crack it. It will take all day today just to find places that sell that kind of equipment. Then I'd need another day to test it out."

Benjamin Frankelyn raises a finger. "Never leave for tomorrow what you can do today."

Arial cannot believe all the aphorisms. She tries to make her point. "That's what I'm saying. I can't get it all done today. I'll need both today and tomorrow."

"One today is worth two tomorrows. Use your downtime to fill in the gaps, but we start tomorrow."

"Look, good thief tools are expensive, and I don't have that kind of money on me."

Benjamin Frankelyn puts an end to the excuses. "Then borrow it from the Templar bank."

Bonus Scene E: Engagement

Betzy Rose Mansion, Red Giant's Base, Shentalpee City
Maundy Thor's Day Nones.
Afternoon, 6th of April, 1284

The humiliating position his soiled, light-brown denim pants put him in forces Lynx's mind to work overtime. His only thought is to head for Dungaree Jeanne's mansion. More than borrowing a fresh pair of pantaloons, Lynx hopes to sort out Inquisitor Sheen's troubling accusations with Johnny Appleseed.

A Justiciar League officer stops Lynx while on the suspension bridge to Dungaree Jeanne's neighborhood on Red Giant's Base. "Halt, this is a high elf only area. You cannot pass here without being accompanied by a high elf unless you have a Thor's Hammer pendant approved by the Council of Perfects."

"Excuse me, Officer, but I am a high elf now. You must have seen the Ivy League Tournament."

The officer looks long and hard at Lynx's soiled pants to grind in his embarrassment. Then he says slowly, "I don't know what kind of shenanigans old Earnestson is trying to pull in order to get his dark-skinned girl elected umpire-in-chief to eclipse the supremacy of light elves, but I ain't going to pretend that wood elf squits like you have any right to walk among high elves as if you were our equals."

Lynx cannot believe the contempt for the umpire-in-chief in the Justiciar League officer's voice. Now that "old Earnestson" praised him so publicly and made himself a sponsoring patron, Lynx suddenly feels a genuine filial affection for the umpire-in-chief. As a matter of fact, Lynx decides to report the disrespectful officer. "Please state your name and rank."

"What?"

"If you truly are a Justiciar League officer, you have the right to order me off this bridge, but I have the right to know your name and rank."

The officer puts his hand on his sidearm and says, "I have several ways to teach smart-mouthed squits like you about manners when addressing a superior officer. Why don't you just scram before I pick one of my favorites?"

Lynx stands his ground—or more precisely, stands firm on the swaying wooden planks of the suspension bridge—and says in a loud voice, "Please state your name and rank, Officer."

The officer pulls out his baton and snarls, "Why, you little squit! I'll give you all the information you need—"

"Officer Bunzi, what's the holdup?"

Lynx looks past the bully and sees Dungaree Jeanne fashionably dressed and walking down the suspension bridge with all the poise of a supermodel, dressed to kill. Behind her swagger five bravos, roguish elf warriors with two sharp blades and a few nasty tricks.

Officer Bunzi quickly jams his baton back under his belt and starts babbling out excuses. "Good evening, Madame Dungaree. I caught this wood elf wandering around in a high elf residential zone that is off limits to the likes of him. He was resisting arrest so I was about to take him down to the station for questioning. Now, if you and your servants there would step aside, I'll carry on with my job."

Dungaree Jeanne takes complete command of the situation. "First of all, Officer Bunzi, Mister Lynx—I mean, *Monsieur* Lynx—is a high elf by public declaration of our umpire-in-chief. Second, I invited Monsieur Lynx to my domicile and as the dungaree of Foreign Trade, I have the right to provide him with my own escort. If you dare intrude upon my privileges as dungaree, it will come to blows with all seven of us here. After we have disarmed you using suitable bodily force, you will have to defend your actions before the new Major Leagues Umpire, Gandorf Mithranderson, who happens to be a close friend of mine."

Officer Bunzi steps past Lynx and once he puts himself at a safe distance from Madame Dungaree, he turns around wagging a finger at her. "Times are changing on Tuscoraura Mountain, Jeanne. You and all your wood elf squits posing as high elves better watch out because the law ain't going to cover you forever."

"Your mouth has gotten you into enough trouble for one evening. I am going to urgently recommend that you shut it before you get on the side where the law won't do *you* any good—forever."

Officer Bunzi spits at them and walks off with a big blob of spittle still dribbling over his chin.

Dungaree Jeanne offers Lynx her arm. He just stands there trembling. She encourages him with a gentle smile until he works up the courage to take it and tuck it under his arm. Together, they walk inside her mansion. The bravos follow and close the door.

He breathes out loud and says, "Thank you for dealing with that bully." Then, turning to her bravos, he adds, "Nice to see you guys, too."

Dungaree Jeanne tugs him deeper into the mansion and says, "We'll deal with niceties later. For now, tell me why you have come."

"Well, I have good news and bad news."

"Let me guess—the good news is that you made it into the Ivy League!"

With a big grin he cannot contain, Lynx beams, "I am a high elf now!"

Dungaree Jeanne gives him a warm hug. "Monsieur Lynx! We are so proud of you! Really! Mademoiselle Zena is talking with Reverend Appleseed now. Come! I'd like you to tell them yourself."

"Um, first could you ask me about the bad news?"

"Oh goodness, Lynx, I was hoping Officer Bunzi was the only bad news I'd have to hear for one night."

"I soiled my Dungaree's . . . my only pair of the light-brown, heavy work edition."

Dungaree Jeanne laughs. "Oh, Monsieur Lynx! Don't worry—I'm not laughing at you. I am just relieved the bad news is nothing serious. So many troubles have befallen us these days. We are going to have to have a serious talk a little later but for now, let's celebrate. I want to see you dressed like a true high elf."

After they make their way through her hallway, Dungaree Jeanne takes him to the storage room and gives him a full outfit of her finest denim products: a sturdy tunic, white denim pants, leather boots and vambraces, and a felt bycocket cap. "Now that you are a high elf, you might as well look the part."

After cleaning up in the wash basin and changing into his new clothes, Lynx walks into Reverend Appleseed's guest room regaled like a prince. Zena's heart flutters to see him arrayed so splendidly and she calls out in Eldric, "My, my, Mister Lynx! Are you on your way to a wedding?"

The backhanded compliment both stings and flatters. Lynx tries hard to repress his sensitive feelings and, forgetting their guest, bravely announces the good news to Zena in Eldric, "Thank you for encouraging me to try out for the Ivy League, Mademoiselle Zena. I'll soon be commissioned an Ivy League junior officer."

"Wow! That makes you a high elf! Monsieur Lynx!" Zena jumps up and clasps her hands, giddy like a schoolgirl. Again ignoring their guest, she navigates around Reverend Appleseed's bed and gives Lynx a hearty bear hug. "I knew you could do it!"

Trying to direct attention from himself, he says, "I have good news and bad news for the colony."

Zena steps back. "Let's hear the good news first."

"The good news is that the longhouse humans captured the hulking, green goblin that we saw at the Shade Gap, and turned him over to Umpire Kibbler. Apparently, he snuck past the Ivy League."

Zena covers her mouth, horrified by the good news.

"What's wrong? They got him!"

After a few deep breaths Zena says, "Oh no! That goblin must have been lurking after us to take revenge on us for ruining the sacrificial ritual. There might be dozens more coming after us."

Lynx shrugs. "There is nothing to worry about. Our umpire-in-chief has the beast in custody now."

"Since when did he become 'OUR' umpire-in-chief?" questions Zena. "Monsieur Kibbler is the bane of high elves—and wood elves too, for that matter—and he's ruining the Magnificent Charter!"

Lynx turns red, but Dungaree Jeanne stops her quickly. "Mademoiselle Zena Jeannesdottir, you will not voice another treasonous phrase against our umpire-in-chief or I will turn you in myself! You certainly have the right to run against his daughter in the upcoming election, but by no means will that sort of pettiness and disrespect be tolerated here—or anywhere else on Tuscoraura Mountain."

Zena diverts the conversation. "If that's the good news, what's the bad news?"

Lynx already knows what she will think about the next piece. "Even though I technically won the tournament, the Ivy League is officially recognizing Mademoiselle Florenz as the winner. That's going to look good for her in the upcoming elections."

Zena laughs it off, "Oh phew! That's not a big deal. If everyone saw you win, that will cut Mademoiselle Florenz down to size. Besides, winning the Ivy League Tournament is nowhere near as special as becoming a magicultor. Mage Nittany will be here next Thor's Day to preside over my magica wand culling ceremony. That will steal all her thunder."

Lynx shrugs, "If you say so."

"Monsieur Lynx, have you spoken to Reverend Appleseed about Inquisitor Sheen?"

"Not yet."

Hearing his name in Eldric, Johnny Appleseed asks in Aenglish, "What can I do for you, Monsieur Lynx?"

Lynx switches to his rough Aenglish and asks with all seriousness, "Is true that blackflame is for to—how do you say—make live again the dead? Is true?"

With a sad nod, Johnny Appleseed explains, "The purpose of the blackflame is to provide cool shade for the feverish and refrigeration to keep food from spoiling. Some dark rituals require blackflame; but every element has both beneficial and destructive uses. Yellow fire cooks food or it burns your hand. Water refreshes you with drink or it drowns you."

"Is true apple seeds are poison?"

"Yes, plant'em, don't eat'em."

"Is true dogfennel kill one who drink firewater?"

"Most medications have side effects," Appleseed explains. "When used in the wrong amounts for the wrong purposes it can be toxic, just like nearly every other herbal medicine available. Why do you ask?"

"You know Inquisitor Sheen?"

"Yes."

"He call you bad Christian because blackflame is not natural and do bad to some people."

"Surgery is not natural but it is sometimes very necessary to save a life. Some people do bad things with money but you can't give alms without it."

Lynx pauses to reflect on his words and then says, "When he speaked, all his words maked sense. Now your words make sense. We not allow inquisitor to come here to hurt you but he ask if you want to speak to a young human monk."

"Who's the monk? Do I know him?"

"They call him Brother Clarke. If you speak with Clarke, he promise Inquisition let you have peace."

Johnny Appleseed rolls his eyes. "That's like asking a dog not to bark at strangers or chase squirrels. But I am a guest here and will gladly speak with anyone Dungaree Jeanne invites to her home."

Lynx turns to Dungaree Jeanne and says, still in Aenglish, "I not want that Christians fight. Maybe with Brother Clarke we solve big problem."

Dungaree Jeanne considers for a while. "Fine," she says at last. "Monsieur Lynx, tomorrow you will bring Clarke here. If Inquisitor Sheen is satisfied, then we have made peace for Christians. If not, then I will send Captain Manzone to teach the dog not to bark."

An uncomfortable silence lingers in the air. To break the heavy mood, Dungaree Jeanne hands Lynx a wicker basket with his soiled clothes and asks in Eldric, "Monsieur Lynx, would you like me to launder these or would you prefer to take them home yourself?"

Slightly embarrassed, Lynx replies in Eldric, "Yes, Madame Dungaree, I can wash them at home myself."

"Very well, Monsieur Lynx. Please accompany me a short distance. I have a request for your ears only." Then she says in Aenglish, "Please excuse us, Reverend Appleseed. There are several urgent matters I must attend to. Regrettably, I must beg my leave."

Johnny Appleseed gives them all a worried smile. "Of course. Thank you again for your kindness and hospitality."

Dungaree Jeanne replies, "You are always most welcome in this house, Reverend Appleseed. Now if you will excuse me, I bid you farewell!"

The evening stars twinkle brightly and a cool breeze brings a quick shiver as they first step out of the Betzy Rose Mansion. Only one elevator operates this late at night so they head back across the suspension bridge toward Thor's Base.

Lynx walks beside Dungaree Jeanne holding his basket of soiled clothes in silence, taking in the natural chorus of the crickets and owls. Not a soul stirs across the bases. All the high elves have locked themselves inside their homes, gossiping furiously about the umpire-in-chief's brazen political moves today.

Not long after they exit the mansion, Captain Manzone and his bravos emerge, keeping a respectful distance. When they arrive at the reflecting pool with the magica tree in the middle, she sits down on the ledge and says, "Monsieur Lynx, would you be kind enough to sit with me for a minute?"

"Gladly, Madame Dungaree."

Captain Manzone and his bravos find suitable positions nearby to stay alert and maintain their macho appearances, picking at their fingernails with their long daggers and leaning vigilantly at corners where hypothetical ruffians might sneak up on them.

The wind blows and the spray of the aqueduct's waterfall sprinkles them. Dungaree Jeanne says softly, "Pardon me if you are getting wet, but I wanted the noise of the waterfall to drown out this conversation. I feel I have to tell you something that not even Mademoiselle Zena knows. You have to promise me you will keep this strictly between the two of us."

"Naturally, Madame Dungaree."

"Very well then. You heard me tell Officer Bunzi that our new Major Leagues Umpire, Monsieur Gandorf Mithranderson, is a close friend of mine."

"Yes," replies Lynx. "I was surprised to hear it."

"It isn't quite true. In his youth, Monsieur Gandorf loved me and was intensely jealous of my husband when I married him. My husband was creative, energetic, happy, and adventurous. Soon after we got married and we realized I was pregnant with Mademoiselle Zena, Monsieur Umpire Gandorf provoked my husband into challenging him to a duel.

"My husband was the greatest swords-elf on Tuscoraura Mountain at the time and Monsieur Umpire Gandorf stood not a chance. Knowing this, he bribed my husband's second to betray him. That is why Mademoiselle Zena has grown up without a father."

Lynx fills the pause with a generic condolence, "I'm very sorry for your loss, Madame Dungaree."

Acknowledging the comment, Dungaree Jeanne continues, "Over the years, Monsieur Gandorf has realized how much pain and suffering he caused and often sends me gifts and tries to do me favors to make up for it. The Bible teaches I must forgive him, but it is hard. At least I know that he deeply regrets his actions and has never gotten himself involved in a duel since."

"That's nice."

"Monsieur Lynx, now that you have become a high elf, I want you to promise me that you will never challenge anyone to a duel and that you will never accept a challenge, no matter how gross the insult."

Lynx looks at the bravos and says, "I don't know that it's so simple, Madame Dungaree. I could get killed for not accepting a challenge."

"Then run away. What use are all the riches and honors of the Tuscoraura elves if you have to kill an innocent elf to retain them?"

Lynx stares hard behind them.

"Monsieur Lynx, are you listening to me?"

Lynx points behind them through the dim light of dusk and says, "Um, I believe we have a problem."

"What kind of problem, Monsieur Lynx?"

"Remember Mademoiselle Zena said she'll regain the campaign advantage when she gets accepted as a magicultor's apprentice at Pinne Mage University?"

"Yes."

"She's not going to get accepted."

"What? It's pretty much a done deal. There's no doubt that she has tamed the magica tree."

"Yeah, but it's dying."

Dungaree Jeanne spins around and examines the magica tree in the pale moonlight. The poor tree just sags there as if gasping for light and joy, shriveling under the chilly shadow of the neighboring blackflame that leeches the life out of it. "Oh my chilly fingertips, Monsieur Lynx, we must put it out."

Lynx boldly stands up and dips new bycocket cap in the reflecting pool. Splashing the water on it, Lynx gets seared with a blast of frost. The blackflame explodes, roars, and crackles into ice. Snowflakes puff in the air. The blackflame grows bigger.

They open the guest room door but the missionary is asleep. Dungaree Jeanne starts lighting the lamps. Johnny Appleseed stirs a little, then, still half-asleep he calls out, "What's all this ruckus about?"

Lynx gathers his courage, sticks out his chest and states firmly in Aenglish, "Reverend Appleseed, blackflame bring death to Mademoiselle Zena's magica tree! I throw water but water only make blackflame more strong. How we stop it?"

"Blackflame doesn't harm trees; it just blocks sunlight. I told them not to put it so close to that magica tree—they are more sensitive to light than any other tree. They need rainbow light to survive."

Lynx replies, "If magica tree die, Mademoiselle Zena not go to Pinne Mage University."

Johnny Appleseed winces. The pain in his leg makes it hard to sleep. They have just robbed him of one of those few precious moments he has had to rest. Putting on a brave face he says, "Just douse it with some whiskey or wood tar, anything that is highly flammable. Whatever puts out regular fire makes blackflame stronger, and vice versa."

Proving herself a true expert at eavesdropping, Zena bursts into the room and demands in Eldric, "What is going on with my magica tree?"

Stunned at her daughter's rudeness, Dungaree Jeanne breaks it to her directly. "The blackflame is killing it. Umpire Kibbler must have known it would destroy your career as a magicultor. Can you cull the magica branch right away before it dies?"

Zena looks at her, dumbfounded. "No. I have to cull the magica branch while Mage Nittany is looking on in person to make sure no one else did it for me. Can't we just extinguish the blackflame?"

Dungaree Jeanne tells her, "Lynx tried to douse it with water, but that only made it grow stronger. Reverend Appleseed says we need tar or whiskey."

Zena says impetuously, "Then let's do it. Let's put out the blackflame!"

Dungaree Jeanne thinks out loud, "I've got a hogshead of whiskey in our warehouse from our last trade convoy. We could hire a team of dwarves to carry it, but they would need a high elf with them to get close enough to the blackflame without the Justiciar League stopping them to ask for passes."

Captain Manzone interrupts, "The blackflame is dedicated to Thor. Putting it out could be considered sacrilege. You cannot run for any public office in Tuscoraura if you have been convicted of sacrilege."

Zena blows off his warning. "Mister Lynx can do it for me. No one will know I had anything to do with it."

Lynx's eyes bulge at how easy it was for Zena to volunteer him to spend the rest of his life in jail or as an outcast from elf society while she blithely pursues her unrealistic career ambitions. Finally starting to realize how much he has allowed her to take advantage of him he says, "I'm sorry, Mademoiselle Zena, but you have to be realistic. OUR umpire-in-chief has proven himself too clever for you. He has destroyed your career in magiculture and exposed your secrets to the public. Worst of all, you are still in love with the elf whom I believe betrayed those secrets to him.

"It's over, Mademoiselle Zena. Withdraw from the election before you destroy yourself and your mother. You can question my devotion to you all you want, but I am not going to allow you to ruin the lives of your friends and family over an election that you have no hope of winning."

Zena's first reaction is to blow up with rage at Lynx but she takes a deep breath to calm herself and looks at the wooden floor for a while so as not to let her eyes betray her true feelings. Once she has gathered her wits about her, she thinks for a moment, then takes the ruby ring off her left hand and holds it out. "Monsieur Lynx, you know me. I play for keeps. You are right—the current umpire-in-chief has maneuvered my campaign into a very dark corner; but I have a plan to turn this around. If you will help me extinguish the blackflame, I will give you what your heart desires most."

She kisses him on the cheek and puts the ring on his finger. "Monsieur Lynx, I will marry you."

BONUS ACT A

A TISKET A KATABASIS

Scene A: Breakfast at Nittany's

Wood Elf Village Green Leading off Wildcat's Base,
Good Frige's Day Prime.
Early Morning, 7th of April, 1284

Tucked in their cozy woodland village, the Tuscoraura wood elves outside greet the morning with cheerful smiles and pleasant salutes as their neighbors pass by. Inside his own bed at last, and after having gone two nights in a row with precious little sleep, Lynx makes a firm resolution to sleep in.

As the sunlight creeps slowly through the shutters of his window, he hears a commotion in the living room. Voices. Strangely familiar voices. He rolls over, guessing he is probably just dreaming.

His mind is fuzzy and his limbs still ache from the exertion of competing in the Ivy League Tournament. Although he does his best to ignore them, the voices chatter on outside his bedroom door.

He suddenly feels the need to relieve himself in the chamber pot, but his fatigue is so all-encompassing that he simply cannot muster up the energy to sit up, let alone walk across the room.

The voices grow more animated outside his door. Guests? His mother, Cougar, has not had any guests over ever since she got remarried to that young murk elf. *A fire elf marrying a murk elf—and a murk elf barely any older than himself! What is middle earth coming to these days?! Seriously.*

Through the door, Lynx hears his mother say, "No, no, don't worry! Lynx is eager to talk with you! Let me get him up!"

Her fist pounds against his door. "Lynx, dear! We have guests. Come out and say hello!"

No, no, no! This can't be happening!

The loud pounding is quickly followed by a dull headache. His mother knocks on his door again. "Lynx! Can you hear me? Are you awake?"

He triest to tell her to let him sleep but his throat is so dry and sore that he only manages a faint groan.

His mother opens the door and says, "Guess what, Lynx dear? Those elves you rescued from the goblins are going to be staying with us! Madame Puma is actually a Highrune relative of ours! They brought two humans with them. Her husband, Master Gulliber, got passes for the humans as well. This is so exciting!"

His mother rushes back to the living room and leaves his door open. Awkward beyond belief; they can all see him in bed. He gets up, wraps his sheets around him and, dressed like a ghost, closes the door.

Barely does he sit back down on his bed before his mother knocks at the door again.

"I'm up!" Lynx grumbles. "Just let me get ready. I can't visit with them without any clothes on!"

"Hurry it up, dear! I would also appreciate your help making waffles."

Accepting the fact that his dreams for sleeping in have been dashed, Lynx slowly navigates his way to the chamber pot. After finally relieving himself, he throws open the shutters and empties his chamber pot out the window.

He then surveys his room. On the desk he made for himself out of a hemlock tree that got knocked over in a storm, he has a small buckhorn comb for his hair, a handheld polished-steel mirror, a medieval version of a toothbrush, a washing bowl, and a few spare utility knives. His only other furniture besides the wicker bed and goose feather mattress is a chest with a warded lock where he keeps his clothes, some family heirlooms, and the jewelry he uses for special occasions, like graduations, weddings, and funerals.

It is then he notices the ruby engagement ring Zena placed on his finger the night before. Part of him still thinks he is dreaming, and the other part of him warns him about how volatile Zena can be. Unfortunately, both parts of him assure himself that he is still madly in love with her and veto any attempt that his rational brain makes to convince him that he should just return the ring and have nothing more to do with her.

With reality coming back into focus, Lynx has to decide what to wear. With only two wood elf outfits, it has never been a problem before. Although he will not officially be a high elf until Umpire Kibbler completes the purchase of his commission, both sets of wood elf clothing need laundering, so he convinces himself to wear Dungaree Jeanne's stylish high elf clothes instead.

In addition to the bycocket cap, which is still a little damp from dipping it in the reflecting pool last night, Dungaree Jeanne gave him an ornate belt buckle, a bracelet made out of copper wire and amber beads, a silver clasp for his small, new shoulder cape, and an ornate lapis lazuli necklace strung on silver filigree that he claims he only accepted because it looks very masculine but really the deep blue and gold flecks fascinated him from the first moment he laid eyes on it.

Once appropriately attired and with his hair combed down, Lynx winces as he opens the door, actively dreading comments about his new outfit.

When the door opens all the way, all pretenses drop as he sees Missus Puma and Master Gulliber seated in the guest chairs waiting for breakfast while they chat with his young new murk elf stepfather, who is setting up the large guest tabletop on sawhorse stands.

His mother is bustling around the kitchen, pulling out their spare clay bowls and extra wooden spoons, mixing the waffle batter and pouring deer milk and fresh well water into cups. Louis and Clarke sit on a small pile of hay covered with a woven mat in the corner because elven chairs are too small for humans.

Lynx shakes his head to try to get his brain in the right place again before speaking. Firming up his smile, he says in Eldric, "Health and happiness! Welcome! All of you! You bring light to this place! It is such a pleasant surprise to take you in as guests. I hope you can stay with us as long as possible."

His mother chimes in, "They just might stay with us for a while. When they went back to the house they used to live in before they were taken as slaves to that evil shoemaker, they found that another wood elf family has been squatting in their home. They didn't have the heart to sue for an eviction, since the poor couple has several small children. Besides, they have been gone for so long that our Wildcat umpire might just rule in favor of the squatter family anyhow.

"It turns out I remember Missus Puma from before she got married to Master Gulliber. She was one of the prettiest ladies in our clan. She even asked me to be a flower girl at their wedding. They have been asking all about you and have been telling all the neighbors how you shot the dagger out of the goblin king's hand and slew him with it. What was it, like, a three-hundred-yard shot?"

"Wait, what?" Lynx blinks.

Master Gulliber explains himself. "I know you are too modest to tell the whole tale yourself, but you heroically saved those monks on the altar, didn't you?"

"Yes, but I . . . I . . ."

Master Gulliber finishes his sentence for him, "But you have more urgent news to share with your mother—isn't that right? I think you'd better explain your new outfit."

Missus Cougar looks at him. "Yes, son, how on middle earth did you afford that outfit? Even if you took all the loot from the goblin king, we all know that goblins just wear crude trinkets—nothing to pay off an outfit like that."

"Well, Mom, a lot has changed since yesterday evening. As you can probably guess, I am a high elf now," Lynx proclaims feigning modesty but bursting with pride.

"What!?" Missus Cougar shouts with sheer startlement. Then she starts bouncing on her toes like an excited chipmunk as the realization sinks in. "You are a high elf now! How did that happen? Did you marry Mademoiselle Zena? Don't tell me one of those obnoxious leagues finally gave you a fair chance to prove yourself in their tournaments."

Lynx shakes his head and beams with pride. "Mademoiselle Florenz Kibblersdottir was awarded first place in the Ivy League Tournament, even though I technically should have won. The Ivy League adjudicators ruled against me because I did a flagpole at the top of Tiw's tree and disqualified me for it, claiming it would set an impossible precedent. Our noble Umpire-in-Chief Kibbler berated them publicly for treating me so unfairly and offered to pay for my commission out of his own purse."

Missus Cougar runs up to Lynx and gives him a big hug. She fusses over him while his stepfather awkwardly gets up to pat him on the back and shake his hand as if he were Lynx's real father, but clearly the young stepdad lacks the acting skills to pull it off.

Master Gulliber stands up and adds his own commentary in Eldric. "We must celebrate! This lad is a hero. The goblin king was about to sacrifice that human cleric over there to one of their demon gods, Poodoo, but Mister Lynx—I mean, *Monsieur* Lynx—shot the sacrificial dagger right out of his hand from nearly three hundred yards away. The other goblins took the miraculous shot as a bad omen and started a vicious round of infighting—as goblins are wont to do. That distracted them long enough for Lynx to sneak in and stab the goblin king in the heart with his own dagger while Missus Puma and I went around freeing the other prisoners.

"Mademoiselle Zena tried to help but she was surprised by a goblin lurker and took a nasty blow that nearly bought her a one-way ticket to Valhalla. Lucky for her, Monsieur Lynx was strong enough to carry her halfway through the forest to where a dwarf cleric was able to pray over her and heal her completely."

Missus Cougar clasps her hands in admiration. "Oh, my pointy ears, Master Gulliber! That is such a bracing story and you tell it so well! Perhaps you should give a Thor's Enlightenment Discourse on it."

Holding his lapels and looking up as if pondering her suggestion seriously, he says, "You know, I just might put in a petition to the council about it. Our community deserves to hear the full story."

Missus Puma covers her mouth and squeals, "Oh, please don't, Gulliber! You'll embarrass us for the rest of our lives. We've just gotten back home and now you'll make us too ashamed to live in fire elf society."

"Oh, don't worry! I'll just tell them what they want to hear," Master Gulliber explains confidently. "People like you when your words match their expectations."

"You aren't going to lie, are you?" Missus Puma quickly asks with a worried look.

"Who, me? Lie? Never! I'll just spin it a little so it fits their preconceptions."

Lynx observes that the guests are all waiting for their waffles. "Mother, sorry for sleeping in, but I was exhausted. Let me make the waffles for our guests, and Master Gulliber can tell you all about his travels."

Lynx puts on an apron to protect his fancy new outfit and starts managing the waffle iron with the skill of a master chef. His love of waffles has forced him to learn a number of tricks to ensure that the waffles come out crisp, golden brown, light, and fluffy every time. His mother pulls out their best maple syrup.

Master Gulliber loves to talk, and he is so skillful at it that he is able to hold the attention of Madame Cougar and her young murk elf husband, Mister Stallion the whole time. His stories keep getting better.

With Louis and Clarke excluded from the conversation by the language barrier, Lynx takes the opportunity to serve them some of his perfect waffles as he sorts out his doubts. Lynx says in Aenglish, "Brother Clarke, Madame Dungaree invite you to speak to Reverend Appleseed to fix problem."

Clarke replies, "Reconciliation with the Church is the only way Johnny Appleseed will be able to preach freely in Vinland. I have heard many good things about him, and I am sure this whole nonsense about the blackflame heresy is a simple misunderstanding that will be easy to clear up."

Lynx wrinkles his brow in agitation. "Reverend Appleseed is good man but blackflame kill elf magica tree. We must stop blackflame. We must say to Mage Nittany that she come before magica tree die."

Clarke says, "According to Inquisitor Sheen, the main reason your leader invited Johnny Appleseed here is that he wants to use the blackflame to reanimate the dead. Delawaerr and Ottowa scouts are sending in frequent reports of elf-like wendigos roaming out of Tuscoraura Mountain."

Louis asks, "What's a wendigo?"

Clarke says, "Inquisitor Sheen explained to me that when used skillfully, there is a certain blackflame ritual that can send the living and the dead into an undead state where they wear their own flesh like a coat instead of having body and soul being joined as a harmonious entity while alive.

"In this transmogrified state, the undead can become dependent on its master and obedient to his will. Such an undead wight is called a thrall. The thrall can have superhuman strength, great speed, and incredible resistance to earthly weapons, as long as its spirit has a strong will. Only three elemental attacks can harm it—fire, holy water, and silver.

"That is the necromancer's goal, but it doesn't always work out that way. When used incorrectly, especially if attempting to recall the dead from the afterlife, that same blackflame ritual can miscarry and create an undead wight, which Algonkian loremasters call a wendigo. A wendigo has an untamed appetite for violence, murder, and desecration. The strength, speed, and endurance of any particular wendigo may vary from feeble to indomitable.

"Inquisitor Sheen believes your umpire-in-chief has been experimenting with the blackflame ritual on the bodies of dead elves. He must have learned too late that trying to create a thrall is extremely difficult."

Louis sums it up. "So, the Tuscoraura elves have been performing the blackflame ritual on dead elves, but he keeps messing it up so instead of creating obedient thralls, he is creating savage wendigos."

"Yes."

Lynx gets defensive. "Fire elves not make winnebagos."

Clarke shakes his head. "Hare Gipper, I'm not going to tell you what to believe, but time is running out. The wendigos could overrun these beautiful wood elf villages you live in now if no one stops them. Our job is to get rid of the blackflame so he cannot perform this ritual anymore and you want to get rid of the blackflame to save your colony's magica tree. I propose we work together."

Lynx thinks for a moment and replies, "My love elve, Mademoiselle Zena, ask me that I put out blackflame in Thor's Base and that I say to Mage Nittany that she come to Tuscoraura Mountain before magica tree die. I help you with your quest and then you must help me with my quest for Mademoiselle Zena. We stop blackflame and ask Mage Nittany to come right away."

Clarke smiles broadly, "Absolutely! We both need to put out the blackflame. We'll go from there. Waffles for breakfast today and breakfast at Nittany's tomorrow."

Scene B: The Reluctant Saint

Betzy Rose Mansion, Red Giant's Base, Shentalpee City
Good Frige's Day Sext. Noontide, 7th of April, 1284

Lynx takes Louis and Clarke up to Thor's Base on the public elevators. His purse is empty and there is an extra charge for full-sized humans. Fortunately, Louis has a few farthings that he pitches in for the fees. The dwarf takes the human coinage and the battleaxe off Louis's back as collateral against a future payment in respectable elf or dwarf coins.

Once up top, the magnificent wooden architecture dazzles Clarke's attention while the fabulously pretty young elven maidens distract Louis from appreciating the other fine arts with their giggles. Meanwhile, Lynx cannot take his eyes off the dying magica tree whose resplendent colors have always made the reflecting pool the centerpiece of cheerfulness and uplifting enchantment in Thor's Base. Now in the shadow of the blackflame, the tree looks depressed and haggard.

Dungaree Jeanne, having agreed to the interview between Clarke and Appleseed this morning, has posted several of Captain Manzone's bravos on Thor's Base to escort them to her home. Whether it be the bravos' confident demeanor, lavish clothes, or the deadly weapons hanging from their belts, the Tuscoraura elves suddenly pretend not to notice the two humans as soon as the bravos walk up to them.

Once inside Betzy Rose Mansion, the bravos make the trio wait in the parlor until Dungaree Jeanne, wearing a day gown that does not fail to impress, comes downstairs to greet them in Aenglish, "Good morning, Monsieur Lynx, dear! I see you have brought your friends. Wonderful! I do sincerely hope this solves the problem for our guest, Reverend Appleseed, once and for all. Shall we go in to see him?"

Lynx bows to her and says, "Hale ant sail, Madame Dungaree! I present Mister Louis and Brother Clarke."

Dungaree Jeanne holds out her hand for Clarke to kiss it but having never left his monastery since childhood, he completely misses the cue and holds his hand out to her in the same way, as if trying to imitate a special handshake. Louis, with a little more life experience under his belt, takes her hand and kisses it. Seeing his attention to protocol, Clarke grabs her hand awkwardly and tries to replicate the gesture with significantly less success.

Going with the flow, Dungaree Jeanne says, "Mister Louis and Brother Clarke, I welcome you as guests in my home. Please walk this way."

Clarke, wearing his monk's robe, copies Dungaree Jeanne's elegant gait until Louis jabs him in the ribs. She knocks on the door to Johnny Appleseed's room and from inside a voice calls out, "Come in!"

She opens the door and introduces the human visitors. "Good morning, Reverend Appleseed! These gentlemen are Louis and Clarke. Clarke is here to broker an understanding with the Inquisition."

"Good morning, Madame Dungaree!" Johnny Appleseed props himself up in his bed, grimacing with pain as he moves his leg. As soon as he recovers, he smiles up at the two visitors and says, "Good morning, gentlemen. How can I help you?"

Clarke asks, "May I pull up a chair?"

Hearing his request, Dungaree Jeanne claps her hands and gives instructions to her bravos. They arrange the chairs in the room and bring in another big chair so Louis can be comfortably seated as well.

Clarke begins, "Are you the famous missionary known as Johnny Appleseed?"

"I am."

"My understanding is that you do not wish to see Inquisitor Sheen in person because you are afraid he would unfairly arrest you, is that correct?"

"Nothing personal against Father Sheen, but I'm not so sure I can trust the Inquisition after some downright frightening episodes of torture and false condemnations I've seen with my own eyes."

"Understandable. Although I am not an inquisitor, I have received extensive training as a cleric. In that capacity, he has deputized me to mediate your reconciliation with the one, holy, catholic and apostolic Church. If we come to an agreement today, he has given me his solemn word that the Holy Office of the Inquisition will allow you to continue your preaching in Vinland undisturbed. Do you understand?"

"I do."

"There are three simple conditions the Holy Office requires of you. First, are you willing to make a public profession of faith as formulated in the Creed?"

"Excuse me, Brother Clarke, but I am not a well-educated, formally trained cleric as you are. I do not know the Nicene Creed by heart. Will you accept it if I recite the Apostle's Creed?"

Clarke nods, and Johnny Appleseed recites the Apostle's Creed.

When the recitation finishes, Clarke asks him, "Second, are you willing to restrict the gifts you distribute to apples or apple seeds?"

Johnny Appleseed looks surprised. "What's wrong with dogfennel? It cures addiction to strong drink."

"Well, it does, but according to Inquisitor Sheen, if someone relapses and drinks firewater with dogfennel in their blood, it will kill them."

"That's regrettable, but for some people, dogfennel is the only way to defeat their demons in a bottle."

"Humans are weak. You may continue to preach, promote, and encourage abstinence from strong drinks, but you may not directly or indirectly bring about the death of someone who fails to live up to that ideal through dogfennel. Do you agree to halt the distribution of dogfennel?"

Johnny Appleseed shows dismay on his face. "I agree; but what about the Bible? How am I supposed to preach the word of God without the word of God?"

Clarke replies, "Jesus alone is the Word of God. Books are easily misinterpreted outside of a proper context. You may continue to quote Scripture from memory when you preach, but the Christian faithful must go to a monastery where a suitable theologian can explain obscure passages if they wish to read the Bible for themselves. Do you agree to halt the distribution of unauthorized copies of the Bible?"

"How big does the monastery have to be?"

"I don't understand your question."

"If I gave a copy of the Bible to a suitable theologian who lives in a monastery of only one person and directed the faithful to visit that monastery, would that satisfy your condition?"

"Yes, I suppose it would."

"Then I agree."

"Excellent!" says Clarke enthusiastically. "We only have one condition left. Do you agree to help undo the harm you have inflicted upon the Tuscoraura elf community on account of the blackflame that you brought here?"

Johnny Appleseed is taken aback. "What harm?"

At that moment, Zena comes bursting through the door screaming, "Your blackflame kills magica tree!"

"I am confined to bed with a broken leg; what do you expect me to do?"

Clarke goes on, "Inquisitor Sheen explained to me that several years ago, the leader of the Tuscoraura elves got his hands on a grimoire that describes various rituals to transmogrify the living and recall the deceased into an undead state as thralls—incredibly powerful, nearly invincible, and perfectly subservient to the will of their master. More often than not, however, those rituals are done improperly and cause the victims to become mindless, ferocious, and uncontrollable wendigos who murder arbitrarily and inflict pain and suffering wherever they go.

"Last year, the Holy Office of the Inquisition paid a party of adventurers a small fortune to steal this grimoire and cut off all accesses to blackflame on Tuscoraura Mountain. For a while, new elf wendigos stopped appearing; but the Inquisition believes that the umpire-in-chief has been conspiring to resume his experimentation with blackflame. In order for the Holy Office to lift its ban on your preaching, you must agree to help destroy all copies of this grimoire and remove any trace of blackflame from here."

Shocked at this news, Johnny Appleseed takes a moment to recover his breath and then says, "I will do whatever I am capable of to halt the production of wendigos but right now that won't amount to much with my leg broken as it is. As we say in Kentikie, I couldn't even hit a snake with a belly full of rabbit stuck in a mouse hole."

Zena immediately steps in and says, "I have plan that we go in Kibbler's house and find book you call grimoire. Then we put out all blackflame."

Clarke looks up at Zena happily. "Awesome! That would solve everybody's problems. What's your plan?"

Zena says proudly, "I have friend, garden gnome. His name is Master Jack Spriggins. He have very big beanstalk that go up to Kibbler's house. We go inside and we find the book. You agree, Brother Clarke?"

"Agreed."

Zena turns and says, "You agree, Mister Louis?"

"Would this quest make me a hero?"

Madame Dungaree says, "Technically, yes."

Louis gives them a mischievous grin, "I've always wanted to be a hero. I guess the time is now."

Johnny Appleseed says, "That's the spirit! I wish every Christian would start their day with those words on their lips. Evil wouldn't stand a chance."

Zena then leans over to Lynx and gives him a big kiss on the cheek. "You agree, Monsieur Lynx?"

Lynx resents the pressure she puts on him but he gets caught up in her loveliness and confidence. Besides, he has to admit to himself that he has always wanted to be a hero too. He allows himself to kiss her on the cheek says in Aenglish, "Agree."

Scene C: Jack and his Beanstalks

Wood Elf Trails, Tuscoraura Mountain
Good Frige's Day Nones. Afternoon, 7th of April, 1284

A dwarf wagoner lashes his bored donkey to head left off a narrow forest path toward a tumbledown farm at the outskirts of the wood elf village trails. After fussing over the next three hundred yards, the donkey finally provides the dwarf wagoner with a reasonable excuse to stop pulling the wagon—a gate. Next to the gate stands a large, well-crafted sign written in the Ogham alphabet and below it in the Latin alphabet: SPRIGGNS GAIRDDNS.

The dwarf lets out a loud, deep-bellied grunt that sounds sort of like a yeehaw but without any of the fun-loving, hard-riding, adventuresome spirit the word carries today. It draws the garden rabbit's attention.

A downtrodden halfling gardener is hard at work nearby, wearing a dirty apron over his plain, white shirt and faded, green dungaree overalls. On his shabby outfit a well-worn, striped, yellow silk scarf cleverly complements his frayed straw hat as if the last reminder of the comfortable wealth that at one time used to be his.

The halfling was once an aldernome in the Tuscoraura bailiwick of garden gnomes but you would not know it by looking at him. Once where success and prosperity were written all over his face, crow's feet and drudgery are now plant their cares between the laugh lines. As a member of the gentry, he used his clout and coins to convert this land, originally zoned as a wood elf farm, into a gnomish garden. Sadly, poor sunlight and inadequate irrigation have depleted the soil and taken their toll on his spirits. None of the tidiness that gives garden gnomes their name and the source of their pride makes a showing here.

Alert to the dwarf's grunt, the halfling's rabbit goes running up to the fence and snorts at the dwarf noisily while staying safely behind the gate. The halfling gardener looks up from spreading feed for his geese and knits his brow with worry . . . dwarves are often employed as debt collectors.

The gardener draws up his courage and comes ambling up to the gate, but the dwarf wagoner completely ignores him and just hops off the wagon. The halfling starts to speak to him in halting Medifskar, the dialect of Dwarvish most common on Tuscoraura Mountain, but the dwarf simply walks away. The halfling stands at the gate completely confused.

When the dwarf seems to have wandered out of earshot, the garden gnome's curiosity gets the better of him. He opens the fence. His large garden rabbit and his barking dog shoot past him to the wagon, sniffing and hopping excitedly. Suddenly, a pretty young face pops up from under a canvas cover and says cheerfully in Eldric, "Hello, Master Jack Spriggins!"

Startled at first, a friendly smile replaces the worried timidity and he returns her greeting in perfect Eldric, "Oh, Mademoiselle Zena! Welcome!"

She rips off the canvas covering and hops out of the wagon. Exuding the full extent of her charm with her body language, Zena says, "These are my friends."

Louis and Clarke lift their heads up and behind them, Lynx and the leader of Dungaree Jeanne's bravo squad, Captain Manzone, all climb out of the wagon. The bravo captain walks over to take up a protective stance next to Zena but seeing the bunny charging at him, he jumps back into the wagon. The attack bunny snorts and wags his tail, bouncing in circles.

Seeing the fearless bravo beat a hasty retreat, Clarke panics, "Run away, run away!"

Large, muscular, and aggressive, the rabbit's huge incisors could easily snap off a few fingers, and one charge with his powerful hind legs could break a few ribs. The garden gnome grabs the guard bunny's blue harness and calms him down in Gnorrachi, the colloquial language of the garden gnomes. "Settle down there, Peter. These people are our friends."

With the guard bunny restrained, Captain Manzone recovers his machoism and makes his way around the cart to lead the donkey inside the gate. Captain Manzone claims to be the best swordmaster on Tuscoraura Mountain. Dungaree Jeanne hired him knowing boasting is par for the course with sellswords like him but to his credit, there are no elves alive in Shentalpee City who dare so much as insinuate that they have bettered him in a contest of blades.

After Louis and Clarke regroup, Master Spriggins gives Zena a warm, friendly hug. "Welcome to you and your friends. I was just feeding the geese. If only I had a goose that could lay one egg a day, she would be worth her weight in gold, I tell you. Even with all these geese, I'm lucky to get three eggs a week. Anyhow, enough about me; how are you doing?"

"Fantastic!" exclaims Zena. "I'm doing fantastic. How are you?"

The farmer looks down at the ground and pats his hands on his dungaree overalls as if to remind her that he is loyal to her mother's clothing brand. "Oh, you know how it is for a gnome gardener living too far above the topsoil. Some seasons are better than others. Mama's health problems are making her a bit ornery these days, but we still got a clean burrow to sleep in safe and sound at night, so I am not complaining."

Louis decides it's time to make overtures to the guard bunny while Clarke looks down tentatively from the safety of the wagon bed. Like an old pro with animals, Louis reaches down and allows the bunny to sniff his fingers. That's all the bunny needs to decide that he and Louis are going to be best friends forever. He pets him, rubs his back and scratches behind his ears. For his part, Peter Rabbit licks Louis's fingers and smears his dirty paws all over his britches.

Seeing it's safe, Clarke climbs down from the wagon. That same instant Master Spriggins's dog runs up to sniff him out. Clarke pats the doggie's head and woof—the start of a wonderful friendship.

Clarke looks up at Louis and says in Aenglish, "I wonder what his name is."

The garden gnome says in his heavily Gnorrachi-accented Aenglish, "Bing-oh is his name-oh."

Louis looks up delighted that the garden gnome speaks some Aenglish and tells Clarke, "I think the farmer said his dog's name is Jango."

The halfling gardener corrects him. "We are gnome-oh. We do not be farmer-oh. We say gardener-oh."

Louis replies, "So you're saying that halflings don't call themselves farmers, they call themselves gardeners. Is that right?"

"Garden gnome-oh is only gardener. Other halfling is yes can be the farmer-oh. You know Derry-oh halfling? The farmer in the dell is high-oh the Derry-oh in garden gnome-oh esteem, like my wife."

Louis looks puzzled and tries to sort out what Master Spriggins is trying to say, "Oh, right, so the farmer takes his wife from the Derry-oh halflings?"

"No! Me not farmer-oh, me is gardener-oh."

Clarke plays with the dog. "How old is Jango?"

The halfling corrects him, "Bing-oh."

Clarke is not sure he heard that right. "He's bingo years old? I don't know how to count in Gnorrachi."

"No! Dog is five years-oh. Dog's name is Bing-oh."

Louis tries to help. "He said the dog is five years old but the dog's name is Dingo, not Jango."

The halfling gardener gets frustrated. He says, "No, no, no! Gardener has dog-oh and Bing-oh is his name-oh: B-I-N-G-" and he finishes the spelling with a clap of his hand to indicate there is no *O* at the end.

Zena cuts in and says in Aenglish, "He try to say that name of dog is Bing."

The garden gnome lights up with joy at finally being understood. "Yes! That is what I say-oh."

Invading his personal space, Zena interrupts the conversation and puts an arm around the gardener's shoulders and says in Eldric, "Master Spriggins, do you remember how you told me if there were ever a favor you could do for me, I shouldn't hesitate to ask?"

"Absolutely, Mademoiselle Zena."

"Well, I'm hesitating. This is a big favor to ask."

"Please, Mademoiselle Zena, come under my roof and have some tea. We can discuss your problem. Master Spriggins will fix all your troubles."

Zena looks around carefully and studies the property outline. To the southeast corner of Master Spriggins' farm are the three giant sequoia trees that hold up Umpire Kibbler's mansion. Due south is a much lower platform held up by a grove of sycamores that extends Vandsee Estates to over thrice the size of any other estate on Tuscoraura Mountain.

Real estate in a sequoia grove is so precious that even the richest industrialist who serves as the umpire-in-chief of the Tuscoraura fire elf colony does not get a single extra square foot of living space on a sequoia platform. What his money and influence have allowed is a permit to construct an extra base on a sycamore grove, giving the Kibbler family an unheard-of degree of privacy and luxury—they are the only high elf family in all of Tuscoraura Mountain that does not have to share living space with servants and workers.

Kibbler's one-hundred-foot-high sycamore base cut off much of the sunlight needed to grow crops to the north. The fire elf who sold it to him knew that but Master Spriggins had no clue since garden gnomes normally only cultivate underground crops.

When the farm failed year after year, Master Spriggins went to the Council of Perfects to complain. They were largely unsympathetic to his plight but to appease the angry garden gnomes at his back, the council voted to grant him permission to grow bean vines on the support cables leading up to the platform as compensation—a small consolation . . . until today.

Zena says, "My friends and I were hoping to put on a little play. It is extremely important for us that we have complete privacy, and I was wondering if we could use your farm to rehearse."

"Oh, no trouble at all, Mademoiselle Zena. You go right ahead. I'll just be getting a few chores done and staying out of your way."

"Well, see, there's the rub, Master Spriggins. When I say complete privacy, I mean no one, absolutely no one, can see this play before we put it on or else the effect will be ruined."

Master Spriggins gives her an anxious look. "What kind of play is this, if you don't mind my asking?"

Zena's face turns conspiratorial and she whispers, "The play will be a satire wherein we'll catch the conscience of the umpire."

"Oh, that kind of a play, is it?"

"Yes, and for your own sake, I don't want you to have to answer any entangling questions about it, if you catch my drift."

"Oh, I do, Mademoiselle Zena! I do! I catch your drift like this." He does a catching motion with his fist.

Mademoiselle Zena fingers a few golden Tuscoraura double eagles into his palm and says, "Here are a few tokens of gratitude to compensate you for the lost time and productivity, but we don't want anyone on this farm at all. I hope Dame Spriggins is well enough to travel."

"Oh, Mademoiselle Zena, this is too much! I don't make that much in a week with this lousy old farm."

"Keep the difference as a contract fee. We want you to make sure no one knows we are using your farm. I don't want you going into the village or visiting a tavern. No one sees you. No one asks questions."

Master Spriggins lightens up and points his finger in the air. "How about fishing? Everyone knows I love fishing! I've still got my big old sign that says gone fishing! No one will wander onto my farm if they see that sign up. They all know not to look for good old Master Jack Spriggins when he goes fishing. The missus hasn't been a big fan of fishing so far but when she sees these eagles, I'm sure she'll learn to like it fast. How does that sound, Mademoiselle Zena?"

"That sounds just fine, Master Spriggins."

"Just let me finish feeding the animals and then my garden is your garden."

The poor old gnome heads off to finish up his chores and Zena gathers her party of adventurers for a huddle. She calls the play in Eldric, even though only Lynx and Captain Manzone can understand her, "Okay, listen up, people! Master Jack Spriggins grows his beanstalks on these support cables that stabilize an intermediary platform between Umpire Kibbler's mansion on that sequoia platform over there and the Kibbler workshops and servant quarters on that sycamore platform just above us. The entire complex is referred to as Vandsee Estates.

"The weak point is right there. That intermediary platform has only one building on it—the brownie warehouse."

Lynx asks, "What is a brownie?"

Captain Manzone tells him, "The brownies are gnomes from the southern part of Albany. Those from the north are pixies."

Zena continues, "Apparently, they are indentured servants who take the night shift for most of Kibbler's workshops, so they'll be asleep when we get there. Their sleep schedule will be crucial to our success."

She unrolls a map. "Getting up to the sycamore platform is going to be a long and arduous climb, but that will be the easy part. Making our way from there into Umpire Kibbler's mansion on the sequoia platform will take precision, coordination, and an ability to improvise if the situation changes.

"These two bridges here both connect to Kibbler's private residence, where the grimoire and any spare braziers of blackflame will be, but most workers walk along the lower bridge on their way home and the scouts usually only take the upper bridge. Once the workers are all across the lower one, we will cross that bridge when we get to it.

"Once inside Umpire Kibbler's mansion, we will have to move quickly. In general, Umpire Kibbler is very secretive about what goes on in his house but there is only one room that no one is allowed to enter, ever. Right over here. That's almost for sure where he keeps the grimoire. We grab it and go.

She finally looks up and realizes Louis and Clarke have not understood a single word of what she said. As if on cue, Clarke asks, "Are you going to translate that into Aenglish?"

She says in Aenglish, "Too much that I explain again. You two humans just follow us. No problem." Then Zena points to the wagon they rode in on and looks at Louis. "You, big fellow, take rope from wagon and carry it up there. When we finish, you tie rope and we all go down. Understand?"

Louis and Clarke both nod.

"All right, team! Grab your gear. It's on!"

Zena goes first, but even with the best elf climbing gear supplied by Dungaree Jeanne, one hundred feet up a beanstalk is a struggle for everyone. Lynx is still sore from the last tournament and the fortysomething Captain Manzone starts to feel his age. Clarke, having spent most of his life at a manuscript illumination desk, has no aptitude for climbing at all and only makes it to the top thanks to Louis's help. His robust physique and strong fingers from years of cutting and sewing tough pieces of leather give him the vigor to haul Clarke up the last stretch of the climb.

Still, the task saps Louis of his grit. He collapses at the edge of the platform and pants wildly. Zena yanks his arm and tries to get him back onto his feet before a passing patrol should ruin all that hard work.

Zena's unrelenting urgings gets them all safely inside the brownie warehouse before any vigilant eyes land on them but the day is not won. Zena takes her team into the kitchen's pantry. "This should be a safe hiding place where we can observe the lower bridge until it is all clear to cross. Captain Manzone, I want you to keep a lookout just in case—"

With a hiss, Captain Manzone raises a hand to remind her to keep her voice low. He points two fingers to his eyes and then swings his fingers out into the brownie kitchen. They follow his gaze and see a yawning gnomid girl wearing a brown kilt, sporran pouch, and a bodice with a brown sash over her right shoulder down to her left hip. She heads for the pantry.

Improvising, Lynx grabs a blob of dough, plunks it in a half-empty jar of honey and powders it with a handful of cocoa powder. He sticks it out on a plate just before the brownie girl opens the pantry door. Curiosity gets the better of the little girl and she sniffs the treat. She looks around cautiously then sticks her finger in for a taste. Immensely pleased with the result, she stirs it with a cooking spoon and dumps the mix onto a baking stone. The oven embers start warming it to perfection.

While she waits she pours herself some deer milk and pulls her bakery invention out of the oven, cutting them into squares before sampling them.

With a smile a mile wide, she runs off to share these cocoa bakery squares with her closest friends and family. From that point on, they would become the signature treat coming from the brownie community indentured at the Kibbler workshops.

Waves of relief pass over the adventurers seeing the kitchen now clear. Zena sees another door and waves the team over, saying in a low-pitched voice, "We have to find another way out of here."

They follow her to the door but instead of an escape route, they discover a larder filled with seafood hanging from hooks. In the middle of the larder at the base of the thrawl stone burns a brazier of blackflame, chilling the enclosed space aggressively. A one-eyed cat snacking on a squid yowls at the interruption and skitters off past the icebox.

Zena sees the crack of light where the one-eyed cat escaped and says, "If we could just move that block of ice off the icebox, we'd be able to get out of here."

Captain Manzone objects, "It's too big!"

Zena points to Louis and says in Aenglish, "Big fellow, move ice, please, so that we go out."

Louis moves up through the small larder, getting his face slapped with fishtails, eel caudal fins, and octopus tentacles. He presses hard against the ice block until his fingers sting, but it will not budge.

They all look at him expectantly, so instead of giving up, he unstraps his battleaxe and starts chipping at the corners of the ice block. The ice actually chips off bits of his axe blade but with a little patience and some dedicated effort, he dislodges the ice block until it slides out far enough for them to squeeze past.

And not a moment too soon! The excitement over the girl's cocoa bakery squares has a large number of brownies flooding into the kitchen to whip up a batch of their own.

The rest of Zena's plan for getting into Umpire Kibbler's mansion flows without a hitch. The party of adventurers tip-toe across the bridge leading to the upper part of Vandsee Estates without being seen.

Having visited often enough as a child thanks to her friendship with Florenz, Zena knows the layout of Kibbler's residence and guides them quickly to an attic adjacent to the mysterious chamber the umpire-in-chief has marked as strictly off-limits to outsiders.

The door to the gallery is boarded up with chains and wooden beams. Zena looks back at Louis and whispers, "Psst! Big fellow! Open this wall."

In the cramped attic space, Louis struggles to get the two-handed battleaxe off his back again. Once ready, he gently taps the axe-head against the plaster wall. The thin support beams, mud, and straw, soon crumble away. The hole is big enough for even Louis' wide shoulders to fit comfortably through so Zena leads the party of adventurers inside.

As Zena expected, the room was originally designed to be the great hall of the mansion, specifically for receiving guests and holding feasts. They find themselves up in a cramped servants' gallery designed for lighting the chandeliers, which no longer have candles in them, nor any sign of melted wax.

For all his caution in boarding up the servants' entrance to the gallery, Umpire Kibbler never seems to have considered the possibility that his intruders might break a hole through the wall.

Zena, Lynx, Captain Manzone, Louis, and Clarke creep along the gallery silently and peek over the walkway's barrier to survey the great hall below. Everything about the room tells them it has been reconfigured for dark rituals. A table in the center is draped with a black cloth and marked with variegated sands, glowing crystals, strange symbols, and bloody tools that look more apt for torture than religious rites.

A brazier of blackflame burns darkly in the middle of the table and all around the room are cages and boxes of various shapes and sizes. A few coffins lie open with the embalmed bodies of wood elves visible. What really makes them squeal with fright is the medium-sized cage that holds the dead body of old Mother Hubbard's dog. One small cage holds a nervous little guinea pig and a stinky box holds a dead skunk, while an enormous cage not far from the brazier imprisons the hulking goblin while he sleeps. The native hue of his green skin is sicklied-over with the pale cast of the blackflame's shadowing.

All around the room are racks of contorted instruments and unsavory costumes. On the table, a bookstand lies open with a codex that must be Umpire

Kibbler's coveted grimoire. Despite their supposed friendship, Florenz did not hesitate to go public with a scandal involving her mother. Zena is more than eager to even out the score by embroiling Florenz's father in a juicy scandal of necromancy. With any luck, the lurid details inside that book will capture the imagination of the voters and horrify them away from supporting Kibbler's dynastic ambitions.

"Psst!" She grabs Louis's attention. "Big fellow, give me some rope."

Louis unravels a length of rope. He hands her an end and lowers her down over the gallery's ledge.

Lynx hisses in Aenglish, "Pull her up! Now!"

Louis stops and looks at him, confused. Lynx pops his head up and waves his arms for Zena to come back but, eager for her prize, she waves him away.

Moments later, everyone else hears the approaching footsteps and chattering voices and they all lend a hand pulling her up. The ruckus and the delay caused by the numerous locks and bolts on the main door give Zena time to scamper back up to the walkway in time.

They all lie low while the footsteps enter the ritual chamber. Someone clanks at the goblin's cage. Among the chatter, Umpire Kibbler's voice is unmistakable, but the other voices are harder to pick out. One of the elves in Kibbler's company seems to be able to speak Gobbledygook, the language of the Magog goblins, saying, "Phlip phlopin phleye."

The goblin barks back, "Phee pheye pho phum!"

Umpire Kibbler asks, "What did he say?"

The translator hesitates and then says, "He's telling us that he smells the blood of an Aenglishman."

"What is that supposed to mean? Does he want to

kill Johnny Appleseed? Is that the real reason he trespassed onto Tuscoraura Mountain?"

"I don't know, Monsieur Umpire."

"Well, ask him!"

The translator attempts to speak to the goblin again. "Phiddle dum phiddle dee phum Johnny Appleseed?"

The goblin just roars again, "Phee pheye pho phum!" Although bound hand and foot, he shakes the cage and spits at his captors.

Umpire Kibbler says in disgust, "The savage! Never mind negotiating with brutes like that. Tie him up over the ritual table so we can perform the blackflame transmogrification on him. Soak his ropes in linseed oil. If anything goes wrong, we'll have to burn him alive. We can't risk having the likes of him rampaging around Shentalpee City as a wendigo."

"Monsieur Umpire, I am not so sure the rafters of this hall will be able to support his bulk. He must weigh over twenty stones!"

Umpire Kibbler says dismissively, "Run cables to all the rafters and gallery arches. As long as you distribute the weight evenly, it'll be fine. I'm going to dinner now. I want the ritual to be ready by the time I get back. Tell Monsieur Gandorf that I hope for his sake that he's figured out the stormcrow by now."

Lynx's eyes open wide at the mention of Enganyon's father and the newly appointed Major Leagues Umpire. He looks directly at Zena but she shows no reaction whatsoever.

Amid the brisk footsteps exiting the ritual chamber and a voice calls out, "Quickly, fetch some cables. As if this place wasn't creepy enough, the umpire-in-chief wishes to turn the ceiling into one giant spiderweb."

The door reopens Umpire Kibbler comes back in saying, "Oh, and uh, Blunderbore, summon the captain of the scouts. I want to know if Johnny Appleseed has been snooping around the premises."

The voice of the one called Blunderbore barks out, "The rest of you, get to work! We'll need to take down those boards blocking off the servants' entrance to the galleries. I will worry about contacting the monsieur Umpire Gandorf and searching for Appleseed."

As soon as the footsteps leave the ritual chamber, Zena peeks over to see if anyone is left standing around. The room is empty, so Zena starts to move. Captain Manzone hisses at her, "No time! We have to leave before they catch us."

Zena leaps over the gallery railing with the rope and zips down saying, "Not without that grimoire!"

She grabs it as the goblin watches her with hate in his eyes and then shimmies back up the rope, with the rest of the adventurers hauling her in at the same time.

They all crawl on hands and knees out through the hole Louis cut in the wall. Clarke feels a tug on his monk's robe and he looks back to see Captain Manzone slicing a sizeable piece of fabric off his Carmelite habit with a dagger. Its cream color almost perfectly matches the plaster, and Captain Manzone carefully hangs it over Louis's hole to make it less visible.

They clamber over the creaking attic boards as swiftly as possible in hopes of avoiding a run-in with Kibbler's servants.

Too late!

They hear footsteps coming up the stairway they are supposed to use as their escape route. Lynx points to a stack of crates and says in Aenglish, "Go there!"

Captain Manzone does not speak a word of Aenglish but he catches on to Lynx's meaning. Once again he pirates Clarke's robes and pulls the long, brown scapular off over Clarke's head. When the team crouches behind the crates, Captain Manzone drapes the brown scapular over their heads. Its color perfectly matches the old wooden crates and saves them from certain punishment and death as the attic door bursts open and agitated servants comes up lugging crowbars and huge spools of cable.

For nearly half an hour Kibbler's servants tear at the planks and boards, totally oblivious to the hole in the wall only a few feet away or the party of adventurers hiding behind the crates. At last, they pry open the old door and start setting up ropes to suspend the goblin.

All clear, Zena hustles the down the steps and navigates efficiently through the halls and corridors of Umpire Kibbler's mansion. Louis, Clarke, Lynx, and Captain Manzone follow tight on her heels until she takes them into an old cloakroom and they all have a moment to catch their breath and think.

Zena announces proudly in Eldric, "Almost there, adventurers! Down the hall to the right is the servants' back entrance. From there it's a straight shot to the ledge of the sequoia platform. We'll just slide down the big fellow's rope and ride the donkey cart out of here."

Lynx looks at her. "There's only one problem."

"What's that?"

"Guard dogs. Lots of them."

Zena huffs, "Kibbler doesn't use any guard dogs."

Captain Manzone says, "Before you shoot his contribution to the planning phase down, let's take a look for ourselves. He seems to have pretty keen ears."

"What do you mean, planning phase? I've already done all the planning!"

Before an argument arises, Captain Manzone heads out and sneaks up a nearby flight of stairs to take a peek out the windows. He waves the party of adventurers to follow and they leave Zena by herself in the closet. Not appreciating the challenge to her leadership, Zena eventually gives in and follows them. Captain Manzone points out the evidence confirming Lynx's suspicions. As soon as Zena sees it she exclaims, "Whoa! Who let the dogs out?"

Lynx exclaims in despair, "We're stuck up here!"

Zena does her best to reassure the others—and herself. "No problem! We'll just toss the doggies a bone and they'll let us go."

Captain Manzone asks, "Why would trained guard dogs let us walk by just because they've got a bone?"

Zena says, "A doggie's nothing if he's got a bone."

They cannot see the servants' back entrance from the window, but Lynx hears another noise and reports it to the party. "There is a scout posted just outside the door, probably a girl scout by the way she coughs. If we open it, she'll raise the alarm at once."

Zena gets defensive. "What are you trying to say about the way girls cough?"

Captain Manzone jumps to his rescue. "Nothing. He's just saying there is an armed scout out there and that she's a girl. Not that her gender matters much because we'll get killed either way if we don't figure something out."

Zena looks back at Lynx. "How did you know about the guard dogs?"

"I could hear them."

Captain Manzone pats him on the shoulder. "Like I said, pretty keen ears. Keen as a kid with a hand in old aunt Arazone's cookie jar before she lost her hearing."

Zena gets defensive again. "What are you trying to say about the way girls hear?"

Captain Manzone puts his arms up. "Nothing! It's just an expression. I'm just saying I'm glad Lynx hears well. Walking into the girl scout at the door or the dogs on the bridge would have cost us our lives."

Zena says, "Okay, look, everybody! It's me who's been doing all the thinking so far. That's what girls are good at. Would you boys mind showing that you're good for something other than complaining?"

Captain Manzone grimaces. "Boy, that got personal real fast."

Zena shoots back, "What are you saying about the way girls get personal?"

Louis finally interrupts, "Would anyone mind translating this argument for us in Aenglish?"

Zena is in no mood to go over the conversation so Lynx tries to explain it in his broken Aenglish, "I hear dogs and Captain Manzone says cost of girl scout cookies is our lives. Mademoiselle Zena thinks like girl and we boys no think. Get it?"

Louis mutters, "No."

Suddenly, Lynx perks up and then exclaims with muffled jubilation, flip-flopping between Eldric and Aenglish, "Guess! Goose! Egg hair guess! I hear goose."

Clarke catches on and comes up with a plan. "Hey, Louis! Remember when you were trying to find the elf jewelry in the shoemaker's mansion and you let your goose run around as a distraction? What if we set the goose loose from the coop?"

Louis says, "That's a brilliant idea!"

Captain Manzone asks for a translation in Eldric. "Fifth saga hen?"

Zena says in Eldric, "Time till at ran outer henny."

Lynx starts to translate but Clarke says, "Don't worry. We caught on to that one."

Zena snaps back in Aenglish, "Will you boys please keep mouth shut? You talk as much as room full of schoolgirls!"

They all keep quiet and follow Zena out.

The place is crawling with scouts and trained guard dogs. Zena turns to Louis and Clarke, saying in Aenglish, "Louis, you open chicken house. When chickens run, we all go on chicken run too."

Clarke objects, "I thought it was a goose coop."

Captain Manzone asks, "Fate thither that?"

Unsure of the plan now, Clarke asks, "What does that mean?"

Lynx replies, "What does that mean?"

Clarke says, "I don't know any Elvish; that's why I'm asking you."

Lynx slaps his forehead. "No, I tell you, 'fate thither that?' means, 'what does that mean?' in Eldric."

Louis puts a hand on Clarke's shoulder and says, "Let it go, Clarke. I'm going on the chicken run."

While the party of adventurers stares at each other in total incomprehension, Zena keeps a close watch on the movement patterns of the scouts and at the right moment, she hisses, "Now!"

Louis jogs out through the kitchen door and starts hacking away at the coop with his battleaxe. Hens, roosters, geese, and ganders come flapping and squawking out. He runs back inside as soon as the dogs arrive and closes the door a hair's breadth before the first snout snags him.

Without hesitating, Zena waves them to follow her all the way back through the house to the servants' back entrance past the cloakroom. Zena opens it a crack and sees the elve scout has left and no dogs are in the vicinity. It seems the distraction worked.

After they all make a mad dash to the ledge, Louis spins desperately to unravel the full length of the rope. In order to make a clean getaway, they cannot leave the rope behind, which means they have to tie a special knot in the middle of the rope that makes one end the escape route and the other end the safety release.

Captain Manzone sees Louis fumble with the rope anxiously, then pushes him aside and ties the knot all by himself. Not a moment too soon, once removed from the temptation of chasing the wild goose, the dogs lead the nightwatch scouts straight to the platform ledge, where they hear the zipping of the adventurers' descent.

The girl scout peeks over and sees them all sliding down on the taut rope while another rope right beside it hangs slack. Familiar with knots, she realizes that the slack rope is the safety release and gives it a quick tug, long before it is safe for the adventurers to do so. The rope drops and with it, the party goes into free fall.

Now, judging from the length of this story and the fact that you have many pages yet to read, o most perspicacious reader, you can probably guess that our heroes do not die from that fall. Providence must be watching over them tonight because Louis is nearly to the ground by the time the rope drops free. He is the meatiest and heaviest one in the party and cushions their fall. Still, they all sustain minor injuries—sprained ankles and wrists, bruised bottoms, aching backs, and a case of whiplash here and there.

Knowing the pursuit is not over, they all help each other up and start limping off in whatever direction Zena takes them. Had that been the only escape plan, they would now be dangling over Umpire Kibbler's blackflame brazier like marshmallows over a bonfire—or like popsicles over a freezer vent, to be precise.

Lo and behold, Master Jack Spriggins has had a successful afternoon fishing and the ornery Missus Spriggins has convinced him—or more precisely, henpecked him—into returning home early. Seeing the poor donkey harnessed up to the wagon all day, he felt sorry for her, fed her, watered her, and combed her down. The grateful donkey and the kindhearted gardener have been keeping watch for Mademoiselle Zena and her friends ever since.

Noticing their silhouettes dropping to the earth, Master Spriggins exclaims to his elderly mother, "Look, Mama! The sky is falling!"

With utter common sense, she replies, "No, the umpire's little chickens have flown the coop."

Almost instantly he surveys the field and sees dozens of delicious, dinner-table fowl flopping and flying around his farm. Then, far off, Master Spriggins catches sight of Zena and her friends limping towards him. He hops into the donkey cart and steers her over rough terrain to greet them. He calls out in Eldric, "Need a lift?"

Zena, bruised and shaken but still holding Kibbler's grimoire safely in her backpack, throws her fists into the air and shouts, "That's uber-friendly of you!"

Lynx, Captain Manzone, Louis, and Clarke all manage to get their sore limbs aboard the wagon. The elf scouts are already taking potshots at them and attempting to lower ropes down so as to join in hot pursuit. Master Spriggins gets the picture real fast and knows exactly where to go to shake them.

Incidentally, Umpire Kibbler's prized egg-laying goose lands right in the middle of Master Spriggins' yard. His elderly and wise mother hobbles over there to embrace the golden opportunity.

Scene E: Orpheus

Garden Gnome Burrow, Tuscoraura Mountain
Good Frige's Day Vespers.
Evening, 7th of April, 1284

It's a rough ride, to say the least. Bumping their way across the field, the rigid wagon wheels jostle the carriage, aggravating their sore bones and bruised joints in new and devilishly painful ways. The rough-planed wood of the wagon bed chafes against their skin and their elbows clatter against each other as Master Spriggins snaps the reins for the donkey to go faster.

At first, the scouts chase after them on foot, and although elf scouts are extremely fleet-footed, the motivated donkey outpaces them.

Then the horns. Shrill horns are heard all over the colony. They call out to the League of Licornes, the reindeer-mounted elf military league. Unlike mounted humans, who consider the coordinated, heavily armored knights' charge as the pinnacle of mounted tactics—an unstoppable wall of steel and meat crushing everything in its path—the ideal elf cavalry is a shadow; silent, lonely, dream-like.

Master Spriggins sees mounted elf reindeer riders pursuing him in the far off distance. It won't be long before they're right on his tail. Unless he finds a good hiding spot soon, none of them will have the slightest chance of survival.

It is, however, the special blessing of gnomes that they always know where to hide. Master Jack Spriggins takes a shortcut leading to a garden gnome burrow entrance. The reindeer riders stop several yards past the burrow entrance where the path grows pitch black. It's not that they are afraid of the dark. They are afraid of provoking a war with gnomes they can't see.

We need to correct another common misperception about elves. Although they have some of the keenest ears for hearing among all the clayborn races and generally have sharp eyesight, they have no special aptitude for seeing in the dark as do the gnomes and dwarves, who are fundamentally subterranean peoples.

Elves are all diurnal. Their small, wispy frames, wiry muscles, strong hands, and long fingers reflect adaptations to running through forests, slipping through craggy rocks, and climbing trees and cliffs. Elves thrive in open-air environments with lots of clutter for them to hide behind, leap over, or artistically rearrange. Consider how the Great Plains have never had any significant elf populations.

Within moments of steering the wagon down into the entrance of the garden gnome burrow, Master Spriggins has to get down off the wagon and lead the donkey from the front because of the burrow's low ceiling. The main highway through the garden gnome settlement is just barely wide enough to fit the wagon. Underground, every corridor is a cave-in hazard, so they dig sparingly. Every forty yards or so they build a niche for wagons to pass—but only wide enough for them to squeeze alongside each other nimbly pressed against the burrow wall.

After a quarter of an hour's journey, they reach their first garden gnome precinct. The deputy warden on night shift halts them at the gate. He has heard the creaking wagon wheels and felt its vibrations from so far off that by the time Jack waves his greeting, the deputy warden has already lit an extra torch, posted it, and gotten bored enough waiting for the wagon that he has already started on some of the paperwork.

"Anything to declare?" asks the deputy warden. To his credit, despite the boredom of night watch, he does not in the slightest look tired. Gnomes do most of their activities during the daytime but underground it can be easy to lose track of the day and night cycles above.

"Uh . . ." Jack Spriggins scratches the back of his head, wondering what kind of story he is supposed to make up to explain his strange cargo. The truth is always the best excuse, so he goes for it. "Three elves and two humans."

The deputy warden brings his torch around the wagon and sees the party of adventurers sleeping uncomfortably. He grimaces. "These your friends?"

"Absolutely."

"Are they going to tell me that when they wake up or did you . . . you know—"

Master Spriggins is offended by the insinuation. "No, I don't know! I saved their lives!"

"I'm still going to have to write up a report for the bailiff and they'll have to corroborate your story."

"Not a problem. Is there anywhere they could sleep for the night?"

The warden returns his torch to its sconce. "You want my advice, Jack? They're best off where they are. Just let 'em sleep. You already owe me a dollar just for parking the wagon in our lot and stabling the donkey. No sense in paying for a full night's lodgings if by the time you get them into bed, they only get another hour or two of sleep out of it."

"Can you break change for a double eagle?"

"You can leave the eagle with the office as a deposit and when you want your wagon and donkey back, they'll refund you whatever you overpaid. The bookkeeper keeps a chest in the office when he's on duty, but he only works during the day cycle."

Master Spriggins reaches into his pouch and hands the deputy warden one of the double eagles Zena gave him. The deputy warden steps into the office and fills out the parking permit on a strip of birchbark and hands it to him. "You mind answering a few questions while I fill out this report for the bailiff?"

Master Spriggins wiggles nervously. "I'd rather they answer the questions for themselves. I just came home and saw them fall from this rope they had set up. They said they were rehearsing a play. The must have got too close to the umpire-in-chief's property because he sent some scouts after them. I just brought them here because they looked hurt from the fall. Would you happen to know of any clerics or physicians taking patients this late in the night cycle?"

"Yeah, but the nightly rates are doubled and your friends here don't look too bad off. Again, take my advice and wait until the day cycle. Healers are overpriced enough as it is. Let me help you unharness your donkey and we can push your wagon into that parking stall over there. You're lucky one's actually available. Parking down here is always a botheration, even at this hour."

The two gnome grooms unharness the donkey and brush her down, then give her some alfalfa and water. She has taken such a liking to Master Spriggins that when he leaves her, she starts braying wildly.

The donkey's braying wakes the party of adventurers up in a state completely disoriented by the dim light and muggy smells of the gnome burrow. Master Spriggins pets the donkey to calm her down while the deputy warden questions them in Gnorrachi.

Not a single one of them knows any Gnomish dialects except Zena, whose grasp of the language slips when the deputy warden starts throwing out all the legal jargon required by his paperwork.

The tension eases when the exhausted donkey finally falls asleep and Master Spriggins comes over to translate, since his fluency in Eldric extends to business transactions. Once back in her native language, Zena immediately starts rattling off everything on her one-track mind about how important it is to get the book in her backpack safely up to Shentalpee City.

The deputy warden stops her from speaking and says in Gnorrachi, "Look, I'm sorry, Master Spriggins, but this sounds like it's above my pay grade. I'm going to have to take the lot of you to precinct headquarters, where your friends can be interviewed by properly licensed interpreters."

Master Spriggins raises his hands as if to protest his innocence. "That's fine with me. I'm a law-abiding gnome. I just want to make sure my friends can get the healing arts they need in a timely fashion."

"Oh, don't worry! I've got a feeling the warden is going to declare this a public case. They will get all the aid they need—and a little help from the community purse if we play this one right. Just follow my lead."

"Yes, sir, deputy warden, sir!" says Master Spriggins with the first smile he has worn all night. Forasmuch as he is willing to help Zena, he would really prefer not to waste all the gold eagles she gave him on this episode.

As the deputy warden unlocks the gate to the Deagle's Den Precinct, he warns Master Spriggins, "Tell the missy elve to be extra watchful with all that jewelry. I ain't gonna lie to you—we just haven't been able to put the kibosh on all the sticky fingers in here. We've got cutpurses, pickpockets, urchins, pilferers, and burglars aplenty down here. The bailiff even thinks the Thieves' Guild must have its headquarters down here."

Master Spriggins translates and word goes around the group. At this point, Zena cares little for her jewelry. She cradles her grimoire like a baby, fearing only that their bold incursion onto Vandsee Estates would all be for naught if she does not end up using her hard-won political ammunition against Florenz.

The garden gnome nightwatch is still prowling the narrow thoroughfares of this wealthy trading post. Gnomes in general are industrious and creative, but also a bit unadventurous. Without a vigorous trade center attracting merchants to their burrow, they would have no luxury goods to make getting rich through gardening and artisanal crafts worthwhile.

Deagle's Den is close enough to the high bailiff's manor to make going to market a convenient outing, but far enough away to keep all strangers, swindlers, and other sorts of hooligans at arm's length.

To everyone's relief, they all arrive at the precinct headquarters with their belongings intact and sit in a waiting room for a very long time before the warden shows up. No one complains. The sofas are cozy, and the sweet pastries and hot chamomile tea make for a particularly reinvigorating breakfast.

When the warden finally does come in, he impresses them all. He is an exceptionally large gnome, nearly five feet in height, and rolling in folds of flesh that at one time covered heavy-duty muscle. His badge of office sits proudly on his left collar, pinning a vestigial cloak that barely covers his shoulders to a white linen shirt brocaded with green, yellow, and brown thread. Hugging his portly waist, an ample brass belt buckle depicts the Battle of Deganwy in which a band of courageous knockers, Welchland gnomes, defeated an invading Aenglish army by robbing them of all their supplies. His boots seem exceedingly soft and well-cushioned. He walks on them with a slight wince and shows relief when he sits down.

He speaks in Gnorrachi as translators repeat his words in Aenglish and Eldric. "Welcome, visitors! Warden Grayer is my name and on behalf of High Bailiff Harfud Fellowhide, it is a pleasure to grant you these access passes to Deagle's Den as honored guests of our esteemed Master Gardener Jack Spriggins."

They all murmur their thanks and Zena begins to speak but Warden Grayer holds up his hand to let her know he has not yet finished his speech.

"Deputy Warden Stoor has informed me that you were injured in an accidental fall while rehearsing for a play beneath the Vandsee Estates. While I would like to believe that, I have received a missive from the high bailiff's reeve asking all precincts to keep an eye out for a group of intruders who were chased off Umpire Kibbler's property last night. Am I to understand that those intruders are you?"

Zena is more than eager to explain her side of the story. "Monsieur Warden, we are very grateful for your kind welcome. Before we begin, I must make it clear to you that the conflict at hand puts at jeopardy the safety and security of us all on Tuscoraura Mountain. As the leader of the opposition party to Umpire-in-Chief Kibbler's tyrannical regime, I assembled a party of adventurers to raid Vandsee Estates—"

Gasps of shock and surprise arise not only from the garden gnome officials in the room but also from the other adventurers in her party, who were kind of hoping to stick to the play-acting story.

Zena holds out the book. "We invite your loremasters to examine its authenticity. This book is the first solid piece of evidence to prove that the current umpire-in-chief is causing the wendigo infestation. His experiments with blackflame rituals in an attempt to raise up for himself a private army of undead warriors have gone terribly wrong."

Warden Grayer thinks for a moment. Gnomes have always prided themselves on their intelligence and sagacity. He takes a sip of chamomile tea and then says, "A crisis of this magnitude cannot be taken lightly. You claim that your umpire-in-chief is an evil necromancer and that you are the only elve fit to replace him. If what you say is true, I ought to bend my knee to you and kiss your hand as the savior of Tuscoraura Mountain."

Zena waits for him to say more, but Warden Grayer clearly wants to see how she handles herself at this exceedingly awkward part of the conversation.

"Monsieur Warden, I am not a goddess seeking your veneration. I am a hardworking, dedicated elve who sees her beloved kin and neighbors in grave peril. I cannot but act and do my best to save them. The consequences of inaction . . . I tremble at the thought."

He puts the teacup down. "Well spoken! I can see you are not a stranger to the realms of politics; but I must ask you a more important question. Can you produce witnesses?"

"Yes, Monsieur Warden. You can depend on it."

"No, mademoiselle elve, it will be your life that depends on it."

The high bailiff of the Tuscoraura garden gnomes has managed to pack his courtroom with emotional onlookers sitting in every corner along with a large number of officials, security wardens, and snack vendors. The box seats in the gallery near the ceiling of the courtroom are standing room only.

Clearly, this trial will make great sport for the nosy and prying gnomes who want to be first in line for the juiciest bits of gossip in the bailiwick. The courtroom is designed to hold large numbers in such a cramped space and has a series of beehive chimneys that are designed to pressurize the room evenly so as to freshen the air by forcing currents of wind up and down the vents and across the crowd.

Even so, the air is stifling with the press of bodies and constant shouting from a few hundred big mouths with bad breath. Immediately upon entering the courtroom, Zena starts to sweat from the oppressive atmosphere. Dour, barrel-chested gnomes and dwarves are well-adapted to the small pockets of stale air that come with living underground, but only with copious gusts of fresh air can slender-boned, spritely elves maintain their mental and physical health.

Zena's gnomid jailer sits her on a bench politely but then immediately after that Louis, Clarke, Lynx, and Captain Manzone are shoved down next to her so hard they nearly topple over. The only reason they don't fall is that the gnomes in the front rows are more than willing to lend a hand and push them back upright.

As she sits and watches the scene, Zena makes two important observations. First, the roughness of the gnome jailers is mostly for show. For the legalistic and intellectual gnomes, the mind games of a trial are about as thrilling and theatrical as a wrestling match for dwarves. Second, she immediately sees a special guest star is in attendance—Lawspeaker Sturl Snorrison of the Tuscoraura Mountain dwarves.

A brilliant dwarf by all accounts, Lawspeaker Snorrison has won fame for his legal knowledge and poetic accomplishments as much as for his touchy and easily offended temperament.

According to the laws of the bailiwick, Zena has a right to a lawyer and after consulting with the first gnome lawyer assigned to her case, she requested that Inquisitor Sheen be summoned as a witness to testify that her breach of Vandsee Estates was well warranted by suitable authorities.

In an extraordinary stroke of bad luck, Zena's key witness happens to be a dwarf. Summoning a dwarf to testify in a Tuscoraura courtroom without an indult from the Tuscoraura Mountain Dwarves is a legal gaffe of catastrophic proportions. Lawspeaker Snorrison caught wind of it and has come to vindicate the dwarves rights.

Having fired her lawyer, Zena insists that the gnomes appoint one with greater circumspection. Her new counsel coaches her to hew to a fine line: she must comport herself in a dignified manner, not to grovel nor cast blame. "Respect the system and the system will respect you."

Through the excited chatter in the courtroom, the high bailiff bangs his ridiculously large gavel. Its concave face is ingeniously designed to create an ear-popping boom when struck against its sound block.

The audience immediately quiets down as they all cover their ears. The high bailiff keeps booming out enough noise pollution with his gavel to make their ears ring for a long while afterward. Lynx writhes with pain as he clutches his sensitive ears but Lawspeaker Snorrison and his dwarf delegates take the auricular punishment stoically.

After having thoroughly deafened everyone in the room, the high bailiff carelessly starts rattling off his legal mumbo-jumbo in such muffled and garbled tones that anyone in the courtroom must lean forward with cupped ears to catch his words.

The party of adventurers sits there on their bench waiting nervously—all except Zena, who takes advantage of the first pause in the high bailiff's ramblings to stand up and begin her oration.

If ever a gnome showed annoyance at a mosquito buzzing around his ear, I assure you he did not wrinkle his face with such pure and unadulterated irritation as the high bailiff does now. He picks up his gavel and slams it with such intensity as to make Lynx believe his ears are going to bleed.

The high bailiff puts the gavel down and everyone uncovers their ears. With a quick snatch, he picks it up again and gives it one last crack like a peal of thunder so that the whole crowd releases a simultaneous whimper at the pain.

Her lawyer runs over to Zena saying in fluent Elvish Runic, "Please, Mademoiselle, speak not until it is thy turn lest the high bailiff to hold thee in contempt of court."

Reluctantly, Zena sits down and allows the boredom to wash over her as the gnomes carry out their procedures and protocols. Each gnome has a role and insists on carrying it out with the greatest degree of dignity and decorum, like a series of has-been movie stars trying to milk their cameos for as much screen time as possible.

Finally, a senior under-bailiff reads the charges against the defendants in Gaodelin, the language of legal transactions among gnomes. He then passes the scroll to a warrant beadle who translates it from Gaodelin into Elvish Runic and then Dwarvish Runic. That warrant beadle hands the scroll to a young gnome who serves as acting petty warrant catchpole. The young gnome reads those same charges again, but this time in Aenglish with a flawless Lunden accent.

"Whereas Mademoiselle Zena Ranglursdottir and her party of hired retainers, hereafter the defendants, stand accused of trespassing on the private property of Umpire-in-Chief Kibbler Earnestson, hereafter the plaintiff, and smashing his chicken coop, which either intentionally or unintentionally led to a diminution of chattel rightfully appertaining to the plaintiff.

"Whereas the defendants are accused of burglary for removing from the aforesaid mentioned property of the plaintiff a certain book which the plaintiff disavows any knowledge of other than the fact that it happened to be on his property the night of said trespass.

"Whereas the plaintiff is suing for restitution of that same book, which is not his but was on his property, and thus is his by right of eminent domain.

"Whereas the plaintiff accuses the defendants of seeking unlawful access to state secrets by entering upon those parts of his private property which are used exclusively for business and governmental purposes.

"Whereas the plaintiff wishes to extradite the defendants to stand trial in an Elvish court of law for stealing state secrets, even though he asserts that no state secrets were uncovered or stolen during said trespass of that part of his private property which is used exclusively for business and governmental purposes."

Even after hearing the translation into Elvish Runic of all this legalese, the charges are so convoluted that Zena does not understand the half of it. Her main takeaway is that Umpire Kibbler is trying to sue her for the book and have her arrested without incriminating himself.

Zena waits until the senior under-bailiff instructs the warrant beadle to ask for her response. After the warrant beadle has delivered his formulaic request in Gaodelin and then repeating it in Elvish Runic, she dares not speak. Standing there in awkward silence, the warrant beadle eventually mumbles to her in Eldric, "You can get up and talk now."

Zena bows respectfully and enunciates her speech in Elvish Runic slowly so they can translate her words into Gnorrachi. "Worthy Monsieur High Bailiff Harfud Fellowhide of the noble House of Stoar, on behalf of Shentalpee City's dungaree of Foreign Trade, I wish to thank thee and acknowledge thee for allowing Master Jack Spriggins, a dear friend of our family, to give us aid and succor within your burrows after we fell from the rope hanging down from the sequoia platform supporting the upper section of Vandsee Estates.

"My companions and I stand accused of trumped-up charges aimed primarily at discrediting my bid for the chief umpirage of the Tuscoraura elves.

"The court should be aware that this is the plaintiff's second attempt to do so. The first was a public accusation leveled by the plaintiff's daughter, Mademoiselle Florenz Kibblersdottir, that a highly respected member of this community, Miss Bartlebee Scrivener, used her employment in my mother's household to steal a secret recipe for elf fire.

"The plaintiff's daughter provided no evidence to substantiate her accusations and her act of defamation has brought great harm to Miss Bartlebee's person and her professional credibility. as is testified in the documents prepared by my defense counsel and signed by the family of the wrongly accused gnomid."

The gnomes in the audience break out into animated side conversations until the high bailiff slams his gavel down a few times.

Zena continues. "Worthy High Bailiff, esteemed jurors and upstanding members of the courtroom audience, the book that we willingly submit to thy loremasters for inspection proves the plaintiff has been conspiring to create an army of undead warriors as weapons of mass destruction."

More chatter erupts and more gavel bangs follow.

"As for the accusation that we stole the book, I point out that this edition does not belong to the plaintiff, nor to his estate. It is merely the copy of a book that was stolen from him long ago by the dwarf cleric who has come to—"

Lawspeaker Snorrison stands up and shouts with quivering lips as his face goes red with outrage, "Objection, Your Supreme Worthiness! Objection!"

The high bailiff smashes his gavel onto the sound block enough times to finally calm the lawspeaker down. Everyone keeps their ears covered until after the high bailiff moves his hand away from the gavel. "State your objection, Noble Lawspeaker Sturl Snorrison."

The lawspeaker takes such a deep breath that his nostrils flare out wide. He says in a resounding voice, "The Tuscoraura Accords forbid a member of one community from summoning a member of another community to speak on their behalf in a community that neither of the two belongs to without the permission of the community that the summoned member does belong to."

The gnomes in the audience are deeply sympathetic to his complaint and nod to each other as if his objections were perfectly logical.

The lawspeaker continues. "Speaking on behalf of the Great Dainn of the Tuscoraura Mountain dwarves, Dvalinn son of Duneyrr of the line of Durathror, I categorically deny that we have given the dungaree's daughter any such permission and therefore I petition you to declare him an invalid witness and to invalidate any testimony or evidence he provides on her behalf."

"Objection sustained." The high bailiff slams the gavel and says, "Please continue, Mademoiselle Zena."

"Worthy High Bailiff, please let the court know that I would never summon a witness in violation of the Tuscoraura Accords. The dwarf cleric in question, Inquisitor Sheen, is a spiritual guide to me and I merely summoned him to comfort my soul and to take counsel on personal matters.

"It just so happens that he is also the same dwarf who, acting upon orders of the Holy Office of the Inquisition, stole the book that the plaintiff claims he has no knowledge of but wants back so desperately.

Although Inquisitor Sheen would corroborate my claims, the defense does not call him to the stands.

"Instead I ask one of thine own loremasters to affirm or deny my claim that the book in my possession has been copied from the original stolen book in question into Runic half-uncials, an elvish scribal hand, and not any human rotunda or chancery script as would be befitting for such a book of rituals.

The high bailiff nods and says, "Junior under-bailiff Regibald Inkling, would you please submit artifact A to Loremaster Gerrof Gernumble for his forensic analysis? Please continue, Mademoiselle Zena."

"I thank thee, worthy High Bailiff. Furthermore, I state that although we deny any unlawful trespass on any governmental property of Vandsee Estates, we do affirm that the aforementioned chickens flew the coop.

"It was strictly in self-defense. The plaintiff neither properly restrained his dogs nor gave adequate warning of the dogs' vicious propensities. Were it not for the defective coop, he would be guilty of criminally negligent attempted manslaughter.

"Therefore, worthy High Bailiff, I ask thee to consider the charges leveled against us by the plaintiff as spurious, inaccurate, and politically motivated.

"For as long as this generation can remember, elf-gnome relations on Tuscoraura Mountain have been marked with a firm and profound trust. The plaintiff's current accusations and those leveled against our friend and stewardess, Miss Bartlebee Scrivener, strain those relations and have already endangered the job security of many garden gnomes in Shentalpee City."

"In conclusion, I have full confidence in the cleverness and perspicacity of the gnomes and dwarves assembled here this day to see through the plaintiff's red herring arguments, to rule in our favor, and to lay the foundations for even stronger intercommunity relationships under my leadership as the next umpire-in-chief of the Tuscoraura elves."

Applause breaks forth from the box seats above the defendants' bench and spreads through the stands as gnome after gnome takes his hat off to honor Zena's eloquent defense of the serious charges leveled against her and her companions. The gnomids whistle their approval and ululate a victory chant for her.

A uniformed gnome approaches with a polite bow and says in Eldric, "I am Junior Under-Bailiff Grouse and I shall escort your party of adventurers out of the courtroom and back into the waiting room to await the high bailiff's verdict. May I add, Mademoiselle Zena, that you delivered quite a stirring speech."

Zena thanks him and Lynx asks the junior under-bailiff in Eldric, "Is there a privy nearby where I could use a chamber pot?"

The junior under-bailiff points down the corridor. "End of the hall. The gentlemen's privy is on the left and the ladies' privy is on the right."

After that important message gets translated into Aenglish as well, the adventurers all go off to relieve themselves.

When they get back, they find Inquisitor Sheen sipping chamomile tea with their bitterest enemy in the courtroom, Lawspeaker Snorrison.

The irascible old dwarf stands up and bows to them all. Bald on the top, the long hair falling down from the sides and back of his head is all gray but the hair on his beard is almost entirely a bright copper red with only a few white streaks through it. The loud, red beard does not make him look any younger, just a little more eccentric. Of only medium build for a dwarf, his chest is covered by honorary medals clanging around over his puffy-sleeved red coat, awarded for his credits as a lawyer, but he also wears commemorative pins and merit badges that he has won in poetry competitions.

None of the adventurers misses the gist of it all—he is important and he wants them all to know it.

The dwarf lawspeaker turns to Zena and says in Elvish Runic, "Masterfully spoken, Mademoiselle Dungaree. I think it is safe to assume that the high bailiff will rule in our favor."

Without flinching at the volte-face in attitude he is now evincing, she replies in Elvish Runic, "Thank you, famed Lawspeaker Snorrison. That thou hast come up from the Dwarrow Delves to take our side in the courtroom has filled me with comfort and confidence. But, wilt thou allow me to compliment thee on thine impressive facility with the Elvish Runic tongue?"

"Not at all!" bellows the old dwarf. "In fact, I strictly forbid it. I do not even consider Elvish Runic to be one of the twelve languages I speak fluently. Rather my studies in your mother tongue are just enough to enjoy the harmonies in thy poets' verses."

Zena takes him by the hand and says, "Oh, then at least thou must allow me to sing for thee sometime. I have been told that my recitals are pitch-perfect and my interpretation of certain Runic odes reflect some of the subtleties of the ancient meters; but I won't believe it until thou canst either affirm or deny it."

Lawspeaker Snorrison kisses her hand and says in Elvish Runic, "It would be an absolute delight, my lovely demoiselle; but first we have some very serious business to attend to. Please have a seat in my donkey cart for this long and unexpected journey. Coming at such late notice, there is only room for the two of us. Thy servants will have to walk behind us."

Zena nods to the other adventurers. Lynx and Captain Manzone start to leave but when they realize Louis and Clarke have set themselves down for a second round of snacks, Captain Manzone reaches down and grabs them by the collars to drag them away.

Masking her anxiety as pleasantly as she can, Zena asks in Runic, "Will Thy Magniloquence be so kind to as to hint where our journey shall take us?"

But Lawspeaker Snorrison is already on his way out of the waiting room. His serving dwarves bring a stool to help him step up into the luxurious donkey cart. Baffled, Zena turns and asks, "Inquisitor Sheen?"

Inquisitor Sheen smiles broadly. "As you recall, my main goal in coming to Tuscoraura Mountain was to quash the Blackflame Heresy. Now that Johnny Appleseed has agreed to stop its distribution, I am happy to report to you that the Holy Spirit has revealed to me a plan that will solve all your problems—and mine—tonight."

"All our problems? I'm sorry to deflate your joy but the monsieur umpire-in-chief has blackflame braziers all over Vandsee Estates. We only stole his grimoire.

"In terms of stopping your Blackflame Heresy we have only begun to realize its vast extent. In terms of my problems, they have no end. So, with all due respect for your prayers, I do not believe that all seven gods of Tuscoraura combined have the power to grant so many favors in one night."

Coming down the corridor, two dwarf guards walk in holding none other than Florenz Kibblersdottir, wrapped in chains. Inquisitor Sheen winks at Zena and says, "With all due respect for your faith in the seven gods of Tuscoraura, Mademoiselle Zena, but to work a miracle of such epic proportions, I only need the power of the One True God."

After riding a hundred yards or so down the gnome burrow grows dark and harsh, more like a mineshaft than a residential avenue. Breaking the silence, Zena asks the lawspeaker gently in Runic, "Ought we not wait for the high bailiff to hand down his verdict?"

Lawspeaker Snorrison chuckles to himself. "Ah, I forgot what it was like to be young and so afraid of the opinions of the elders. Good old Harfud just needed to put on a show to get Kibbler off his back, and thou gavest him ample excuse to do so.

"The gnomes down here are already furious about the little stunt Florenz pulled last week by publicly accusing a garden gnome of the worst kind of perfidy without coming down here to ask for a trial. The only reason Kibbler's daughter is still alive is that she didn't formally accuse Bartlebee in an elf court of law."

Zena asks innocently, "Thou wouldst kill her without a trial for putting someone on trial without consulting thee? 'Tis an unruly form of justice."

He raises his eyebrows. "How old art thou, Mademoiselle Zena?"

"Seventeen, Thy Magniloquence."

"Then I easily forgive thee for asking such an obvious question. High elves have a bad reputation for only caring about the world in the treetops. If thou wishest to be a good leader someday, thou must consult with the humans, dwarves, and gnomes who share Tuscoraura Mountain with thee whenever it comes to issues so vital for survival.

"Permit me to ask thee this; how wouldst thou feel if thou didst discover that an elf thou lovest came down to Dwarrow's Delve and was executed for stepping on an ingot vent?"

"I would be outraged!"

"And thou wouldst have good reason. To the elves, stepping on an ingot vent is a trivial offense. For a dwarf, it is mass murder. No jury of dwarves would believe that someone could accidentally step on an ingot vent; but a jury of elves certainly would.

"The point is that to condemn a foreigner for violating laws without representation from their own people is an act of war. Mademoiselle Florenz only did this informally, but the consequences were severe."

"What dost thou mean?"

"Within hours of announcing Bartlebee's sabotage, opinions among elves, gnomes, and dwarves were so polarized that even if she were innocent, she could never get another job or hold her head up in public again. Mademoiselle Florenz destroyed Bartlebee's life without giving her a fair trial. As a result, many gnomes who work for high elves considered quitting their jobs before their livelihood could be destroyed with such a reckless stroke."

"I never thought of it, but thou art right—'tis vile."

"No, 'tis much worse. By airing the case publicly to the elves and not communicating with the proper authorities, Mademoiselle Florenz has tipped off all of Bartlebee's accomplices about a possible investigation long before a proper inquiry could be set up."

"Thou art saying that Bartlebee is guilty?"

"Fractionally; she was nothing but a pawn. But all the real criminals behind the plot got away. If Mademoiselle Florenz had not acted so rashly, we would have ensured that the secret to Athabask fire stayed on Tuscoraura Mountain. Now we know it has been auctioned off to the highest bidder."

Zena says, "But 'tis not too late; we can stop them."

"Oh, 'tis too late. Immediately upon getting their hands on the recipe, High Bailiff Fellowhide offered to share it with our Great Dainn, Dvalinn. Not only does the mercenary Tom Thumb possess the secret to Athabask fire for his own reckless purposes, we have already begun perfecting our own version of dwarf fire in collaboration with the sewer dwarves of Fort Detroit that thou wilt find ten times more powerful than thy current *shentalphur* elf fire.

"With a slip of the tongue, Mademoiselle Florenz ruined all her father's grand ambitions to put fire elves ahead in the arms race. Thanks to her, ye shall soon be decades behind. Weaponizing blackflame is the last thorny issue we must address.

"Until I am elected umpire-in-chief, I have no authority to resolve such issues."

The lawspeaker thumbs over his shoulder. "That is where Inquisitor Sheen comes in."

The inquisitor joins in, using the gift of tongues so that she hears his words in Eldric. "In researching necromancy with the blackflame, Umpire Kibbler has unleashed dozens of elf wendigo on neighboring communities. The Inquisition has now been forced to partner with the gnomes, humans, and dwarves of Tuscoraura Mountain to put a stop to his madness. The papal legate has even assigned Dwarrow Delve its own chapter house of the Knights Paladin."

"Who are the Knights Paladin?"

"Ever heard of the Knights Templar?"

"I think so."

"When the Crusaders conquered Jerosolym, they realized they could never hold it without a large number of fanatical warriors ready to give their lives for the cause. Three groups emerged.

"First of all, the Knights Hospitallers established themselves at the Hospital of Saint John in Jerosolym. They are warrior monks who specialize in healing. Next, the Knights Templar established themselves at the Temple Mount in Jerosolym. They are warrior monks who specialize in winning wars—everything from preparing an unstoppable frontal assault to the nitty-gritty, behind-the-scenes aspects of war, like covert operations, logistics, financing, and diplomacy. Finally, when the fighting got real ugly in the Holy Land, the Knights Paladin established themselves at the Palace of David in Jerosolym. They are warrior monks who specialize in supernatural warfare—breaking curses, exorcisms, and repelling the undead.

"The papal legate in Vinland has issued Umpire Kibbler an ultimatum—stop the necromancy or face a Crusade against the Tuscoraura elves."

Lawspeaker Snorrison resumes speaking in Runic. "Naturally, we dwarves do not want a Crusade on our mountain any more than thou dost. Although our underground colonies would be relatively safe from direct assault, the default Crusader strategy is simply to destroy everything in sight with fire and steel. As neighbors on Tuscoraura Mountain, we depend on each other in more ways than I can enumerate.

"Ah, smell that sulphur in the air? Those are the forges welcoming us home. Come, let us hope thou wilt be elected umpire-in-chief before Umpire Kibbler can menace our homeland with his blackflame devilry."

As they approach Dwarrow Delve, the road gets narrow, gravelly, and steep. An abrupt change of décor takes place—concrete arches brace lead pipes with hissing valves and steaming junctions.

For being the same continuous hole in the ground, the gnome burrows and the dwarf tunnels have little else in common. Gnome burrows have evenly spaced wood beams that support walls of dirt—made of dirt, but not dirty. Everywhere you go has stuffy but warm, inviting smells, as if you'd just arrived home.

Dwarf tunnels, instead, are hewn of stone, and are somehow much less clean, with harsh, acidic smells and ubiquitous clanging noises traveling up and down the corridors, as if reminding you that somewhere down below is a dwarf that is decidedly too busy to talk with you.

Until now, Zena had considered Lawgiver Snorrison's impressive array of medals as his prized prestige possession, but as she walks through the door of his apartment, she instantly smells his most enviable status symbol—fresh air.

After Zena goes inside the lawspeaker's apartment, the guard dwarves uncuff Florenz and lead her inside like a prisoner. Captain Manzone approaches her and asks in Eldric, "How did these dwarves get past your father's security?"

Florenz replies. "They didn't. I came here on behalf of my father to demand your extradition and they arrested me. Trust me, there will be payback."

Inside the lawgiver's apartment, Zena is rather surprised to see the exact same racial stereotypes played out so far below the earth as high above it in Shentalpee City: the waitstaff are all gnomes and the guards, grooms, and cellarers are all dwarves.

Lawspeaker Snorrison waves his large hand, inviting them to sit. "Please, Mademoiselle Dungaree, allow me to introduce thee to the solution for all thy problems. I shall return shortly."

Instead of leaving out platters overflowing with every different treat imaginable for them to choose from, as in the gnome waiting room, the servers in the lawspeaker's dining area bring out small plates of what looks like dark bread and a large mug of a pungent, amber-colored liquid.

Captain Manzone takes a sniff of the mug and wrinkles his nose, asking, "What is this?"

The garden gnome maître d'hôtel says in a rough Eldric, "It's whiskey from rye. It's a drink for the good old boys like you."

Pushing it away, Captain Manzone comments to the dwarf cellarer in Eldric, "Oh, boy, that'll be the day that I die. Can I get a milk? I've heard Dwarrow Delve has some mighty fine goat's milk down here."

The dwarf cellarer looks at him awry and turns to the gnome maître d'hôtel for a translation. Hearing Captain Manzone's comment, the dwarf cellarer makes a loud comment in his mountain dwarf language known broadly as Medifskar.

Captain Manzone looks at the maître d'hôtel, demanding, "What?! What'd he say?"

Inquisitor Sheen seems to be enjoying this so he does the translation for Captain Manzone using his gift of tongues. "He can't believe you just asked for milk. He said that by the way you carry yourself, he was just about to put you on his list as the first elf he's ever met whom he actually considered tough."

Unoffended, Captain Manzone replies, "Well then, tell him to put it in a dirty mug."

Zena says, "I'll have some milk too but in a clean mug, please."

Lynx says, "Can I get some milk too? I'll take mine in a dirty mug as long as he doesn't spit in it. Dwarves don't drink spit to prove they're tough, do they?"

Inquisitor Sheen chuckles. "No, but you do have to at least try the acorn pie to prove you are polite."

Thanks to the inquisitor's gift of tongues, Louis and Clarke finally understand a piece of the conversation. Louis takes a bite of the acorn pie. After he chews it down a bit, he exclaims with a few crumbs flying out of his mouth, "My, my, this is an acorn pie? A little heavy on the berries but the heaviness isn't dry."

Clarke moans, "I can't eat acorn pie!"

"Why not?"

"A long, long time ago—I can still remember the day—I ate a few acorns. While I was eating them, a widowed bride came out and told me acorns are poisonous. I started to shiver. I couldn't take one more step. I can't remember if I cried but someone heard me and had to carry me inside. Only after several weeks in bed and a lot of prayers did I make a full recovery."

The gnome maître d'hôtel answers his concerns. "Acorns are toxic when raw, but if you soak them and drain off the water a few times, then they are good to eat. The nicest part is that leather tanners pay a good price for the drained-off water, called tannin. So that delicious pie you are eating now is very economical and easy to make. Just add some milled grains to the acorn flour and leaven them with eggs, maple syrup, and a pinch of salt."

Captain Manzone stuffs the last piece of his acorn pie into his mouth and licks his fingers. "I can't believe I'm eating this after all the food those gnomes gave us before the trial, but it's delicious."

Lynx adds, "It almost tastes like gingerbread, but the last time I had it, it ran away with me."

Zena quips, "Are you saying your little gingerbread cookie man got up off the plate and ran away?"

"No, darling, I am trying to communicate discreetly the dangers of gingerbread, which caused me to run off to the privy as fast as I could."

Zena rolls her eyes. "Sweetie, there's no discreet way to say such things. They're better left unsaid."

Captain Manzone asks, "Speaking of things left unsaid, did the high bailiff rule in our favor or are we going to be trapped down here for the rest of our lives? Bad news generally spoils my appetite."

He says that just as Lawspeaker Snorrison comes walking into the room after a brief conference with Florenz. He motions to her, "Please have a seat, noble lady, and explain."

With an emotionless face, Florenz says in Eldric, "I will issue a formal apology to Mademoiselle Zena for accusing her stewardess without evidence, saying that she sold Tom Thumb a recipe for acorn pie, not elf fire."

Zena looks at her with triumphant eyes and says, "Aw! Your sincerity is so touching."

"Shut up!" Florenz snaps back. "We both know your mother gave Bartlebee the Athabask recipe to keep the details of your birth defect from going public. You don't deserve to be umpire-in-chief and the fact that these *goyar* are forcing you in proves it."

Though he doesn't understand Eldric, the lawspeaker can guess Florenz isn't happy with the arrangement. "This is for thine own good," He announces with an air of a cop. Then he says to Zena, "Mademoiselle Florenz shall deliver a formal apology after the Thor's Enlightenment Discourse tomorrow. We shall also extinguish all trace of necromancy in Shentalpee City."

Inquisitor Sheen nods. "Now that Johnny Appleseed has agreed to abide by the Inquisition's rules, my only task left is to get rid of any ritual books Umpire Kibbler might have left and extinguish all sources of blackflame. Mademoiselle Florenz will lead me as her guest through the Vandsee Estates so I can use my gift of prophecy to locate any more grimoires or blackflame braziers."

Zena gets anxious. "Wait! What about the brazier dedicated to Thor that is killing my magica tree."

"Lawspeaker Snorrison informs me that your mother has offered us a hogshead of cask strength whiskey from her warehouse to put it out."

Captain Manzone interrupts. "That'd take a dozen elves to carry."

Inquisitor Sheen replies, "Or one very strong goblin. While on Vandsee Estates, we will free the captured goblin if he agrees to carry the cask to the peak of Tuscoraura Mountain. We'll use a special dwarf tunnel to get it there unseen.

"After Florenz gives her speech recanting her accusations against Bartlebee and the Dungaree family, Lynx will ride down the aqueduct on this special dwarf shield and stop right above the blackflame brazier. A few taps on the lead piping will tell the dwarves below it's time to cut off the water to the aqueduct and then the goblin will dump the whiskey down the aqueduct and Lynx will use the shield to redirect the flow onto the blackflame brazier.

"Once the last of the blackflame is extinguished, Florenz will enter the mountain dwarf tunnels and go into voluntary exile."

Zena asks, "What if Mademoiselle Florenz refuses?"

Captain Manzone has an answer for that. "Excuse me, Mademoiselle Zena, remember the part where the dwarves cut off the water supply to Shentalpee City? If the dwarves really control our water, then they can say jump and we have to say how high. Isn't that right, Mademoiselle Florenz."

Florenz shrugs. "Unless we have an undead army that doesn't need to drink water."

Inquisitor Sheen replies, "I pray for all your sakes that it doesn't come to that."

With the plan explained, the party breaks up and the lawspeaker brings suitable donkey carts so that everyone can ride back up to the surface in style. Before setting out, Inquisitor Sheen pulls Lynx aside, saying, "Lynx, may I speak to you a moment?"

"Yes."

"In private."

"No problem."

The go into the kitchen and the inquisitor says, "I'll get straight to the point. I have two sealed letters of inestimable importance. The first must be delivered to the rangers encamped in the marchlands. You must hand it to the leader of the rangers personally. His name is Sir Robert Roger. It certifies that he successfully guided me to Tuscoraura Mountain.

"The second letter must be sent directly to the Holy Office of the Inquisition in Salim with all haste, by Pony Express if possible. It contains my official report reconciling Johnny Appleseed with the Church and approving his return to ministry.

"People's lives depend on these letters. Timing is of the essence and I must purge Shentalpee City of the Blackflame heresy now, while I have the chance. Many people will want me dead so I need to be sure these letters will get into the right hands even if I die. Can I count on you, Monsieur Lynx."

"Yes, Reverend Sheen, but please remember that I am just a poor elf. Only a wealthy elve like the Madame Dungaree of Foreign Trade would have the kind of money to send a letter by Pony Express to Baston."

"Would Dungaree Jeanne be willing to send it?"

"If this letter solves all the troubles for her guest, Reverend Appleseed, then yes, she would."

"Good. And remember not to tell anyone else about these letters. Those who seek to end my life, if they knew you had these in your possession, would end yours just as eagerly."

SUGAR AND HEISTS
AND EVERYTHING NICE

Scene 3: The Oregan Tale

Amphitheater at Thor's Base, Shentalpee City
Hock Moon Day Terce. Morning, 10th of April, 1284

"Monsieur Lynx, I wanted to thank you for saving my life at Tiw's Tree. My father was right, even though I didn't want to hear it at the time. You deserved to win. You improvised a new solution to an old problem, and I'm sure you will make one of the finest officers the Ivy League has ever seen."

Lynx's eyebrows soften and he stares at his feet for a few moments. When he recovers, he looks Florenz straight in the eyes and says, "I was wrong about your father. I assumed he was just a dishonest, power-hungry politician, but your father had the courage to break every social convention among the Tuscoraura elves to stand up for me in public. You have that kind of courage too. You'd make one of the finest umpires-in-chief the Tuscoraura elves have ever seen."

Zena stomps up from behind them both and says, "Mister Lynx, dear, what was it you were saying about becoming the finest umpire-in-chief? The mademoiselle umpire-in-chief's daughter is just about to deliver an important announcement, isn't that right?"

"Mademoiselle Zena!" Dungaree Jeanne calls out from the middle of a crowd of her bravos pushing Johnny Appleseed up in a medieval version of a wheelchair. Though he puts on a brave face, it's clear his leg is still in a lot of pain. "Keep it down, Zena dear! I can see that you're gloating from way back here!"

Zena gives her mother a full-on teenager huff and says, "Mother, we were simply having a discussion about future policy here. There is no mudslinging involved, is there, Mademoiselle Florenz?"

Florenz hesitates. She knows she's supposed to play dumb but Zena's gloating gets under her skin in a way that would make lice and maggots jealous.

Zena presses on. "We've been best friends since childhood. We wouldn't sink so low as to make baseless accusations against each other, would we?"

Dungaree Jeanne is humiliated by her daughter's behavior and says sharply, "Mademoiselle Zena!"

Struggling to maintain her self-control, Florenz decides it's time to change topics. "Why, Reverend Appleseed, what happened to your leg?"

Johnny Appleseed doesn't understand a word of Eldric, so Dungaree Jeanne translates into Aenglish.

Before he has a chance to respond, Lynx says, "The monsieur Enganyon pushed him over the edge."

Florenz forces a laugh. "Oh, that jokester tries my patience all the time; but what happened to his leg?"

Lynx presses on. "No, he literally shoved the good reverend over the edge of Thor's Base. Miraculously, a branch caught him, but the fall twisted his leg bad."

Florenz can't believe it. "He can be devious at times but the monsieur Enganyon would never do anything like that!"

"Never say never, dear!" With a big, cocky grin, Enganyon rushes forward on his crutches to greet them. At Enganyon's heels walks Old Mother Hubbard's dog.

The shock has not washed off Florenz's face when she stammers, "But . . . you could have killed him!"

"You know, the thought had occurred to me," says Enganyon, as if he were incapable of taking anything seriously. "I was just giving him a friendly pat on the back to welcome him to Shentalpee City and I slipped."

Lynx looks at Enganyon's leg and asks sarcastically, "So is that why you decided to fake a leg injury? After all, misery loves company."

Enganyon cannot be outdone in sarcasm. "Exactly. Mister Lynx, you are the only one who understands the way I think. Besides, these crutches happen to match my new jacket."

He is wearing a plain, black leather coat. As the scion of a family of immense wealth, he normally wears a considerably more elaborate white coat, studded with jewels and embroidered with gold filigree.

"Are we supposed to ask what happened to your old coat, Monsieur Enganyon?" asks Dungaree Jeanne.

"As a matter of fact, I sold it and used some of the money to buy this one, and I gave the rest to poor old Madame Hubbard. She was so happy that she ran to the baker to buy her dog some bread, but it died while she was out. Then she called the undertaker to measure it for a funeral, but the dog just got up again and started laughing. She was too spooked-out to keep him, so I told her I'd look after him for her."

"That's quite a story, young elf," says Dungaree Jeanne skeptically.

Johnny Appleseed points to the dog and rambles on in Aenglish. Enganyon asks, "What's he saying?"

Dungaree Jeanne looks at him seriously. "He says your dog's undead. He's worried that if the Inquisition finds out that certain Tuscoraura elves have been using his gift of blackflame to dabble in necromancy—"

Enganyon interrupts her, "You don't say! I'd love to hear all about it except that I want a good seat for this Thor's schtick. Those three magi look nerdtastic."

After the group wanders off their separate ways, Dungaree Jeanne breathes a sigh of relief. Her hired bravos roll Johnny Appleseed into the amphitheater while she hustles after Florenz. Johnny Appleseed loves children, and he asks the bravos to wheel him closer. The big human and the scuzzy bravos make some parents nervous, but Johnny Appleseed comes ready with tricks to delight them all. He pulls the tip off his thumb, plucks coins out of their pointy ears, and snaps a rope in two then connects the halves back together.

When she catches up to her, Dungaree Jeanne pulls Florenz aside. "I just want to apologize for my daughter's behavior. She seems to think that she'll appear more confident in herself if she walks around as smug and haughty as—"

"As the monsieur Enganyon?" Florenz finishes her sentence. "I know that the mademoiselle Zena looks up to him in every way: the good, the bad, and the ugly. But I am the one to owe you an apology because I accused you publicly of treason without there being an official case against you. The high bailiff is furious that I ruined the trust that many high elf families put in their garden gnome employees. He has demanded that I resign from the elections."

"Posh! What do garden gnomes have to say about our electoral processes?"

Florenz looks at her with a grim seriousness that ages her face far beyond her nineteen years. "Reverend Appleseed was right. My father has been toying with necromancy, and the Inquisition is here."

"Impossible!"

"Well, it turned out well for your daughter—the inquisitor healed her from a nasty injury. For the rest of us, it's not going so well. The Inquisition is demanding that we extinguish all our blackflame braziers and that my father turns over all his necromantic artifacts."

"And what did your father say?"

"He planned to kill the inquisitor, but the inquisitor is a dwarf, and now the dwarves are angry as well. They insist we comply with his demands."

Dungaree Jeanne touches her lip. "Oh dear, this is serious. How can the mountain dwarves and garden gnomes help an outsider encroach upon our rights and our sovereignty? We have an ancient alliance."

"Apparently, they consider necromancy a weapon and feel that we have violated the terms of our alliance by secretly developing a new weapon without sharing that information with them."

"Oh. This is very serious," says Dungaree Jeanne pensively, "Still, Mademoiselle Florenz, you can't quit the race. You've come too far!"

With studied calm Florenz replies, "Yes, I can."

Inside Tuscoraura Mountain, two hired dwarf city mercenaries (*statmalalthi*), brothers named Bremmer and Blainn, lead their goblin captive up a narrow spiral stone stairway toward the mountain peak.

Carrying a hogshead of whiskey, the hulking goblin sweats under the weight of the huge barrel. His skin has freezer burns on it from Kibbler's experiments with blackflame. Although he carried it with rebellious pride, the hulking goblin now barely manages to swivel the six-hundred-pound barrel up one step at a time, tilting it from side to side as he goes.

Quite a ways behind the hulking goblin, Inquisitor Sheen trudges up the spiral staircase followed by Captain Manzone, Louis, Clarke, and a hired halfling sorcerer named Flobbin. They keep their distance lest a rolling barrel should sweep them down into the dwarf-made chasm below them.

Clarke's physical endurance climbing the steps is nearing its end. He asks, "Are we there yet?"

Inquisitor Sheen replies, "Hold on, Brother Clarke, you can make it. It won't be much further now."

Louis asks, "Why did that goblin follow us to Tuscoraura Mountain. Is he seeking revenge?"

Inquisitor Sheen answers, "He needs the ceremonial dagger to reclaim his father's title as war chief."

Clarke reaches into his breast fitchet and pulls out the sheathed phoenix talon dagger. "You mean this?"

The inquisitor stops and hushes him. "If the goblin knew you had that, he would kill you for it."

Clarke looks at it glimmer in the torchlight. "It's so bright . . . so beautiful. It must be precious."

The inquisitor hisses, "Put it away, and never let it see the light of day until the goblin is long gone!"

Not understanding a word of Aenglish but sensing the inquisitor's anxiety, Captain Manzone asks in Eldric, "It's nice that the goblin agreed to carry that for us, but how do we know we can trust him?"

Using his gift of tongues Inquisitor Sheen explains, "There are some mighty clever fellows living under this mountain, Captain Manzone. As part of the deal for his freedom, the goblin had to drink a slow-acting dwarf poison. He feels none of its effects right now, but if he does not hold up his end of the bargain, it will eventually kill him. Once he dumps the whiskey down the aqueduct, I will administer the antidote to him."

Captain Manzone says, "You have the power to heal him; why do you need an antidote?"

Inquisitor Sheen says, "First of all, I do not have the power to heal anyone. It is a gift. The Lord chooses whom to heal and when, not I.

"Second, we have a rule never to pray for supernatural intervention when God provides a natural means. The devil tempted Jesus to turn stones into bread in the desert and Jesus refused because there was plenty of bread in the closest market. Later on in his ministry, Jesus multiplied bread and fish because—and only because—it was not possible to obtain what they needed at the market.

"To trust in God and love him through ordinary circumstances is the first and most important act of faith. If you do not believe that, then you have no business asking him for miracles."

"I'm glad you'll ask. We'll need a lot of miracles if we're going to survive this day."

As luck would have it, Clarke's breathless lungs and palpitating heart has kept half the party back. Umpire Kibbler and a dozen Justiciar League elves stand with bows drawn, encircling the goblin and the two mercenary dwarves, but they do not suspect that Inquisitor Sheen is back inside the mountain vault along with the halfling sorcerer named Flobbin, Captain Manzone, Louis, and Clarke.

Umpire Kibbler shouts out in Eldric, "Surrender now and you will get a fair trial!"

The dwarves and goblin have no clue what he is saying but Captain Manzone calls out from the safety of the vault, "Unfortunately for your sake, I am not overly fond of being treated fairly! I've been playing kicks-and-giggles too long to expect any reward from civil authorities except a noose around my neck!"

Umpire Kibbler replies, "Then how about one more round to see who's the better player?"

At once, the Justiciar League warriors loose their arrows. The goblin spins with superb reflexes and none of the arrows penetrate deeply. The dwarves' shields stop a few arrows but several poisoned arrows find the chinks in their armor from behind.

Though the elf poison is fast-acting, Bremmer charges forward and shield-bashes one elf off the mountain cliff while Blainn tosses his hand-axe right into the chest of another elf archer who sees it coming but does not manage to dodge it in time.

Bending low and attacking from behind, Captain Manzone leaps off a rocky outcrop, spinning in the air until he lands between two Justiciar League warriors.

Taken by surprise and outclassed by his swordplay, they fail to parry the bravo's flurry of blades. He runs the first through the armpit with his rapier and hamstrings the second with his main-gauche dagger. The goblin flings the wounded elves off the mountain.

Louis unslings the large battleaxe from his back and charges into the midst of the elves, but they are all gone by the time he gets there. Hiding behind rocks, crevices, and outcrops, the Justiciar League warriors start peppering the inquisitor's party of adventurers with poisoned arrows.

Flobbin has his lodestone staff ready and quickly polarizes it to deflect the incoming arrows, giving the party of adventurers time to regroup. Not a moment too soon! Falling to the ground, the goblin and two dwarves cough, wheeze, and spasm as the poison spreads through their bloodstreams.

Inquisitor Sheen bends down and heals them one by one. With four elves down the odds are looking significantly better going into the second round. Captain Manzone struts out in front. "Hey, Kibbler! Did I mention that if you want to play kicks-and-giggles with me, you're going to need the big boy expansion set? Your team has all archers. We've got a sorcerer and a healer. What's your play?"

Umpire Kibbler asks, "How about silver arrows?"

While the elfin archers switch out their arrows, the goblin uses the opening to flee, but the two dwarfin mercenaries charge, yelling in Medifskar, "Breska!"

They sprint up the steep mountain path in full armor while Umpire Kibbler and four of his Justiciar Leaguers retreat upwards toward the peak, leaving two elves on each side to flank the party of adventurers.

The dwarves' helmets limit their peripheral vision but they both stop halfway up, sensing the elves' encirclement. Panting, they have a look all around and see the two teams of elves moving down behind them. Bremmer mutters, "Drassil! We've got no archers."

The two sides stare at each other, crab-walking here and there to gain better positioning. The dwarves can't let the elf archers work their way around their backs, and the Justiciar Leaguers don't want to waste their precious silver arrows unless they have a sure shot.

This is the origin of the term *Tuscoraura standoff*.

In the blink of an eye, Blainn whirls around and flings his backup hand-axe with blinding speed toward the Justiciar League archer who has worked his way farthest down their flank. The elf is peering over a sizeable rock but the axe explodes the rock, blinding the elf with its fragments.

The blinded elf writhes and Flobbin uses his lodestone staff to pull three elven steel-tipped arrows off the ground and hurls them at the blinded elf. This famous battlesage technique is known today as the magic missile, though it has nothing to do with magiculture and everything to do with sorcery. Regardless of the terminology, Umpire Kibbler is now down to seven archers against the six adventurers.

Another Justiciar Leaguer dashes toward a crevice where he can sneak around the party's back, but Flobbin digs his heels into the rocky turf and pulls at all the metal on the elf—his elf blade, a boot dagger, and his quiver of arrows, and yanks the brave elf out of cover before he can take them off.

Bremmer jumps out into the open, blocking silver arrows with his shield as the Justiciar League archers desperately try to save their colleague. One expertly placed silver arrow makes it past Bremmer's shield but misses the gap in his armor. Even Justiciar League patrol bows stand no chance to pierce double-linked dwarven mail.

The exposed elf draws a silver elf blade to engage the charging dwarf, but Bremmer's war hammer attacks are fast and furious. Unable to regain his footing, the exposed elf succumbs to the blows. Umpire Kibbler is now down to six archers.

The surviving Justiciar League officers unstrap any metal on their persons that they can think of and desperately charge out into the open with their silver arrows notched, hoping to swarm the sorcerer.

With Bremmer still making his way back to the inquisitor's battle line, Blainn is out of throwing axes but he helps shield Flobbin from their silver arrows.

Amidst a frightful onslaught of silver arrows, one strikes Flobbin in the neck and a roar of cheers erupts among the elves. Inquisitor Sheen kneels down to pray over him and pushes the arrow all the way through the wound. The blood dries up at once and the pierced flesh mends. The mood among the Justiciar League elves sours.

Umpire Kibbler shouts, "Will no one rid me of this turbulent priest?"

On the jog back to his brother, Bremmer has gathered a handful of silver arrows and snaps them, yelling, "Their left flank has exposed! Now is the time to cut them off!"

Blainn waves to the party to follow him but Flobbin has a different plan. He sends such a burst of polarized earth energy to clear all the loose elf weapons off the mountaintop. The Justiciar Leaguers have nothing but one or two silver arrows left each and they all point them at the inquisitor. In response, the city mercenaries shield him all the more tightly.

Umpire Kibbler nervously thumbs through a book and starts reciting an incantation in the dark speech of Caldor. Moments later, a column of blackflame shoots out from his hand and sets a slab of stone on dark fire. The blackflame billows up, sending blasts of cold air.

In an instant, Umpire Kibbler has sealed off his left flank with a black firewall. Instead of executing their final victory charge, the adventurers shrink back from the biting cold of the unnatural fire and find themselves dead-ended out on the open rock face.

The surprise blackflame attack takes the adventurers by surprise. With that one moment of weakness, Officer Bunzi's instincts as a bully kick in. He looks straight at the adventurers and senses their hearts beat with fear at the black fires, exults in their wild-eyed confusion, laughs at their momentary helplessness.

He pounces. His only silver arrow flies past the dwarves' shields and strikes Inquisitor Sheen through the chest.

Scene 4: Quest: Impossible

Templar Priory, Town of Rofchester
Woden's Day Prime. Morning, 19th of April, 1284
Feast of Saint Aelfheah, Bishop and Martyr

The next morning, Benjamin Frankelyn and his team start off early with the sunrise. The Templar priory is a modest fort made of brownstone. Ariel wants to get her sweet girl act over with as fast as possible so she'll have the rest of the day for purchasing a nice set of vault-cracking tools. Her leather armor and daggers do not exactly match up with the sweet and innocent stereotype. She ditches the armor but keeps the daggers, tucking them in even more intimately than before—after all, a nice girl can never be too cautious these days!

Visiting a few shops, she finds some surprisingly stylish and zesty outfits, but she does not indulge in trying any of them on. A long, modest dress calls to her. Imagining what a nice girl should look like, she asks herself, *All self-respecting, sweet, and innocent girls wear modest clothes, right?*

To resolve her doubts, Ariel shows the half-goblin/half-dwarf cleric a dress and asks, "Do I have to wear a modest dress to look innocent and sweet?"

Monsignor Meyer raises his hands like it's a police holdup and says, "Don't ask me. I don't check out girls anymore. But before I became a cleric, my mommy told me that shapely hips won't guarantee a happy family life. Even if I were in the marrying business, I wouldn't let a little skin overly influence my decision."

"Just answer the question about the outfit."

"That's more like a nun outfit than a sweet girl next door outfit. Not sure that's what you're supposed—"

She squints her eyes. "Okay, let's start over. Tell me this outfit makes me look frumpy."

"That outfit makes you look frumpy."

"Perfect! That's exactly what I wanted to hear."

Together, they go to the rendezvous point. Benjamin Frankelyn takes one look at Ariel and frowns. "I said innocent and sweet, not a nun!"

"Nuns are innocent and sweet—at least they're supposed to be."

Benjamin Frankelyn pulls at his sideburns dramatically and moans, "But even if they're not innocent and sweet, they know a lot about religion. If you get jittery about the liturgy or snarky about the hierarchy, they'll see through you at once. The Templars aren't just warriors, they're monks! That's like walking into a wine shop dressed like a vintner and asking where's the grape juice."

Monsignor Meyer says, "Oh, that reminds me of the time we caught an old lady walking out of the sacristy with a bottle of altar wine. The abbot stopped her and asked, 'Where are you going with that?'

"She pointed to an old guy snoring on the church steps and said, 'I got it for my husband.'

"The abbot looked at the snoozing old man for a moment, then said, 'Good trade.' And he let her go! Ha! Uh-ha! Uh-ha! *Snort*!"

They all start laughing—some because they get the joke, others because his snorting laughter is contagious. It takes the monsignor a while to recover from his own joke. He says, "Don't worry, Ben. I'll cover for her."

Frankelyn looks at him awry. "How did you figure out my name?"

Monsignor Meyer shrugs his huge shoulders. "I might be a bad one, but I'm still a cleric. Once you have the gift of prophecy, you always have the gift of prophecy. God didn't take it away when I . . . er . . . fell from grace. He's funny like that. How do you think I got signed on to a party of adventurers that specializes in hide-and-seek quests like this?"

Benjamin Frankelyn gets cheeky. "I always figured it was just your big nose. But that's not important now. Can you just use the gift of prophecy to figure out which vault the sword is in?"

"No, I can't. The Templars have clerics of their own. They've got special protective blessings that keep guys like me from taking advantage of the system."

"Well, I can tell you that the sword is evil. Can't your gift of prophecy detect evil?"

"Yeah, but it's still a long shot. It's a bank, after all, and money is the root of all evil. I'm going to get a lot of false positives if I send up a detect evil prayer. Let's get moving. Whoopee's in position and doesn't want this to take any longer than it has to."

Ariel adds, "I second that."

"Wait. Where's Whoopee?"

"He's already hanging onto my belly, and the leather pouch is strapped on as a cushion for him to fill up with air once he drops off so I won't walk out of there looking like I lost a hundred pounds after one dump."

"Right." Benjamin Frankelyn pats the cleric's fake belly and calls down to the dark elf inside, "How you doing in there, buddy?"

From under the monk's robes a voice moans, "Let's just get this over with."

Monsignor Meyer says, "Ariel, you go in first and I'll come in a few moments later to make it seem like we're not traveling together. While I'm waiting for you to finish up your business, I will ask to use the privy and then I'll let Whoopee out. You're going to have to try to delay them long enough so they don't bring the fake gold bars into the vault until after he's ready to sneak in after them."

Ariel snaps her fingers and psyches herself up. "Okay, I got this. Innocent and sweet. What could possibly go wrong if I just do the sister act?"

Ariel walks into the brownstone Templar fort. The inside is dark and stuffy. The few narrow windows are barred with heavy iron rods, allowing little light or air to get in. Wealth is apparent everywhere. The large number of candles burning all day long, polished hardwood floors, and granite teller counters were all extravagant luxuries in the Middle Ages, even though they would be considered standard for a bank these days. Two Templar clerks, one human and one dwarf, sit at separate desks.

Ariel groans to herself as she realizes Benjamin Frankelyn's plan will get shot to pieces as soon as Monsignor Meyer steps in. *There is only supposed to be one clerk! How am I supposed to distract both of them?* She turns around to go out and warn him.

The human clerk on the left looks at her quizzically and says in Latin, "Pax Domini tecum."

Remembering she is wearing a nun outfit and is supposed to know Latin, she plays dumb and answers in Aenglish, "Ah, yes, holy brother! I think I'm not supposed to be here."

He switches to Aenglish and asks, "What have you got in the sack?"

"Oh, you know, just some silly old gold bars, but it's none of your business, really."

"Actually, I'm a banker. Gold bars *are* my business. There's plenty of thieves out there and you just walked into one of the safest banks in Vinland. You won't get to the end of the street before they steal it. God has brought you here, not by accident. Take the hint."

"I'll take my chances. Thanks. Bye! I mean, God be with you." She opens the door and Monsignor Meyer walks right in and exclaims with a cheerful outspreading of his hands, "Sister!"

The dwarf clerk on the right says to the lumbering half-goblin/half-dwarf brother in Dwarvish Runic, "Lakunto Tesaged."

Monsignor Meyer replies in Aenglish with his porcine Santa-Claus-like jovial manner, "Peace of Christ be with you, brothers. Sister Wendy here is really an extern—a novice extern—so we'll speak Aenglish for her sake."

"There are two of us. We can help you both in your own languages."

Ariel says, "Well, that's a blessing, isn't it, Brother . . . uh . . . Brother Francis . . . Footer?"

Monsignor Meyer tries to stall, saying, "What a blessing indeed! God's providence is everywhere if only we have the faith to see it."

The human clerk says, "Would you like me to take a look at those gold bars, Sister Wendy?"

Ariel shakes her head. "Oh, no need. My abbess told me I needed to be as discreet as possible about this. I'll just get a safe deposit box."

"Small, medium, or large?"

"What would be the right size if I, say, wanted to store a sword in a safe deposit box?"

Human clerk doubts he heard that right. "Do you have a sword with you as well?"

"No, no, no! Our convent is hoping to obtain the sword of Saint George from the Holy Land. You know, the one he slew the dragon with? So I might as well get one big enough to fit a sword, just in case."

The dwarf clerk squints his eyes. "You just said your abbess."

"My abbess what?"

The dwarf clerk voices his suspicions. "How can you live in a convent if you have an abbess? An abbess is the head of a monastery, not a convent. In any event, I recommend you bring the sword in for authentication before your abbess purchases it. There are many hucksters in the relic trade these days. We have a very thorough authentication team."

"What, you think I took vows yesterday? I know a real sword when I see one!"

The dwarf clerk grows very suspicious. "So your abbess trains the nuns in your convent in the use of swords? Is this a convent for adventurers, perhaps?"

Monsignor Meyer slaps Ariel on the back. "Goodness gracious, no! I guarantee you she is no adventurer! Sister Wendy is a famous artifact critic. Nuns from all kinds of different convents and monasteries bring her in to consult about the authenticity of various relics and artifacts. That's why she got confused and called her mother superior an abbess! She is from a monastery, but she is temporarily on assignment in a convent."

The dwarf clerk replies, "Sister, you ought to ask your mother superior for a penance to curb your haughty attitude."

Ariel goes at him. "Why, I oughta—"

Monsignor Meyer covers her mouth and says, "Speaking of penances, a guy walks into a canonry and tells the prior, 'I want to become a canon regular, the monastery up the road is too strict.'

"The prior tells him, 'My son, you are welcome to join us, but we use the discipline daily here.'

"He says, 'No problem, when can I begin?' The prior says, 'Today, thanks be to God!'

"For the rest of the week, the prior notices his new postulant's back is all wet every morning and finally he asks him, 'Brother, why is your back all wet?'

"The postulant points to the sacristy and says, 'You said to use the discipline every day!'

"The prior follows his finger and says, 'Oh, that's not a flagellum, that's an aspergillum!'"

The two Templar clerks roar with laughter and Monsignor Meyer can hardly contain himself laughing and snorting. Ariel's face is stone cold until Monsignor Meyer looks right at her. She pretends to laugh.

Whoopee can hardly take it anymore and makes a splurting noise with his lips.

When his laughter calms down, Monsignor Meyer groans and says, "Excuse me, gentlemen, I was fasting for a novena in reparation of sins when our provincial visited us. I ate a full meal with him and now it's disagreeing with me. Do you have a privy I can use?"

The human clerk says, "I'll show him the way. Brother Bifur, would you tend to the young nun over there? Those gold bars look heavy."

The dwarf clerk waddles over to Ariel, still chuckling to himself, and says, "Okay, so you'd like a medium safe deposit box for the gold bars, correct?"

"Yes, Brother Bifur."

He looks up at her. "How do you know my name?"

"The other brother just said it."

"Right, and what is your name, Sister?"

Ariel looks away from him for half a breath.

"Uh . . . Sister Shensi."

"Brother Frank Footer over there just called you Sister Wendy. Which is it?"

"Um . . . both, really. He knew me before I entered the convent, I mean monastery. Wendy's my baptismal name and Sister Shensi is my name in religion. Saint Shensi is the patron saint of . . . er . . . adventurers."

"So you *are* an adventurer?"

"No way!"

The dwarf clerk takes the sack of gold bars and says, "That'll be fourpence. Do you have a groat?"

Ariel deeply regrets trying to pull off this sister act. "Absolutely. It's great for prayer."

The dwarf Templar shakes his head. "A groat is the new four-pence coin. Since you seem to get around, I figured you might have one on you."

Ariel says, "Actually, about that—I heard Templars are great money lenders. Can I borrow, say, twelve dollars? You know, one for each of the apostles."

"For that kind of loan, you'll need collateral." In the blink of an eye, the dwarf Templar unstrings the sack and dumps the gold bars on the counter before Ariel can stop him.

She grabs for the bars and starts stuffing them back into the bag, saying, "Oh, never mind then."

He takes one look at the pyrite and says, "These are fake. I don't know what you're playing at, but this ain't real gold and you ain't a real nun."

Ariel gathers her bars up and storms off in all the mock outrage she can muster. "Well, I never! How dare you disrespect a woman of the cloth like that!"

Around the corner, Benjamin Frankelyn, dressed as a Knight Paladin, asks her eagerly, "How did it go?"

Ariel curls her lip. "What's an aspergillum?"

Frankelyn's face falls. "Oh no! That bad, was it?"

"Monsignor Meyer got into the privy, so at least Whoopee's in place, but they wouldn't take this stupid fool's gold back into the vault."

"Hopefully, the monsignor got some useful intel."

A few moments later, Monsignor Meyer comes out smiling and says, "By all the saints, those Templars are swell guys, let me tell ya!"

Benjamin Frankelyn looks at him expectantly and asks, "What happened to Ariel?"

"Yeah, so, the sister act didn't quite work out, and we have no idea where the vaults are. The good news is, I lowered Whoopee into the cesspit. He'll have to hide out there until we can cook up a plan to get him out. I say we start first thing in the morning."

"It's first thing in the morning right now."

"I meant tomorrow. No sense pushing our bad luck now. Dark elves are comfortable in cesspits—it reminds them of home." Monsignor Meyer laughs until his face turns red and tears well up in his eyes.

Benjamin Frankelyn gets worried. "Did your gift of prophecy reveal anything about the sword?"

"Well, I spoke with the tongue of angels, but it felt like I was holding the hand of a devil. All I got was a cold, brooding evil."

"Yes, yes, that must have been it. The sword has a cold evil to it. It is a blackflame sword, after all."

"But I still haven't found what we're looking for."

"Why not?"

"You, Mister Silent Willy Dogood, have told us nothing about it. How am I supposed to find it if I have no idea what I'm looking for?"

Flurrrppp.

Benjamin Frankelyn asks, "What was that?"

Monsignor Meyer removes the inflated leather wineskin from under his robe and says, wiping a tear from his eye, "Oh, it's Whoopee's cushion. It makes this annoying sound, but it only helped lend credibility to my story about needing to use the privy. That's the only part of your plan that's gone right so far."

Benjamin Frankelyn looks at Willis. The white-haired adventurer is wearing blue robes with a silver cross, signifying the order of the Knights Paladin. "We can still pull this off. Ready for part two, Willis?"

Willis moans, "Are you sure it's a good idea to be posing as warrior monks? I don't know what an aspergillum is either."

Benjamin Frankelyn shakes his head. "Just follow my lead."

The two phony Knights Paladin walk into the bank. The human clerk asks, "May I help you, brothers?"

Benjamin Frankelyn puts on his most authoritative voice. "We have come here urgently from Salim. Our patron has reported that a vault slip has been stolen from his residence. He paid an ungodly fortune so that the Templars would get the item to him safely. We're here to ensure that sloppy security procedures don't endanger the safe transfer of the item."

The dwarf puts his elbows on the desk as if offended and says, "So the big cardinals in Salim are sending Knights Paladin to make sure the Knights

Templar are doing their job right. Is that how it goes these days?"

Benjamin Frankelyn keeps his calm. "The fact that we are Knights Paladin is irrelevant to the matter. We just happened to be the only trusted sons of the Church that were heading toward Rofchester."

The dwarf Templar keeps interrogating them. "And what business brings you to Rofchester?"

"We're investigating reports of wendigo elves wandering out of Tuscoraura Mountain."

The human Templar says, "Yes, I have heard such reports. It's getting worse, not better."

The dwarf Templar is not appeased. "Did the cardinals in Salim trust you enough to tell you precisely what item it was that had its vault slip stolen?"

Benjamin Frankelyn leans in close and says, "This is for your ears only. Gather around."

The human and the dwarf Templars huddle in together. Willis leans in as if he were in on the secret. Benjamin Frankelyn raises an eyebrow and whispers slowly, "The Sword of Layban . . ."

Willis stands back slowly and squints his eyes, nodding as if that just made total sense to him. The dwarf Templar genuinely seems relieved to hear it and says, "Well then, we have good news for you. We got the warning by Pony Express before Goldilocks arrived. She presented the vault slip and we arrested her. She came in wearing a red cloak and an elven dagger. Tomorrow we will cart her off to Salim for trial.

"You can tell the cardinals our security procedures are quite rigorous. We will not hand over the item until a fully authenticated vault slip is reissued."

Benjamin Frankelyn gawks. "Goldilocks is here?"

The dwarf points to a cabinet overhead. "Her cloak and dagger are up there in the evidence chest. We removed them carefully so as not to spoil any clues."

Benjamin Frankelyn slaps his hands together and starts to head out. "Splendid! You know what we Knights Paladin always say . . . leave the cloak and dagger stuff to the Templars. Well, that'd be all. Thank you so much! God bless us, everyone!"

As soon as Benjamin Frankelyn reaches his party of adventurers, he starts jamming out on an imaginary air lute. Ariel looks at him as if he's crazy. But Monsignor Meyer has seen it all before and does not betray the least bit of surprise. He says, "So, I'm guessing that part went better than the first. I don't need the gift of prophecy to know you walked out of there empty-handed. What's got your spirits up so high?"

Benjamin Frankelyn strums a fast-paced cadenza on his imaginary lute and says, "They captured Goldilocks and she's right inside there with Whoopee!"

Ariel looks around, trying to feel the joy. "Whoopee! Yeah that's great, I think. What'd you have in mind? You want Whoopee to kill her?"

"No, no, no! Don't you see? She'll steal it for us."

"Why would she do that?"

Benjamin Frankelyn recovers his calm and announces solemnly, "I'm going to make her an offer she can't refuse."

Scene 5: Lynx to the Rescue

Amphitheater at Thor's Base, Shentalpee City
Hock Moon Day Terce. Morning, 10th of April, 1284

"Yeehaw!"

Leaning back on the dwarven shield, Lynx sticks out his feet and trails a hand behind him to brake his speed down the watercourse. He's going too fast. Two ornate wooden flowers guard the lip of the aqueduct and his feet slam into them so hard the wooden petals fly off. The shield gets swamped with water on one side, flipping him upside down. As his legs dangle over the reflecting pool, Lynx grips the base of one wooden flower with his right hand and keeps hold of the shield, flapping in the spray, with his left.

Down below, the spectacle upends the audience, but the three polar elves prove their scholarly prowess by pulling out source stones and magica wands to help Lynx back up onto the aqueduct.

Florenz knows exactly what he is doing so she announces to the crowd, "Illustrious fire elves! I beg you, keep your calm. In the wake of the goblin's attack, my father has decided to tighten up our security procedures and introduce some radical reforms. He has received credible reports that the Inquisition has arrived at Tuscoraura Mountain and has contrived a number of ingenious traps to ambush them.

"Please remain seated and calm. All these measures will make sense shortly. Monsieur Lynx, do you have a progress report for us?"

"Um . . . yes. I've got an important public service announcement to make. Our noble umpire-in-chief, who has personally sponsored my commission in the Ivy League, has come up with a cunning plan in mind to . . . ah . . . eliminate the threats to our homeland security. Right now, the current project I'm working on is top secret but will. . . ah . . . eliminate those threats."

His words make no sense, but public service announcements rarely do, so no one notices. He continues, "Right now, we are experiencing some technical difficulties, so you can go right along with the program for this Thor's Enlightenment Discourse, and I'll–I mean, we'll—finish up this important public service project shortly."

Florenz resumes. "So now, without further ado, I introduce three elves renowned for their wisdom—Hakeem Melchior, Mage Gaspar, and Sage Balthazar."

With brown skin and black hair, a stout chest, long arms, and pointy ears, Hakeem Melchior's physical characteristics defy all ethnic stereotypes. On his head sits an ornate red silk turban and he wears a decorated red leather vest and red velvet sash over a green silk shirt. His green pants are puffy, while his red shoes stick out far enough to flop at the toes. He says in Runic with a thick polar elf accent, "May the gods bless ye, merry fire elves of Tuscoraura Mountain! Tidings of comfort and joy to one and all! We three elves from Oregan are bearing gifts—we have traveled from afar. Across snowy tundra, through torrid valleys, and over grand canyons we have followed the northern star, leading us unto ye, our cherished fire elf cousins.

"Instead of one big gift to your community, we decided to hand out a few little gifts to each of your families. To keep them together, we tucked the gifts into a new stocking, which we offer as a bonus gift.

"Now, let us explain the first gift—a needle. Beneath the earth run ley lines that harness and channel the power of the elements. Sorcerers call the site where these ley lines converge the North Pole.

"The needle we bring unto ye is actually a thin piece of lodestone. When perfectly balanced and suspended from a string, it will unerringly point the way to the convergence of those ley lines.

"We, the Yulenisse, now call ourselves polar elves because over a century ago, a group of dedicated mages, philosophers, sages, alchemists, geomancers, and astrologers teamed up and founded an underground city with a complex of workshops on our pole, the northernmost convergence of ley lines.

"This oasis of learning includes an observatory, a prismatic greenhouse for growing magica trees, a vast library of books in every field of learning, and a research station with workshops in the fields of sorcery, alchemy, noetics, tectonics, and astrology.

"Any scholar would need nothing more than to follow that needle and the light of the North Star to calculate where to find us at the North Pole. For nearly a hundred years we have given each visitor a share in our knowledge, without price.

"In recent years, the number of visitors to our workshops has declined drastically, for several reasons. In the first place, most races prefer to dwell in middle earth, where clement weather prevails and seasonal changes are pleasant. Polar north can only be found in upper earth, that inclement region of our world where adventurers seldom dare explore.

"Several well-meaning scholars have hired parties of adventurers to escort them out to the North Pole to visit our workshops. Since these needles will always point to the convergence of the ley lines until they crisscross over the North Pole itself, they assumed that they would traipse across upper earth along the Oregan Trail until their needles fell into an X shape.

"Unfortunately, their calculations were off. Their learning was superficial, and their adventurous spirit was easily chilled. They did not heed our maps, which clearly stated, 'Warning! Ley lines pulse and shift.'

"Each year the convergence of ley lines migrates and, unlike the adventure tales, in real true sorcery, X never, ever, marks the spot.

"The most important part of sorcery is done in the library. A hundred years ago, our workshops were directly over the North Pole. Had they done their research, they could have tracked the ley line drift over the years and traced it back to our exact location.

"Instead, they found the polar wastes barren and empty. Disappointed, they returned home and began spreading rumors that our sorcery, alchemy, noetics, tectonics, and astrology workshops do not even exist."

Hakeem Melchior steps down off the stage and Mage Gaspar moves forward and speaks in a melodious voice. "In order to revive the flow of visitors, our nomocratic prefect, the monsieur Kris Kringleson, has decreed that every year on the winter solstice we will distribute an updated almanac containing articles on our research, star charts, current maps of ley lines, and geomantic fluctuations, and a mail-order catalogue of our latest inventions.

"Therefore, our second gift unto ye today is a copy of this year's almanac. At the back, we have a current list of all the known elf communities in Vinland that will be receiving a free almanac this upcoming winter solstice. This knowledge base is for non-military purposes only. Weaponizing our ideas is forbidden.

"So remember, we are making this list and checking it twice to ensure that all those receiving these almanacs are truly committed to playing nice with our new technologies. Likewise, naughty elves who dabble with necromancy or carelessly release toxins into the environment or provoke unjustifiable wars will be removed from this list."

Mage Gaspar steps down and Sage Balthazar replaces him on the stage. "Finally, since those gifts already mentioned are not enough to stuff those stockings full, we added a special treat from the North Pole for the children—a sweetened mint stick with a hook at the end."

The little elf children burst into a joyful noise as they dig their hands into the nearest stocking and pull out candy canes. They are made from two sprigs of peppermint, one red, the other white, twisted together, soaked in sweetened honey water, and sunbaked until crispy. These original candy canes were not edible. The children all quiet down to suck on their treat and chew on the ends without swallowing.

Now that the three wise elves have finished, all eyes look up to Lynx, who is still sitting at the lip of the aqueduct awkwardly waiting for something. Feeling the audience's attention on him, he waves at them.

Inquisitor Sheen groans with pain as his blood pressure drops. From the copious bleeding, Bremmer and Blainn instantly recognize that the arrow has pierced a major artery. Inquisitor Sheen collapses.

Friend and foe alike observe a moment of silence for the great cleric—all except Umpire Kibbler, who babbles away as he reads his notebook in preparation for another blast of blackflame.

Bremmer and Blainn charge at the umpire, knowing their only hope for victory is to cut him down before he readies a second blackflame attack. Seeing the large, angry whites of the dwarves' eyes, Umpire Kibbler sticks out his hand once again and spews out a cone of blackflame that envelops the brothers. Their double-linked steel mail offers little protection against the freezing flames and if not for their padded gambesons underneath, the deep cold would have shocked their circulatory systems into hypothermia.

Their numbed hands can barely hold onto their weapons and their chilled joints hamper their reflexes. In no condition to fight, they abandon the party and run away. They are not cowards, but they are here for the pay, and they know when a fight is lost.

With the city mercenaries gone, Flobbin stands no chance against all those silver arrows. He blows the small conch shell on his necklace and kicks up a fierce but short wind storm to cover his own retreat.

Hustling back into the vault before the Justiciar Leaguers can target him Captain Manzone calls to the humans, "Tame till at ran outer henny!"

The dwarf mercenaries are already sealing up the vault but Captain Manzone stops them and looks back with genuine concern at the two humans still standing out there as helpless, exposed targets, calling to them, "Kum an . . . kum an!"

Instead of retreating, Louis brandishes his battleaxe and says, "Follow me, Clarke. We are only going to get one shot at this." Taking off at a full-speed run up the hill, Louis makes a mad dash toward the umpire-in-chief, who begins reading his notebook for a third time.

One of the Justiciar League warriors jumps out and does a somersault downhill, tripping Louis with his bow as he rolls by. Clarke, unarmed, follows close behind Louis and leaps over his tangled-up legs. Exclusively focused on the task at hand, Clarke reaches out with his long arms to snatch the notebook out of Umpire Kibbler's hand.

Louis gets up as quickly as he can and swings at the nimble elves with his battleaxe. They hop out of the way and laugh as if taking delight in the harmless exercise. Instead of shooting out one last deadly blast of blackflame, Umpire Kibbler's left hand catches fire—black fire.

Although it goes out at once, since flesh is not black flammable, the flare is enough to deaden his left hand with frostbite. Umpire Kibbler screams in pain and tries to grab at the book with his right hand but Clarke holds it high above the elves' reach. Running out of laughter, Officer Bunzi grabs Clarke's robe from behind, kicks his knees out, and puts him in a headlock.

With Umpire Kibbler and two Justiciar League officers occupied with Clarke's antics, the remaining three officers make sport of Louis. One has a silver dagger and wagers with the others that he can finish Louis off with the dagger alone.

Louis swings the huge battleaxe at the elf but the Justiciar League officer manages to slip by and deliver a slash on Louis's arm. Instead of swinging the battleaxe, Louis attempts to poke at his opponent with it. Another Justiciar League officer pokes back with his silver dagger and delivers a nasty cut on Louis's left hand.

Justiciar League Officer Bunzi rips the book out of Clarke's hand. He holds it out to the umpire-in-chief, but Umpire Kibbler, a lefty, instinctively reaches out for it only to realize that his left hand is too numb to hold it. The book drops.

Just as Umpire Kibbler bends down to pick the book back up the hulking goblin comes lurking out from behind him, yanks Umpire Kibbler off his feet by the scruff of his neck and flings him over the steep mountain precipice.

At first sight of the goblin, Justiciar League Officer Bunzi switches back from confident bully to abject coward. He flees to the aqueduct and dives into it, sliding down head-first.

The hulking goblin continues his rampage with a quick grab at one of the three Justiciar League officers and uses his hostage as a meat sack to slap another elf over the edge. The remaining Justiciar League officer shoots his last silver arrow at the goblin but his hostage absorbs the arrow instead.

Charging down the shooter, the goblin shoves him off the peak of Tuscoraura Mountain and throws the hostage down after him.

The last remaining Justiciar League officer tries to make a last stand against the goblin but Louis grips his double-handed battleaxe and strikes him from behind. The rampaging goblin vents his frustrations on the fallen elf and tears him limb from limb. The battle ends with indescribable brutality.

Having given up hope after the failure of their last-ditch effort to take on Umpire Kibbler, Louis and Clarke are bewildered and shocked at their sudden victory. All they can do is watch as the goblin lets out a mighty roar as he heaves the hogshead of whiskey over to the aqueduct.

In the original plan, the two city mercenaries were supposed to tap some kind of code onto the lead pipe that serves as the spring's spout. Only the mountain dwarves deep down below can cut off the spring water from the aqueduct. Instead of a secret code, Louis and Clarke improvise by banging the pipe as loudly and desperately as their impulses direct them.

The mountain dwarves must have gotten the memo that improvisations might be the order of the day because the spring water ceases to flow down the aqueduct almost instantly. Without a word, the goblin takes a large rock and smashes the barrel's top open, then pours the whiskey down the aqueduct.

Without caring about the results below, the goblin prince puts the empty hogshead barrel down and holds out a hand to Louis and Clarke, expecting his due.

They look at him, puzzled for a moment, until Clarke snaps his fingers and remembers. "Inquisitor Sheen said the dwarves gave him a slow-acting poison to ensure he wouldn't double-cross them."

Louis says, "The antidote must still be on him."

Louis climbs back up to where the inquisitor's body lies and searches his belt purse but finds nothing. The goblin hangs over the two anxiously, ready for another round of brutality if they fail to deliver the antidote.

Louis gives up and the goblin takes his turn searching but his big, clumsy, green fingers are even less successful. As Clarke watches him, he considers how the goblin's huge muscles, big jaw, and green skin make him seem threatening as a first impression. Yes, that first impression also included being made part of a ritual human sacrifice; but that all has changed.

He remembers how this goblin has been betrayed and abandoned by friends and family, has suffered through several nights of torture, was held captive and forced to perform exhausting and dangerous work. Clarke begins to see him not so much as a scary monster anymore but as a vulnerable person like himself. That goblin will either have to rebuild his life around those who betrayed him or wander as an outcast in unfamiliar and hostile lands.

He remembers Inquisitor Sheen's warning that the goblin has come to Tuscoraura Mountain seeking the phoenix talon dagger—the only item that could help the goblin restore his legitimacy among his fellow tribesgoblins. Clarke instinctively reaches for his breast pouch where he stores his most important items and almost gives the phoenix talon back . . . almost.

The mounting rage and frustration of the goblin bring him back to his senses. Clarke tells Louis, "Wait! A monk keeps his most important and vital items in his breast fitchet."

Pockets, as previously mentioned, had not yet been invented. At the time they had fitchets instead. Sure enough, there is a little slit in the side of Inquisitor Sheen's robe for him to slip his right hand into a small leather pouch. Clarke pulls out a small vial the size of the tip of his pinky and hands the drink to the goblin.

The goblin looks Clarke in the eyes and a pang of fear stabs through Clarke's heart. *What if he knows I am hiding the phoenix talon dagger from him?*

After a moment of contemplating Clarke's guilty gaze, the goblin lowers his eyes and inspects the vial. It is too small for the goblin's large, powerful fingers to open. Dropping it or crushing it accidentally would mean certain death for the goblin.

Clarke looks up at the sky and sees the setting sun to his left. It means he is facing north. He recalls a sermon he once heard about facing "true north"—doing the right thing. At last he relents and obliges the goblin by pulling out the miniature stopper and pouring the antidote into the goblin's mouth for him.

The goblin presses a hand to his chin in a gesture of thanks, then walks away. Suddenly, he starts to run. Louis and Clarke look around and see a large company of Justiciar League officers and sergeants rushing toward them; a few are already testing the range of their arrows in their direction. The goblin returns to the empty barrel and holds it behind his back as a shield as he leaps down the steepest side of the mountain, drawing the attention and the arrows to himself.

Louis says to Clarke, "I don't think they are in a mood to listen to our explanation of how their umpire-in-chief got killed, even if we could speak Elvish."

Clarke looks down the aqueduct with a grin. "Agreed. I see only one way out of this."

"Honestly," says Louis, "I've been wanting to try that out for a while."

The water is up and flowing again so they leap in.

The crowd is about to leave when a Justiciar League officer comes shooting down the aqueduct headfirst, barely managing to keep his face above water. Lynx bounds to his feet and lets the officer zing past him, splashing down into the reflecting pool below.

While the Justiciar League officer flopping around in the pool draws the crowd's attention, few notice that the water from the aqueduct suddenly stops flowing. Taking his cue, Lynx sets the dwarven shield down and positions it above the blackflame brazier.

In a few moments, a stream of amber liquid flows down the empty aqueduct. With the shield, Lynx diverts its flow onto the blackflame brazier. Snap, crackle, and pop! The blackflame fizzles out.

When they notice the blackflame has been quenched, an uproar surges through the crowd. Some elves are relieved—finally able to voice their fears about the blackflame. Others writhe with indignation at the quashing of a gift dedicated to the statue of Thor. Arguments break out throughout the plaza; a few elders call it sacrilege and demand atonement—with Lynx's blood.

To make matters worse, two humans come sliding down the aqueduct and get dumped in the reflecting pool soon after Lynx himself jumps down into it. New outrage flairs up. How did those humans get here? What are they doing in our water? It's not a swimming pool! It is the primary source of drinking water and aesthetic peace for the colony. Now confusion reigns.

Seeing Florenz, the Justiciar League officer trudges out of the pool and says to her, panting, "The goblin! The goblin killed your father!"

Down below on Thor's Base, Justiciar League Officer Bunzi flops around in the reflecting pool. Lynx, thanks to the help of Sage Balthazar and his water sorcery, has stayed up top above the blackflame brazier, claiming to be there on orders. Florenz confirms his story and no one bothers him. With the help of a well-designed dwarven tower shield, Lynx has successfully diverted the whiskey that the goblin dumped down the aqueduct onto the blackflame.

With a snap, crackle, and pop, the last blackflame brazier on Tuscoraura Mountain has fizzled out. Quest complete!

Hearing Louis and Clarke yelling their way down the aqueduct Lynx jumps down into the pool and swims furiously out of the way just barely in time before the two splash down behind him. Weaponless, Officer Bunzi is scared stiff of the large humans.

The commotion of the events at the peak of Tuscoraura Mountain, as well as Mademoiselle Florenz's unexpected apology and Lynx's derring-do in extinguishing the blackflame, have generated a good-sized crowd of onlookers motivated by curiosity and at least a little suspicion.

Several of the elder elves fear retribution from the seven gods and are genuinely offended by the sacrilege. They demand expiation with Lynx's blood.

Arguments break out throughout the plaza, with some elves jamming up the elevators trying to get themselves and their children out of the brewing storm and other elves riling up more trouble.

Just when the crowd reaches its breaking point and verges on anarchic violence, Major Leagues Umpire Gandorf Mithranderson shows up with a large contingent of armed elves combined from the Justiciar League, the League of Licornes, and the Ivy League.

Elf standard bearers from each of the leagues blow their horns furiously, demanding that the crowds quiet down. Officers and sergeants from the leagues wade into the reflecting pool to bring Lynx, Officer Bunzi, Louis, and Clarke before the Major Leagues Umpire, who gets a translator to ask them in Aenglish, "Is the Monsieur Umpire Kibbler still alive?"

Louis and Clarke both answer, "No."

The officers and sergeants press through the crowd using their swords, elbows, and batons to get the hysterical elves to quiet down. Enganyon's father shouts above the crowd, "Reports have confirmed that our umpire-in-chief has died in defense of his homeland. As Major Leagues Umpire, I am exercising my prerogative to declare martial law and assume leadership of the government until the Council of Perfects decides on a provisional head of state!

"Due to the current state of political crisis, the Council of Perfects will be holding an emergency council session at sundown. All those not invited to the session are ordered to return to their homes until the council has announced its decision. Anyone found roaming the walkways after sundown without a pass will be arrested as a rabble-rouser."

Followed by Old Mother Hubbard's undead dog, Enganyon cheerfully walks over to Dungaree Jeanne and Johnny Appleseed and says, "My recommendation is that we head over to the council chambers right now so we can get some good, front-row seats. Don't worry, they'll have refreshments available inside."

Dungaree Jeanne looks at him suspiciously. "By my bushy eyebrows, you do seem to be taking this unexpected catastrophic turn of events rather well."

Enganyon gets behind Appleseed's wheelchair and starts pushing him toward the council chambers as the shocked and panicked crowd jostles and frets all around them. "Oh, Madame Dungaree, you are always so dramatic! There is nothing catastrophic or unexpected about this turn of events. My father's been planning this all out ever since he took office."

Scene 6: Handcrank Redemption

Templar Priory, Town of Rofchester
Woden's Day Compline. Night, 19th of April, 1284
Feast of Saint Aelfheah, Bishop and Martyr

The security has been much tighter than anything he could have imagined. Templar sergeants follow a tight schedule keeping watch over every imaginable corner of the vaults—the corners inside the latrines happily escaped their imaginations.

After the Templars locked it all up for the night and after having stewed in feces all day, the dark elf code-named Whoopee cautiously creeps out of the cesspit and washes his hands and face off with the pitcher and basin provided for the privy. Monks were some of the cleanest people in the Middle Ages, and washing the hands and face regularly was required by their rules.

Now he begins the impossible task of trying to locate the vault that might contain this blackflame sword. Benjamin Frankelyn has been so tight-lipped about the whole operation that Whoopee would not even recognize the sword if he tripped over it. Still, he is a professional and knows his business well. He looks around, memorizing every detail of the walls, the doors, and the layout of the vault. He paces out the hallways and scans for potential access points, making a mental note of one spot ideal for an escape tunnel.

With impeccable timing, a small section of that very section of wall starts making a harsh grinding noise.

The wall starts to shake and then crumble until a six-inch bore bit pokes its way through. It retracts, leaving a cloud of powdery dust and a small tunnel just big enough to fit his fist into. A voice calls through the hole, "Whoopee!"

Still miffed about the cesspit, the dark elf calls back, "Glad you're having fun, Benny. I spent the day crouching in poo. You humans always make us dark elves do the dirty work."

The hole is too long and narrow for them to see each other but it carries the echoes of their voices well. Benjamin Frankelyn says, "You can take it up with the complaints department. Right now, I need to know if you've figured out which vault has the sword."

The dark elf hears a movement. Something black and furry skits around a corner. Benjamin Frankelyn calls out but the dark elf hushes him. "Shhhhhhh!"

Benjamin Frankelyn calls out again, "What is it?"

"I thought I saw a kitty cat. I'm going to go check it out." Whoopee sneaks over and peers around the corner. He sees a big, bushy mop of curly, blond hair on a girl with furry, black boots locked behind some bars. She seems to be asleep. He tiptoes back to the hole and says, "It's a little girl with curly, blond hair."

Ariel's voice comes piping through the hole. "Goldilocks! You found the cat burglar we need!"

Benjamin Frankelyn says, "Listen, this girl knows where the sword is. We need to cut a deal. Can you get her over to this hole to negotiate?"

"She's locked in a cage with iron bars."

"Use the wire I gave you. It's made by the Akmy dwarves. It should cut through iron fairly easily."

"Don't worry! I got this." The dark elf goes back and asks in Aenglish, "Hey, you! Goldilocks! You awake?"

No response.

She must be really tired because she does not look all that comfortable the way she is sleeping. He looks around and sees a tin plate with leftover corn and lima beans on it. He reaches in and bangs the plate against the bars and it makes a racket.

The girl is not happy to be woken up and she moans. When her eyes focus in on his dark face, she instinctively addresses him in Drowish, the language she spoke with her mother, "Peh-peh-le-pee yew! It smells like you spent the day in a cesspit."

A huge smile broadens across his face as he realizes the blond, curly hair hides a young, cute, aristocratic, dark elf lady. He loosens up and reaches out a hand and replies in Drowish, "I did, sister! I'm a dark elf too and I'm here to rescue you. Give me some skin!"

She whips him with her chains so hard it hurts.

"Suffering succotash! What was that about?"

She warns him sternly, "No touchie! There's one rule when talking to princesses and it's no touchie!"

"You're a princess?"

"Technically, yes. My mother was a dark elf commodore. If you knew anything about sea elves, you'd know that makes me a princess."

Whoopee applies the charm. "Indeed, it does, Princess. Indeed it does. So then, how did a gorgeous princess like yourself end up in a nasty cage like this?"

"I took a wrong turn at Albuquerque."

Trying to make friendly with her, he chatters away in Drowish. "Well, you see, I'm a member of the Ducaine Magicultors' Guild—named Magicultor of the Month last December. Anyhow, I'm with this cool group of adventurers who want to crack a vault that's got a dark flaming sword inside it. The chubby human peeping through the hole back there wants to talk."

"If you haven't noticed, I'm behind bars."

"That's the nice thing about magic. Locks, bars, traps, guards—no big deal." He takes out his magica wand and sings a magic word, "Poisson!"

Nothing happens. The princess wrinkles her lips and says, "Very impressive, Magicultor of the Month."

Whoopee chuckles, "Obviously, it's warded. No big deal. As they said in magic classes, 'Your magica wand is only the first of many tools it takes to be a great magicultor.' Check this out. This is a wire that can cut through iron bars. If you agree to hear the human out, I'll cut you out of that cage. Deal, sister?"

"Fine, but I am not your sister. Now cut this lock."

"Aye, aye, Your Highness."

He files furiously back and forth at the lock with the Akmy wire. Once he has cut through most of the lock, she leans back and gives the cage door a tremendous kick. The door slams into Whoopee and knocks him off his feet with a loud, "Ouch! That hurt."

She walks past him without offering to help him back onto his feet and finds the hole on her own. She calls down through in Drowish, "So what's the deal?"

Unruffled, Whoopee gets himself up and shouts past her to his friends, "So your human Goldilocks girl is actually a beautiful Drowish princess!"

Benjamin Frankelyn replies in Aenglish and Whoopee translates his words into Drowish, "Princess, we are honored to make your acquaintance. I am a frankelyn to a very important personage in Vinland and it has come to the attention of my patron that you are seeking the Sword of Layban."

The dark elf princess snaps back, "I didn't come all the way out here to get the sword for you!"

"Oh, agreed!" says Benjamin Frankelyn. "When I get into a bind like this, I like to find a solution that is, shall we say, a win for the both of us."

The princess folds her arms and says, "Before we even begin, tell me how this is all supposed to end up as a win-win scenario. Other than my leftover succotash, I don't have anything to offer you except the sword, and that's the one thing I'm not willing to negotiate about. I'm not seeing a win here."

Whoopee relays her concerns to Benjamin Frankelyn, who continues, "Well, you see, I did some reading up on the Sword of Layban, and apparently it means a lot to the Ammonite Christians. A group of them are here in Rofchester and they are willing to help you. The only price they are asking is that you listen empathetically to what they have to say."

"Fine. Get me out of here."

Whoopee tells her, "Good, now step back a bit."

"Why?"

"This is going to be loud and messy."

Before Whoopee gets her to stand back, the stones of the wall crumble and disintegrate. A tunnel opens all the way out of the Templar vault. It's a long and uncomfortably narrow passageway, just wide enough for a skinny elf to wiggle through like a worm. The rocks inside are still crumbling.

The princess orders Whoopee, "You first."

Whoopee isn't even paying attention. He's upset. He sticks his head through the hole shouting to his fellow adventurers, "Where was the kaboom? There was supposed to be an earth-shattering kaboom!"

Slithering through the tunnel is twice as awful as it sounds and doesn't help the princess's sour mood any.

Once she gets through to the other end, she sees a jovial Benjamin Frankelyn dressed in plain medieval civilian clothes; the broad-shouldered half-goblin/half-dwarf Monsignor Oscar Meyer wearing his clerical robe; Ariel, who has dyed her hair red and stuffed some wool fleece around her gums to change her facial features; and the white-haired Willis, now back in his suit of reinforced mail armor, singling him out as a fighter-class adventurer.

Benjamin Frankelyn smiles proudly. "You've heard of elf fire, right? Imagine what happens to solid stone when you heat it with elf fire then quickly freeze it with blackflame. Impressive, isn't it?"

Around them stand four figures in simple, white robes—two women and two men. Their faces are austere but gentle. An older woman introduces herself using the mystical gift of tongues so all can understand each other despite the language barriers. "I am Sister Elmyra and this is my associate, Sister Penelope. We think you ought to know the truth about Jesus Christ."

Goldilocks snaps back, "Oh, don't worry, I already know all about him. Can we move on to discussing why you are going to give me the Sword of Layban or should I just start running now?"

Sister Elmyra's gift of tongues is powerful enough that all present hear Goldilocks's Drowish words in their own native language. Benjamin Frankelyn replies to her in Aenglish, but she hears his words in Drowish. "The deal was for us to break you out in exchange for empathetic listening. You're just assuming you already know what they're going to say. Give them time to explain and we can find a solution where we all win." Benjamin Frankelyn bows to Sister Elmyra and yields the spotlight—or in this case, the moonlight—to her.

Sister Elmyra resumes speaking. "No worries, my dear. Let's talk about what matters most to you right now—the Sword of Layban. It is significant to Ammonite Christians because without it, the true faith would never have come to Vinland. Layban had it forged as a weapon capable of great evil, but God has used it by his command to accomplish a greater good.

"We are a peaceful people, and we are not here for the sword itself, but our prophet believes God has a plan to use it to lead us to a treasure without price."

"What makes you think I know anything about this treasure you are seeking?"

"Pure faith. A certain prophet, seer, and revelator foretold evil on a scale that would make the Thieves' Guild look like a gathering of modern-day saints unless we follow this path. The Sword of Layban is worthless to us, but we believe its bearer will save Vinland."

The blond-haired dark elf princess looks at her intently. "So you're saying you would agree to let me have the Sword of Layban because of some prophecy, but I have a hunch this guy over here wants it too."

Benjamin Frankelyn puts a hand on her shoulders but she snaps, "No touchie! Rule number one with princesses—no touchie!"

Frankelyn backs off and says, "You're right, princess. All I'm saying is that we agreed to some empathetic listening. You keep assuming you already know what we're going to say. Do you know a way to get the sword out of that vault? Because if you do, by all means, go ahead. It's all yours."

"No, I don't know how to get it out."

He continues. "You know which vault it's in, but you don't know how to get it out. We have a plan to get it out, but we don't know which vault it's in. Let's figure out our differences before the Templars find us."

Sister Elmyra says, "This is going to take some trust. All of us, including Mister Frankelyn here, fear the evil of the Sword of Layban. But if we give it to you, you must promise to lead us to the bronze plates that contain the Law of God. Only by learning and obeying the Law of God can we hope to keep this nation from dwindling and perishing in unbelief.

"The power of the blackflame is enough to engulf this entire continent from sea to shining sea in war, strife, and sin, but our prophet has told us that although you seek it for the evil powers it will grant you, you will eventually turn from your evil ways."

The princess crosses her arms and states, "So let me get this straight; you know I am going to use this sword for evil, but you are going to help me get it anyway because your prophet says that I'll eventually lead you to some kind of bronze plates."

"Yes. It's the only way."

The dark elf princess suddenly becomes apologetic. "So let's just say hypothetically that I have no idea where these bronze plates are. Do I still get to keep the sword—hypothetically speaking, of course?"

Sister Elmyra replies with great patience and kindness in her eyes, "We know that you are ignorant of the bronze plates right now but we firmly believe in God's plan that you will lead us to those plates one way or another."

She turns to Benjamin Frankelyn and asks, "Okay, but it kind of sounds like a stretch to me. Is that what you believe too, Mister Frankelyn?"

Benjamin Frankelyn smiles cheerfully. "Nope. Not at all. I work by reason, not by faith. Let's just say when it comes to the battle between good and evil, I steer the middle course and keep neutral about it all."

Goldilocks groans. "I've heard that line before."

Frankelyn continues. "The reason I invited the Ammonites here is that they have preserved in their oral traditions important information about how the sword works. Getting the sword to work is key to our plans for getting it out.

"The Sword of Layban has the power to billow out freezing blackflame, even in small, confined spaces without fresh air. All we have to do is ignite the blackflame inside its vault and it will freeze-burn the vault. Once the metal has frozen through, we'll heat it with elf fire. The alternation will make it brittle enough to shatter it as easily as if it were made out of glass. If you agree to turn over the Sword of Layban to us so we can complete our quest with it, we'll give it back to you when we're done with it."

She squints with suspicion in her eyes. "And how long is that going to take?"

"A few days, perhaps; a few weeks at most. Once we complete our quest, we won't need the sword anymore. It'll be all yours. Win-win scenario."

"How am I going to know you'll keep your end of the bargain? You could just keep telling me, we need one more week, and before you know it, years go by."

Benjamin Frankelyn cuts to the chase. "Think of it this way. You get your hands on the sword first, so we're the ones taking the biggest leap of faith in trusting you. If you don't trust us, you're welcome to go back and take your chances with the Inquisition."

"So why are you taking a leap of faith with me? You just said you work by reason and not by faith."

"That's my ideal. As a realist, I accept the fact that ninety percent of our decisions are based more on faith in someone or something than hard facts or rational explanations. That's just the way life goes."

"So let's fit this deal into the ten percent that makes perfect sense to our reason."

"No, the other ten percent is pure emotion."

The princess thinks for a while. "Fine, what are the magic words to make the Sword of Layban work?"

Sister Elmyra says, "They are not magic words at all, but rather a dark incantation for an unholy ritual—words that bring great evil upon those who speak them. Consider well before you—"

Goldilocks interrupts, "Yeah, yeah, blah, blah, blah. Just tell me the words and let's get this over with."

"By the power of Layban . . . I have the power!"

Goldilocks shrivels. "That's kind of dorky."

Willis cuts her off. "Don't knock it! For some people, it's really cool. Maybe it's a guy thing."

Benjamin Frankelyn resumes. "You and Whoopee are the only ones who can fit through the tunnel. He'll bring the elf fire. All you have to do is put your hand on the safe box holding the Sword of Layban and recite the ritual words. After he heats it with elf fire, just keep tapping at it and it'll break."

"What if I had a hammer and I'm hammering until morning? I wouldn't hear the Templars coming back."

"Don't worry, we've got a hammer of our own. We'll hammer out a warning if there is danger around. Once you break through, stop the sword from flaming by calling out, 'Let the power return!' Be careful, it'll be extremely cold in there."

Goldilocks thinks for a moment. Despite all her misgivings, she runs out of objections. This frankelyn has answers to everything. She says, "I don't like it, but whatever—I'm going to go with it. You have a deal."

"Splendid!" exclaims Benjamin Frankelyn. "Let's shake on it!"

"Tut, tut! No touchie!" She points to herself and reminds them, "Princess. No touchie!"

They all look at her silently. She remembers she once heard a preacher say that the path to evil starts from 'whatever.' With those words still ringing in her ears, she intentionally chooses to brush aside all the warnings of her conscience. "Whatever."

She then shakes hands with the devil.

Scene 7: Dear Lynx

Council Chambers at Thor's Base, Shentalpee City
Hock Moon Day Vespers. Evening, 10th of April, 1284

Suspecting foul play, Florenz gives instructions to Officer Bunzi, the soaking-wet Justiciar Leaguer who told her about her father's death. "Go tell the monsieur Major Leagues Umpire that I am too distressed over my father's death to attend the emergency council session; then, meet me at Woden's Tree."

After delivering the message, Officer Bunzi looks for Florenz at Woden's Tree but can't find her.

"Psst!" she hisses at him. "Over here."

He moves to where the sound came from and a hand grabs him into the tree trunk. "Where are we?"

"This is a secret entrance into the council chambers that only the umpire-in-chief knows about."

"Then how do you know about it?"

"Duh! You really think Zena could win the election? My father started showing me the ropes early."

"Yay democracy! And why take me along?"

"My father told me once, 'That Officer Bunzi is a low-life thug, but you can count on his loyalty.'"

"Thanks for the compliment, I think."

"Climb this ladder. I suspect the Council of Perfects is going to be a lot more honest about what happened to my father if they think I'm not listening."

"So you have a secret room where you can spy on everything that goes on in there?"

"Exactly. And if you betray that secret, you'll be put to a horrible death."

"Don't worry. Your father was right about me."

"That's reassuring; but not at all comforting."

"Hey! I'm loyal, okay? The other part—"

"Shhhhh!" Florenz puts her hand over his mouth.

Through the spy holes they hear Dungaree Jeanne say, "By my bushy eyebrows, you do seem to be taking these unexpectedly catastrophic events rather well."

It's Enganyon's voice that responds. "Oh, Madame Dungaree, you're always so dramatic! There's nothing catastrophic or unexpected about this turn of events. My father's been planning it out all along."

Florenz blurts out, "That rat!"

Officer Bunzi jumps back. "Where?"

"Shhhh! Keep it down. It was only a metaphor."

"Do metaphors bite?"

Florenz waves him to follow. "Only when you don't want to hear the truth. Come on!"

They climb through some tight tunnels and walk over rafters until they reach a dusty, unpolished, dark room with a screen that allows them to look down into the council chambers and hear what is going on. There are no chairs or cushions, so they sit on the raw planks.

Officer Bunzi gets antsy. "So how's a rodent supposed to know if I don't want to hear the truth?"

"Shhhh!" Florenz breathes right into his ear. "They'll hear us down there with all your chatter."

Still trying to digest Enganyon's comments, Florenz settles herself against the screen to watch and listen.

Dungaree Jeanne sits in the front row next to Johnny Appleseed in his wheelchair. The civic summoner reads the names of those summoned to the council session. To Florenz's surprise, the names Johnny Appleseed, Zena, and Lynx are on the list.

Zena is seated next to Enganyon's father, Major Leagues Umpire Gandorf Mithranderson, who has taken his place next to the umpire-in-chief's chair. Once the civic summoner has finished issuing summonses, the high commissioner commissions the meeting by going through the formality of inviting the umpire-in-chief to speak. Then, at his request, the entire council chamber pauses for a moment of silence out of respect for the umpire-in-chief's death.

The high commissioner announces, "In the absence of our dearly departed monsieur umpire-in-chief, I call upon the acting head of state for the Tuscoraura Elves, the monsieur Major Leagues Umpire Gandorf."

A burst of applause erupts as Umpire Gandorf makes his way onto the stage and addresses the high elves in the audience (no wood elves were invited) in Runic. "Mesdames, mesdemoiselles, and messieurs, esteemed high elves of our noble race around whom the cosmos turns, on this day, a tragic day, we gather to honor the life of our dearly departed monsieur Umpire-in-Chief Kibbler Earnestson, and to ensure that the fire elves of Tuscoraura Mountain will carry on his legacy.

"Superlative high elves, read through the history books to understand what this great elf accomplished. Never has our military felt more confident. Never has our economy been so strong. Never have our relationships with the longhouse humans, the mountain dwarves, and the garden gnomes been so reliable and productive as they are now at the end of these twelve years of his umpirage. Ask yourselves: would the longhouse humans have turned over a lurking goblin to Monsieur Drayton while he was umpire-in-chief?

"He was a second father to me and appointed me Major Leagues Umpire because he knew that our military needed a strong leader to unify its power.

"I remember the day when Mademoiselle Florenz announced to him she would run for umpire-in-chief. At first, he refused. He wanted her to take over his business and have a happy life with no other concerns than taste-testing chocolate chip cookies.

"'What's the point,' I asked him, 'of spending thy whole life fighting to open the path to happiness for thy children when thou must bar them from the career they see themselves most happily pursuing?'

"I reminded him that, although it goes against precedence for the children of umpires to run for office, no law forbids it. By the time the sorbet was served at that dinner, our dearly departed monsieur umpire-in-chief promised his daughter he would support her candidacy in private as her father but not in public. If she was going to win the chief umpirage, she would have to earn it on her own merit.

"Her dedication to the campaign trail and her stellar performance in the Ivy League Tournament proved that she was a worthy candidate. However, superlative high elves, it pains me to say that Mademoiselle Florenz is no longer on Tuscoraura Mountain. She has gone into voluntary exile."

Florenz gasps. "What? I never said that!"

Umpire Gandorf continues. "The first reason is obvious: her grief at her father's loss. The second reason is less obvious but equally public: her embarrassment over the Bartlebee affair."

Florenz can't believe her ears! "Why that—"

Officer Bunzi leans into her ear. "Shhh! They'll hear us down there with all your chatter."

"When her staff first intercepted the letter implying the garden gnomid Bartlebee leaked the secret recipe for elf fire, she did not want to act on it out of her love for her dear friend, Mademoiselle Zena. The poor taste of her campaign manager pressured her to go public with the scant information available, claiming that it would be the only way to protect Shentalpee City. After hours of agonizing over it, she felt she had no choice.

"We now know Bartlebee handed over a simple acorn pie recipe. In a single day, Mademoiselle Florenz realized that she lost both her best friend to dirty politics and her father to a security breach. Such strokes of misfortune one at a time have shattered stronger persons, but all together on a single day . . .

"She needs time to grieve. But that timing leaves us in a delicate predicament. Right now, Mademoiselle Zena Jeannesdottir is the only candidate for the chief umpirage left in Shentalpee City."

A few gasps ripple through the audience as the ramifications of the current political situation sink in.

After a rhetorical pause, Umpire Gandorf continues. "Without a second candidate, according to the Magnificent Charter, we cannot hold an election. If we postpone the elections, it could be months, perhaps years, before candidates of sufficient quality step forward."

Florenz rolls her eyes. Now she sees where Umpire Gandorf has been going with this. He is going to angle the whole situation so that his indecisive son can get back on the ballot, even after spitting on the opportunity when it was first presented to him.

Umpire Gandorf calls out, "Mister Lynx Highrune, wilt thou please approach the stage?"

Surprise and shock hit every last soul in the council chambers. Absolutely no one saw this coming.

Lynx stands, surprised and nervous. When he walks up onto the stage, Umpire Gandorf turns him around with an affirming pat on the back and announces, "To honor the memory of our dearly departed monsieur umpire-in-chief and to fulfill one of his last promises, as acting head of state, I hereby grant Monsieur Lynx Cougarson of Clan Highrune a paid commission as a junior officer in the Ivy League and enfranchisement as a high elf of Tuscoraura Mountain."

Umpire Gandorf hands him a scroll and the chamber hall offers a reluctant round of applause.

"Monsieur Lynx, all the other high elves on Tuscoraura Mountain have declined to run for the office of umpire-in-chief. Wilt thou be willing to put in thy bid for candidacy to maintain the democratic process?"

Lynx hesitates. It's all too much to take in.

Zena stands and asks publicly in a loud voice, "Monsieur Major Leagues Umpire, art thou not intending to prosecute him for sacrilege? After all, the blackflame was dedicated to Thor."

Lynx looks at Zena with bulging eyes, feeling utterly betrayed. *How could you bring that up at a moment like this? With a friend like you, who needs enemies?*

Umpire Gandorf announces to the council chambers in Runic, "If thou dost accept the candidacy, Monsieur Lynx, as acting head of state, I would grant thee an umpirical pardon for thy act to keep these disruptions from scuttling the ship of democracy."

Her glare makes Lynx realize Zena doesn't want him to become her equal. He rebels. "I accept!"

Satisfied, Umpire Gandorf ushers Lynx off the stand with the disinterest of a newspaper reader suddenly realizing the edition in hand is yesterday's news. He nods to the civic summoner, and the warder goes down and wheels Johnny Appleseed to the front. Dungaree Jeanne stands next to him as his translator.

The high commissioner asks Johnny Appleseed, "Dost thou swear to tell the truth, the whole truth, and nothing but the truth, or else invite the wrath of Woden upon thy head?"

After hearing Dungaree Jeanne's translation, Johnny Appleseed replies, "The good Lord in the Bible forbids us from swearing, but I solemnly affirm before the One True God that I will tell the truth, the whole truth, and nothing but the truth."

Dungaree Jeanne translates his statement word for word. The high commissioner looks to Umpire Gandorf with worry on his face.

The Major Leagues Umpire nods and asks him in a commanding voice, "Reverend Appleseed, the two humans have informed us that before his death, our dearly departed monsieur umpire-in-chief figured out a way to weaponize the blackflame by shooting it out of a siphon. Armed with this advanced technology, he used it to ambush and destroy the inquisitor. Little did he suspect that the captured goblin had forged an alliance with the Inquisition and brought death to many brave high elves, including our dearly departed monsieur umpire-in-chief.

"In thy expert opinion, is it possible to weaponize blackflame in a manner similar to what the two humans claim our dearly departed monsieur umpire-in-chief managed to do?"

Dungaree Jeanne waits for Appleseed's reply and says in Runic, "Yes, Monsieur Major Leagues Umpire."

The chamber audience mumbles and comments to each other. Umpire Gandorf continues interrogating him through Dungaree Jeanne. "Canst thou replicate the military applications of blackflame that the two human witnesses described?"

"No, Monsieur Major Leagues Umpire. He cannot."

Umpire Gandorf calls out, "I propose legislation establishing a commission to thoroughly investigate the blackflame findings of our dearly departed monsieur umpire-in-chief. These discoveries could be the key to maintaining elf military superiority in the near future!

"My thanks to thee, Reverend Appleseed, for thy testimony. Thou mayest return to thy place."

She starts to roll Appleseed back to the front row of the audience but he whispers to Dungaree Jeanne and she says in a loud voice, "Begging thy permission, Monsieur Major Leagues Umpire, Reverend Appleseed wishes to make a final statement regarding his gift of blackflame to our community."

"Permission granted."

Johnny Appleseed speaks as Dungaree Jeanne translates his words into Runic. "In my childhood, famines were common in Vinland. Our soil is fertile, but nutritious food often spoils quickly. I have seen families and entire communities on the brink of starvation because their vast supplies of food had rotted before anyone could eat them.

"When I learned of apples—how easily they grow in almost any climate and how easy they are to preserve as apple jelly, apple sauce, apple butter, and dried apple chips—I decided the first step to combatting hunger in Vinland would be to make apple seeds readily available. I traveled far and wide, offering the gift of free apple seeds and using my family's patrimony to establish apple orchards across Vinland.

"Through my travels, I saw how alcohol drove mothers and fathers to spend money that should have gone to feeding their hungry children on inebriating drinks instead. Dogfennel was the only effective remedy to alcoholism I could find, so I began to distribute it along with the apple seeds.

"But when I came upon a group of outcasts who fostered the secret to blackflame, I realized I had discovered the best solution to keeping food from spoiling. It seemed to me that hunger and famine were on their last legs in Vinland. If only I could make blackflame available to every community, then we could support twice the number of people with half the food production that is required now due to the amount of spoilage that wastes food stocks so easily.

"Regretfully, the military applications of blackflame have caused quite an uproar among Church authorities. The Inquisition has tracked me down and forbidden me to distribute dogfennel, blackflame, or even the Bible.

"If you do choose to cultivate blackflame and investigate its military applications, understand that you must prepare for a terrible war. The Crusades have brought to their knees fortresses previously considered impregnable. Think of what happened to the town of Donora when it tried to shut its gates to the crusaders."

Hearing his grave warning, the high elves break out into laughter. They hold the pope's battalions in utter contempt. Umpire Gandorf quiets them down and asks, "Is it not true that the Inquisition fears most the power of blackflame to recall the dead from the netherworld?"

"It is."

"Could blackflame recall our dearly departed monsieur umpire-in-chief from the netherworld?"

"Not without the Sword of Layban."

The high commissioner smacks his gavel. "I wish to second Monsieur Major Leagues Umpire's proposal to establish a blackflame commission. Any opposition?"

Silence.

"All in favor, say aye."

The raucous shouting of the power-hungry high elves drowns out the gavel.

"Motion carries!"

Satisfied with how that went, Umpire Gandorf turns to Lynx. "Now then, there remains only the formality of Monsieur Lynx's candidacy. Please repeat after me. I, Monsieur Lynx Cougarson of Clan Highrune, high elf of Shentalpee City, do hereby tender my candidacy for the position of umpire-in-chief over the fire elves of Tuscoraura Mountain."

Lynx repeats the formula, but barely does he sit down when one high elf stands up. "Objection!"

The high commissioner bangs his gavel. "Your objection, Monsieur Toadly?"

With bombast on his lips, Toadly says, "A good number of us are wondering why we are banking the future of Shentalpee City on a nouveau riche, former wood elve mademoiselle and a young upstart, former wood elf monsieur when we have before us in these very council chambers the perfect candidate: one who has merited his commission in a major league through his own competence and who has never committed a sacrilege or been embroiled in a scandal, and one whose bloodlines do great honor to our elfin pedigree—Monsieur Enganyon Gandorfson."

Murmurs of agreement make Toadly even bolder. "I make a motion to draft ad hoc legislation in this emergency council session allowing Monsieur Enganyon Gandorfson to reconsider his candidacy for umpire-in-chief!"

Applause washes over the assembly. Before the hand-clapping stops, the high commissioner has already seconded the proposal and the audience has carried it.

All of a sudden, the Toadly Act paving the way for Enganyon to offer his candidacy for umpire-in-chief is now law under the Emergency Provisions Act of 1284.

When Enganyon walks up to his father's umpirical chair, he acts as if he is totally taken by surprise and has no idea what to do. Enganyon steps up to the stage, where he addresses the chamber audience in Runic. "Mesdames, mesdemoiselles, and messieurs! While I am deeply honored by the high regard ye hold me in and I would do anything within my power to honor the legacy of our dearly departed monsieur umpire-in-chief, my heart desires to see only one elve in that role—Mademoiselle Zena Jeannesdottir."

He kneels on one knee before her and pulls out a ring. In a loud, manly voice he says for the whole assembly to hear, "Mademoiselle Zena, thou art the only elve I ever truly loved. Wilt thou marry me?"

Jumping up and clapping and flushed red in the face, she says, "Yes! Yes!"

Some elves in the chamber audience take no delight in this spectacle. Lynx, hurt, confused, and humiliated, storms out of the council chambers. Florenz fumes.

Officer Bunzi taps Florenz on the shoulder and says meekly, "Maybe we should get going, Mademoiselle."

Straining every nerve to calm herself before speaking, Florenz states, "Please tell the Major Leagues Umpire I've gone away. In my absence, you must recover my father's body, put it in a barrel of vinegar, and hide it here. Take the key to my father's coffer and bribe anyone who tries to stop you."

"You're not leaving for exile, are you?"

"No. I'm going on a quest to bring back the Sword of Layban—and my father's soul."

BONUS ACT B

EENY MEENY
MEINY MOE

Scene A: Betzy Rose Mansion

Betzy Rose Mansion, Red Giant's Base, Shentalpee City
Hock Moon Day Compline. Night, 10th of April, 1284

Dungaree Jeanne and Johnny Appleseed are eating a late dinner in the kitchen. They hear a knock at the door. Dungaree Jeanne stands up. "Oh, I really must get a new stewardess!"

She walks over and opens the front door. It's Zena. Floating in like a ballerina Zena whispers, "Good evening, Mother dearest!"

Irate, Dungaree Jeanne cries, "Mademoiselle Zena! How could you? You're engaged to Monsieur Lynx!"

Zena twirls with delight. "Mother, you and I both know that what he really wanted was to become a high elf. Our Major Leagues Umpire finalized that for him, so *Monsieur* Lynx has nothing to complain about. Besides, it was all so romantic! Did you see the way he got down on one knee in front of all the most important high elves on Tuscoraura Mountain?"

"You promised Lynx you would marry him if he saved your magica tree, and he risked his life for you!"

"Yeah, Mom, but it was dwarf cleric's plan. Besides, the two humans and the goblin did most of the work."

Dungaree Jeanne slaps her hands against the sides of her face and exclaims, "Oh, my dimpled cheeks! I completely forgot about the two boys! Reverend Appleseed hasn't even finished dinner and I'll need more food. My house is becoming a zoo for humans!"

Zena takes advantage of the situation to avoid any more confrontations with her mother. She walks back out the door and says, "I'll go find them."

Dungaree Jeanne returns to dinner with Johnny Appleseed. Without a stewardess or cook, Dungaree Jeanne has had to order Narnese takeout: sack-wise lark fritters and murried mulberry dish coney. She also got a side order of hedgehog sticks in yellow sauce with hominy and a pot of cold sage soup.

Still, it is hard to keep up. Even with the extra hedgehog sticks, she can tell that Johnny Appleseed is still hungry but not taking any more, just to be polite. What's she going to do when two human teenage boys arrive at the table?

Johnny Appleseed observes meekly in Aenglish, "Mademoiselle Zena seems quite happy."

Dungaree Jeanne snaps back sternly, "Her mother is not happy. She promised to marry Monsieur Lynx and now she forgets all about him!"

Johnny Appleseed, unconsciously eyeing the last lark fritter, asks, "Am I safe to guess that Enganyon proposed to Zena at the council meeting tonight?"

"Yes. You are interpreting that correctly."

"And what did they decide about the blackflame?"

Dungaree Jeanne puts the last lark fritter on Appleseed's plate and says, "Go ahead. Eat it. They will try to figure out how the late Monsieur Umpire-in-Chief managed to shoot blackflame from his hands."

"They want to make it a weapon?"

Dungaree Jeanne is disgusted. "Yes. And they want to make more undead horrors."

Right then, Zena comes bursting through the front door, screaming hysterically and jumping up and down and shaking her hands. Right behind her, Louis and Clarke come racing in and slam the door behind them.

Dungaree Jeanne hops up. "What is it?"

Louis, holding his axe and reeking with a foul odor, says in Aenglish, "Don't open that door!"

Johnny Appleseed starts to wheel himself over, asking, "What's out there?"

Louis, out of breath, huffs, "It's a zombie skunk! In the dim moonlight we saw a cat. I was going to pet it until I got close and realized was a skunk—not just any old skunk, but a zombie skunk! It hissed at us, so I took out my axe and chopped it in half. The back half just stood up and squirted me and the front half bit the tip of my shoe! Fortunately, it was a good, hard leather shoe so I kicked it off before it got my toes."

Johnny Appleseed wheels himself over to the door, stands up, balancing on one leg, and opens the door. The zombie skunk hisses and comes crawling inside in two separate halves.

Johnny Appleseed begins praying, using the mystical gift of tongues, saying in an angelic language, "Sleep, brother skunk. Rest eternally."

The two halves of the zombie skunk seem to grow tired and then stop moving entirely.

Clarke asks, "What did you do to it?"

"Turn undead prayer. It is a form of exorcism that comes with prayer and fasting."

Clarke asks, "You performed an exorcism on it?"

"Not exactly. An exorcism refers specifically to expelling an evil preternatural spirit that possesses the physical body of an unwilling victim. The undead skunk's mortal spirit was possessing its own physical body against its own will. It was scared and panicked; that's why it seemed to be attacking you—it was really just trying to escape from its undead coil."

Clarke tries to wrap his head around all that and expresses his puzzlement out loud. "But Inquisitor Sheen said he went through Vandsee Estates and extinguished all the blackflame braziers."

Johnny Appleseed says, "Obviously Umpire Kibbler wasn't the only one interested in blackflame necromancy in Shentalpee City."

Zena, only marginally calmer, says in Aenglish, "First we put that thing away, then I tell you."

"Tell us what?"

Zena points at the two halves of the skunk on the porch and says, "Away!"

Louis uses his battleaxe like a broom and sweeps the two halves of the skunk off the porch and knocks them over the railing down to the forest floor below.

"Now tell us what you know!"

Zena points at Louis and says in Aenglish, "You smell bad! Very bad! You go out too!"

Dungaree Jeanne says in Eldric, "Mademoiselle Zena! Is that any way to talk to our guests?"

Zena whines, "But the smell is so bad! Do you want him to stink up the whole house?"

Dungaree Jeanne pauses and sighs. The rules of hospitality prevent her from kicking out a guest over body odor but really, the stench from the putrefied undead skunk's spray is far worse than any natural skunk. It will already take a lot of effort to get the smell out of her foyer. She definitely does not want Louis spreading it all over her mansion.

Dungaree Jeanne relents and says in Aenglish, "Mister Louis, may we ask you to step outside for a moment? We need time to think how to handle this."

Louis nods and heads out the door.

Zena says in Aenglish, "After big meeting, Umpire Gandorf says to Perfects and to me that we stay. He was showing us something important. Everyone else go out and we stay. Umpire Gandorf has many servants. They bringed funny black robe like stormcrow, blackflame, big book, and dead skunk. He said words and skunk get up. Perfects very happy. Servants tried to put skunk in cage but skunk run out."

Johnny Appleseed looks grim. "This is serious. I did not suspect that the elves would all be so intent on necromancy. I promised I would undo the damage done by the blackflame. I will abide by my word."

Dungaree Jeanne asks, "What can we do?"

Appleseed holds his nose. "First, we need to get some peanut butter to get that smell off Louis."

Dungaree Jeanne says, "You won't find any here. There is a Laymanite merchant at Carlyle Fair who stocks exotic goods like peanut butter."

Clarke reaches into his breast fitchet for the leather pouch where he keeps his most valued possessions and says, "Reverend Appleseed, would this help?" As he pulls out Kibbler's notebook, the goblin ceremonial dagger falls out.

Johnny Appleseed leans over and picks it up. "Ah, a phoenix talon dagger!"

Clarke snaps with an irrational panic, "It's mine!"

Johnny Appleseed gives it back to him gently. "This has great power against the undead, but of course it's yours. What did you want to show me?"

Clarke takes the goblin dagger back and shows him the notebook, saying, "The head elf that shot the blackflame at us with his hand was reading from this book. It got a little wet when we went down the aqueduct but maybe you can make sense of it."

A knock at the door calls Dungaree Jeanne's attention. "What do we do with Louis? I don't want him to stink up the house."

Clarke says, "Don't worry! It's a warm night; we can sleep out on the porch. Do you have a pillow?"

The knock at the door turns into a low-grade bang. Clarke throws open the door and says, "Wait a little, Louis! We're getting some bedding."

Instead of Louis, he looks down and sees Major Leagues Umpire Gandorf Mithranderson standing on the threshold.

Umpire Gandorf sidesteps Clarke and walks inside without waiting for an invitation. He sees Zena and throws his arms around her, saying in Eldric, "Good evening, my dear daughter. Sorry to see your home invaded by all these humans. Where's your mother?"

Dungaree Jeanne steps forward. "I'm right here."

Umpire Gandorf turns to her and tries to give her the same warm hug he gave Zena, but Dungaree Jeanne remains stiff. He says with his most charming voice, "Madame Dungaree, you will have to excuse the importunity of visiting at this hour, but the matter is pressing and really cannot wait for morning."

Dungaree Jeanne walks to the parlor and says, "Please have a seat, Monsieur Umpire. As head of state, this matter must be truly important, given how many issues demand your attention at the moment."

Umpire Gandorf sniffs the air and comments, "There's quite an overpowering odor of skunk in the air. I sincerely hope one of those abominable creatures has not made its way to your doorstep."

"A large number of abominable creatures have made their way to my doorstep of late. It would hardly be fair of me to complain of just one more."

Umpire Gandorf laughs pleasantly and elbows her with a wink. "What a noble spirit you are, Madame Dungaree!" He then takes a seat on the sofa in the parlor and stretches his arms up in the air and starts speaking, animating his ideas with an abundance of hand gestures. "Our dearly departed monsieur Umpire-in-Chief's astrologer really messed up! He had Umpire Kibbler believing he would live at least another twenty years, surrounded by grandchildren, et cetera, et cetera, et cetera. I swear there was an ascendant conjunction that he missed or something.

"Anyway, I don't know much about astrology, but I do know business, and the Vandsee Estates are in total disarray right now.

"His head steward, a brilliant gnome by the name of Blunderbore, came to me before the council assembly and told me they have a shipment of cocoa beans they are supposed to pick up at Carlyle Fair. The shipment is so important that our dearly departed monsieur Umpire-in-Chief always led the convoy personally.

"Having been kept out of the loop on this one, Mister Blunderbore is afraid that if we miss this pickup at the Carlyle Fair, the Laymanite merchants won't risk hauling their precious cargo all the way to the fair next year. With both our dearly departed monsieur Umpire-in-Chief and Mademoiselle Florenz unable to manage the Vandsee Estates, you, Madame Dungaree, are poised for a spectacular business opportunity—the profit margins are in the tens of thousands of dollars."

Dungaree Jeanne looks at him skeptically. "If it's such a great opportunity, Monsieur Umpire, why are you asking me to do it? You could do it yourself."

"My inner greedy pig would certainly want that, Madame Dungaree; I assure you. With my sudden and unexpected promotion to head of state, and in this time of severe crises for the Tuscoraura elf community, I am shorthanded on staff as it is.

"This convoy is too important to leave to one of my junior underlings and I simply cannot attend to it personally. Not only does the financial solvency of the Kibbler workshops depend on that cocoa shipment, but with so many workers on his payrolls, the entire economy of Tuscoraura Mountain would be hit with a severe recession if his business shut down suddenly—hundreds of Tuscoraura elves, gnomes, humans, and dwarves would go unemployed in a single day. Financial crises would spark up from here to the bowels of the bedrock below us.

"I am not just asking you to get this job done, Madame Dungaree. I am asking you to assume control of the Vandsee Estates during Mademoiselle Florenz's absence. In view of our upcoming marriage alliance, your family's success is my family's success. As the Dungaree of Foreign Trade, no one would question why I handed this lucrative deal to you—you have the business savvy to pull this off. What do you say?"

Dungaree Jeanne leans back on the parlor sofa. "I'll think about it, Monsieur Umpire."

Umpire Gandorf shakes his head. "I'm sorry, Madame Dungaree, but it's too late for that. Carlyle Fair ends on Frige's Day next. Whoever goes has to start preparations immediately. If you don't accept my proposal right now, I'll have to offer it to Clan Chamara. It would be a pity, though, because I don't think they are nearly as capable as you."

"I don't like getting pressured into major commitments like this without knowing all the facts."

Flinging his hands around, Umpire Gandorf says, "Madame Dungaree, talk about getting pressured into major commitments without knowing all the facts! Our dearly departed monsieur Umpire-in-Chief asked me to head the Major Leagues hours after he found out about the captured goblin. Then he goes off and gets himself killed, leaving me the head of state.

"I know I'm offloading a major crisis from my plate onto your plate, but I have seven other major crises to deal with before I'm going to get any sleep tonight. Please, at least let me rest easy over this one."

Dungaree Jeanne looks at the top of his head as if trying to see if there are any horns or a halo sprouting out above it and then says, "Fine. Against my better judgment, I'll do this for you and for the colony. What are the details?"

Umpire Gandorf claps his hands together and says, "Atta girl! I knew I could count on you! It's all very simple really. Just head out to Carlyle Fair and ask for a Laymanite merchant who goes by the name of Zelph. Have your agent tell him the password, *swordfish*, and he'll show you the wares—ten loads of cocoa beans in sacks of eighty thousand beans each. Each sack weighs about two hundred pounds, so you'll need to figure enough pack animals to carry a ton of cocoa beans."

"How much is he expecting me to pay him?"

"Right now, cocoa beans are worth their weight in gold and the price is not negotiable—ten thousand dollars—and he won't accept Vinland coinage. You will have to bring either twenty-four thousand gold florins or twelve thousand silver marks or eight thousand pounds sterling. However, he is very interested in parsley, sage, rosemary, and thyme. He'll give you very good rates on those for bartering. Also, he pays well for cambric shirts."

Dungaree Jeanne likes this deal less and less. "Beans that expensive! Where's the profit?"

"The Vandsee Estates have a workshop that will process the beans into cocoa powder. It will cost you about two thousand dollars to cover the cost of processing the beans, but this shipment of cocoa beans will make enough powder to sell on the market for over twenty-four thousand dollars. You will double your investment on the cocoa powder alone, but you could triple your profits if you roll your product over into cookies, cakes, pastries, et cetera, et cetera, et cetera."

Dungaree Jeanne says, "That's all fine and dandy, Monsieur Umpire, but do you realize how much money is at risk? If my convoy goes south, or if any other incident occurs, I'd be ruined financially!"

He stands up and starts to leave. "Our dearly departed monsieur Umpire-in-Chief pulled this operation off flawlessly every year for the past twenty years. What could possibly go wrong under your expert management? Now if you'll excuse me, I have the remaining six major crises to handle before getting to bed tonight."

Dungaree Jeanne stands up, resigned to her fate. "Naturally, Monsieur Umpire. Mademoiselle Zena will show you to the door."

With a beaming smile, Zena offers her arm to Umpire Gandorf, who accepts it gracefully. They walk to the door and he looks back at Dungaree Jeanne saying, "Oh, and I do hope you get a new stewardess soon. Once Mademoiselle Zena is married to my son, she'll be treated like a princess. I certainly do hope the transition won't come as too much of a shock to her."

As soon as he walks out the door, Zena exclaims, "Oh, Mother! Isn't he simply charming! He'll make us the richest family in Shentalpee City!"

Dungaree Jeanne folds her arms. "Or ruin us. Mademoiselle Zena, I know you don't want to hear this, but I don't trust him one bit. Not one little bit."

Scene B: A Picnic to Remember

Wood Elf Village Green Leading off Wildcat's Base
Tiw's Day Prime. Early Morning, 18th of April, 1284
Eve of the Feast of Saint Aelfheah, Bishop and Martyr

Lynx's mother, Missus Cougar Highrule, knocks on the door to her only son's bedroom.

No answer.

This time she knocks and says loudly, "Knock! Knock!"

A weary voice calls through the door, "Who's there?"

"Your friend, Ben."

"Ben? Ben who?"

"Ben waiting for you to open this door!"

"Are you joking?"

"No! Reverend Appleseed and Madame Dungaree are waiting in the living room, along with those two humans. One of them smells like he got sprayed by a dead skunk."

Lynx calls out, "Oh snap! I'll be right there."

He throws on his wood elf clothes—now laundered and cleaned, thanks to his mother—since the high elf clothes that Dungaree Jeanne gave him are still too damp to wear. No matter how hard he combs, Lynx can't get the bed-head out of his hair. He puts on his bycocket cap (even though it is rude for elves to wear hats indoors) and walks out with a big smile. "Welcome to our humble home, dear friends!"

Johnny Appleseed, still in a wheelchair, gets lost in thought at how cozy this "humble" wood elf cottage is compared to the really humble homes he has seen in his travels. Poor halflings live in dugouts that are little more than nasty, dirty, wet holes, filled with the ends of worms and an oozy smell. Poor humans living above ground don't have it much better. They often cram six or more persons in a one-room cottage with compacted mud for flooring and that thatched roofs that only keep out the rain when fresh. Over time the thatching grows moldy, rotten, and gets riddled with wasp nests.

Despite being at the bottom of the elfin social strata, wood elves not only have well-worked wooden floors and lacquered wood shingles on their roof, they also have several rooms separated with wooden walls and wooden doors that afford a great deal of privacy. Though wood elves cannot afford high-elf-style upholstered furniture, they have enough tables, chairs, cabinets, and beds to make life comfortable. Nothing Appleseed sees here counts as "humble" in his mind.

Missus Cougar Arminsdottir of Clan Highrule welcomes them all in but the offensive odor relentlessly wafts off Louis in every direction. According to the rules for hospitality in elf culture, Missus Cougar cannot uninvite Louis from her house but she stews in frustration thinking how it might take several days with all the windows and doors open to eliminate the smell completely.

Dungaree Jeanne sees the conflict between politeness and horror on Missus Cougar's face and intervenes with great social grace. "Good morning, Monsieur Lynx! My friends and I are planning to picnic by the lake and we were wondering if you would care to join us. Naturally, your parents are more than welcome to join us if their schedule is not tied up."

Relief washes through Missus Cougar's brow and she replies theatrically, "Oh, Madame Dungaree, you are so kind; but we are so tied up that there is absolutely no way to untie it all. Even if we took a big knife to chop right through the knot we'd have more untying to do. We'll have to content ourselves with the knowledge of how greatly you honor our beloved son, Mister Lynx . . . I mean, *Monsieur* Lynx . . . with your august company."

"We then demand that you honor us with your company on some other occasion."

Missus Cougar starts walking them out of the house. "Oh, yes, Madame! I promise, and a promise is a promise. Well then, no sense standing around. You've got a lovely picnic to go to and we've got plenty of untying to do. Isn't that right, Mister Stallion."

From the couch, her young murk elf husband calls over, "Absolutely, my love."

With that, They head out to the lake.

After a pleasant stroll a little less than half a mile to the north, they reach Lake Fortinbras, named in honor of the great gnome sheriff of Nordland who established the alliance between the *hamnet knamar*—rock pile gnomes—and the *eldralfar*—fire elves. Together, they overcame the invasion of the flatland humans under King Claudius.

Poor Johnny Appleseed has to endure the undead skunk smell the whole way because Louis is the only one strong enough to wheel the chair over the rough trails of the wood elf village. Lynx, ever the brave elf, decides to stick with Johnny Appleseed to keep him company while Clarke and Dungaree Jeanne walk a comfortable distance ahead.

Knowing that Lynx is heartbroken after getting dumped by Zena in such a humiliating way, Johnny Appleseed asks, "Monsieur Lynx, would you mind if I speak to you a few words about Zena?"

Lynx nods. The broken, vulnerable look on Lynx's face is enough to make the heart of any father cry.

Johnny Appleseed struggles to hold back his tears. "When I was young, I fell madly in love with every beautiful maiden who noticed me. I was tall, rich, and loved music, so I got a lot of notice for my part, but I also got a lot of heartbreak out of it too. Several young ladies loved me for the wrong reasons and when I didn't play along with their romantic fantasies, they treated me with studied cruelty.

"As I got older, I realized that I was looking for love in all the wrong places. Instead, I started to focus on pleasing the Lord. It brought me a new freedom."

Lynx grows dour and slightly resentful. "You say I no love any elve anymore and I will be happy? It not happen that way. I do not choose elve I love. I cannot stop that I think about Zena."

Johnny Appleseed says, "You are right, Monsieur Lynx. You can't just stop thinking about Zena because then your heart would be empty and, as we say in Kentikie, nature abhors the void.

"All I'm getting at is that when you've got a second chance lined up, losing your first big chance at love isn't such a big deal. You've got something wonderful lined up for you, I'm sure; something much better."

Lynx replies, "You love Christian God so your heart not hurt anymore. But I am only new Christian. Now my love to Mademoiselle Zena is here." He pounds his chest. "My love to God is here." He taps his head. "Maybe when I become old like you I love Christian God and forget Mademoiselle Zena, but not now."

The pained and pensive eyes of his brave little elf friend wander off. Johnny Appleseed decides that he has said his piece and then keeps silent through the smelly ride out to Lake Fortinbras.

Just before they arrive at the lake, Dungaree Jeanne notices that Lynx has wandered off on his own. She catches up to him, takes his arm, and says, "Monsieur Lynx, I wish that congratulating you on earning your place in the Ivy League and becoming a high elf were an unmixed joy. My disappointment at my daughter's behavior can only be a fraction of the disappointment you feel. We shared heated words over it but her head is like a clay pot—the hotter the fire the harder it gets.

"However, I can make it up to you in a small way that will bring great profit and happiness to us both. As you know, our Magnificent Charter gives you eighty days from the time you are elevated to the rank of high elf to register suitable accommodations in Shentalpee City with the Council of Perfects or risk demotion.

"So, I am offering to hire you as the steward of my mansion. Bartlebee's old room is small, but it connects to the guest room as a suite. Once Reverend Appleseed is well enough to journey on, I can offer you his room as well. We can turn it into quite a respectable apartment if you allow me to help you with the furnishings and decorations. I will train you into your responsibilities little by little, aware that your commitment to the Ivy League comes first for the next four years. What do you say?"

Lynx brightens up like a lost kitten that has finally found a home. "But . . . but . . . I don't know what to say, Madame Dungaree."

They are already close to the lake so she says, "Good, then tell me you accept and I will explain your first quest for me as my steward."

Lynx, deeply touched, says, "I accept."

Dungaree Jeanne immediately switches to Aenglish and announces to the whole party, "Good. Now we must eat. Mister Louis, could we ask you to sit back some distance so the unfortunate cologne you are wearing does not spoil our appetites?"

Louis says, "No worries. I wanted to go swimming anyhow. Maybe it will take some of the stink off me." Louis unstraps his axe and his purse and leaps into the lake with all his clothes on.

With Louis splashing off in the background, Dungaree Jeanne huddles up the team and divvies out the trenchers of bread holding bits of cooked duck eggs, leeks, walnuts, and eel, flavored with salt, vinegar, mustard, onion, and garlic. Believe it or not, it never occurred to anyone to eat such a meal with an extra slice of bread on top until the Earl of Sandwich came along in Aengland several hundred years later. Back then, they just had to bite into their bread was more like a plate to hold the meat and vegetables.

Dungaree Jeanne announces in Aenglish as they eat, "Monsieur Lynx has accepted a position as my new steward. I put him in charge of my entire household. In that capacity, he will be in charge of this next quest. The Major Leagues Umpire asked me to pick up a shipment of cocoa beans from a Laymanite merchant at Carlyle Fair. This bodes well for Louis because that merchant also happens to sell peanut butter.

"The Major Leagues Umpire knows that many fire elves do not like us because we put out the blackflame. They believe Umpire Kibbler was a hero because he weaponized it and used it to summon the undead.

"Therefore, I believe this quest is a trap. Umpire Gandorf wants to use this 'business opportunity' to destroy the Dungaree family once and for all. I do not know what he plans to do with Mademoiselle Zena but as her mother, I am afraid."

Lynx says impetuously in Aenglish, "Then we not go. We stay here and stop Umpire Gandorf."

She pulls out another basket from the pouch on the wheelchair and says, "Look, duck eggs are fragile. I've intentionally put some in your basket and some in his basket so that if one basket should accidentally drop, we'd still have some duck eggs for our lunch. Umpire Gandorf never puts all his eggs in one basket. He has two plans—one if I say yes, and one if I say no.

"I'm taking my chances with saying yes because I have a good idea what he might be planning for us at Carlyle Fair. I have no clue what he'd be up to if I said no. We will buy the cocoa beans, but we will move the payment to Carlyle Fair from many directions. If he attacks us on the way out, I can call the whole business off with only a small loss.

"Monsieur Lynx, you will go to Carlyle Fair with Captain Manzone, Louis, and Clarke ahead of the main trade convoy. You will bring parsley, sage, rosemary, and thyme. You will give everything to my agent, Master Leevai Strauss. He will also bring a large number of cambric shirts to negotiate the price of the cocoa down and bring back to Tuscoraura the cocoa beans along with his regular shipment of denim.

Johnny Appleseed speaks up. "Madame Dungaree, you have been so kind to me during my period of convalescence that I would like to offer to pay you back with some little favor. As it happens, one of my apple orchards is not far from Carlyle and my orchard keepers usually sell their surplus there. I will give you as many fresh apples, dried apple chips, applesauce, apple butter, and apple seeds as I can spare."

Dungaree Jeanne bows deeply and says, "Reverend Appleseed, I wish I could decline such a generous offer, but for the sake of my family, for the sake of all the elves in Tuscoraura, I cannot."

Clarke interrupts, "Wait, how do you own an apple orchard? Don't you have a vow of poverty?"

"Jesus said, 'Blessed are the poor in spirit.' I live the life of a poor man like our Lord Jesus Christ, who, though he was rich, became poor so that through his poverty we might become rich. I inherited substantial landholdings from my father and invested the income wisely. My farms, estates, and apple orchards now stretch across Vinland. My right hand does not know what my left hand gives out but it might be enough food to feed one hundred twenty thousand persons and much livestock."

"Wow!"

"Reverend Appleseed, you are always full of surprises. Now, Monsieur Lynx and Mister Clarke, you will have one day to arrange the payment of the cocoa beans with Master Leevai. While you are seeing to that, all the bravos under Captain Manzone will be going to the highways and the byways hiring adventurers, mercenaries, and anyone who can hold their own in a fight. When we all join up, we will travel as swiftly as possible to the Tuscoraura marchlands.

"We will only have half of the cocoa shipment with us. Master Leevai will hide the other half in sacks of corn, squash, and beans, and ship them on a boat to Harrisburgh. Again, two baskets for our eggs."

"How will we know Master Leevai Strauss?"

"I sent a message by Pony Express to him with a detailed description of this plan. He is smart, and he will find you. He will say the password, *Blue Danube*."

Lynx says in Eldric, "Speaking of the Pony Express, I have two letters that must be sent out urgently. The first is for the Holy Office of the Inquisition in Salim in the duchy of Masswachoosut Bay, confirming Reverend Appleseed's reconciliation with the Church. The second certifies that the rangers encamped in the marchlands completed their quest for the inquisitor."

Dungaree Jeanne takes them. "Of course, Monsieur Lynx, I will make sure they get to their destinations."

Johnny Appleseed, looking up, says, "That reminds me. Clarke, do you remember that ritual book you gave me? You said Umpire Kibbler used it to shoot blackflame. It was stolen from my room last night."

Dungaree Jeanne snaps her fingers and looking up she says, "That's right! Umpire Gandorf came in moments after Clarke gave it to you. He must have recognized it. No doubt he has played a part in Umpire Kibbler's attempts to summon the undead."

Lynx says in Aenglish, "We know so. In Vandsee Estates we hear Umpire Kibbler say that Umpire Gandorf must play stormcrow."

Appleseed gasps, "Stormcrow? Ugh!"

"What is it?"

"This situation is dire—far worse than I had imagined—and it's all my fault. I must write the Holy Office of the Inquisition and let them know that the Sword of Layban must be here."

"The what?"

Johnny Appleseed explains, "If Umpire Gandorf knows about the stormcrow, then he very likely has the Sword of Layban. The Hill Dwarves of Cumorah hid it, along with the Breastplate of Layban, long ago to prevent it from unleashing untold evils across Vinland, but with their recent change of leadership, nothing is sacred—if the price is right."

Lynx speaks up despite the knot in his throat. "What if Inquisition keep Sword of Layban for Inquisition? We have big problem, no?"

"Impossible," states Johnny Appleseed. "For as much as I don't like their heavy-handed style, I am quite sure the inquisitors would never be so foolish as to meddle with the Sword of Layban."

Scene C: Carlyle Fair

Village Green, Town of Carlyle
in the Aenglish Lordship of Vinland
Woden's Day Sext. Noontide, 19th of April, 1284
Feast of Saint Aelfheah, Bishop and Martyr

The scene of gaiety and mirth at Carlyle Fair is no stranger to Lynx and Captain Manzone but as for Louis and Clarke, who have spent their childhoods in a sweatshop and a monastery, respectively, the colors and liveliness on the fairgrounds mesmerize them.

Until recently, fairs have been a church hosted and organized event. But King Eddard has decreed this kind of romping fun inappropriate for a churchyard and now all Aenglish fairs are held out in village greens or open fields.

Carlyle Fair lies just outside the city walls, so people can come and go as they please. The event is heavily policed by armored sergeants, and non-violence is strictly enforced by ecclesiastical and civil authorities. Even the thieves are limited to stealing nothing more than a coin or two from each mark. They can never steal enough to ruin someone's day or else a reported theft could provoke a shakedown of the entire Thieves' Guild, leading to torture-extracted confessions from anyone who might remotely fit the description of a possible thief. When King Eddard means business, he is as efficient in cruelty as in counting coins.

Across the Carlyle plains jugglers, musicians, acrobats, and troupes of strolling players do everything from slapstick comedy routines to reenacting famous scenes from the Bible. They don't all work for tips. Some are employed by the wealthy vendors to attract customers to their stalls like live-action television commercials, complete with slogans and jingles.

At the edge of the fairgrounds, chaos greets Lynx's party of adventurers. A cranberry and apple juice seller with a huge ceramic jug in a wicker basket strapped to his back comes up to them and offers them a free swig of juice as a sample. He has four wooden cups latched to his belt. He offers Clarke a free sample of his juice, but the wooden cup has mud caked around the rim.

Coming from a monastery, Clarke is used to clean cups and says, "It's dirty."

The vendor rubs his fingers along the edge, mixing the mud into the juice. "There you go! All clean now!"

Clarke is thirsty but he just says, "Thanks. I'll pass."

The juice vendor passes the muddy cup to Louis, who gulps it down. The juice is cool, refreshing, and tasty, despite the mud flavor. Wiping his mouth with his sleeve he asks, "How much?"

"A dime for a small cup and a quarter for the big."

"Wow! That's expensive."

"It's a fair fare for a fair."

Louis grunts, "Whatever, I'm just really thirsty. You got change for a penny?"

"Big cup or small cup?"

"Big cup."

Louis hands him the penny and the juice vendor hands him three large silver farthings. Louis gulps the juice down and the vendor walks away.

Captain Manzone mumbles something to Lynx in Eldric and Lynx tells Louis in Aenglish, "Captain Manzone say coins no good."

"What do you mean?"

Lynx confers with Captain Manzone and tries to explain the difference. "Big silver farthing from Lunden have only little silver in it. No one take it. Small silver farthing from York is good or big copper quarter from Baston is good. He say if you want to buy at fair you must get good coin from moneychanger."

Dungaree Jeanne has given them all a generous spending allowance in Tuscoraura gold eagles and silver dollars. Even at the wildly inflated prices at the fair, most vendors refuse to make change, and those that do just rip them off by handing them debased or clipped coins. On top of those difficulties, Tuscoraura coins are prized locally for their purity but are unknown abroad, so foreign merchants refuse to accept them. The florin, a one-pound gold coin from Firenze, and the sterling silver penny from Lunden, enjoy the best international reputation so despite the fees charged at the moneychanger tables, it's well worth the price to have the right coins to enjoy the fair.

While Captain Manzone and Lynx try to help Louis exchange his coins, Clarke stands by a circle of dancers doing a rondelet accompanied by an older woman fiddling on the viol and a young man strumming on a lyre. A heavyset dwarf woman plays the portative organ while a group of halflings slap their tambourines.

The dance is simple. Everyone faces right, holds hands with the person in front and the person in back, and takes two steps forward and then leans back and takes a half step behind, following the rhythm of the music and tambourines. Clarke feels guilty merely for watching the dancers because he is still wearing his shredded clerical monk's robes.

Suddenly, he gets an idea. No need to maintain appearances. He's not a real cleric anymore. Clarke visits some clothing merchants and finds a readymade tunic and a pair of hose (pant legs that you tie to your belt—definitely not tights). He invests in a nice pair of boots and then visits a barber.

Technically, it's illegal to trim away a monk's tonsure since the bald spot helps ecclesiastical authorities in tracking down runaway monks, but Clarke's hair has been growing in for several weeks. An upfront payment with a big tip overrules all curiosity from the barber. A few snips later, Brother David has cut the last of his ties with his former life as a monk.

By the time he checks in with Louis, Lynx, and Captain Manzone, they don't even recognize him. Guessing his new look is complete, he goes off and watches the rondelet up close. A pretty young halfling opens up the circle and he joins in the dancing, making merry until he drips with sweat and runs out of breath.

Having lost track of time, he takes a break and heads over to the stalls where pushy vendors are selling snacks. He buys a small blackbird pie and a big mug of sage water, mostly because the meat pie vendor seems to be the only one willing accept the change the clothing merchants gave him.

As Clarke munches and sips, wanders past a pair of jugglers. The first wobbles on stilts while tossing tomahawks back and forth with a partner on a large, round barrel. Farther afield he sees a fire sorcerer impressing the crowd with floating fireballs and giant, colorful explosions.

Closer to the central green, a bear dances to a happy tune. Acrobats pole-vault and tight-rope their way onto impossibly small makeshift towers and then leap down from them. Instead of breaking their legs, they tumble, roll, and execute even more impressive backward falls, forward handsprings, and flips.

Only now does Clarke begin to realize the full commercial significance of a fair. He sees spice merchants dressed in exotic articles of clothing that he does not even have names for. Other foreign merchants specialize in perfumes, rugs, expensive fabrics, specialty weapons and armor, scrolls and books made out of paper, amate, papyrus, parchment, and vellum.

Craftsmen of every imaginable guild are present, but those who specialize in high-end, luxury-priced goods are most likely to consider renting a stall at this fair worth the expense. Chandlers have wax candles available at a premium price and tallow candles for sale in bulk. In some of the more modest stalls away from the central fairgrounds, coopers proudly display their wares—casks, barrels, buckets, tubs, and butter churns. Yet a little farther afield farriers, loriners, and saddlers stand ready like a pit crew to smooth your ride on any type or size of hoofed mount, including ponies, horses, donkeys, mules, reindeer, moose, and boar.

Some races seem to dominate certain crafts. Elves from Tuscoraura and elsewhere overrepresent the Broderers' Guild with embroidered caps, saddle pads, blankets, capes, shirts, dresses, and stockings available in astoundingly intricate patterns. Several journeyman broderers stand ready to enhance any fabric you bring to them, like tattoo artists for your clothes. Elf cordwainers offer the finest quality leather shoes with revolutionary technologies in converse fitting, extra wide footwear for halflings and dwarves, and sizes that extend from tiny toddler elf shoes to sandals huge enough to fit any Sasquatch troll with a big foot. Naturally, with the great importance of expensive ornaments in their culture, elf jewelers have no peer.

The halfling branch of the Mercers' Guild offers the very best in traveling provisions, such as preserved cheeses, salt, biscuits, raisins, and dried meats. They are a little pricey, but the flavor they imbue into hardtack borders on gourmet quality as opposed to the maggoty, dried-up bread some goblins try to sell. Bakers, butchers, and fishmongers have an almost religious status among halflings and bring the highest standards of quality to those fields. They are also the finest brewers, dyers, and apothecaries available. Herbal remedies, healing mushrooms, and poultices made from various roots and berries are all common knowledge among most gnomes in Vinland, so the corresponding guild standards among gnomes are much higher than with other races.

By far and away the majority of human Vinlander stalls are piled high with furs. Some humans enjoy being uprooted, living in the wild, and tolerate isolation and the constant stress of danger better than all other races except trolls and goblins. The abundance of furry creatures in Vinland has become a major source of wealth for many of the native and colonial explorers in this land. Only recently have they begun to realize that stocks are dwindling, but the rugged individualism that makes them so brave and hardy prevents them from seeing any value in missing out on profits for the sake of abstract concepts like ecology and environmentalism, which hadn't yet been invented. So, they continue to overhunt our poor, furry friends.

At the other end of the spectrum, humans excel at farming, husbandry, and orchard-keeping. Along with those come vintners, wool men, spinners, and weavers. Fabrics are the mainstay of many human communities, especially those from Aengland and Vlameers. Humans generally corner the fruit markets but the vegetable trade is split, since halflings all excel in cultivating underground vegetables like leeks, onions, turnips, carrots, radishes, garlic, beets, and the recently arrived Nawak cash crop, potatoes.

Dwarves, of course, are famous for their smithies. Dwarf steel mail is the strongest armor in the world and offers the best protection with minimal restrictions on movement. Dwarves obsess over swords and blades of all types and love to contrive devious and lethal new bladed weapons. A significant minority of them prefer to give the hurt with wicked bludgeon weapons instead—clubs, maces, hammers, mallets, mauls, batons, staves, and flails. Their masons, plasterers, and plumbers have enough advanced engineering skills to build sophisticated housing with hot and cold running water. Believe it or not, thanks to the dwarves, pipes with running water and on-demand faucets, as well as sewage, have been available in Vinland throughout most of its history after Leif Erikson—for those willing and able to invest their large fortunes in domestic comforts instead of war. Granted, in those war-like times, such individuals were few and far between.

Dwarves are without doubt the most relentless and efficient miners, skinners, tanners, and smelters, but they do not always become the best curriers or leather armorers. Leatherworking is an industry where equal opportunity allows a dedicated artisan of any race to rise to the top. When it comes to fletchers and bowyers, the best crossbow makers are dwarves. Goblins make the best self-bows (flat bows), humans make the best composite bows (war bows), though human longbows are seeing a revival, especially in Welchland and Aengland, and elves make the best recurve bows (short bows). Halflings specialize in slings.

After checking out the various merchant stalls, Clarke sees Lynx and runs over to greet him. Not recognizing the new haircut and clothes, Lynx starts moving away until Clarke calls after him, "Wait up, Lynx! It's me, Clarke!"

"Oh, Brother Clarke," replies Lynx. "I not know you like that. You have new hair and new clothes."

Lynx says, "In elf culture we say *authur* when you cut hair, like to say, you look more rich now that your hair is so nice."

Clarke sticks his hand in his purse. "Thank you, but actually, I'm quite a bit poorer now. I've used up almost everything Dungaree Jeanne gave me. What have you been up to, Hare Gipper?"

Lynx replies, "I see archery tournament and I pay one penny to do it. On first round we are one hundred yard and I shoot all three arrow on middle target. I say to myself that I am good and will shoot two eye at fifty yard, but it was not like this. On second round we shoot one hundred fifty yard. On third round we shoot two hundred yard and I only hit target one time."

Clarke says, "At least you tried. Where's Louis?"

"Louis does good. Look there!" Lynx points to a tournament where a pitcher tosses an apple and the contestant has to split the apple in half with an axe as it flies through the air. Louis has just beaten the high score of twelve apples in a row. He splits number thirteen and then takes a slice out of fourteen. A judge comes in and inspects apple fourteen and declares it good. The crowd throws its hands up in a wild cheer.

Overcome by the unexpected burst of support from the crowd, Louis grows a bit self-conscious and whiffs the fifteenth apple. The contest rules entitle him to keep all the apples he split but he calls out to the crowd, "Anyone want some free apples?"

The mad rush of apple eaters suddenly stops when the wall of foul skunk odor coming from Louis hits the crowd. Their enthusiasm for him dies instantly and they clear the field, shaking their fists at him. Disappointed at the fickleness of the crowd, Louis has to pay for a burlap bag to gather up his sliced apples and then rejoins Lynx. Louis doesn't recognize Clarke at first. "Hi, I'm Louis of Joliette. How about you?"

Clarke laughs and says, "I was Brother David the Clarke this morning, but after this haircut, no one seems to even recognize me. I guess I'll be plain old Clarke from now on."

Louis's eyes pop open and he gives Clarke an affirming look of recognition. "Yeah! I like the new look. So where did Captain Manzone go?"

A man with a wide-brimmed, tall, yellow hat with a white jerkin around his shoulders and a royal-blue overcoat approaches, followed by Captain Manzone. The man in the yellow hat bows with a flourish and says, "You, gentlemen, look like you'd be up for a waltz down the *Blue Danube*."

They all look at him with crossed eyes until Clarke says, "Oh yeah! The password!"

The man with the yellow hat has a capuchin monkey riding on his shoulder and says in good Aenglish with a barely perceptible Avrith accent, "Good to meet you, friends. Now, please come with me. There are too many open ears on these fields."

They walk to the edge of the fairgrounds and as they proceed, they notice a growing number of professional sergeants and men-at-arms tailing them until they arrive at a large tent fenced off by five fully loaded wagons linked together in the shape of a pentagon.

Entering the tent, he touches a mezuzah sewn onto the tent flap and then kisses his hand.

Clarke asks, "Am I supposed to kiss that too?"

The man with the yellow hat replies, "Inside are the words, 'Hear, O Israel: The Lord our God, the Lord is one. Love the Lord your God with all your heart and with all your soul and with all your strength. These commandments that I give you today are to be on your hearts. Impress them on your children. Talk about them when you sit at home and when you walk along the road, when you lie down and when you get up. Tie them as symbols on your hands and bind them on your foreheads. Write them on the doorframes of your houses and on your gates.'"

Clarke touches it and kisses his hand. Lynx copies the gesture and so does Louis. Captain Manzone is not a religious elf but he decides to go with the flow.

Telltale signs of wealth abound around the man in the yellow hat—the pet monkey, the white ermine fur jerkin around his shoulder, the numerous and well-armed bodyguards—but inside the tent it is as plain as a soldier's barracks. A few cots line the edge of the tent, which is easily spacious enough to fit twenty people comfortably and perhaps thirty uncomfortably. The only other furniture is a fold-up writing desk, a few chests, and three collapsible benches.

The side flaps are left open to allow daylight inside. The pentagon-shaped wagon fort is the main barrier against prying eyes that will allow them to discuss confidential military secrets.

The man with the yellow hat gestures to the benches with a sweep of his hands and they all sit down. Their host welcomes them and asks them to introduce themselves. After Lynx, Louis and Clarke tell him a little bit about themselves. Master Strauss says, "My name is Master Leevai Strauss, Grand Master of the Merchants' Guild in Harrisburgh. Only yesterday, I received the letter from Madame Jeanne Ranglursdottir explaining in great detail the situation confronting the Tuscoraura elves and the Inquisition's threat to call a Crusade for dabbling with necromancy.

"My heritage is Jewish, so such religious disputes among Christians generally do not concern me, but I also have little interest in seeing Vinland overrun by armies of undead elves and revenant wild monsters.

"A few of my convoys have already suffered attacks from these elf wendigos and if Dungaree Jeanne says this quest is vital to stopping more crazed undead wights and monsters, then I will do everything in my power to make sure it succeeds. My business deal with Dungaree Jeanne has been extremely profitable and has helped me amass one of the top five hundred largest fortunes in Vinland.

"Once upon a time, when I was a young fabric merchant just starting out in the business world, I agreed to give Dungaree Jeanne all the free denim she should want in return for half of the pants and jackets she designed and tailored with those materials. My profits on the open market from the fancy clothing she produced started trends and fads that put over one thousand percent profits into my company with each exchange. I began shipping Dungaree Jeanne's sturdy and fashionable clothes across Vinland. Although we branded them officially as Dungaree Jeanne's denim pantaloons, coats, and overalls, Aenglish men and women started to called them Leevai's.

"Enough about me. We have a quest to complete. Captain Manzone has already delivered to me the shipment of parsley, sage, rosemary, and thyme. Mounted scouts from my private guard are going out to link up with Johnny Appleseed's shipment of produce from his apple orchard nearby.

"So far, so good—everything has gone according to plan. But Dungaree Jeanne guessed that no one would try to interfere with our setup. We'll be most vulnerable on the way into the marchlands, so that is probably where Umpire Gandorf will strike—"

Clarke interrupts him, asking, "If you know where and when you will be attacked, why go?"

"Dungaree Jeanne is in a delicate position. If she does not carry through with this shipment, she will be blamed for allowing the Kibbler family business to collapse. It is clear from her letter that Umpire Gandorf is doing his best to discredit the Dungaree family in order to smooth the way for his son, Enganyon, to become the next umpire-in-chief instead of Zena.

Louis asks, "So what do we do next?"

Master Leevai Strauss raises his eyebrows. "For now, go and buy whatever armor and weapons you think you will need to acquit yourself well in a fight."

Clarke objects, "I spent my life in a monastery. I don't know how to fight!"

Master Leevai gets up and goes into a chest. He pulls out a crossbow and says, "Here, take this. This crossbow is powerful enough to pierce even dwarf steel mail with a direct hit and it's got a winch to crank it, in case your arms get tired. Just point and shoot, and if you hit the bad guys, you'll do some damage. In my employ is an expert marksman named William Tell. Ask for him by name when you get outside and he'll give you a little basic training on how to use it effectively in battle."

Scene D: Superstitions of Freedom

Village Green, Town of Carlyle
Thor's Day Prime. Early Morning, 20th of April, 1284
Morrow of the Feast of Saint Aelfheah

The next morning, Master Leevai Strauss informs the party of adventurers that he has successfully purchased all ten bags of cocoa beans and he brings Louis a jar of peanut butter and some rags. Louis, Clarke, and Lynx go down with Master Leevai to the watering hole to help him lather him up with the peanut butter and scrub off the smell that has been plaguing him for the past few days.

Oddly enough, Master Leevai's monkey, George, follows them down to the watering hole but keeps his distance. After the peanut butter has removed the skunk smell, the monkey's curiosity overwhelms him and he jumps onto Louis's shoulder and snatches the jar of peanut butter out of his hands. Leaping away to the safety of a mulberry bush, the curious little monkey scoops out a handful of peanut butter for a snack.

Lynx chases the monkey but Louis calls out, "Don't scare him! He'll drop the peanut butter jar! I want the rest of that."

Clarke joins the chase. "Oh, it's all in good fun!"

The monkey stops to scratch his nose. Lynx and Clarke are about to sneak up on the monkey when a traveling vendor comes up and yells, "Half a pound of tuppenny rice! Half a pound of treacle! Mix it up and make it nice! Thruppence for a pound is my bargain price!"

Alerted by the vendor's caterwauling, the monkey notices Lynx and Clarke sneaking up on him and jumps back into the mulberry bush.

In frustration, Louis shouts, "No thank you! We are not interested in any treacle!"

The three adventurers chase the monkey around the mulberry bush until Lynx says in Aenglish, "I hide behind mulberry bush. You chase and I jump out."

The trap is set, but once Louis and Clarke make their move, another itinerant vendor steps us and says, "A penny for a spool of thread! Another for a needle! Together for seven quarters."

"Oh no!" they moan.

Frightened by the vendor's publicizing, the monkey runs past them all and climbs up a tent pole with the peanut butter jar cradled under his left arm.

While these antics go on, Dungaree Jeanne arrives at the fair, riding up at the head of an elf warband through the forest of tents and stalls. One dozen moose riders stick out high above the crowd carrying long, thin lances and recurve bows.

A well-bred war moose averages twenty-one hands from hoof to shoulder, offering the heavily armored elfin moose riders perches that start off seven feet above the ground. Adding to the effect with their high saddles and tall, colorful helmet plumes, the imposing moose riders reach in height two or three feet higher than even the tallest human knights on their warhorses.

They are the most expensive of all mercenaries and not always worth the cost. Although moose can charge at high speeds with their eight-foot-wide antlers, they are not endurance animals and cannot gallop for long. They are especially lethargic in warm weather, when they risk overheating. They cannot sweat like horses, so their riders must constantly cool them off with water during a battle. Their saddles are crafted with built-in wooden shields like compact mobile towers to protect the rider but the moose bulls themselves cannot tolerate body armor because the insulation makes regulating body temperature even more difficult. Slow, huge, and unarmored, they are easy targets for ranged troops.

For all their liabilities, a well-timed moose charge can crush heavily armored infantry and can bowl over even the best human knights on their large warhorses if handled with expert precision. Some moose riders also have an extra ace up their sleeve, or rather, on their back—a tank of elf fire with a pressurized siphon hose and hand pump that can shoot bursts of flames up to twenty yards.

Riding on a stout and noble reindeer, Dungaree Jeanne herself wears elf leather armor with a war spear in hand and a short sword at her side. A round shield, a recurve bow, and a quiver full of poisoned arrows are strapped to her saddlebag. Another fifty reindeer outriders follow close behind her, similarly armed. Behind them on foot jogs a contingent of forty or so Ivy League scouts.

Dungaree Jeanne and the captain of the Ivy League scouts approach the mulberry bush where Louis, Clarke, and Lynx have been chasing the monkey. The captain looks at Lynx, stripped down to his britches. When Lynx sees him, the laughing dies down.

The Ivy League captain calls to him in Runic, hoping the wood elf will not understand his elevated speech, "Art thou Mister Weasel Cougarson of Clan Highrune? I am Captain Bucklead!"

The monkey at the top of the tent pole finishes the peanut butter and drops the clay jar.

POP!

The jar shatters. The Ivy League captain jolts, then does his best to look calm and dignified. Lynx salutes and says in one of the few Runic phrases he knows well, "Junior Officer Lynx Cougarson of Clan Highrule reporting for duty, Monsieur Captain."

The captain replies in Runic, "A correction is in order. Mister Lynx Cougarson of Clan Highrune, I am Captain Bucklead Yallson of Clan Boneswen. This affidavit testifies that the Monsieur Major Leagues Umpire himself has sponsored thy commission into the Ivy League. Unlike some reports that thou hast heard, admission into the Ivy League is not an empty token of privilege that can be bandied about by any spoiled brat who has the family ties or political connections to obtain it. It must be earned. The Magnificent Charter allows us the right to demand an admission test. Listen carefully to the dean's decree."

Captain Bucklead pulls out a scroll, unravels it, and reads in Runic: "Hear ye, hear ye! To help protect and honor the legacy of our dearly departed monsieur Umpire-in-Chief, the Monsieur Dean of the Ivy League Halvard Prinson has offered to escort this shipment of cocoa beans and by this means hopes to keep the Kibbler workshops running for the benefit of the entire colony of Tuscoraura elves."

He then rolls up the scroll and tells Lynx in Runic, "The condition for thy membership is to keep to the trees without descending to the forest floor from Green Spring to the Tuscoraura marchlands. Buy whatever equipment thou may need for the journey quickly and fall in with the company within the hour. We shall set out from the western road of the fairgrounds."

Though he misses a few words here and there, the general sense of Captain Bucklead's message is clear as day to Lynx. Shocked at hearing the draconian requirement for his admission to the Ivy League, Lynx forces himself to look brave and unintimidated. He salutes and says in a mix of Runic and Eldric, "Yes, Monsieur Captain, I will gear up at once."

Dungaree Jeanne gasps. She halts the Ivy League captain and says in Runic, "Monsieur Captain, dost thou realize how much this shall slow down our convoy? There is a reason the mercenaries I hired are all mounted. If thou wishest to help us with scouting thy help is welcome, but I shall not endanger the lives of my employees and the economy of Tuscoraura simply to accommodate thy puerile attempt to haze my friend and fellow high elf, Monsieur Lynx."

Captain Bucklead hardens his face. "May I remind thee, Madame Dungaree, that Mister Lynx is still technically a wood elf until he has passed his admission test. If the Ivy League refuses his application for a commission, which we have the right to do, then he cannot be considered a high elf and his candidacy for umpire-in-chief will be invalidated."

Dungaree Jeanne nods her head. "And with only one candidate left, the Council of Perfects shall cancel the upcoming election which my daughter, Mademoiselle Zena, is now sure to win."

Captain Bucklead puffs up his chest. "Admittedly, my political allegiances oppose the concept of an *arriviste* umpire-in-chief, Madame Dungaree, but permit me to assure thee that I have nothing to do with these orders or their political consequences. I am a soldier and I obey orders whether they conform to my inclinations or not."

Dungaree Jeanne replies, "Whether it conforms to thy inclination or not, thou art the key pawn in a very dirty game of power. Permit me to remind thee that at this level of the game of politics, there are only two outcomes—win or die. If thou dost anything—anything at all—to sabotage the safety of my people, as leader of this military expedition, I will have thee summarily executed for treason. I would rather take my chances defending my actions in a court of law than risk us all fending for our lives trapped in an ambush."

"So be it, Madame Dungaree. Orders are orders, and I act according to the best decisions of my conscience. I hope thy conscience is as clean as mine at the end of this quest."

Dungaree Jeanne does not wish to speak to the knave any longer. She looks up and sees a shirtless Lynx, having washed himself in the waterhole, emerging dripping wet with rippling muscles shining in the warm rays of the morning sun. She shuffles off the awkward spell by asking him in Eldric, "Monsieur Lynx, do you need more money for the equipment?"

Lynx grimaces. "I have no idea how much that kind of equipment is supposed to cost."

She says briskly, "Put your shirt on and follow me. I will make the necessary purchases for you. We leave within the hour."

By the end of that hour, Master Leevai has already transformed his wagon fort into a mobile battle convoy. Having divested himself of most of his goods, he sends his most trusted party of adventurers east disguised as poor farmers carrying vegetables to Harrisburgh. In reality their sacks contain all his coinage and half the shipment of cocoa beans. For now, his wagons now no longer serve as mobile trading posts, but are boarded up and reinforced like tanks. His foot soldiers hang onto the sides like riders on a downtown trolley.

Louis and Clarke purchase some leather vambraces, greaves, and a reinforced cuirass each. Louis likes the look of the crossbow Master Leevai gifted to Clarke but can only afford a small, secondhand, manual cocking crossbow for himself from a human bowyer merchant. Having spent his pennies lavishly or gotten ripped off at nearly every end of the fairgrounds, Louis cannot even afford crossbow bolts.

Dungaree Jeanne confers with Master Leevai in Aenglish. "Bad news—we have to take to the forest route from Green Spring to the Forge Hill Gap."

"Why don't we go over Blue Mountain? It won't be easy, but we could hold off a much larger force if we get attacked there."

"Apparently the monsieur Umpire thought of that too. He sent the Ivy League to 'escort' us but they are really here to force Monsieur Lynx to shadow our convoy from the trees. If he touches the forest floor, they will refuse to admit him into the Ivy League.

"The only forest dense enough for Monsieur Lynx to follow us from the trees is Lurgan Forest. No doubt that is where the ambush is planned."

Master Leevai scratches his head. "Too bad for the kid, but I'm not getting us all killed for his career."

"Monsieur Umpire Gandorf has us boxed in. If Monsieur Lynx fails, they will have to cancel the elections. As acting head of state, Monsieur Umpire

Gandorf will have plenty of time and leverage to make sure his son gets elected instead of Mademoiselle Zena. Once Monsieur Enganyon takes control of the government, he will not need the excuse of a trade convoy to have us all killed. As I said before, when it comes to the games of elf politics, we either win or die."

Moving around her, Master Leevai opens a tent flap and presents a large party of armored dwarves. "Okay, since it's going to be all or nothing, let me introduce you to a famous company of mercenaries—the Magnificent Eight. Oberst Schneevitchen, a dwarf warmaiden who performs well both in open battle and in games of intrigue, is their leader. They will have an important and nearly impossible quest to accomplish."

Dungaree Jeanne shakes her head uncomfortably. "If Oberst Schneevitchen and her seven dwarves are such magnificent warriors, you should not divert them away from our convoy on a quest. At this point, I have to ask what quest could be more important than getting those cocoa beans to Tuscoraura Mountain intact?"

"Their quest is getting you back to Tuscoraura Mountain alive."

The morning is still young and the entire convoy assembles on the west road leading out of the Carlyle fairgrounds. In addition to reinforcing his five regular wagons for combat conditions, Master Leevai has rented out two battlewagons. All the wagons have arrow slits and resealable loopholes in the sides, but the battlewagons are reinforced with steel bands and have crenellated ramparts up top for ranged soldiers.

Dungaree Jeanne moves out along the road close behind him, surrounding herself with her regular employees, all trusted friends and relatives, riding reindeer, and well-equipped for battle.

Together, their setup very much resembles a chessboard. Master Leevai's command wagon is like the king piece insofar as Master Leevai himself is not a combatant, but his army is powerful and depends on his presence for their cohesion and direction. Master Leevai's own battlewagon serves as the command center. In addition to the standard military features, this command center battlewagon has an artillery scorpion fixed up top with adjustable sights for anti-personnel targeting on the run.

Dungaree Jeanne resembles the queen piece on a chessboard in the sense that, as a reindeer rider, she is highly mobile, but the troops under her direct command are not the mainstay of the army.

Two companies of clerics represent the bishop pieces. On Master Leevai's side is a mobile synagogue for Jewish clerics. Though we do not normally refer to Jewish religious leaders as clerics, the role they play on the battlefield puts them in a similar class as clerics in the Christian and Islamic traditions. Moreover, this unit of Jewish clerics, who refer to themselves as Bikur Holim, based on a Hebrew term for extending aid to the sick, do not all qualify as rabbis—some are cantors, scholars, or holy lay men and women.

The Jewish clerics have a variety of roles. There are hakamim, or wise men—wisdom-based clerics who delve deep into the mysteries of the Torah—and hazanim, or cantors—charisma-based clerics who invoke and evoke God's power with their melodious voices, good looks, and popularity in the community. Like the Augustinian clerics on Dungaree Jeanne's side, the Bikur Holim clerics focus first and foremost on healing wounded soldiers, but unlike Christian clerics, all Jewish clerics also have the ability to invoke God's wrath to smite their foes—causing them to get suddenly ill or confusing them to the point where they attack each other. Some have even called upon the angel of death to strike down the firstborn among their enemies, and others have made city walls crumble at the sound of a shofar.

For her side, Dungaree Jeanne has hired Christian clerics, both male and female. Despite being dressed in sacred robes called habits, they are not monks or nuns. They are actually canons and canonesses—whose community way of life follows the rule of Saint Augustine—thus they are known as Augustinians.

Although they receive wages for their services, these gnomish, dwarven, and human clerics are not technically mercenaries but rather stipendiary clerics. Stipendiary clerics do not receive tithes from the people of a parish or tenants of lands owned by a monastery. Instead they must travel, hiring out their religious services to the highest bidder. Although this may seem a trivial distinction to modern readers, it is important in the eyes of canon law, which strictly prohibits clergy from hiring themselves out as battlefield mercenaries.

Canon law does not bar clerics from combat, but it does forbid them from attacking first and requires them to carry only blunt melee weapons for self-defense. Under these restrictions, their contributions to the battlefield are said to be oblique rather than direct, as represented by the bishops' diagonal movements on a chessboard. Essentially, they pray for the healing of wounded warriors, invoke special blessings to buff those who are in combat, and ward off attacks by enemies who dabble in the spirit realm.

The cavalry units represent the knight pieces. For that purpose, Master Leevai has hired a company of mercenary heavy cavalry who call themselves the Knights of the Round Table, after the famous Arthurian legends. Their roster includes humans on huge war horses, dwarves on powerful war donkeys, and gnomes on stout war ponies. With them are a few lighter support cavalry—human squires to replace equipment and ferry any dismounted knights out of the combat zone, as well as gnome hound jockeys to hunt down any mobile or hidden ranged units the slow-moving knights cannot neutralize. Dwarves do not have light military units of any type but their donkey-mounted crossbow dwarves, though heavily armored, serve a similar role, since they are a mobile missile unit.

Dungaree Jeanne's cavalry constitutes the bulk of her mercenary army. They are a company of mercenary reindeer scouts calling themselves the Rough Riders. Their roster is the inverse composition of the Knights of the Round Table—nearly all light cavalry, with a few moose heavy cavalry and armored boar riders in reserve. Captain Gunnar Sveltson is a war-scarred elf who got elected leader of the Rough Riders by his peers for being without a doubt the roughest of them all.

At the flanks, the specialist troops represent the rook pieces. On his side, Master Leevai has hired an outfit of human battlemages and battlesages calling themselves the Skybrim. To avoid confusion, allow me to clarify the differences between battlesages and battlemages. Battlesages are sages, master sorcerers, who specialize in the use of lodestones on the battlefield—drawing in or driving away metallic objects. Earth sorcery works best on iron and steel but also affects other metals except silver and gold.

Battlemages are mages, master magicultors, who specialize in the use of a branch (a magica wand) or a stem (a magica staff) from a properly cultivated magica tree to trigger locomutation—a vanishing mechanism locked deep in the biology of the magica root. Essentially, battlemages can make any object except silver or gold disappear from one location and reappear at another instantly.

The farther away the locomutation, the more concentration it requires. A small, pure metal object will travel to its newly assigned location with few objections, but a great mass of pure metal requires a significantly greater assertion of willpower to overcome its inertia. We could visualize the difference by picturing the way a small metal ball will roll uphill with a simple flick of the wrist but a large metal ball might roll back and crush you if you are not properly braced for its weight.

Stone and composite metals are harder to locomutate, analogous to the way a roughhewn chunk of ore will not roll uphill but has to be shoved or dragged every inch of the way because of its shape. Inert organic material is even harder to locomutate. Living plants require more willpower than lifeless ones and living animals require still more. Usually, living persons must eat a few magica leaves before a mage can successfully locomutate them.

Research has shown that intoning certain syllables at certain pitches helps sync the magicultors' connection with their wands or staves. A magic word or phrase is useless when sung in the wrong key, and hence magicultors must carry a pitch pipe unless, like Zena, they are born with perfect pitch.

Way in the back, on Dungaree Jeanne's side of the convoy, is a battlewagon of gnome slingers calling themselves the Warband. Their leader is a far-sighted gnome named Captain Armigan. Capable of raining stones and pellets on target up to five hundred yards away, gnome slingers have the longest effective range of any missile troops in a medieval army. The top of their battlewagon is crenelated like a castle wall so the slingers can pop up, hurl a sling stone, and then quickly duck back under cover. In addition, they have a few armored gnome magicultors and sorcerers in a purely defensive role to protect the slingers.

The effectiveness of the Warband and the Skybrim special forces units is well summarized in the unlimited front, back, and side motion of the rooks.

As with a chessboard, the most numerous troops on the battlefield are the frontline foot soldiers. In ancient Roman armies the infantry, known as *pedites,* were glorious. They were the backbone of a military machine that conquered half the civilized world. By the Middle Ages, foot soldiers had lost their prestige and battle effectiveness to the point that the word *pawn* today means someone you push around and who cannot stand up for himself.

Master Leevai's foot soldiers are no pawns.

They call themselves the Glorious Dastards. These forty Jewish men are entirely composed of refugees who occupied the best years of their lives seeking out and executing vengeance on those who masterminded pogroms or committed hate crimes against individual Jews. After a while, they realized the skillsets they'd developed made readjustment to civilian life hard, if not impossible.

Many of these men have escaped from prison towers and dungeons to mingle with the dregs of society. Under the leadership of Master Leevai they have survived, and now thrive, as soldiers of fortune.

They come from all walks of life and have such diverse combat skills that they are more like a very large party of adventurers balancing their natural talents, training, and class skills to work together as a coordinated and complementary fighting force. The Glorious Dastards keep on their roster street tramps that used to make a lonesome living through begging and petty crimes, as well as thugs who worked together to organize criminal rackets to carry out their own street version of justice (and sometimes indulge in a little profitable injustice). Hence the name stems from their hard-earned righteous but dastardly reputation.

Exceptional individuals among their ranks include Leonard Benjamin, a meaty pugilist who uses the strength and speed of his fists, sleek armor, and keen instincts to break into an enemy formation and wreak havoc at close quarters where long weapons would get tangled up. They also have a bard, whose nom de guerre is Sholem Aleichem. This retired swordsman uses his love of music and skill with the fidel, a medieval violin, to inspire his comrades to epic feats in battle and to disorient his enemies. The duelist, Bruce Mandel, is a skilled swordsman who drained his family's fortunes training under the best sword masters money could buy for the sake of protecting a lost code of honor. Mandel's precision sword work complements perfectly the raw fury of the berserker, Shimshon Roth. Shoulder to shoulder, they are unstoppable in battle.

Dungaree Jeanne's foot soldiers are less reliable. To gather infantry for her division, she assigned Captain Manzone's bravos the quest of gathering as many fighters to bolster the front ranks of her army as possible. Accordingly, each one of his bravos split up and visited every tavern, village green, and back alley to recruit anyone and everyone willing to prove their worth with a weapon. The resulting unit decided to call themselves the Behooved but they look more like a circus troupe than professional infantry.

One bravo came back with a group of hoodlums who swagger around in colorful costumes and too many tattoos and ring piercings. They are bored teens looking for mischief and a free meal rather than dedicated fighters. Another bravo decided to rent tavern brawlers who work as bouncers on the weekends. Most of them are big guys with bigger inferiority complexes who feel a need to skulk around looking for someone to intimidate.

All the bravos put together, however, barely come up with as many recruits as Trelany, the only female bravo in the group. (Technically, she is a brava, not a bravo). Anyhow, she came back with a group of misfits that both impressed and worried Captain Manzone from the start—a Trakota shaman called Crazy Bull whose secrets seemed more dangerous than his tomahawk; an exiled Fox chieftain, whose name is Kahnawroke but everyone calls Karaoke, singing songs of lamentation with no words that utterly unnerve his comrades; a javelin-throwing picaro from Salamanca named Lazarillo de Tormes whom no one takes seriously; an itinerant jester named Babyface Nelson, whose ridiculous antics they all seem to take too seriously; a discredited dwarf politician whose bitterness at life has earned him the nickname Grumpy; a brutish brigand with a big scar on his face by the name of Al Carbone, who is famous for corrupting civil authorities; a fearless Aenglish frontiersman baptized as Nate Bumpo but raised among the Delawaerr as Straight-Tongue; a tumbler using the show name Barnum; a desperado fleeing the law under the alias Dutch; and a gnome con artist using the sobriquet Atlas, who pretends to be a magicultor except that the only things he seems able to make disappear are silver coins—the one trick real magicultors cannot pull off.

Having set the pieces in place, Dungaree Jeanne and Master Leevai knowingly move forward into Umpire Gandorf's trap.

Scene E: Brilliancy

Shippen Forest in the Confederacy of the Seven Nations
Thor's Day Terce. Morning, 20th of April, 1284
Morrow of the Feast of Saint Aelfheah, Bishop and Martyr

The convoy moves forward at a brisk pace for five hours. Eventually, the sultry afternoon brings occasional rain clouds, swarms of gnats, sweaty foreheads, and itchy skin. When they reach Green Spring Creek, Dungaree Jeanne calls a halt for the troops to drink from the streams, take a snack, relieve themselves, and rest up before the final drive home. The journey has been so peaceful that she almost wants to believe all her misgivings have been for naught.

Instead of allowing his troops to rest, Captain Bucklead shouts, "Ivy Leaguers! To the trees!"

The Ivy Leaguers wade across the creek and do their best to dry themselves off before having to climb the trees with wet gloves and slippery boots. Once in the foliage, they camouflage themselves. Lynx drinks from the stream by the wayside and lifts his head.

From the canopy above, Captain Bucklead drops down right next to him and says in Eldric this time, "Mister Lynx, here is your horn. It makes the sound of a blue jay. Blow it if you spot danger. Each Ivy League scout has a horn that makes a different sound. Mine is the sound of a black-capped chickadee. Listen—

Chickadee-dee-dee-dee-dee.

"When I send out this call, all the Ivy League scouts must report in. If you are the last one in the company to respond, you fail. The rules don't specify an exact distance, but I expect you to keep far enough away from the team to be an effective scout. Understood?"

Lynx understands too well. "So the rules allow me to stay close to you so I don't fail, but you want me to stay as far away as possible so I do."

Captain Bucklead does not like his smart answer. "One more comment like that from your mouth and you fail. The bottom line is that you don't belong. But since I seem to be the only one smart enough to know that, my orders are to give you a fair chance at passing. Fair and easy are not the same. Understood?"

"Understood, Monsieur Captain."

"Your trial ends at Lake Letterkenny, just through the Forge Hill Gap. When concealed, you are also allowed to swim as long as you don't make too much noise splashing around. We usually recommend that you bring a leafy branch into the water to provide a floating hiding spot.

"If something happens to me, the mademoiselle Senior Officer Onashelf will assume command of the company and take over my horn. In that case the decision about passing the test is hers. Understood?"

"Understood, Monsieur Captain."

"Dismissed, Mister Lynx."

Lynx decides not to let Captain Bucklead out of his sight. He can just imagine that the prejudicial captain will try to pull away from him as far as possible and summon all the other Ivy Leaguers one by one so as to claim that Lynx did not respond to his call. The other consideration is that the captain's horn is such a faithful imitation of a chickadee call that if Lynx cannot physically see him, he might spend the rest of the ordeal chasing after real chickadees instead.

It is one of those hot, wet afternoons when you can still see the sun between dark, puffy clouds. The rain falls hard and heavy in big drops. Not long after that, the sunshine peeks through the clouds and steams up the soggy ground.

As a result, the trees are wet, hot, and slippery.

Somehow, he had imagined that his ardent love for Zena would carry him through this ordeal on angel's wings. Instead, it feels like he can only slide around on jabberwarg spittle. The conditions in the trees are so slippery and steamy that all the other Ivy Leaguers except Captain Bucklead are spending half their time walking on the ground.

Captain Bucklead puts on a stern face as he wrestles his way from branch to branch. He will not tarnish his reputation or lessen his own opinion of himself by demanding of Lynx a task he himself cannot accomplish. Madame Dungaree has posted scouts of her own watching his every move, seeking some legal ground to ditch the Ivy League altogether.

Try as he might, Captain Bucklead cannot put any distance between himself and Lynx. For a seasoned professional these conditions are brutal, for Lynx the ordeal is a painful and exasperating nightmare.

Swinging down from a mighty oak, Lynx's grip slips off the wet bark of a peeling birch tree. He lands solidly on a birch branch below, but then his left boot slides and his knee smacks into the trunk hard. Nerve pain shoots up to his brain and does not let go.

The shock of the slip allows Captain Bucklead to get ahead. Lynx knows that the captain is itching to blow his chickadee call as soon as he falls out of earshot, so Lynx presses on like a squirrel with its tail on fire.

Soon, he reaches the river that the Albo-Erinish settlers here call the Letterkenny River, but the local Susquetoga have named it Conodoguinet—the long, bending river. The finish line for his trial, Lake Letterkenny, lying just through the Forge Hill Gap in the Blue Mountain chain, is now in sight.

Pausing to survey the area, Lynx catches sight of Captain Bucklead rushing across the river underneath a small waterfall. He recalls that Dungaree Jeanne wanted to meet with him under the aqueduct's waterfall so the loud noise it was making might drown out their conversation from prying ears. Captain Bucklead's intention seems clear—with Lynx's trial coming to an end, he wants to blow his horn on the far bank of the Letterkenny River so the crashing waters of the cataract will mute his chickadee horn.

Lynx spots an elm tree with a branch extending well into the river. He figures it goes far enough out to safely jump into the river, then cross quickly.

The ordeal has been exhausting. Salty sweat streams into his eyes from under his green cap, stinging them fiercely. He cannot wipe off the sweat fast enough. Lynx flips his cap around and takes a running jump for the elm tree. The pain in his knee seems to drain the vim from his legs and his falls short of the elm's main bough, banging his chin against a thin branch with enough oomph to knock loose his grip.

He pinballs from branch to branch until a lower branch finally dumps him into the river. As it turns out, this little accident has saved his life because the river is too shallow for high jumping. The lower branches broke his fall well enough, but the rocky bottom of the river sends a nasty shock to his already aching knee.

Realizing how close he came to getting seriously injured or killed, he lifts up a silent prayer, *Thank you, God, that you allowed me to fall into this river.*

Lynx knows that if Captain Bucklead sees him coming, the captain will try to run away, so Lynx decides to hide himself underneath the waterfall. Once he gets a good footing on the slippery rock, Lynx hauls himself underneath the rushing waves. The waters are painfully cold. The breakers sweep over his limp body. The waters roar as they crash onto the rocks.

Dungaree Jeanne has been keeping an eye on them both. Seeing Lynx fall behind, she grows suspicious and orders the convoy to come to a halt on the far bank.

As soon as he emerges from the water, Captain Bucklead puts the chickadee horn to his lips and blows. Lynx cannot hear it, but he can see it. There's no time to lose! He cannot allow himself to report in last or all this agony will have been for naught.

Drawing on every last drop of strength in his soul, Lynx strains his way through the stony shallows beneath the falling waters. The effort wipes him out. His limbs pulse with pain and he loses his lunch in the river. With his back aching, hands blistered and knees electrified with pain, Lynx forces himself to climb up a shoreside willow tree, huffing and puffing.

He looks for Captain Bucklead—vanished! To come this far only to allow that scheming highbrow the chance to give him the slip . . . ugh!

Amid the splashing and burbling rush of the river, he hears a deep note calling out to something deep inside him. Not a chickadee horn but a clarion call. He hears it not with his ears but buried inside his soul. The deep note calls to a sudden loneliness inside his heart.

On the open riverbank, the bright sunshine warms and caresses his face. His eyelids droop. It's over. He has failed. The humid, warm air lulls him to rest, but he refuses to give up. He climbs a willow tree and scans the tree line for any sign of the Ivy League.

Pffeeeet!

His brain reechoes with the sound planted deep within. To Lynx, the piercing whistle has no direction or vector. Panic and confusion rise within his heart. Voices in his head accuse him of flunking his test.

Then a gentle breeze, a wind in the willow, carries those accusing voices away and he hears a conversation coming from the west that explains it all. Bringing his mind to full alert in this world, he zeroes in on a giant boy playing a flute.

"Your pipe is broken, Babyface," says the heavily armored dwarf, Grumpy.

Upon closer inspection, Lynx realizes that Babyface is a full-grown man, piping away at his tiny flute with a Bacchic lilt in his step but only making that deep sound that he hears more with his bones than with his ears.

It is not hard to deduce that Lynx is the only one picking up on the pipe's tone. The big, baby-faced mercenary dances and wiggles his tush to pretend music. Tooting away at his pipe, he leads a conga line for his followers—a rogue, a brigand, and a tavern brawler all hop along behind him.

Pffoooot!

The pipe only sounds one note and it is the same note that Lynx heard deep inside his head beneath the cataract. Pheasants slap their wings and take to flight.

A crow caws and skims away over the treetops. Below, a deer hightails it out of there as the crow flies.

"What on middle earth are you trying to accomplish, Nelson?" asks the armored dwarf, noticing the escaping birds with alarmed eyes.

Babyface ignores him and keeps up the merriment. His babyface is not the only unusual visual trait that makes him stick out of a crowd. His leather armor is not tanned dark brown like everyone else's. Rather, it retains the original piebald pigmentation of the cow's fur—white with black splotches.

While the pied piper dances, the skies open and dump out another short but heavy rain. Babyface Nelson sneers, "Well if it isn't always the grumpy dwarf to make it rain on our parade. If you didn't feel such a constant need to kill our fun, we wouldn't need to make it up with another round of short jokes."

The brigand named Al Carbone says, "Oh, oh, I got one! So, I was waiting down the road to rob a rich dwarf when I saw a cutpurse sneak up behind him and make off with all his coins. I couldn't imagine how anyone could stoop so low. Heh, heh, heh!"

The ruffians laugh hysterically. The grumpy dwarf just tears the soundless pipe out of the piper's hands.

The desperado using the name Dutch grabs the dwarf's fist and tries to wrestle the pipe back, saying, "Leave off, Grumpy! This pipe belongs to my friend. Don't let his babyface fool you—he's a vicious fighter."

Despite the difference of two feet in height, the dwarf is stronger. He locks both hands together and pulls down hard, shifting his weight to interfere with the desperado's footwork. The big oaf flips over the dwarf's shoulder and lands flat on his back.

Blades come out with a swish.

Lynx sees the escalation and knows he has got to stop the pied piper. Something big is going down and the pied piper is obviously orchestrating it. Lynx leaps down from the willow tree and runs with all the speed his exhausted body can muster toward them.

Dungaree Jeanne rides by on her magnificent war reindeer. "Monsieur Lynx, what are you doing on the ground? If he sees you Captain Bucklead will fail you on your test. We're only a few yards from the Gap!"

Lynx does not stop to chat. He runs past her shouting in Eldric, "We need to stop Babyface!"

Before Lynx gets there, the seven-foot-tall exiled Fox chief, Kahnawroke, readies his tomahawk and war knife to back up the dwarf.

The desperado, Dutch, points a finger threateningly at the Fox warrior. "Stay out of this, Karaoke!"

Lynx draws his short sword and stands in the middle of the face-off. Lynx sniffs the air, then points to Babyface's boots, and says in Aenglish, "Dead rabbit on your foot! Dire wolf smell it from three miles away."

Taken off guard, the whole group looks at the pied piper's boots. He gets defensive. "What? That's my lucky rabbit's foot!"

The dwarf inspects the pipe and then holds it up, saying, "Hobgoblin whistle."

Karaoke's eyes widen at the revelation of the betrayal. He yells, "You filthy traitors!"

Dutch smacks the back of Grumpy's helmet hard with his mace before he runs away saying, "Correction—we're *filthy rich* traitors!"

The pockmarked Fox war chief whips his tomahawk, spinning it in the air and its axe-head buries itself deep into Dutch's back. By the time they all look up, Babyface Nelson has already sprinted out of effective range for throwing a war knife. As he runs away, Babyface calls back, "You'd better watch your back, Grumpy!" With that, he disappears into the forest, with Al Carbone right behind him.

Dungaree Jeanne rides up and sees the dead desperado, asking in Eldric, "Monsieur Lynx, what is this all about?"

As if on cue, horns sound in the distance and the growling of dire wolves ripples behind the forest curtain.

Lynx says in Eldric, "Madame Dungaree, the trap has sprung."

As soon as she hears the dire wolves, Dungaree Jeanne shouts to Lynx, "Quick! Follow me!"

But she does not wait for Lynx. She gallops as fast as her reindeer can carry her to Master Leevai's command center. The hatch goes down and she rides her reindeer directly up into the battlewagon. The guards close the hatch, shutting Lynx out.

Lynx contemplates banging on the hatch but he sees hobgoblin dire wolf riders coming over the ridge. His best chance for survival is to climb a nearby tree with thick foliage and hide.

From way up high at the top of that hundred-foot-tall oak tree, Lynx gets a good look at all the disposition of troops. Seeing the hobgoblins surrounding the convoy, he cannot help but think that Dungaree Jeanne's enemies severely underestimated her. Such hobgoblin raiders could easily wipe out an ordinary merchant convoy, but Dungaree Jeanne has at her back a full-fledged army capable of conquering a small city.

Back in his command wagon, Master Leevai Strauss calls a war council with Dungaree Jeanne and all the unit captains. He points to the dead body of Dutch and the other members of Captain Manzone's Behooved mercenaries and shouts, "Who hired those troops? They are undoubtedly the seediest harvest of nut jobs, corn flakes, and cesspool scum I have ever seen gleaned from a crop of lowlifes."

Captain Manzone raises his right hand lazily. Master Leevai asks, "What? Your right hand hired them without you knowing?"

"No, that's ridiculous. I told my bravos to go out and hire anyone they could find for a big fight. Hiring lousy soldiers is usually not a problem in battle since anyone not worth his salt will be dead soon enough."

"This time they did *not* die soon enough. They just gave away our position to a horde of hobgoblins!"

Captain Manzone does not apologize. "At least the rest of them seem pretty solid."

Madame Dungaree takes the blame. "Those were my orders. I thought the risk was worth it. The enemy would have found us sooner or later, and I agree with Captain Manzone—the ones that are left are the kind of soldiers I like to have on my side in a serious fight."

Master Leevai lets it drop. "Okay, people, here's the plan. We're going to use the bend in the river to castle up our wagons. Madame Dungaree, I'll let you personally lead all the cavalry, including your household guard, the Rough Riders, and my Knights of the Round Table, out and around the battlefield in a long loop. We want the enemy to think there are far fewer of us so they commit all their troops. If you see them attack, charge them from the rear!"

"What about the Ivy League?"

"There is no doubt in my mind that they betrayed us as well. The whole point of having scouts is to give us advance warning of approaching hostile forces. Captain Bucklead must have seen those hobgoblins a long time ago and he never warned us."

Dungaree Jeanne frowns and says, "I don't like it, but you're right, Master Leevai. If I see Captain Bucklead again, I'll have him executed on the spot!"

With that, Master Leevai sets his opening gambit into motion—the wagons castle up next to the river, the Glorious Dastards up front, and the Skybrim battlemages and battlesages anchoring his left. Tucked safely behind them, a deep bend in the river protects his right flank and rear. The wagon drivers unharness the horses and take them inside to keep them safe.

The hobgoblins must know that a powerful army awaits them because they all rein in their dire wolves as soon as the wagons come into sight. Hobgoblins have the same green skin, fanged overbite, pointy ears, large brows, wide cheekbones, protruding nose, and long cleft chin as goblins, but they are as short as halflings.

They are generally smarter than ordinary goblins, speak a more complex language, and have devised military tactics specifically to counteract their mortal enemies—elves. Like elves, they prefer to live in treetop settlements and tame forest animals to support their livelihood. Like goblins, their ironworking skills are primitive, and they still rely on wood, stone, copper and bronze for most of their tools and weapons. They are hunter-gatherers who know how to plant some vegetables in clearings and groves, but they do not clear fields for cultivation.

Though the hobgoblin vanguard prowls over two hundred yards away, the halfling slingers inflict several casualties with their first volley. Hobgoblins know better than to stand around in the open with gnome slingers in range. They tug the wolves' collars to turn back and dissolve back into the forest out of sight.

Although dire wolves are deadly sprinters, reindeer can easily outrun a dire wolf in a prolonged chase, so as scouts, they do their best to hover at the edge of visibility to keep an eye on the hobgoblins' movements. The moose riders, on the other hand, flee at once. As long as they are outnumbered by the wolves, they stand no chance of contributing anything useful to the battle.

A war moose can easily clobber several dire wolves in a single charge but after that they are helpless against the coordinated hit-and-run tactics of a pack. Moose are surprisingly fast but they are primarily adapted for cold climates. They cannot maintain top speeds for long without overheating. If a pack of dire wolves encircles the moose riders, even elf fire cannot save them. The mercenary moose riders take off at a brisk trot southward and hope to find their way to Fort Loudon before the hobgoblins give them chase.

The mercenary elf boar riders stick around. They are heavily armored—the only steel-armored units in the entire elf military system. As such, they are vulnerable to battlesages but as a trade-off, their armor is tough enough to make them invulnerable to most other types of attacks. They can take on dire wolves, even when outnumbered.

With the opening moves made, the ambushers have already put to flight twelve moose riders, while the convoy has only taken down a handful of hobgoblin wolf riders. Most importantly, the ambushers have had to call off their initial surprise attack. They severely underestimated the convoy's military strength.

Dungaree Jeanne exits Master Leevai's command center mounted on her reindeer and calls the leader of the Rough Riders, Captain Gunnar, to her side. She points the last known position of the hobgoblin dire wolf riders and says, "They're giving us too much space. My hunch is they're waiting for reinforcements. If we can find out which direction those reinforcements are coming from, we can set our slingers up to give the newcomers a warm welcome.

"I'll take a contingent west to scout out the Forge Hill Gap, then we'll head south to make sure nothing is coming from that direction. Meanwhile, I want you to check out what's over that ridge to the north and then double back east to make sure no one has been following our trail from behind. We'll regroup here. If you see the Ivy League, order them to report in with me. If they don't comply, consider them hostile."

From up at the top of his oak tree, Lynx can see the shock on Captain Gunnar's face at the thought of considering fellow elves as belligerents fighting on the same side as hobgoblins. It would be no less shocking for beleaguered sailors to find out that some of their shipmates are working for the sea monsters.

Dungaree Jeanne heads west with her reindeer scouts and Captain Gunnar cautiously approaches the ridge to the north with his. The boar riders stay in reserve, tucked safely behind the frontline wagons for now. For a while, it seems the hobgoblins are mere specters sent to spook the convoy into sitting tight.

Captain Gunnar's reindeer scouts gallop back from over the ridge, racing furiously with a few extra wounded elves on their hind saddles. Lynx climbs down to see for himself. On his way, a reindeer scout gallops in his direction and Lynx shouts to her in Eldric, "What's going on?"

The elve rider slows down a little and tells him, "It's a disaster out there! Hobgoblins have treeshadows lurking over that ridge. The Ivy League is taking heavy casualties and we have already lost six reindeer and one rider trying to help evacuate the wounded! Captain Gunnar has ordered a full retreat."

Lynx asks, "Does the madame Dungaree know?"

"Yes, she said the Ivy League forced us to come this way, so they are going to have to deal with the mess they created. No one is allowed to risk their life to extract any more Ivy Leaguers."

Lynx starts to sprint toward the ridge while the scout shouts after him, "Hey! I said orders are to let the Ivy Leaguers take on the treeshadows themselves!"

Lynx yells, "I *am* an Ivy Leaguer!"

With that, he jogs up the ridge and climbs a large sycamore tree. It does not take long for him to hear the hobgoblins rustling through the leaves. With anxious eyes, he spots a few hobgoblin treeshadows. They are able to climb directly up tree trunks with bronze claws attached to their fingers and toes and use blowpipes which they can shoot with one hand, so they have better mobility than elves but limited range.

Hobgoblin blowguns make no noise. They shoot envenomed darts fletched with owl feathers. Elves prefer plant poisons to taint the tip of their arrows, such as mountain wolfsbane, white snakeroot, and manchineel, whereas hobgoblins raise water moccasins and rattlesnakes to harvest their fast-acting venoms.

Elf hit-and-run tactics only work against an enemy you can see. Hobgoblins are masters of stealth. Elf reindeer scouts can outpace all other clayborn in the thick of a forest but even they fall victim to a hobgoblin booby trap on occasion. In many ways, the rivalry between elves and hobgoblins is the deepest between any two races of the clayborn in Vinland. It certainly is the nastiest and most vicious when it comes to laying on the hurt—casualties will be high today.

Lynx does his best to approach the combat zone keeping a low profile. Not long after he comes over the ridge, he hears the groaning of an elve nearby on the forest floor. He crawls over carefully and does his best to use the forest underbrush as cover while he sneaks over toward the wounded elve.

It's none other than Senior Officer Onashelf! Lynx asks, "Where are you wounded?"

She groans in delirium.

Lynx rolls her over and finds the dart in the back of her leg. The entry wound is going black with necrotic flesh from the venom. Ivy Leaguers always carry a pouch of antidotes. Lynx knows the procedure—he is supposed to cut away some of the dying flesh and suck out as much of the venom as possible, then apply the antidote. The problem is that he does not know which vial in the pouch contains the proper antidote!

He rummages through the pouch on her belt and pulls out a random vial. He notices the Futhark letter "⍰"—Dagaz—on the stopper. Realizing the antidotes are in Runic alphabetical order, he puts it back and looks for the letter "⍰"—Kauna—which would signify "kamputer" or "hobgoblins" in Eldric. He sees three vials marked with the same letter.

Lynx uncorks one of the three at random, debrides the wound with his knife, and applies the antidote. He then hoists her up and walks back up the ridge. Senior Officer Onashelf's moaning suddenly stops.

Fearing she might be dead, he slips her off his shoulders to check her pulse and feel her breath. The moment he does, a blowgun dart flies over his shoulder and hits the ground in front of him.

A new level of panic gives him the energy to pick her up and sprint in a random zigzag pattern up over the ridge and back to the battlewagons.

He carries the downed officer to the Augustinian hospital wagon and the clerics immediately take over caring for her.

One more time, he climbs back over the ridge and surveys the area until he sees another wounded Ivy Leaguer. This time around he sprints the whole way and back, not even checking the injury until they are both safely inside the hospital wagon.

By time he gets back with this second Ivy Leaguer, the clerics' prayers have been answered and Senior Officer Onashelf is sleeping peacefully. As he walks by, she opens her eyes and Lynx asks gently, "How are you feeling, Mademoiselle Senior Officer?"

Onashelf replies, "I'm covered in my own scat, but otherwise, I think I'll live. Brother Camillo told me you carried me here by yourself."

Lynx curls his lip. "Word is that the madame Dungaree is so mad at the Ivy League for forcing her to take this route that she has forbidden any of her troops from risking their lives to carry the wounded to safety."

Onashelf says, "She's right and she's wrong. Captain Bucklead herded us straight into a trap and switched sides. He's working for the hobgoblins; but the rest of us are innocent. We're the only ones who can fix this mess anyway." She sits up, almost fully healed. "Let's get going."

On the way back toward the ridge, they spot Dungaree Jeanne coming back from her recon of the Forge Hill Gap. When she sees Senior Officer Onashelf, Dungaree Jeanne is not in a good mood and demands, "Where is Captain Bucklead?"

Gathering up her strength, Onashelf replies, "He betrayed us! He led us straight into an ambush of hobgoblin treeshadows!"

"Then tell me where he is so we can make him answer for his actions."

"He's gone. He blew his horn to gather the Ivy League. Then he said he had special orders from the Major Leagues Umpire. We were to abandon the convoy and follow him. It wasn't long before we were surrounded by hobgoblin treeshadows. He went over to their side and started attacking us."

Dungaree Jeanne wrinkles her brow. "It's worse than I thought; but why did he want to kill innocent elves? It would have been enough to flunk Monsieur Lynx out of the Ivy League to destroy my daughter's candidacy. This is treason of the highest order."

Onashelf says, "Dungaree Jeanne, you are the only one that can answer that question. These games of politics make no sense to us ordinary folk."

Lynx interrupts, "Still, there are a lot of innocent Ivy Leaguers who are cut off by the hobgoblins out there and they need our help!"

Dungaree Jeanne replies, "It's too dangerous! Our reindeer scouts cannot see the treeshadows. I cannot risk losing them to the hobgoblins. Without our reindeer scouts, we'll be blind! The Ivy League will have to pay with its blood for what they've done."

Onashelf says, "Please, Madame Dungaree, at least lend us a few halfling slingers or crossbow dwarves. The hobgoblins' blowguns cannot shoot very far. As long as we act as spotters for them, the slings and crossbows will easily be able to take down the hobgoblin treeshadows long before they get close enough to be a threat."

Lynx adds, "Madame Dungaree, I know you are mad because the Ivy League used my vulnerable position as a wood elf to betray us, but it wouldn't be right to let innocent elves die for the wrongs committed by their leaders."

"Unfortunately that is the burden of leadership, Monsieur Lynx. The innocent perish at their whim." She looks into Lynx's eyes. There is an innocence and child-like idealism that abates her anger slightly. She relents and says, "Still, if there is a safe way to rescue the innocent Ivy Leaguers, we'll take it. Pick a safe spot and move into position along the ridge and I'll send you halfling slingers from the Warband and crossbow dwarves from my own personal retinue to commence the rescue operation. If any one of them takes a single casualty, you call off the entire rescue operation or I will hold you personally responsible for their deaths. Is that understood, Senior Officer Onashelf?"

Once she makes her way back to Master Leevai's command wagon, she starts dictating orders to her runners in Aenglish.

Louis and Clarke overhear Dungaree Jeanne's request for backup. Louis says, "Clarke and I want to come with you!"

Clarke looks at him, surprised. "We do?"

Louis holds up his cheap crossbow. "Yes, we both have crossbows! We'll be able to help out."

"Fine. Go! You know the risks."

Louis turns back to Master Leevai. "Um . . . Master Leevai, could I borrow a few quarrels from you? I didn't have enough money to buy any at the fair."

Master Leevai smiles. "Very well, Louis. Make them count! Madame Dungaree, I will also send an apprentice magicultor along as well. According to the battlemages, this one is particularly skilled at making leaves and branches disappear at long distances."

"Very handy skill right now!" agrees Dungaree Jeanne. Then she turns to the enthusiastic young men and says, "Oberst Schneevitchen's Magnificent Eight dwarves are all skilled at the crossbow as well. I'm sending them up to the ridge."

Master Leevai looks angry. "But they are your personal bodyguards! The whole reason I hired them was to protect you. We cannot risk your life, Madame Dungaree, or else we jeopardize the entire game plan!"

"Agreed," says Dungaree Jeanne. "Until they come back, I'll play it safe here with you."

"Fine," concedes Master Leevai. "But Oberst Schneevitchen herself stays with you at all times. I'm sure the remaining seven will be just as magnificent without her."

Dungaree turns around and says in Aenglish, "Okay, Louis and Clarke, off you go! It's time to save the day."

Up at the ridge, the situation is reaching a critical breaking point. Envenomed elves languish up in the tree branches, moaning in their delirium, while others have fought hand-to-hand in the trees. A few hobgoblin corpses testify to their fighting spirit, but outnumbered and stuck with the serious tactical disadvantage that Captain Bucklead left them in, the Ivy League scouts have gotten the worst of most of the exchanges. They are down to a few well-hidden survivors.

While the crossbow dwarves, gnome slingers, and human auxiliaries hang back, Senior Officer Onashelf belly-crawls up to the crest of the ridge with Lynx, hoping to study the lay of the land without tipping off the hobgoblin treeshadows. The hobgoblin wolf riders keep moving farther off into the distance, avoiding arrow range of the elf reindeer scouts.

Once she has a sense of where her fellow Ivy Leaguers are and where a few of the enemy hobgoblins might be hiding, she calls up the seven dwarves. They form a semicircle with their tower shields affixed to the ground with spikes. With their defensive position set, the apprentice magicultor and halfling slingers take up their positions under the cover of the tower shields.

Senior Officer Onashelf points to a thick tree some fifty yards to the northwest and the apprentice magicultor proves his worth instantly. With a wave of his magica wand he says, "Shizzelam!"

The branch suddenly loses its foliage and the halflings and dwarves spot the hobgoblin right away.

They launch quarrels and pellets and the hobgoblin drops to the forest floor.

Rinse and repeat. After clearing out the closest hobgoblin treeshadows, Senior Officer Onashelf declares in Eldric, "Okay, I'm going out there to rally the survivors and carry the wounded out of the combat zone. Monsieur Lynx, please tell them in Aenglish."

Lynx does his best to explain the plan in Aenglish, but the second-in-command of Oberst Schneevitchen's dwarves, Otzan Merdoc—Otzan being the Dwarvish Runic equivalent of Lieutenant—puts his huge hand on Senior Officer Onashelf's shoulder and says in Aenglish, "You're our best spotter. Without your trained eyes, we'll never be able to provide an adequate covering barrage for a runner. I'll send Sneezy."

After Lynx translates what he says, Senior Officer Onashelf seethes. "Are you crazy? He's already sneezed up a storm. If he sneezes once out there, he'll blow the whole rescue operation!"

Lynx argues with her in Eldric, "I'll go. I've already done it twice without a covering barrage."

"Look at you! You're drenched in sweat, limping, and worn out. I can't let you go in that state. I'll go."

Seeing the fuss, Louis volunteers. "I'll go. My crossbow is jammed and I don't even know how to use it. I can carry the wounded easier then you."

Otzan Merdoc says in Aenglish, "Good idea. I've seen your shooting and, you're right, it's not helping. Lynx, are you okay with this boy tagging along?"

Lynx informs Senior Officer Onashelf. "The dwarves agree that the two humans would be most helpful out there. I'll guide them out there."

Onashelf sees the logic and nods. One of the Warband halfling slingers says to Louis in Aenglish, "Take this rope. It may come in handy."

As Louis tucks the rope over his shoulder, Lynx points to Clarke, "Okay, you come with me."

Clarke is not so sure but before he can object Lynx and Louis are running toward a wide oak tree.

A hobgoblin dart barely misses them. Fortunately, Senior Officer Onashelf stays alert and points the hobgoblin out. With another shizzelam and a barrage of missiles, the hobgoblin is dead before he can reload.

Panting but determined, Lynx leads Louis and Clarke out to recover three bodies of the fallen Ivy Leaguers on the forest floor. By the time they make it back to the ridge, only one is still breathing. Clarke volunteers to carry her to the hospital wagon.

By this time, Senior Officer Onashelf has spotted five more Ivy Leaguers who seem to be alive but are hidden and too wounded or too afraid to move. Others lie up in the branches inert, and their grisly postures convince her they are no longer alive.

After discussing the situation with Otzan Merdoc, Lynx announces in Aenglish that Senior Officer Onashelf has decided that the only way to rally the surviving Ivy Leaguers is to take to the trees.

Otzan Merdoc refuses to lose his spotters, but Clarke comes back from the hospital wagon with a limping elve, Junior Officer Freya. The clerics are drained, and their prayers were only able to heal her up enough for her to think straight but she cannot walk on her own. Still, she insisted on being carried back to the front line to help in whatever way possible. Otzan Merdoc agrees to appoint her spotter and they let Lynx and Senior Officer Onashelf climb the nearby trees.

They wait for quite a while but not much happens. A branch shakes here and a group of leaves rustle there but back on the ground in the tower shield fort, none of it makes any sense to anyone except Junior Officer Freya. She does not speak a word of Aenglish but from her excitement, the fighting must be vicious.

Time passes. Otzan Merdoc whispers to the group, "If they take too long, our daylight hours will burn out. We'll be sitting ducks come nightfall."

An uncanny silence looms. Birds, chipmunks, and squirrels chirp out false alarms that unnerve the halfling slingers.

Suddenly, Junior Officer Freya points their attention to the forest floor frantically. The dwarves, halflings, and Clarke get ready to shoot, expecting wolf riders. Instead, they see Lynx running toward them with a wounded elf on his shoulders. Lynx's face is red and pouring with sweat. He pants and moans like a cross-country runner trying to squeeze his last ounce of endurance toward the finish line at a marathon.

Just short of the tower shield fort, Lynx collapses. Louis and Clarke run out to help. Louis carries the wounded elf, Junior Officer Jormungand, on his back while Clarke hoists Lynx to his feet and props him up on one shoulder. Lynx has lost all control of his breathing and hyperventilates. When he is safely behind the tower shields, Clarke starts to set Lynx down but he immediately gets back on his feet, wheezing out the sound, "Zo . . . zo . . . zora."

"What is he trying to say?" asks Louis.

"*Zorro* means 'fox' in Spanish," replies Clarke.

Otzan Merdoc slaps one of his dwarves on the arm. "Dopi, wur!"

The dwarf named Dopi pulls out his large waterskin and Otzan Merdoc dumps it all over Lynx's head, shoulders, and arms. Lynx's breathing starts to calm down. Merdoc comments in Aenglish, "He was just overheated. Now then, Hare Gipper, what did you want to say?"

Still breathing heavily, he points back. "Zoramites!"

Clarke asks, "What are Zoramites? Insects?"

Otzan Merdoc says, "Only the fiercest warriors in Vinland. I'll tell you what—if someone offers you a job to defend a castle when the Zoramites go marching in, you don't want to be in that number."

The crippled elf spotter, Junior Officer Freya, starts tapping Otzan Merdoc's shoulder urgently. They all look over the tower shields. Out from the tree line, Zoramite warriors step forth—hundreds of them.

Running out in front of the columns of their warriors, Zoramite archers send bronze-tipped arrows up into the trees. Their bows are neither longbows nor short bows, but war bows. Longbows are made of a single piece of wood and reach the full length of a human's height. Their primary goal is range, and thus they require long, thin arrows. Longbows are difficult to use properly, requiring long, powerful arms and a lifetime of training. But they are cheap to manufacture, lightweight and durable, making them ideal for equipping a peasant army going on a long campaign.

Contrary to the popular misconception, short bows, or recurve bows, are not all that much less powerful in terms of draw weight than longbows, but they are designed to inflict maximum damage rather than to carry as far as possible. Thanks to their recurve shape and their two or more types of wood glued together, they can withstand incredible amounts of draw tension and usually work best with stout broadhead arrows.

A recurve short bow's compact size makes it the perfect sidearm for militia of all races to carry around and inflict some damage during the skirmish phase of a battle or for light cavalry to punish enemy ranks without risking an engagement at close quarters. Their initial production cost restricts their use to professional soldiers and their efficacy degrades quickly with use, making them too expensive for dedicated archer units. Still, their usefulness as a secondary weapon for infantry or cavalry units has proven decisive time and again over the course of history.

War bows, also known as reflex bows, are by far the most expensive bows and must be made of wood, horn, and sinew laminated together. These bows have roughly the same draw weight as short bows but their power is oriented toward accuracy and armor penetration. Their expense alone makes them impractical for amateurs, but a professional adventurer who specializes in archery will find that for its durability, accuracy, and armor penetration, a war bow is a necessary expense.

The Zoramite archers shoot up into the trees with frightful efficiency. The tops of the trees shake fiercely as the Ivy Leaguers scramble down onto the forest floor to flee. There is no point in hiding, since the hobgoblins know exactly where they are and no point in keeping to the trees, since it is clear the Zoramite archers are skilled enough to hit anyone in range.

After a few volleys, all the Ivy Leaguers trapped deep within enemy territory are dead. The Ivy League counterassault on the hobgoblins is over. All that is left for them to do is run!

Seeing the Zoramite archers chasing the Ivy Leaguers, Lynx pants out a few words in Aenglish. "We must help them!"

Otzan Merdoc nixes that idea at once. "We stay here! The Dungaree forbids us from risking our lives to save those traitorous elves. You elves can go you're your own but the rest of us will stay put!"

For the first time in this battle, Lynx takes his recurve bow off his back, strings it, and notches an arrow. He shoots at the Zoramite archers to get their attention but his arrows don't even reach, but he notches another arrow and jogs forward.

By now, Senior Officer Onashelf and her Ivy Leaguers are on the forest floor, booking it with all their might toward the tower shield fort. Eight survivors in total; six running and two wounded elves being carried on the backs of others.

With Lynx recklessly running out in the open, hoping to divert some of the attention away from the six elves running for their lves, Louis does not want to miss out on the action and he follows close behind Lynx, setting off a chain reaction. The apprentice magicultor follows Louis. Soon, the halfling slingers, the only ones who can reach the Zoramites with their missiles, are moved by their courage and leave the safety of the tower shield fort as well. They start pelting the Zoramite archers with stones to keep them at bay.

Otzan Merdoc boils with anger but he sees the elves' desperate plight and shouts out new orders. His dwarves pick up their tower shields and charge forward. The dwarf called Dopi carries Junior Officer Freya on his back, protecting her with his tower shield. He knows they will need her now more than ever since the hobgoblins are rallying to wipe them out.

Meanwhile, Clarke carries the elf Sergeant named Jormungand back to the hospital wagon.

By the time the dwarves reach the halflings, the fleeing elves are about one hundred yards away and the lead Zoramite archers are still about two hundred yards behind them. At a full run, the Zoramite archers have lost all semblance of accuracy in their shooting, but their swelling numbers are enough to terrify even the bravest of elves.

Lynx, still all red in the face and soaking wet, starts to stagger on his feet and swoon.

Despite the distraction provided by the halfling slingers, the sheer volume of Zoramite arrows takes its toll on the fleeing Ivy Leaguers. An unlucky Zoramite arrow lodges itself into one Ivy Leaguer's thigh and the elf trips and face-plants into the ground on account of the sudden pain in his leg and the inhibition of his mobility. The other fleeing elves, either out of fear or out of ignorance of his fall, leave him in the dust.

If that were not bad enough, Senior Officer Onashelf, weakened by her first injury and trying to carry a comrade to safety on her shoulders, slackens her pace to a desperate jog. Zoramite arrows slam into the dirt all around her and eventually hit the elf on her back. To make matters worse, hobgoblin treeshadows start moving around to flank the dwarves and gnomes. Despite the bold rescue effort, it does not look like any of the wounded will make it out alive.

Hark! Here come the cavalry! The heavily armored Knights of the Round Table in shining armor come charging forth to the rescue! Clarke tipped them off on his way to the hospital wagon and without orders, they decided to do the gallant thing as chivalrous knights and rescue the elves. Despite the storm of arrows, their hardy war horses, war donkeys, and war ponies keep running even after the arrows start hitting them.

Reaching down a hand, Sir Lancelot locks grip with a pretty elf and hoists her onto the back of his steed. Galloping deep into the forest near enemy lines, Sir Galahad dismounts and lifts up that unlucky elf who got left in the dust, then carries him onto the back of his noble horse. Dame Kay wheels her mount around and grabs Senior Officer Onashelf by the scruff of her neck with her right hand as she passes. In an incredible display of physical strength, Dame Kay carries both Senior Officer Onashelf and the wounded elf wrapped around her shoulders out of the combat zone with just the one hand. One by one, the knights-errant carry off the fleeing Ivy League elves.

Unfazed, the Zoramite archers turn their attention to Lynx and Louis. Realizing their predicament, Lynx slaps Louis on the back and says in Aenglish, "Now we run! Look, like me!"

Lynx runs in a zigzag pattern to throw the archers off and, though arrows fall all around them, they manage to confuse the Zoramite archers with their random scramble and make it back to the dwarves' tower shields unharmed.

But they get no rest, for as soon as the dwarves start to withdraw from the combat zone, hobgoblin treeshadows start blowing darts at them. The dwarves' armor has almost no gaps in it, so the envenomed darts bounce off harmlessly; but one of the halfling slingers gets stung on his bare foot.

Junior Officer Freya grunts out loud, bouncing up and down to point out the hobgoblin on their flanks despite the language barrier. The apprentice magicultor follows her finger and cries out, "Shizzelam!"

The entire branch under the sneaky hobgoblin disappears and he falls through the air. For good measure, the halflings send a volley of stones at him as he drops down, killing him before he hits the ground.

Halflings are tough, sturdy, and unrelenting. Even with the venom working its way through his body, the halfling slinger does not give up. Admiring his resolve, Otzan Merdoc hoists the stricken halfling on his shoulders and sprints in full armor with unimaginable speed back to the hospital wagon—almost catching up with the mounted Knights of the Round Table.

Not long after all the injured are safely inside the Bikur Holim and the Augustinian wagons do the Zoramite archers appear on top of the ridge in clusters. Between the clusters of archers appear three units of Zoramite infantry in phalanx formation. Their spear tips crackle with electric sparks.

"Into the wagons!" yells Master Leevai. Louis and Clarke join Dungaree Jeanne and Master Leevai in the command wagon while Lynx and the eight other surviving Ivy League elves mash themselves into the crowded Augustinian hospital wagon.

The Zoramite spearmen march out from the woods onto the ridge and form a tight phalanx square, with all their shields interlocking. They bang their bronze-tipped spears against their bronze shields, tapping out a strange cadence: *bang, bang, swipe; bang, bang, swipe*. They chant, "Nachnu nachnu nshlamlech!"

They keep chanting and rhythmically bang their spears against the top of their shields then swipe along the sides. Dungaree Jeanne asks, "What are they saying?"

Master Leevai says, "What a strange dialect of Avrith! It sounds like they're saying 'we will, we will, subdue you' or 'petrify you,' or something like that."

To the utter befuddlement of the convoy, the cloth-armored Zoramites with chest plates of reinforced leather or horn scales tied together with heavy ropes just stand there banging and chanting. Archers, slingers, and crossbow dwarves shoot at them from the five wagons, inflicting a steady stream of casualties. As one Zoramite falls, another steps up to take his place.

Master Leevai looks up to the hatch leading to the artillery scorpion turret on the roof of his command wagon and barks, "Someone get up there and teach those Zoramites a lesson!"

No one moves.

Master Leevai looks around. The sorcerers and magicultors all shrug sheepishly. Master Leevai moans, "I've got to send someone! Who will go for us?"

Clarke raises his hand. "I'm here. Send me."

Master Leevai looks at him and says with a fatherly tone, "With the Zoramites all bunched up in that phalanx formation, you'll nail two or three of them with each shot but you'll be an obvious target. Grab some heavy armor from that chest and Davy Copperfield over here will show you how to operate the artillery scorpion."

The journeyman magicultor does not want to waste his time showing Clarke how to use such a boring weapon. He is so close to becoming a master in the New Amsturldam Magicultor's Guild and his masterpiece—qualifying project to become a master—is precisely a new technique to make huge quantities of copper or bronze disappear. If only he could have a few more moments to scribble out the tuple that will help him calculate precisely the right magic words and tones to make all that bronze out there disappear.

When Clarke comes to him after picking out a huge war helm and some iron pauldrons from the chest, Journeyman Copperfield says, "Just climb the ladder and pull out the safety pin. You should be able to figure it out on your own. Holler if you have any questions, I'm kind of busy right now."

ZAP!

ZAP!

ZAP!

Three huge bolts of lightning streak forward from each of the three phalanxes, blasting open the Skybrim's wagon, the Behooved's wagon, and Warband's battlewagon. Other than sending a few halflings flying through the air and covering everyone's faces with black soot, the lightning bolts cause few serious injuries to the wagons' occupants. But the blasts leave all those companies exposed to the Zoramite archers and the big noise from the spectacular scattering of splinters and burning embers everywhere, has terrified the entire convoy to the soul.

Barely do they take a moment to survey their destructive handiwork before they start up their war chant again—*bang, bang, swoosh; bang, bang, swoosh*—"Nachnu, nachnu nshlamlech!"

The Zoramite archers loose a volley of arrows on the vulnerable and disoriented warriors with stinging effect. The defending sorcerers amplify the polarization of their lodestones like an invisible umbrella to knock the next round of arrows off course while the magicultors locomutate a few bows off of some archers.

Dungaree Jeanne shouts, "We have to charge them down before they blast us again!"

"Impossible!" Master Leevai shouts back. "It's suicide to attack a phalanx head-on!"

Covered with his own blood on his face, Battlemage Shabtai Zephathai, the leader of the Skybrim, crawls out from the wreckage and says to the hydrotheurgic sorcerer Arthur Currie, "Can you make it rain?"

The hydrotheurgist wipes the mud from his face and says, "Yes, sir! A hard rain is going to fall."

Back inside the command center wagon, Journeyman Magicultor Davy Copperfield waves his magic wand and shouts, "I got it! I figured it out! Watch this—pucka pucka squiddly boink!"

His magic words have little effect. The Zoramite war chant goes on—*bang, bang, swoosh; bang, bang, swoosh*—"Nachnu, nachnu, nshlamlech!"

Out of the darkened sky, a downpour of big, heavy drops washes over the battlefield. Electric sparks leap and sputter, shocking some of the Zoramites. Those who are not properly grounded wiggle and shake, bare their teeth and open their eyelids as the current travels through their wet bodies.

A Zoramite hydrotheurgic sorcerer polarizes his salt crystal to repel the rainwaters. With some of the built-up energy diffused thanks to the rain, the defenders have a few more seconds to come up with a way to stop the next zap.

Inspecting the Zoramite ranks, Battlemage Shabtai figures out why Davy Copperfield's spell failed. "Copperfield! The answer is blowing in the wind! Look to the far left—that Zoramite waving his banner all over the place. It's tangled up in orange—the shields must come from the Viscount of Blakkendecker!"

The metalleurgic magicultor hears Battlemage Shabtai's words and it comes together in his mind. Blakkendecker shields have a different alloy makeup to maximize their aethereal conductivity. He runs a few more tuples and then waves his magic wand, shouting, "Bukka bukka bukka sweetily poink!"

All of a sudden, the front row of Zoramites find themselves without shields, spears, or swords—all of their bronze weapons have completely vanished.

The Glorious Dastards shout a war cry. "Bonsai!"

They charge up the ridge at the unarmed Zoramite phalanxes and the whole formation dissolves. Recognizing an easy victory when they see it, Captain Manzone's Behooved bound forward to challenge the fleeing hoplites, but not one of the unarmed Zoramites chooses to keep on fighting.

Once at the top of the ridge, the bravos and swashbucklers jump and yell, "We are the champions!"

Master Leevai turns to Dungaree Jeanne and shouts, "Quickly! Gather all your troops. Now is the time to make our escape, before they regroup!"

Both leaders head out of the central command wagon and blow their horns, recalling all troops. They hitch up the horses and start rolling out.

They do not celebrate long before the Rough Riders come flying in and report to Dungaree Jeanne. Hearing their report in Eldric, she calls to Master Leevai in Aenglish, saying, "Another human army is marching in from the south and a halfling army is coming at us from the east. We must get through the Forge Hill Gap before they reach us!"

Master Leevai gazes and replies with the color draining from his face, "Uh . . . they guessed that would be our next move. Look!"

Over the treetops a huge shadow, like that of a dragon, sweeps through the Forge Hill Gap and sprays fire across the entrance. A few short breaths later, the Gap to the west becomes an impassable inferno. They look north and see the hobgoblins and Zoramites begin to rally. Fenced off in every direction, it looks like a checkmate is only a few moves away.

Everyone knows dragons don't exist. Dragons are imagined to have two arms, two wings, and two legs. Whether you suppose a dragon to be related to a serpent, a lizard, or a bird, you will find no vertebrate animal in nature with a pair of wings that also has two arms and two legs. The huge, serpent-like creature flying above their heads right now is a wyvern—it has a pair of enormous webbed hands that it uses as wings and a pair of legs. No arms.

A wyvern cannot breathe fire but the renegade fire elf riding on its back has a syphon of elf fire and a special pump that uses the flapping motion of the wyvern's wings to propel the flaming ooze over enormous distances. All it takes is one pass to effectively cut off their retreat through the Forge Hill Gap. The wyvern flies high above the convoy so as to avoid the risk of having magic or sorcery or a stray bolt bring it down to earth.

Master Leevai groans, "Jeanne, this is not good. Please tell me you have a backup plan."

Dungaree Jeanne frowns. "I did, Leevai, but that wyvern just ruined it."

"How much time do we have before the gnome army across the river gets here?"

A gnomish stone rolls up to Dungaree Jeanne's foot. "None," she replies to Master Leevai. She turns to Battlemage Shabtai. "Can your sorcerers do anything to stop these sling stones?"

"A bit. I have a wind sorcerer that can help blow these stones off course, but he gets dizzy after a while. Master Leevai, perhaps you can have the dwarves set up some tower shields so the Skybrim can get in place. I have a feeling the Zoramites and the hobgoblins will hold back on the top of the ridge and just shoot at us until the main human army arrives from the south. For now, I'll send our two pyrotheurgists to work on parting the firewall at the mouth of the Forge Hill Gap so we can escape through it."

Dungaree Jeanne points. "They're over there! Those garden gnomes are almost at the river."

Master Leevai voices his surprise. "Those aren't just your ordinary, garden-variety gnomes! Those are the Metro Gnomes—a professional outfit of the best mercenary halfling sharpshooters in Vinland. Whoever set this up didn't want to leave anything to chance!"

The Metro Gnome slingers are so accurate that even from three hundred yards they do some harm with each volley. As they march forward, their aim gets more and more deadly.

"We need to take out those slingers or we'll get overwhelmed from all sides!" says Dungaree Jeanne.

Captain Manzone shouts, "Get me Karaoke!"

An Algonkian-speaking bravo relays the summons and Karaoke runs back to report in, covering ground with astonishing speed. For all his huge frame, he is as light on his feet as a pronghorn antelope and he dodges all incoming sling stones as if he were just doing his favorite song and dance.

Captain Manzone confers with Karaoke through the Algonkian-speaking elf bravo. Satisfied with the conclusion of the conference, he says to Dungaree Jeanne in Eldric, "As I suspected, this is the giant for the job! He claims that Crazy Bull has had a vision. According to the vision, as long as he holds a certain black rock, no sling stone can harm him. Karaoke believes him and has agreed to lead the charge against the Metro Gnomes."

Dungaree Jeanne takes a long look to size him up and then gets right down to business, saying, "Visions are beyond my scope, but we need all the light infantry available to swim across the river under the cover of that clump of trees over there. The Metro Gnomes are launching their sling stones in volleys. If you time it right, you can make short runs out in the open without taking any casualties.

"I want you to run past the ford in the river so the Metro Gnomes won't figure out what you are doing. Then once you are out of sight, swim across the river, double back, and sneak up on those Metro Gnome slingers from behind. We will never live through this if they continue to threaten us. Bring all the Behooved and Glorious Dastards who can swim and move undetected with you. We need every soldier available to ensure the success of this quest."

Back in the hospital wagon, Lynx is fast asleep. His injured knee, the heat exhaustion, his damp, chafed, and blistered skin, his tired and sore limbs, the disappointment at failing his test, and the betrayal of the Ivy League all take their toll and leave him utterly exhausted in mind, body, and spirit.

One of Master Leevai's wounded halfling slingers speaks Eldric and translates the plan for crossing the river to knock out the gnome slingers to Senior Officer Onashelf. She decides to lead the five remaining uninjured Ivy League elves along with the eight Rough Riders who lost their reindeer to the hobgoblin treeshadows' envenomed darts.

A senior officer from the Rough Riders named Elvmore takes charge of the dismounted elves and they join up with Captain Manzone's Behooved, who are now down to ten elf bravos fit for battle, three human swashbucklers—Porthos, Aramis, and Athos—and two tavern brawlers—a civilized Sasquatch troll they call Big Foot and an uncivilized human named Mearl.

Through a complicated chain of interpreters, the elve brava, Trelany, explains the plan to her recruits—Crazy Bull the Trakota Shaman, Karaoke the exiled Fox chieftain, Lazarillo the picaro, Barnum the tumbler, Nate Bumpo the frontiersman, and Atlas the gnome con artist. Although Grumpy is one of the best all-around warriors on the field after Karaoke, his heavy armor makes swimming not an option so he joins up with Oberst Schneevitchen's Magnificent Eight, who welcome him readily.

By the time the strike team assembles, the Metro Gnome slingers have taken up positions behind trees and boulders barely seventy-five yards across the river. There are no more volleys. They send their sling stones pounding in at a syncopated beat to the point where they have the entire convoy locked down. Their stones fly in with such accuracy that anyone who ventures out in the open gets hit with a pellet.

Master Leevai calls to Captain Kolfack, leader of the Glorious Dastards, saying, "We need a distraction!"

Captain Kolfack yells back, "One grand distraction, coming right up!"

The Jewish bard Sholem Aleichem climbs to the top of a battlewagon then dances and plays his fidel. Obsessed with the musical taunting of the bard, the Metro Gnomes redirect their aim to him, but nimble and whirling to the beat of his own wooden clogs tapping on the roof of the command wagon, he somehow evades all their sling stones with outrageous good fortune.

The enchantment only lasts a short while but by the time he leaps down for safety, the battlesages are in position and begin blowing their conch shells and whirling their salt crystal staves.

Suddenly, a wind turbine and a jet stream of water kick up the riverbed, blowing sand and spraying water into the eyes and faces of the baron's army and the Metro Gnomes across the river. Viewing the sandstorm with satisfaction, Captain Kolfack shouts, "Make every grain of wet sand count, yiddishe koepfe!"

Taking advantage of their blindness, Crazy Bull leads his band of light infantry south over the next ridge and out of sight from the rest of the combatants.

The battlesages can only keep up the sandstorm for so long but when the winds and the waters die down, the remaining wagons not destroyed by the Zoramite lightning bolts are driving hard toward the Forge Hill Gap, even though it is still engulfed in flames. The baron of Hershel has his herald blow a horn, signaling the shoot-at-will command to his missile troops.

The wyvern and its renegade fire elf rider, seeing their work undone by the pyrotheurgists, swoop down for another pass. After finally figuring out how to make the dumb thing work, Clarke takes a shot at the wyvern with his artillery scorpion but misses. The elf rider steadies his syphon and sprays the entrance to the pass once more. Although the pyrotheurgists are frustrated to see that they will have to start all over again from scratch, they are otherwise relieved that the wyvern rider has not attempted a direct attack—clearly, he has orders not to destroy the convoy's valuable cargo.

With the bardic trance lost, all the Metro Gnome slingers once again target the convoy with deadly accuracy while the baron of Hershel sends the Zoramite archers and hoplites west to cut off the retreating battlewagons. In this rough terrain, the horses pull valiantly but progress is slow, and it soon becomes clear that the swift-footed Zoramites will outpace them before they reach the Gap. The hobgoblin dire wolf riders and treeshadows hover behind the forest ridge to deny the convoy the right to pass northward.

Just as the hail of sling stones from the Metro Gnomes grows unbearable, Karaoke and Crazy Bull lead the light brigade into the river. The dismounted Rough Rider Senior Officer Elvmore whistles and chirps to call the attention of some nearby mounted Rough Riders. By now they are very familiar with the terrain and show Karaoke and Crazy Bull the best place to cross the river. It is slightly too deep to count as a ford but the taller humans can touch bottom and help the weaker swimmers among the elves make it across the river without getting swept downstream.

Believing in his vision, Crazy Bull keeps the protective black rock clenched in his fist and commands his light brigade to creep up as quickly as possible. The moment the Metro Gnomes notice him, Karaoke yells out in Aenglish, "Forward!"

The light brigade charges forth. Crazy Bull runs out ahead of them with a huge, spiked crossbow-stock club in his right hand and the protective black stone in his left. A swift runner, he reaches the Metro Gnome slingers well ahead of the rest of the light brigade, but he holds his own in the combat—outnumbered thirty to one—without a scratch.

Despite the distraction provided by Crazy Bull, the Metro Gnome slingers see the light brigade coming and storm at them with shot and stone. One after another falls, but the light brigade runs boldly and well into the jaws of death. Although the Metro Gnomes are competent swordsgnomes themselves, once the light brigade closes in for a melee, their skill with leaf-bladed short swords cannot stand up to the artistry of the swashbucklers and bravos. They flash their bare rapiers in the air, slicing down the slingers. The Metro Gnomes reel from the quick strokes; their formation shatters and desynchronizes. In panic, they flee.

A small detachment of Rough Riders has been watching the charge of the light brigade from a safe distance. Now that the Metro Gnomes have been put to flight, they spur their reindeer to swoop in for the attack. Chasing fleeing troops is the Rough Riders' primary calling card. Within moments, the rout is complete—all the Metro Gnomes are either captured or dead on the battlefield.

Dungaree Jeanne and Master Leevai have no time for jubilation over the light brigade's victory over the Metro Gnomes. The hospital wagons are teeming with wounded soldiers and their primary escape route through the Forge Hill Gap has been cut off by an inextinguishable elf fire wall and a large phalanx of Zoramite pikemen supported by sorcerers, magicultors, and heavy archers.

Before the light brigade has time to catch up with the convoy, a full-fledge feudal army reaches the battlefield from the south. Master Leevai recognizes the heraldry on their banners at once. It's the baron of Hershel, an ambitious man and a long-time competitor of Kibbler's commercial interests.

The first ranks of Hershel's army consist of levy infantry—serfs drafted (or levied) to fight in his army. They carry mostly farm implements as weapons, except for a scattered few who are able to afford a cheap sword or bow.

Most of these peasants have no armor but some have stitched together coats of cloth armor. To make cloth armor, you twist rags tightly together and stuff them into four inch tubes. Sew the tubes together around your neck, chest, and waist. Voila! You now have four inches of padding between you and death.

Behind the levy of human light infantry marches a rank of heavily armored gnome infantry. These gnomes have immigrated into the barony of Hershel from the Hungarian province of Luempa-Wuempa after the Cuman Rebellion stirred up fears of a second Tartar invasion.

The Luempa-Wuempa gnomes wear steel mail over padded leather armor with a coat of plates over top. This is the armor many fans of medieval war gaming call plate mail. It is literally a coat with thick plates of steel sewn onto the chest and back. These plates are very heavy but can stop every weapon except a well-placed couched lance in a cavalry charge.

For weapons, and are all armed with swordstaves. Although these Luempa-Wuempa heavy infantry gnomes are vulnerable to sorcerers, they have their own small squad of battlesages to negate the polarization of any opposing lodestones.

On the left flank of the baron's army rides a company of mailed knights, the baron's feudal retainers. A squad of light armed Luempa-Wuempa hound riders holds the flank on the right.

After appraising the battlefield, the baron of Hershel is infuriated by the large army fielded by the Dungaree Jeanne's convoy. With the hobgoblins repulsed, the Zoramites disarmed, and the Metro Gnomes routed, the baron decides it's time to end this game. He orders his herald to blow the horn for the wyvern to incinerate the convoy.

Hearing the horn sound out the code for a full attack, the renegade fire elf torques his wyvern's trajectory hard to come around for a steep strafing run with his elf fire. This time, he starts his fire run from the east and hopes to spray the light brigade, still running out in the open, with elf fire in passing. Nimble on their feet, the light brigade dives and roll out of the way to avoid getting incinerated.

The renegade fire elf rider, in his eagerness to wreak revenge upon the light brigade takes his wyvern closer for a second spray but she has to flap her wings strenuously to avoid cannoning into the river. The sharp upturn in her flight path gives Clarke a clear shot at her chest with his artillery scorpion on top of Master Leevai's command wagon. Unused to the weapon, he points it in the right direction but does not compensate enough for the trajectory of the fletched bolt's arc due to its heavy steel head. The bolt dips faster than Clarke had anticipated and instead of hitting the wyvern's heart, the bolt grazes her belly, causing the creature more pain than permanent harm.

The shot is enough, however, to disrupt her flight pattern. She crash-lands into Master Leevai's command wagon, knocking it over. The pain of the scorpion's bolt ticks her off. Clarke jumps clear as she lunges for the artillery scorpion, chews it, and rips it out of the turret.

Sir Galahad, always fantasizing about fighting a dragon up close, charges at it with his sword-of-war held tightly with both fists. Without a horse, the full suit of double-linked steel mail armor slows his stride to a trundling jog. She snaps at him with her teeth, drawing a precipitated swing with his sword that misses and leaves his guard overextended.

The wyvern bats Sir Galahad back with a sweep of her left wing and locks him in her jaws. His armor is sturdy enough to keep her teeth from sinking into his flesh, but the sheer pressure of her bite squeezes the wind from his lungs. Only the reckless charge of the rest of the knights-errant convinces her to let go, but she thrashes him about one last time for good measure.

The Warband slingers and the other archers launch all they have got at the wyvern, but her thick hide and her savage fury keep the huge creature from feeling most of it. The dwarf crossbow bolts, on the other hand, bite into the wyvern's thick scales and she rears in pain.

The renegade fire elf, angered at the cruel torment his beloved wyvern suffers, sprays a stream of elf flame at Oberst Schneevitchen's Magnificent Eight. The hardy and well-trained dwarves stop, drop, and roll until they smother the flames.

The light brigade, having crossed back over the river, runs up behind the wyvern. They hurl daggers, tomahawks, and clubs at the renegade fire elf. Strapped into his saddle securely, he cannot dodge the incoming projectiles. First one, then two, then a dozen metal objects stick out of his body. He slumps over, lifeless. The enraged and grieving wyvern sweeps half of them off their feet with a single swipe of her tail.

The one who bears the brunt of the tail's impetus is Senior Officer Onashelf, who was trying to maneuver her way onto the wyvern's back to deliver a killing blow between the shoulder blades. With her feet clipped out from under her, Senior Officer Onashelf flounders on the ground, disoriented and exhausted.

Although his artillery scorpion is a wreck, Clarke wants to get back into the fight. He pulls the goblin king's ceremonial dagger out from his leather breast pouch and runs out to slash the tail as it slides by. The wyvern howls with pain and smacks Clarke so hard that he loses his grip on the dagger. Lynx and Louis are shocked at its effectiveness against the thick, scaly hide, but Clarke only rejoices that his precious phoenix talon has a chance to prove its worth in battle.

Crawling on the ground, Senior Officer Onashelf unsheathes a poisoned knife and stabs the wyvern's underbelly. The knife pierces but just barely.

Livid, the wyvern swats Senior Officer Onashelf down with the back of her wing and shambles around to bite the elve to pieces. Seeing the sympathetic senior officer in trouble, Lynx grabs the phoenix talon that has spilled out of Clarke's hand and charges.

Once again the talon proves its worth and punctures the wyvern's scaly hide.

Lynx's tactic works! The wyvern forgets about Senior Officer Onashelf and wheels its head to snap at Lynx. He dives aside but the wyvern readjusts its aim and snatches Lynx up by the midriff.

Seeing Lynx in danger, Louis notices that although the scorpion has snapped its the turret, the arms are still intact. He calls Clarke over and together they set it upright, crank back the winch, and reload it.

Louis hoists the artillery scorpion's slider beam onto his back. Taking careful aim, Clarke launches a well-placed bolt and pierces the wyvern in the side. The scorpion bolt, the crossbow dwarves' quarrels, the poisoned long knife and the phoenix talon dagger have all taken their toll, the wyvern staggers and drops Lynx—at least, what's left of him.

Dungaree Jeanne, Louis, and Clarke run over to Lynx to see if he's all right. As soon as they get there, they realize they'd hoped for too much. Tears fill their eyes as they look at a brave elf, chewed up and spit out by a wyvern. He's a bloody mess, with gaping wounds across his abdomen and legs.

Louis bends down to pick him up but Clarke stops him and says, "No, wait! If you don't carry him the right way, you'll make it worse. It doesn't look good, but the clerics can still fix him up. We've got to hurry!"

Clarke nudges Louis aside and uses his medical training as a cleric to staunch the blood and avoid aggravating any broken bones. He gets his arms around Lynx in a delicate manner to hoist him up and get him to the healers as quickly and as gently as possible.

They are so distraught over Lynx's condition that they don't even notice that Hershel's cavalry is moving into position for the final charge.

Senior Officer Onashelf shakes her head and staggers to her feet. Still stunned by the wyvern's blow, she stands there dazed until she sees Clarke carrying Lynx to the hospital wagon. Blood is dripping everywhere. Onashelf screams, "Nooooo!"

Turning around with tears in her own eyes, Dungaree Jeanne snaps back into command of the situation. "Senior Officer Onashelf, rally the Ivy League and tell Captain Manzone to gather up his Behooved! Report to Master Leevai's command wagon with all the captains you can find on the double."

Senior Officer Onashelf sobs and then recovers her breath enough to say, "What about Monsieur Lynx?"

Dungaree Jeanne shakes her head. "Nothing in this world can help Monsieur Lynx at this point."

Not knowing why, but feeling it's important, Senior Officer Onashelf runs over to the dead wyvern and extracts the phoenix talon dagger that Lynx plunged into its neck. She then heads out to comply with Dungaree Jeanne's orders.

Master Leevai runs out and says hurriedly, "They're surrounding us, Madame Dungaree! Our escape route through the Forge Hill Gap is a burning inferno. If there are any more tricks up your sleeve or any options at all that I have not considered, now is the time to tell me about it. I'm out of backup plans."

Dungaree Jeanne says, "Yes, I've still got one move left—it's called a pawn promotion. All we have to do is make it through the firewall in the Gap. Get your strongest soldiers to tip the command wagon back onto its wheels. Let's move!"

Master Leevai thinks she's going mad. "At least two hundred Zoramites are blocking our way to the Gap!"

Dungaree Jeanne does not waver. She says, "Once the Glorious Dastards engage the Zoramites from the southern flank, I'll send the Behooved around their flanks to the north. With the Zoramites split, the Skybrim will push through the middle and split the firewall open wide enough for the wagons to pass through. We'll be safe once we're inside the Gap."

Putting his faith in her, Master Leevai asks no more questions but sends his Glorious Dastards to face off against the Zoramites. No sooner do they get into position to make a rush at the Zoramites than the baron's feudal knights line themselves up, knee to knee, for a couched lance charge at their rear.

Check!

Dungaree Jeanne cannot allow those knights to break the Glorious Dastards from behind. She tells Captain Gunnar to send the elf boar riders whom he's been holding in reserve to challenge Hershel's feudal knights. There are only six boar riders against Hershel's twenty-seven feudal knights. They don't flinch.

Seeing what is happening Master Leevai orders Sir Lancelot to bring his eleven remaining Knights of the Round Table to back up the boar riders. Seventeen heavy cavalry cannot hope to win a head-on charge against twenty-seven feudal knights but seventeen are enough to give them pause.

Hershel's knight banneret in command, Sir Rhys, waffles between clearing out the Knights of the Round Table first and obeying Hershel's orders to charge the Glorious Dastards once they get into position. A knights double-linked mail armor is tough enough to withstand most infantry weapons, even attacks from behind, but a couched lance in the back is death.

Heavily armored warhorses are hard enough to turn around on a parade ground. Once they commit to their attack against the Glorious Dastards there's nothing they can do to keep themselves from getting skewered from behind.

The baron of Hershel counters the Knights of the Round Table by sending his heavily armored Luempa-Wuempa swordstaff infantry forward. Although human bred warhorses are so large the gnomes' fingertips can't reach the riders, their swordstaves can. In fact these swordstaves are specially designed to find gaps in knights' armor with their blades and rip knights off their saddles with their hooks.

Unless the Knights of the Round Table and the boar riders charge soon, Luempa-Wuempa swordstaff infantry will shred them to pieces.

Check!

Dungaree Jeanne has no choice but to order the gnome slingers of the Warband to hold them at bay. Although the Luempa-Wuempas barely feel the Warband's sling stones and pellets against their coat of plates and visored helmets, their armor has gaps. In particular, gnomes despise shoes. Once the Luempa-Wuempas get close enough to threaten Dungaree Jeanne's heavy cavalry, the Warband will be able to dislocate elbows and cripple shins with studied aim.

Seeing the Luempa-Wuempa infantry come to a halt, Dungaree Jeanne is about to give the order for the Glorious Dastards to attack the Zoramites when a large pack of hobgoblin dire wolf riders swoop down from the northern ridge.

They toss their deadly war darts at Dungaree Jeanne's Behooved light infantry and at the Glorious Dastards. These hobgoblin war darts have three-foot shafts, barbed tips, and fletching to help them fly straight. Leather thongs attached to the back, called catkins, enhance the speed and distance of a throw, similar to an atlatl. A well-thrown war dart can pierce ordinary steel mail from thirty yards. The Behooved and the Glorious Dastards suffer ugly wounds.

Although many of the Behooved are skilled at throwing daggers and hatchets, they've been fighting all day and few have any to spare. The dire wolf riders don't allow themselves to approach within effective rang of throwing weapons anyway, since the catkins on their war darts give them plenty of range.

Check!

Dungaree Jeanne calls Captain Gunnar and instructs him to lead the Rough Riders against the hobgoblins. They are the only unit she has left that can move fast enough to run them off but it's a big risk. Reindeer scouts are auxiliary troops—they are mostly active before and after a battle, gathering intelligence about the lay of the land and troop dispositions and then chasing down fleeing troops.

They are equipped with short recurve bows for hit-and-run tactics when necessary, but other than elf long knives and a small, round leather shield with a metal boss called a fender, they generally don't carry any other weapons. Dire wolf riders, instead, are the hobgoblins' primary shock troops.

As a rule, sending reindeer scouts against dire wolf riders is foolhardy at best. But rules have exceptions. The Rough Riders are not just scouts fulfilling their community service obligations in a military league, they are mercenaries whose main goal in life is being deadly. Captain Gunnar, is a specialist in the elf *apgar,* or hewing spear and has trained his followers in its use. The hewing spear mounts a seax blade on a long sturdy pole so that it can chop, slash, and stab with one hand or with two depending on the foe's tactics. Captain Gunnar excels in all three techniques.

The Rough Riders sally forth peppering the hobgoblins with broadhead arrows from their recurve bows but the hobgoblins only take it as in invitation to dance. It is only when the reindeer charge at them directly with their sharpened antlers do the dire wolves take notice. They snap back with sharp canines but quickly get a mouthful of elven *apgar* blade.

In melee combat, hobgoblins do not have a standard weapon and can use anything from a crude spear to a bladed gauntlet. The most common weapon for hand-to-hand combat among dire wolf riders is the hobgoblin sickle-sword, which crudely resembles an ancient Egyptian *khopesh*. They carry a round shield that is a smaller version of an infantry targe, called a target, which is almost always exactly twenty inches in diameter and could be made of anything from wicker-woven vines to solid steel.

Medieval elves often prized the wicker-woven versions of captured hobgoblin shields for use in archery practice, hence deriving the meaning that the word *target* has taken on today.

The Rough Riders inflict a heavy toll in casualties upon the hobgoblin dire wolf riders with their initial assault, but once the hobgoblins wisen up to the sting of a reindeer's antler the fight turns into a face-paced skirmish with both sides cautiously awaiting the opportune moment to strike at their foes and neither side drawing enough blood to disable the other.

That's good enough for Dungaree Jeanne. She turns to Master Leevai and asks, "Are the Glorious Dastards ready to attack the Zoramites now?"

Master Leevai glances around the battlefield and says, "No! Look!"

The baron of Hershel has sent his gnome hound riders to break the stalemate between the hobgoblins and the Rough Riders. The hounds are even bigger than dire wolves but much less ferocious. Instead they are bred for speed and heartiness. They can run fast and for a long time. Hound riders, like jockeys today, must be small, slender, and indomitable.

Their speed is mind-boggling, even for swift reindeer scouts. They are the lightest of all cavalry troops in Vinland, carrying no weapons other than a small stack of javelins and no protection other than a round shield (*targe*). Their main tactic is to spot unsuspecting foes and pick them off with a javelin strike mid-stride in a high speed pass.

The alert Rough Riders would normally not have trouble returning the favor with a few well-placed arrows but with hobgoblins to worry about dodging in and out of the forest to the north, the gnome hound riders take their toll in blood without retribution.

Check!

With their tactical situation deteriorating quickly, Dungaree Jeanne cannot redirect the Warband's attention to the hound riders without allowing the Luempa-Wuempa heavy infantry to get within striking range of her heavy cavalry who in turn are keeping Hershel's feudal knights from charging into the Glorious Dastards' rear.

"I must ride out against those hound riders myself."

Master Leevai is appalled at the idea. "You can't risk your life like that. If we lose you, we're all lost. The Skybrim can take care of those hound riders."

Dungaree Jeanne gives him a stern look and says, "Correction, if we can't get past that firewall, we're all lost. The Skybrim pyrotheurgists are the only ones who can do that and the rest of the Skybrim are needed to keep them safe. I'll ride with my household guards. The Magnificent Eight can cover us with their crossbow bolts from the top of the Command Wagon."

Master Leevai resigns himself. "It's our last desperate hour. Go and may God be with you."

Dungaree Jeanne mounts up with her personal retainers, relatives, and household guards and leads the attack. Her reindeer riders make their first shots with their recurve bows count before the hound riders see them coming. Realizing they have been outflanked, the sleek gnome jockeys loop around Dungaree Jeanne's back, easily outrunning her retinue's reindeer.

As the gnome hound riders hustle to their new vantage point, the Magnificent Eight loose a withering volley of crossbow bolts. Six hounds drop and their riders take a nasty spill. Unnerved, the remaining gnome hound riders clear off the field of battle entirely.

Dungaree Jeanne joins up with the Rough Riders. Together they drive the hobgoblin dire wolf riders over the ridge. As the hobgoblins fall back, Dungaree Jeanne raises her arm signaling for her light cavalry to follow.

Experienced military professionals all, they wheel around in good order and descend upon the Luempa-Wuempa heavy infantry. They never get close but they harass the heavily armored gnomes with arrows, attacking from the rear and feinting charges.

Master Leevai needs no further cues. He orders the Warband to switch their sights from the Luempa-Wuempas to the hobgoblin dire wolf riders who are just now emerging from the forest to attack Dungaree Jeanne's light cavalry in the rear. Thanks to the river, they can't get to here without passing close by the Warband's battlewagon. Not a single one would survive, so the hobgoblins hover behind the northern ridge, waiting for a suitable opening to resume their attack.

With the hobgoblins and the Luempa-Wuempa's tied down, Master Leevai blows his horn for the Knights of the Round Table and the elf boar riders to attack Hershel's feudal knights. Sir Lancelot has already worked out a plan with his elf allies. The Knights of the Round Table will attack with swords, not lances to hold the attention of Hershel's much larger cavalry force. If any of the feudal knights break their couched lance formation to counter properly with swords, the boar riders will dart into the fray to clip the legs of the warhorses as they pass. Heavy double-linked steel mail only makes getting thrown from a giant horse more lethal a fall.

Barely do the Knights of the Round Table make contact with Hershel's feudal knights when Master Leevai signals the Glorious Dastards, along with the heavier armored members of Captain Manzone's Behooved, to charge at the Zoramites simultaneously. The Zoramite archers loose a volley of arrows into their midst to break their momentum but the Skybrim battlesages and metalleurgic sorcerers ply their skills well enough to deflect the incoming arrows above their heads or into the ground.

Despite their courage and the Skybrim's protection, Master Leevai's light infantry troops all stop in their tracks before they engage the Zoramite hoplites in phalanx formation. The Zoramites' spears are long enough and their ranks are tight enough that the Glorious Dastards and the Behooved would have to bypass three rows of spearheads before they even make contact with the enemy.

The Skybrim do their best to repel and locomutate away those bronze spearheads but the Zoramites have battlemages and battlesages of their own who, though not as powerful, are still skilled enough to negate their attempts with strong defensive techniques.

Observing the impasse, Master Leevai calls up one of the Bikur Holim for some good, old-time smiting. Walking forward, Hakham Jehoshaphat takes off his large headdress and puts on a small skull cap, revealing his completely bald head. He starts praying.

You have probably observed some rabbis swaying forward and back while in prayer—apparently, prayerful rocking is a tradition that stretches back to the Middle Ages and beyond. Hakham Jehoshaphat demonstrates a unique spiritual tradition whereby once he really gets into his prayer, he then starts jumping.

The Zoramites foolishly take the bait and start mocking the man of God for his bald head and his odd method of prayer. The jumping Hakham Jehoshaphat calls down upon them the curse of Elisha, and two huge cave bears suddenly come charging out of the forest. To get a sense of how big an eleven-foot cave bear is, try to imagine that the bear's paws are so big enough to scratch the top of a gnome's head with its thumb and tickles his toes with its pinky at the same time. The cave bears charge in, kill forty-two Zoramites, then wander away.

Following the bear attack, the terrified Zoramites lose some of their cohesion. Barnum the tumbler does a diving roll underneath the three rows of spears and slashes some ankles with his long knives before scampering away. Taking his cue, the Elf bravos and Glorios Dastards smash, bash, hop, skip, and jump about their foes, determined to provide the Skybrim with the distraction they need to part the firewall.

"Jumping Jehoshaphat! He did it!" cries Master Leevai. "Quickly, it's now or never!"

The Skybrim battlesages and battlemages focus with all their might. In one coordinated surge, they invest all their will and strength into blasting a magnetic hole in the middle of the Zoramite phalanx.

The berserker, Shimshon Roth, leaps into the hole at the head of a triangle of the Glorious Dastard's toughest warriors. They drive a wedge of meat and steel into the Zoramite phalanx so that the pyrotheurgist can get close enough to the firewall to open it.

Realizing what is happening, the Zoramite captains urge their hoplites to take down Shimshon Roth's squad before they split the middle. They poke, slash, and gauge out flesh but the berserker continues dealing blows with unmitigated ferocity. Shimshon Roth draws so much attention to himself that the Zoramites fail to notice the pyrotheurgists slip through.

The firewall parts.

Sir Robert Roger's rangers come pouring through the Forge Hill Gap like lions leaping toward their prey.

Leading the charge are the rangers' three big heavies—Sir John Henry of Big Bend, the escaped Aphrican slave with bulging muscles who wields a giant sledgehammer of war, also known as a maul; Sir Paul Bunyan, the Frankish-Canuck woodcutter who stands seven feet tall, brandishing a double-edged lumberjack axe; and Sir Casey of Mudville, the husky warrior armed with a large, two-handed oaken bat.

These three specialize in breaking through enemy ranks. The three ranger heavyweights smash into the Zoramites from behind long before Hershel's cavalry or infantry can complete their charge. They stiff-arm their massive weapons sideways and bowl over as many unsuspecting Zoramites as possible in the initial rush. From there, they push and shove their way forward until they meet up with the Glorious Dastards.

With a large wedge of rangers following the big three into the gap, they shatter the Zoramite phalanx with the combined vigor of unified, fresh troops breaking into an exhausted battlefield.

Sir Robert Roger of Methuen, their leader, Sir Jon Stark, the unit's first lieutenant, the bear fighter Sir Davy Crickett, the "Swamp Fox" Dame Frances Marian, who would eventually be credited as the founder of the United States' special forces; the famous knife fighter Sir Jim Bowey, who would later amass a great fortune manufacturing and selling the war knives he relied on most; and Sir Cotrel Walker, the ranger from the Principality of Texico famed for his combat skills both with and without weapons; all plow into the Zoramite ranks in unison with the big heavies.

Following close behind them is a second wave of rangers, including the pioneer, patriot, and politician Sir Daniel Boon; Sir Ethen Allan, who later founded his own company of rangers during the War of Independence called the Green Mountain Boys along with Sir Seth Werner; the halfling ranger Sir Kip Karlson, who later stole from the rich and gave to the poor (keeping a small finder's fee for himself).

Sir Benedict Arnald, the faithful leader of the rearguard follows up with his three heavies—Sir Febold Feboldson, Sir Joe Magarac, and Sir Joseph of Montferrand, also known as Big Joe Mufferow. Behind them march the future mayor of Baston and regent during the interregnum Sir Jack Hancock; Sir Humbert of Denk, whose failed marriages made him the subject of much gossip; Sir Daniel Morgon, hailed as the most brilliant tactician in the War of Independence; Sir Gilbert Sullivan, the Erinish ranger who went on to a prominent career in theater after his retirement from adventuring; Sir Rip van Winkel, who lived to a very ripe old age thanks to his vigorous regimen of mid-afternoon naps; Sir Frankl Stein, the tall Ashkuzi ranger famed for his intellect; and the infamous dwarf magicultor, Sir Rumpel Stilton.

Seeing the Zoramite phalanx shattered, the baron of Hershel commits all his reserves consisting of his peasant levy, which pose little threat and a pawn promotion of his own, whose threat no fire elf could have imagined.

Dungaree Jeanne and the Rough Riders have done their best to stall the baron's swordstaff heavy infantry gnomes but the Luempa-Wuempa captain has displayed sound tactical judgment. Deducing that the reindeer riders attack was aimed at distracting them from defending Hershel's feudal knights, he orders his beleaguered gnomes to ignore the incoming arrows and march double-time towards the Knights of the Round Table and the elf boar riders.

Although the toll in casualties is heavy, the Luempa-Wuempa's gamble pays off. Keeping an active awareness of the field of battle, Sir Lancelot spots the armored gnomes bearing down on his rear and orders his knights and boar riders to withdraw.

The captain of the company of feudal knights is the baron of Hershel's cousin, Sir Goodbar. Although Sir Lancelot's charge has taken down seven of his knights, he does not allow his men to seek revenge while they withdraw. Instead, he points to the Glorious Dastards and shouts, "See there, my brave companions! Those ruffians have dispersed our Zoramite allies. Let us punish their arrogance before they have a chance to reform their ranks! Charge!"

With that he canters off, whirling his sword high above his head. The feudal knights themselves are in disarray. A cavalry charge with heavy warhorses lined up in a tight rank, knee to knee, is a superbly destructive force on a medieval battlefield. Charging one at a time without coordination lessens the impact considerably but timing is everything. With the Glorious Dastards focused on the fleeing Zoramites and unprepared to counter a cavalry charge, Sir Goodbar sees an opening and he means to seize it.

As for Hershel's peasant levy, pawns in every sense of the word, they race forward with the baron close behind. They bypass the fighting entirely. The baron is using them as a mere screen to hide a small cart drawn by a boar.

It turns out the Baron wanted to leave nothing to chance and was well prepared to fight fire with fire. He has hired not one but two renegade fire elves. This second one slips into the Forge Hill Gap undetected thanks to the cover provided by the peasant levy and pours out an incendiary ooze across the entrance. Dungaree Jeanne's retreat is cut off once and for all.

Checkmate!

Watching horror-struck as the curtain of firewall closes, Dungaree Jeanne races back to the command wagon and announces to Master Leevai in Aenglish, "We are surrounded, cut off, and outnumbered. We cannot win this fight. Our best hope is a stalemate. If the baron of Hershel wants our cocoa beans, he can have them." She kicks one of the cocoa bean sack over and splits it open with her leaf-bladed sword.

Dungaree Jeanne continues, "The Rough Riders and I will will scatter the rest of the cocoa beans across the field. His mercenary army is fighting for riches, so we'll give them more than they ever dreamed of."

"While I provide the distraction, Battlemage Shabtai, but I'm also going to you to breach that firewall just one more time so you can all escape."

Battlemage Shabtai tugs his beard, "Impossible! We exhausted all our resources to open the first time."

Dungaree Jeanne will not take no for an answer. "I can stall them. Tell your company to reach deep inside and put all they've got into it. We need to break through the firewall for us all to survive. It's do or die."

"Then we die, Madame Dungaree. If you overload a donkey's back, it breaks. If you overload a sorcerer's mind, it breaks. Elf fire is resistant to sorcery. Your own people designed it that way. They have no chance of surviving another effort against it. Getting hacked to pieces by a sword would be a gentler death for them."

"But we have no alternative. There must be a way to crack that firewall."

Silence follows. The terror on the battlemage's face makes it clear to them all that his refusal is not mere stubbornness. They have reached limits of nature that even the most powerful clayborn cannot cross. In the quiet, despair sinks into their hearts.

"I have a way."

All eyes in the room turn to Master Leevai, who pulls out a small silver box attached to his neck by a silver chain and offers it to her. "Here, take it. This amulet is worth more than all my other assets combined. All my riches are thanks to you, so this amulet is rightfully yours.

"The centerpiece is an archon stone. It can maintain the polarization of any source stone that touches it. Surrounding the archon stone in that silver box are three powerful source stones that are permanently polarized to repel fire, aether, and metal. It will allow you and anyone within ten feet of you to walk through the firewall unharmed."

Dungaree Jeanne gasps, "Ten feet! That's barely enough for one wagon! Surely you're not expecting me to run away and leave you all here to die!"

Master Leevai says calmly, "If your distraction works well enough we can all survive. You take the wounded in two hospital wagons of the Augustinians and the Bikur Holim through the Gap. Everyone else who can still run or ride will race south with me to Fort Loudon until we're sure we're safe. Then I'll fetch the other five bags of cocoa beans from Harrisburgh and bring them to you in Shentalpee City."

"But you said ten feet! That's only enough to get one wagon through."

"Unhitch the horses. They wouldn't walk into the firewall anyway. You ride the wagon up front while a few stout humans and dwarves push the wagons from behind. Once the first is through move back and jump onto the second. If you do it right you could get both wagons through quite quickly. Then the fire wall will close behind you and seal off your escape.

"Depending on how greedy the baron of Hershel's troops are we might need to pull off a fighting withdrawal. His side has suffered numerous casualties as well, so chances are good he'll let us go as soon as he sees his mercenaries running off with all his loot."

Dungaree Jeanne holds up the silver box with the archon stone inside and says, "Thank you for being a faithful friend all these years, Master Leevai. When that firewall closed, I almost succumbed to despair, but this archon stone has given me a new hope."

Master Leevai pushes her out. "We can get all sentimental next week while sipping tarberry juice at the gazebo. For now, let's hand out some cocoa!"

The Rough Riders gather around to fill pouches and helmets with scoops of cocoa beans. Master Leevai asks Louis and Clarke to relay the plan to the rangers in Aenglish and get them to lend a hand unhitching the horses and pushing the hospital wagon.

Meanwhile, the Glorious Dastards fight with all their might and main to survive. The feudal knights' charge into their ranks was poorly coordinated and they saw it coming but it still battered a good number of Dastards. After all, lacking spearmen, they couldn't do much to stop the knights other than spread out a bit to give themselves some room to dodge.

However, several Skybrim battlemages were able to locomutate away buckles and saddle straps so that when the battlesages set their lodestones to repel metal, several armored knights flew off their horses.

Moreover, the Behooved and the rangers joined the Glorious Dastards in taking on the feudal knights with all sorts of unorthodox fighting methods, everything from grabbing riding boots to tossing cloaks over their helmets.

For his part, although Sir Lancelot couldn't stop Hershel's feudal knights from attacking the Glorious Dastards, he did order his Knights of the Round Table and the elf boar riders with him to swoop down upon the feudal knights in the rear while the Luempa-Wuempa swordstaff infantry were hustling across the field to catch up with them.

The Luempa-Wuempa captain again shows his prowess in warlike tactics. He splits his company into two ranks. The first company turns volte-face to form a spear wall, protecting their rear from a cavalry attack, while the second company continues on towards the Glorious Dastards and the Behooved to help the feudal knights scatter them off the battlefield.

The baron of Hershel is thoroughly impressed with the Luempa-Wuempa captain's ability to improvise on the go and follows up that initiative by ordering his levy peasants to charge the rear flank of the Behooved.

Timing is everything. Hershel's poorly trained and poorly equipped farmers wouldn't have stood much of a chance against those ferocious fighters except that the Behooved was a motley bunch to begin with, many of whom already got going when the going got tough. Down to fourteen soldiers and having committed themselves to the battle with the feudal knights, the remaining Behooved fighters pale with terror hearing fifty desperate peasants with long, pointy objects shouting vehemently behind them.

Likewise, the only eighteen uninjured Glorious Dastards are left in the fight. They are profoundly exhausted and shaken by the loss of so many of their comrades in arms. Now that they see another wave of well-equipped and well-trained gnomes coming to the attack, the Dastards lose heart.

Tasting victory so close, Hershel orders his musicians to pound their kettledrums and blast their trumpets, a rallying call for all his troops to join in the final drive to crush the convoy's last dram of resistance.

The baron laughs to himself as those coveted sacks of cocoa beans pathetically tossed out of the convoy wagons in an act of abject desperation. He waves his hand in the air and shouts, "Finish them!"

What? Where are they? His army is gone! Hundreds of warriors have vanished! What foul magic has worked such a wonder?

Cocoa beans! Millions of pennies' worth of cocoa beans just lying about the battlefield! The levy foot soldiers are the first to see the cocoa beans and grab for them immediately.

Who could blame them? A few handful of those would make for a decent retirement fund! No sense in putting their lives in grave danger when they could grab dollars' and dollars' worth of cocoa beans!

The hobgoblin dire wolves only need one sniff and they faithfully race to the closest stash of cocoa beans. The treeshadows descend on the battlefield to join the feeding frenzy. Tipped off that there might be other sacks of cocoa, the fleeing Zoramites double back to scavenge for loot. Each sack of brown gold sets off a new scrum—the various conscripted and mercenary groups wrestling each other for control over the cocoa.

Even the baron of Hershel has enough economic sense to recall anyone loyal enough to heed his voice out of combat to help him seize the beans for himself. If those mercenaries escape with all that cocoa, the financial loss from assembling an army with borrowed money will ruin him.

Master Leevai has experienced the fickleness of fortune firsthand too many times to believe they are safe. It is time to cut his losses and get out of there as fast as possible. He steers his battlewagon south and whips the horses to give it everything they've got to get them out of there. Seeing that the loyal Luempa-Wuempas are still exchanging blows with his Glorious Dastards, he calls out to Captain Kolfack, "Retreat! Get the wounded onto the wagons! This is our only chance to escape with our lives!"

The Luempa-Wuempas have no intention of letting the Glorious Dastards get away but the baron of Hershel calls them off. Reluctantly they obey orders.

Deeply relieved that Master Leevai has successfully disengaged from combat, Dungaree Jeanne orders her hospital wagon to move west through the firewall. Huddled within her archon stone's bubble of protection, the rangers and the Magnificent Eight dwarves push the wagon into the raging wall of elf fire. The fire stone in the amulet, powered by the archon stone, parts the firewall before them.

Once she and the two hospital wagons have passed through, the firewall closes back in on itself, sealing off their flight through the Forge Hill Gap from pursuit.

But pursuit is the last item on the baron of Hershel's agenda. He paid a small fortune for the information about the cocoa bean shipment and for the mercenary contracts to secure it. Thanks to their magicultors, the Zoramites take control of nearly two hundred pounds of cocoa beans and load it on their supply wagon. With the hobgoblins dashing about to collect the beans and the peasant rabble grabbing whatever they can for themselves, Hershel is running out of options.

Most of his feudal knights have all been killed, injured, or unhorsed. They are in no shape to run around the battlefield picking up tiny beans. The only loyal units left intact are his Luempa-Wuempas, the hound riders and the swordstaff infantry. They follow his orders, dash quickly about collecting cocoa bean sacks and driving off looters.

In the end, the baron and his loyal Luempa-Wuempas eventually quit the battlefield with nearly five hundred pounds of cocoa beans. Bitter at the betrayal of the vast majority of his army, the baron of Hershel retreats to his castle to live the life of a recluse, thoroughly resolved never to trust anyone except his Luempa-Wuempa gnomes ever again.

For their part, when it comes to processing and marketing cocoa beans, the Luempa-Wuempas prove themselves as dependable in their sweatshops as they were in the heat of battle, making the baron a very wealthy man indeed.

Scene F: All Quiet on the Western Face

Forge Hill Gap in the Confederacy of the Seven Nations
Thor's Day Vespers. Evening, 20th of April, 1284
Morrow of the Feast of Saint Aelfheah, Bishop and Martyr

As soon as the firewall closes behind them, Dungaree Jeanne opens the hatch to get an update on Lynx's condition from the clerics. "Sorry, Madame Dungaree, but that elf was dead on arrival."

"No, no, no! I'm paying you to heal him. Now get to work and make him better."

Speaking for the group, a dwarve nun by the name of Mother Elvira puts a hand on her arm and says, "Madame Dungaree, this has been a traumatic day, with many serious losses. Having treated so many wounded and prayed so many prayers, we are all at the limits of our physical, mental, and spiritual endurance. We knew he was a Christian and had him anointed. That's all we could do for him. I'm very sorry for your loss, Madame Dungaree."

The loss of Lynx brings a bigger emotional shock to her psyche than all the other disasters of this ordeal put together. She cannot admit to herself that he is gone. She sits there stunned and bursts forth with a flood of tears until she is too tired to even cry.

For a while, a somber silence pervades the wagon but eventually, a light banter develops. She hears the name Lazarillo and remembers the Bible story where Jesus raised Lazarus from the dead.

Maybe a Christian healer powerful enough might be able to bring Lynx back. Her thoughts turn to

Johnny Appleseed. She is not sure exactly how the system works in spiritual realms but she figures she has done enough good in her life to try negotiating with God. *I've done so much for your holy man, the least he could do for me would be to resurrect Lynx.*

By the time Dungaree Jeanne's hospital wagon arrives back at Tuscoraura Mountain it is late at night, but she orders Captain Manzone and two of his bravos to carry Lynx's body up to her home as quickly as possible. The dwarf elevator operator on night duty is asleep and she shakes him vigorously to wake him up.

Coming out of his sleep the dwarf murmurs, "What? Oh . . . you want to get up to the top. That'll be a nighttime fee of five dimes or two quarters."

Dungaree Jeanne almost chokes. "Look, I'm not in any mood for haggling. My friend needs urgent medical attention. Here's a dime. Get us up there now!"

"I'm sorry, madam, but a dime only covers one passenger during the nighttime."

Dungaree Jeanne's veins start popping on her neck and temples. "Passengers are a dime a dozen, day or night. Now get us up there at once or I'll take this up with Lawspeaker Snorrison. He happens to be a personal friend of mine."

Apparently dropping a name like Snorrison's makes an impression on this sleepy dwarf and he pulls the lever that releases the counterweight stones. The elevator bounces up and down, then slowly climbs as the dwarf pulls down on the weighted rope.

Once up in Thor's Plaza, she orders the bravos carrying Lynx's body to follow her at a jog. She knows that rushing about is not going to change anything but somehow, when it comes to someone you love, you feel like you need to do something . . . anything . . . rather than roll over and let them slip away from you without fighting back. Observing the commotion, the Justiciar League night watch elves approach.

"Halt!" calls out Justiciar League Officer Bunzi.

Dungaree Jeanne calls out, "Quickly, send word to the Major Leagues Umpire that I'm back. If you still have any hopes for your future, make sure you inform him yourself."

Officer Bunzi resents being brushed aside, but aware of the dramatic political crises afoot, he obeys.

Arriving at her mansion, Dungaree Jeanne fumbles for her keys and finally finds the spare key in the flower pot but not in the exact location she left it. Someone must have been fiddling with it. She tells herself she will worry about that later.

Bursting into Johnny Appleseed's room, she takes a candlestick out of its holder and lights it with Captain Manzone's torch. She hates to wake him up rudely and hopes that lighting the various candelabras and lamps around the room will pull him out of sleep gently, but Appleseed just rolls over and keeps snoring.

Addressing the bravos, Dungaree Jeanne points to the bench in the bay window. "Put him on that bench."

The bravos lay Lynx on the bench while Dungaree Jeanne tries to awaken Johnny Appleseed by slapping him on the shoulder. She says in Aenglish, "Help me, Reverend Appleseed. You are our only hope."

Captain Manzone does not allow his bravos to slouch one bit. Utterly exhausted from a very long and hard day but aware of the delicate emotional circumstances, he lines up with them respectfully and makes them stand at attention.

Dungaree Jeanne takes the hint and says, "Thank you, Captain Manzone. Company dismissed."

Captain Manzone bows respectfully and his bravos do their best to imitate his demeanor, though a respectful and humble attitude does not come to them naturally. They eagerly leave for some well-deserved rest. Although slouches when it comes to hard work, these bravos lived up to their name today and all performed bravely on the battlefield. They are good and ready to pamper themselves for the next few days.

Still hunched over Johnny Appleseed, she looks back to check on him one more time. By now his eyes are open and his face shows how much of a struggle it is for him not to fall back asleep right away. Confused, he greets her with a feeble smile. "Good morning, Madame Dungaree."

Dungaree Jeanne stands up and filled with courage, fear, hope, and despair all mixed in one, says, "Pardon me, Reverend Appleseed, but it is not yet morning. I need you to look at Lynx. The clerics and healers we hired said they couldn't do anything for him."

"Sure," says Appleseed, still not catching what's going on as he struggles to sit up. Lynx is completely motionless and soaked in blood. Without thinking, goes to stand up and puts his weight on his broken leg. The pain nearly makes him faint. With a tremendous effort of will Johnny Appleseed takes two painful hops on his good leg and sits on the window bay next to Lynx.

Appleseed closes his eyes and begins to pray silently with his hand on Lynx's head. Dungaree Jeanne stands next to him, waiting. The silence of the room and the peace of the night opens her repressed sentiments and tears start to drip from her eyes.

After a good while, Appleseed opens his eyes. "I'm sorry, Madame Dungaree, but the boy is dead."

Dungaree Jeanne tries to say something but instead she lets loose with sobs and tears and bitter groans of lamentation. He puts a hand on her shoulder to comfort her but she remains stiff and unbending.

Eventually, the sobbing calms down and she tries again to speak but instead only lets loose a new round of tears. Finally, the third time around, she manages to say, "If you had been there, he would not have died. But I am sure anything you ask of God, God will give it to you."

"Madame Dungaree—" Johnny Appleseed begins to say something, then stops.

"Yes?"

"Never mind. I can see your mind is made up. I will pray and ask God to raise him from the dead."

A loud sigh of relief escapes her lips and the exhaustion and strain of the day smack her like a reindeer rider smacking her head on a low-hanging branch. She wobbles on her feet and walks over to his bed. She sits and waits.

And waits.

After a long, deep prayer, Johnny Appleseed opens his eyes as if he were not quite sure where he is at present. Dungaree Jeanne looks at him, expectantly awaiting his pronouncement. He gives her a long, blank stare. Dungaree Jeanne loses patience and asks, "Is he alive again?"

As if coming to his senses, Appleseed looks around and recognizes the room, the bed, her face, and says, "Oh yes, he is alive—but in another world."

"Bring him back to this world!"

Compassion and sadness wash over his face with a tinge of celestial happiness and he says, "He does not want to come back, Madame Dungaree. He died well, sealed with the blood of the Lamb."

She looks at him, baffled, angry at the words she is hearing and says, "He's covered in his own blood. There was no lamb."

"He died to save the life of another, to save many lives. He was willing to lay down his life for his friends and there is no greater love than that."

She shakes her head. "There's got to be something you can do: restart his heart or put air in his lungs!"

Appleseed looks down for a moment, then looks her straight in the eyes. "Madame Dungaree, I'm a miracle worker, not a doctor. The whole point of my job is to help people get to heaven, not to fix their bodies. I don't know any easier way to say this but he is where he belongs, and he doesn't want to come back."

"Yes, but God hears your prayers when you ask for something. Ask God to send Lynx back to us."

"I did ask and God said no. He allowed me to talk to Lynx personally, and Lynx asked me to convey to you two favors that he would like to ask of you."

Dungaree Jeanne looks at him, not quite sure if she wants to believe his words or not.

Appleseed continues, "He asked that you burn his body on a funeral pyre so Umpire Gandorf cannot try to recall his soul through a blackflame ritual."

She gasps.

"He also asks that you keep Zena's engagement ring on your finger. He says he sees now that there was a lot that was selfish about his love for Zena, but that his love was always sincere and always real. He wanted what was best for you both and was willing to undergo whatever risks and sacrifices it would take to make it happen. He cannot take the ring with him but he can keep the love. Whenever you see it, you will think of him—and perhaps yearn for your heavenly home together with him."

Dungaree Jeanne weeps to the very depths of her soul. The sobs gush out so that she feels the pangs in her ribs; it scrapes her throat raw and burns her eyes.

Johnny Appleseed gets up and puts his arm around her and holds her for a while until she falls asleep in his arms. The discomfort to his leg is so great that he eventually relents from his compassionate support and lays her down on his bed. He puts a sheet over her and grabs a pillow and cover for himself and goes back to sleep on the maple hardwood floor.

Scene G: Counting Magpies

Betzy Rose Mansion, Red Giant's Base, Shentalpee City
Saturn's Day Nones. Afternoon, 22nd of April, 1284
Eve of the Feast of Saint George, Martyr

Hearing a knock at the door, the new stewardess opens it and says, "Monsieur Enganyon! Welcome to Betzy Rose Mansion!"

The shock on his face could hardly be less than seeing a ghost—Dungaree Jeanne's new stewardess is none other than Miss Buttercup of Clan Chamara!

With his innate social grace, Enganyon smooths over his initially shocked reaction with a cordial but distant smile. He addresses her in Runic to create even more emotional distance since he's quite sure she won't understand him all that well but she'd be too proud to admit it. "Ah, Miss Buttercup! It brings me great relief and comfort to be greeted by the familiar sight of thy face on this occasion. What more might one ask than the company of honored friends in these difficult and sad times. Is the madame Dungaree at home? I do wish to condole with her over the loss of our dearly departed monsieur Lynx."

Buttercup at least caught the last part and instantly corrects him, telling him in Eldric, "I believe you mean *Mister* Lynx. According to reports, the Ivy League rejected his commission. It breaks my heart to think he had to deal with that kind of rejection in his last moments." Buttercup gives him a courteous but bitter look directly in the eyes, then says, "Yes, the madame Dungaree is at home, as well as the mademoiselle."

"If it pleases thee, inform them that I have come to call on them to lend my comfort and support."

She recognizes the Runic phrase *to call on* as "heimsaek," which is a close cognate to the Eldric phrase meaning *home seek*. Maintaining her pride and putting on airs, she says in Eldric, "Very well, monsieur. I will be back shortly with their reply."

Contrary to the rules of elf etiquette, she leaves him standing outside the door. She should have shown him to the parlor. Enganyon would prefer to believe that the slight is due to her inexperience in her new position so he steps inside, closes the door, and takes a seat in the parlor by himself.

Miss Buttercup comes back and the expression on her face hints at her surprise upon seeing him in the parlor, but she does not press the issue. She simply says with stiff courtesy in Eldric, "The madame and mademoiselle are visiting with Reverend Appleseed but they would be delighted if you cared to join them."

Enganyon says in Eldric, "A delight indeed! I hope the good reverend is recovering speedily!"

"Remarkable man," replies Buttercup, indulging in a bit of small talk. "He always seems happy and at ease no matter how much pain he's in because of his leg."

Not wanting to allow her the familiarity of small talk but not wanting to insult her either, he switches back to Runic and says, "Let us hope that his cheerful countenance can carry us through this period of mourning for our dearly departed monsieur Lynx."

She opens the door to Johnny Appleseed's room, curtsies, and then leaves without further comment.

Laying her hand of playing cards on the table, Dungaree Jeanne stands up and says in Runic,

"Welcome, Monsieur Enganyon. It is very kind of thee to come condole with us over the loss of our dearly departed monsieur Lynx."

"Indeed, my deepest condolences, Madame Dungaree. His passing is a bitter blow to the entire colony. Whenever a wood elf moves up in rank to the order of high elves, it is a cause of rejoicing and celebration for every last elf on Tuscoraura Mountain. It assures us that the Magnificent Charter remains as strong and efficacious as our Founding Mothers and Fathers intended it to be, even after all these many decades. For indeed, their ideal was to found our vibrant society on the principles of meritocracy rather than aristocracy or dynastic tyranny."

Zena pulls up an elf-sized chair next to her and says in Runic, "Please, Monsieur Enganyon, wilt thou not have the kindness to join us? This chair next to me is unhappily vacant."

"I could imagine no greater pleasure, beloved mademoiselle, but first permit me to salute the Reverend Appleseed. I shall never be able to forgive myself for the peril to his life that my carelessness caused him and for the pain and suffering he has undergone on my account."

Zena says, "He is a human of magnanimous spirit and has forgiven thee completely. Please study his example and learn to forgive thyself."

Enganyon moves around the bed and shakes Johnny Appleseed's hand warmly and he greets him with the only Elvish greeting he knows, "Hale ant sail."

Enganyon speaks for a while in Runic then Dungaree Jean translates. "Monsieur Enganyon says he is happy to see you are getting better and is sorry for the pain, suffering and . . . delays . . . that you have endured because of him. He says he has learned much from the words of wisdom you have given him during his visits. He hopes to visit you as often as his servant, Sarman, or his fiancée, Mademoiselle Zena, may be available to translate for him."

Knowing that Enganyon's family is of such old, aristocratic stock that they speak Runic even at home, Zena says to him in Runic, "Please, Monsieur Enganyon, have a seat and join us for a game of cards. Reverend Appleseed's proficiency in this game during his convalescence has advanced to such a degree that he soundly beats us every round. Perhaps thy skill will give us a chance at winning."

Enganyon sits down next to Zena and gives her a gentle kiss on the cheek. He says, "To see thee win, my dear Mademoiselle Zena, is all my heart ever yearns for. I have so many fine thoughts and memories about Monsieur Lynx, but I wish to beg thy pardon and ask thy permission to discuss some mundane but urgent matters while we play cards."

Not a fan of aristocratic pretensions, Dungaree Jeanne says in Eldric, but still maintaining a very formal tone and posture, "We defer to your discretion that these matters must indeed be serious and pressing. May I ask that we conduct our conversation in Eldric to ease the burden of translation? To be polite to our guest, we rigorously maintain the habit of asking his opinion in Aenglish so that he doesn't feel left out."

"Agreed," replies Enganyon. Dungaree Jeanne apologizes to Reverend Appleseed for holding a conversation in a language he doesn't understand but he begs her not to worry about it.

Zena deals the next hand. Enganyon talks while they play their cards. Dungaree Jeanne takes mental notes on the cards he plays and his body language.

When everyone folds their cards, Dungaree Jeanne says in Eldric, "Please allow me to translate for Reverend Appleseed."

"Naturally."

Using the stack of cards placed in the middle as a mnemonic device, she says in Aenglish, "Reverend Appleseed. I value your opinion highly. Let me see if I can remember all that Monsieur Enganyon has said."

She places an ace of hearts down and says, "One for sorrow. Monsieur Enganyon has informed us that the Council of Perfects has scheduled a state funeral for all seventeen fallen elf warriors who died in the ambush—including Monsieur Lynx—for next Moon Day."

Johnny Appleseed says gently, "Poor, unfortunate souls—so much senseless loss of life."

Dungaree Jeanne thinks for a moment and places the two of bells on the little table. "Two for joy. They also scheduled a state wedding between Monsieur Enganyon and my daughter, Mademoiselle Zena, on *Freyfax*—I think in Aenglish you say, 'Lammas Day.' They want all the elves of Tuscoraura to make an offering to the god Ingvin in thanksgiving for our survival and to show the meaning of love to all elves."

Appleseed comments, "So this is love . . ."

Zena is giddy already. "It is biggest wedding of all elves in Tuscoraura! With silver bells, and cockle shells, and seven bridesmaids all in row. Wait, seven? I think we need more, maybe twelve bridesmaids . . ."

Dungaree Jeanne holds her hand to calm her and says in Eldric, "Mademoiselle Zena, please calm down and let me finish." Then she says in Aenglish, "Don't worry, Reverend Appleseed, you will be our guest at the wedding."

She puts two more cards on the table and, pointing to the three of acorns, says in Aenglish, "Three for a girl. They will make Senior Officer Onashelf a captain in the Ivy League, because she was a strong leader at the Forge Hill Gap. She fought hard and she brought a large number of them home. She deserves to be a captain. Very much so."

Appleseed says, "Indeed, it sounds like she wasn't afraid to go the extra mile to save others."

She points to the next card, the four of hearts, and says, "And four for a boy. The monsieur dean of the Ivy League claims that Monsieur Lynx failed his test but the council has overruled his judgment and has given him a captain's promotion because Monsieur Lynx died heroically—rescuing so many elves, including Senior Officer Onashelf. How do you say that in Aenglish?"

Johnny Appleseed comments, "We call that a posthumous brevet promotion to captain. It sounds like the Council of Perfects has changed their minds about Lynx . . . I mean Monsieur Lynx. He has gone from zero to hero in their estimation. I wonder if it was worth it to struggle so hard to win the favor of a people who didn't want him to succeed in life."

"That was Lynx's dream."

"A dream is a wish your heart makes."

"Yes, he wished his dream with all his heart," says Dungaree Jeanne. She puts the five of leaves down and says, "Five for silver. Umpire Gandorf wants to make a new league of elf warriors. He calls it the League of Nations. This league is for fighting wars beyond

Tuscoraura's marchlands. All the current elf leagues train to fight here on Tuscoraura Mountain exclusively. The Council of Perfects says that we lost the battle against the hobgoblins and the humans and the halflings because we do not train to fight against the clayborn beyond our borders.

"The problem is that the old leagues already fight fiercely over recruits—especially the good ones who win tournaments—so they have refused to allow the League of Nations to hold a recruiting tournament. The trick is, the old leagues only want high elves. The natural solution would be to allow the wood elves to join the League of Nations.

"Since the order of high elves was founded specifically to provide defense for elf society, it would be a deep violation of our social code not to promote those wood elves serving in the League of Nations to the order of high elves. But, high elves must live up here in Shentalpee City. The flood of newcomers would bring turmoil, resentment, and conflict among the old guard, not to mention severe overcrowding.

"The solution that Umpire Gandorf has proposed is to create a new order of silver elves who would have most of the rights and privileges of the high elves without the requirement to live in Shentalpee City."

When she puts down the next card, the six of bells, she looks at Appleseed nervously. "Six for gold. Despite the losses in the ambush, we managed to ship five bags of cocoa beans back to Tuscoraura. It should be enough to recoup our losses and keep Shentalpee City's economy from entering an economic depression.

"Umpire Gandorf has announced to the council that if Mademoiselle Florenz does not return before the election next month, then the Council of Perfects will sell Vandsee Estates for six million dollars and use the profits to continue Umpire Kibbler's research into blackflame technology. As a reward for my valiant service to the state in transporting the cocoa beans under such difficult circumstances, the council will offer the sale of Vandsee Estates to me first.

"If I do purchase Kibbler's residence and workshops and take over all his businesses, it would open the way for me to become the richest elve on Tuscoraura Mountain. I do realize that I would indirectly be funding necromancy and other uses of the blackflame, which you promised the Inquisition you would oppose, so we would need to discuss this."

Johnny Appleseed stays silent and keeps listening.

Dungaree Jeanne places a seven of acorns on the table and says, "Here is seven for the secret never to be told. Zena has a minor birth defect. Her right hand is smaller than her left, just a tiny bit. Her right arm is shorter than her left, just a tiny bit, and so forth. If I don't tell you, you don't see it; but when she puts her hands together and you look closely, you see it. She is also missing her right chest muscle but since no one is allowed to look there, no one has noticed.

"To be on the Council of Perfects, an elve must be perfect. The umpire-in-chief is head of the Council of Perfects. She must be perfectly perfect. If anyone learns about her birth defects, she cannot be umpire-in-chief. Bartlebee knew about it so she forced me to pay her ten dollars each month to keep it a secret.

"She put all the information about Zena's birth defect in a black box and gave it to a Pony Express rider gnome with special instructions. She paid in advance for the box to be delivered to the Council of Perfects but told them to keep it in storage in an undisclosed location. She promised to send them one penny a month as rent for the storage space and if she failed to pay the rent for any reason, they should just send the black mail package to the council."

Johnny Appleseed says, "Maybe Zena should just admit it. Otherwise, her world will always involve hiding who she really is in order to be someone she's not. That kind of lying wears you down over the years. She'll have to pay a heavy price for all the deceptions and disappointments she created and I guarantee you—that day will come."

Zena does not like that idea. Instead she informs him, "Maybe we pay price today and then we are done. Thieves' Guild in Tuscoraura say they find black mail first and they sell us black mail. If we do not buy, then they deliver it to Council of Perfects."

Johnny Appleseed replies, "If there's a Thieves' Guild operating in this area, then whoever stole Kibbler's notebook with the secret to shoot blackflame from his hand had to get their okay to steal it. Can you tell Monsieur Enganyon I'd like to get it back."

Dungaree Jeanne translates for him and says, "Monsieur Enganyon says they won't negotiate unless we pay their price for the black mail."

Appleseed asks, "How much are they asking?"

"Ten thousand dollars."

Johnny Appleseed does not flinch and informs her, "Don't pay it—that's extortion. If you pay the Thieves' Guild now they will tie knots around your weak spots and make you dance however it pleases them. You might as well just tell your secret now."

Dungaree Jeanne says, "As we say in Eldric, *hidaho patata,* Reverend Appleseed, no worries—we cannot pay such a sum. It is the alternative that frightens me. There's another option but it makes me question if it's worth the price."

"What is the other option?"

Dungaree Jeanne says, "Near the end of the battle, Master Leevai and I agreed that our best chances for survival were to split up. Since I had no sorcerers or magicultors to protect my wagon, Master Leevai gave me a source stone that he called an archon stone. He said it was more valuable than all his other possessions combined. I am inclined to take the time to study sorcery and discover what this is all about."

Johnny Appleseed's eyes go wide. "That archon stone is much more than a source stone. It is a life stone. It taps into the very foundations of what it means to be alive. It is worth far more than ten thousand dollars. Don't let anyone know you have it."

Dungaree Jeanne raises her eyebrows. "You know about this stone? Please tell us everything you know."

"I am no expert. All I know is that it has two main uses. The first is the one you are talking about—to hold the polarization of any other source stone permanently. In that sense alone, any sorcerer would be willing to pay a small fortune for one of those.

"The second use is to render an undead wight invincible. Normally fire is a natural way to banish the undead. Burning the body disintegrates it enough to evict the undead spirit from its home. This is only an imperfect solution because the undead spirit will then be exiled in this world, wandering around restlessly until it finds a way back to the netherworld.

"Attacking a wight with ordinary weapons only slows it down—cut off its arm and it will reach down and stick it back on. Striking a wight's limbs off with silver weapons will make it take a lot longer to reattach but eventually, it will come back recomposed and angry as ever.

"A cleric with an adequate grounding in prayer and fasting can turn an undead creature back to the realms of the dead. If no cleric is around, throwing holy water will weaken the undead spirit's hold on its mortal body for a short while.

"Once an archon stone is planted in an undead wight's heart, it can no longer be banished from this world by fire or the prayers of a cleric. Moreover, normally the undead cannot perform magic or sorcery but a wight with an archon stone can use a magica wand or a source stone as well as any mage or sage.

"Any necromancer who has successfully reanimated a thrall would pay a king's ransom to get their hands on an archon stone.

"Those stones are so powerful that the Knights Paladin have a buyback program to get them out of circulation, although the ransom they pay is not as kingly as a necromancer's price.

"Given the history with dabbling in necromancy here in Shentalpee City, the Thieves' Guild can have only one purpose in mind for that archon stone . . . they will sell it to Umpire Gandorf—if he is even telling the truth. My instincts tell me that Umpire Gandorf already has the black mail and is using it as leverage to get us to hand over the archon stone. If the Thieves' Guild really wanted the archon stone, they would focus first on taking it for free, not bargaining for it."

Zena does not like the turn this conversation has taken and says, "Monsieur Enganyon says truth. I know if he is lying because I myself am good at lying."

Appleseed disagrees. "With all due respect, mademoiselle, I'm not so sure it works that way. Lying only blurs your affection for truth. In general, the more you lie, the easier it gets to believe the story you want to hear . . . especially when you are in love. As we say in Kentikie, love is blind."

Dungaree Jeanne feels torn. This whole affair can only go in one direction—ugly. She plays an eight of leaves. "Eight for a wish. The Council of Perfects wishes you would help them in their blackflame research. They are promising to pass a law allowing high elves to become Christians if you help."

Zena takes the cards from her mother's hand and plays the nine of hearts. "Nine for a kiss." She gives Enganyon a kiss and says, "Monsieur Enganyon is now in election with me but he will let me win."

Dungaree Jeanne explains, "The Council of Perfects was just about to cancel the upcoming election on grounds that there was only one candidate left when Monsieur Enganyon stood up and reminded the council that they had passed legislation allowing him to tender his candidacy.

He never officially declined it when he proposed to Mademoiselle Zena, so he announced that he was going to run for umpire-in-chief to keep Mademoiselle Zena in the race. He has already told a crowd of high elves that he is only in the election to support his fiancée and has warned them sternly not to vote for him."

Enganyon stands up as if to excuse himself. Johnny Appleseed takes a turn and plays the ten of leaves and says, "Ten for a word you must not miss. Madame Dungaree, I realize you are in a sticky situation but please take my advice. Tell Enganyon that we will consider giving him the archon stone in exchange for the black mail only if the Thieves' Guild returns to us Kibbler's notebook first."

Dungaree Jeanne says, "Perhaps we should consider such a proposal more carefully."

With urgent assertiveness Johnny Appleseed says, "No, tell him right away. I will explain why this is your best course of action shortly.

"Trust me, madam, I've been in similar situations before. If Enganyon is not capable of coughing up that notebook, then you all would be wise to leave Tuscoraura Mountain before your real enemies destroy you completely."

Dungaree Jeanne defers to Johnny Appleseed's judgment and tells Enganyon that she will not deal with the Thieves' Guild unless they return the stolen notebook. If they did not steal it, then they will just have to figure out who did.

Enganyon agrees to convey her condition to the Thieves' Guild and as far as Zena is concerned, the matter has been settled. Jealous of any contact Enganyon might have with Miss Buttercup, Zena offers to show him to the door herself.

Dungaree Jeanne starts to leave as well but Appleseed calls to her, "A word, Madame Dungaree?"

"Naturally."

Johnny Appleseed says, "I need to remind you that Lynx has requested that his body be cremated. He does not want a necromancer to forcibly recall his soul back to his body."

Dungaree Jeanne replies somberly, "Yes, yes. I will make sure the council respects his last wishes."

Johnny Appleseed speaks up again before she leaves. "Please excuse me for butting into your private family affairs, but if Enganyon truly loved Zena and wants to see her win, why doesn't he just pay off the Thieves' Guild himself? I mean, an aristocratic rich boy like him could fork out ten thousand dollars."

Dungaree Jeanne snaps her fingers. "Good point. It never occurred to me. It wouldn't be easy but, yes, Monsieur Enganyon has the wealth and connections to come up with that kind of money."

Like a super sleuth, Johnny Appleseed presses on with his deductive reasoning. "So he comes talking to us like getting rid of our archon stone is going to solve all our problems. Remember, this is the son of the man who reanimated Old Mother Hubbard's dog.

"Umpire Kibbler had been meddling with necromancy to animate an army of undead thralls but he kept messing up and turning all the dead elves crazed wendigos instead.

"Umpire Gandorf comes along and suddenly he's using my blackflame braziers to enthrall dead dogs and skunks. Now as I said before, if he knows about the stormcrow all he needs is the Sword of Layban to properly enthrall rational persons. Once he has the Sword of Layban, he will only be one archon stone away from making himself immortal and invincible.

"The quest for immortality has driven nobler minds to embrace pure evil. I wouldn't be surprised if he organized the entire ambush first and foremost to get at Master Leevai's archon stone and the hullabaloo about those cocoa beans was nothing more than a sideshow to distract attention away from his real purpose."

Dungaree Jeanne nearly starts hyperventilating at this overwhelming news. Johnny Appleseed reaches over to put a hand on her forehead to pray over her. Eventually her breathing returns to normal and she says, "So you're saying this has nothing to do with black mail or the Thieves' Guild. It's just one more piece in a well-planned conspiracy by Umpire Gandorf to usurp the chief umpirage and use the desire among Tuscoraura elves for military supremacy to make himself an immortal undead warlord."

Johnny Appleseed leans back. "Madame Dungaree, I am so sorry, but I had no idea that was the real reason they invited me to preach the word of God to the high elves up here. Who could have suspected that the Holy Office of the Inquisition had a good reason to order me to halt the spread of blackflame?"

"O my tingling tongue!" groans Dungaree Jeanne. "If that's true then what about my dear Zena?"

"Elf politics are new to me, Madame Dungaree, but I have a good guess. Maybe Umpire Kibbler considered Enganyon a serious threat to his daughter's candidacy and bullied him out of the race. Your daughter Zena was the only high elve in Shentalpee City he did not take as a serious threat because of her wood elf origins. Now that Umpire Kibbler is out of the way, Umpire Gandorf is free to put his son back in the race."

Dungaree Jeanne raises her eyebrows. "Perhaps that is what the monsieur Enganyon meant when he said that his father has been planning this all along."

Johnny Appleseed keeps going. "Here is my thought on the notebook. If he doesn't have it, he's lying about the Thieves' Guild. If he does have it and hands it over to you, then you know he cares about Zena. If he holds back on handing it over to you, demanding the archon stone first, then his sympathies lie with your enemies."

Dungaree Jeanne yanks at her hair. "O my dizzy brain! What is this world coming to? Is everybody evil and power hungry? I can't trust anyone these days."

Seeing her so crestfallen, he pleads, "Madame Dungaree, please don't give in to despair. There is good in this world and it's worth fighting for. I have a plan that might just set things right."

Scene H: Unto the Last Days

Reflecting Pool at Thor's Base, Shentalpee City
Sun Day Terce. Morning, 23rd of April, 1284
Feast of Saint George, Martyr

With nearly all the high elves of Tuscoraura giving her a standing ovation, Zena walks down the aisle dressed in a white robe and flowery garland with all the cute smiles and confident glances of a celebrity—and she loves every moment of it.

Handshakes and cheek kisses go out with timed precision so as to be sure every last elf in the crowd clapping along knows exactly whom they are applauding for. Up on the podium, a halfling mage in blue velvet robes with white silk frills stands up front beaming with joy and ready to officiate the ceremony.

The famous halfling—half-leprechaun and half-hob—Mage Nittany O'Martix, beams a smile at Zena filled with motherly pride. For as much as Zena wants everyone to pay close attention to her, Mage Nittany's opinion of her is the only one that matters today. It has been a unique privilege for Zena to receive so much personal attention from the prestigious Chancellor of Pinne Mage University, whose mentorship and tutoring have brought her to this moment.

An elven string quartet thrums gently in the background. It is a beautiful day in the neighborhood. A golden sun in the big, blue sky warms the bright-eyed elves decked out in elegant suits and plush gowns and oodles of intricate jewelry studded with precious stones and gems.

They all know how important this moment is for Zena and for the whole Tuscoraura colony. She does not merely feel special . . . she *is* special—for the first time in a hundred years, a Tuscoraura elve will head to Penn Mage University as an apprentice magicultor.

Puffy clouds and fluttering angels seem to surround Zena as she paces with deliberate steps to the front. But when she catches sight of the reflecting pool, she screams with a deep-bellied rumble.

"Aaaaaaaaaak!"

Everyone looks at her, befuddled. Not taking her eyes off the reflecting pool, she lets out another ear-splitting, shrill squeal. "Eeeeeeeeeek!"

The crowd soon figures out the reason for her breakdown. The magica tree is gone!

Zena gasps and buckles over onto her knees and bursts into sobs. The flowers in her bouquet smoosh across the wooden platform. The crowd shuffles and hums with shocked chatter.

Mage Nittany turns to see what's troubling Zena and notices that the magica tree, which has been there all along this morning, is suddenly gone. An expression of cognition hits her face and she races over to Zena to comfort and encourage her. She puts her hand under her chin and says in Aenglish, "Darling, look at me. Look at me, dearie. It'll be all right. Everything is fine. Have a seat and I'll explain everything. There, there."

Enganyon comes over to let Zena cry on his shoulder as he helps her to a vacant seat in the audience—not the special seat reserved for her up front with the guests of honor.

The crowd quiets down when Mage Nittany calmly walks up onto the podium. She addresses them in

Runic, "Mesdames, mesdemoiselles, messieurs, ladies, and gentelves, all ye audience members, please have a seat! No need to panic! Please sit ye down and I shall explain presently.

"I begin with an apology; not for Mademoiselle Zena, but for myself. It has been quite a while since I lived among elves so my tongue is now quite rusty. Ye shall hear some tedious grammatical errors in my halting Runic speech. For that, I apologize, and for any other unintentional harm done to your beautiful language whilst I explain the disappearance of your colony's magica tree.

"But before I do that, I wish to say that I am extremely happy to be here with ye all on this occasion. From the first trepid steps upon Vinland's soil of those elves who debarked from the longboats *Grimm Sweeper* and *Mother of all Geese,* the New World elves have developed a strong tradition of magica cultivation, and some have even rivalled the greatest mages in Europa.

"They say a little elfin magic goes a long way. Your own fire elf colony up here among the giant sequoias can boast of the achievements of Mage Oleron Astari, who first developed the technique to concatenate the locomutation of metals. In the first century of its founding, Eldric mages from Tuscoraura Mountain were commonly employed as professors, mentors, and coaches at Pinne Mage U.

"It saddens me to think that only through the chronicles of our great university can I remember a time when Tuscoraura elves were a common sight, playing snookball on our campus greens and monopolizing the fantastic beasts and unicorns section of our pastures. We—myself and all the august faculty—are so excited to once again open the doors to Mademoiselle Zena here and thereby restore the amity and familiarity that once existed between us.

"As ye know, the primary requirement for admission is that a clayborn youngling should have the ability to crop a branch off of a living magica tree under the supervision of a faculty member. Now your only magica tree is gone. What happened?

"When I first arrived, I noticed that the magica leaves were starting to recover from the rot caused by the blackflame, but it was still in a very fragile state. The excitement and tension of this day, especially combined with these sonorous stringed instruments, must have pushed the poor tree past its breaking point and triggered its locomutative defense mechanism.

"Before I leave, I will inspect the patterns in the soil left by its roots, but I am not worried. The tree will find a new habitat and once Mademoiselle Zena finds it, I'll come right away to officially observe her culling her first magica branch. Once at Penn Mage U, she will learn how to turn it into a powerful magica wand.

"As a professor of magiculture for over twenty years, I can assure ye all that her natural talents are unparalleled. I have no doubt she will be successfully admitted to a very promising apprenticeship with some of the finest magicultors in Vinland."

Zena stands up and calls out, "But wait! Where did it go? Where exactly am I supposed to find it?"

Mage Nittany's blustery personality overrides Zena's stress and exasperation. "No worries, dear. The winds are blowing due north strong and steady. Go to Fort Niagara and ask the Magicultors' Guild there to give thee a tour of the magica trees under the falls. If it overshoots the Niagara Falls, thou canst try visiting the Tahquamenon Falls. Just check in with the Magicultors' Guild in Fort Michilimackinac."

"Wait! Wait! Niapanera Falls? Tahquobel Falls? Fort Michikfilaysnack? Quick! Someone get me a scroll and a quill to take notes. I'll never remember all this."

"It isn't that simple, my dear. A crosswind could come along and sweep it off in another direction entirely. Contrary to popular opinion, being a good magicultor is not all about making large objects vanish—it's about the journey.

"In other trades, 'journeyman' is little more than an intermediate title before mastership, but after thy apprenticeship at Pinne Mage University thou wilt be traveling across Vinland, visiting magica trees and the clayborn who tend them, be they elves, dwarves, goblins, or trolls. By the time thou art ready to prepare thy masterpiece, thou wilt know half the magica trees in Vinland by name and their cultivators.

"So mayhap thou wilt circumnavigate the shores of all the Great Lakes. Some magica trees love to hide in the spray of the breakers along the banks of the choppier waters out there. Mayhap thou wilt to travel east to the Bushkill Falls among the wigwam humans along the Delawaerr River.

"The wigwam humans are simply so lovely to their guests and extra friendly toward elves. I just know thou wouldst enjoy every moment with them. They have matriarchs and sagamores knowledgeable in every field: magiculture, sorcery, and the spirit realms.

"Before I go, I wish to admonish ye, o illustrious fire elves of Tuscoraura Mountain. Regarding the lack of magicultors and sorcerers coming from this community of Tuscoraura fire elves, I cannot help but suspect that high elves pressure their children to follow only the most lucrative career paths, while the nether elves have few career options."

Enganyon tugs on Mage Nittany's sleeve to interrupt her and whispers into her ear. She continues, "Oh, excuse me. I am told that ye refer to nether elves here as wood elves. Pardon me if any faux pas or slip of the tongue offends anyone here. Runic for me has always been a dearly beloved but demanding academic study. I hope not to embarrass her by reminding ye all that Mademoiselle Zena was born a wood elf and if her mother had not been awarded high elf status, she would never have discovered her aptitude for tending magica trees.

"Thus it seems that only through a narrow twist of fate has Shentalpee City been spared the ill fortune of going yet another hundred years without a magicultor. If the Council of Perfects is willing to invest the time and money into bringing more magica trees to Tuscoraura Mountain, I assure ye, we have several young magicultors that would be happy to educate ye on caring for them for free. Given your illustrious history with magic, I have no doubt we can bring about a revival of the magica culture here in Tuscoraura.

"As a parting gift, Mademoiselle Zena, I shall leave with thee a parcel of some of the best magica chewing leaves we cultivate at our Pinne Mage greenhouses. This is from a large-toothed Appalachian magica tree we call Bob. After eating one of Bob's leaves ye need only wait a quarter of an hour for the sap to mingle with your four humors. Then sing the appropriate song and poof! Thou canst locomutate thyself."

She wiggles her fingers at the crowd of baffled elves with a smile on her face and says, "Well, the Notus is starting to pick up and I need to catch an appointment this afternoon. Toodle-oo! On my way out, please pay close attention to the song I sing to locomutate out of here. Thou must needs sing the song exactly as I do to make it all the way to the village at Mage College."

With that, she waves her magica wand over her head singing, "Shalajadoola nitchicka poola . . ." She starts disappearing and then waves goodbye with a true optimist's smile. At last she sings the coda, "Pibbity pobbity goo," and disappears completely.

Scene J: Antigone's Agony

Training Grounds at Thor's Base, Shentalpee City
Moon Day Terce. Morning, 24th of April, 1284
Eve of the Feast of Saint Mark the Evangelist

Mothers weep hysterically.

Fourteen elf bodies lie in state on the steps of the council chambers along with three empty coffins commemorating those whose bodies were never found. Nearly all the elves on Tuscoraura Mountain have made their way to Thor's Base, with the crowds spilling over onto the suspension bridges and neighboring bases.

Criers are placed strategically throughout Thor's Plaza and on its edges. They repeat the words of the eulogists in loud, booming voices so the elves on the fringes can hear as well. With such large numbers of wood elves, the Council of Perfects has decided to allow all the eulogies to be given in Eldric, with only the scripted ceremonial parts being conducted in Runic.

After several elves who fell in battle have been eulogized, Zena steps up to deliver her eulogy for Lynx. The high commissioner officiating the ceremony looks at her a little agitated and announces, "At the request of Clan Highrune, Monsieur Enganyon Gandorfson will now give the eulogy for Captain Lynx Cougarson."

Zena looks around with mouth wide open, at a loss for what to do. Enganyon walks up past her on the way to the podium, gives her a quick pat on the rump and whispers, "Don't worry, babe, I got this."

Left hanging in the middle of the council chamber steps with several thousand eyes watching her, Zena needs to think quick. It would be bad form to storm the podium and usurp center stage from Enganyon, especially at a funeral, but it's kind of humiliating to come all the way up in front of the crowd for no reason and then return to her seat after having wandered around up there aimlessly like a total doofus.

Her political instincts prove sharp enough to smooth over the gaffe when she walks over and gives Lynx's mother, Missus Cougar, a theatrical hug and kiss on the cheek. She whispers into Cougar's ear, "Did you really ask Monsieur Enganyon to give the eulogy?"

Cougar looks at Zena sternly. "You broke my poor Lynx's heart!"

Zena looks at her for a moment and nods apologetically. She then respectfully shakes hands with Lynx's young murk elf stepfather. Just before Zena steps off the stage, Missus Cougar adds, "Besides, Monsieur Enganyon paid good money for the privilege of giving that speech. Their friendship obviously meant something to him."

Standing there at the podium, Enganyon's whole demeanor is different. Gone is the snarky young man with a cavalier glint in his eye. In an instant he has transformed himself into the perfect picture of respect for the dead and patriotic fervor.

He begins his speech in Eldric with a tear in his eye. "Our dearly departed Captain Lynx was a hero to me long before he came to the attention of the public. Back then, he was Mister Lynx, an ambitious wood elf coming to me for coaching on his archery techniques. He aimed to be the best archer among the fire elves and win a commission in the Justiciar League.

"He was cock-sure of himself and ready to work hard. I told myself, 'I like this guy.' And so, I started giving him a few pointers. Even though I had trained under the best archery instructors money could buy since childhood, under my guidance, he got so skilled that he nearly beat me out of the commission I won at this last Justiciar League tournament.

"It is true that some friction developed between us because we both set our hearts upon the same beautiful young elve, Mademoiselle Zena. But that healthy competition between us did not stop me from wanting the best for my wood elf protégé.

"Impressed by his immense natural talents and skills, I assured him he would win the Justiciar League tournament next year, but figured he should give the other tournaments a whirl.

"As it turned out, I was right. Many of you saw how he heroically saved Mademoiselle Florenz Kibblersdottir's life from that broken branch at the top of Tiw's tree. He did this awesome upside down flagpole up there and yet somehow, Mademoiselle Florenz was declared winner.

"Our dearly departed Captain Lynx showed no bitterness or resentment at being treated unfairly and when our dearly departed monsieur Umpire-in-Chief announced that he would pay for the commission out of his own personal funds, the monsieur Lynx welcomed his new benefactor with deep gratitude.

"Since he did not win his commission in the tournament officially, the Ivy League sent our dearly departed Captain Lynx on a quest to prove his skills as an Ivy League officer. In a cruel twist of fate, it just so happened that the Ivy League assigned him as a scout to escort the doomed trade convoy led by the madame Dungaree of Foreign Trade.

"Perhaps they underestimated the value of their cargo and the capacity of humans for treachery, but the ambush took the convoy by complete surprise. Hobgoblin mercenaries fought our valiant Ivy Leaguers from tree to tree. Naturally, we won the fight, but at a heavy cost in blood. Risking his life time and again, our dearly departed Captain Lynx singlehandedly carried out of the battle zone a large number of wounded Ivy League officers and sergeants.

"An elf is not finished when he is defeated. He is finished when he quits. The fatigue of carrying his wounded comrades did not stop him from rallying the troops and counterattacking the hobgoblins to wipe them out completely.

"Just when they thought it was safe to withdraw from the battlefield, a renegade fire elf came riding down upon them on a wyvern equipped with elf fire.

This renegade destroyed the madame Dungaree's wagons, losing half the shipment of cocoa beans. In a heroic act of self-sacrifice, our dearly departed monsieur Captain Lynx ran up to the wyvern and stabbed it in the neck, even as it chewed him to pieces.

"His valiant charge defeated the enormous beast but it also inflicted grievous wounds upon him. They carried him back to Shentalpee City. As soon as I heard the news, I rushed to his side and pleaded with him, 'Old friend, you can't die on me now. Hang in there!'

"But he looked me in the eyes and said—"

Enganyon chokes on a sob and tears well up in his eyes. "I'm sorry . . . it still gets me to remember what kind of guy he was. He said, 'Monsieur Enganyon. I'm done for, but my story isn't over. I promised Mademoiselle Zena I would help her win that election. If I die, the council will be forced to cancel the election. Please, run for umpire-in-chief in my name to keep Zena in the race.'

"I told him that I already refused my nomination but he reminded me of a very ancient fire elf law that allows a dying or incapacitated elected official to appoint a regent from his own clan to fill his post until the next election. It sounded like a long shot but I said I would do my best to make his final wish come true."

Enganyon pauses briefly to weep and says, "My father, the Major Leagues Umpire, loved him like a son, so when I told him the last words of our dearly departed monsieur Captain Lynx, he immediately got a team of lawyers working out the legal ramifications to make it happen. Clan Highrune has issued me enfranchisement into their clan so I can qualify as regent for Lynx's candidacy until the election.

"Now, some ungracious elves have claimed that because our dearly departed Captain Lynx did not complete his initiation quest on account of the ambush, he never officially got accepted to the Ivy League and therefore never formally acceded to the order of high elves. If so, as a wood elf, his candidacy for the chief umpirage would be invalid.

"In response, I want to admit to my own shame that I have been unfairly prejudiced against wood elves myself. The courage and skills demonstrated by our dearly departed monsieur Captain Lynx in life began melting away my stubbornness, but his heroism has shattered my blindness and has proven me flat-out wrong about wood elves. I have learned that whether we are high elves or wood elves, we all bleed the same red blood of patriots.

"And so, it gives me great joy to announce to all the fire elves of Tuscoraura Mountain that the Council of Perfects passed legislation in its emergency session this morning confirming his rank as an Ivy League Captain and his enfranchisement in the order of high elves.

"Can I ask that any elves here in this crowd whose lives our dearly departed monsieur Captain Lynx saved please come up here and stand beside his casket?"

At first one or two healthy-looking elves walk up and then a few who are all bandaged up. Others hobble up on crutches. One is still on a stretcher. More come up with splints on their legs and bandages around their arms, chests, and heads.

Enganyon starts clapping. The elves in the audience are not sure what to do. Inviting these cripples and invalids up showcases how bad the battle was. Elves are supposed to win always. Many are embarrassed.

However, random high elves seated at strategic locations throughout the crowd stand up and applaud these wounded heroes.

Soon the applause spreads as the fire elves, particularly the wood elves, begin to feel moved not only at the hardships these elves endured but also at the sincerity of Enganyon's change of heart. Such an elitist, aristocratic young elf finally rooting for the trampled-down lower order of wood elves will have ripples throughout the entire structure of fire elf society at Tuscoraura.

There it goes again . . . Zena hears it. It is the sound of those same elves who started the clapping, she is sure of it. They voice their support in words such as these: "Oh, my fuzzy chin! Monsieur Enganyon would make a fine umpire-in-chief, wouldn't he?"

Although she has no solid proof, Zena is quite sure that Enganyon—or maybe it is his father—is angling for a real chance at winning the election.

For as much as she loves Enganyon, she has no choice but to fight back.

Before the applause comes to an end, Zena presses through the crowd to fetch Senior Officer Onashelf, now promoted to Captain, whose grief and mourning have kept her back.

Zena says to her, "Captain Onashelf, if you ever want to make this right, now is the time to act."

She looks at Zena and says, "But I already gave your mother the phoenix talon back."

Zena replies, "Yes, but now it's time to tell the Tuscoraura elves your story."

"You told me to keep quiet about that."

Zena replies fiercely, "I told you to not say anything until the right moment. Monsieur Enganyon has called up those whose lives Monsieur Lynx saved during the ambush to stand up there with him at the podium, as if to endorse his candidacy for umpire-in-chief. Now is the right moment. Go up there and ask him if you can say a few words from the podium."

Onashelf shakes her head. "Why would he let me do that? I'm not on the list to give an elegy."

"Just tell him that because Monsieur Lynx got you to the hospital wagon in time, you were able to save other lives and you want to call those people up to the podium as well, since they are now part of Monsieur Lynx's legacy. He'll go for political rhetoric like that."

"Hey, that's pretty good. Where do come up with that stuff?"

"Call it a gift. We have to move quickly, before he sends everyone back to their seats."

The two fire elves get up and make their way through the crowds. In the pushing and jostling, they get separated. Zena's body language is that of a woolly mammoth trampling over peons, but the highly trained and limber physique Onashelf has forged through intense training flutters through the chaos like a sparrow through a the bush.

Onashelf slides up onto the podium just as Enganyon is about to dismiss the survivors and she whispers Zena's message into his ear. To her surprise, he nods cheerfully and steps aside. Onashelf freezes for a while when the full impact of the size of the crowd hits her. Thousands of elves stare at her with curiosity and even contempt. She is not on the program. What right does she have to command their time and attention this way?

She has no experience at all with public speaking, but she remembers how annoying it is when you cannot hear an elf speak so she vociferates like a drill sergeant shouting at new recruits, saying in Eldric, "Mesdames, mesdemoiselles, messieurs, ladies, and gentelves! I am Ivy League Captain Onashelf Aebersdottir of Clan Elkbell. The monsieur Junior Officer Lynx—now brevet Captain Lynx—saved my life twice. In the first moments of the ambush, I was hit with a hobgoblin blowgun dart. In the heat of battle I did not feel it until the venom incapacitated me.

"The monsieur Captain Lynx found me and administered the antidote I had in my belt. He carried me on his shoulders under threat of attack back to the hospital wagon where a team of clerics was able to restore me to fighting form within a few minutes.

"Captain Lynx saved the lives of not only the fire elves you see here, but by his timely intervention, he allowed me and several others to evacuate our downed team members. Monsieur Enganyon has kindly permitted me to also invite up to the podium those elves whose lives he saved secondarily. Please come forward now."

Another seven, then eight elves come up to the podium and stand with the original six, for a total of fourteen elves. Enganyon is about to retake the podium when she holds up a finger and continues, "I also wanted to set the record straight regarding the ambush. We were a unit of forty Ivy League scouts supported by fifty mercenary reindeer scouts.

"We were all professionals. How is it possible that we got ambushed when the whole point of scouting is to avoid ambushes? The answer is quite simple—we did not fall into an ambush. We were betrayed."

Shocked gasps and horrified squeals rise up from the crowd like a wave as the criers finish repeating her words to the audience members.

"Captain Bucklead was assigned to be the leader of our expedition. He forced our dearly departed Captain Lynx to prove himself worthy of his commission because it was purchased. When we first encountered the hobgoblin treeshadows, Captain Bucklead went over to their side and started attacking us, his own brothers and sisters, with them.

"The program for the funeral says that this is also a memorial service for the missing, whom we consider casualties. Nowhere on any of the lists of those we commemorate today appears the name of the leader of our squad, Captain Bucklead Yallson of Clan Bonesalp.

"Someone behind the planning of this ceremony obviously hopes we will forget about him. He was a fire elf of unflinching loyalty and total dedication to the supremacy of our colony. I have traveled with him on over twenty unique quests for the Council of Perfects. He has succeeded time and again where other elves have failed. He epitomized the Ivy League's ideals of athletic discipline, broad scope of mind, and attention to detail.

"Nearly all elves can stand adversity. But if you want to test an elf's character, give him power. Captain Bucklead came from a wealthy family and won appointments to posts that gave him great authority and power. He was criticized by many for his elitism, for the low esteem he held wood elves in, for his rigid devotion to antiquated traditions. But never once in all his years of service could anyone accuse him of using his power for personal gain.

"So I ask you again, how were we ambushed? It was not an accident. His orders were clear—we were not supposed to follow standard protocol. He made us leave vast swathes of our trek unscouted. Obviously, the enemy's location was already known to him.

"We all knew *he* was setting up an ambush. What we could never have imagined in a thousand years was that the ambush was intended for us!

"Before betraying us he gave me a scroll, which he said contained vital information to the survival of the Tuscoraura fire elves, which I was only to open if he failed to return. When I opened it, what struck me as most odd was that there was nothing unusual about it.

"It was a standard quest-giving scroll. Then I read the quest. It went something like this: 'As dean of the Ivy League, I hereby issue Order 66: you are to aid the hobgoblin mercenaries in destroying the convoy. No member is to return alive except yourself.'

"Then it all made sense. Captain Bucklead was the only fire elf on Tuscoraura Mountain loyal enough to betray his own people. His rigid authoritarian principles and his rules-oriented mentality were known to all, especially to Dean Halvard Prinson. Any other elf would have violated the oath of obedience we take upon initiation to the Ivy League rather than betray fellow elves to hobgoblins."

While she is talking, Zena stays mingled in with the crowd. Whether because she possesses the strange quality called serendipity, whereby someone's good luck never seems to desert them, or because her political instincts are engraved at such a primordial level of her being that she always ends up at the right place at the right time but right in front of her she spots Justiciar League Officer Bunzi.

Knowing him to be the perfect bully, Zena murmurs in her blending-into-the-crowd voice, "Her words are treason! She is making the Major Leagues Umpire look really bad. Isn't there a Justiciar League officer in this plaza with guts enough to arrest her?"

The browbeater in Justiciar Bunzi takes over at once and he rushes forward, cuffing Captain Onashelf. As she is dragged away, she breaks free from Officer Bunzi's grasp. She runs up to Lynx's coffin and shouts, "O Captain, my captain!"

Officer Bunzi slams the back of her head with his baton and hisses, "Quiet, traitor!" He locks her arms in an elbow bar behind her back and hauls her, dazed, up the steps toward the council chambers.

As she is coerced to climb those stairs, one by one the survivors of the ambush stand up on their benches and call out, "O Captain, my captain!" They hold up their fists with their thumbs and first two fingers extended out sideways—the elf hand gesture signifying, 'we will not forget.'

Soon the entire crowd has their two fingers and a thumb in the air. They all salute Lynx, declaring out loud, "O Captain, my captain!" It is clear to everyone that the fire elves of Tuscoraura are upset and ready for a regime change.

Within a few breaths, Enganyon's endearing speech in honor of Lynx is forgotten and the magnanimous gestures decreed by the Council of Perfects elevating Lynx to the order of high elves and brevetting him to the rank of captain now appear as little more than a smokescreen to hide a sinister and pervasive high-level governmental conspiracy to murder him.

As Zena planned, Officer Bunzi's arrest only confirms that this is an official cover-up. The crowd is now thoroughly agitated.

Major Leagues Umpire Gandorf Mithranderson races over to Officer Bunzi and rips Captain Onashelf out of his arms. After a theatrical show of anger at the unwarranted arrest, he carefully escorts Captain Onashelf back to the podium and announces in Eldric, "There are risks and costs to action. But they are far less than the long-range risks of comfortable inaction. Thus, I applaud Captain Onashelf for her courage in coming up here to speak out. She has identified a problem and has taken upon herself the burden of rebuking guilty authority figures.

"I do not know who ordered her to be arrested, but as Major Leagues Umpire, I declare her to be released and will personally offer her an indemnity for the inconveniences and rough treatment she has suffered."

With a paternalistic pat on the back, Umpire Gandorf encourages Captain Onashelf to go back into the audience and take her seat. He continues, "This is the first I have heard of Order 66, and you will forgive my ignorance of such a vital matter if for no other reason than I have been in this post for barely two weeks now. As I am the first to fill this office, my time has been spent working with other key government officials to define exactly which duties belong to me and which ones lie outside of my jurisdiction.

"Regarding the issuance of orders in the various military leagues, I have not been included in a single directive from any of the deans. My secretaries can all vouch for that. Maybe in light of this scandalous revelation, it is time to change that and add a little oversight to the way deans issue orders to the loyal and faithful soldiers of our colony.

"There is no way to say this softly, so I will speak boldly and honestly with you, o skillful and comely fire elves of Tuscoraura Mountain, confident in your dedication to the democratic principles this colony was founded upon. Our colony has endured enough disasters and humiliations in the past few weeks to make us question whether the Magnificent Charter is respected any longer, or is it a forgotten scrap of paper floating away in the wind as our democratic ideals collapse around us.

"On New Year's Day, Reverend Johnny Appleseed brought us blackflame, a new element capable of preserving food and delivering devastating frost attacks. What happened?

"The Inquisition showed up, extinguished all our blackflame, murdered our umpire-in-chief, and intimidated our guest into such profound silence that he is afraid to even mention the word *blackflame* around elves anymore. What have we done to teach our enemies a lesson for picking a fight with fire elves?

"Nothing!

"What happens when outsiders attack our convoys?

"Nothing!

"Aggression unopposed becomes a contagious disease. Not only have we taught the Inquisition they can mess with us and get away with it, but we announced to all the greedy, bloodthirsty leaders in Vinland that the Tuscoraura fire elves move around untold wealth in their trade convoys and we are too weak to stop them from taking it all for themselves.

"Where has our fighting spirit gone? We have petty legal squabbles to sort through, agreed. We have an educational gap to deal with, agreed. But right now none of any of that matters, because unless we show Vinland that we are strong by this time next year only one-third of us will be left alive in the smoldering ruins of our city, mourning the loss of the other two-thirds who will have been either killed or sold into slavery.

"If Tuscoraura Mountain is going to be the homeland for the next generation of fire elves, then we must restore the proud and ancient military traditions of our ancestors. We must teach our children to resolve their conflicts with swords, not legal arguments. Weapon handling must be their daily curriculum.

"A free people ought not only to be armed, but disciplined. To this end, a uniform and well-digested plan is requisite, and their safety and interest require that they should develop new weapons and new tactics to counter and defeat heavy infantry head-on, stop a massed cavalry charge, drive off dire wolf riders, et cetera, et cetera, et cetera.

"The best way to predict a better future is to create it. And so, it is with great pleasure and confidence in a better future that I announce to you the resolutions passed at the emergency council session this morning.

"In the near future, I will deliver a Thor's Enlightenment Discourse to fully explain the extent and limitations of my new role, but before we go into details, I would like to address Order 66 and proclaim that henceforth, all orders issued by deans must be submitted immediately upon issuance to the office of Major Leagues Umpire, who shall have veto power over them. Furthermore, the Major Leagues Umpire will have the right to audit all current military leagues to assess their efficacy and recommend new training regimens, upgrades to weapons, equipment and tactics, recruitment procedures, et cetera, et cetera, et cetera.

"Of greatest concern to the Council of Perfects was Dungaree Jeanne's report stating that we elves, having specialized exclusively in the hit-and-run tactics that have proven effective in grinding down invading armies in the past, have no stopping power when it comes to holding a field of battle or a key strategic position of any sort.

"To remedy this serious strategic defect, the Council of Perfects has voted to create a new military league, which we will call the League of Nations. This new league will specialize in analyzing the military weapons, technologies, tactics, and strategies of foreign powers and seek ways to neutralize them, especially ways to defend trade convoys and hold ground against heavy infantry and massed cavalry charges, et cetera, et cetera, et cetera.

"The League of Nations will hold military jurisdiction over any Tuscoraura fire elf who travels past the marchlands. The Justiciar League will hold military jurisdiction over any fire elf or visitor in Shentalpee City, and the League of Licornes will hold military jurisdiction over any fire elf or visitor leading off a base. The Ivy League's jurisdiction will be limited to the marchlands proper.

"These juridical boundaries are by no means static. After having studied each military league individually and the impact of all military leagues taken together after my appointment as Major Leagues Umpire, my first and most striking conclusion is that their effectiveness is severely limited by their lack of collaboration. In fact, there is no procedure or protocol whereby they could even initiate any form of collaboration. Fostering this collaboration will be my primary duty as Major Leagues Umpire.

"Finally, I remind all the fire elves here present that Madame Dungaree only undertook this disastrous trade quest upon my insistence that, due to the untimely death of our dearly departed monsieur Umpire-in-Chief and the self-imposed exile of his daughter, Mademoiselle Florenz, this quest would be vital to the economic survival not only of the Kibbler workshops, but also to the entire economy of our homeland. On this account, the madame Dungaree herself has been led to the brink of economic disaster due to the losses from this ambush.

"Therefore, I hereby appoint the madame Dungaree of Foreign Trade, Jeanne Ranglursdottir, as our first dean of the League of Nations, with a full living salary provided by the state. Her duties will be to research and explore new military weapons, technologies, tactics, strategies, troop types, unit configurations, et cetera, et cetera, et cetera."

The proposal is met with great applause. Umpire Gandorf continues, "The deans of the current military leagues strenuously opposed the creation of a new one on grounds that the eligible military-aged elves have almost all already been spoken for and that removing soldiers from their current leagues could have disastrous consequences for the colony. I, however, won their support by pledging to forbid any new recruiting tournaments or transfers from the current leagues into the League of Nations.

"Where will we get our new National Leaguers?

"The solution to this dilemma came when a brilliant young fire elf lawyer proposed an amendment to the Magnificent Charter. Amendments are rare because they require a unanimous vote from the Council of Perfects. When are politicians ever happy unless they are bickering about something? Both fortunately and unfortunately, this crisis threatens our existence to such a degree that the council was able to overcome party rivalries and personal differences to pass this amendment unanimously.

"As acting head of state, I hereby announce the creation of a new order of elves recognized by the government of Shentalpee City. This new order will grant to its members the title of silver elves.

"The order of silver elves will solve the problem of military advancement. Our dearly departed monsieur Captain Lynx is a hero to our people. He attained the rank of high elf through his military prowess. Despite his worthiness, many high elves have complained that military achievements alone run the risk of creating groups of high elves who lack the educational background or intellectual achievements necessary to handle their civic responsibilities. The ignorance of one voter in a democracy impairs the security of all.

"Military advancement through merit will no longer be blocked due to education or housing concerns, but it will be limited to the order of silver elves. From now on, only great cultural achievements can earn an elf a place among the high elves for those not born into it. Liberty without learning is always in peril, and learning without liberty is always in vain.

"Where, then, will the silver elves live? Once again, the genius of our dearly departed monsieur Umpire-in-Chief will have a lasting mark on our society. He was the first to conceive of building an elf base upon a sycamore grove. Vandsee Estates proves that sequoia groves are not the only suitable bases for fire elves.

"We shall construct new bases on sycamore groves. Where will we get the money to fund all these projects? Read my lips—no new taxes. If the mademoiselle Florenz Kibblersdottir does not return by the election, then we will consider the Vandsee Estates public property and auction it off to finance our reforms.

"Creating a new order of silver elves will also foster student exchange programs between elf colonies. Agreed—a high elf from Appalachia is not entitled to the privileges and rank of high elf in Tuscoraura if he or she has not merited it here, and vice versa. However, demoting high elves to the order of nether elves when visiting other colonies has all but cut off any interchange between light elf colonies.

"We will send ambassadors, diplomats, and envoys to all the Runic-speaking elves in Vinland and Europa to encourage them to officially recognize this new order of silver elves as well. Traveling high elves and silver elves will be able to stay with and enjoy the rank and privileges of silver elves in other colonies without posing any threat to established political or cultural traditions. This will be a great benefit to all elves throughout the world because it will raise the level of professionalism among our military personnel in a similar way that the guild system has raised the level of professionalism among the various crafts and trades by fostering the interchange of ideas through travel.

"And so, to conclude this funeral oration, we return our attention to the seventeen fallen heroes lying in state before us. As we express our gratitude to them, we must never forget that the highest appreciation for their ultimate sacrifice is not to utter words about them but to make sure their sacrifice counts.

"And so, I am happy to announce to you that we have indeed learned to weaponize blackflame. I promise to bring back our fallen heroes as Shentalpee City's first dedicated unit of undead warriors. In life, they gave it all to serve the patriot's dream and now they will serve that dream in undeath."

Ringing applause fills the treetops of Tuscoraura Mountain. Not a single elf realizes they are all cheering their own enslavement.

Having their fears and suspicions of political scandal and intrigue temporarily swept aside by this rousing speech, and thinking only of the wild hopes for military glory Umpire Gandorf has promised, the elves applaud with uncontrolled fervor.

Johnny Appleseed, having heard the translation of all these speeches from Dungaree Jeanne, surprises her and all the elves present by rolling his wheelchair out to intercept Umpire Gandorf. To Dungaree Jeanne's greater surprise, he calls her over and asks her to translate. Johnny Appleseed strikes a deal with the Major League Umpire to deliver a few words.

Dungaree Jeanne wheels Appleseed next to the podium and he speaks with heartfelt sincerity. Taking a moment to think, she begins her translation of his words into Eldric for all present to understand. "Mesdames, mesdemoiselles, messieurs, ladies, and gentelves. First of all, I wish to thank Dungaree Jeanne for inviting me to Tuscoraura Mountain and for welcoming me as her guest up here in Shentalpee City.

"The primary goal of my quest in coming here was to bring you the truth. Truth is probably the only valuable and elegant commodity the Tuscoraura elves seem to have no interest in.

"The great enemy of truth is very often not the lie—deliberate, contrived, and dishonest—but the myth—persistent, persuasive, and unrealistic. Too often we hold fast to the clichés of our forebears. We subject all facts to a prefabricated set of interpretations. We enjoy the comfort of opinion without the discomfort of thought.

"Truth is prescience. Forewarned is forearmed. Sometimes we can want something so badly that we ignore the warnings and leap into risks that ought to have been given careful deliberation. I brought the blackflame here to fight the war against hunger, not to empower the races of middle earth with new weapons of mass destruction.

"However, seeing that your Council of Perfects seems so determined to create a legion of undead warriors, I have just promised your Major Leagues Umpire to help you research the non-violent applications of blackflame in exchange for the chance to warn you about the dangers of its military applications. You must know the truth about the undead before you attempt to transmogrify or reanimate any more persons or creatures.

"Necromancy is the science of using supernatural forces to control the wills of the undead. When one has done evil in life and refuses to face up to the truth of their evil deeds, then as spirits, they see with utter clarity the insanity of their lies, the true horror of what it means to deface the divine beauty stamped upon each living being. To recall a soul who has gazed upon pure evil and been captivated by its allure creates a frenzied wight, insane, with cannibalistic, bloody violence, called a wendigo.

"The former umpire-in-chief already created enough wendigos to tip off the Inquisition that something is rotten on Tuscoraura Mountain. If word gets out that more wendigos are on their way, they will send a whole Crusade will descend upon the elves of Tuscoraura Mountain as numerous and as destructive as the plagues of locusts in Pharaoh's Aegypt.

"Your Major Leagues Umpire's premonition of a future filled with military defeats will come true sooner than even he has imagined. It is not a question of cowering before Church authorities but merely a reasonable sense of caution before recklessly tampering with forces of nature that are beyond the comprehension of mortal minds.

"My final word to you is this. When Lynx's body arrived in Shentalpee City after the battle, Dungaree Jeanne asked me to pray to bring him back. He came to me in a vision and told me that he is happy now. As his last request, he asked for his corpse to be burned so his soul may rest in peace for good."

With the speech finished, Umpire Gandorf goes back up onto the podium. He addresses the crowd one final time in response to Appleseed's challenge. "Ask not what your colony can do for you . . . ask what you can do for your colony. In life, our heroic Captain Lynx was marked with a sincere desire to serve his colony. I find it hard to believe that in death he would refuse the awesome privilege to fight for his colony. He will be among the first cohort of undead fire elf warriors."

On cue, Zena comes back and hands Appleseed twelve small stones. He gets up out of the wheelchair and walks over with a painful limp to Lynx's coffin, arranging the twelve small stones around it.

"Lord, you are the God of Abraham, Isaac, and Jacob," he prays. "Prove to them that you are the God of Israel and that I am your servant. Show these elves that you will accomplish what you have commanded me to do. Lord, answer my prayer and let these elves know that you, Lord, are God, and that you alone can change hearts and minds."

A raging fire pours down from the heavens and reduces Lynx's coffin to ashes. Although standing close to the coffin and completely engulfed in the flames, Johnny Appleseed walks out unharmed, and better—his leg once was broken, but now it is healed.

ACT IV

I SPY

WITH MY ELFY EYE

Scene 1: Meet the Heresiarch's Family

Village of Carthage, Long Falls
in the Confederacy of the Seven Nations
Tiw's Day Vespers. Evening, 25th of April, 1284
Feast of Saint Mark the Evangelist

Ariel's party of adventurers has new-found respect for Benjamin Frankelyn. For a nineteen-year-old, he has unbounded energy, dazzling people skills, and an uncanny knack for improvisation. Not only did his plan for cracking open the vault work, but he got Goldilocks to hand over the Sword of Layban without issue.

After a week of journeying, they reach an Irokian village called Long Falls where a group of Aenglish Blackflame Cultists has taken refuge from the inquisitors seeking to put them on trial for heresy. They have named their settlement Carthage.

Once inside the cultists' secret temple, Frankelyn tells Whoopee, "Introduce the princess to her new best friends, if you please. This is Heresiarch Joagbert, the head of the Blackflame Cult in Vinland. His archdeacon is Elmer the Fadet. The Fadets are cliff elves from Vaucluse in Languedoc, now controlled by the Frankish king. His other deacon is Hugo the Troll. Unlike the stereotypes about trolls from his Sasquatch tribe, he is a very sensitive and philosophical believer who was deeply touched by the religion of Heresiarch Joagbert."

Whoopee translates the introductions for the princess into Drowish. When Deacon Hugo notices the conversation turn to him, he holds an undead rabbit in his hands and says in simplified Aenglish, "I always wanted my own little bunny rabbit. I like to hug him and pet him and squeeze him. I named him George. One day George stopped moving, but Joagbert made him good again. I like Joagbert."

Whoopee explains the gist of the troll's conversion story and she stares up at the giant, hairy deacon. She's not quite sure how to respond so she just smiles and agrees. "Right . . ."

Deacon Elmer says in Runic, "Princess, our beloved heresiarch would like to see thee ignite the sword to test if thou truly hast the power."

She replies in Runic, "What is it with ye people and power?" She asks Whoopee for the Sword of Layban and at his request Frankelyn hands it to her.

She holds it up and exclaims, "By the power of Layban . . . I have the power!"

Black puffs of flames like dark thunderclouds crackle with blue sparks. She then recalls the flame saying, "Let the power return!"

The sword's flaming blade settles down to a low rumbling of shadows at play which then disappear completely.

The heresiarch smiles with sinister satisfaction and speaks to Deacon Elmer, who then tells her in Runic, "The heresiarch is greatly pleased with thy mastery of the sword. He still has much to teach thee before thou canst unlock its full potential. He shall teach thee how to reanimate the dead with it, if thou art willing to call him thy master."

The princess tries to stifle her smile of eagerness and says modestly, "I am ready to learn, master."

The heresiarch guides them deeper into the secret temple. They come to a crypt, and the heresiarch orders the troll to open the large, stone slab covering one of the sarcophagi. Deacon Hugo puts down his undead bunny and slides the stone away to reveal a decaying giant dwarf. His shoulders alone are nearly five feet wide and he stretches from head to toe roughly six and a half feet tall. His massive body makes him seem much more powerful than any giant she has encountered.

"Behold! The last of his kind," says Deacon Elmer. "The Jintel were a race of dwarves of unusual size. Their language and facial features are similar to their cousin Pyrinoak dwarves, but their colossal strength made them reckless and slower to apologize than common sense would dictate. They fought war after war and their population dwindled in Europa. A century ago, a Jintel clan sailed to Vinland but they fared no better.

"Their race has since finished. Markest thou my words, this Jintel is a good candidate to become thy thrall not because of his large size, but because of his strong will. In the undead state, a thrall's abilities in the physical world depend more on their qualities of mind and spirit than any physical characteristic. A strong will translates into great physical strength, and an agile mind grants a body that was once clumsy in life more dexterity than Gordo the Thief. A weak-minded ogre in life becomes a weak-limbed ogre after reanimation.

"This Jintel you see here, Balrock, was strong-willed. It is not by coincidence that he survived longer than any of his kinsmen. The heresiarch offers thee the gift to enthrall him so he may serve thee in thy noble quest of seeking revenge against the Inquisition that slew thy father. In return, thou wilt welcome missionaries of the blackflame into thy homeland."

"Fine. Now show me this ritual."

Deacon Elmer says, "Before we begin, thou must know the rules. Thou shalt not allow thy thrall to get wet with holy water. Thou shalt not subject thy thrall to get sliced or diced with silver weapons. Thou shalt not allow thy thrall to get blessed by holy clerics or druids. Thou shalt not snack after midnight."

The princess grimaces and says, "I thought joining up with the evil side would mean that I do not have to worry about the thou-shalt-nots anymore."

"Not snacking after midnight is just my personal recommendation for thee. The rest of these thou-shalt-nots have more to do with the immutable nature of the cosmos. There is nothing good or bad but that thinking makes it so; but there are some rules you just cannot break without breaking thine own coccyx bone."

She huffs and says, "Okay, fine. Let's just get on with the part where I enthrall this giant dwarf."

"Thou must first learn the Dark Tongue of Caldor."

"Drat! And how long will that take?"

"An instant but it shall reveal thy secret thoughts."

"I only have one thought on my mind—revenge."

Deacon Elmer says in Aenglish, "She is ready."

Heresiarch Joagbert lays a hand on her head and says, "Receive the power to speak the Black Tongue of Caldor, Florenz Kibblersdottir."

Suddenly, the princess is able to speak directly to the heresiarch in the Black Tongue of Caldor. "Okay, you figured me out. Now show me how to use this dumb old sword to bring back my father."

"Call me master."

Florenz shrugs and says, "Okay, master. Show me."

The heresiarch goes through the ritual in the Black Tongue of Caldor. Her memory is keen, and it is not long before she is able to perform it perfectly by heart.

Once she is ready, Florenz taps both shoulders of the giant dwarf with the Sword of Layban, saying, "Arise, Balrock! I dub thee a servant of the black fire, a dread knight of the flame of Layban. I bid thee come back from the shadows. Arise, Sir Balrock!"

The dull-yellow eyes of the reanimated giant open. His throat gurgles and a convulsive motion agitates his limbs. Oh, his twitching fingers! The humungous body shivers as his yellowed skin tightens. It scarcely covers the work of muscles and arteries beneath.

His lustrous, black hair hangs limp from his head as he sits himself up. His mouth opens with a garbled moan, displaying his pearly white teeth, but there is nothing healthy about them. Behind his shriveled lips, the whiteness of his teeth only forms a lurid contrast against his dried-out eyes, sunken back into dun-yellow sockets and emitting a strange, reddish glow.

Breathless horror and disgust fill Florenz's heart until a rush of power intoxicates her mind. "Arise, Sir Balrock!" she shouts. "Bow to thy new master!"

The giant studies her for a moment, then works his way out of his sarcophagus and bows before her. A surge of pride and superiority wells up in her. She swears to herself she will bring back her father and gather a great army of undead warriors against the Inquisition who orchestrated his death.

As if reading her thoughts, the heresiarch lets out a sinister laugh. He speaks to her in the Black Tongue of Caldor. "Good, my young apprentice. I can feel thy anger. Take up thy weapon. Strike down the next inquisitor thou seest with all of thy hatred, and thy journey with the blackflame will be complete."

Not wanting to ruin the moment but needing the Sword of Layban back, Benjamin Frankelyn announces cheerfully, "Welcome to the family, Balrock! It's been a real treat to watch you two bond so quickly. Now, Your Highness, could you please return to me the sword so we can complete our quest?"

The heresiarch tells him in Aenglish, "According to the power of blackflame gathered within the Sword of Layban, this giant dwarf is now a Dread Knight and as such, deserves the style of respect *Sir* Balrock."

Clearing his throat, Benjamin Frankelyn corrects himself. "Ahem. Yes, well, then. My apologies, Sir Balrock. We are glad to have you with us. And thank you for the clarification, Your Holiness . . . um, Your Evilness . . . how should I address you, Heresiarch?"

"Please, please, just plain Joagbert. We despise hierarchy and aspire to create an egalitarian society."

Benjamin Frankelyn does not appear unsettled in the least by his words. "Wonderful! Just wonderful! You must send me a pamphlet someday about all those ideals and aspirations you have. In the meantime, I should really like that sword back so I can complete my quest. You know the deal. We'll only release the funds for our contribution to your cause if we succeed in our quest as well.

"So how about it, Joagbert?"

The heresiarch turns to Florenz and nods, but she seems to like possessing the sword too much to give it up. Benjamin Frankelyn gets edgy. Ariel and Willis put their hands on their weapons—they are not in the least inclined to let this quest fail after they have come so far.

The heresiarch commands her in the Black Tongue of Caldor. This time, the sound is horrible. She screams and covers her ears until she gives in. "Yes, master."

Clearly battling with her own will, she drops the Sword of Layban with a clank upon the stony ground. Wrapping it in a cloth, Benjamin Frankelyn asks politely, "Excuse me, Joagbert, one last question. Um . . . with no hierarchy and all, I'm just curious why everyone keeps calling you master."

"I said we despise hierarchy, Mister Frankelyn, but make no mistake about it—once a person fully commits to evil, I am very much the master."

Bonus Scene A: Double, Double Toil and Trouble

Betzy Rose Mansion, Red Giant's Base, Shentalpee City
Frige's Day Prime. Early Morning, 28th of April, 1284
Feast of Saint Vital, Martyr

Breakfast at Betzy Rose Mansion is much more pleasant with a stewardess, and Buttercup is very conscientious about her responsibilities.

Dungaree Jeanne sits down at table with Johnny Appleseed. Buttercup brings out an odd tray of a certain type of ringed bread with cream cheese and smoked salmon garnished with tomato, sliced onion, cucumbers, and some capers.

The next tray has a more traditional elf breakfast from Alfheim—lefse topped with rakfisk, served with onion and sour cream and dried cod treated with lye, called lutefisk.

Dungaree Jeanne samples the smoked salmon and revels in the flavor with true culinary ecstasy. "Miss Buttercup, I dare say, this is one of the most delicious breakfast foods I've ever tasted. Where did you get it?"

"Thank you, Madame," replies Buttercup. "Your dry dock keeper, Mister Steve Dore, found a cookbook in the hospital wagon that you brought back with you after the ambush. He brought it down to the garden gnomes' burrow and had a translation made for us for free. They call that recipe lox."

"For free! How did Mister Dore manage that?"

"He gave the original to the gnome copyist. New and exotic cookbooks sell faster than hotcakes among gnomes. He said the revenue from the cookbook would more than pay the fee for the translation."

"Brilliant, Miss Buttercup! Your skills in the kitchen are legendary. Whoever marries you, I account the luckiest elf in Tuscoraura. This lutefisk and lefse are absolutely to die for." She then tells Johnny Appleseed about the free cookbook in Aenglish and asks his opinion about Buttercup's cooking skills.

He grimaces and says, "Well, you see, Madame Dungaree, it's all a bit fishy."

Dungaree Jeanne replies quickly, "You are right; a free translation is too good to be true. I don't trust gnomes much either anymore, not after what happened with Bartlebee. But what do you think about the breakfast? Isn't it marvelous!"

Johnny Appleseed says, "Yes, it surely is, but you see, we Midwesterners are not used to eating so much fish for breakfast."

"Oh, I understand. Have you ever tried tynnlefse?"

"Never heard of it."

"It's an elf dish made with a thin flatbread rolled up with butter, brown sugar, and cinnamon. Would you care to try some?"

"Yes, please! That sounds delicious."

Dungaree Jeanne rings the small silver handbell for Buttercup and requests her to make the tynnlefse for Johnny Appleseed. As soon as Buttercup exits, Dungaree Jeanne gives him a conspiratorial look. "Reverend Appleseed, I realize that you probably wish to leave Tuscoraura Mountain now that your leg has miraculously healed, but I'd like to hear your plan to solve this trouble with Monsieur Enganyon.

"Given the recent turn of events, I have begun to doubt even more seriously the sincerity of his feelings toward my daughter and I was hoping you might impart some final blessing from your vast stores of wisdom to help her see what we all see so clearly—that she is being used."

Johnny Appleseed chuckles to himself and says, "Oh, I wouldn't call it vast wisdom, just a little trick I picked up when living among the Passamaquoddy, whom you would call one of the wigwam humans. They gave me the recipe for a love potion. You know teenagers . . . half their love is little more than an onset of melancholy humors mixed with pure stubbornness to do exactly what their parents say they can't do."

My dear reader, allow me to interrupt the good Reverend's conversation to clarify a point about teenage love. Nowadays we call it hormones, but in the Middle Ages they still followed the Galenic tradition of medicine, which classified most feelings and illnesses as an imbalance of the four humors. Many modern readers have a hard time imagining why the ancient Graec physician Galen would put a thrilling teen crush in the same category with clinical depression. They feel so different on the surface but deep down, there is much that binds them.

Remember that emotions are seesaws (or as Midwesterners would say, teeter-totters) whereby a swift elation at one end always brings a crash down at the other. For the ancients, the blood had four chemical components that they referred to as humors. When one humor gained predominance over the others, it affected our moods and caused various illnesses.

As we have pointed out, black bile caused a melancholy mood that manifested itself either as infatuation or depression. Yellow bile caused a choleric mood that manifested itself either as anger or fear, which we now call the fight-or-flight response. Phlegm, a fancy word for snot, caused a phlegmatic mood that manifested itself either as emotional detachment or as a snotty, smug paranoia. Finally, our red blood caused a sanguine mood characterized either as a cheerful optimism or as a bloody obsession.

Getting back to our story, we overhear Johnny Appleseed as he explains his plan. "Just whip up a flagon of the love potion and give it to our little mademoiselle. Once she's drunken it all down, wait a day or two and then tell her that you've changed your mind—not only do you approve the marriage but you insist that she should marry Enganyon as soon as possible. She'll dump him, guaranteed."

Dungaree Jeanne calls out in Eldric, "Miss Buttercup, please fetch me a quill and some parchment. I need to write this recipe down." As soon as she has the writing implements she says to Johnny Appleseed in Aenglish, "I do have your permission to write down the ingredients to this love potion, don't I?"

"Absolutely! You start off with about half a cup of apple verjuice."

"Apple verjuice? What's that? Ver apple juice?"

"Actually, verjuice is slightly different. It's made with sour apples. This only works if you follow the recipe exactly, so no substitutions. Sorry."

"Okay, apple verjuice. What else?"

"Then you add perry cider."

"Perry cider? What's that?'

"It's like apple cider but made out of pears."

"What's apple cider?"

"Hmm, why don't I write this all down? Then you can have Buttercup take it down to that gnome to translate for you. Let's see now . . . half-cup of apple verjuice, half-cup of perry cider, seven cress shoots, five chervil buds, twelve tarragon roots, a drop of porpoise unguent, about a spoonful of conger gelatin, and the liver of a dowitcher. Actually, you are allowed to substitute the dowitcher liver for the liver of any wading shorebirds, like a sandpiper.

"Mix that all together, then you just add three hairs of the person you want Zena to fall in love with next and it's all over. It's a pity about Lynx—I would have liked to see him happily married to Zena."

Just at that moment, Zena walks in and snatches the parchment off the table, asking, "So who am I supposed to fall in love with next?"

Dungaree Jeanne stands up. "Mademoiselle Zena, how rude! Were you eavesdropping on us?"

She gives her a sneer. "Well, Mother, I would apologize if I didn't have the good fortune to discover that you have been plotting to poison me with a love potion! I'm engaged to the elf of my dreams and all you can think of is ruining my happiness by making me fall in love with some loser. Who's it supposed to be . . . Officer Bunzi?"

"Mademoiselle Zena, can't you see what Monsieur Enganyon is doing to you? He's manipulated events perfectly so he can be elected the next umpire-in-chief. This engagement isn't about his love for you—it's about elbowing you out of the way."

"Mother, all that manipulating is not Monsieur Enganyon's fault. It's his father. I'm starting to suspect that he planned Umpire Kibbler's death all along. Maybe he's been in touch with the Inquisition and was just waiting for Umpire Kibbler to appoint him Major

Leagues Umpire before doing him in. Besides, Monsieur Enganyon emphatically does not want to be umpire-in-chief."

"But, Mademoiselle Zena, the way events are rolling, most elves are going to vote for him. The prejudices of the high elves against Mademoiselle Florenz for her dark elf heritage were working in your favor, but those same prejudices are going to work against you because he is from an old, established high elf family. I was born a wood elve and for a lot of high elves that makes you a fake."

Zena looks at the paper and says, "You know what? This little love potion might come in handy. If we manage to stoke Monsieur Enganyon's passion for me a little hotter, he might just build up the nerve to stand up to his father." She then turns to Johnny Appleseed and asks in Aenglish, "If Monsieur Enganyon drink my three hairs in love potion, he love me more, no?"

Johnny Appleseed says, "If he manages to get them down, all the better; but you know how it is—hair sort of tickles as it goes down and might trigger a gag reflex. If there is no hair in the love potion, he will simply fall in love with the first girl he sees after the potion touches his humors—about a quarter of an hour later."

Zena calls Buttercup over and hands her the paper with a few coins, commanding her imperiously in Eldric, "Miss Buttercup, go ahead and have your gnome translate this and see if he can brew up a batch for us as well. Here are a few golden double eagles; that should cover any expenses you might incur."

Only Johnny Appleseed notices Buttercup's nasty glare at Zena when she curtsies and gives her a formal reply. "As you wish, Mademoiselle Zena."

Dungaree Jeanne adds, "Oh, by the way, Miss Buttercup, could you please swing by Lathspell Mansion and inform Monsieur Enganyon that we have come to a decision regarding the . . . um . . . exchange he requested? We would like him to come here in person to discuss it. Thank you, dear."

"As you wish, Madame Dungaree." A cunning smile breaks upon her lips. "As you wish."

Later that afternoon, Enganyon knocks at the door with a small black box tucked under his arm. Buttercup opens the door with enthusiasm and greets him in Eldric, "Why, Monsieur Enganyon! It's so good of you to call on us."

He stiffens and says, "Yes, unfortunately, this is not a social call. We have some very urgent and serious matters to discuss. Is the madame Dungaree at home?"

"Indeed she is!" says Buttercup, as if today were the best day in her life. "I'll call her at once. Please have a seat in the parlor."

No sooner does he reach the parlor than Zena comes running down the main stairwell, dressed lavishly, and throws herself into his arms. The impact almost knocks the wind out of him but he recovers quickly and twirls her around with grace and charm. He gives her a little peck on the cheek and says, "You make my heart spin every time I see you, my dear."

Zena calls up the stairs as her mother comes down, "You see, Jeanne, he is so in love with me!"

Dungaree Jeanne starts to scold her, "Mademoiselle Zena, how many times have I told you not to address me by my—" She sees the black box tucked under Enganyon's arm. Instead of admonishing Zena for her indiscretion, she speaks to Enganyon in Runic. "Why, Monsieur Enganyon! How wonderful! Thou wert able to recover the black mail for free!"

Enganyon sets Zena down on the couch and sits himself next to her. He places the welcome table (a medieval elf version of our coffee table—but coffee would not be popularized for another two centuries) and says in Eldric, "Let's get right down to business, then. This is indeed the black mail that Bartlebee had stowed away in the Pony Express post in case she should be discovered. It was only by extreme good luck that my friend from the Thieves' Guild intercepted it. Naturally, just stealing it would only have alerted the halflings working at the Pony Express to the fact that they had been robbed. Aware of this problem, the Thieves' Guild broke in, looked at it, left, and created a minutely exact copy of the box it was in. Then they had to break in again, replace it, and deliver this original box to me."

Slightly impatient, Madame Dungaree tells him in Eldric, "Yes, Monsieur Enganyon. We have already been over all that. The last time you were here you also mentioned that they were demanding the exorbitant price of ten thousand dollars, which I could not pay even if I extended my credit with every lender I know."

"Did I mention an affordable alternative?"

"The archon stone? Out of the question! Do you have any idea how much that stone is worth?"

Enganyon loosens his collar and says in Eldric, "Well you see, Madame Dungaree, I would like to put the archon stone back into the question. My friend from the Thieves' Guild said the guild received an offer for twenty thousand dollars. He said the guild master would force him to sell it unless we came up with the archon stone immediately. Hence, I agreed to his terms and am rushing over here from that conversation in hopes of delivering the archon stone right away."

"But we never agreed to give him the stone!"

"There are no two ways about it. I had to make a decision to save Mademoiselle Zena's reputation."

Dungaree Jeanne looks at him sternly. "Then go ahead and release the black box to the Council of Perfects. Mademoiselle Zena's disqualification from the race means little to me. In my opinion, she has little chance of winning as it is, so the only one who stands to lose anything by her disqualification is you."

Enganyon wipes his forehead. "It doesn't work like that, Madame Dungaree. I already promised him I'd get him the archon stone. The Thieves' Guild does not take it lightly when someone breaks a contract with them. They'll kill me if I return empty-handed."

"Monsieur Enganyon, you made the deal. You can pay for that black box out of your own funds if you are so afraid for your life."

Zena stands up and says, "Mother, this is inconceivable! He has put his life on the line for my sake and now you are going to throw him to those wolves!"

Dungaree Jeanne folds her arms and says with dignified calm, "To be honest, Monsieur Enganyon, I am not so sure this friend of yours is on our side at all. How did they even think to snoop around Pony Express posts looking for unsent packages? The Pony Express mostly sends letters that have no worth over and above their sentimental value.

"Besides, if the Thieves' Guild really wanted the archon stone that badly, how come they have not stolen it from us by now? Monsieur Enganyon, I think you are a spy for your father and the Council of Perfects."

Zena exclaims, "Inconceivable!"

Dungaree Jeanne replies with a sour look on her face, "Dear, I don't think that word means what you think it means."

"I know what it means, Mother! It means it's not even worth considering, beyond comprehension, implausible, impossible!"

Dungaree Jeanne continues, "Not one jot of his story makes any sense, Mademoiselle Zena. If that really is the black mail that Bartlebee intended to send, then I say it has caused enough damage as it is. I think it is time that you are just going to have to publicly face up to the fact that you have a birth defect."

Zena screams wildly, "What kind of mother would say that to her child? I can't believe what I'm hearing . . . I'm . . . I'm leaving! You're not my mother anymore!" Zena bursts out of the parlor and slams the door behind her.

Dungaree Jeanne sniffs but maintains her composure. She turns her head to Enganyon and says, "Well then, Monsieur Enganyon, do you have anything else to say? I believe this discussion is over."

Enganyon licks his lips and his eyes dart back and forth quickly, as if he is forcing his mind to overclock all its resources to come up with a way to convince her to give him the archon stone. He says, "Yes, Madame Dungaree, my friend—his name is Mister Mephistopheles—told me that Bartlebee sold the recipe for the Athabask fire to a mercenary company of dwarves led by Master Chief Engineer Tom Thumb. We—my friend Mister Mephistopheles and I—can help you steal the recipe back from this Tom Thumb character if you just let us have the archon stone."

Dungaree Jeanne folds her arms. "Young elf, I said the discussion is over."

Enganyon falls to his knees. "Please, Madame Dungaree, you don't understand! Working with the

Thieves' Guild is like cutting a deal with the devil. They don't take no for an answer. If I don't deliver the archon stone, they'll kill me!

"I know the archon stone is worth a lot more than ten thousand eagles. I will pay you back if you just give me time. Please, I am begging you. The Thieves' Guild is powerful. I can run but I can't hide from them. Sooner or later, they will catch up to me and put me to a horrible death as an example to keep anyone else from double-crossing them."

Dungaree Jeanne looks over to Johnny Appleseed and does her best to explain what happened. When she finishes explaining and venting her feelings, Johnny Appleseed pauses, then asks, "Did he bring me back the notebook I asked him about?"

Dungaree Jeanne asks Enganyon about the notebook. Absentmindedly he pats himself down, then reaches into a leather pouch behind his belt and pulls out the notebook. Without hesitation, Enganyon hands it over to Johnny Appleseed and gives him a weary smile. Appleseed then says to Dungaree Jeanne, "I did say that if he did not hesitate to give it to me, we would know he is telling the truth. But I did not predict that he would try to force your hand in such an obvious manner with this whole death threat story.

"Still, I agree with you. The fundamental problem is that whoever wants the archon stone, whether it be his father or his friend from the Thieves' Guild, Mephistopheles, has no sense of moral responsibility and will certainly use the archon stone for evil ends. We cannot let it fall into their hands. It would cause more damage than you or I could ever undo in a lifetime."

Dungaree Jeanne asks, "So what do we do?"

"We have to call his bluff. We can use the special chewable magica leaves that Mage Nittany left us to locomutate him to a place where the Thieves' Guild will never be able to find him—if his life really is in danger. If he refuses, then we can safely assume the death threat is make-believe."

Dungaree Jeanne thinks for a short while. She then rings the bell for Buttercup and tells her in Eldric, "Miss Buttercup, dear. Please bring a round of hot cocoa for us all. Reverend Appleseed is recommending that I fetch a special gift for Monsieur Enganyon."

Relief washes over Enganyon's face and his color returns. He puts his hands together and keeps repeating, "Oh, thank you, Dungaree Jeanne, oh, thank you! Please tell Reverend Appleseed I say thank you!"

Miss Buttercup asks, "Shall I bring a mug of hot cocoa for Mademoiselle Zena as well, Madame?"

"Yes, Miss Buttercup. She is prone to fits if distemper but usually recovers shortly afterwards. Thank you."

Buttercup curtsies with a strange, leering smile at Enganyon. Again only Johnny Appleseed notices but he keeps it to himself. Dungaree Jeanne excuses herself from the company

The wait is awkward but mercifully brief. Buttercup carries a tray of piping-hot mugs with large saucers so the guests can hold them. On each saucer she has placed two elegant butter cookies shaped like sea shells. Just as Buttercup offloads the last mug from her tray, Dungaree Jeanne returns with a small silver box and hands it to Enganyon.

Dungaree Jeanne dismisses Buttercup. "That will be all, Miss Buttercup. Feel free to take some time off until dinner."

"As you wish, Madame." With another curtsy, Buttercup takes her leave from the parlor with a light skip in her step.

Dungaree Jeanne takes a seat on the sofa and Enganyon sits down next to her. Barely containing his eagerness over the silver box, he asks, "May I see it?"

Dungaree Jeanne nods. Enganyon eagerly opens the box and his face pales. Picking up the leaves, he looks around nervously. "What's this?"

Dungaree Jeanne smiles and says, "Magica leaves. Surely with your father's sizeable library, you would have found a book or two on the topic."

"I don't get it."

"We are offering you a chance to escape. Chew this, and Reverend Appleseed can locomutate you to a location where the Thieves' Guild will never find you."

"Impossible. The Thieves' Guilds around Vinland are all connected. Once they put out a bounty on my head, every lowlife in Vinland will know about it."

"This is a place where lowlifes cannot go, Monsieur Enganyon. Don't worry—you'll be safe."

"I'll be bored! That would be worse than a death sentence! You're basically going to exile me to some hillbilly, Podunk town where I will have nothing to do for the rest of my life and will never get to talk to any of my friends or family ever again!"

At that precise moment, Zena walks into the parlor with a gleaming smile on her face. She addresses her mother with the most pleasant and formal tone she has ever used with her mother; that she has ever managed since becoming a teenager. She says in Runic, "Madame Dungaree, I would like to say I am sorry for my outrageous behavior. Thou art the head of the household and thou alone makest the decisions that thou deemest best for our family. Thou art the best mother an elve like me could have and I appreciate all the sacrifices thou hast made for me over the years. Wouldst thou please accept my apology?"

"Why, Mademoiselle Zena!" replies her mother in Eldric. "That is the nicest compliment you have paid me for as long as I can remember. What brings about this sudden change of heart?"

Zena looks up to the ceiling for a moment and then smiles slightly and says in Eldric, "Let's just say that I overheard your proposal to use the magica leaves to help Monsieur Enganyon escape Tuscoraura Mountain and it got me thinking. Please give me a moment in private with him. Perhaps an early wedding and an extended honeymoon is exactly what we need as a couple. I am assuming that when this crisis blows over and the dust settles, we would be allowed to return to Shentalpee City."

Dungaree Jeanne consults with Johnny Appleseed and he voices his suspicions at such a sudden change of heart but assures her that Zena could go with Enganyon to the refuge if she wanted and that they could come back if they truly felt it was safe. Armed with that information, Zena ushers Enganyon out of the parlor for a private, heart-to-heart discussion.

After a short wait, both young elves come back into the parlor glowing with reassurance and cheerfulness. Enganyon sits back down on the sofa in the same spot next to Madame Dungaree and raises a mug of hot cocoa, saying, "It is all settled then! What a wonderful honeymoon it shall be! Madame Dungaree, may I propose we drink a toast of this exquisite hot cocoa to your daughter, Mademoiselle Zena?"

Dungaree Jeanne can hardly believe it. "But . . . you have to be married to go on a honeymoon."

Enganyon says, "Indeed we do. Next Saturn's Day cannot come too soon. I'm sure I'll be able to stall the Thieves' Guild until then."

Dungaree Jeanne looks at Johnny Appleseed and tells him about Enganyon's sudden change of heart. He says, "Unexpected, but let's roll with it."

Dungaree Jeanne says, "Well then, Mademoiselle Zena, we raise a cup of hot cocoa to you and your fiancé. May your marriage be happy and blessed with all the children your hearts desire!"

Before taking a sip, Zena does a double-take when she sees something floating in Enganyon's mug. In a near panic she says, "Wait! Don't drink that!"

Enganyon gives her a surprised look. "Whatever is the matter, my beloved Mademoiselle Zena?"

"Um, I saw three hairs floating in your drink."

Enganyon picks up the saucer with his left hand and holds the mug handle with his right, saying,

"Nonsense, there is nothing in my drink except pure chocolatey goodness."

He is about to take a sip when Zena grabs his arm, spilling the hot drink on his hands. "Ouch!"

Zena does not relent and insists, "Wait! Right there. See! Three hairs!" She points into his mug.

Enganyon chuckles politely to offload the awkwardness of the situation. "It is nothing but a trifle, my love. Once I clean this spill up with my handkerchief, we'll drink to our future and not belabor the matter any further. Some pressing errands await."

Zena seizes hold of the mug and the saucer and pulls them away from Enganyon. She puts them on the table, saying, "Love, the cocoa is much too hot to drink right now. Please visit with us just a short while longer. I will fetch us some cool, refreshing sweetened mint water for now."

He pulls back on the saucer, creating a little tug-o-war. This scenario perfectly demonstrates the expression *high elf standoff*. Enganyon insists, "No time, my beloved Mademoiselle Zena. I must prepare for this journey before Mephistopheles gets wind of our plans."

Enganyon's grip slips and Zena pulls his mug in front of herself, spattering a splash on the welcome table. She offers Enganyon her own mug, saying, "Oh dear, I spilled it! Please, Monsieur Enganyon, take this one in front of me so you can have a full cup of this hot cocoa. Besides, there were no hairs floating in mine. As you are our guest, we must offer you the very best."

Johnny Appleseed snatches the mug from Zena's hand, then slides his own mug in front of Enganyon and says in Aenglish, "No problem. He can drink mine. I saw those hairs too. Don't worry, it won't bother me."

Now two mugs sit in front of Enganyon.

Dungaree Jeanne grabs the mug from Johnny Appleseed's hand and slides the one in front of herself over to his place. She says courteously in Aenglish, "Please, please, you are our guest too! I cannot allow you to drink that. As the lady of the house I am responsible for our new stewardess's carelessness in letting these hairs fall into the brew. I will drink the tainted mug, Reverend Appleseed."

Seeing the tainted hot cocoa safely in front of her mother, Zena interrupts and says, "Wonderful, let's all drink now!" She takes a sip of her hot cocoa and puts it down, anxiously expecting Enganyon to do the same.

Enganyon quickly grabs the one in front of Madame Dungaree and says, "Oh, it matters not. We are all family now."

He is just about to drink it when Zena slams her mug down in the middle of the table and starts to wrestle with him for the cup again. "But it does matter, darling!" she hisses through clenched teeth.

Madame Dungaree stands up as well and insists, "No, please, Monsieur Enganyon, please, the problem is resolved. Look, I fished out the hairs floating in the other one. No harm done."

By now Zena has lost track of which mug had the three hairs in it. As she examines the mugs Enganyon takes one at random and downs it rather quickly to end the feud, even though it burns his mouth. He winces. "That was delicious indeed. Now if you'll excuse me, I absolutely must make my preparations for our imminent departure. A fond adieu to you all!"

He gives Zena a deep kiss right in front of her mother and Johnny Appleseed and rushes out.

Zena rushes out after him to see him to the door, saying, "I'm coming too!"

Pondering the situation, Johnny Appleseed turns to Dungaree Jeanne and says with a worried brow, "You know, it just dawned on me. Zena has already proven her skill at eavesdropping and snooping around. What if she found the archon stone?"

Dungaree Jeanne looks at him, alarmed. "Oh no! I will check at once!" She runs out of the parlor.

Johnny Appleseed inspects the hot cocoa mugs and then sees Zena floating back through the house, intoxicated with love, humming and dancing as she walks by without even noticing Appleseed.

Dungaree Jeanne storms down the stairwell yelling in Eldric, "Zena Jeannesdottir! You stole the archon stone! Do you have any idea what you have done?"

Zen wears a wispy smile. "I saved my fiancé's life."

"No! You just destroyed our family and brought certain ruin upon Tuscoraura Mountain. Now Umpire Gandorf is going to make himself an invincible undead wight. When word gets out, the Inquisition will surely send a Crusade to destroy Shentalpee City!"

Zena puts her hands on her hips and says, "If Umpire Gandorf is invincible, then we won't have to worry about the Crusades, will we?" She struts past her mother, who is trembling with anger.

Johnny Appleseed, seeing Zena heading upstairs, says, "Um, excuse me, Madame Dungaree! It looks like Enganyon just drank the hot chocolate the stewardess intended him to drink. You don't think it had any—"

Zena's face drops. She whirls around and runs out the front door, moaning to herself, "Oh no! Monsieur Enganyon! Enganyon darling, wait! Come back!"

Scene 2: War Never Changes

Township of Salim
in the Aenglish Duchy of Masswachoosut Bay
Woden's Day Terce. Morning, 3rd of May, 1284
Holy Rood Day (Crouchmas)

They travel by day on a horse-drawn wagon and at night they load the horses onto the wagon and let Sir Balrock pull the harness. After another week of journeying, the party of adventurers reaches the township of Salim, the seat of the Holy Office of the Inquisition in Vinland.

Benjamin Frankelyn holds one last huddle to make sure the plan is clear in everyone's mind. Relying on his dark elf Whoopee to translate his words into Drowish, he says, "Princess, thank you for your cooperation so far. I'm glad this is working out for you. Ariel has a replica of the Sword of Layban, which the Hill Dwarves of Cumorah forged for us after we left Rofchester.

"We won't be able to fool the high inquisitors with a fake sword because of their prophetic gifts, but right after presenting the real Sword of Layban, Ariel will switch it out using sleight of hand with the fake one. If that fails, Whoopee will swap it out using magic.

"Sir Balrock has been very useful so far but the downside to having an undead giant in our company is that he won't escape the notice of the guards at the city gates. He'll have to stay here. We'll use this place as a rallying point to fall back on in case of an emergency.

"Princess, please make sure he knows he is supposed to stay put right here. If we get caught outside the residence of the high inquisition with an undead thrall—yeah, I don't even want to think about it. So I'm only going to ask this once—can Sir Balrock obey orders and stick to this spot?"

Confident, Florenz replies, "He can."

When he hears Whoopee's translation, Frankelyn snaps his fingers. "Good! That's what I like to hear!

"Monsignor Meyer, you will come with us to lend a veneer of holiness to our group. Meanwhile, Willis, here's a few pennies. Take Whoopee and the princess to dinner at a tavern called the Leaky Carvel, my treat. You'll find it down the road on the right from the high inquisitors' residence at the Holy Office headquarters.

"Princess, once we get the real sword back, you're free to head home with the Sword of Layban. Any questions? No? All right, let's move out."

Almost from the first moment, the plan falls apart. Benjamin Frankelyn, Ariel, and Monsignor Meyer approach the Holy Office headquarters and the security measures are about triple in size and scope of what Frankelyn was expecting. A Swiss guard patrol snags them from behind and interrogates them. "Who are you two, and what's this tramp doing here with you?"

Benjamin Frankelyn turns around with a patient smile and says, "Good evening, dearly beloved brothers in Christ. We are friars seeking an audience—"

The Swiss guard interrupts. "Dolts! This is the precinct of the high inquisitors' residence! No women!"

Assessing the official heraldic markings on the patrol and the unbending expressions on their faces, Benjamin Frankelyn quickly calculates the most likely outcomes for various responses that come to mind and he says, "We are grievous sinners and have been told that only one of the high inquisitors in person can absolve us from our unspeakable crimes. Can you point out to us the way?"

"For starters, you have to show proper penitence for your sins by disassociating yourself from the company of women."

As casual as can be, Benjamin Frankelyn turns to Ariel and says, "My dear, treat yourself to some dinner at a local tavern. It seems this will be our last conversation before we enter a life of righteousness."

She shrugs her shoulders and heads off, still carrying both the fake and the real Sword of Layban. Immediately, Benjamin Frankelyn realizes he made the right call. The patrol leader escorts him to the high inquisitors' residence himself and calls on the captain of the inquisitorial household guard to receive them. The captain comes out with a halfling master thief who pats them all down. No way would they have gotten away with the old switcheroo in front of a guy like that.

The captain looks like he is ready to have them all locked up in the stockade. He shouts, "You gentlemen have guilty looks on your faces!"

Benjamin Frankelyn smiles as if the captain were his long-lost rowing buddy from the Cambridge crew team and says, "Tell the high inquisitor that we are very guilty indeed. We have stolen from the Templars of Rofchester and have come to do penitence."

"Come back in the morning. The Holy Office closes after Vespers."

"Let us say that restitution for our sins must be made immediately."

The captain folds his arms. "I said tomorrow."

"Tell you what, Captain. We'll be on our way. We'll come back in a few days after the high inquisitor has executed you and made his choice about your replacement. In the meantime, we're not going to guarantee that we will be able to return the object we stole so iniquitously from the Templars. I can only guarantee you that the high inquisitors will be furious with you when they hear they missed out on this opportunity to get it back for the Church."

The captain stares at him, trying to assess if he is bluffing. He asks the master thief, "What have they got of value on them?"

"These guys are used to playacting and they have nothing of value on them, but that doesn't mean they're bluffing. If they had something truly valuable, they wouldn't be carrying it on their persons. If I were on the beat, my instincts would tell me to follow these guys around for a while. They'll eventually lead us to something extremely valuable."

The captain huffs, "Wait here while I get your story checked out. What's your name anyway?"

"Mister Silence Dogood."

The captain goes in and comes back out a short while later. He says abruptly, "Walk this way."

The captain leads Benjamin Frankelyn and Monsignor Oscar Meyer inside with four guards surrounding them as if fearing them to be assassins. They walk through hallways paneled in carved wood with scenes from Graec and Roman mythology—not all of them are as pious as one might presume for a residence of clerics. The guards open the door to a dining room with a long table capable of entertaining a large number of guests. Instead, there are only three men seated—one in a large chair, the next in a middling chair, and the third in a small chair.

From their cardinals' robes and obvious family resemblance, Benjamin Frankelyn does not need more than one guess that the three men facing him are the Cardinals Orsini—the three bears of the Holy Office of the Inquisition in Vinland. They are eating a meal. The shortest of the three, Piccolo Cardinal Orsini, seems the friendliest. He says, "Ah! Mista Dogood, so kind of you to pay us a visit. Pwease, you and ya fwiend awe wewcome to join us fa suppa. Any good news?"

Benjamin Frankelyn takes a seat, unfolds a napkin, and places it on his lap as if he ate here every night. He says in his most charming voice, "Good news indeed, Your Eminence! The Templars have once again proven themselves reliable bankers. Your Rofchester refund is ready and awaiting your approval."

The serving boy brings him three dishes. One is piping hot, the other is cold to the touch, but the third looks and smells deliciously warm. Benjamin Frankelyn indulges in a nice, warm bowl of porridge.

The biggest of the three brothers, Paterno Cardinal Orsini, puts on a sour face and says, "That is not the way we understand it. We received an urgent message by Pony Express from the Templars that the bank was destroyed by blackflame and nearly all the valuables inside turned to glass and shattered. Our investment was lost."

Benjamin Frankelyn pats his lips with the silk napkin and says, "Your Eminence, the line 'nearly all' is the most important one to take away from that brief. Since the Templar clerks were being less than reasonable with our honest request, we took liberties with the quest details and found a way to recover for you what is rightfully yours. It's not a sin to steal what belongs to you in the first place, is it? As for the blackflame, it's not our fault the vault lacked a proper sprinkler system or um . . . flamethrowers to put it out."

The middle brother, Maderno Cardinal Orsini, joins in. "Not at all. The captain of our guard informed us you claim to have something for us. Our loremasters and a few monks with special gifts in these matters would like to examine it. Where is it?"

Benjamin Frankelyn gulps down another spoonful of delicious porridge, then leans back and says, "Nearby, Your Eminence. Before we get to that, may we discuss the reward you had offered my patron? It would be foolish of me to deliver the goods before making sure that no misunderstanding of the quest reward should inhibit our working relationship. After all, my patron went to great expense to hire an adventurer of my caliber for this quest; at this late stage, it's not my policy to bungle it for him."

Instead of responding to this kind of petulance, the three Orsini brothers begin to pray. They open their eyes and Maderno Cardinal Orsini says, "The gift of prophecy is telling us that the Sword of Layban is not far away. And also, the girl."

"What girl?" asks Benjamin Frankelyn, putting on an innocent face.

"Goldilocks. The Templars apprehended her when she was trying to collect the sword, but she escaped the wreckage. No doubt your handiwork as well."

"The name does not sound familiar."

"The size of a child; blonde, curly hair. Please do not delude yourself that you could get away with lying to us. Even a low-level cleric could use the gift of prophecy to see through a flat-out lie like that."

Benjamin Frankelyn strokes his chin and looks up into the air as if thinking intently. "*Familiar* then is probably not the best term. Yes, indeed, we found a dark elf there, but she is not a child and she does not go by that name. She identifies as a princess."

Paterno Cardinal Orsini says, "Play all the word games you please, Frankelyn, just deliver to us the sword and the girl. Life is always simpler and less painful when you cooperate with the Inquisition."

Benjamin Frankelyn measures his words carefully. He cannot get away with lying to such powerful clerics but he cannot tell them the truth, either—too dangerous. He says with deliberately constructed wording, "The Sword of Layban is in the possession of some of my associates who are waiting to hear word from me that you are going to uphold your end of the deal for my patron. As for the girl we rescued, I have a feeling she is not far from here, doing everything in her power to recover the Sword of Layban for herself."

Maderno Cardinal Orsini says, "Perhaps she has tempted you to betray us."

Benjamin Frankelyn holds up his hands and says with a defensive chuckle, "Every day I pray the Lord's Prayer, 'Lead us not into temptation.'"

Paterno Cardinal Orsini says, "Stalling is futile. Our household inquisitors will easily locate them. The Holy Office of the Inquisition is not just another faction—it's the mother of all factions and we can destroy your reputation across Vinland. You'll never receive another quest from anyone again if you so much as think about double-crossing us."

Benjamin Frankelyn does not flinch at how easily their prophetic gifts cut through his schemes and he immediately goes on the offensive. "Speaking of double-crossing, we must discuss my patron's new status as viceroy. When will he be crowned?"

Maderno Cardinal Orsini says, "As soon as we receive the sword and take Goldilocks into custody, you will receive a royal decree appointing the baron of Amhirst Aengland's crown governor-general of Vinland. He will have extensive authority but no crown, no royal privileges, and no hereditary title."

Benjamin Frankelyn is visibly flustered. "That wasn't the deal. He was supposed to be *crowned* Aenglish viceroy of Vinland."

Paterno Cardinal Orsini says, "We are altering the deal. Pray we do not alter it any further. We have an agent in Ithica who described how overeager the baron of Amhirst was to usurp the Crown's authority for his personal interests. A viceroyal crown in Vinland would tempt even the most loyal servant to declare independence from the royal crown in Mother Aengland. King Eddard is an honored Crusader and a friend of the Holy Office of the Inquisition. He looks after our interests, and we look after his."

Benjamin Frankelyn leans forward and says intently, "If loyalty is your basis, then you will appreciate the fact that I look after the interests of my patron. I repeat—no deal until I receive word from him that he agrees to your changes."

"Too late," says Paterno Cardinal Orsini. "Our household inquisitors have just used the gift of tongues to report that your friends are already in our custody."

Benjamin Frankelyn replies, "How do you think the people would respond to hearing that the Holy Office of the Inquisition is using blackflame necromancy in its war against heresy?"

Maderno Cardinal Orsini laughs dismissively, saying, "No one would be so bold as to believe you—not in public, anyhow. Up until this point you have handled yourself well, so it comes as a surprise that you should risk all on such a clumsy threat. However, it does seem that you are exactly the kind of efficient, loyal, and unscrupulous adventurer we are looking for to fulfill an important quest. Perhaps we can compromise."

"I respectfully decline. I am actually a student of sorcery and must return to my studies."

"We beg to differ, young Frankelyn," replies Paterno Cardinal Orsini. "You have come this far. I regret to inform you that you have crossed the point of no return. From here on out, you will do as we say or join the next crop of heretics being burned at the stake."

"This deal is getting worse all the time."

"Glad we can all agree. Captain Ronaldo, bring Miss Sacagawea in, if you please."

"Right away, Your Most Reverend Eminence."

A beautiful young woman with bronze skin and black eyes appears from the inner hallway. Her gentle steps and deliberate gait tell Benjamin Frankelyn and Monsignor Meyer that she has endured many hardships and pulled through them with great courage. Instinctively, they both stand up to greet her when she walks into the dining room as if she were royalty. Her bearing is confident but modest, devoid of pretension but evincing a strong sense of self-worth.

Maderno Cardinal Orsini explains, "A confederacy of Algonkian and Irokian nations allied with the former Frankish viceroy Samuel de Champlane a long time ago and are not happy that the new Aenglish settlers flooding into the west are refusing to honor the treaties they brokered with the Franks. The situation is escalating rapidly, and they have sent Miss Sacagawea to us as the representative of their cause.

"The unofficial leader of the confederacy, Sagamore Pontiak, has written down sworn statements from a large number of leaders inviting us to send missionaries and agreeing to a military alliance with the Holy Office of the Inquisition if we help them recover from custody the former Frankish viceroy, whom they call the Great Uncle."

Piccolo Cardinal Orsini says excitedly, "This is a wunce-in-a-wifetime chance fa us in Vinwand! We want you to intwoduce Miss Sacagawea to the bawon of Amhiwst and teww him how gweat she is!"

Maderno Cardinal Orsini continues, "After you vouch for her, she will recover Uncle Sam and deliver him to Pontiak's confederacy. In return, we will overlook your indiscretion in trying to threaten us—and pay you thirty pounds sterling for your troubles."

Benjamin Frankelyn groans, "Thirty silver pieces to betray my benefactor. I'm loving the irony here."

Maderno Cardinal Orsini says, "The Lord chastises the son he loves with an iron rod indeed. We had promised the baron of Amhirst the privilege of denouncing any of his political enemies to us. We will honor that pledge and extend a custom offer to you.

"On that table is a signed and sealed unconditional pardon with papal authority. If you ever find yourself detained or in trouble with the law for any reason, you have only to present that pardon and you will be freed from custody or punishments immediately."

Piccolo Cardinal Orsini adds, "That's a huge gift fwom us, Mista Fwankewyn. Just think of aww the things you can mess up and just wak wight out of the dungeon! Besides, you can wash ya hands of tweason—you awe not gonna betway the bawon, we awe . . . I mean, Sacagawea is."

Piccolo draws stern looks from his brothers, who both shout at him, "Stai zito!"

Maderno Cardinal Orsini says, "You are not betraying the baron of Amhirst. He wanted supreme authority in Vinland, and that royal edict on the table confers it to him. He wanted the friendship of the Holy Office of the Inquisition and he shall have it. By doing this little favor for us, you guarantee that the baron of Amhirst gets what he wants. If you refuse, we keep the sword, Amhirst's title as governor, and throw you in our dungeon, just to keep our little secret safe."

Frankelyn asks, "What do you intend to do with our princess, whom you call Goldilocks?"

Paterno Cardinal Orsini replies, "She will stand trial. If we uncover any foul play, she'll be burned at the stake. If she's innocent, we'll cook something up to burn her at the stake. Get it? Cook something up—burn at the stake! Ha, ha, ha!"

Piccolo Cardinal Orsini joins in laughing but Maderno Cardinal Orsini does a facepalm.

When the one-sided laughter dies down, Maderno Cardinal Orsini concludes the discussion. "The choice is yours, Mister Frankelyn. Behind door one is the royal edict declaring the baron of Amhirst Aenglish crown governor-general of Vinland, thirty pounds sterling silver, an unconditional pardon for any future misunderstandings, and the friendship of the Holy Office of the Inquisition."

Paterno Cardinal Orsini wipes the drip from his nose and adds, "Behind door two is our dungeon. We feel confident we've already got all we need to know from you, but I do have a few techniques for extracting confessions that I'd like to try out. You could give us feedback from your firsthand experiences."

Benjamin Frankelyn gulps. "Well, Your Eminences. It's been a tough decision, but I've decided to go with door one."

Benjamin Frankelyn stands up and bows. "This has been a pleasure, really, but I must be going. Miss Sacagawea, would you care to join Monsignor Meyer and myself on a tranquil stroll through this beautifully moonlit evening?"

She bows her head gently.

"You can lay out in detail all you need from us to complete your quest as we walk, my dear. Come along, Monsignor Meyer, we have work to do for our new friends."

Once they reach the Leaky Carvel tavern, Sacagawea asks, "Where's your party of adventurers?"

"Over here, come meet them. You already know our cleric, Monsignor Oscar Meyer. This is our fighter, Willis, our rogue, Ariel, and our magicultor, Whoopee."

Sacagawea looks at them. "Those names sound kind of fake."

Willis raises his hand. "Mine doesn't."

Whoopee mutters, "That's 'cause it's your real name."

"Come on!" he huffs. "You keep giving it away. She would have thought it was a clever code name if you hadn't said anything. You want me to come up with a name as silly as yours?" He takes a sip of his drink and says, "How about we call you Heiniekin?"

Benjamin Frankelyn asks, "Where's the princess?"

A wave of shame washes over Ariel's face. "They took her and the real sword. They had powerful clerics with the gift of prophecy. I had no chance."

Monsignor Meyer grunts, "What does it matter to us? We fulfilled our quest and now that the princess has been arrested by the Inquisition, that cancels our obligation to fulfill our promise to her."

Ariel shoots him an angry look. "Is that the kind of drivel you learn in your theology classes?"

Seeing the party about to explode in an ugly argument, Sacagawea says, "Do not worry. I know where she is."

They all look at her, astounded. Sacagawea continues, "I understand that my current quest requires you to steal something from your quest-giver. You are a man with a deep sense of loyalty, Mister Frankelyn. So here's the deal—if I help you rescue the princess and steal this sword back from the Inquisition, will you help me rescue Uncle Sam from captivity?"

"Deal."

Ariel is confused. "So you are going to steal from your patron? That's bad business in my book."

Benjamin Frankelyn replies, "Monsignor Meyer was on to something. You see, my patron agreed to engage my services only occasionally while I study sorcery at Silvermorn. Now that I have completed the quest he assigned to me, I am no longer in his service."

Ariel huffs, "I don't like it, but if we have to resort to technicalities to rescue the princess, then technicalities will have to do for now. I'm in."

Sacagawea cuts off any further discussion. "Deal. Now listen. There's no time to waste. I overheard the inquisitors say they intend to send the sword on the next ship to Frankland. There's a dwarf whaling vessel docked at Baston heading back to Bayonne at dawn."

"Bayonne? That derelict port city in New Gersey?"

Sacagawea acknowledges Ariel respectfully and says, "Actually, I was referring to the port city in the Duchy of Aquatania in Europa at the northern base of the Pyrinoak Mountains. The high inquisitors have already sent for a messenger from the Pony Express post in Salim. If we can intercept the Pony Express rider after he makes the pickup, your magicultor can locomutate away this sword of yours."

Whoopee says, "Brilliant plan. Unfortunately, I'd have to be within fifteen feet to get it right the first time. I could probably pull it off from as far as sixty feet, but I might just as easily flub it up."

Benjamin Frankelyn says, "Don't worry, Whoopee. We'll get you close. What about the princess?"

Sacagawea says, "She'll be in the dungeon. There's a chimney that leads all the way down to it from the roof. It's only wide enough to fit a skinny elf."

They all look at Whoopee and he puffs out his chest proudly. "You guys make fun of me for being skinny all the time, and now you see how many times I get to rescue the princesses on these quests!"

Willis says, "You've only done it once so far. I see two problems with going down a chimney. First, we have to get up on the roof without being noticed. Second, there's usually a fire going on at the bottom."

Whoopee says, "Don't worry! I can work my magic with the fire, but getting past the guards will be a real problem. We cased the joint and there's no gap in the patrol routes. If one false step of ours tips the guards off that something funny is going on, they'll call in their high-level clerics. We won't be able to hide from their gift of prophecy."

Ariel says proudly, "Leave that to me. I grew up in a castle with overprotective parents. Sneaking past guards is what rogues like me do best."

With that, they commence the first part of their plan—recovering the Sword of Layban. Ariel and Whoopee jog back to the Holy Office without drawing too much attention. They maneuver themselves behind an empty butcher's stall and arrive just in the nick of time; the Pony Express rider is knocking on the door.

Ariel says, "Quick! They're handing her a package."

Whoopee says, "Okay. I'm doing my best. Let's see, the metal seems to be a more ancient version of steel—probably just wrought iron—with a gold hilt. It'll be sloppy, but this magic word just might do the trick . . . presto change-o!"

He waves his magica wand.

"Nothing happened," says Ariel.

Whoopee looks closely and whispers, "That pony rider's got an apotropaic charm."

Ariel gasps, "What does that mean?"

"See that dreamcatcher on her saddle? It's made of unicorn ivory—very powerful at warding off magic. We've got to get rid of it."

Ariel rolls out from under the butcher stall and walks across the intersection to make it seem like she is coming from the next alley over. She staggers and sways as if she is drunk and walks up to the halfling pony rider. "My family lives in Baston and I haven't got a dime. Can you give me a lift to Baston? I'm in no condition to walk."

The halfling Pony Express locks the package in a security saddlebag and mounts up quickly. She flips Ariel a dime and snaps her reins.

Ariel throws her body in front of the pony and it rears. "How about a quarter?"

She pretends to stumble over the spooked pony and swipes the dreamcatcher as she falls to the cobblestone.

A guard calls out, "Wait! Arrest that woman!"

Two Swiss guards come out and apprehend Ariel. The guard in the doorway calls to the Pony Express rider, "Let me inspect the package to make sure she didn't steal the sword."

The rider unlocks it and hands the package to a Swiss guard who takes it back inside for inspection. After a close examination from their cleric and master thief, the Swiss guard hands the authenticated package back to the Pony Express rider.

No sooner does she secure the Sword of Layban back into her saddlebag than whoopee sings out from behind the butcher stall, "Presto change-o."

The other Swiss guard puts manacles (the medieval version of handcuffs) on Ariel and starts leading her inside for interrogation. Weary of trouble, the Pony Express rider gallops off into the night while two Swiss guards head over to the butcher stall to investigate.

The next instant, Whoopee displays the full scope of his virtuosity as a magicultor. Seeing his friend about to get tortured, he whips his magica wand around and chants, "Mancala hexa hold'm, mancala niney morris."

Ariel's manacles are gone! The Swiss guard next to her is now wearing them.

Whoopee whirls around and intones, "Hnafatafl chataranga latrunclarum, majong bagammon go!"

The fake sword on her hip vanishes and the real Sword of Layban takes its place. She elbows the Swiss guard in the nose and scampers off into the shadows.

Whoopee turns around to dash away, but the Swiss guards catch up to him. He barely has enough time to reach into his pouch and shove a few magica leaves in his mouth before the Swiss guards corner him and take him into custody.

Knowing when a situation is lost, Ariel does not stick around for the swarming Swiss guards to detect her hiding spot. As quietly and swiftly as she can, she slips from shadow to shadow until she makes her way back to the Leaky Carvel.

When Ariel sees her companions in the tavern, they ask, "Where's Whoopee?"

"They arrested him."

Benjamin Frankelyn asks, "Did you manage to swap the swords?"

"No, but Whoopee did say a lot of magic words before he got caught. I think he locomutated the real Sword of Layban into my scabbard."

Benjamin Frankelyn draws the sword from her hip and comments, "I put a little scratch into the real one to help me tell the difference." He inspects the blade briefly. "Yep! This is it. Whoopee pulled it off before they got him! Now that's team spirit. I'm really starting to like that little guy."

Ariel snorts, "Well, we don't just like him; we all love him because he's family. We're going back!"

Benjamin Frankelyn is too practical for chivalrous rescue attempts. "Wait! We need to get the Sword of Layban far away from here before those snooping clerics start doing their prophecy trick again."

Ariel argues, "You might be okay with waiting for them to torture him until you work out your plan, but I'm not going to wait. As leader of this party of adventurers I call the shots, and I say we move out now. You're just here to spy on us, remember?"

"Okay, fine, I guess I did say that," concedes Benjamin Frankelyn. "We'll split up. You go find Whoopee without a plan. I'll go bury the sword at our regroup point so Sir Balrock can keep a watch over it. Then I'll meet you back here."

Ariel groans. "What adventurers' guild did you train in? Haven't you heard the old adage, 'Splitting up is the best way to turn a questline into a horror story'?"

It's starting to get late enough that the tavern empties. The innkeeper puts his big hands on the table and says, "The inn's closing, so unless you're going to rent a room, I'm going to have to ask you to leave. It's a penny a night per person; a tuppence each if you want your own room."

Benjamin Frankelyn hands the innkeeper a groat but the innkeeper asks, "What's this?"

"A groat. Newly minted fourpence piece. We won't stay long, but this should cover your discretion."

The innkeeper eyes the coin to figure out if it is legit or not. Benjamin Frankelyn adds, "Or we can leave."

The innkeeper takes the groat and walks away.

Benjamin Frankelyn smiles and says, "Now then, where were we?"

Ariel takes charge of the rescue operation. "Monsignor Meyer, pray and see if your gift of prophecy can tell you where they've taken Whoopee."

Monsignor Meyer prays for a while, then looks up and says, "Halleluiah, praise the Lord!"

Benjamin Frankelyn comments, "Monsignor Meyer, your piety is inspiring, but we really haven't got the time for a worship service at the moment. Did you find Whoopee or not?"

"Had a vision," replies Monsignor Meyer. "Whoopee got some magica leaves in his mouth before they arrested him. He managed to locomutate himself away before they put him in a warded cell, but he didn't get very far. He's still hiding behind a butcher's stall adjacent to the high inquisitors' residence.

"The place is still crawling with guards. They're sending a group here to apprehend Ariel. We don't have much time before their clerics find Whoopee too."

Willis pounds his fist in his palm. "Let's move out!"

Sacagawea interrupts their fervor. "I'm your best chance for getting in and out of there alive. I know the butcher stall you're talking about. Follow me."

Monsignor Meyer and Willis look to Ariel for her say in this. She nods and motions with her hand for Sacagawea to take the lead.

Sacagawea looks at Ariel and says, "We'll draw less attention if it's just the two of us. Mister Frankelyn is right. You need to get that sword as far away from here as possible. I suggest the two big guys stay with him in case he runs into any trouble. Ariel and I need to go alone if we are going to sneak past all those guards."

Willis objects, "What if it's a trap? She works for the Inquisition. How do we know she's not going to hand us over to them one by one?"

Ariel swallows hard and looks Sacagawea straight in the eyes to get a sense of her motives. She sees nothing but a young woman who is an expert at masking her own feelings.

After a short pause, Ariel says, "We don't have time to come up with another plan. It's all or nothing. Willis, Monsignor, escort Mister Frankelyn and the sword back to Sir Balrock. I'm with her."

Willis hands her the party's climbing rope. "The Monsignor will know if you get double-crossed. We'll come for you even if we have to raise an army."

They split up and head out to face the dark terrors of the night.

The guard dogs are already sniffing around the butcher stall and barking. One of the Swiss guards smashes open a barrel and they all cover their noses at the stench. Another guard kicks it over. Oozing intestines, gooey brains, dangly sinews, and stinking entrails spill across the floor. The puddle of muck seems to take the shape of a little person.

Ariel tosses a coin across the cobblestones. The sudden *clink-clank* startles the edgy Swiss guards and she dashes off in the other direction.

"It's her!" One of them yells and the rest of the Swiss guards ply their skills at parkour in chasing after her. In full armor, they display less skill than a stack of sixty-gallon steel drums.

Sacagawea scoops Whoopee out of the sludge he's been hiding in and they slink off into the darkness.

When they come to a secluded spot along the Salim harbor walk, Whoopee whines. "Next quest I sign up for is going to including a clause stipulating extra pay if I get stuck with all the yucky work again."

Sacagawea points to the waterfront and says, "You need to get cleaned off."

Whoopee is not thrilled about a cold dunk. "Wait! Where's everyone else? What happened to Ariel?"

"I'm right behind you, you little stinker. Sacagawea's right. You'd better wash yourself off. I could smell you from two blocks away."

Whoopee knows she's right and takes his chilly bath like a brave dark elf. After drying off for a bit in the cool night air, Sacagawea leads them back towards the high inquisitors' residence.

"Ariel, if you can pick this lock, the attic of this house leads out to a scaffold. We can use it to get onto the roof of the residence."

Ariel twirls a lockpick in her fingers and says, "Let me show you how it's done, sister!"

Her pick does the trick. Soon they are on top of the high inquisitor's residence. Sacagawea points out the chimney that leads to the dungeon. Still wet and feeling the evening chill, Whoopee says, "It's mighty nice of them to keep their prisoners warm like that at night."

She replies, "I think the purpose is to heat up the hot pokers for their victims' feet."

Whoopee gulps as he pulls out his magic wand. "Sound like nice guys. I'm going to have to assume they'll be hard at work when I get down there. All right, give me some room to concentrate. Making all that fire locomutate from way up here will be a chore."

Whoopee closes his eyes to concentrate, then he swirls his magic wand around and sings, "Oo ee oo ah ah ting tang walla walla bing bang."

The smoke from the chimney thins out and Ariel lets down Willis's rope. "Quickly, before they relight the fire."

Whoopee slides down the rope swiftly but cautiously. As he gets farther down, the bricks inside the chimney get hotter and hotter. He drops down the last few feet, singes his fingertips on the way down, and rolls out of the fireplace into a dimly lit torture chamber.

A torturer and his assistant are getting two fire pokers ready, having already tied Florenz to the rack. Fortunately for her, Whoopee's appearance interrupts the torture session before it really heated up.

Drawing his dagger with his right hand and keeping his magic wand ready in his left, Whoopee charges at the torturers with the wild ferocity of a momma bear defending her cub. The torturer's assistant's first reaction is to swipe his hot poker at the raging dark elf, but it is a slow and clumsy weapon and he swings wide. The torturer himself grabs some hooks with extremely sharp points attached to chains and swings one at the dark elf with deadly accuracy.

The attack is spot-on. The hook buries its tip into the back of Whoopee's left leg. The torturer yanks him off his feet but once on the ground, Whoopee waves his wand, chanting, "Izzy wizzy!"

The hook disappears. Whoopee gets back up and runs with a limp at the torturer, who blocks a chop from the magica wand in Whoopee's left hand with the length of chain he has been holding. The torturer realizes too late that a magica wand isn't sharp. Having diverted his foe's guard in the wrong direction with the feint, Whoopee slashes the torturer from hand to elbow with the dagger in his right hand.

The assistant torturer decides to help his mentor, stabbing at Whoopee with his fire poker, but the dark elf uses his small size to roll underneath the bed of a torture rack. Whoopee watches the assistant's feet carefully and when the assistant walks past, Whoopee slashes at the back of the assistant's ankle, hamstringing him. The assistant tumbles to the floor and lands on his own hot fire poker. It hisses against his skin and burns in deep. The big baby cannot stand the pain and rolls on the floor, crying hysterically.

The torturer, seeing the dark elf's skill with his wand and his blade and the dexterous movements that took his assistant down so quickly, realizes he cannot win the match by force of arms, so he resorts to a different tactic. He grabs the other hot poker and holds it over Florenz, shouting, "If you want to see your girlfriend live, drop your weapons!"

Whoopee looks at him anxiously and raises both hands in the air. The torturer smiles with cruel satisfaction, reassured his ploy worked—but too soon! Whoopee flicks his wrist and trills, "Jantar mantar!"

Not bluffing, the torturer jabs the poker toward Florenz, but it has disappeared. With another flick of his wrist Whoopee sings, "Jadu mandu!"

The hot poker reappears above the torturer's head. He looks up and it drops down onto his face. Whoopee dashes forward and drives his dagger between the screaming torturer's ribs, quieting him for good.

Whoopee frees Florenz and says to her in Drowish, "Hey, Princess, welcome to our party of adventurers! We've got the Sword of Layban for you, as promised."

Florenz is in no mood for cheerful reunions. Immediately after her hands are loose, she sees the blubbering torturer's assistant trying to flee, grabs a fire poker, runs over, and finishes him off.

Whoopee is horrified by the act of vengeful violence and waves her toward the fireplace, warning her, "Okay, that's enough. Let's split before anyone comes to check out who's been doing all that screaming."

Florenz looks at him sardonically and says, "Seriously? It's a torture chamber. People scream down here all the time."

"Right, let's just leave. All this freaky torture stuff makes me want to go home and unwind with a nice cup of hot cocoa."

At last, she smiles. "Ever heard of the Kibbler workshops? I'll get you a lifetime supply of hot cocoa if we make it out of this alive."

"Seriously, girl! You're my hero."

She gives him a wink and heads into the still-hot fireplace to climb the rope up the chimney.

Once they make it to the top, Sacagawea is already worried that their escape route has been cut off. "It's getting bad down there. The Swiss guards are edgy and the captain just sent someone to wake up a high-level cleric to make sure that there are no intruders left in the vicinity. We are going to need one heck of a distraction to get out of here in one piece and we need it now."

Whoopee says, "Oh, don't worry, lady. Just sit back and relax. You know all that fire in the chimney? I had to put it somewhere."

It doesn't take long for the smoke to start puffing out the windows of the high inquisitors' residence. Soon enough, the inquisitors are racing out of the house in a panic and barking instructions to the guards. More worried about the priceless works of art going up in flames than their own safety, they instruct the Swiss guards to form a fire brigade.

For an expert like Ariel, adding misinformation and misdirection to the smoky confusion is second nature and the adventurers walk out of the vicinity unnoticed while the guards scramble about all around them.

Sacagawea leads them through Salim's back roads and dark alleys to a house built next to the town wall. The owner is an entrepreneur who moonlights as an escape artist. For three dollars he hoists up a ladder onto the wall after the night watchman paces past the house and lowers a rope down the other side.

When they reach Sir Balrock's hiding place, their fellow adventurers greet them with warm hugs. Benjamin Frankelyn notices Florenz backing away from the profusions of affection and switches to a love language that he knows she'll appreciate. He gives her a gift—the Sword of Layban. He asks Whoopee to translate for him and says to her, "Now you see that we have kept our end of the bargain. We consider you our friend and we hope that you will count us among your friends. Please know that you can call on us for a favor in the future if you ever need anything. We just might do the same."

Whoopee talks to her in Drowish briefly and looks up at the entire party of adventurers and tells them her answer. "She says she only needs one thing—revenge."

Scene 3: The Return of the Martinet of War

Malarkey Market at Thor's Base, Shentalpee City
Whit Sun Day's Eve Compline
Night, 27th of May, 1284

Gone is the sweet, loveable young elve who was so pampered by her father. Tonight, a different Florenz steps onto Thor's Base. There is anger in her eyes, a mystically evil sword on her hip, and a party of undead thralls at her back. Her red cloak is dirty and prickled with dead leaves and broken twigs. Her curly, dyed-blond hair has lost its bounce and its black roots show.

"Hey, beautiful! I heard my girlfriend's back."

It's Enganyon, dressed in a dashing military uniform. Not far behind him stand Officer Bunzi and another Justiciar Leaguer who was one of Enganyon's former cronies when he was nothing but a rebellious teen. Enganyon's got a confident and affectionate smirk on his face, hiding his guilt behind a romantic mask.

"Hey, liar. Your girlfriend's back and you're gonna be in trouble."

Enganyon looks around as if Florenz must be calling someone else a liar. It's late at night. The plaza is empty, but Enganyon feels the need to put on a show.

Florenz isn't in the mood for nonsense. "I've been gone for a long time, but I know about your cheating."

"Has someone been spreading lies that I was untrue to you, darling?"

"Let's put it this way: if you don't break off your betrothal to Mademoiselle Zena tomorrow, you're going to be sorry you were ever born."

"Tomorrow? The paperwork alone'll take a week!"

Sir Balrock grabs his cheeks, lifts him, and squeezes.

Florenz's patience runs thin. "Monsieur Lynx was engaged to Mademoiselle Zena when you proposed to her. Should we ask him to sign off on your registry?"

Enganyon struggles but cannot break Sir Balrock's grip on his face. He tries to speak, "Hey la day la!"

"What did you say?"

"Hey la day la!"

"What's the matter? A wight's got your tongue?" She snaps her fingers and says, "Drop him."

Sir Balrock lets go. Enganyon gasps for air and mutters, "He's kind of big and he's awful strong."

Florenz sneers, "So what about the paperwork?"

Enganyon is still clutching his face. "Monsieur Lynx died in an ambush on an Ivy League quest."

"That's a pity. I really liked that kid. Hmmm, that means that Mademoiselle Zena is the only candidate left. Did they call off the election yet?"

"Actually, there *is* another candidate."

"What? Who?"

"Me."

"You? But you were like, 'Oh, I don't want to be umpire-in-chief. I only want to see the love of my life, Mademoiselle Zena, become umpire-in-chief.'"

"That was the love potion talking! She gave me a love potion. I wasn't in my right mind. You know that I only—"

She slaps his face. "Stop! In the name of love, before you break my heart. That really hurt, and your lame excuses are only making it worse. Never mind how it started. End this infatuation or Sir Balrock here will cut you down to size. I've tried so hard to be patient, but it's over. Capisce?"

"Oh, darling, you know I only have eyes for you! Are the stars out tonight? I can't tell. You sparkle—"

"Oh, cut out the poetry. Just hold me tight and tell me you love me."

"I love you, and I promise I'll never let you go."

Florenz gives him a sly grin. "Never say never."

"I'll never win with you."

"Never."

Their tender reunion is interrupted by Officer Bunzi, who points to his comrade. "Excuse me, Mademoiselle Florenz, but do you want Junior Officer Parris and I to, you know, mosey on home while you two enjoy your moment in the still of the night?"

She unfurls herself from Enganyon's arms and asks, "Actually, Officer Bunzi, you are exactly the person I need right now. Did you recover my father's body and hide it where I asked?"

"Yes, Mademoiselle, I did. It ended up costing—"

"Never mind the cost," she snaps. "Now I'm back and things will be fine. Follow me."

She takes them all into the secret room overlooking the council chambers and has them open up the barrel full of vinegar.

Florenz ignites the Sword of Layban and chants, "Arise, Kibbler! I dub thee a servant of the black fire, a dread knight of the flame of Layban. I bid thee come back from the shadows. Arise, Sir Kibbler!"

Her pickled father emerges from the vinegar barrel with his flesh bleached white. The damage from the fall has marred his face, having knocked out all his front teeth except his canines. The damage to his mouth is so severe his words are all garbled. Instead, he projects his thoughts to those nearby using the Black Tongue of

Caldor. To ordinary folks it just sounds like a horrid, shrieking noise inside their minds. Only Florenz understands what the Dread Knight is saying.

She replies in Eldric, "When I left you, I was but the learner. Now, I am the master. Even the heresiarch will have to bow to the power of the Sword of Layban."

The undead Umpire Kibbler points to Enganyon and speaks to him forcefully in the black tongue of Caldor. Enganyon writhes in pain at the cacophonous utterances ringing inside his head.

Florenz stops her father, saying, "He's as clumsy as he is stupid. He *must* obey me as his master."

Her father speaks again and she replies, "I will go speak with the high elves. They will not rebel. This will be a day long remembered. It has seen the return of the monsieur umpire-in-chief and it will soon see the end of the Inquisition." She turns to Officer Bunzi and says, "Tomorrow call all the high elves of Shentalpee City for a special Thor's Enlightenment Discourse."

Enganyon does not like the way events are developing and he points to the monstrosity that was Umpire Kibbler and asks, "How do you know it's really him? I mean, that could be some kind of demon or foul spirit animating your father's body."

Florenz growls and chides him. "I find your lack of faith disturbing. My father wishes to punish you for your faithlessness, but I have other plans. You will bring us Dungaree Jeanne's archon stone."

"It's a priceless treasure, darling! She'll never—"

"Never say never. Failure is not an option."

Officer Bunzi cringes. Enganyon tries to blow it off and pretends to be joking, "Yes, master."

No one is fooled.

Bonus Scene B: Saving Face

Malarkey Market at Thor's Base, Shentalpee
Woden's Day Terce. Morning, 3rd of May, 1284
Holy Rood Day (Crouchmas)

Dungaree Jeanne is shopping at the Malarkey open-air market trying to buy fresh vegetables at a discount rate. Until recently, she would never have even considered going shopping for her own groceries—it's a stewardess's job. After the hot cocoa incident, Miss Buttercup has disappeared, probably hoping to lie low until Zena's anger over the episode blows over.

Now that Zena has given away the archon stone, her mother's last plank of economic security has been swiped out from under her feet. That mug of hot cocoa they drank to Zena's future now feels like an ill-omened toast to a bleak future sicklied over with a pale cast of only two thoughts: doom and gloom.

Buttercup had been using the shopping lists that Bartlebee came up with, never a thought about discounts or bargains in any of them. Once upon a time, Dungaree Jeanne had been poor and she had come up with quite a few money-saving measures to eat well on a low budget. Perhaps because shopping relaxes her or perhaps because she wants to practice being poor again, she hits the Malarkey Plaza with an eye out for good deals.

The first item her eye catches is the tall figure of Johnny Appleseed walking toward her. She greets him cheerfully in Aenglish, "Good morning, Reverend Appleseed. What brings you out here?"

He breathes in the fresh morning air and says, "You know me, Madame Dungaree. I've lived out in open nature for so many years. It has been really hard on me having to stay cooped up inside, playing solitaire."

"I'm very sorry we've been so neglectful as hosts."

"No, Madame Dungaree, don't even apologize. You have been quite busy and I feel that since I have arrived, nothing but misfortune has befallen you. I hope to make it up to you someday."

"You have already more than made up for it by trading all your apples and apple seeds for those bags of cocoa beans. I don't know how I will pay you back."

Johnny Appleseed shakes his head and says, "Oh, no worries! Your friendship is the greatest recompense I could hope for. In the meantime, I must send a letter to the Inquisition arguing that this notebook proves there is nothing mystical about Umpire Kibbler's ability to shoot blackflame. The diagrams suggest that his workers found a way to reconfigure the elf fire syphons to shoot blackflame. The mechanism is extremely complicated, and he was probably using the notebook to remind himself of the proper procedure rather than invoking evil spirits or anything like that."

"What about the Sword of Layban?"

"Thanks to the Thor's Hammer pendant you lent me, I was able to pace through Vandsee Estates and all thirteen bases yesterday, praying with the gift of prophecy. I'm quite certain they don't have it. If you could help me send this letter by Pony Express to the Holy Office of the Inquisition explaining my findings, perhaps we could avert an impending Crusade."

Dungaree Jeanne looks sad. "You know, it has been very comforting having you at my house during these difficult times. You have not only the gift of giving wise advice but also a gift for empathetic listening. I'm going to miss having you around."

They notice the hubbub of an overly curious gathering in Thor's Plaza. She says, "It looks like our dear friend, Master Gulliber, is going to give a Thor's Enlightenment Discourse. Would you care to join me for one last event in Shentalpee City before you take your leave?"

"It would be an honor." Johnny Appleseed holds out his arm and Dungaree Jeanne wraps her elbow around it. Together they take their seats on the edge of the outdoor theater so as to avoid disturbing the other elves while she translates for him.

In the absence of Umpire Gandorf, the high commissioner introduces the event in an overly stylized and thoroughly unexciting manner. Master Gulliber steps up to the podium and says with a resonating voice, "The Council of Perfects has graciously allowed me to give this Thor's Enlightenment Discourse about our experiences among the wall humans. The secrets they hide behind those walls are mind-boggling. I feel it is my patriotic duty to expose their depravities so you can be prepared for the kind of dangers Missus Puma and I faced while among them.

"Unpatriotic elves say they have nothing to be thankful for. Such elves live by excuses. They blame all their own shortcomings on others and never take responsibility for their actions—or their own lack of action—refusing to admit the real reasons for their failures. They see the rewards other elves obtain from their hard work and call it pure luck.

"In fact, my wife, Missus Puma, and I had a successful shoe business leading off Oriole base. We worked all day and all night and produced wooden clogs, deer-hide sandals, and vellum shoes. Our shoes were so sought after that whenever a trade convoy would go out, elf merchants would order human- and dwarf-sized shoes to increase their profits ten- or twenty-fold at the various trade fairs.

"Several years ago, we decided to go to the Grand Freedrich Fair to sell our wares ourselves, so as to cash in on the exceptional marketability of our shoes among other races. We brought along a large quantity of ready-made shoes that we had crafted in advance, as well as material to make custom shoes on location. We were the only workshop to produce shoes with converse designs for the left and right foot. Everyone else had a one-size-fits-all approach.

"A Bastonian shoe merchant named Master Nikephoros Spaulding came to us and said he would buy out our entire stock of shoes and all our raw materials for five thousand pounds sterling. If he had been honest and respected us, we would have made him rich by selling to him every year. Instead he betrayed us, kidnapped us, and enslaved us."

One of the high elves in the crowd asks, "How did they do that? Were they that much taller than you that they could overpower you so easily?"

"Humans taller than us?! Missus Puma, did you hear that?! You don't get out much, do you, monsieur? Oh no, humans are much shorter than elves. We call them lily-livered puny humans. Our portmanteau for them is lilliputians.

"This is how those sneaky creatures captured us. Missus Puma and I parked our wagon along the banks of the Antietam Creek and fell asleep as we sat out by the campfire under the stars. The Lilliputians tied us up while we were sleeping on the sandy beach there."

Another elf asks, "How were they able to get away with such a crime? Didn't the authorities intervene?"

"What authorities? Wall humans have bullies in charge of them who do nothing but collect taxes and send them off to fight in wars! Their clerics and religious authorities do little to help, either, obsessed as they are with their petty doctrinal squabbles."

Another elve says, "But clerics are in charge of maintaining harmony and order with clear teachings."

"Indeed they are supposed to, but wall human clerics care nothing about the faith and morals of the people they serve. Instead, they condemn each other over trivial precepts. One time my poor wife, Missus Puma, cracked an egg on the narrow end. The Inquisition found out and condemned us both for not cracking our eggs on the wide end. They arrested us, tied us hand and foot to stakes, and set a pyre of kindling wood under us on fire."

"Wait, how did you escape that one?"

"I had a plan. I drank as much water as I could the night before and relieved myself in the fire. While the steam and vapor billowed up, I cut the ropes that bound my hands with a nail and then freed my wife. We escaped in the smoke and confusion, and the dim-witted lilliputians thought we disappeared by magic.

"It was our good fortune that Missus Puma and I had only recently invented a special pair of spiked athletic boots that enabled us to run away faster than they could catch us. We have two varieties. The first is a running boot that we are calling Adidazar's shoes, after my clan. Its spikes are dull so that you never get stuck to the forest floor while running, but are long enough so that you won't slip on muddy or loose turf.

"The second type has short, sharp spikes for tree climbing. These we are calling Puma's shoes. Tree scouts from the Ivy League will find that they have a huge advantage when keeping to the tree with a pair of Puma's on their feet. You've all heard how the treacherous Captain Bucklead forced our dearly departed monsieur Captain Lynx to keep to the trees for over fifty miles while the rest of the army rode comfortably on mule-drawn wagons."

Holding up a pair of spiked shoes, Master Gulliber continues, "If he had not been wearing his new Puma's, he would never have reached the Battle of the Wyvern in time to save the lives of dozens of fire elves.

"Finally, our honorable dean of the League of Nations has been working closely with us to develop a third shoe for her new military league, specially designed for stealth and covert operations. We call them sneakers. These will enable you to walk softly and carry a big stick. They are now on sale at Gulliber's workshop, conveniently located in Missus Cougar's house leading off of Wildcat Base.

"Madame Dean and Dungaree, I yield the podium."

Bewildered, Dungaree Jeanne says to Johnny Appleseed in Aenglish, "I barely know him. How could I have worked with him on those shoes? I don't even know what to say."

Appleseed replies, "You had better go up there and wing it. That elf has rallied up a remarkable degree of enthusiasm for your military league. It's a good time to take back the initiative. Seize the day!"

Dungaree Jeanne sighs. "Your wisdom extends to every facet of life. If I have to make it all up on the spot to stop the monsieur Gandorf, I'll just do it."

She goes up to the podium and says, "Thank you, Master Gulliber, for all the help you provided our dearly departed Captain Lynx during his lifetime. And I sincerely hope that the line of footwear products you have contrived will aid us in developing our new military's infrastructure."

Taking a formal stance, she addresses the crowd in Eldric with these words: "Mesdames, mesdemoiselles, messieurs, ladies, and gentelves, many of you are curious about how I plan to accomplish the revitalization of our military as outlined by our esteemed Major Leagues Umpire in his last public speech. He has entrusted me with the task of developing several specialized military units that will fill tactical roles that have hitherto been lacking among fire elves—most noticeably, heavy infantry.

"Umpire Gandorf has also enjoined upon me the task of incorporating new technologies, particularly the blackflame, into our arsenal of fire weaponry. New gadgets, however, are not enough. I maintain that we need to incorporate new mentalities as well if we are going to survive. Our slender elven physique makes the heavy infantry role impractical.

"However, our ancestors in Mount Ragnarök had special relationship with the dwarves there. Dwarves love heavy labor and are physically well built for it. The dwarves of Mount Ragnarök lived inside the volcano, mining open new rooms and corridors while the elves used their artistic skills to beautify those spaces.

"The ancient fire elves could not have colonized the rocky mountain walls without the dwarves, and the dwarves could not have earned the kind of pay they received without the fire elves. What if we could return to the ways of our ancestors? What if we could have heavy infantry dwarves serving as regular soldiers in our League of Nations? What if we could recruit not only elves from other colonies, but halflings and humans as well? The new order of silver elves provides us a way! It shall mark the rise of all the clayborn in Vinland in the fight against evil.

"My first act as dean of the League of Nations is to extend eligibility for the new order of silver elves to all military recruits from among the wood elves, garden gnomes, mountain dwarves, and longhouse humans living on and under Tuscoraura Mountain.

"Many of you are shaking your head, clearly convinced that such openness is impossible. Do you realize how much our closed-mindedness has cost us thus far? Monsieur Lynx, a wood elf, saved the lives of a great many high elves during that ambush. They would all be dead if the naysayers against social mobility had their way.

"The facts prove that Monsieur Lynx actually won all the military leagues' tournaments this year and was disqualified from first place simply because he was a wood elf. Some of you, particularly the high elves in the audience, believe the grounds for disqualification were valid. But no one can dispute that he did win all the tournaments. It was only by the magnanimity of our dearly departed monsieur Umpire-in-Chief that Monsieur Lynx finally earned a commission.

"No more! Every deserving wood elf will be admitted to the order of silver elves without hesitation and without undo roadblocks from technicalities and rule-bending. Mark my words, the moment I see four silver elves of merit, I will send them off as a party of adventurers to other elf colonies, to gnome burrows, to human walls, and to dwarf mines to recruit the best and the brightest to this new world order.

"As we grow the number of colonies that officially recognize the order of silver elves, we will—"

Suddenly, Dungaree Jeanne gawks and all but screams, "Oh my squinty eyes, it's Mademoiselle Florenz Kibblersdottir!"

Florenz steps up onto the stage and says in Runic, "Mesdames, mesdemoiselles, and messieurs. I am here to set the record straight. I left Tuscoraura not because of my grief at my father's death, but because of the overwhelming evidence piling up before my eyes that my father was intending to subvert our democracy.

"In public, he encouraged all elves to collaborate in unlocking the secrets of the blackflame to update our military technology. In private, he had been secretive about his own experiments with the blackflame so that he could raise up an undead army with unquestioning loyalty to him alone."

The crowd gasps.

"My father intended to use me as a puppet umpire-in-chief. To that end, he bullied all my rival candidates out of the race except Mademoiselle Zena, because he figured he could use the scandal involving her gnomid stewardess to discredit her without knocking her out of the race. That tactic backfired. It so enraged the garden gnomes and mountain dwarves that they aided the inquisitor in orchestrating my father's death.

"During my exile, I endured many hardships and have had much time to think about the injustices my father was committing. I have resolved to set them all straight. There is no time to go into all the details now. The bottom line is, I succeeded. I have mastered the blackflame and I intend to share that power with you, o superlative high elves of Shentalpee City."

Florenz draws the Sword of Layban and intones the words, "By the power of Layban . . . I have the power!"

As the blackflame erupts from her blade, wild applause and cheering erupt for the return of their exiled princess and her newfound power.

Florenz continues holding the flaming sword above her head and says, "I have paid a heavy price to obtain this weapon for ye, o famed high elves of Tuscoraura Mountain. Our enemies resent our superiority. Even now, the Inquisition is gathering a Crusade to take this sword away from us. Who among ye chooses to surrender this new technology and throw ourselves on the mercy of the Inquisition?"

The audience looks at her, watches her, listens to her, and hears her, utterly stunned. *Is this the same Florenz who left Shentalpee City only a few weeks ago?*

The skin on Florenz's hand holding the flaming sword starts to redden. It cracks and blisters. She pays no attention, nor does the crowd. Instead, she shouts, "With this blackflame, I have reanimated long-lost warriors, including my father. Behold!"

From the back of the crowd, a heavily battered version of Umpire Kibbler, with white skin and no teeth except his canines, presses through the audience. The giant dwarf is right behind him, crushing benches and scuffing the polished hardwood floors with his heavy boots as elves dive out of his way in panic.

In the giant dwarf's wake follow twenty or more undead wights. Umpire Kibbler and the giant dwarf, Sir Balrock, go down on one knee and bow their heads to the blackflame. Florenz shouts, "Who among ye chooses to surrender these new undead warriors and throw ourselves on the mercy of the Inquisition?"

Now hisses and boos circulate through the crowd at the thought of cowering before the Inquisition.

Florenz shouts over their voices, "I say let the fire elves master both the unquenchable elf fire *and* the mystical blackflame. Who among ye chooses to stand with me and fight?"

The crowd gets up on their feet and applaud wildly.

Louder she shouts, "Who among ye chooses to stand with me and fight?"

The elves are jumping up and down and screaming in a mad frenzy—delusions of grandeur infect their minds and they are ready to relinquish all their rights as elfin persons for the sake of latching onto the power they now see before their eyes.

As if thundering with the voice of Thor himself, Florenz places an amulet into her undead father's mouth. It has an archon stone in the middle inlaid next to a large chip of pyrite, a big glob of amber, and a dark clump of lodestone. Her father dutifully swallows it.

Florenz shouts, "I have obtained an archon stone, which will render my father invincible. Shall we surrender it to the Inquisition or shall we fight?"

They claw at their faces and wriggle around hypnotically, letting loose a wide range of emotions. They cheer and hoot and holler. They weep and cover their faces. They chant, "Florenz, hail! Florenz, hail!"

At last, she sheathes the freezing-cold sword and states with the dignified authority of a war-hardened commander, "Your choice is made. As of today, I declare martial law. We prepare for war."

Scene 4: Bend it Like a Buttercup

Shentalpee City on Tuscoraura Mountain
Whit Moon Day Terce. Morning, 29th of May, 1284

As his background in blackflame, miracle-working, and magiculture attracts more gossip on Tuscoraura Mountain, Johnny Appleseed receives an ever-growing stream of visitors. He is honoring his promise to instruct the elves in the non-military applications of blackflame, and thanks to his generosity and humble service in helping the colony, a good many elves are open to hearing him tell them stories from the Bible. A few even request baptism into the Christian faith.

On this fine, sunny morning, Florenz knocks on the door at Betzy Rose Mansion and Enganyon stands proudly behind her. Dungaree Jeanne opens the door and says in Runic, "Why, Mademoiselle Florenz! Such a pleasure to see thou hast returned. Please come in!"

She steps in but Enganyon politely waits outside. Florenz notices the slight at not inviting him in and seeks to rectify it. She asks in Eldric, "Would you mind if the monsieur Enganyon joined us?"

Dungaree Jeanne wears a stern face. "I don't believe the monsieur Enganyon and I have any business to discuss. If he wishes to apologize to my daughter for his behavior of late . . . ah, here she comes now."

Zena creeps down the steps, red-eyed from hours of crying. She sees the visitors and whimpers, "Monsieur Enganyon . . ."

Enganyon steps forward and says in Runic, "I do wish to apologize, Mademoiselle Zena. I have treated thee most unfairly. What business had I to propose marriage to thee when my heart was all along bound to the mademoiselle Florenz? I have come to set things aright and call off our hasty engagement."

Straining to hold her nerve together, Zena replies in Runic, "Thou canst not, Monsieur Enganyon. I have not agreed to a cessation of our betrothal contract."

Enganyon shows no pity or remorse. "As it stands, thy consent is irrelevant. Since thy betrothal contract with Monsieur Lynx was on record when I proposed to thee, the scribe at the council chambers never even entered the contract we submitted to the registrar. For the future, please remember that before thou wilt be free to enter into a new betrothal contract, thou must obtain a public copy of Monsieur Lynx's death certificate and present it to the registrar."

Zena's eyebrows curl with intense frustration. She switches back into Eldric. "But that's the love potion speaking, not you! I have the recipe; I can fix this!"

Dropping down into Eldric as well, Enganyon waves it all away, saying, "Oh, don't be ridiculous! Most love potions are fakes, hawked to unsuspecting and desperate teenagers who cannot deal with rejection." He then looks at Florenz lovingly and says in Runic, "Even the real ones can at best simulate a passing ardor. My love for the mademoiselle Florenz, I assure you, has never faltered since the day I first laid eyes on her."

To wonder if Zena is crushed at hearing those words is like wondering if a crusty pretzel sitting on an anvil is still edible after a grand piano has fallen twelve storeys down upon it. If only Enganyon were frantic and emotional, she could process his reaction as a gut-wrenching predicament that he is struggling to escape with a bout of bizarre, erratic behavior. But the dispassionate rationality behind his words makes her realize it's over for good.

Her normal reaction to not getting her way is to throw a temper tantrum, scream and shout, and say hurtful words to her loved ones. This time around she just stands there, dizzy and unable to speak.

With the unpleasant formalities accomplished, Florenz steps forward and says in Eldric, "Madame Dungaree, Master Leevai and Captain Gunnar have arrived from Fort Loudon with their mercenary companies. The Council of Perfects would like you, as acting dean of the League of Nations, to convince them to stay and help us fight off the Crusade. You will have a budget of five hundred dollars for their expenses.

"The council is also willing to promote non-elves to the order of silver elves if they prove themselves exceptionally valiant in battle, but please be aware that as of now, no official protocol for inducting them has been approved. No guarantees.

"You have come up with some clever ideas. I hope for your sake that you manage to put them into effect to aid Shentalpee City in this upcoming war."

Dungaree Jeanne says, "That sounds like a threat."

Florenz continues in Eldric, "It is. By the way, if we do survive this attack by the Crusade, the Council of Perfects is now convinced that Bartlebee did in fact sell the Athabask recipe to Master Chief Engineer Tom Thumb. Before confirming you in the office of dean, they want you to kill him and make sure no one else has gotten a hold of that recipe. If you fail, you will be executed for treason and your family will be banished.

"That is also a threat."

Dungaree Jeanne stares wide-eyed and speechless at Florenz while her heart skips a beat or two. What happened to the sweet girl who was Zena's best friend for so many years? Zena, for her part, is still so stunned that she shows no reaction whatsoever.

Dungaree Jeanne finally finds her voice. "You publicly announced it was all a big misunderstanding."

"The Council of Perfects would not allow me to publicly humiliate your family without hard evidence. Since I could not produce any, they forced me to come up with some excuse to recant my accusations. Thanks to the Thieves' Guild, we now have conclusive evidence—and other information damaging to your family's good name. If you eliminate Tom Thumb, we'll lock that all away in the secret archives and confirm you as dean of the League of Nations."

"Lock it away? Why not destroy it?"

Florenz cannot fathom why such an intelligent person cannot see the obvious, so she states it clearly with fire in her eyes. "To make sure you do not give them a reason to unlock it."

They gaze at each other in silence for a menacing moment like two lionesses pacing in circles around each other without breaking eye contact to so much as blink. Dungaree Jeanne's mind spins furiously to come up with a counterattack and then she pounces. "The Monsieur Major Leagues Umpire has stated that the League of Nations is to include a unit of undead warriors. Will you be transferring the undead warriors you summoned at Thor's Base to my command?"

"Yes," says Florenz with a snarl. "As soon as this issue with Tom Thumb is resolved and the Council of

Perfects officially confirms your appointment as dean of the League of Nations. Not all the Perfects are convinced the League of Nations is a good idea. Since its only official member right now is a spellbound Pinne Mage University dropout," pointing to Zena, "I highly recommend you take the council's advice to recruit Master Leevai and Captain Gunnar for the war effort before they figure out that your leadership here is nothing but a waste of time and resources."

Dungaree Jeanne gasps at the rudeness of the insults and presses on. "In Thor's Base, after Master Gulliber's talk, you placed an archon stone in your undead father's mouth, rendering him invincible. They are quite rare and hard to come by. May I ask where you got that particular archon stone?"

"No." Florenz waves her hand and dozens of Justiciar League police barge into Betzy Rose Mansion. Dungaree Jeanne's hired bravos intercept them with their swords and knives drawn. They are all brilliant duelists but have no discipline for fighting in ranks, and their fancy footwork would be useless in such confined quarters. Dungaree Jeanne orders them to stand down.

The Justiciar Leaguers seize Johnny Appleseed's wheelchair and push him out to Florenz, who holds up a letter and announces in Runic, "Johnny Appleseed, I hereby place thee under arrest for espionage and subversion against the Tuscoraura elves."

Johnny Appleseed asks, "What's she saying?"

Dungaree Jeanne ignores him and speaks directly to Florenz in Eldric. "What is the meaning of this? Reverend Appleseed is our guest. Arresting him is an insult to our honor as his hosts."

"Precisely." Florenz grins and flaps a letter in front of her face. "We have intercepted a letter written by Johnny Appleseed informing the Inquisition of our military technology. He will be hanged as a spy."

"No! He wrote that letter to avoid a war! He was trying to save Tuscoraura Mountain from a Crusade! How could you do this to a sweet, old man?"

"You may recall that he affronted my father's honor after he delivered his TED."

Zena chokes, then cries out, "That was me! You never figured it out, but I put him up to it."

"If I have learned anything from your two-timing ex-fiancé, never say never. I knew all along."

"So you knew all along and never had the nerve to do anything about it?"

Officer Bunzi shackles the crippled missionary and wheels him out.

Florenz concludes, "Never say never. I just did something about it. Aren't you proud of how grown-up I am now?" She walks out the front door.

Bonus Scene C: Ronin

Thor's Plaza, Shentalpee City on Tuscoraura Mountain
Whit Moon Day Nones. Afternoon, 29th of May, 1284

Dungaree Jeanne and Johnny Appleseed find Master Leevai and Captain Gunnar sitting on the ledge of the reflecting pool closest to Thor's statue. Dungaree Jeanne calls out to them in Aenglish, "Master Leevai! Captain Gunnar! It is such a joy to see you both safe and sound! Why ever did you not call upon me at Betzy Rose Mansion?"

Master Leevai hugs her. "Madame Dungaree! What a relief to see you alive! You were right—Hershel did not pursue us. I assume your 'pawn promotion' was a code word for calling the rangers to came to your aid."

Dungaree Jeanne replies, "It shames me to say it, but I twisted their arms into it. The inquisitor had written a note to the mayor of Ithica guaranteeing that the rangers had fulfilled their quest. Monsieur Lynx asked me to mail it to Ithica by Pony Express. Instead, I sent word to the rangers telling them that unless they shadowed my convoy as guards, I would not send the letter. To be fair, I also paid them handsomely for their services."

Captain Gunnar stands up and says, "Hale ant sail, Madame Dungaree! Speaking of getting paid, my Rough Riders are getting restless about the second half of our contracted payment. They were making merry in Fort Loudon to celebrate surviving the battle. They were counting on the danger pay mentioned in the contract to cover their bills when they would get back."

Dungaree Jeanne says, "Gentlemen, I invite you for some refreshments at the Gazebo while we discuss business."

They sit down at an open-air table. Master Leevai orders blueberry juice while Captain Gunnar has grape juice. Johnny Appleseed is impressed that they carry papaya and orders some.

Across from the garden restaurant is Tiw's Square, the training grounds for all the military leagues. It is unusually busy today, with elves of all levels sweating and slashing away to train themselves up to their best fighting form against the upcoming Crusade.

Dungaree Jeanne is still not quite convinced this war is anything more than a publicity stunt on the part of Florenz to make her newfound military technologies seem vital to the survival of the Tuscoraura elves.

Dungaree Jeanne gets some cranberry juice mixed with apple juice and says with a calm, reassuring tone, "Master Leevai . . . Captain Gunnar . . . you both fought well at the Forge Hill Gap and there can be no doubt that had we relied upon the leadership of less-qualified warriors, none of us would be alive today. We all know you've earned your pay and the bonuses I promised.

"We also know that throwing away those cocoa beans ensured our survival, but it brought about significant financial loss. I have already overextended every line of credit available to me to process the remaining cocoa beans in the Kibbler workshops and keep my denim factories open.

"The return of Mademoiselle Florenz Kibblersdottir has tied up all my funds since now we have to sort out in court how much I owe her for the use of her workshops. So right now, I simply do not have the coin to cover everything I owe you. However, the Council of Perfects has said it will grant me five hundred dollars if you all agree to stay and defend Tuscoraura Mountain against the crusading army."

Since his command of Aenglish is rudimentary, Captain Gunnar switches to Eldric, which he speaks fluently thanks in part to its similarities with Klipsk, his native language. "Madame Dungaree, it was only by great teamwork and your heroic leadership that the Rough Riders only lost one elf in the combat zone. Even so, a good number have been seriously injured, and we lost many thoroughbred reindeer in that action.

"If I don't come back with their hard-earned wages, plus compensation for the injuries and lost animals, plus a payment to the family of the elf who died in battle, I'm going to have a mutiny on my hands. You don't need me to remind you how unruly soldiers can get when they feel they've been treated unfairly.

"So I'm only telling you this because I respect you. We are going to sign whatever contract we need to get what's owed to us, but when that Crusade shows up we are moving on unless you can pay us in full for the next contract in advance. Five hundred dollars will just barely cover what you owe my troops—if I throw in some of my own money. That's where it stands."

Dungaree Jeanne takes a sip of her apple-cranberry juice and swallows hard. "I understand where you're coming from, Captain Gunnar, and I appreciate your honesty. On top of the pay, the Council of Perfects will admit all the Rough Riders to the New World Order."

"What do you mean by New World Order?"

"If you stay and fight with us, your Rough Riders will be granted all the rights and privileges of high elves but without having to live in Shentalpee City, and without the right to challenge a high elf to a duel.

"We have worked together for years and you know my caliber—I always pay my debts. I will give you the five hundred dollars to cover your expenses and will personally compensate you for whatever comes out of your own purse as soon as I have the funds.

"You are free to go if your elves insist but surely you understand that it will look very bad for me. It might mean the end of my career as a military dean."

Captain Gunnar sighs, "I cannot state enough how much we, the Rough Riders, respect you. We accept your offer of five hundred dollars and admission into the New World Order, but we won't to fight the Crusade without payment in full before the battle.

Captain Gunnar leaves it there and Dungaree Jeanne does not know what else to say. He is basically taking every bargaining chip she has to offer just to maintain their working relationship. She had meant to withhold admission to the New World Order until after he'd given a promise to fight the Crusade but she lets him take that for free when she realizes that without an official induction ceremony from the council, she can write the taking of an oath of loyalty to her as supreme commander into the rubrics—a useful fall-back plan just in case Florence decides to move against her.

It dawns on her that she is becoming the kind of person she always criticized bitterly—a government official using her position for personal advantage.

Master Leevai has picked up enough Eldric over the years to catch the general sense of Captain Gunnar's words. He sees the turmoil on Dungaree Jeanne's face so he says as delicately as he can in Aenglish, "Madame

Dungaree, as you will recall, you asked me to hire as many mercenaries for this job as possible. I've exhausted all my funds hiring the Knights of the Round Table, the Skybrim, and the Bikur Holim. For all the camaraderie and team spirit we have built up over the years in your service, my Glorious Dastards are still fundamentally mercenaries and they work for pay. They bore the brunt of the fighting and nearly half got killed or seriously wounded.

"I'm sorry if this is distressing you, but I am fundamentally an accountant, not a warrior. As each soldier dashes about the battlefield dreaming of glory and renown, I cannot help but see all the bills for their equipment and services popping up in the back of my mind. My innate business sense overrides the fantasies that adventurers rely on to drive them on to complete their quests.

"With all due respect, my gut reaction is the same as Captain Gunnar's. We will do whatever is needed to get what's in arrears, but don't expect us to stick around to fight a Crusade without a significant cash advance."

Johnny Appleseed interrupts, "Excuse me, Master Leevai, but may I point out that the Glorious Dastards have a reputation for setting wrongs aright. If they defeat the Crusade here, the Jewish people of Vinland will be safe from the Inquisition."

Master Leevai responds, "We are already safe from the Inquisition. It only has jurisdiction over Christians. As long as we do not claim to be Christians, they cannot hurt us.

"Right now our biggest worry is King Eddard, who keeps raising taxes on Jews and with his last edict, he has put all Jewish bankers out of business. He wants the Jews to become farmers, but no one will sell good, arable lands to Jews in Aengland. More and more of my kin are having to cross the Ocean of Atlantis to make a living here in Vinland.

"Where does that leave me? My wife's cousin needed a job so I hired him as a bodyguard, even though he doesn't know which way to point a crossbow. Then an old buddy from Yeshiva tells me his son needs a job. You see where I'm going with this? I'm fabulously rich thanks to you, but every day I load up the wagons I'm still stressing out about how I'm going to pay all of King Eddard's taxes and get everyone the wages I promised them."

Dungaree Jeanne tries to pick up Johnny Appleseed's line of argumentation. "That's just it. If we defeat the Inquisition, we can push back against King Eddard's policies on religion in Vinland."

Master Leevai wears a heavy look on his brow. "As it is now, there is no mechanism in Canon Law that would allow the Inquisition to bring any harm against Jews. If we fight on your side against the Inquisition, it just might become an excuse to bring down a new pogrom against us. Madame Dungaree, you have been so good to us and we are grateful. But, I am sorry, this is not our fight.

"It pains me to say this, but our bill is going to be a lot higher the Captain Gunnar's. We fronted you all the herbs you asked us for. We paid to ship half the cocoa beans out and got them back safely to Tuscoraura Mountain. We fought a big battle. We took some significant losses and we weren't able to hold the battlefield, so we left a lot of loot lying on the ground.

"The total comes to three thousand dollars. We appreciate all you've done for us and admire and respect you immensely, but now is just not a good time to ask us to pick a fight with the Inquisition. We need our money and we need to go."

Dungaree Jeanne takes another hard swallow of her cranberry-apple juice and says, "I simply can't pay."

Master Leevai sighs and says, "There is one option. I know a wealthy arcanist who is obsessed with figuring out how to produce an archon stone. He has offered to mortgage it for thirty thousand dollar. We both need the coinage; I'll keep whatever I need to cover expenses and lend you the rest. You can pay me back in instalments over the next three years."

Dungaree Jeanne leans back and, unable to hide it any longer, tears well up in her eyes. "They tricked my daughter into giving them the archon stone. Now Umpire Kibbler keeps it in his chest to make him an invincible undead wight."

Master Leevai cannot hide his emotional response either—pure horror. He mutters, "I can only hope the Crusade wins this fight after all. The thought of an immortal Kibbler will soak my pillow with hot sweats at night. This is much worse than I thought. Don't you think you should cut a deal with the Inquisition to get the archon stone back?"

Dungaree Jeanne says, "Even though the highest government officials betrayed me, I cannot bring myself to betray my own colony."

Johnny Appleseed tries to be helpful, "I owe an immense debt to Dungaree Jeanne and have business contacts scattered all over Vinland. Perhaps I could go around to see if I could—"

"You're not going anywhere!" says a voice in Eldric.

The startled group looks up and sees Florenz, suited up in the leather armor of an Ivy League officer, leading a squad of Ivy League sergeants. Captain Enganyon marches right behind her at the head of a troop of Justiciar League officers and sergeants.

The elf warriors surround Johnny Appleseed. Florenz holds up a letter and announces with a loud voice in Runic, "Johnny Appleseed, I hereby place thee under arrest for espionage and subversion against the Tuscoraura elves."

Dungaree Jeanne cannot believe her ears. Johnny Appleseed looks at her confused and asks, "What is she saying?"

Dungaree Jeanne ignores him and speaks directly to Florenz in Eldric, "What is the meaning of this? Reverend Appleseed is a guest at Lathspell Mansion. He has done nothing wrong and even if he had, arresting him is an insult to the monsieur Major Leagues Umpire's honor."

Florenz flaps the letter in front of her face. "You should know better than to remind me of Monsieur Gandorf's honor. We have intercepted a letter written by Johnny Appleseed informing the Inquisition of our military technology! He will be hanged as a spy!"

Florenz then turns around and calls out, "Listen up, fire elves of Tuscoraura! My father declares a state of martial law! Go now, and prepare for war!"

Scene 5: Cleanup Hitter

Vandsee Estates
Shentalpee City on Tuscoraura Mountain
Ember Woden's Day Vespers
Evening, 31st of May, 1284

Florenz is sitting at her father's desk while Umpire Kibbler stands unblinking behind her. His eyes have a faint glow of red in them, but he does not move them to look at any of the people sitting in the room. In fact, he does not move at all. His chest does not heave to breathe, his feet do not shuffle, and his face does not twitch a muscle, even when flies land on his eyelids.

In front of her desk, like two schoolboys sitting in silent detention before the principal, Enganyon and Umpire Gandorf fidget while Florenz reads through a scroll on her desk.

When she finally rolls up the scroll, Enganyon jumps in first and says in Eldric, "My beloved Mademoiselle Florenz, Reverend Appleseed is clearly favored by his God. His God listens to him when he calls upon his name. Is it really wise to antagonize both the Inquisition and his God over a trivial letter? He insists he wrote it to dissuade the Inquisition from sending the Crusade against us."

Florenz gives him a stern glare and says harshly, "First of all, Captain Enganyon, during the state of martial law, the Magnificent Charter bids us address each other by our military ranks. Since the Ivy League and the Justiciar League were wise enough to promote us, we must address each other as captains.

"Second, Johnny Appleseed should not have survived that fall. The Tuscoraura elves were to be the last nation to learn the secrets of blackflame. Not only did you let Mister Appleseed live, but you let him report information on our military technologies to the Inquisition. He must die.

"Third, my father appointed your father Major Leagues Umpire for one purpose and one purpose only—to orchestrate the ambush at Forge Hill Gap and rid the colony of the madame Dungaree and her daughter. The madame Dungaree's daughter was more popular than expected and her network of business and military contacts could enable her to spark a rebellion after my father is declared supreme umpire for life."

Enganyon hems and haws, saying, "Technically, your father is dead now, so supreme umpire for life would be a rather short term. I was expecting us to change tack and slot you in as supreme umpire for life instead, after you get elected through the normal—"

Florenz cuts him off abruptly. "It's too risky. The monsieur Lynx was supposed to be the only non-viable candidate left on the ballot by election day. Instead, the mademoiselle Zena is still alive and has too many supporters. She could easily sway her constituency into her mother's camp in case of a civil war. We'd be forced to execute half the colony for sedition. It's no fun being the supreme ruler over the fire elves and if there are almost no fire elves left to rule over."

Enganyon bobs his head around as if trying to be modest. "Well, there's always my constituency. You wouldn't have to execute them since we'd support—"

"Yes! Thank you! Thank you for bringing up the most painful topic of all. What in the sigelwar fires of lower earth possessed you to run for umpire-in-chief? You made yourself my rival instead of my ally. Do you know how I deal with my rivals?"

Enganyon puts his fist to his mouth and clears his throat. "Your flair for getting rid of them inspires awe."

Florence gives him a patronizing nod. "Good. Good. That's exactly the way it should be. So how are we going to fix this?"

"Well, you know, I could always speak to—"

She cuts him off. "For starters, we're going to require your father and all the Shentalpee City umpires to transmogrify into undead thralls."

Up until now, Umpire Gandorf has been lolling his head in boredom, aware that nothing he says will make any difference. Suddenly, at that last statement, he looks up with terror in his eyes. "You can't! I'm still in my prime! My mind is sharp as an assassin's blade.

"After all, I was the one who figured out the whole stormcrow thing. Without it, your father would never have gotten the blackflame siphon to work. It would be a horrible waste of my technological genius to turn me into an expressionless zombie like your father—no offense intended."

"None taken, Monsieur Umpire," replies Florenz. "But don't be too proud over that technological terror you introduced as the stormcrow. The ability to squirt blackflame is insignificant compared to the true power of the Sword of Layban.

"After you transmogrify into my undead thrall you will be in charge of monitoring your own son's activities. If the monsieur Enganyon fails me again, you shall execute him with your own hands. Your will shall be unable to resist my commands as Master of Layban."

Enganyon looks at his father's face rising with anxiety and says, "The solution is simple. I'll just announce that we've come across a legal technicality that makes my candidacy invalid. Now that you are back, I don't need to be on the ballot anyway."

Umpire Gandorf adds, "Besides, your blackflame nearly killed off that magica tree that the mademoiselle Zena was counting on to get admitted into Pinne Mage University. It vanished to save itself and Johnny Appleseed claims he can help her find it.

"So there it is. We just tell Johnny Appleseed to take the mademoiselle Zena off to search for her magica tree. Bam! It's that simple. Everyone is happy and our plan . . . I mean . . . your plan, gets back on course. No one has to die."

Florenz stares with an expression that tells them she is deeply unimpressed with their thinking skills.

She says, "There's going to be a new rule around here—you don't throw your useless opinions at me unless I ask for them. And when I do ask for them, it will just be for show—to make it look like I actually care what other people think, this being a democracy for the time being and all that blibber-blabber.

"In the future, you'd better learn how to come up with opinions that sound a lot more like the ones coming from my mouth than the drivel coming from yours. Appleseed has to die so no one else can get their hands on the blackflame. The mademoiselle Zena has to die because your son made the mistake of proposing to her in a plenary session of the Council of Perfects. The madame Dungaree has to die because she has the power and influence to rally the fire elves against us.

Enganyon runs his fingers through his hair and leans back for a deep breath before saying, "Captain Florenz, this is not you speaking! It's the Sword of Layban! It's corrupting your beautiful soul!"

She narrows her eyes at him. "No darling, it's the angst speaking. You liked me a lot better when I was naïve and easy to manipulate. You and your father have been playing games behind my back this whole time doing anything and everything you could think of to seize power for yourselves.

"Now you wonder why a girl like me doesn't trust you? I've just come to terms with the fact that I was born into a powerful family. That was reason enough for Umpire Drayton and his goons to deprive me of my mother as a child, for my best friend to humiliate my father in public, and for my boyfriend to propose to her on the day my father was murdered.

"So it comes down to this—you and your father learn how to take orders, or I'll kill you both and find friends that won't be so quick to stab me in the back."

Enganyon gulps. Umpire Gandorf puts a hand on his son's shoulder and stands up, saying, "We understand our instructions and we will obey, master. Let's get out of here, son. We've taken up enough of Captain Florenz's time for one day."

Bonus Scene D: Meddling, Wheedling, and Yodeling

Shentalpee City on Tuscoraura Mountain
Thor's Day Terce. Morning, 1st of June, 1284
Feast of Corpus Christi

Knock, knock.

Dungaree Jeanne opens up but when she sees Umpire Gandorf and Enganyon standing on her threshold, she starts to slam the door in their faces. Enganyon catches it and begs, "Please, Madame Dungaree! Mademoiselle Zena's life is in danger."

A tear wells up in Umpire Gandorf's eye. He steps forward and says, "Madame Dungaree, I have done many evil things in my lifetime, including my part in your husband's death. It's time for me to right the wrongs I have committed, even if it costs me my life.

"My main concern is for the lives of our two children. No price would be too high to see them live out the rest of their lives happily married and surrounded by their own children.

"But my conscience forbids me the luxury of living to see my grandchildren. Monsieur Enganyon and I are the only two elves who know Umpire Kibbler's full plan to destroy the government of Shentalpee City. He intends to murder Mademoiselle Zena and make himself supreme umpire for life. Now that he's undead and has the archon stone, that'll be a very long time!"

Upon hearing the warning, Dungaree Jeanne stops wrestling with Enganyon to close the front door and says, "He can't possibly get away with that!"

"He got away with attempting to murder Reverend Appleseed."

Dungaree Jeanne's eyes burst wide open. "Monsieur Enganyon! Are you saying that you *meant* to kill Reverend Appleseed?!"

Umpire Gandorf says, "Umpire Kibbler ordered me to murder Reverend Appleseed, but my son came up with a plan to save his life without disobeying the orders. Base-jumping was a trick he and his more reckless friends have pulled off several times before. He orchestrated the fall so it would look like an assassination attempt but at the same time, ensuring that the good reverend would survive—I swear!

"Now Captain Florenz wants Mademoiselle Zena dead as well. If we don't murder her, she'll kill *both* Mademoiselle Zena *and* my son."

Enganyon jumps in. "Captain Florenz forced me to break off my engagement with Mademoiselle Zena with death threats. That's the only reason I did it—to save her life. But now it doesn't matter. She wants Mademoiselle Zena dead anyhow."

Dungaree Jeanne takes a breath and says, "This is a lot to take in. Come in. I'm assuming you have a plan to spare Mademoiselle Zena's life."

They go into the parlor. As soon as they sit down, Umpire Gandorf explains, "As you know, in times of emergency, the Council of Perfects has the right to appoint a supreme umpire with emergency powers until the crisis is resolved. However, a loophole exists in the Magnificent Charter. It says that the supreme umpire must hold emergency elections by the next summer solstice unless it's already an election year.

"The Founding Mothers and Fathers meant by that to say that the regular elections would supplant the emergency elections, but Umpire Kibbler has a team of unscrupulous lawyers that have already written a brief arguing that in an election year, the incumbent umpire-in-chief who is appointed supreme umpire does not have to hold any elections at all."

Dungaree Jeanne asks, "Won't the honest lawyers be able to overturn such an obviously erroneous interpretation of the Magnificent Charter?"

"There are no honest lawyers in Shentalpee City, Madame Dungaree."

Dungaree Jeanne is fighting in her mind through the incomprehensible mess they are throwing at her and can only exclaim, "No one in their right mind would buy such an argument!"

Umpire Gandorf continues, "It's not up to anyone in their right mind; it's only up to the Council of Perfects to decide how the Magnificent Charter gets interpreted. Umpire Kibbler will resort to any threat or intimidation to bend them to his will."

Fumbling to prepare some chamomile tea, Dungaree Jeanne says, "This is bad . . . very bad. What were you planning to do about it?"

Umpire Gandorf says with new energy and enthusiasm, "Beat him to the punch. Elves in Vinland now use the Christian Julian calendar, but when the Magnificent Charter was written they used the old Alfheim calendar.

"No one is sure when exactly Shentalpee City switched calendars, but if you calculate by the old elvish calendar, then the summer solstice—election day—is in twelve days. All we have to do is get the high commissioner to agree to the change and we can have a new head of state before the current monsieur Umpire-in-Chief can execute his plan."

"That sounds kind of risky. What if the high commissioner refuses?"

Enganyon perks up as well, saying, "We will tell the high commissioner that Umpire Kibbler has decreed a series of reforms, including the restoration of the old Alfheim calendar. If anything goes wrong, he can claim he was merely following orders."

"So what do you need from me?"

Enganyon says, "We'll need Mademoiselle Zena to put on her game face. I know my change of attitude came as a bit of a shock, but she's all weepy and shaken up. If she wants to be umpire-in-chief, she's going to have to act like she's in control. She needs to look like a good candidate if we are going to pull this off. We have to make sure the winner is Mademoiselle Zena or me."

Dungaree Jeanne corrects him. "You mean 'or I.'"

"Whatever. If both of us lose this election, all kinds of bad will turn over on Tuscoraura Mountain. I don't even want to try to imagine it. Can we count on your support, Madame Dungaree?"

Dungaree Jeanne takes a moment to process the whole prospectus, but Enganyon does not need to wait long for a reply. Zena, with her typical skill at snooping, barges into the conversation from out of nowhere and says, "Health and happiness to you, Umpire Gandorf! As for you, Captain Enganyon, I must state that, although I had a good cry over your despicable conduct, I am not at all weepy.

"This is your bid for power. Your lives are in more danger than mine. My only condition for going along with this is that, whether you win or I win, you must break off this betrothal to Captain Florenz and reinstate your commitment to me."

Enganyon moves his hand over his heart and says in Runic, "There was never a question that I would come back to thee, my dear. Although I have been strong-armed into a marriage contract with Captain Florenz, my love for thee is constant and true and has never faltered."

Umpire Gandorf looks at Madame Dungaree and asks in Eldric, "What say you, Madame Dungaree?"

Dungaree Jeanne replies, "Mademoiselle Zena's head is still full of romantic notions. My conditions are two-fold. First, you must release Johnny Appleseed from jail. Second, the mercenary companies I hired to defend my convoy still have not been paid. I'll need three thousand dollars before tomorrow. That way, we'll have some military backing in case this all blows over the wrong way. No money, no support."

Umpire Gandorf looks at her seriously and says, "If we don't win this gamble, I am dead anyway. I will give you the three thousand dollars as a loan, which you can pay back with three percent interest over the next five years either to me or to my son. Is that acceptable to you?"

"When can I have the money?"

"Within the hour. Just specify a delivery location that's not in Shentalpee City."

Dungaree Jeanne's expression of worry lightens up for the first time throughout this conversation and she says calmly, "Very well, Monsieur Umpire, you have just bought yourself an ally. Let the constitutional revolution begin!"

Scene 6: The Democratic Big Bang

Shentalpee City on Tuscoraura Mountain
Tiw's Day Sext. Afternoon, 13th of June, 1284
Morrow of Saint Gervase (Nordlandic Midsummer)

Two weeks later, Captain Florenz is sitting at her desk, reviewing reports and writing briefs to various elected officials and clan leaders reassuring them that her undead father is still perfectly capable of ruling Shentalpee City as umpire-in-chief. Blunderbore enters her office. "Kindly excuse the interruption, Madame Captain, but Johnny Appleseed has escaped."

"Send out search parties."

"No need. We know where he is."

"Why haven't you arrested him?"

"It seems elections were held today. We did not want to infringe on the jurisdiction of the electoral deputies."

"But it's not Election Day."

"Someone convinced the high commissioner that Election Day should be held on Midsummer as reckoned by the old Alfheim calendar instead of the Julian Calendar of Roma."

"I'll put a stop to that! Bring me my armor."

Florenz marches into the square dressed in a new suit of black leather armor and followed by her undead warriors robed in black with silver death masks hiding their decaying faces. Florenz breathes heavily, seething with anger. Johnny Appleseed is sitting with Zena by the reflecting pool, while Umpire Gandorf harangues the crowds from the amphitheater stage.

Enganyon and Dungaree Jeanne stand near Zena as if waiting to congratulate her. Deducing from the scene that Zena has won these fake elections, Florenz points the Sword of Layban at Umpire Gandorf, clearly the mastermind behind it all, and yells, "Arrest him!"

Her undead warriors take off, shambling toward him. Some shuffle like elderly convalescents in long pajamas, but others sprint forward with the ferocity of saber-toothed tigers. Umpire Gandorf runs.

Whizzing by Johnny Appleseed and Zena, Umpire Gandorf is drenched with sweat and flushed red on his face and neck. A few steps after having passed them, he turns back and looks at them, bewildered. His cheeks twitch as he croaks out the words, "Run, fools!"

Madame Dungaree, Enganyon, Zena, and Johnny Appleseed feel the heat of Florenz's anger breathing down at them. They join Umpire Gandorf and flee.

Having anticipated undead resistance, Enganyon and his father are armed with silver blades. They push their way through the crowds and run into the outdoor Malarkey Market. One undead warrior gropes for Dungaree Jeanne but Umpire Gandorf doubles back and strikes off its hand. The undead warrior stops and picks up its hand. It tries to jam the hand back onto its wrist but the silver in the blade impedes it from bonding. The undead warrior gives up in short order and chucks its own hand at Umpire Gandorf.

The hand nails him square in the back of the head and Umpire Gandorf topples over. Within a few heartbeats he is swarmed by undead warriors, grabbing his ankles, poking at his face, and twisting his arms.

Enganyon is the swiftest runner of the group but he hangs back with his leaf-bladed silver sword to protect the others. For all his bravery and for all his skillful strokes severing limbs, he is quickly overwhelmed too.

The undead warriors claw at his face and tangle their limbs between his arms and legs. Subdued, Enganyon is dragged back through the crowd as a vengeful Florenz walks toward him imperiously.

Johnny Appleseed sees what is happening and begins to pray his restoration prayers. Each undead warrior tries to resist him in a battle of wills but they are no match. One by one, the knot of undead limbs wrapped around Enganyon and Umpire Gandorf untangles. Soon, Enganyon hacks his way out.

He runs over to help his staggering father back up onto his feet. Umpire Gandorf, frightened out of his mind, somehow manages to push his body back into gear, fleeing with a heavy limp and a wheeze.

Enganyon and Umpire Gandorf follow Dungaree Jeanne and Zena across the bridge to their home base—Red Giant's Base. With the undead warriors stunned, Johnny Appleseed finds the silver sword that Umpire Gandorf abandoned on the floor and uses it to start cutting away at the ropes on the bridge connecting Thor's Base to Red Giant's Base.

Ashamed that he did not think of such a heroic idea himself, the injured Umpire Gandorf calls out to Madame Dungaree, "Tell Reverend Appleseed that I can cut off the bridgehead. Let him keep praying or doing whatever he did back there to save my life."

Johnny Appleseed replies, "That kind of miracle requires prayer and fasting. I'm getting exhausted."

Hearing Dungaree Jeanne's translation of that last comment, Enganyon shouts, "Now's the time to give it all you've got, Reverend! I'm too young to die!"

Seeing the next round of thralls making their way toward the bridge, Johnny Appleseed sits on Dungaree Jeanne's front porch so he can concentrate in prayer.

The undead thralls come charging at them and Appleseed prays with all his heart. The first few thralls drop like bags of bones but shortly afterward, Johnny Appleseed collapses from the strain, unconscious.

From behind the basilica, Florenz marches forward shouting, "Traitors!"

Enganyon desperately saws at the suspension bridge ropes with his silver sword. (Silver doesn't hold its edge as sharp as tempered steel, so cutting those tough ropes takes a little extra elbow grease.) When he sees Florenz storming her way across Malarkey Plaza toward him he shouts out to her, "But, my love, you won! The Tuscoraura elves elected you their umpire-in-chief! I was just helping you win the election!"

Florenz looks shocked. "Wait, what?"

The Ivy Leaguers stop in their tracks. Florenz can't help but think out loud, "The high elves are all too arrogant and conceited to vote for someone who does not look like them or who fails to live up to their superficial and unrealistic standards of perfection."

Enganyon says, "Apparently not . . . I mean . . . of course, you look like us and live up to our superficial and unrealistic standards of perfection."

That was not the answer Florenz wanted to hear.

Umpire Gandorf redoubles his efforts to cut the bridge cables. Meanwhile, one undead thrall drags itself forward with a total lack of enthusiasm, as if it would rather be taking a hot bath right now. Florenz is too flustered with conflicting emotions to give a clear command to direct its enslaved will decisively. It simply obeys her last command halfheartedly and steps onto the suspension bridge, wiggling its arms like a slug in a purple finch's beak.

The frayed cables holding up the suspension bridge start to snap. Umpire Gandorf shoves him across the bridge toward safety while he himself runs back to intercept the thrall, shouting, "You shall not pass!"

Seeing the turmoil, Florenz tries to resolve the conflict in her heart. She asks tentatively, "Wait, wait! Are you trying to say that you really love me for who I am, Captain Enganyon?"

Enganyon fumbles to find the right words. "It didn't hurt that your father was the most powerful elf in Shentalpee City, but I could genuinely see us marrying and living happily ever after."

Apparently, that was not the answer either. Her lips curl, her nose wrinkles, her fingers clench the bare skies. She gives a mental command to Sir Balrock, the giant dwarf now holding a whip. It comes lumbering forward from behind the basilica, picking up impressive speed as it goes. When the Ivy League sergeants realize what is coming their way, they dive to the sides to avoid getting trampled.

Enganyon shouts, "Quickly, Father! Come back!"

Umpire Gandorf sees the giant dwarf hurtling at him and hacks ever more vigorously at the last few strands of the suspension bridge cables. The giant dwarf's huge bones and rotting flesh still weigh an incredible amount. Seeing it coming, Umpire Gandorf makes a dash for safety on the far end. Sir Balrock's first ponderous step snaps the last cords. The suspension bridge gives way and the giant dwarf plummets down to the forest floor.

As for Umpire Gandorf, he feels the bridge boards slacken and leaps forward just as his feet start to lose traction. With a lucky reach, Umpire Gandorf grabs hold of the ledge with his two hands and hangs on for dear life.

BUT!

Before Enganyon and Dungaree Jeanne can reach down to pull him up, the giant dwarf Balrock lashes out with its whip and snags Umpire Gandorf's ankle, pulling him down with it. They both fall one hundred fifty feet to the forest floor.

Enganyon screams, "Noooooooo!"

Dungaree Jeanne pulls Enganyon, screaming and crying hysterically, away from the ledge. Meanwhile, Zena plies every muscle in her body to drag the unconscious Johnny Appleseed into Betzy Rose Mansion but makes little progress.

Once the hysterical Enganyon is safely inside, Dungaree Jeanne runs out to help her drag the unconscious human inside her front door. Zena locks the front door while her mother dashes from room to room, bolting and reinforcing all the doors and shutters.

Dungaree Jeanne looks at Johnny Appleseed and says, "Zena, dear, please bring me a pillow and a blanket. When he wakes up, he may be our only hope of getting out of this one alive."

"Great idea, Mom! We can use some of his magica leaves to locomutate out of here."

Dungaree Jeanne looks at her daughter grimly. "Mademoiselle Zena, magic won't be enough. We need a miracle."

Bonus Scene E: Mustering the Achaeans

Shentalpee City on Tuscoraura Mountain
Frige's Day Nones. Afternoon, 23rd of June, 1284
Nativity of Saint John the Baptist (Christian Midsummer)

The three Cardinals Orsini ride in a large litter carried by twenty-four chained prisoners. Litters are not prone to the bumps and jostles of hard-wheeled wagons, especially over the rough forest terrain they are now covering. The Cardinals consider the litter an indispensable luxury so as to help them use the travel time for devising battle plans and making important decisions about the conduct of this Crusade. Their entourage on horseback includes a flock of clerics, monks, and mercenaries ready to protect the important cardinals with their lives.

Piccolo Cardinal Orsini says, "Oh, wook! We are coming over a hill. I absowutewy wove it when we can see the whowe awmy in one gwimpse. Quite a fowmidible sight, if I do say so mysewf."

Maderno Cardinal Orsini rebukes him gently, "Brother, God has assembled this army, not you. It is not for vainglorious boasting but to stamp out the great and abominable Blackflame Cult."

Piccolo Cardinal Orsini sighs, "Oh, those hewetics! I hope this is the wast of those pesky vawmints."

Cardinal Maderno Orsini comments, "Pity how many innocent lives will be lost. I was hoping to convert those elves to Christianity, not wipe them out."

Paterno Cardinal Orsini bounces his fingers together in glee. "They will all become Christians in the afterlife, brother. Ah, we must have arrived. I see some log cabins burning off in the distance. Wood elves live in log cabins, don't they?"

Maderno Cardinal Orsini opens the door to the litter and sees the sign for Spriggins Gardens. He calls out to the Knight Hospitaller riding next to them, "Elect Radisson, can you please instruct the heralds to assemble the leaders of the Crusade? I think it is time to hold a war council before we proceed any deeper into fire elf territory. This would be a good place to fortify as a camp. Post guards. Every soldier not on guard duty must aid in the construction of wooden walls around our camp."

The slaves put the litter down and the cardinals step out. Paterno Cardinal Orsini waves his hand. "Caliban, unchain the prisoners and have them set up our meeting tent. Invite the nobles to a war council."

While the prisoners get to work, the cardinals' attendants pour them mint water to refresh themselves from the journey—of course, none for the prisoners who are exhausted and dripping with sweat.

With their throats moist, the Orsini brothers take out their breviaries and in choir with the clerics in their entourage, chant out the liturgy of the hours in Latin.

As they finish up, the baron of Amhirst approaches the tent before any of the other lords. He is in a foul mood. "Your Eminences, now that I have delivered to you the Sword of Layban and diverted my soldiers and resources to go on this Crusade for you, I believe it is about time you announce to the other Aenglish lords that I have been appointed Aenglish viceroy of Vinland, don't you think?"

Maderno Cardinal Orsini replies, "Come now, Lord Amhirst. That sour face will get you nowhere. A resounding victory at Tuscoraura Mountain will fill your coffers with treasures beyond your wildest imaginings and establish your place among the greatest lords of Vinland."

Amhirst does his best to maintain a respectful tone when he says, "Your Eminence, mortal men soon forget the victories that are supposed to win them immortality. What I need is a title that won't let them forget who I am. You promised to obtain for me the title of Aenglish viceroy of Vinland in exchange for delivering to you the Sword of Layban. I have done my part of the deal; it's time for you to do yours."

Paterno Cardinal Orsini shrugs and says, "Very well then, Lord Amhirst. Stay calm. Bring your captive, Viceroy Samuel de Champlane, to the meeting tent and we shall officially remove his ring and crown and place them on you."

Amhirst turns to Sir Robert Roger and says, "Bring the captive to this tent and have the men build a stockade barrier around our camp."

Sir Robert Roger bows. "Right away, my lord."

Once the meeting tent is set up, Amhirst accompanies the cardinals inside. He chuckles to himself at the thought of going in a lowly baron and walking out the highest royal personage in Vinland.

The cardinals' tent is more like a huge carnival pavilion. For all its ample size, it soon fills up with a surprisingly large number of lords that the baron of Amhirst does not recognize. Having been ambitious his whole life, he has always made a point of getting to know the movers and shakers in Vinland and finding ways to get them to owe him a favor or two in case he should need to call upon them at a crucial moment.

The parade of unfamiliar nobles painfully reminds him how far he still is from that goal. The other contender for Viceroy—the duke of Philadelphia—is making his rounds, keeping tabs on the other nobles.

Maderno Cardinal Orsini sees the intimidated look on Amhirst's face and picks just that moment to call attention to him. "My lords, by the grace of God you have been chosen as the leaders of the new world, Vinland, not merely for your own benefit, but to assure that the kingdom of God will stand firm on earth. Today, God's kingdom is threatened by heresy—the great and abominable Blackflame Cult. You are the ones who have responded to God's call to wipe it out."

"Before we begin our council of war, I invite two Vinlander lords to introduce themselves and their contingents. First, I introduce to you, Lord Geoffrey, baron of Amhirst and conqueror of Montreal."

Polite applause spreads throughout the tent. The baron of Amhirst does his best to look confident. "Esteemed lords of Vinland, this holy Crusade has brought us together to purify our land from the taint of heresy. As you are well aware, our Frankish neighbors have been harboring heretics within their borders for years beyond counting, and His Holiness Pope Martin has asked us, the faithful sons of the Church, to remove that blight from Vinland.

"And so, it gives me great honor to bring to this Crusade the army that conquered Louisburg, Fort Ticonderoga, and Montreal. In the course of these conquests, we captured the recalcitrant Frankish viceroy of Vinland, Samuel de Champlane, and have laid claim to his heritage by right of conquest.

"Having marched here directly from Ithica, I wish to make special mention of two elite units in our company. First and foremost, we bring with us a detachment of sorcerers, graduates of Silvermorn College of Sorcery, led by Battlesage Mickey Oswald.

"Second and just as illustrious, I present to you the Queen's Rangers led by Sir Robert Roger, who will join us shortly. Before the rangers arrived here, no one dared cross the forests of the Allegheny Valley for fear of the ferocious Magog goblins. Thanks to them, King Gog is no more, and the goblin tribes of Magog have scattered far and wide in fear.

"Next, I introduce the Fort Pitt militia, led by Sir John, baronet of Fourbes—"

Sir Sean Madigan leans over and whispers a correction into Amhirst's ear. Amhirst turns around and announces, "Excuse me, my lords, I meant to say, Sir Henry Garland, one of my most brilliant commanders. Just the man to lead the Fort Pitt militia."

Recovering his poise, Amhirst says, "Next, I would like to introduce Lord Samuel Maverick, newly appointed viscount of New Yourke City—"

Again, Sir Sean Madigan leans over and whispers a correction. Amhirst looks around and says, "Of course,

Lord Maverick will be arriving with his troops shortly. As you can imagine, the great responsibility on his shoulders for pacifying Manhatten after the riots by Petur Styvesant's unruly Vikings was bound to entail some delays.

"Finally, I would like to introduce some notable and trustworthy members of my staff—my herald and a great coach for our troops, Sir Sean Madigan, and my newly appointed frankelyn, Benjamin Chandler of Baston, an apprentice sorcerer specializing in aethergy. Benjamin is the leader of a party of adventurers with a brilliant record in successful quests for both myself and the Holy Office of the Inquisition.

"And now, I believe the Cardinals Orsini have an important public service announcement to make."

Maderno Cardinal Orsini steps up in front of the gathering and says, "Yes, yes, of course. Lord Amhirst's faithful service to the Aenglish Crown and the Holy Office of the Inquisition has merited for him the thanks of the Church and the people of Vinland. Before we make our announcements, we would like to invite Lord William Pinne, duke of Philadelphia, to introduce the lords of his contingent."

Lord William Pinne steps to the front with a jovial smile and says, "Thank you, Lord Amhirst, for your support on this Crusade that I have undertaken for the sake of the faith in Vinland. With me are some of the finest and most accomplished nobles in Vinland; but you will all excuse me if I introduce first my son, Sir William Pinne the Younger, whom I have placed in charge of the Philadelphia militia. Many of you have already heard of his exploits.

"Though he has not yet reached his majority, he has earned his own spurs through his valiant actions at the Battle of the Plains of Abraham. Lord James Wolf, moments before his tragic death, personally knighted my son as a reward for his key role in assuring the victory before the walls of Kaybec. What father would not be proud of such a son?

"Equally proud am I of my daughter, Lady Philippa, who has made quite a name for herself as the leader of a party of adventurers. With all due respect to the baron of Amhirst, my daughter is the real leader of the adventurers whom he mentioned presently. His young frankelyn was merely the liaison for the last quest they were on—a quest, I might add, Their Eminences the Cardinals Orsini would say the said frankelyn managed to bungle after my sweet Philippa and her party had completed its objectives with much skill and cleverness."

Amhirst starts to look combative over the insult, but Maderno Cardinal Orsini intervenes. "My lords, there can be no doubt that Philippa and her party of adventurers have completed several invaluable quests for the Holy Office of the Inquisition. We are not at liberty to discuss the particulars of any specific quest, but we insist that the baron's frankelyn has shown a remarkable intelligence and resourcefulness that will no doubt make him a pivotal player in the future of Vinland. We very much wish to retain his services."

Lord William Pinne continues. "Yes, well, his potential did very much impress my fair Philippa as well. I hope he will continue to hone that promise.

"Now, it is my pleasure to introduce some of the greatest nobles in Vinland. First, I introduce my esteemed gnome vassals and dear friends, Lord Hugo Aramingo and Lord Richwell Kensing. We Philadelphian humans share our boundaries with two brilliant and important halfling cities, Northern Liberties and Southwark.

"Lord Hugo Aramingo is burgraff of Northern Liberties, a vibrant community of Nordlandic Kabouter gnomes famed for weaving fabrics of the finest quality. Both in industry and warfare, Vinland's Kabouter gnomes are highly revered. None can equal them in marshaling such large and well-equipped companies of both hound riders and heavily armored infantry.

"And this is Lord Richwell Kensing, bailiff of Southwark. The Warwick Hobs came over from Aenglish soil with many of the human colonists under my banner. The bonds of friendship have been strong between them on both sides of the Ocean of Atlantis.

"With us today, and giving us great confidence for the success of our endeavor, is Lord Fredrick Maryland, earl of Baltimoor. He and his noble father have been the most generous lords in granting headrights to colonists from Aengland. Generations of munificence and loyalty have borne fruit for his family in the number and caliber of knights that he brings with him to the battlefield—the largest contingent on this Crusade.

"And next I am honored to introduce the son of the most famous gnome in the British Isles, Lord Bodo Fraggins, high sheriff of the Wilming halflings who live in peace among the Delawaerr tribes. The Wilming gnomes are proud to call themselves halflings, representing the finest traditions of both Albany's pixies and Erinland's leprechauns. No doubt Lord Fraggins will win great glory for himself and his people here in Vinland to carry on his uncle's noble legacy.

"We also welcome Lord Felker Sinbolt, ancient noble of the Ramapough Trench dwarves. His renown on the battlefield is already so far-reaching that his war cry alone is enough to put enemies to flight, as happened at the Battle of Sideling Hill when he came to the aid of his Delawaerr ally, War Chief Shingas.

"To our great honor, some Christian Ashnabeks have joined us under the leadership of Sagamore Tsheetz, known in Aenglish as Leaps-the-Ships for his boarding maneuver to capture the Frankish cog *Alcide* at the naval action of June 8 in the Saint Laurence Gulf of back in 1275. He holds the title of Beloved Man of the Altoona tribe, and his war chief is reckoned as an elder and wise man. Altoona War Chief Mallow Club has found a means to secure victory in every trial of combat he's led as war chief through the past two decades.

"The Pinne family has relied upon the loyalty of the Harris family for generations and Lord John Harris, count of Harrisburgh, shows himself the worthy scion of noble stock. With him today he brings his feudal knights, sergeants, and a levy of archers and spearmen.

His eldest son, Sir John Harris, acting as castellan of Fort Harris, stands at the head of the militia there and his daughter, Lady Aelfreda Harris, is an accomplished battlemage leading a company of colonial marshals.

"In his entourage comes the famous 'Fighting Bishop,' His Excellency John Elder of the diocese of Paxton and his volunteer militia, known as the Paxton Boys. His Excellency Bishop Elder brings fire to the hearts of all who hear him preach and inflicts deep bruises with his war mace.

"My lords and ladies, do not let the small stature of Lord Gustavus Thornbury, provost of the Trent Knockers, deceive you. In the use of the swordstaff he excels all the humans and the gnomes of Vinland, and his heavy hauberk is made of the finest double-linked mail. He deals mighty blows, but only the arrows of true love can pierce his armored chest. He is truly the ultimate warrior who has won—"

Rrriiipppp!

The sound of tearing canvass behind them makes all the gathered lords turn around. As a sword cuts a slit from the top to the bottom of the tent, they draw their arming swords, waiting anxiously. On hostile soil, the dangers of an assassination attempt to destroy the leaders of the Crusade loom constantly in their minds.

Two black-gloved hands part the canvas flaps and an odd-looking knight steps through the opening, bringing the light of day upon their smoky gathering.

Guards come around back shouting, "Halt!"

Amhirst frowns and waves off the guards, saying, "Let him go. Lord Maverick, could you please for once be like everyone else and enter the tent through the flaps that are designated as the entrance?"

"Begging your pardon, my lord, but the guards said I was too late and they wouldn't let me in. I told them I'm a big-shot viscount and all but they were like, 'We don't care if you are the president of the United States of the Holy Land, you're not getting in there.' So I was like, 'Try to stop me.' And you know what?" He points to the big slit in the tent's wall. "They didn't see that one coming."

Maderno Cardinal Orsini intervenes to allay the feelings of indignation, especially among the dwarf lords who are always so easily offended, and says, "Welcome, Lord Maverick! Your presence on this Crusade is a boon to all the lords of Vinland. You will forgive me if I interrupt your grand entrance, but the baron of Amhirst already introduced Your Lordship. Once again, congratulations on your elevation as viscount of New Yourke. Now let us turn our attention back to the duke of Philadelphia as he finishes introducing his contingent."

Unable to wipe the smirk off his own face at Amhirst's unruly protégé, Duke William Pinne resumes his introductions, saying, "Yes, of course. May I present Lord Heathe Skorr, count of the Korrigan gnomes of Barres County. He is a young man but old in the ways of courage, having fought nobly while outnumbered three to one at the Battle of Braddock's Field. Without him, not a single Aenglishman would have escaped. He rallied the gnomes to Sir George Warshington's side.

"His father, Count Daym Skorr, was a good friend of mine and though I mourn his loss, I also rejoice that he has raised such a worthy son to lead his people.

"In addition to these Crusaders who fight to safeguard the faith in Vinland and have received a plenary indulgence for taking up the Crusader vow, I have also called up several companies of non-Christian warriors who have agreed to come on this Crusade as allies. In my profusion of zeal and as a show of my piety, I have offered to add half my share of the spoils to their regular share in compensation for the spiritual benefits of the Crusade they are missing out on. I trust that Their Eminences the Cardinals Orsini will find ways to reward my generosity."

"Indeed we shall," replies Maderno Cardinal Orsini. "Indeed we shall."

Duke William Pinne continues, "Well, then, I am proud to introduce Elder Patufet Stromfis, peerless grand schwurf of the Payo Schwurfs—the most powerful of all the gnome communities in Vinland. Though they still cling to the pagan gods of the Ancient Vlameer Order, Elder Stromfis has agreed to allow Christian missionaries to operate within their borders.

"Next is my great friend Oconostota, the red war chief of the Punxsutawney tribe. Although not yet a Christian, he has been favorable to Christianity throughout his tenure as leader of his people. The Aenglish call him Philip, and many Aenglishmen and people of the Ohio Valley seek the counsel of his seer, known as Buckeyed Woodchuck. He has seen a vision with the path to Vinland's future paved with gold as a result of our war with the Tuscoraura elves.

"Over here, I am honored to introduce Lord Nybling Dankwart, great dainn of the Allegheny Mountain dwarves, who quarreled with his father, the famous and valiant Lord Etzel of the White Mountains. His father's second wife, Kremhild, brought ruin to his people through her schemes to provoke a war against her family who had disowned her decades before. Lord Nybling led a group of White Mountain dwarves who refused to fight such a patricidal war into the Allegheny Mountains where they paved Nemacolin's Trail and became immensely wealthy through the income of the tolls they now collect.

"Finally, last but not least, Lord Sander Brandson, prince of Scarsdale. The Korrigan gnomes of Scarsdale are Ammonite Christians. As such, they have yet to resolve the status of their recognition with the Holy See in Roma, but they have come here with us to honor an ancient treaty between our peoples."

Piccolo Cardinal Orsini claps his hands. "That's gweat!" Turning to his brothers he asks, "Do I get to tell them how many battawions the pope has?"

Paterno Cardinal Orsini groans but answers politely, "Little brother, I think it's Maderno's job."

"Fine," huffs the little cardinal.

Maderno Cardinal Orsini announces, "Lords and ladies of the Blackflame Crusade, allow me to introduce to you Brother Pierre Radisson, the elect of Saratoga Springs, a practicing brother of the Knights Hospitaller. He has been elected commander of the hospital at Saratoga Springs but has postponed his official installation ceremony to join us on this Crusade."

Piccolo Cardinal Orsini pats a large knight on the back and says, "This guy is Bwotha Jack de Molay—a big, meaty knight if I eva saw one!"

"Thank you, little brother," interrupts Maderno Cardinal Orsini. "Please welcome the preceptor of the Rofchester Temple, Brother Jack de Molay, a man both brave and large of stature, leading twenty-four unshakable knights of the temple and thirty brother sergeants on horse.

"Here is Brother Oliver Roland, commander of the Knights Paladin from the Masswachoosut Bay Colony."

Piccolo Cardinal Orsini butts in, "These guys got it all figuwed out how to bust some baddies. If thewe is eva something stwange in ya neighbahood, these awe the guys you'w gonna caww."

Maderno Cardinal Orsini forces a laugh. "Thank you, brother. May I proceed without interruption?"

"Fine."

"My lords and ladies, please welcome Sir John Hathorne, captain of the Salim colonial militia and chief magistrate of the Masswachoosut Bay Superior Court of Judicature, a noble, praiseworthy knight who is also knowledgeable in letters.

"Sir Glover Marmaduke, chief inspector of the docks for the city of Marblehead, is a gnome famed for his exploits at sea. Although he was recently convicted for piracy, the Inquisition has seen fit to commute his sentence in return for his wholehearted participation in this Crusade.

"Finally is Sir Gunthar Ortwin, landseer of the Pocono Mountain dwarves and a fervent son of the Church. He brings with him fifteen dwarf prospectors and thirty dwarf pioneers. Dwarf pioneers scout land masses for potential veins and then call in the prospectors to assess it. The landseer takes the prospectors' recommendations and determines if the dwarf community should commit miners to breach a shaft on that vein."

Piccolo Cardinal Orsini holds up the landseer's enormous hand for all to see and says, "These dwaves awe tough, man alive! You shouwd see how big they hands awe! Wow!"

Paterno Cardinal Orsini says without emotion, "Thank you, little brother, for all the extra information you are supplying, but we have a meeting to run. Why don't you hold your comments until the end?"

"Fine."

Maderno Cardinal Orsini immediately moves on to the next issue, saying, "Now, my lords, Lord Geoffrey, baron of Amhirst, and Lord William, duke of Philadelphia, have both petitioned King Eddard and

Holy Mother the Church to confer upon them the title of Aenglish viceroy of Vinland—Lord Amhirst by right of conquest, since he conquered Montreal and captured the Frankish viceroy of Vinland, and Lord Pinne by right of preeminence, since he commands the allegiance of more vassals and holds right of lordship over more subjects than any other noble in Vinland.

"The Holy See, in consultation with the curia, has decided that the right of conquest precedes right of preeminence in conferring titles. Due to the large number of Aenglish lords who participated in the conquest of New Frankland, the conquest of Montreal is not sufficient to claim the right of conquest. However, the capture of the Frankish viceroy of Vinland does grant you a claim to his title.

"However, there has been some dispute as to the legitimacy of the prisoner. Some say he is merely an innocent, poor old man who happens to resemble Lord Samuel de Champlane. I have in my company several high-level clerics who know the viceroy well. If, after a brief interview they can verify his identity, I have been invested with the authority to crown you, Lord Geoffrey Amhirst, Aenglish viceroy of Vinland. Please bring the prisoner forward."

The baron of Amhirst nods to Sir Sean Madigan, who approaches him and whispers to him.

Amhirst turns red with anger and humiliation. He calms himself and announces, "It seems the viceroy is indisposed at the moment. Could we resume this meeting at another time?"

Maderno Cardinal Orsini says, "If you are afraid your prisoner will not pass the interview, we must declare your claim to right of conquest null and void.

We do have the right to appoint a governor-general in the name of King Eddard of Aengland. We propose a compromise. Whichever of you two lords has his troops make it up first onto one of the elf tree-lofted platforms will be named governor-general. Agreed?"

Duke William Pinne turns to Baron Geoffrey Amhirst cheerfully. "Indeed; that sounds fair to me."

Barely able to hide his outrage, Amhirst walks out of the tent—through the exit made by his Maverick. Sir Sean, seeing the ploy and not wanting to get squeezed out, quickly says, "We agree."

Sir Sean then races out of the tent to catch up with the baron and confesses, "My lord, I took the liberty to speak on your behalf and told the cardinals we agree. My fear, quite honestly, is that they will use the missing viceroy as an excuse to offer the title to the duke of Philadelphia instead of you, to whom it rightly belongs. That goes without saying, but I thought—"

Struggling to control his anger, Amhirst snaps, "You thought wrong, Sir Sean. As a matter of fact, we are all going about this wrong. All wrong."

Sir Sean trembles a little as he asks, "What do you mean, my lord?"

Amhirst stops and looks Sir Sean fiercely in the eye and says, "Of all the years of schooling that I spent learning Latin, only one phrase really ever stuck in my head."

"What was that, my lord?"

"Velle est posse. Do you recall what it means?"

Sir Sean does not want to upstage the baron right now but he does not want to look dumb either. He says tentatively, "Something like 'where there's a will, there's a way,' my lord."

Amhirst sneers and says, "In your world that would be a good translation. In my world, a more appropriate translation would be, 'when someone gets in your way, find out which one of his relatives is most eager to read his will.' I assure you, every powerful man has at least one close family member who wants him dead."

"You can't possibly mean—"

Amhirst cuts him off and demands, "Get me Ariel!"

Scene 7: The Grand Detour

Shentalpee City on Tuscoraura Mountain
Tiw's Day Sext. Afternoon, 13th of June, 1284
Morrow of Saint Gervase (Nordlandic Midsummer)

The red-and-white striped bedsheet grabs Florenz's attention as soon as Enganyon carries it out of Betzy Rose Mansion. She calls out to him, "What's that?"

Enganyon says, "We wish to parley."

Florenz scratches her ear and calls across the chasm, "You know I'm such a soft touch that I'll probably regret it later on, but right now the only terms we're going to discuss regard the manner of your execution."

Dungaree Jeanne yanks the flagpole out of Enganyon's hands and waves its star-spangled banner. "Excuse me, Mademoiselle Umpire-in-Chief-elect, but you must have gotten the wrong impression. We're not here to surrender; we're here to share some good news.

"Both Master Leevai and Captain Gunnar have agreed to join the League of Nations. I'm not going to let the heresiarch and his undead minions overrun our beautiful colony on my watch."

Florenz glares. "Oh yeah? You and what army?"

Horns go off beneath them.

The anxious elves all rush to the ramparts of Thor's Base to see what's going on down below.

Haughty hosts of Crusaders are mustering in a pell-mell of mad confusion in the wood elf villages on the forest floor. Trumpet blasts burst in the air, signaling the oncoming havoc of war.

A dread silence reposes over Shentalpee City.

At length, Florenz looks up and rages. "Your blood will wash out the pollution of their foul footsteps."

Dungaree Jeanne still gazes over the railing. "Praise the power that has preserved us from your cult!"

Florenz is so angry she spits as she shouts, "Traitor! I should have known you've been siding with our foes all along!"

"Not at all, Mademoiselle Umpire-in-Chief-elect. You are the one who has allowed outsiders to seize control of our fair city. We will not let the heresiarch dictate our freedoms. Until a moment ago, the League of Nations was the only group of elves brave enough to stand up to you with that blackflaming sword of yours but now heaven has rescued our land.

"Swear that you will expel the heresiarch and I will summon the League of Nations to assist in the defense of Shentalpee City. Refuse and I'll rally every freedom-loving elf on Tuscoraura Mountain to depose you."

Florenz fidgets with the scabbard of the Sword of Layban, calculating a solution to her predicament. If Dungaree Jeanne starts a civil war now, she just might win. Florenz decides to cut a deal. "Okay, okay, fine. He has terrible bad breath anyway. If you bring the League of Nations into the fight on our side, I'll kick the heresiarch out of here after we win—I swear it."

"Kick him out now."

"That would be foolish. We've been preparing to fight the Crusade ever since he got here. He's got a bag of nasty tricks all ready for them. Let him unleash the Aeolian winds upon our enemies before he leaves."

"Agreed, but remember—we will fight for you only as long as your cause is just."

The earth groans under the trampling feet of dwarves, men, and gnomes as each company of warriors seeks a place of honor on the battlefield without exposing themselves to too much danger. Dozens of heralds go about shouting orders amidst the tumult until at last they are arranged in a formidable battle line.

Although Amhirst's contingent is small in number compared to the duke of Philadelphia's many vassals, allies, and mercenaries, the cardinals immediately notice the baron's absence. Suited up for war in armor adorned with the papal insignia, Paterno Cardinal Orsini canters briskly into Amhirst's camp on his warhorse and calls out, "What is going on here? Didn't you hear the trumpet call for the general muster?"

Amhirst exits his tent and casts a smug glare at the cardinal, saying, "I'm sorry, Your Eminence, but you have failed to deliver on your promise to make me the new viceroy. Fool me once, shame on you. Fool me twice, shame on me. I'm sitting this one out."

Paterno Cardinal Orsini growls, "Be warned, Amhirst—if you abandon this Crusade, you will incur an excommunication."

"Abandon the Crusade? Heavens no! I promised to *accompany* the Crusade, not to fight in it."

Paterno Cardinal Orsini is not amused. "Suddenly you think you can go playing at being a lawyer with me? I could destroy you in the course of a leisurely afternoon's siesta if I wanted to."

"Your Eminence," sighs the baron of Amhirst, "The memory of the killings at Fort William Henry has engraved in my mind a deep caution about war leaders who feel bound to nothing more than the letter of a treaty. We all have to do a better job in managing expectations if we are going to work together."

The cardinal clenches his fists. "This is treachery!"

"At least I'm an honest traitor who plays by the book, Your Eminence. My herald, Sir Sean, is still trying to make sense of your playbook. Until then, no game."

Paterno Cardinal Orsini gallops off, seething with rage. Sir Sean turns to the baron and asks, "My lord, do you think it was wise to irk the cardinal thus?"

Amhirst shrugs. "The man betrayed me. The world is not big enough to hold both of us. My Achilles' heel is my ambition, and he holds Paris's arrow in his quiver. We can't both walk out of here alive. Right now, we should be looking into every possible stratagem to make sure the elves crush the cardinals."

Unlike the high elves up in the imposing tree-lofted bases and towers, the wood elves have no protection against the invaders. Some flee toward the marchlands, but most crowd around the elevators, screaming for a chance to be hoisted up to the safety of Shentalpee City. The dwarves working the cranks strain to get the overloaded elevators up while shoving off desperate hangers-on, slowing the process down. Parents pass their screaming children to anybody lucky enough to make their way onto an elevator. Chaos rules over their terror with gloating tyranny.

The wind smells slow and sour while the high elves watch the crusading army march toward them in unending ranks, trampling down the scutch grass and uprooting the dandelions. A few old crows caw out the sounds of their morbid curiosity and add to the palpable tension.

The high elves safely tucked inside their thick wooden barricades lean over the railings to mock the invaders, but the panicked squeals of the wood elf refugees take away some of their thunder. The Justiciar League officers busy themselves knocking on doors, asking for high elf volunteers to take the unsheltered wood elves into their homes—vagrants can become a security liability in the event of an assault.

Leading off Thor's Base, the major dignitaries of the non-elf communities arrive—the mountain dwarf Lawspeaker Sturl Snorrison; the garden gnome High Bailiff Harfud Fellowhide; and the longhouse human War Chief Skaruren—also known as King Hancock to the Aenglish.

Representing the high elves, High Commissioner Kordon Bleuson rides down in one of the larger elevators. He steps off before touching down and it jangles behind him. A detachment from the League of Licornes rides over to him and helps him mount his battle reindeer.

Once the green-and-brown League of Licornes' reindeer honor guard has formed up with the high commissioner, they unfurl their white flags and escort him across the scorched wood elf village to a parley with the duke of Philadelphia and the Cardinals Orsini.

With his teeth sounding gray, Maderno Cardinal Orsini greets each delegate in his own language. "Hale ant sail, Monsieur Kordon! *Se'g Honyaweh,* Skaruren agigo rekweh! *Kaishu,* andrea nanoa Sturl! *Beannach,* tighern Harfud gnormach!"

Then he says in Latin, relying on his translators to make his words understood, "The Holy Office of the Inquisition has no ill feeling toward your peoples. We are only here to arrest the heresiarch and his blackflame cultists, including the renegade Florenz Kibblersdottir. We personally assure you that she will get a fair trial. We will offer the fire elves a truce and safe-conduct to our tent and back for the sake of negotiating terms."

The elf high commissioner, compared to the others, is shortish, brownish, oldish, and mossy. With a voice that is sharp and perfunctory, he says in Latin, "Salve, patres conscripti cardinales!" Sensing he didn't get it quite right, he switches to Elvish Runic, saying, "We accept your offer to negotiate, as long as you withdraw your army past the marchlands. We demand restitution for all the mayhem and destruction you have caused before we discuss terms."

The lawspeaker's command of Latin is quite strong, so he delivers his words entirely in Latin. "Your Eminences, we do not recognize Florenz Kibblersdottir as the legally appointed umpire-in-chief, and we have no love for the wendigo-creating cult leeching off her opulent city-state. Nonetheless, you have recklessly violated our territorial sovereignty and threatened our blood-sworn allies without inviting us to mediate the conflict. A diplomatic affront of such epic proportions cannot be ignored."

King Hancock says in the Irockian dialect of the Tuscoraura tribes, "You say that the fire elf leader walks with the turtles and runs with the rabbits. Today the rabbit sleeps and the turtle finishes the race. You bring axes to chop down our trees and torches to raise our homes, but the sequoias above do not burn; the caves below do not split. United we stand."

Maderno Cardinal Orsini sneezes with a sawdusty sneeze and says in Latin, "Our armies have merely chopped down a few trees. We have done no harm, esteemed lords of Tuscoraura Mountain, and we have not invaded your territories. We are the high inquisitors of Vinland, and our business is hunting down heretics. Princess Florenz harbors the heresiarch of the great and abominable Blackflame Cult. As soon as we arrest them, we will—"

The high commissioner cuts him short. "We will not discuss terms unless you withdraw your army and make restitution! You have no hope of winning a war against us. Leave, before we demonstrate our fury."

With a grim look on his face, Maderno Cardinal Orsini suddenly lapses into his Italian dialect, common only on the city streets of Roma. "All right then, here's our condition—unless you hand over Princess Florenz Kibblersdottir and the other blackflame heretics, we'll whack them down off every scrofulous tree growing on top of Tuscoraura Mountain and smoke them out of every smogulous hole beneath it."

The translators struggle to decipher the message. When they communicate the gist of it, the high commissioner is so enraged he can only gargle and croak out a few nonsense words. Suddenly he looks behind him and says in Eldric, "You're asking for it and boy oh boy, you're gonna get it. Here's our umpire-elect on her way now to show you what's what."

Florenz trots up on a war reindeer followed by her father on foot in a dark cape. His face is pale and his jaw hangs open. The whiteness of the two canines on his upper jaw spooks them from afar.

Lawspeaker Sturl Snorrison turns around and seethes with outrage, shouting in Elvish Runic, "Mademoiselle Florenz! How dare you violate your parole by returning to Tuscoraura Mountain!"

Florenz keeps a stony-hard face and rebuts his accusation. "You condemned me without a trial for condemning Bartlebee without a trial. I have come back to set the record straight. Now the fire elves have elected me umpire-in-chief. Any attack on me as head of the state is an attack on Shentalpee City itself."

The lawspeaker's fury boils with exasperation. "We told you we would not recognize you as head of state. A political stunt like this is reckless in peacetime and sheer madness in time of war."

The high inquisitor's translator tries to explain to the cardinals what is going on, but it is all hopelessly confusing.

Maderno Cardinal Orsini shouts out, "Enough! War has been averted. Mademoiselle Florenz and her father are here. The Holy Office of the Inquisition always gives heretics a chance to repent. Come with me, heretical elves, and answer to the tribunal."

The lawspeaker turns back to the high inquisitor and declares, "If you have a mind to vacate our lands, we won't stop you. But, be warned! Dwarves hold grudges. If you bring any more pandemonium to our homeland we will roll you over so hot and heavy that your widows will use your corpses as yule logs."

The dwarves and gnomes send their criers who speak Eldric to the panicking throng of wood elves around the elevators, asking them to calm down and proceed in an orderly fashion to the burrows and tunnels beneath Tuscoraura, where they will be given refuge until the crusading army withdraws.

Most forget about the elevators instantly and head for safety among the dwarves and gnomes underground. Those wood elves who desperately sent their children up the elevator now plead with the dwarf operators to help get them back down again.

The undead umpire-in-chief, Kibbler Earnestson, walks toward the high inquisitors imperiously. The high inquisitors are well prepared for dealing with the undead, and low-level clerics bring out a pair of silver manacles. They chain the umpire's wrists together behind his back. A pair of silver manacles come out for Florenz as well, just in case. The Inquisition's guards escort the two prisoners into the tent.

Once inside the tent, the gathered lords all have a common language, Aenglish, so the high inquisitors order the proceedings to be conducted in Aenglish. They form a tribunal and give Florenz an opportunity to publicly confess her wrongdoings and declare her repentance. Her testimony is long and complicated.

The Inquisition's translator, a Toutonic cleric who knows Latin, Elvish Runic, and Dwarvish Runic perfectly—though his Aenglish is still a little weak—tries his best to explain to the gathered lords the convolutions of her political discourse through his thick Toutonic accent.

It comes out something like this: "Mademoiselle Florenz, she says zat she vants no schlaughter of innocent lives. She says zat zee Eldritch elves voted her . . . how do you say . . . First Vampire, but she is schtill no vampire. She says zat she vill come to schtand judgment. She says zat her fazer is zee eldritch First Vampire. Her fazer vill also come to schtand judgment. Her fazer vill say to us about ze schvartz fire."

The duke of Philadelphia looks at him, baffled. "What is an eldritch vampire?"

The translator points at Kibbler and says, "Zat!"

The duke of Philadelphia shrugs. "Whatever. Just tell the eldritch vampire that we accept his repentance, but unfortunately cannot leave without an indemnity. Fighting this pesky heresy is expensive—two hundred silver marks for my battalions, two hundred for the Inquisition, and two hundred for our allies and mercenaries should be sufficient."

Florenz hears the translation and asks, "How about a fist full of dollars?"

The translation has less spunk, but Paterno Cardinal Orsini catches the drift and says, "Don't get too cocky with us, miss! With one wave of my hand I can turn your undead father back to the realms of oblivion forever."

Florenz replies, "Don't try to frighten us with your clerical ways, Inquisitor. Your sad devotion to that ancient religion has not helped you conjure up the Sword of Layban, or given you clairvoyance enough to find the heresiarch's hidden base—"

Before she has a chance to finish that thought, her eldritch vampire father darts forward with incredible speed and force. Though his arms are still chained behind his back, they forgot to muzzle him. He leaps over a tall guard in a single bound and bites Paterno Cardinal Orsini in the neck.

Duke William Pinne shouts, "That eldritch vampire is biting the cardinal's neck! Someone get it off!"

Using the power of the archon stone in his chest, Vampire Kibbler polarizes the three source stones in the amulet to repel fire, lightning, and metal. The steel-clad and steel-armed soldiers around him flip backwards as if an invisible fist has punched them where it counts. The braziers and candles in the tent flicker out and the darkness adds to the chaos while the eldritch vampire wreaks bloody havoc.

Before any guard reaches the tent flaps to let more light in, Florenz jumps back over her chained wrists to bring her hands to the front and she draws the Sword of Layban from a special concealed sheath she had constructed specifically for this payback strike. "By the power of Layban . . . I have the power!" she thunders.

Having memorized the middle cardinal's position and rehearsed this covert operation with her father many times, she strikes Maderno Cardinal Orsini in the thigh with the Sword of Layban, freezing his innards and setting his armor ablaze with the blackflame surging out from its blade.

Hearing the commotion, the outside guards pour into the tent. Once sunlight shines in through the open flaps, the light infantry guards—immune to the sorcery because they wear no steel—step forward. One brave swashbuckler with leather armor, a wooden buckler, and a silver sword chops at Vampire Kibbler just before a cleric uses his Turn Undead prayer. The silver sword severs his right arm at the shoulder.

Although the Turn Undead prayer cannot destroy the vampire's unnatural bond of soul to body thanks to the archon stone, the effect of the prayer sends Kibbler flying back as if he got hit with a wrecking ball.

Florenz quickly realizes that in a den of clerics, Knights Paladin, and fighters who specialize in countering magic, sorcery, and the undead, her father's invincibility has severe limitations.

Florenz beats a hasty retreat behind her father just in the nick of time. The leather-clad swashbucklers and a few light-armored guards lunge in to attack with wooden and silver weapons. Vampire Kibbler whirls his severed arm on the silver chain like a flail and smacks the nearest swashbuckler with tornado force, flipping him over the inquisitors' lunch table. Florenz reaches back and drags her father out of the tent.

Not a moment too soon, because a Knight Paladin steps forward with a blessed cross. The power of the cross clobbers Vampire Kibbler and knocks him senseless. His body slumps over his daughter's, but she does not stop. Florenz hoists him up onto her shoulders and carries him off at a run.

Before pursuing them, the Crusaders turn to the last surviving high inquisitor. Clutching his dying brothers, Piccolo Cardinal Orsini crumples his tear-washed cheeks and shouts, "Kill them all!"

Duke William Pinne objects, "But, Your Eminence, many of these wood elves are good Christians!"

Suddenly having lost his speech impediment, the hysterical inquisitor screams, "Kill them all, and God will recognize his own!"

The horns blow and the Crusaders rush forward to a terrible massacre of innocents.

ACT V

YOU'RE IT

Scene 1: Monstrous Mash

Shentalpee City on Tuscoraura Mountain
Tiw's Day Sext. Afternoon, 13th of June, 1284
Morrow of Saint Gervase (Nordlandic Midsummer)

At the reckless command of the enraged little cardinal, all the Crusaders rush forward to attack the helpless wood elves who have not yet reached the safety of the dwarf tunnels or the gnome burrows. Even without the elaborate jewelry of a high elf, a wood elf's day-to-day getup still has enough linen fabrics, copper buckles, high-grade steel tools, and homemade finery to make looting their belongings a profitable business model for the rank-and-file Crusaders. Moreover, elves always earn a good price on the slave market.

Back at the cardinals' tent, Florenz and her father run for their lives—or in the case of her father, for his undeath. She mutters breathless curses upon the heresiarch who severely overestimated the archon stone's effectiveness in rendering her father invincible. The Inquisition proved itself quite capable of dealing with the threat. Even the legendary Sword of Layban failed to make her the kind of super-warrior the heresiarch led her to believe she would become.

As they retreat, her father's will revives little by little. Still, the active source stones inside her father's chest provide little protection against the gnome sling stones and the human silver arrows from the cardinals' elite guard. Her father tries but fails to reattach his right arm, severed with a silver blade. He runs close behind her but staggers around as if punch drunk from the Turn Undead prayers and the blessed crosses they have directed at him. As he runs, he does manage to position himself to absorb the missiles flying in at Florenz.

Thanks to his protection as a mobile meat shield, Florenz only suffers a few minor grazes on the way back to Shentalpee City, despite the torrents of arrows, crossbow bolts, and sling stones falling down upon her.

But her luck soon runs out. Several light-armored swashbucklers from the high inquisitors' tent catch up to her before she reaches Thor's Base with her father. They are armed with silver swords and know how to use them well . . . very well.

Unable to outpace them in the footrace, Florenz desperately parries their blows with the Sword of Layban. Her father does his best to ward them off by flicking his chained hand at them, but his imprecise swings offer little relief. Her swordsmanship is simply not up to par, and she knows it will only take them a few more strokes to bypass her guard.

But Florenz has never put much stock in swordplay —a waste of time. Organization and planning, as far as she is concerned, will always win the day, and she has carefully laid out and rehearsed a plan for escape.

The elevator operator dwarves have been keeping one elevator, reinforced with sturdy boards, dangling about ten feet above the battlefield with a large brass bell buried upside down directly beneath it. The swashbucklers move to corner her just as Florenz hops down into the bell with her father holding onto her tightly. He then uses the archon stone to flip the polarization of the lodestone in the amulet to repel metal as vehemently as possible.

Kibbler's lodestone magnetically propels them both upward out of the bell's skirt like a railgun or a sorcery-charged blunderbuss. A dwarf elevator operator makes ready to reach out and grab them as they fly by, but their trajectory is so perfect that they both make a clean landing inside the elevator's platform without any help at all. Impressed, the dwarf compliments her in Eldric, saying, "Quite a bell hop, Mademoiselle Umpire!"

Crossbow bolts, longbow arrows, and sling stones come flying up at them. Florenz does not want to wait around to chitchat. She gives him a terse reply. "Okay, bellhop, just get us out of here."

The operator dwarves ply their muscle strength and quick hands to the pulleys. The elevator glides upward swiftly. Vampire Kibbler continues to swat at sling stones and intercept arrows aimed at his daughter until they rise up beyond their range.

Once they're at the top, the heresiarch walks over to them, surrounded by his entourage of cultists and blackflame fanatics. With triumph in his eyes, he curls his fists together and announces, "Welcome back, Lord Vampire and my young apprentice, Florenz. From here you will witness the final destruction of the Inquisition and the last of its pathetic Crusades."

Florenz grabs her father's arm, still dangling from the silver chain, and says in the Black Tongue of Caldor, "What gives with this? My father's not as invincible as you promised. The high inquisitors had a lot more tricks up their sleeves than you ever bothered to tell me about. I'm starting to doubt the blackflame will do much good against this Crusade."

The heresiarch ignores her doubts and says, "Little combat tricks are nothing compared to the true power of the blackflame. Behold!"

With a grandiose wave of his hand, the heresiarch summons undead reinforcements. Out of the forest charge hundreds—nay, rather thousands—of undead animals, big and small; woolly mammoths, cave bears, saber-toothed tigers, moose, deer, opossums, rabbits, squirrels, chipmunks, field mice, and garden snakes.

The stampede of undead animals crashes into the Crusader front lines like gusts of hurricane winds—it flattens them, but does not completely destroy them. The Crusaders desperately attack the undead animals only to find themselves gored, clawed, bitten, gnawed, trampled, and butted by that monstrous fury.

The valiant soldiers hack the undead animals to pieces, but only those appendages severed by silver blades stay severed. Those animals attacked by steel recompose themselves into strange new horrors.

The duke's son, Sir William Pinne the Younger, bravely chops the antlers off an undead antelope lunging toward him. At that moment, a scalped jackrabbit hops by and attaches the antlers to its own head. The undead jackalope harries the Crusaders with such speed and precision with its antlers that it leaves a trail of death and destruction in its wake.

The battlesages in the duke's employ conjure up ensorcelled tornadoes with their wind and water source stones to vacuum up the monsters while the battlemages whip around their magica wands uttering every manner of incomprehensible magic incantations to locomutate the monsters away from the battlefield. But the vast number of undead animals overwhelms their endurance, and soon the front lines of Crusaders are put to flight in a mad panic.

Only the three orders of military monks keep their calm as they strive to devise a tactic to clear these abominations of nature away. The Knights Templar are renowned for their prowess with weapons and use blessed maces and silver swords combined with brute force to break the forward momentum of the monstrous onslaught. True to their untarnished military fame, the Templars follow Brother Jack de Molay into the jaws of hell and pass through unharmed.

The Knights Hospitaller, the pious warrior monks of compassion, add prayers and holy invocations to their attack. They protect not only the Crusaders but also—and especially—the innocent, unarmed wood elf refugees. Though bound by their vows to obey the high inquisitor, they conscientiously object to war crimes. Peace and healing follow wherever they go.

For all the hard work and the valuable tactical achievements of the other military orders, it is the Knights Paladin who save the day. Their temperate lifestyle allows them to heroically wade their way into the worst of the fighting. Armed with prayer and fasting according to the Lord's command, they burst through the festering horde of monsters with righteous fury in their eyes.

The human Paladins ride warhorses, the dwarf Paladins ride war donkeys, and the gnome Paladins ride war ponies. They all couch their holy lances and hone in on the largest and most ferocious monsters before them. When their lances break, they pull out holy water and blessed crucifixes, silver blades and relic-filled maces, staves carved with saints' effigies, and shields painted with icons.

Though surrounded by unnatural beasts that outnumber them a hundred to one, they cast themselves into the fray fearlessly. Still, the odds are so dismal that it would take a miracle for them to succeed—and yet, somehow, these holy warriors dish out just such miracles with sugar and spice.

After an hour of brave strokes, fervent prayers, and mighty miracles, they demolish and scatter the frenzied undead before them. Body part after body part, slabs of meat, dismembered limbs, splattered organs, gristle, and bone twitch and ooze across the forest floor—a horrid sight but a threat no more.

Having retreated back to their camp, the bloodied Crusaders stand together, huddling against each other and trembling like children under a blanket having just come inside after being caught in a thunderstorm.

The duke of Philadelphia can almost hear all the coins tumbling out of his coffers while picturing for himself a protracted siege. He hopes they can give it one last hurrah and says, "We still have the element of surprise! If we press our advantage—"

"Whoa, whoa, whoa!" interrupts Brother Radisson, the Commander-elect of the Knights Hospitaller. "The elves have been preparing for this attack long before you even summoned us. There is no surprise here and we have no advantage—we are getting picked off like mosquitoes in a flock of bats . . . uh-oh!"

"What?"

The Elect Radisson points to the skies. "Holy bat guano! Look up there!"

Along the edge of Thor's Base, Vampire Kibbler leads the other notables and high elf leaders whom he has forced to undergo transmogrification into the undead state. Among their ranks is the enthralled revenant Gandorf Mithranderson, the unwilling but subservient Major Leagues Vampire. Wearing long, black capes as a sort of primitive parachute, they throw themselves off Thor's Base one after another.

Riding next to Duke William Pinne of Philadelphia, the rogue adventurer Ariel—whose real name is Lady Philippa, the duke's daughter—sees their black capes flutter as they come flying down and turns to the Hospitaller knight. "Look up there! Are they sending undead bats to attack us? They look too big to be ordinary bats—they're like bat . . . men."

The Elect Radisson follows her finger and the undead umpires come quickly into view. "Holy Adam laid to rest west of paradise! Those aren't bats; they've got more undead elf vampires!"

The first to crash to the ground, Vampire Kibbler's flattened body billows out and upward like a tube man sky dancer at a luxury car dealership. Likewise, as if reinflated by the electric fans of their own willpower, the other sky-fallen vampires uncrumple their limbs to a macabre rhythm.

"Look! They're dancing!" The Crusaders stand around mesmerized, watching the pulverized vampires wriggle and churn as if featured artists in some horrific ballet. No sooner do they recompose themselves than the vampires smash, rip, fling, and batter the Crusaders with no mercy. They spin them around, pound them down, and toss them up in the air like a pizza man kneading thin-crust pizza dough.

Suddenly Ariel, *alias* Lady Philippa, calls up her party of adventurers. Monsignor Oscar Meyer charges to the rescue. His war mallet comes down with such force that it knocks one vampire's right arm clean out of its shoulder socket. He then chants a Turn Undead prayer that immediately drains the battle frenzy out of another vampire.

Ariel wedges herself between two vampires and severs a left arm off the first and a right arm off the second with her silver knives. Before the one-armed vampires can retaliate, Willis chops off the legs of the first with his longsword while Whoopee taps his magic wand on the second's knees to make them disappear, humming out his magic words, "Ekki tang zoo boing!"

Hard behind Ariel's party rides a detachment of Knights Paladin. They are armed with clay bombs filled with holy water, exorcism oils, and blessed salts. They foist these sacred petards on the vampires and neutralize their ferocity.

Even from afar, Vampire Kibbler senses the strength of this group's holiness. His bloodlust has not been slaked, but he knows that another assault by the Knights Paladin will annihilate his undead thralls.

He simply does not have enough vampires to put up a fight against such a holy foe. Far too few elves volunteered to undergo transmogrification. He uses the Black Tongue of Caldor to order his thralls to retreat from the battle.

Next time, he will return with a massive undead elf army. It will take time, patience, and most of all, a brilliant lie to convince enough high elves in the power structure to force transmogrification upon the citizens of Shentalpee City whether their private, individual consciences agree to it or not.

Not far away, Vampire Gandorf seethes with loathing as he watches Vampire Kibbler run away. His heart burns to take revenge for his death and political demise but his mind allows him no respite except to obey Vampire Kibbler's commands. Vampire Gandorf retreats and the other vampires follow close behind.

Seeing the vampires retreating, Ariel shouts to the surviving Crusaders, "Fall back to the camps!"

They unanimously follow her.

Scene 2: The Odyssey Policy

Shentalpee City on Tuscoraura Mountain
Saturn's Day Nones. Afternoon, 24th of June, 1284
Nativity of Saint John the Baptist
(Christian Midsummer)

"Amhirst!" shouts the little cardinal as he storms into the baron's camp. "Your little pouting session will come to an end right this instant. We're languishing here and the Duke of Philadelphia doesn't have enough troops left to mount a proper assault. Those undead monsters and vampires crippled his army. This is the last time I'm going to say this. You'd better put your troops in the field or I'll excommunicate your army and release them from their feudal vows to serve you."

"Tut, tut, Your Eminence," replies Amhirst, sipping his wine by the campfire. "If the rest of Vinland does not hear about it, your excommunication won't bother my career aspirations much. You are deep in enemy territory, surrounded by elves and cultists who are hell-bent to reap vengeance upon you; I wouldn't give you one chance in thirty to make it out of here alive.

"In my business as a successful military leader, one in thirty makes for some very shabby odds and in war, the only bookie is the grim reaper. The last I heard, he doesn't extend credit to anyone, not even clerics. What this Crusade needs is coordination. Appointing a single leader as, say, crowned viceroy of Vinland, might streamline the chain of command, allow us to drive home the final punch—the coup de grâce, as the defeated Frankish viceroy of Vinland would say."

Piccolo Cardinal Orsini stomps his feet and pouts. "Okay, okay already! I get your point. It was all just a big misunderstanding. The capture of the Frankish viceroy of Vinland does grant you a claim to his title, but my advisors have been telling me that the man you captured is not the viceroy, merely an innocent, poor old man who happens to resemble Lord Samuel de Champlane. After a brief interview to verify his identity, I will crown you Aenglish viceroy of Vinland. Please bring the prisoner forward."

The baron of Amhirst nods to Sir Sean Madigan, who approaches him and whispers into his ear.

Amhirst turns red with anger and humiliation. He calms himself and announces, "It seems the viceroy is indisposed at the moment. Could we resume this meeting at another time?"

"If you are afraid your prisoner will not pass the test, I must declare your claim to right of conquest null and void. The duke of Philadelphia, however, has proposed a compromise. Even though he is the highest-ranking noble in Vinland and most deserving of supreme command, whichever of you two lords is first to have his troops seize one of the elf tree-lofted platforms shall be named governor-general. Agreed?"

Barely able to hide his outrage, Amhirst walks out of the tent. Sir Sean, seeing through the ploy and not wanting to get squeezed out, quickly says, "We agree."

Sir Sean then races out of the tent to catch up with the baron and confesses, "My lord, I took the liberty to speak on your behalf and told the cardinal we agree. He obviously wants to offer the title to the duke of Philadelphia even though it rightly belongs to you. That goes without saying, but I thought—"

Struggling to control his anger, Amhirst snaps, "You thought wrong, Sir Sean. As a matter of fact, we are all going about this wrong. All wrong."

Sir Sean trembles a little as he asks, "What do you mean, my lord?"

Amhirst stops and looks Sir Sean fiercely in the eye and says, "Do you know how I translate *velle est posse*?"

Sir Sean does not want to upstage the baron right now but he does not want to look dumb either. He says tentatively, "Something like 'where there's a will, there's a way,' my lord."

Amhirst sneers and says, "In your world that would be a good translation. In my world, a better translation would be, 'when someone gets in your way, find out which one of his relatives is most eager to read his will.' I assure you, every powerful man has at least one close family member who wants him dead."

"But the cardinal's brothers are already—"

As they walk, Amhirst sees Sir Robert Roger directing his troops in building stockade walls and storms up to him. "Sir Robert Roger! How could you lose my most valuable prisoner?"

Sir Robert Roger looks at him, befuddled. "My lord, you did not entrust the viceroy to my custody, if that is whom you are referring to."

"Someone was sneaking around our camp and took him away. You're supposed to detect intruders. That's what I pay you big dollars for! At the crucial moment, you come up empty-handed!"

Benjamin Frankelyn walks up boldly. "Excuse me, my lord, but we're not entirely empty-handed at the moment." Benjamin Frankelyn bows with great deference, attempting to soothe the wrath of his patron.

"You will find that the missing viceroy is just one of many schemes the Cardinals Orsini have been playing on you. After sniffing around the right places, I found out Piccolo Cardinal Orsini himself sent an agent to abduct the Frankish viceroy from your custody.

"It seems the high inquisitors promised the duke of Philadelphia appointment as crown governor-general of Vinland as well. You should have listened to my advice and accepted the appointment when we first got back from Salim. Now we're back to square one, dancing around while the Inquisition chuckles. The cardinal arranged this whole charade about demanding to see the Frankish viceroy in person, knowing full well you did not have him."

Sir Sean Madigan immediately backs him up, saying, "You see, my lord! It's nothing but a childish ploy to get both you and the duke of Philadelphia strung along on this Crusade without fulfilling any promises to either of you."

Amhirst glares at Benjamin Frankelyn and says, "So now you're going to tell me that your trusted fellow adventurer Ariel—or should I say Lady Philippa Pinne, the blasted duke's own daughter—helped the Frankish viceroy escape even though I paid her a small fortune to retain her services because she's really been working for her father all along!"

Frankelyn responds confidently, "Lady Philippa's integrity is irreproachable, my lord. You hired her to deliver the Sword of Layban to the Holy Office of the Inquisition and she completed that quest admirably. Not even her father knows that she carried out this quest for you. Still, I assure you she was not assigned the quest to rescue the viceroy for the cardinal."

"What makes you so sure?"

Benjamin Frankelyn polishes his fingernails on his tunic after a quick breath and says, "I happen to have stumbled across the identity of the adventurer who did it; also a young woman, like Lady Philippa, and also a frankelyn like myself, but in service to the Ottowan Lord, Sagamore Pontiak."

Skeptical about such a lucky find, Amhirst folds his arms and asks, "So where is the viceroy now?"

Benjamin Frankelyn raises his eyebrows as if deeply sympathetic to the baron's plight. "Alas, could it not be more obvious? The viceroy is resting in the cardinal's tent as we speak."

"Sir Robert Roger!" Amhirst snaps. "I want you to get that viceroy back for me. Do whatever you have to."

Benjamin Frankelyn clears his throat and raises a hand. "A word of caution, my lord. You have already introduced Sir Robert Roger to all the lords of this Crusade as a trusted member of your retinue. If he is caught, or even noticed, while engaged in this quest, it could prove disastrous to all your ambitions."

"So how do you suggest I get the Frankish viceroy back from the cardinal?"

Frankelyn raises his eyebrows. "Forget the Frankish viceroy and forget the Aenglish viceroyship. It was never on the table to begin with. King Eddard's priority is to reassert his authority in Vinland, as you discovered when you met his coroner at Ithica. He has no interest whatsoever in sharing royal prerogatives with a viceroy in Vinland. None. You will only make him your enemy if you press this issue any further.

"Look at the whole landscape with a level head, my lord. The Church was furious with kindhearted Uncle

Sam because he wasn't tough enough with the blackflame heretics. The whole reason they agreed to let King Eddard conduct his war against fellow Christians on Vinland's soil was that Uncle Sam was using his position as Frankish viceroy to block the Inquisition from executing heretics.

"The pope does not want a noble who can stymie his orders here or anywhere else in the world. There will be no viceroy of Vinland. Never again. Period."

Amhirst cannot argue with Frankelyn's logic but does not like the picture he is painting. He asks, "So what do you suggest I do instead?"

"Take up their offer to be Aenglish governor-general. I have certain information that both King Eddard and Pope Martin have approved the title since it's not hereditary and it doesn't include any royal privileges. A governor-general has the power to enforce the Crown's wishes, but can be removed instantly by the king's decree. There *will* be an Aenglish governor-general and, with all due respect, unless you act quickly, it won't be you."

Welling up with anger once again, Amhirst says, "Isn't it perfectly obvious that the duke of Philadelphia has a much larger and better-equipped army than I do? He got decimated on his first try. We don't stand a chance of seizing those elven platforms. The whole offer is a ploy to deliver the title to him instead of me."

Benjamin Frankelyn's natural charisma works wonders at calming the baron back down when he says, "Indeed, it *is* perfectly obvious! But why not beat the duke and the cardinals at their own game? All you have to do is be the first one to reach the top of one of the tree-lofted elf platforms."

"Impossible."

"As the Good Book says, all things are possible with God—and I might add, with a little ingenuity. It just so happens that in my adventures, I stumbled across a certain young elve who is the daughter of the leader of the Tuscoraura elves. Send me on a quest to negotiate with her and I am sure we could work out a winning solution to the cardinals' challenge.

"However, my one condition is that you grant me full authority to speak in your name. If I have to run back and forth to get your approval for every stage of the negotiations, it won't work."

Amhirst's reluctance grows softer—but not too soft. He says, "My word is my honor. If you bind me to a treaty in my name, I will honor it. If, however, the treaty costs me too much, you will pay the difference with your head. Are you willing to bet your life that this arrangement will win me the title of governor-general without promising away more than it's worth?"

"Indeed I am!"

Amhirst is not sure how he came around to trusting Benjamin Frankelyn so completely but he says, "You have full authority to speak in my name. Sir Robert Roger, get our frankelyn whatever he needs."

"Thank you, my lord. You might as well start appointing your new gubernatorial staff now. The next time you see me, Vinland will be yours."

Bonus Scene A: Three Elves and a Druid

Betzy Rose Mansion, Shentalpee City
Sun Day Prime. Early Morning, 2nd of July, 1284
Feast of Saint Swithun

Boarded up in her mansion as both prisoner and refugee, Dungaree Jeanne has been trying to find a diplomatic solution to this ordeal, all the while dealing with Zena's bitterness toward Enganyon and his desperate grasping at some hope for survival.

While the three elves scrounge around for a decent breakfast, Johnny Appleseed is still asleep in the guest room. Madame Dungaree had planned to convert that room back into an elf-sized living quarters for Lynx to move into as her steward but after he died, she could not bring herself to make any changes to the room. At least Buttercup washed the linens while she was here.

The trapped elves fidget in an awkward silence around the breakfast table—not because they have nothing to say, but because they have so much that needs to be said that they do not know where to begin.

Enganyon, used to being doted upon, cannot comprehend why they do not begin the day talking about him, at least to offer him their sympathies on the loss of his father. Zena finds herself incapable of such courtesies and Dungaree Jeanne is too busy.

A huge thump on the door jolts them from their thoughts and Enganyon is the first to voice his fears. "They're coming! Madame Dungaree, let's wake up Reverend Appleseed right away. We need to wake up him up now so he can locomutate us out of here before they break down the doors!"

Madame Dungaree tries to keep a calm head. "Captain Enganyon, it was nothing more than a bird crashing into the shutters."

Sensing his panic and faintheartedness, Zena decides it is time to resume hostilities with Enganyon. "Frankly, Mother, few eventualities would please me more than never having to look at Monsieur Enganyon again for the rest of my life. In fact, I will specifically ask the good reverend to direct our magica trails away from each other."

Enganyon defends himself in Runic as if to distance himself from emotion. "Mademoiselle Zena, I understand that from all appearances, thou feelest that thou hast been treated rudely, but I assure thee that there is an explanation. Right now it is not the best time to go into it with the loss of my father and our state of siege and thy changeable moods—"

"My changeable moods!?" shouts Zena in Runic, itching for a fight. "Hast thou ever considered that I am merely reacting to the drastic alterations in thine own behavior? It is as if I were speaking to a completely different elf every time I see thee!"

"Mademoiselle Zena, if thou must harry me so, then I can only state in my defense that I have had to pretend to be a different person every day to survive in this corrupt colony. Shentalpee City was once known as the sparkling colony, the Venice of the Skies. Now, darkness and danger have wrapped themselves all around it like a mummifying shroud. Once we leave this bedeviled colony, thou shalt discover that the real me loves thee ardently and permanently."

Dungaree Jeanne questions him in Runic, "Why art thou so eager to quit Shentalpee City? Where is thy courage, Captain Enganyon? Moments before the election, thou sworest that thou wouldst stay here and fight to the end."

Enganyon fiddles with words to make sense of his cowardice. "I so firmly believed in the good sense of the voters that I never imagined myself in any position other than that of the duly elected umpire-in-chief . . .I mean . . . I thought for sure—"

Angry eyes poke him like red-hot irons. Dungaree Jeanne gloats in the uncomfortable truths Enganyon is unwittingly exposing, but Zena's fury and indignation mount with each word.

Realizing he is only making matters worse, Enganyon slurps his eyeballs back deeper into his skull, like a turtle retreating into its shell. A few blinks later, he summons the old, cocky self to help him and says in Eldric, "What I'm really saying is that I meant for Mademoiselle Zena to win the election all along. My dream was never more than to be a faithful, supportive husband to you, my beloved, as the mademoiselle Umpire-in-Chief of Shentalpee City, and I felt certain that you would be the one—"

Zena, all red in the face, bares her teeth and says in Eldric, "—and if not, you figured you could always fall back on Florenz, except for the fact that you already tried to overthrow her and she's not taking it too well. Now you want to scamper out of here like a mouse when the pantry door opens."

"No, no, no!" Enganyon claws through his long, flowing, blond hair with his fingernails and moans in Eldric, "Shentalpee City is just no fun anymore. I'm not a coward, I just don't want to live in the dark all the time, hiding from people who want to destroy my family and force me to pretend to be someone I'm really not."

With long, radiant lashes, Dungaree Jeanne bats her eyes and says with profound conviction in Runic, "Tuscoraura Mountain has indeed become a dangerous place, and in it there are many dark places. But still there is much that is bright and beautiful, and I want Shentalpee City the way our ancestors dreamed of. I, for my part, believe that standing firm and being the real me is the only way to make that happen. Thou ought to try it for a change."

All at once, Zena and Enganyon start yelling over each other's voices, hurling accusations, recriminations, justifications, and exculpations. Their ruckus stirs Johnny Appleseed. His bushy, gray eyebrows wiggle and he takes a deep breath. It's not until they all quiet down that he abruptly opens his eyes.

They all stare at each other for a few moments until Johnny Appleseed gives them all a big smile and says in Aenglish, "God bless you all for visiting me in my illness. I'm feeling much better now."

Dungaree Jeanne pulls out the magica leaves Mage Nittany gave to Zena and tells him in Aenglish, "Florenz has surrounded Betzy Rose Mansion with undead warriors, scouts from the Ivy League, and sharpshooters from the Justiciar League. The only way to escape is locomutation with these magica leaves."

She hands the pouch to Johnny Appleseed. He opens it as they look on eagerly. With the simplicity and the calm demeanor of a curious child, he takes out a pinch of magica leaves, crumples them, pulls them, and sticks them back in. Then he pronounces, "Sorry to disappoint, but the leaves are all dried out."

"What's he saying?" asks Enganyon in Eldric.

Dungaree Jeanne ignores him and asks in Aenglish, "You mean it won't work?"

Johnny Appleseed answers, "It means that this stuff in here is only enough to locomutate one elf far enough to get away from here safely. I have my own stash and I could divide it among two of you, but unless I go with you, there is no telling where you'd end up. Your most likely terminus would be the Crusader camp, seeing as how they got so many magicultors down there." He reaches over and puts the tin pot back on his head and comments, "As we say in Kentikie, out of the frying pan and into the fire."

Dungaree Jeanne announces in Aenglish, "Then there can be no question about it. You must take Mademoiselle Zena to safety." She then switches to Eldric and says, "New plan, Captain Enganyon. Reverend Appleseed can only take one elf with him. The rest of us will hold out here and find a way to help the Crusaders free Shentalpee City from the tyrannical grip of Florenz."

Enganyon looks at Dungaree Jeanne as if she has just stabbed him. "But, Madame Dungaree, you can't seriously mean . . . I mean . . . it almost sounded like you were suggesting that we . . . you and I . . . stay here and help overthrow our own government while Zena escapes to safety with Reverend Appleseed."

Dungaree Jeanne comments, "Captain Enganyon, in general, you have keen political instincts, but your need to state the obvious is a serious liability."

Enganyon shakes his head and says in Eldric, "But, but you're basically planning to fight to the death!"

"Again, Captain, obvious."

Enganyon's courage shrivels at the implication and he screams, "No! I'm too young to die!"

Zena looks at him and says coolly, "Ah-ha! Now there's the real Enganyon! I've been waiting so long to finally meet you without one of the many masks you feel obliged to wear."

Without another word, Enganyon gets up and leaves the room.

With sad eyebrows, Dungaree Jeanne sighs and pronounces solemnly her verdict on him in Runic, "The great clan of Rashbold has fallen low. Their ancestors were so brave that some called them rash, while others called them bold. They were so proud of their famed courage that they combined both labels into their clan name. They have no worthy scion to carry on the tradition of risking everything for the sake of saving the colony. Mademoiselle Zena, one hundred fifty feet below us enemies surround our colony, hoping to plunder our wealth, but our own duly elected umpire-in-chief hopes to enslave all the fire elves on Tuscoraura Mountain.

"The future of Shentalpee City now depends on you. Go with Reverend Appleseed. Learn from him. Perhaps someday, you will return to Tuscoraura Mountain with the wisdom and skills to restore Shentalpee City to its former greatness."

Standing up and saluting her mother with the respect due to her as dean of the League of Nations, Zena replies in Aenglish so Johnny Appleseed can understand her, "Yes, Madame Dean of the League of Nations, I am ready."

He gives her the dried leaves to chew and meditates, concentrating his will on the layout of the earth and mountains and forests and trees around them. At long last he looks up at her and says the magic word, "Mellon!"

In the blink of an eye, they are gone.

Dungaree Jeanne stares at the empty space where her daughter was for a while with sadness in her heart, fearing she might never see her daughter again. From day one after her birth, Zena has always been a high-maintenance elfling but of all the creatures to walk the face of the earth, Dungaree Jeanne has always loved her the most. Zena's departure with Johnny Appleseed gives Dungaree Jeanne, for the first time in her life, the feeling that the future will be all right.

"Ahem!"

"Ahhhh!" Dungaree Jeanne is startled by the sudden intrusion.

Enganyon announces in Runic, "Madame Dungaree, I have resolved to surrender myself to the authorities and plead for clemency. I shall wave this white flag out the front window and request a parley with the mademoiselle Umpire-in-Chief-elect."

"Monsieur Enganyon, that's not a white flag! That's my best quality red-and-white striped guest bedsheet!"

"If I hold out a dirty old dishrag, what do you think my chances of obtaining a favorable audience with Mademoiselle Florenz will be?"

Getting up, Dungaree Jeanne wipes the tear from her eye and grabs the striped sheet from him. "Okay, okay. If we're going to demand a parley, we might as well do it in style. Go grab the starry blue pillowcase from the linen closet and meet me in my sewing room. We are not going to surrender, we are going to wave the flag of freedom!"

A blurry light pierces the darkness. When it all comes into focus, Zena and Johnny Appleseed find themselves sitting next to a stream running down a gentle hill in a wide-open meadow. Johnny Appleseed stands up and laughs, "Well how about that? It worked! I reckon we are far enough from the fighting to stroll off to make it all the way to Lake Eerie."

Zena rubs her eyes and says in Aenglish, "I no think we are too far. This is marchlands. Shentalpee City is that way." She points off east, the housetops of lofted buildings still faintly visible through the distant foliage.

Johnny Appleseed follows her finger and says, "At least we're sure where we are. The first magica grove we ought to be visiting is that-a-ways across the stream. If we walk quick, it'll only take us twelve days."

Zena stops abruptly and says, "Wait! We can't just walk off! We have no food, no blankets, no waterskins."

Johnny Appleseed points to the stream and says, "It's summer—we don't need blankets. We don't need waterskins either. Just take a sip from the river."

"No good. We get thirsty again after little hours."

"The Lord will show us another place to drink."

"We get hungry too."

"The Lord will provide us with food as well. Just place your trust in him. In God we trust. That's what I always say, and it works."

Zena buries her face in her hands. "You not understand. We not go far without food, water, and stay warm."

Johnny Appleseed looks at her seriously and says, "Mademoiselle Zena, I've walked across Vinland from sea to shiny sea with no walking stick and no traveling bag, no bread and no waterskins. I've got no sandals on my feet and never carry a second tunic, just like the good Lord tells us. If you want to be a good magicultor, the first lesson you've got to learn is how to live off the bounty of Mother Nature."

Zena takes in his words for a moment, speechless. She sniffs and starts wading into the stream. "Fine. We go as you say. No food, no water but this." With that, she scoops up some water with her hand to drink, but Johnny Appleseed just puts his face to the surface and laps it up with his tongue.

She looks at him with one eyebrow raised and asks, "Why you do that?"

He says, "In the Bible, the Lord told Gideon that only the men who lap up the water from the stream like a dog would be chosen to serve in the Lord's army and give him glory."

She shrugs and keeps going. No sooner do they cross over the stream than Johnny Appleseed suddenly turns around and grabs Zena's arm, saying, "There! He's there, wearing a white robe!"

Zena looks at him, confused. "Who?"

"Lynx—standing right there! Don't you see him?"

"No."

Johnny Appleseed says in Aenglish, "He's saying something like 'quo vadis.' Does that mean anything in Eldritch?"

Zena replies, "In Latin it means 'Where are you going?' but why Lynx says that I do not know."

Johnny Appleseed points again. "They tell an old story about Saint Peter. Emperor Nero had just started a fierce persecution against the early Christians, and

Peter abandoned his flock in Roma to save his life. On the road outside of Roma, the Lord Jesus asked Peter where he was going. That was enough to remind him that the people of Roma needed a shepherd to encourage them, not a ruler to tell them what to do and abandon them in their hour of need."

Zena sighs, "But what can we do?"

Johnny Appleseed looks up as if listening for a while and says, "Lynx wants us to take the Sword of Layban back from Florenz. He says it will point the way to something of great importance for the future of Vinland."

"Take it from Mademoiselle Florenz? Impossible! We are just two clayborn with no power."

"Mademoiselle Zena, if I have learned anything in my long years of life it is that when God asks us to do something, he will provide the means. Great deeds are accomplished with his strength, not our own. In God we trust."

Zena's face turns red; not a cute, rosy blush shade but an angry, vindictive sort of crimson. "But why? They kill us, you know? I try to help elves of Tuscoraura Mountain and they only vote me off show. It is no good to help elves. They only treat you bad in return for good you do."

Johnny Appleseed looks at her seriously and says, "Do you remember how Jonah did not want God to forgive the Ninevites? He could only see and feel his petty grievances against them. He forgot to see that forgiveness makes the world go round, makes it grow better and more beautiful. Indeed, there is some good in this world, Mademoiselle Zena, and it's worth fighting for."

"God, that sounds so corny!"

He slaps her across the cheek and scolds her. "That's for blasphemy! The quest for the Sword of Layban is not poetry. This is a race against evil! If the Sword of Layban is controlled by the Blackflame Cult, the armies of darkness will march all over the face of the Earth! Do you understand me?"

Visibly angry, she shakes her finger at him and says, "Why you obsess about Sword of Layban? So what if it is evil? Good and evil are always part of life. You say you fight, but you know you never win. I not understand it. Never! And not my father."

He looks at her and says, "Umpire Gandorf sacrificed his life to save Shentalpee City."

Zena's face twists with anger. "Umpire Gandorf betrayed my father. Why do I care if he go dead?"

Johnny Appleseed replies, "Umpire Gandorf *is* your father. Your mother wanted to marry him but Umpire Gandorf's family would not allow him to marry a wood elf. Umpire Gandorf helped your mother find a unicorn so she could become a high elve but even after she attained the rank of high elve, his family refused. They pressured her to forget Umpire Gandorf and marry someone else instead.

"When your mother's husband found out that you were really Umpire Gandorf's daughter and not his, he challenged Umpire Gandorf to a duel. Umpire Gandorf stood no chance against him in a fair fight, so he took the only path he could see for his own survival and cheated by paying your own father's friends to turn against him. So yes, he betrayed the man you knew as your father, but Umpire Gandorf indeed is your father."

"No!! Lies! All lies!"

Johnny Appleseed puts his arm around her as she weeps uncontrollably from the shock of the news. "Your mother asked me to tell you the truth when I thought you would be ready to hear it. Perhaps you are not yet ready to hear it, but we have no more time to waste fostering delusions.

"Florenz has used the Sword of Layban to enthrall many innocent people to her will in an undead state. Her next victim will almost surely be Umpire Gandorf. I firmly believe Lynx is trying to tell us that God has called us—you and me—to take a stand and rescue them from a fate worse than death."

"What if we suffer this fate worse than death too?"

Johnny Appleseed replies, "The consequences of failure are indeed calamitous for us as well, but it's the right thing to do. Besides, danger is overrated anyway. As we say in Kentikie, I'll take my chances."

Zena hears him out and finds the strength to lay down her life for her friends somewhere deep inside her. "Then as they say in Latin, *alea jacta est.*"

"What does that mean?"

Zena faces him and says, "We probably gonna die but what the heck."

Scene 3: The Vandsee Conference

Vandsee Estates, Shentalpee City on Tuscoraura Mountain
Moon Day Nones. Afternoon, 3rd of July, 1284
Morrow of Saint Swithun

Back up on Shentalpee City, umpire-in-chief-elect Florenz Kibblersdottir has invited the deans of the military leagues to her mansion on Vandsee Estates. She addresses them with these words: "Esteemed deans, as you know all too well, we have not been able to drive the Crusade off our lands as quickly and as easily as you originally thought. I have spent the last few days planning the final solution."

Dean Norwall, head of the League of Licornes, interjects, "With your permission, Mademoiselle Umpire-in-Chief-elect, the League of Licornes would like to participate in the final assault against the Crusaders, even if we have to fight dismounted. We believe that our unflagging—"

Florenz cuts her off. "There will be no final assault."

"But you just said—"

"I just said that I have finished planning the final solution to the Crusade, not the final assault against it."

"Excuse me, Mademoiselle Umpire-in-Chief-elect," says Dean Kallel, head of the Justiciar League. "We must attack. Ever since the bankruptcy of the Kibbler workshops, our economy has teetered on the brink of ruin. Our treasury cannot endure the financial burden of a protracted siege! It is better to expend a few extra lives and reduce the surplus population than to have our standard of living collapse."

Florenz chews her nails while the dean talks. When she is done, she spits out the distal edges. "This is why the high elves elected me umpire-in-chief. It seems everyone else fails to see the obvious. The Crusaders are not attacking us because they know *we* will win if they do. We are not attacking them because we know *they* will win if we do. If we do nothing, it comes down to whoever runs out of resources first. High elves are heavy consumers, and the wood elf refugees up here are only making it worse. Right now, the Crusade is poised to win the waiting game.

"As you so clumsily put it, Shentalpee City is encumbered with surplus population. Throwing their lives away will certainly stretch out our supplies a lot longer, but your reports all agree that ridding our city of enough population to win the waiting game would leave us with too few defenders to repulse an assault."

Dean Halvard, head of the Ivy League, points out, "And even if we do defeat the crusading army below us today, they'd just send another one in a few months' time. Is it really worth—"

Florenz cuts in. "As I was about to say before you so rudely interrupted me, I've just made a deal that will keep the Crusaders out of here forever."

She opens the door and behold! Benjamin Frankelyn steps out and delivers an elaborate bow to salute the shocked elf military leaders.

Bonus Scene B: Diomedes in the Dark

Shentalpee City on Tuscoraura Mountain
Moon Day Compline. Night, 3rd of July, 1284
Morrow of Saint Swithun

Smeared with camouflage face paints and huddled behind a thicket of brush, Zena surveys the Crusader camp in the pale moonlight. She whispers her observations out in broken Aenglish to Johnny Appleseed with a conspiratorial tone. "They cut down all trees and bushes around camp. Humans think they can stop elves to sneak up at night."

Johnny Appleseed cautions her, "Begging your pardon, Mademoiselle Zena, but it's too dangerous to just waltz in there. We need a better plan."

"Little elves sing song, 'Elves are stealthy made out of jelly. Humans are cloddish made out of hogshish.'"

Appleseed fails to see the tactical significance in her little jingle. "Playground taunts aren't going to save your life when they catch you and put your head on a chopping block."

The camp is densely packed with Crusaders, and a good many of them are too jittery or too rambunctious to sleep. Zena surveys the area until she sees one knight sleeping outside his tent clad in the skin of a gray wolf, while on his head he has set a cap of ferret skin. He lies upon the skin of an ox, with a piece of fine carpet under his head. Four squires snooze and snore around him using their shields as pillows.

The squires have planted his lances upright with the rear spikes driven into the ground. They have each stacked their mail armor on the ground in orderly rows. Each squire keeps the warhorse under his charge tethered right next to him.

Zena recognizes the knight as none other than Sir Dolon of Meadville, the famous herald—a man rich in gold and silver. Sir Dolon won fame for himself as a good runner, taking many ribbons and trophies in foot races at the various fairs and tournaments that a merchant's daughter such as herself is wont to attend growing up. Sir Dolon's father, the baron of Meadville, befriended the nearby Delawaerr leader, Chief Custaloga, thanks to the efforts of a prosperous merchant from the Island of Rhodes, Nathaniel Green, whose son of the same name later became the famous general we all know and love.

Sir Dolon is the only son among five sisters and has made his father proud with his achievements. Such is the man Zena intends to kill and use his tent as a base of operations to spread death and destruction among the Crusaders attacking her homeland this night.

When Zena approaches, she hears voices inside the tent. One human is telling another of a dream he had. "In my dream, a cake of gingerbread tumbled into the tent of the high inquisitor. The gingerbread man struck it so hard that it fell over. The whole pavilion turned upside down and collapsed on the cardinal's head."

Zena takes this as a sure sign of her impending victory and says to Johnny Appleseed in Aenglish, "You hear? The stars say we bring down cardinal."

In the dark, it takes her a moment to realize that Appleseed is gone. Instead, a female human rogue holds a dagger to her throat and hisses, "One false move, missy, and you're a goner."

Zena holds up her hands and wants to demand a fair trial but she is not sure how to say that in Aenglish. She settles on a simpler demand, "Take me to your leader."

The human rogue leads her out and Zena sees Johnny Appleseed restrained by a beefy half-goblin cleric. A white-haired human fighter points a crossbow at her and a dark elf magicultor points his magica wand at her with his right hand, holding a dagger in his left. Zena lifts her hands high up in the air.

The white-haired human says, "Uh-oh, Philippa, you don't think this elve girl is—"

Ariel interrupts, totally exasperated. "Terry, how many times have I told you not to use my real name when we are on quests? My code name is Ariel, all right? How difficult can it be?"

Terry gets defensive. "They wouldn't have known it was your real name if you didn't just tell them that."

"Whatever; it doesn't matter. The *doyen* will probably have them all executed anyway."

Terry mutters, "You just gave away the name of our leader!"

Ariel groans, "It's not her name, it's her title. Let's just get these punks out of here."

Ariel's party of adventurers leads them out of the camp past the killing fields where the bodies of dead Crusaders lie scattered among the dismembered remains of the undead animals sent against them. The wind whispers of fear and hate in the places where Christian love has perished beneath the weight of political ambitions and greed.

In the middle of the field, shrouded by the dark of night, a hatch opens from beneath the forest floor leading down into a gnome burrow. Tied up as captives, Zena and Johnny Appleseed walk through the dark, sodden corridors until they reach a dwarven stony vault where several important-looking dignitaries of various races are debating strenuously about the best course of action.

In the center, an elve eventually takes notice of the party of adventurers and bangs her gavel, announcing, "Attention, delegates! Spies have been apprehended sneaking around in the Crusader camp. Prisoners, what do you have to say for yourselves?"

Zena looks up at her, totally confused, and can only bring one word to her lips. "Mom?"

Scene 4: Holy War Mania

Shentalpee City on Tuscoraura Mountain
Tiw's Day Prime. Dawn, 4th of July, 1284
Third of Saint Swithun

As rosy-fingered dawn stretches her arms out at the break of the new day, Sir Robert Roger wakes his rangers from their cozy dorms up on Vandsee Estates, the sycamore platform holding up the Kibbler workshops. Although she trusts Benjamin Frankelyn enough to go along with his plan, Florenz has ordered both bridges leading up to Thor's Base destroyed, just in case the rangers have ideas of their own.

Once the rangers are up and ready, Sir Robert Roger orders his bards, Sir Humbert of Denk and Sir Gilbert Sullivan, to sound their trumpets with the fanfare and pizzazz of an epic, earth-shattering struggle. All the rangers carry empty jars and torches.

He calls out to his rangers, "Look at me and do the same. When I go up to the edge of the platform, do as I do. Shout, 'For the Lord and for Amhirst! God wills it!' Smash your jars on the ground and wave your torches."

The blaring trumpets, the din of crashing clay jars, the whirling of torches, and the wild shouting above rouse the sleeping Crusaders. They come out and climb up on the palisade wall of the camp to spectate.

From below, Sir Sean Madigan, having carefully stationed himself in the middle of the crowd, hypes up the battle with a running commentary: "Oh look! I can't believe it! The Queen's Rangers have made it to the top of one of the elven treetop platforms. And what a battle it is, folks! There goes Sir Robert Roger up against the ropes. Ouch! What a punch! That black-masked elf nearly smacked him over the ledge!

"Here comes Sir Benedict Arnald, his faithful friend, to the rescue. If anyone can teach that heel of an elf a lesson, it's Bonking Benny. The black-masked elf climbs up on the ropes and does a backflip. He flattens Sir Benedict Arnald . . . and that's terrible!

"Wait! I see a comeback brewing like a storm. All those rangers up there are teaming up like superstars!"

Suddenly, Sir Benedict Arnald gets up and bangs his derrière into the oncoming dark-masked elf, knocking him over backwards. Sir Benedict Arnald extends a hand to Sir Robert Roger. He tags him back into the fight.

The Crusaders chant, "Vic-to-ry! Vic-to-ry!"

Meanwhile, high up behind the scenes, Florenz watches the choreographed fight at the edge of the platform next to Benjamin Frankelyn. He hollers, "Oh, look at that suplex finisher! The elves are supposed to pretend to lose by now and there goes your fiancé, hijacking the show!"

Seeing Enganyon's stunning performance, Florenz cannot help but root for him. "Take that!"

With one giant, acrofatic [sic] leap, the ponderous ranger, Sir Febold Feboldson, squashes Enganyon, face to the mat. Cheers rise up from the Crusader camp below. As far as they are concerned, the match is a total and complete victory for the rangers.

Scene 5: A String Quartet

Shentalpee City on Tuscoraura Mountain
Tiw's Day Terce. Morning, 4th of July, 1284
Third of Saint Swithun

Back in the tent of the high inquisitor, Piccolo Cardinal Orsini holds a conference with the duke of Philadelphia and the baron of Amhirst. Despite the apparent victory, the cardinal is displeased and rants, "How did your rangers get up there?"

The baron of Amhirst puts his hands together piously and says, "As it says in the sacred Scriptures, we called upon the Lord, our Rock, and he answered our prayer!"

"We have the holiest clerics in Vinland on our team and our prayers were not answered so dramatically."

Amhirst plays innocent. "Oh, you know how it goes; you get some friends to vouch for you, slip a few coins under the table, drop a few names worth mentioning . . . it smooths the process, even in heaven."

Piccolo Cardinal Orsini leans in and consults with his team and says, "My high-level clerics heard the voice of the Lord, your Rock, and they are saying that the Rock says the Rock has not been mentioned yet! Do not forget that you cannot lie to the Inquisition. We specialize in detecting lies."

"I wouldn't dream of it, Your Eminence! If you want to go into specifics, we had help from a high-ranking elve who was disgruntled with the status quo, blah, blah, blah—I don't need to bore you with the details—"

Piccolo Cardinal Orsini interrupts, "God is in the details, Lord Geoffrey."

"Speaking of details, whatever happened to the . . . you know . . . the way you talked before?"

The high inquisitor is in no mood for chitchat. "What do you mean . . . the way I talked before?"

"'Wascawy wabbit' and all that rot. It's gone."

"If you must know, the tragedy of my brothers' loss spurred me to overcome my speech impediment. Where there's a will, there's a way."

Amhirst whispers loudly as if letting the cardinal in on a special secret, "You're absolutely right, Your Eminence. That is how we are going to capitalize on this victory and bring success to the entire Crusade. Great minds think alike."

"Ha!" laughs the cardinal sarcastically. "Speak for yourself!"

"Trust me, I do, Your Eminence, I do. In fact, I was just telling myself that a promise is a promise, and one long overdue promise is enough to ruin—"

Piccolo Cardinal Orsini stomps his feet. "Okay, okay already! I get your point. You want your reward for completing this quest. My clerical advisors, however, still fear you might have entered into league with some unholy powers to pull this off."

Amhirst sits down and sips the beverage laid out on the table for him, soaking up the moment—he knows he's got the cardinal by the biretta. "In fact, I was going to invite our elve special agent for you to interview."

"I'd prefer to meet no more elves in person. The pain at the loss of my brothers is still too fresh."

"Oh, nothing to worry about there, Your Eminence. I will simply describe her to you. After all, the Holy

Office of the Inquisition knows better than any other human institution how to read the secret thoughts of the clayborn. If I were lying, you would find out in short order, would you not, Your Eminence?"

"Go on. Tell us about this special agent of yours."

"A disgruntled politician. Her name is Zena. She aspired to high office among the fire elves and was betrayed by their current vampire-in-chief. When she's not hell-bent on revenge, she is quite a lovely young elve, and very open to hearing you preach the word of God. Who knows? You might make good Christians out of these pagans. Your common policy on vendetta might help you two get along famously."

The high inquisitor rubs his chin. "Hmmm. *Hell-bent* is a strong term among clerics, but not entirely inaccurate in this case. My inclination is to turn their forest paradise into an inferno. There's a certain poetic justice in destroying Fire Elf City with fire."

Amhirst rubs his chin, mimicking the high inquisitor, and says, "Hmmm, I do see the poetry in that, Your Eminence, but I must warn you that setting it all on fire might not be as productive a strategy as your armchair theologians imagine. I highly recommend having a good conversation with our insider elve. She will tell you the REAL weakness of Fire Elf City. She is hell-bent on revenge—"

Piccolo Cardinal Orsini says, "Could we please stop bending hell so much? Revenge is not as effective a strategy as most people think, and hell does not bend over backwards to help you. It only breaks your back with fruitless desires."

Amhirst comments, "If only your wisdom extended far enough for you to practice what you preach."

Piccolo Cardinal Orsini folds his arms and curls his bottom lip. "When it comes to clerics, it's a totally different issue. 'Vengeance is mine,' sayeth the Lord, 'and I will repay them in due time, that their foot may slide. The day of destruction is at hand, and the time makes haste to come.' As the high inquisitor, it's my business to right the wrongs inflicted against the Lord."

"Forgive me for being such a paltry theologian—being such a successful war leader leaves me less time for books than I would hope. But I might propose the thesis that God is quite capable of handling all that vengeance stuff for himself."

Piccolo Cardinal Orsini is irritated. "You might as well nail ninety-five such theses to a door and see how far that gets you. Regardless, let us get back to more pressing issues. His Lordship, the duke of Philadelphia here, has his dwarves ready to set up weapons of mass destruction to bombard fire and doom upon the entire—"

"Tut, tut, tut," interrupts Amhirst. "We still haven't resolved the matter of my appointment as the crown governor-general of Vinland."

The cardinal waves his hands. "That, of course, goes without saying. We'll have an elaborate inaugural ceremony for you after the—"

"Nope," the baron of Amhirst states firmly. He gets up and tosses his drink on the floor. "Not going to happen. Fool me once, shame on you. Fool me twice, shame on me.

"If I leave this tent without your promised appointment, I am going to order my rangers to withdraw from the platform they conquered and I'm taking the rest of my contingent out of here."

Piccolo Cardinal Orsini threatens, "If you abandon us, I'll excommunicate your fanny from here to the place you like to bend so much."

"Excuse me, Your Eminence, you already tried that threat and it doesn't work, especially not here, one hundred fifty feet below an enemy *hell-bent* on bringing vengeance down upon your head. You won't survive."

At last, the duke of Philadelphia intervenes. "Your Eminence, the baron of Amhirst has a point. Wars aren't cheap. As a feudal lord, I pay wages and have to replace fallen horses. A quick victory makes war profitable, while a prolonged siege can lead to financial ruin, even if we do ultimately win.

"You gave your word that whichever of us should make it to the top of an elven platform first should be named governor-general of Vinland. The baron of Amhirst won that race fair and square. I expect you to honor your word and proceed with the appointment. If you keep breaking your promises, none of us will make it out of here alive."

Piccolo Cardinal Orsini consults with his high-level clerics and says, "My advisors concur. If you don't want an elaborate inaugural ceremony, then we'll simply name you as governor-general of Vinland with a handshake. Satisfied, Amhirst?"

The baron of Amhirst, still standing, replies tersely, "No. I want the paperwork."

The high inquisitor's secretaries busy themselves scribbling up an official scroll and seal it with the pope's own sigil. Piccolo Cardinal Orsini hands it to the baron of Amhirst and asks, "Satisfied now?"

The baron of Amhirst takes his time to scrutinize the document and to consult with his advisors.

With Brother Tuck's guarantee that the document is sound, Amhirst finally turns to the duke of Philadelphia and says, "Done. Your Grace, you may instruct your dwarves to commence operations and burn Fire Elf City to ashes."

Duke William Pinne bows. "With your leave, Your Eminence, I wish to oversee preparations in person."

Piccolo Cardinal Orsini nods and then says, "Does anyone have a fidel or a viol? I think we'll also need a lyre and a harp or . . . um . . . a dulcimer, and maybe a gittern as well."

Puzzled, the duke of Philadelphia asks, "What's all that for? It's a little early to celebrate victory, is it not, Your Eminence?"

"Nero played the fidel while Roma burned, to mourn the loss of all the art and culture around him. We'll need at least a string quartet to properly commemorate the loss of all the learning and artistic treasures up there on Fire Elf City."

Scene 6: Seabiscuits

Shentalpee City on Tuscoraura Mountain
Tiw's Day Terce. Morning, 4th of July, 1284
Third of Saint Swithun

Laughter and merriment abound among the rangers and the elves. Putting on a show of such grandeur and import has formed a sense of camaraderie among the actors, directors, and producers of the spectacle.

Officer Bunzi comes up to Florenz. "Mademoiselle Umpire-in-Chief-elect. The heresiarch summons you."

"Did he say what he wants?"

"No, but he has ordered his acolytes to prepare the transmogrification ceremony."

Florenz's heart is heavy. It's easy to be mean and cruel when everyone else has a shovel full of put-downs for you. But here, the rangers and the military leagues are all celebrating her. If the heresiarch wants to transmogrify her into an emotionless undead state, she'll lose all the joy—and her free will.

She sighs. "It's been a great show so far. Perhaps the final curtain call is coming."

Officer Bunzi asks, "You mean, it's time to smash the Crusaders once and for all?"

"Or lose ourselves to the same lust for power that led the Inquisition here."

She excuses herself from the feast and heads into the brownie workshop where the heresiarch has installed himself, transforming the premises into a sort of blackflame temple. When she opens the door, the heresiarch beckons her to approach his throne. She kneels and bows low, saying in the Black Tongue of Caldor, "What is thy bidding, master?"

Hooded and creepy, the heresiarch replies, "It is time to unleash the full power of the blackflame. The entire Crusade Army must be frozen solid at the very stakes where they intended for us to burn alive. With the destruction of the Crusade, our heresy will spread like wildfire across Vinland. Its cooling flames will give umbrage to generations of minds and spirits who have hitherto been sweltering from the oppression and superstition of the Christian faith."

Florenz recites words of submission. "Reveal to me thy plan, master, and I shall see to it."

The heresiarch says, "The Sword of Layban is now the ultimate power in Vinland. I suggest we use it. The Crusaders will be coming; hoping to claim the Vandsee Estates. Order the human rangers and your military leagues to transmogrify into your faithful thralls. When they do, you will order the attack to begin."

Florenz looks up. "I'm confused. How can I induce them to accept transmogrification, my master? They are lusty men and have a strong love of life. They know it will drain away all feeling and emotions."

The heresiarch lets out a maniacal laugh. "They will have no choice. You will use the Sword of Layban to set all of Vandsee Estates on blackfire. They will have to transmogrify or perish!"

Not liking the sound of that plan, Florenz points out the obvious flaw and hopes plan B will not involve annihilating her childhood home. "This platform is made entirely of wood. There is not enough metal or stone to set the entire estate on blackfire."

"You forget, my pretty, that a good dousing with oil will make almost any object burn with yellow fire. So too, soaking Vandsee Estates with water will make it dark-flammable."

"Where will we get so much water?"

"Johnny Appleseed is a Christian druid with a miraculous gift for calling down rain. Once the rains have fallen for a short while, you will go through every nook and cranny of these estates that you know so well and set them adark."

Florenz squirms inside without showing it on the outside. "The Reverend Appleseed would never cooperate with such a plan."

"He will have no choice. One of my most trusted heretics is none other than the last high inquisitor, whom I told you not to assassinate. He has used his position to convince the feeble-minded Crusaders to set Shentalpee City on fire from below."

"Ridiculous!" snaps back Florenz. "Sequoias are immune to fire."

"We are sitting in the colony's only sycamore grove. Sycamores will burn, with enough kindling. You have already ordered the elves to cut off access to Thor's Base because you didn't trust the rangers. When the Crusaders' fire threatens to engulf Vandsee Estates, Appleseed will have no choice but to call down rain from the heavens. They will all come to you begging for an escape and you will transmogrify them into thralls—perfectly submissive to my bidding!" Already tasting complete triumph on his wormy tongue, the heresiarch cackles. "Go and see to my plan."

Florenz walks out of the blackflame temple feeling rather downtrodden. When she first met the heresiarch, it sounded like using the Sword of Layban would put insane amounts of power into her own hands. It hasn't. Now the heresiarch wants her to destroy her own home, betray her friends and allies, and submit them all to *his* will, not hers.

At the bottom of it all, she really hates the person she has become. She thought that she could fix her problems by getting a little more assertive and pushing back on all the bullies. Now *she* is the big, bad bully that everyone hates and she still has no more control over her problems than she did before.

Slouching around under the weight of these thoughts, the first elf she happens upon is her fiancé, Enganyon. For as pathetic as he can be at times, she's still glad she hasn't executed him—so far.

Feeling like a champion from his rousing performance in the staged fight, Enganyon spots her from a distance and comes over to cheer her up. "Hey there, my beautiful dove! What's got you down?"

She snaps at him, "Doves are white. I'm a dark elf. Couldn't you have thought of a better metaphor?"

Enganyon takes it in stride and says, "Always eager to please, my beautiful raven."

"Ravens make a horrible cackling noise."

Enganyon is puzzled but does not give up. "My sweetly singing nightingale!"

"Nightingales never sing when you need to hear their songs the most."

"Never say never, darling."

"Whatever. I need to speak to the madame Dean of the League of Nations immediately."

He holds out his arm and says gallantly, "Then at least permit me to escort you to her."

Together, they walk toward the storage room where Dungaree Jeanne has set up her headquarters for her budding League of Nations. Enganyon has figured out by now that saying anything is only going to make things worse, so he just holds her and hopes that supporting her physically will help her feel supported emotionally.

When Florenz enters inside, everyone comes to attention and salutes her. Dungaree Jeanne welcomes her, saying in Runic, "Mademoiselle Umpire-in-Chief-elect, you bring light to this place."

Hearing the formulaic fire elf greeting Florenz breaks down sobbing. Her orders are to engulf this place in darkness.

When she recovers from her fit of weeping, she reveals to Dungaree Jeanne the heresiarch's plan to force them all to transmogrify into undead thralls.

A woman of action, Dungaree Jeanne gets up and immediately rushes out with Florenz to warn Johnny Appleseed not to pray for rain; but the raindrops are already falling. She smells the smoke and runs over to the ledge of the platform. Down below, she sees the huge Crusader bonfires burning around the trunks of the sycamore trees holding up Vandsee Estates.

It is worse than she expected. The heresiarch's plan is already in full motion. She asks anxiously around for Johnny Appleseed and they point her to the far end of Vandsee Estates. She shouts, "Reverend Appleseed! Can you stop it from raining?"

He looks at her exhausted and says, "I just prayed for rain to put out the Crusaders' fires."

"The heresiarch is going to use the rain to set all of Vandsee Estates on blackfire. You must stop the rain immediately!"

Johnny Appleseed shakes his head and says, "It's not up to me. God performs the miracles, but I must prepare to invoke his holy name with prayer and fasting. I've prayed and fasted to the edge of my endurance. The bonfires are already raging below. Without the rain, the whole platform'd come tumbling down in short order anyway. I suggest we stop the heresiarch before he sets the blackfires."

Dungaree Jeanne exclaims, "That's the whole problem! He wanted Mademoiselle Florenz to do it for him with the Sword of Layban. She wants to give it to me for safekeeping but I don't trust myself with that kind of power. Could you hold onto it for us?"

Johnny Appleseed backs away. "No, druids aligned to goodness shouldn't even be touching an artifact of such evil. We need someone whose alignment is chaotic enough to hold it and yet whose moral character is somehow selfless enough to use it for good."

Veins bloat on Florenz's temples and neck as the internal struggle with the Sword of Layban puts immense strain on her body and soul. "Please, someone needs to take the sword from me. It is ravaging through my mind, trying to force me to obey the heresiarch!"

Johnny Appleseed says, "He must have the Breastplate of Layban."

"What's that?"

"Layban was immensely wealthy, and not at all stupid. He feared that if he imbued the sword with too much power, it could one day be used against him. So, he had a breastplate secretly forged that subjugated the sword's owner to his will as a thrall. Little did Layban suspect that he would be slain in his sleep by his own sword's blade after passing out drunk."

Florenz groans, "It's making me forget who I am!"

"Wait, that's it!" shouts Zena in Eldric. "Let's give it to the human cleric who doesn't know his name!"

Dungaree Jeanne balks. "Who?"

Zena looks around to get everyone's attention. "Our dearly departed monsieur Lynx dragged me out to the Shade Gap to rescue these same rangers that are up here now from getting sacrificed to the goblin god, Poodoo. The goblins had also captured a young cleric who grew up in a monastery that never told him his real name. That's the one they call Clarke."

Dungaree Jeanne thinks for a moment. "There's no evidence that he has adopted an alignment that will allow him to hold the sword without becoming evil, but we're out of options. It's worth a shot."

Florenz's will is giving out. "Find him quickly! The sword . . . it's freezing my heart."

Appleseed says, "I'll use the gift of prophecy to find him." He closes his eyes for a brief moment and says, "I see him among biscuits—seashell-shaped biscuits."

Florenz crumples to the ground as she urges her will to defy the heresiarch's commands. "The seabiscuit workshop! It's right over there, but I'm feeling so weak. I can't walk a single step farther."

Johnny Appleseed lifts her up, saying, "I can't carry the sword, but I *can* carry you!"

With Johnny Appleseed carrying Florenz cradled in his arms and the Sword of Layban in her hand, she points the way to the seashell biscuit bakery. Inside, a few naughty rangers and elves have set up a fight club with spectators smoking longbotham weed and gambling on the outcome of the fights. Clarke, formerly known as Brother David, is sprawled out on the flour bags sleeping like a baby, but Louis is in the ring trading fisticuffs with Officer Bunzi.

Officer Bunzi leaps to one side of Louis and swivels an arm around his neck, putting Louis in a chokehold. Louis does not even gag. Calmly, he plants two feet on the ground, jumps up as high as he can, tilting backwards, and lands flat on Officer Bunzi with a tremendous thud.

With his body weight and the force of the fall, the impact knocks the air out of Officer Bunzi's lungs.

Cheers go up until suddenly the crowd realizes that the dean of the League of Nations is standing there watching them. Guilty looks and shushing hisses ripple through the seabiscuit bakery.

Zena rushes over to wake Clarke from his sleep and to get the Sword of Layban to him before it chills Florenz's heart. The groggy young monk looks around bewildered at all the attention. Johnny Appleseed lowers Florenz down next to him and asks, "Can you take the sword that is strapped to this elve's back?"

Clarke asks, "What is it?"

"It is a very evil sword that is about to destroy us all. We want to get rid of it but none of us can hold it. Please see if you can handle it."

"Why me?"

"Because your're not a cleric anymore and you're still a good person. Perhaps it's evil won't affect you."

"Not very reassuring." His hand trembles as he reaches for the sword's grip and recoils suddenly when it nips him with its cold evil.

"No," Clarke replies. "I can't touch it either."

Zena looks around and sees some of the members of the improvised fight club trying to sneak out before they get caught for their breach of military discipline. Suddenly she takes inspiration from the moment and barges into the ring. With the flourish of a true showman, she holds up Louis's arm, announcing in her elvish-accented Aenglish, "Big winner!"

They all look around, puzzled; most of all, Louis.

Zena grabs his hand and leads Louis to Florenz. Then she says to her in Eldric, "He's the one! I know it. Give him the sword."

Florenz winces and blinks her eyes as if someone were shining a flashlight in her face. Slowly, weakly, she draws the Sword of Layban from behind her back and holds it out to Louis. He kneels down on one knee before her to receive his prize.

The sword hovers above Louis's outstretched hand. Finally, Louis reaches up and grips it. At that moment, Florenz clutches it even more tightly and rips it out of his grasp, growling, "My precious."

Suddenly, a faint glow of red fills her eyes. Her willpower snaps and the sword takes over. With unearthly vigor, Florenz holds up the sword and shouts, "By the power of Layban . . . I have the power!"

She runs out of the seabiscuit bakery and starts setting her home ablaze with blackflame.

Scene 7: Precious Goods

Shentalpee City on Tuscoraura Mountain
Tiw's Day Terce. Morning, 4th of July, 1284
Third of Saint Swithun

Dungaree Jeanne calls out to the naughty rangers and elves first in Eldric, then in Aenglish, "We must stop her!"

Too late!

By the time they open the door, the blackflame is billowing around them in every direction. Barely does the blackflame touch a crate, a wall, or a puddle before it ignites with chilling violence. The water soon freezes with a hissing, crackling sound. Like a patchwork quilt on a winter's morning, sections of Vandsee Estates here and there whiten with frost and slick over with ice.

The rangers and elves start to run after her but they slip and slide all over the place, scattered like marbles, helpless as turtles spinning on their backs.

The heresiarch marches out of his Blackflame Temple with his acolytes carrying torches of blackflame. The glee of triumph encircles his head and his belly jiggles with scorn and gloating chuckles.

Using the power of the blackflame, his voice booms. He speaks in the Black Tongue of Caldor, but his acolytes translate into Aenglish and Eldric. "Today begins a new world order, where you shall become deathless champions of the Blackflame Cult. Forget whatever you heard about good or evil. Fate has in store for you only two alternative roles—masters and slaves. Come to me and become the masters! I will grant you powers that you never before imagined possible. You will have no fear of death and earthly blades; sickness and injuries will do you no harm. Receive the blackflame!"

The heresiarch's eyes glow red and blackflames sprout from his fingertips. As impressive as the show is, no one volunteers. He continues, "The blackflame is coming whether you like it or not. It surrounds us and is closing in on us. There is nowhere to run, nowhere to hide. Death and cremation are all that await you over those ledges. The only way for you to survive this day is to submit to the blackflame."

Despite their aversion to the blackflame, several elves and rangers reluctantly move toward the heresiarch, seeing no other way to escape death.

Dungaree Jeanne pleads with Johnny Appleseed to share his wisdom. "Please, Reverend Appleseed, tell us how we can stop him!"

As if racked with doubts for the first time since they met him, Johnny Appleseed shakes his head. "Only a weapon forged out of a material intrinsically imbued with fire, blessed by a holy cleric, and charged with the relic of a saint renowned for great ferocity in fighting evil will be powerful enough to destroy the heresiarch."

Dungaree Jeanne asks, "A material imbued with fire? Like what?"

Johnny Appleseed says, "Flint or obsidian or pyrite, or even a wyvern tooth or a phoenix talon."

A drowsy Clarke pulls out his ceremonial dagger. "Did someone say they need a phoenix talon?"

Dungaree Jeanne grabs the dagger from his hand and holds it up to Johnny Appleseed. "Will this do?"

"Yes, but we still need a relic."

Dungaree Jeanne pulls a ruby ring off her finger. "This was the engagement ring that Zena gave to our dearly departed monsieur Lynx. He was wearing it when he laid down his life to save his friends from the ambush that Umpire Gandorf set up for us."

Johnny Appleseed winces. "Sort of. It's only a second-class relic. Holy body parts are much more effective in turning the undead. Still, it won't matter unless we find a holy cleric to bless the dagger. As a druid, blessing objects is not a class skill for me. Only clerics sanctioned by the institutional Church can bestow blessings on objects. The holier the better."

Clarke asks, "What about that big, half-goblin cleric in Benjamin Frankelyn's party of adventurers? He's a canon regular, right?"

Johnny Appleseed says, "Yes, I remember him. As a canon regular, Monsignor Oscar Meyer could do it; but he's not particularly holy. We're only going to get one chance at this and if the dagger fails to turn the heresiarch, we're all going to end up undead thralls, enslaved mind, body, and will to his evil whims."

Dungaree Jeanne settles it once and for all. "If that's what we've got, then that's what we've got." She twists Lynx's engagement ring onto the dagger's handle and gives it back to Clarke. Then she instructs them. "Louis and Clarke, you two go get Monsignor Oscar Meyer to bless this as fast as you can. Time is running out. He should be in Benjamin Frankelyn's headquarters at the end of that alley. The blackflame is spreading quickly, and the rest of us need to find a way to put it out."

No sooner do Louis and Clarke take off than Vampire Kibbler and his team of undead vampires surround Zena, Dungaree Jeanne, and Johnny

Appleseed, and drag them kicking and screaming into the Blackflame Temple. The acolytes bring a pillow for smothering victims into an undead state.

The heresiarch hunches over and says, "Come now, Jeanne, it's time to be a good girl. You will be the first to transmogrify and inaugurate the new world order as my undead servant."

ACT VI

ASHES ASHES

WE'RE ALL SMALL NOW

Scene 1: Return of the Vampire

Shentalpee City on Tuscoraura Mountain
Tiw's Day Sext. Noontide, 4th of July, 1284
Third of Saint Swithun

The platform itself protects most of the fires from the rain, and the bonfires are big enough that those that do get wet billow with blinding, gray smoke. Amid the suffocating clouds, the heresiarch uses the Black Tongue of Caldor to announce his plan in a terrorizing, ear-splitting voice while his acolytes translate. "Hear me, my friends! A manifest destiny has brought you all together up here on this sycamore platform today. Now, you will witness your leader undergo transmogrification into the undead state. When you follow her example, you will become more powerful than you could have ever imagined possible.

"Then together, as my undead warriors, we will march throughout Vinland spreading heresy and liberating the clayborn from the mindless superstition that Vinland's Christians now believe in."

"Never!" shouts Dungaree Jeanne.

Behind the heresiarch, the undead Vampire Gandorf picks Zena up by the throat and holds her over the ledge. The heresiarch says, "Submit, or your daughter dies."

Dungaree Jeanne cries out, "No! Don't harm her. Promise me you won't harm her and I will willingly submit to your transmogrification."

Johnny Appleseed, bound up in ropes, warns her, "Don't do it, Madame Dungaree! The heresiarch is a master of lies. He will promise you anything and once you give in, he won't keep his end of the bargain—but he'll make you pay off your end a hundredfold."

"I'm a mother. I can't let my daughter die."

"Better to be dead and to rest in peace than to be undead and enslaved to the will of that monster."

The heresiarch interrupts, "Theologically speaking, I am a wight—an undead person is a wight. An undead animal is a monster."

"Let her go!" The stern voice comes from the duke of Philadelphia's daughter. She is leading her party of adventurers toward the steps of the Blackflame Temple, backed up by Benjamin Frankelyn, Louis, and Clarke.

The heresiarch laughs at Ariel with scorn. "I have nothing to fear from a little old lady like you."

Out of nowhere, Enganyon comes swinging down on a rope, yodeling with all his might. "A liddle ole ladi hoo?" As he whizzes by, he cuts off his father's hand with a silver dagger. Zena drops over the ledge.

After a few feet of freefall, a rope tied around her ankle runs out of slack and yanks her back up for a short rebound. Officer Bunzi underneath the platform tied a lifeline around her foot during Enganyon's distraction with impeccable timing.

For a few moments, Vampire Gandorf stands still, as if computing the unexpected new data to figure out what to do next. Enganyon smiles cheerfully at the undead effigy of his father and says, "It's me, Enganyon! I'm your son."

The undead father draws his sword and brings down its blade upon his living son without any remorse. Enganyon, armed only with his silver dagger, counters his father's attacks with dodges, parries, and jumps. His father's blows are coming in heavy but slow enough for Enganyon to deflect the attacks and maintain his footing.

Enganyon sidesteps in front of a sycamore tree and Vampire Gandorf chops at him with so much force that his sword lodges itself in the tree trunk. Vampire Gandorf struggles to pry it out. Enganyon takes advantage of the distraction to grab a large, wooden board and slap it over the back of his father's head. He hits so hard that his father's eyeballs pop out.

Enganyon swoops down and tucks the eyeballs away into his belt pouch, thinking it will blind his father. Instead, red lights flicker inside Vampire Gandorf's skull and with two glowing, red orbs in place of his eyes, Vampire Gandorf resumes his attack against his son.

Meanwhile, Willis, Louis, and Monsignor Oscar Meyer charge at Vampire Kibbler and the acolytes holding Dungaree Jeanne down. The combined mass of their body weight alone is enough to bowl them over like so many duckpins, and the acolytes all end up piled on top of each other. Wriggling, squirming, scratching, and slashing at the acolytes, they manage to free Dungaree Jeanne from their clutches.

Watching his plans fall to pieces, the heresiarch screams with thunderous fury, "Destroy them!"

Vampire Gandorf lets go of the sword stuck in the sycamore tree and grabs a hook off a pulley from one of the workshop lifts. He jams the hook into his severed wrist and hisses two words, "Die, son!"

Enganyon rolls behind the sprawling acolytes just as Vampire Gandorf takes another swing at him. This time, his hook sinks into the back of one of the acolytes. An unsettling relief spreads through Enganyon's soul to hear his father acknowledge him as his son. Enganyon calls out, "To die would be an awfully big adventure, dad. How's it working out for you?"

Vampire Gandorf flings the squealing acolyte away to free up his hook and snarls, "Fool!"

Enganyon grabs a black banner resting on a crate and throws it over his father, replying, "A fool, am I? Well then, you're a codfish."

Still more nimble than his undead father, Enganyon dances around him, slashing at him here and there with his silver dagger but not managing to land a direct hit.

Not far off, Florenz, exhausted from her blackflame binge, recovers some shard of her normal self. When she realizes what is going on, she shrieks, "Oh no, watch out for father! Run, Monsieur Enganyon, run!"

Enganyon, chipper and lighthearted as ever, tips his hat and says, "Faint hearts never won a fight, fair lady."

Unfortunately, he doesn't realize that Florenz's warning was not about *his* father, but hers. Vampire Kibbler comes up from behind and clobbers Enganyon with an empty crate, splintering it over his back. The surprise attack sends him down for the count.

Vampire Kibbler drags Enganyon to the heresiarch, who sneers, "Now your transmogrification through the blackflame will be complete."

Helpless, Enganyon shouts, "No! I'm too young to be undead! I love life."

The heresiarch grins, "Oh, but you'll love being undead too! You'll have the joy of bowing to my will."

He places the ceremonial pillow over Enganyon's face to begin the transmogrification ritual. The acolytes chant with a strange droning hum in the background while the heresiarch recites formulaic words in the Black Tongue of Caldor.

Throughout the ritual, the other vampires pin Enganyon's arms and legs to the floor. All he can do is tap on the ground with his left hand. Whoopee sees Enganyon's call for help amidst the tumult and confusion of the fight and uses his magica wand to locomutate away the pillow covering his face. The next moment, Enganyon takes in a deep breath and the transmogrification ritual is broken.

That same instant, the three rangers' apprentices—Louis, Clarke, and Hayle—come charging in recklessly to save the day. Louis buries his two-handed battle-axe in Vampire Gandorf's back. The vampire, barely noticing the blow, spins around, grabs Louis's wrists, and flings him away with an ease that frightens even the most seasoned veterans on the front lines.

Hayle attempts to sneak up on Vampire Kibbler with a wooden stake in his left hand and a mallet in his right. The plan is futile. Vampire Kibbler turns casually around and slaps the implements out of his hands so hard it knocks his whole body to the ground. Hayle rolls to avoid a wicked stomp of the vampire's foot.

Eager to save his friends, Clarke charges straight at the heresiarch, holding his newly blessed phoenix talon infixed with the engagement ring relic of Lynx. The heresiarch grabs him by the neck, but Clarke's right arm is long enough to get behind his foe's neck. With a swift sawing motion back and forth, the phoenix talon chops off the heresiarch's head.

Enganyon crawls over and scoops up the severed head. He rolls it towards the ledge of the platform. Like a painfully slow bowling ball, the head barely reaches the last plank, teeters back and forth three times, then drops over. The heresiarch's head laughs hideously as it plummets, slowly rotating one hundred feet down into the crusader bonfires below.

The headless heresiarch, however, does not die, but his undead body runs off the ledge in search of his head. Everyone looks around, not sure what's next.

Enraged, Vampire Kibbler lets them have it. He holds out his hand and shoots a short burst of blackflame, covering Enganyon with a coat of rime frost. Enganyon squeals worse than if someone dropped an ice cube down the back of his shirt on a hot summer day. "Ahhhhhh!"

Vampire Kibbler kicks him again and sends another spray of blackflame at him. Enganyon rolls and writhes in pain. After another burst of blackflame, Enganyon is shivering pathetically. He calls out to Vampire Gandorf, "Father!"

Johnny Appleseed taps deep into special druid prayers and prays for his enemy—in this case, Vampire Gandorf. A moment of grace awakens compassion in his torpid, undead soul.

Amid the agony of his son's torture, something snaps in Vampire Gandorf. A tear trickles down the glowing orb in his eye socket. Spotting Hayle's wooden stake and mallet, Vampire Gandorf creeps up behind

Vampire Kibbler and places the wooden stake between his shoulder blades. With one tremendous blow, he drives the stake through Vampire Kibbler's chest with the mallet. The archon stone amulet bursts out through the front of his rib cage.

Though missing a hand, Vampire Gandorf hoists the now vulnerable Vampire Kibbler over his head and tosses him over the ledge. Staggering to the ground as the druid's continued prayers restore his soul to its natural state—death—Vampire Gandorf says, "Son, let me see you with my own eyes one last time."

Enganyon takes the eyeballs from out of his belt pouch and hands them back to his father, saying with a worried face, "But you'll die—I guess you are already dead, but I mean, like, for good this time."

"Nothing can stop that now."

Vampire Gandorf pops the eyeballs back into his head and looks at him lovingly. "I love you, my son!"

Enganyon starts to cry. "I love you, Dad!"

As he fades, Vampire Gandorf says, "My son, be honest, even when it hurts . . . or your spirit will spend all eternity running from the truth."

With that, his body slumps back, motionless. Enganyon holds his father's lifeless body and weeps. Although the rains have died down, a tickle of cold reminds him that the blackflames are close to freezing over all of Vandsee Estates.

The rangers and elves are getting hemmed in and huddle up closer to each other for warmth and safety.

Enganyon spots a narrow passageway through the bitter-cold flames and quickly formulates a plan to rescue the survivors but first, he must run a gauntlet through the most grueling ordeal of all—the truth.

Scene 2: Fudging the Truth

Shentalpee City on Tuscoraura Mountain
Tiw's Day Sext. Noontide, 4th of July, 1284
Third of Saint Swithun

Worse than having the sky fall on his head, Enganyon realizes it is time to fess up when Florenz puts an arm around his shoulders. With both tender sympathy and outraged menace, she asks him, "What did your father mean when he said that thing about running from the truth? Is there something you're not telling me?"

With the skill of a master chef, Enganyon cooks up some zesty excuses fast. "First, we need to rescue Zena! Look, she's dangling below the ledge, barely hanging on for dear life. Next, we need to get everyone out of here before they all get frozen solid by the black wildfires you set. Then we need to stop the high inquisitor from taking over Thor's Base.

"When all that's done, we'll have a heart-to-heart."

The rangers and major league elves are already hauling Zena up. Barely escaping the blackflames at her back, Zena rushes to Enganyon and comments, "That was like a crazy trust exercise."

Florenz asks, "But how did she not fall?"

"When our dearly departed monsieur umpire-in-chief ordered my dad to kill Reverend Appleseed, Officer Bunzi came up with a plan to use these emergency escape lines to make it look like we tried to get rid of him but that he miraculously survived. I'm at my best when faking it, so I volunteered for the job."

Enganyon polishes his fingernails on his chest with a smug wink.

Zena asks him, "Speaking of faking it. Were you faking that you were in love with me or are you faking that you're in love with the mademoiselle Florenz?"

"That's 'Umpire-in-Chief-elect Florenz' to you!"

Zena ignores her and focuses on Enganyon's eyes as if to read the truth from the subconscious signals of his body language. Florenz gets curious too and asks, "Yeah, how about it, Captain Enganyon? Are you faking being in love with me?"

Enganyon gets back up on his feet. "Now, now, ladies, if you just give me enough time, I can make you both see the big picture. The problem is, we don't have time right now. We've got to get everyone off Vandsee Estates before the blackflame freezes us all!"

Florenz says, "We're stuck! When we allowed the rangers up here, I had all the suspension bridges on Vandsee Estates destroyed as a safety precaution."

The annoying Officer Bunzi walks up as if he were the savior of the day and proudly announces, "The Justiciar League has a series of emergency chutes and ladders spread throughout Shentalpee City. I was the one in charge of installing them on Vandsee Estates. With the Crusader fires burning down there we can't use the chutes, but just crank that lever over there and it will bring up an escape ladder to Thor's Base."

Dungaree Jeanne is already coughing as the frozen air scalds her lungs. She asks Johnny Appleseed in Aenglish, "We're cut off from that escape ladder. With your vast knowledge of blackflame, can you tell us if there is any way to keep these blackflames at bay so we can make it over there before being engulfed?"

Reverend Appleseed wraps a blanket around her shoulders to warm her and says, "The answer is all around you. Ever notice how Kibbler chocolates always seem to melt in your hand but not in your mouth? Refined cocoa beans are highly susceptible to heat but almost totally resistant to the cold. If we just scatter refined cocoa powder, it will create a safe zone where the blackfires can't touch us."

Brightening with hope, Dungaree Jeanne exclaims, "I know exactly where the cocoa powder is stored."

Johnny Appleseed cautions her, "We'd need to spread around quite a bit. A few handfuls won't do much against flames this high."

Whoopee interjects, "As a magicultor myself, we could work as a team. All we have to do is run a spell to disperse water on fire and tweak it just enough so that it will disperse cocoa on blackflame."

Johnny Appleseed strokes his white beard for a moment as a great philosophical paradox comes to mind. "Magic would work the charm but we face Meno's problem—we don't know what the magic word for spreading cocoa powder is, so we wouldn't recognize it even if we guessed it correctly. Normally, trial and error can solve the paradox, but the imminent danger around us doesn't afford us the luxury of guessing wrong even once.

"If we locomutate the cocoa powder incorrectly, everyone either freezes to death from the blackflame closing in on us or burns to death from the bonfires raging below us."

Zena steps forward and says in Aenglish, "I know it! I know what is magic word for spreading cocoa powder everywhere!"

The first to doubt is, of course, her mother. "How's that even possible? You haven't even begun your studies as a magicultor!"

A subtle trembling sound soon turns into a mighty rumble as the wooden flooring shakes beneath their feet. The bonfires down below have weakened major sycamore branches and consumed vital support beams. With the alternations of freezing-cold blackfires up top and burning-hot yellow fires beneath, the very foundations of Vandsee Estates crack and shudder. Large chunks of floorboarding splinter upwards nearby while faraway buildings collapse.

The forces of nature rending wood and toppling sycamores reverberate with deafening fright, like the pulsed shrieks of a blue whale whose calf is beset by orcas. What little space is left to the survivors from the dark wildfires around them just got cut down by one-third from the crumbling planks and floorboards. Rangers and major league elves scramble and roll away from sharp slivers and widening gaps, desperate for a stable place to fix their feet.

Frightened by the upheavals, Zena lets nonsense syllables dribble out of her mouth. "Oh, fudge!"

Keep in mind, dear reader, that as of the year 1284, fudge had not yet been invented, and the word itself at that time had no meaning.

Whoopee looks at Johnny Appleseed, shrugs, and says, "Oh, fudge? Zena's magic words sound good enough to me. On my mark, we will cast her spell in harmony for maximum effect."

Dungaree Jeanne points to a warehouse, now separated from them by a gaping chasm. "All the cocoa bean powder is in there, but we can't get to it!"

Whoopee says, "If the magic word is good enough, we'll be able to grab the cocoa powder from back here and locomutate it in puffs so it spreads evenly along the path to those emergency ladders."

Johnny Appleseed pulls out the magica wand that he stores in the handle of the tin pot on his head and nods to Whoopee. "Let's do this!"

They count to three and together shout out in a commanding but melodious tone, "Oh, fudge!"

POOF!

Suddenly, it is snowing cocoa powder and all the rangers and major league elves let out thrilled cheers as the dark wildfires back off, leaving them sneezing but safe all along the corridor to the escape ladders, with a delicious chocolatey aftertaste in their mouths.

From there, it's not long before Enganyon and Officer Bunzi hoist the emergency escape ladders and start guiding the survivors up toward Thor's Base as the rest of the flooring planks and wooden structures collapse behind them on Vandsee Estates.

Being a noble leader, Dungaree Jeanne makes sure everyone is on their way toward safety before allowing herself to escape. Once she is standing on Thor's Base, she shouts out orders, looping her words in Eldric and in Aenglish. "Listen up! We've got work to do, people! First off, Officer Bunzi, take the Justiciar Leaguers, along with Sir Jon Stark's rangers, to post guards at all the chutes and ladders on Thor's Base that you know of. Make sure no one can sneak up on us, and assess which ones offer us the best escape routes.

"Next, Mademoiselle Umpire-in-Chief-elect, I am going to request that you and your Ivy Leaguers take Sir Robert Roger's rangers to the aqueduct. See if you can jury-rig a way to take all non-combatants to the mountain dwarves' vault at the peak.

"Reverend Appleseed, may I ask you to help Lady Philippa's party of adventurers find a way to counter the threat of blackflame up here? We narrowly escaped Vandsee Estates with the cocoa powder. We don't want to find ourselves in double jeopardy.

"Finally, I will work with the League of Licornes and Sir Benedict Arnald's rangers to build barricades to fence off any points of access the Crusaders might use to assault Shentalpee City. We'll also figure out the best tactical locations to set up elf fire siphons in case it comes down to street-to-street fighting. We're safe for the moment, but in a siege like this, the enemy will probably try to find a traitor to open a way—"

Enganyon tugs on her sleeve as sheepishly and as insistently as a little kid asking for apple juice in the middle of a crowded bus.

He stutters, then says, "Um, we're not all that safe up here at the moment."

The comment makes no sense to Dungaree Jeanne, so she asks tentatively, "What do you mean, Captain Enganyon? As far as I can tell the Crusaders' bonfires have had no effect on the sequoias and there's no sign of blackflame in any—"

"Um," he interrupts. "I'm not worried about fire."

Fearing where that's going, Zena flips the archon stone that came out of Vampire Kibbler's heart up in the air and catches it in her palm, saying, "Mother, I believe I owe you one of these. That's the last of the invincible undead we'll ever have to face." Zena glares at her ex-fiancé and says, "Right, Captain Enganyon?"

"Well actually—now that you mention it—it just so happens that the last high inquisitor is coming up a secret passageway with an invincible undead army to destroy Thor's Base."

Florenz doesn't give Enganyon a chance to speak further. "That's impossible! My father was the only one who knew about the secret passageway and he would never betray that secret—alive or undead."

Enganyon starts to fidget. "Well, you see, where there's a will, there's a way. I found out about it so when your dad was still alive . . . or still undead . . . I was kind of angry with you and him for killing my father, so I sort of—"

"Yes?"

"I sort of cut a deal with the Inquisition."

Scene 3: Three isn't Company

Shentalpee City on Tuscoraura Mountain
Tiw's Day Nones. Afternoon, 4th of July, 1284
Third of Saint Swithun

"You what?"

Staring at the floor, Enganyon mutters under his breath, "I hate telling the truth."

Florenz gets in his face. "You betrayed us to the Inquisition? How could you?"

At last he looks her in the eyes and says, "Well, not us. Just you. I only wanted to betray you."

Florenz throws up her arms. "So you really love Zena after all? I thought you loved me!"

"I do love you . . . and kind of hate you too. You're awfully mean sometimes. This is awkward. Not that you're awkward, but because we're . . . I'm awkward. You're gorgeous. Wait, what?"

Zena tries to help him. "Mademoiselle Florenz, you did send that giant undead dwarf to kill us all. As far as I know, you haven't bothered apologizing yet."

"That's Umpire-in-Chief-elect Florenz to you, missy," she reiterates, and then adds, "Besides, true love means never having to say you're sorry."

Dungaree Jeanne drops her jaw and says, "That's the dumbest thing I ever heard."

Florenz ignores her and continues ranting at Enganyon. "So just because of a little misunderstanding like that, you betrayed me?"

Enganyon starts to find his footing and says more confidently, "Yes! No! I wouldn't call that a little misunderstanding, more like a dynastic feud. I was also pretty peeved that you got elected umpire-in-chief instead of me. Somewhere between revenge and ambition, I figured it was time to make a deal."

Zena pulls his shoulder to point him in her direction and says to his face, "You said that you wanted *me* to get elected umpire-in-chief."

"Well, my political ambitions evolved."

Florenz pulls him in her direction and shouts in his face, "So you made a deal with the enemy? Traitor!"

"No, no, no! I'm a patriot! I couldn't let an undead wight seize control of the government and throw out the Magnificent Charter. My primary goal was to restore our way of life according to the vision of our Founding Mothers and Fathers."

Zena pulls him back her way and says, "Okay, forget all that rhetoric for now. Let's get back to the essentials—what exactly is this deal that you made with the high inquisitor?"

Enganyon turns to look at Florenz straight in the eyes and says, "So I was sort of supposed to show them a secret passageway up to Thor's Base in exchange for arresting you and making me the next umpire-in-chief of Shentalpee City."

Florenz exclaims, "I knew it! You betrayed me!"

Zena interrupts, "Does that mean you really love me? You said your heart always belonged to Florenz."

Enganyon replies, "No! Yes! I mean, my love is really . . . look, can we deal with the fact that the high inquisitor is going to come through that secret passageway any moment now? When we are all safe and alive, I'll tell you both anything you want to hear."

Although she was invested in her relationship with Enganyon, what is really causing turmoil in Florenz's heart is her struggle with the revelation that he might have outmaneuvered her politically.

It's one thing to have a gutless, sleazy, two-timing boyfriend. It's another thing entirely to get outwitted at the game you've always believed you play the best. She looks him straight in the eyes and says, "Look! It's not a problem anymore. My dad's secret passageway has been destroyed by the fires."

"There's another one you don't know about."

Florenz gives him a wry face. "My dad would never build a secret passageway that I don't know about."

"Never say never."

"You just did, twice."

"By Thor's beard, I can't win with you, can I?"

"Nope."

"Unfortunately, I did win this time." Instead of arguing any further, Enganyon throws his silver dagger at the trunk of Frige's Tree. It stands there trembling.

From deep inside, drums pound. The silver dagger keeps on vibrating as the pounding grows louder and faster. *Boom! Boom! Boom!*

Like rowdy football players bursting through their team banner, crazed undead ghouls burst through the bark and rush onto Thor's Base.

Scene 4: A Song and a Dance for the Lord

Shentalpee City on Tuscoraura Mountain
Tiw's Day Nones. Afternoon, 4th of July, 1284
Third of Saint Swithun

For as untamed and as savage as their pep rally seems, as soon as Piccolo Cardinal Orsini makes his entrance, the undead ghouls show perfect discipline in lining up in two straight rows beside him. Arrayed in his red cardinal robes, red satin slippers, and wide-brimmed red cardinal hat, the cardinal has added one piece to his wardrobe that escapes no one's notice—the Breastplate of Layban. It is charred from the heresiarch's plunge into the bonfires but otherwise fully intact and exuding a chilling evil.

When the high inquisitor's eyes fall on Florenz he shouts in the Dark Tongue of Caldor, "Well if it isn't Miss hoity-toity Umpire-in-Chief Florenz Kibblersdottir herself! You've escaped us for the last time! Never again will your pointy ears prickle our plans for the people of Vinland."

Florenz pounds her index finger on Enganyon's chest and says, "I'll deal with you later." Then, turning to face the high inquisitor, she yells in Dark Tongue of Caldor, "Thou art supposed to be a lawful cleric—praying and preaching the word of God. Thou hast no business dabbling in necromancy. How darest thou play at being a god by commanding all these undead thralls!"

The high inquisitor replies, booming his voice out as the heresiarch did. "Oh, they're not thralls at all, dearie. They're *ghouls.*

"Without freedom, you can't inspire a true fighting spirit among the clayborn. The Crusaders learned that lesson from infidels in the Holy Land. Instead of serfs, they rely on elite freed slaves called ghoulams to fight their battles for them. While my brother cardinals were busy fighting heretics, I've been interviewing them.

"My stroke of genius has been to raise up an army of undead warriors behind their backs. But my legions are not abject slaves. These ghouls have embraced their undead condition and fight with free will. They are more than a match for your enthralled vampires."

While he is speaking, Dungaree Jeanne leans into Florenz's ear and says, "Keep him monologuing as long as possible. I've got a plan, but I need you to buy me some time."

Florenz nods and replies to the traitorous high inquisitor in the Black Tongue of Caldor, "You speak the Black Tongue of Caldor so fluently. Only those of an evil alignment can do so . . . it's as if you've been evil for a long time. How could your brothers, the high inquisitors, not notice?"

The high inquisitor takes the hook and he starts to monologue away the element of surprise from his surprise attack. "It started with my speech impediment. None of the holy Christian healers could help me. They said God wanted me to endure this defect as a thorn in my side, like Saint Paul.

"Then one day, a blackflame missionary cured it with a single touch. It was then that I knew there were untapped powers in the Blackflame Cult that I could never master as a Christian cleric, but I had to be cautious. I played dumb. I pretended I still had the speech impediment and intentionally made lots of idiotic comments. My brothers were so convinced I was stupid that in their arrogance, they did not bother to investigate my strange behaviors any deeper. My power grew right under their noses. Now I am more powerful than the heresiarch ever was."

Florenz is playing him, but she is also genuinely curious how he got his powers. "More powerful than the heresiarch? How's that even possible?"

Somehow, he seems to grow bigger and louder. "Ever heard of a wolf in sheep's clothing? By betraying my holy calling, I have reached lower levels of evil much faster than the heresiarch ever could, because he was openly evil. Now I'm a big, bad wolf and I'm going to huff and puff and blow your houses down!"

The high inquisitor heaves his chest and his breath explodes with blackflame—not just one or two feet in front of him, but dark fire streams forward with unnatural power twenty, thirty feet in front of him, igniting the wet planks and merchant stalls around him. As he blows, a hoary frost crinkles over his beard.

"Not by the frosty hairs of your chubby little chin," says Florenz as she raises the Sword of Layban and signals to the remaining vampires to attack the high inquisitor. "Time to avenge this reckless assault on Shentalpee City!"

Though wild and ferocious, the high inquisitor's ghouls nonetheless form up ranks and fight with discipline and coordination. As promised, they are more than a match for the elf vampires who come at them helter-skelter. The elf vampires never counted on fighting undead peers. They have no silver weapons, no holy relics, no fire attacks. The cardinal's ghouls are equipped with all three.

The combat is brief. The best and the brightest from among the undead elves, the vampire avengers of Shentalpee City, the cream of the crop from among high elf society, the fieriest of all the fire elves—lay scattered and dismembered, piece by piece, across the floorboards of Thor's Base. Seeing how easily the high inquisitor's ghouls cut down their vampires, the Major League elves scream to each other in a desperate panic, "What shall we do?"

Dungaree Jeanne reappears and holds up her hands, waving for their attention, and says in both Aenglish and Eldric, "Everybody, listen up! Calm down! I've got a plan that will save us!"

Sir Robert Roger shouts, "Quick, put it into action! The high inquisitor is hell-bent on revenge!"

Dungaree Jeanne says, "As the dean of the League of Nations and the founder of the real New World Order, I encourage you all in this moment of crisis to stick to our motto. In God we trust! We must put our trust in the Lord!"

Sir Robert Roger sours his face. "What kind of plan is that?"

As the high inquisitor's ghouls march relentlessly forward, the Major League elves and rangers step back, feeling utterly helpless. As he goes, the high inquisitor blows forth streams of blackflame across the still wet platforms of Thor's Base. Though the rains have stopped, the freezing darkflames turn the soggy wood into brittle ice. The high inquisitor places his blackflame attacks so precisely that he seems to intentionally herd the survivors into a smaller and smaller area.

Taking up Dungaree Jeanne's rallying call, Johnny Appleseed sings and dances. "Oooooh, the Lord is good to me, and so I thank the Lord for giving me the things I need; the sun and the rain and the apple seed. The Lord is good to me. Amen! Amen! Amen! Amen!"

They mock and insult him for looking so silly at such a crucial time when their lives are nearing the ropes' edge of Thor's Base.

At that moment, Amhirst's independent-minded ally, Lord Samuel Maverick, comes sliding down the aquifer hollering like Tarzan and leading a train of swashbucklers who specialize in combating the undead. It's time to even up the score.

Scene 5: The Battle of the Four Armies

Shentalpee City on Tuscoraura Mountain
Tiw's Day Nones. Afternoon, 4th of July, 1284
Third of Saint Swithun

Lord Maverick's swashbucklers are all equipped with blessed silver blades and bucklers with holy icons painted on them. From behind the high inquisitor and his ghouls, the great dwarf Lawspeaker Sturl Snorrison emerges from the same secret passageway in Frige's Tree that the high inquisitor and his ghouls used. Behind him step forth several ranks of crossbow dwarves equipped with hammerhead bolts doused in holy water.

Johnny Appleseed says, "An answered prayer."

Sir Robert Roger replies sharply, "It had nothing to do with prayer! You just happened to be praying moments before we got rescued."

Lord Maverick calls out, "O ye of little faith! No time for palavering. Let's nip these ghouls in their undead heinies!"

A perfectly coordinated volley of dwarven hammerhead crossbow bolts flies out and blows large chunks off the ghouls' flesh with each hit. The line of ghouls falters and loses cohesion.

Taking advantage of the muddle, the swashbucklers leap at the ghouls with their silver swords. Swaying gracefully around them with the synced rhythms of grandfather clocks, the swashbucklers cut the ghouls down a notch, then fall back while the crossbow dwarves shoot off another volley of holy water bolts.

Keeping focused, the cardinal sends out more blackflame to wreak destruction upon the brilliant art and culture enshrined around him upon Thor's Base.

Seeing their tactical situation deteriorating, the ghouls drop their weapons and tear strips off their shirts to wave as flags of surrender. Lawmaker Sturl Snorrison calls out in Latin, "Your ghouls have surrendered. It's time for you to yield. I wish to thank you, Your Eminence, for monologuing long enough for our warriors to get into position. You are now quite surrounded."

"No, Lawspeaker, it is you who have allowed me time to surround you!" His laugh is more like the high-pitched squeal of a pig eager to roll in manure.

As he speaks, the Knights Templar, the Knights Hospitaller, and the Knights Paladin emerge from the same secret passageway in Frige's Tree behind the dwarves. With the ghouls in front of them and the most elite fighting force in Vinland behind them, the dwarves' tactical advantage evaporates.

Johnny Appleseed calls out to the holy warriors with these words in Aenglish, "O brothers in Christ! You know that the Inquisition has been chasing me for years because I have been distributing blackflame as part of my mission against hunger in Vinland. I knew that blackflame could have destructive applications, but I have never used blackflame for any other purpose than to give relief to the feverish and preserve food from spoiling.

"Your high inquisitor has chosen to use blackflame both as a weapon, though it is banned by Church law, and for necromancy, which God forbids in the Bible. Ask yourselves—are you serving God by killing innocent clayborn for no other purpose than to win for the Church a monopoly on blackflame weaponry?

"By attacking us, you would be making the One, Holy, Catholic, and Apostolic Church no better than the great and abominable Blackflame Cult."

The Elect Radisson speaks for the rest when he says in Aenglish, "Reverend Appleseed, your words ring true and cut us to the heart. However, you must remember that we are both warriors and monks. In both capacities, our highest obligation is to obey the commands of our superior officers, even if they ask us to forfeit our lives. We cannot disobey orders simply because our individual, private consciences tell us that our commander is in the wrong."

While the elect speaks, Brother Clarke runs over to Lawspeaker Snorrison and explains Appleseed's words to him in Latin since he knows almost no Aenglish. The Lawspeaker nods and then calls out to the holy knights in Latin, "As lawspeaker for the Tuscoraura Mountain dwarves, my training has made me proficient not only in the ancient Axenhower Code of the Whaler Dwarves, but also in the Alfheim legal tradition. I am also familiar with Aenglish Common Law and Roman Civil Law. Finally, I spent several months memorizing Canon Law and discussing it with the most learned clerics in Vinland.

"If my memory serves me right, Canon Law states that using blackflame for necromancy is an act that can be punished by excommunication. An excommunicated prelate has no authority to give commands to faithful Christians. That means that Piccolo Cardinal Orsini is no longer your legitimate commanding officer. You are free to decide what is right for yourselves."

Brother Jack de Molay, leading the Knights Templar, replies, "You make a good point, but you forget that he must be tried and found guilty by an ecclesiastical court before we can be released from our vows of obedience to him."

The lawspeaker clears his throat, thinks for a short while, then calls out in Latin, "Correct me if I'm wrong but, as I recall, when Pope Gregory instituted the Papal Inquisition, he had it officially codified in Canon Law and explained in the *Liber Extra* of 1234. In it, he states specifically that anyone who transmogrifies a living person into an undead state, or even oversees any such ritual, incurs a *latae sententiae* excommunication. That means that the act itself automatically excommunicates him without the need for an ecclesiastical trial."

Brother Oliver Roland, leading the Knights Paladin, says, "As you know well, we don't fight for the sake of approval or honors among the clayborn. We fight because it is just and right in God's eyes. Although we have overwhelming circumstantial evidence before us, there is no solid proof that he transmogrified these ghouls or that he oversaw any transmogrifications."

Hearing this, Johnny Appleseed announces in Aenglish, "That's a simple matter to settle! We'll ask them." Johnny Appleseed calls out, "O ye ghouls! Speak, friends, and tell us true. Were you transmogrified to your current undead state by Piccolo Cardinal Orsini? If so, raise your right hand."

Nearly half of the ghouls raise their hands. Johnny Appleseed folds his arms and nods. "Any questions?"

Brother Oliver Roland of the Knights Paladin turns and announces in Aenglish, "There is no more room for doubt. Piccolo Cardinal Orsini has chosen to side with infernal powers and has brought upon himself an excommunication by Holy Mother the Church.

"As the highest-level cleric in the present company, that makes me the commanding officer of the crusading forces at Tuscoraura Mountain." Then, turning to the ghouls he addresses them, saying, "O ye ghouls! Choose your side! The cardinal has no authority to give you orders in the name of Holy Mother the Church. Will you join the Knights Paladin under my command, or will you persist in following this excommunicated cardinal down the path of perdition?"

The ranks of ghouls waver. Eventually, one ghoul steps forward and joins the Knights Paladin. One by one, the voice of reason calls a large minority of ghouls out from service with the fallen high inquisitor to the Order of the Knights Paladin.

Though not all are fully aware of the momentous historic event taking place before their eyes, a loud cheer rises up among the clayborn on Thor's Base—all the rangers, the crossbow dwarves, the swashbucklers, and the Major League elves celebrate the first time in history that ghouls have been counted among the clayborn in the fight against evil.

Scene 6: Ghoul Busters

Shentalpee City on Tuscoraura Mountain
Tiw's Day Nones. Afternoon, 4th of July, 1284
Third of Saint Swithun

Still, the majority of ghouls remain firm to their pledges of service to the fallen high inquisitor. Not in the slightest intimidated at having part of his army of ghouls defect, the high inquisitor claps sarcastically and laughs with scorn. "Oh, very clever. Very clever indeed. You know, choosing evil was a hard decision at first, but what I love most about being wicked is that *I always get to win.*"

With that, he blows a stream of blackflame at the Knights Paladin, staggering them all back and freezing the breath from their lungs until they are gasping for air. The Hospitaller Commander-elect Radisson gets enraged at his insolence and charging in with a spear, surges forward for a personal attack against the high inquisitor. The Elect Radisson jams his spear clear through the Breastplate of Layban.

With mocking derision, the cardinal exclaims, "Oh! Look at that! I've been impaled."

The high inquisitor pulls the spear out of his chest and slaps Brother Radisson on the head with the spear's handle so hard it knocks him out cold. As the Elect Radisson sleeps soundly on the platform floor, the high inquisitor taunts them, "Remember when I said I'm even more powerful than the heresiarch, and nobody believed me? The Breastplate of Layban does more than stop pointy sticks. Watch and weep!"

The whole earth trembles and shakes as the high inquisitor stretches out his arms. From near and far the hacked limbs and chunks of ribs and slabs of raw meat and shattered skulls from all the dead animals and clayborn on the battlefields on high and down below recombine into one huge, hideous collection of rotting flesh and bone, encasing him like armor. So much carnage from the death and destruction of the last two days clings to his body and the padding around him that he grows five feet all around. With the cadaverous armor, the high inquisitor transforms into an undead titanoghoul fifteen feet tall.

"What is that?" asks Zena.

Clarke comments, "It's heinous. It looks like he's covered himself in a million watermelons."

Louis asks, "How does he stay puffed up like that? The body parts should just cave in on themselves, shouldn't they?"

Johnny Appleseed says, "If I remember the lore of Layban correctly, the Breastplate of Layban weaves together carnage to form an undead suit of armor."

The stay-puffed watermelon wight belches out blackflame from its muzzle, instantly freezing all the holy warriors within range. The survivors charge with selfless courage. This time around, the Knights Paladin have met their match. Its huge arms swipe at them with sharp, bony claws, dismembering them instantly. Although their weapons gouge large holes in its meat-bone armor, its dismembered victims are sucked back into the gaps, filling them up and boosting its strength.

Florenz draws the Sword of Layban and asks Dungaree Jeanne, "Can we defeat this stay-puffed watermelon wight with this?"

Dungaree Jeanne consults with Johnny Appleseed and then replies in Eldric, "He says it's too dangerous. If those streams of blackflame from the Breastplate of Layban hit the stream from the Sword of Layban, you would be instantly killed, and it might rain blackflame over the entire span of Shentalpee City."

"But would it kill the cardinal too?"

Dungaree Jeanne repeats Florenz's question in Aenglish and Johnny Appleseed replies, "You bet your bottom dollar it'd kill him; but the sun won't come out over Tuscoraura Mountain for a long time!"

Although the dwarf hammerhead bolts pummel the behemoth wight with each volley, it crashes into them with a horrid stomp, crushing even the finest armored dwarves with the sheer weight of corpses. The Knights Hospitaller clamber forward on the icy floorboards, half of them slipping and skidding on the ground before they even attack.

The stay-puffed watermelon wight spits a long stream of blackflame and freezes one after another. Then it steps on the frozen Hospitallers, shattering them like icicles crashing down from broken shingles and it adds their remains to its abominable hide.

Florenz weighs the options and comes to the only possible conclusion. "So many lives lost . . . we have to cross the streams."

Enganyon butts in, "Wait! Reverend Appleseed just said that crossing the streams is bad. That would be suicide."

With a swat of its arm, the mega-wight knocks over the aqueduct's spout and splashes the water in every direction. It then ignites the growing puddle with its blackflame breath. As the aqueduct pours more water into Thor's Base, the flames rise higher and the chill bites deeper into the bones of the living. With a burst of bulbous laughter, the stay-puffed watermelon wight heaves its belly back as it watches Thor's Base ice over.

Florenz announces without taking her eyes off her adversary, "The evil cardinal is unstoppable. It's the only chance the Tuscoraura elves have to survive this."

Enganyon thinks it over for a second and suddenly grows very supportive. "You know what? I love this plan. I'm excited about this plan. Where do you get these amazing ideas?"

Florenz hoists the Sword of Layban over her head and cries out, "By the power of Layban . . . I have the power!"

Johnny Appleseed waves his arms and calls to her in Aenglish. Dungaree Jeanne translates, "He says the only way to destroy the cardinal is if he blows his stream of blackflame directly onto the stream from the Sword of Layban. If the cardinal kills you any other way, you will have given your life for nothing."

The stay-puffed watermelon wight continues to trash Thor's Base by freezing the outdoor amphitheater with streams of blackflame. Florenz charges in with the Sword of Layban flaming, but the stay-puffed watermelon wight swats her with a backhand and knocks her senseless into the Gazebo Cafe's garden.

Louis and Clarke see her go sprawling. Aware of what's at stake, Louis takes up the sword but he doesn't know how to make it go flaming. He shouts over to Johnny Appleseed, "How do I get it to work?"

Johnny Appleseed tells him the formulaic words and Louis repeats them carefully, "By the power of Layban . . . I have the power!"

The sword kicks up a puny blackflame that soon peters out. Louis tries it again and again with the shaky fingers of a chain-smoker who cannot get a lighter on long enough to keep up his streak.

As the stay-puffed watermelon wight rampages on, it grabs a vegetable stand and hurls frozen tomatoes at the rangers. Louis loses patience and lets out a lion's roar as he charges forth. In his rage, the paltry blackflame of Layban suddenly leaps out and hits a new high with its ferocity.

The stay-puffed watermelon wight belches out blackflame across Thor's Base and Louis swings the sword to cross the streams. Right before contact, Louis steps on a slick patch of ice and his feet go flying up in the air. With a nasty *boink,* the back of his head rebounds off the ground twice before settling and the Sword of Layban goes skidding off in another direction.

Enganyon figures out that Louis's plan B is not going as well as hoped. He cradles Florenz in his arms and slaps her cheeks gently. "Come on, baby! Wake up! Don't leave us yet."

She blinks a few times, then turns to Enganyon with a weak voice. "Yes, you're right. I started this mess, I have to finish it. Before I go, I just want to know if you truly love me, Monsieur Enganyon."

Enganyon stutters, "I'd enjoy kissing you. I mean, I'd like to. Is that love? Wait, what?"

Dungaree Jeanne says, "Love is putting someone else's needs before yours. Lynx charged into the maw of the wyvern to keep it away from Senior Officer Onashelf. Lynx never had romantic feelings for her, but he loved her enough to lay down his life for her."

Enganyon sneaks over and picks up the Sword of Layban. He shivers violently from the cold, then drops it. Wrapping his hat around his hand, he picks it up again and says, "If that's what love is, then some people are worth freezing for. I will cross the streams for you, Mademoiselle Florenz."

His hands tremble and he drops it again. Even using his hat as a mitten, the sword is just too cold and inwardly chilling for him to hold onto it for long.

Tears well up in her eyes and she says, "You can't. Your neutral alignment won't allow it. Only I can do this. Just kiss me before you go."

They share a passionate kiss. Enganyon whimpers as if waking up to a whole new world that he never knew was right in front of him all along.

Zena gives her a deep hug and says, "For all those years we played together as little girls, I've loved you and envied you as only a little sister knows how. Florenz, please don't go. You'll freeze!"

She takes up the Sword of Layban with an unshakable resolution in her eyes and says, "The cold never bothered me anyway."

As the stay-puffed watermelon wight rampages toward the last of the beautiful buildings on Thor's Base—the basilica—it pauses before the colossal statue of Thor as if to admire its workmanship for a brief moment. Then it heaves its putrefied chest and belches forth such a tremendous tidal wave of blackflame that snow flurries billow out like a mushroom cloud around it. Then it pummels the statue until it collapses.

Florenz catches up to her foe just as it lays into the tympanum of the basilica with its right foot. Outraged, she shouts, "Nobody steps on the basilica in my city!"

With that, Florenz Kibblersdottir ignites her sword and charges with unflinching courage at the undead giant. The stay-puffed watermelon wight turns and wrinkles its hideous face with unmitigated hatred. Out of blind spite, it unthinkingly blows out a concentrated stream of blackflame that crosses streams with Florenz's flaming blade.

Both freeze over instantly.

A gentle calm blankets the scene.

Silence.

Clarke's voice rings out, "He said he always gets to win but evil always loses in the end!"

Johnny Appleseed cautions them all, "Step back, everyone! It's not over until the flat navel spins."

"What?"

From the middle of the frozen watermelon wight's belly button, cracks start to appear with a *poing*. They start spider-webbing all over his frozen body. The first part to break away is the flat part around its navel. It starts spinning slowly, then faster and faster.

Johnny Appleseed looks up and shouts, "Run! Run for your lives!"

Scene 7: Fallout

Shentalpee City on Tuscoraura Mountain
Tiw's Day Vespers. Evening, 4th of July, 1284
Third of Saint Swithun

Thanks to Officer Bunzi's Justiciar Leaguers and Sir Jon Stark's rangers, most of the escape chutes have been deployed by now. The survivors evacuate Thor's Base in a quick and orderly fashion. Everyone makes it safely to the wood elf villages below in the nick of time.

KABOOM!

After a long wind up, the high inquisitor's frozen corpse explodes, spewing blackflame up and over the forest canopy. Clouds of dust and frozen vapor stifle the skies.

The force of the explosion rattles Tuscoraura Mountain down to the bedrock beneath the dwarven tunnels. Wreckage from the black wildfires collapses, shards of ice rain down, and frozen debris comes crashing from above upon one and all. Elves, humans, gnomes, and dwarves huddle under whatever shelter they can find.

As the fallout starts to settle, Enganyon sees Louis and Clarke. One of them is carrying the Sword of Layban but he can't tell which one. (All humans look the same to elves.) Though not sure exactly why he is outraged by the sight, it bothers him to the core. He runs over and starts shouting at the human in Eldric.

"He doesn't speak a word of Eldric, Monsieur Enganyon." It's Zena. She stews with anger at him.

"But he's got the mademoiselle Florenz's sword!"

"The mademoiselle Florenz is gone! Why can't you get that between your pointy ears?"

Dungaree Jeanne steps in and says, "Because she's not gone. In fact, she's right here."

Enganyon stares at her in silence for a moment.

Zena gasps, "What?"

Dungaree Jeanne points to the sword and explains in Eldric. "I asked Reverend Appleseed to pray for a miracle to bring the mademoiselle Florenz back to life. He prayed and informed me that she is not dead. Apparently, crossing the streams trapped her soul inside the Sword of Layban.

"It also trapped the high inquisitor's soul inside the Breastplate of Layban when he exploded, but the force of the blast must have flung the breastplate several miles from here. When Florenz's body shattered, the Sword of Layban landed at Louis's feet. It's as if she wanted him to have it next."

Enganyon replies, "With all due respect, Madame Dungaree, I could never believe such nonsense."

Dungaree Jeanne says in Aenglish. "Reverend Appleseed, he says he could never believe that the mademoiselle Florenz is inside the sword."

Appleseed prays for a moment and looks up. "Tell Enganyon that Florenz tells him never to say never."

Enganyon gasps when he hears the translation.

Zena stammers a bit then asks in halting Aenglish, "Mademoiselle Florenz, she is really in sword?"

"Her soul is bound to the Sword of Layban, yes."

"That is so very bad!" says Zena.

"It is a mercy," replies Johnny Appleseed. "She chose to delve into great evils during her lifetime, but the Lord Jesus said, 'There is no greater love than to lay down your life for your friends.' She has been given a second chance at salvation now."

Zena asks, "What can she do from inside sword?"

Anxious to learn more, Enganyon pleads for a translation. When he hears the news, he grabs for the sword, vowing to free her. Before he can take hold of it, blackflame erupts from its grip and flash freezes his gloves. He yelps, "What on middle earth!"

Johnny Appleseed explains, "She can guide and defend Louis as he completes the quest destined for her. She promised to find some bronze plates. She will have to honor that promise from inside the sword."

Enganyon demands, "Tell the humans to give me the sword and I'll make this right."

Dungaree Jeanne conveys his words to Johnny Appleseed and he replies, "No. Florenz saw Louis wield it bravely in an attempt to take her place in sacrificing herself. She wants him to carry it. She feels a kinship with him for tasting the same temptations she had and yet carrying the same spark of goodness that led her to sacrifice her own life to save others."

Enganyon cannot wrap his mind around all this. He asks in Eldric, "But what is Mister Louis going to do?"

Dungaree Jeanne asks Louis in Aenglish what he intends to do with the Sword of Layban. His face draws a blank. "I have no idea."

Seeing his confusion, Johnny Appleseed offers sound advice. "Keep it a secret. We have already seen too many ways that the sword can be used for evil, but it was given to Florenz to be used for good. What good will come of it remains to be seen. Until then, her only advice to you, Louis, is to keep its power a secret so that evil people cannot get their hands on it.

"And this is my advice to you: do not be afraid! You don't have to figure out the great mysteries, or even your purpose in life, before adventuring out there. Just go forward with a heart full of trust in God's goodness. The hand of Providence will lead you to wherever you're supposed to be one blind step at a time. As followers of Christ, we walk by faith, not by sight."

Clarke says, "Louis and I decided to join up with Sir Robert Roger's rangers as apprentices. Is that okay?"

Johnny Appleseed replies, "You don't need to ask me. As long as you keep praying every day, you'll find what it is God's calling you to, sooner or later."

Louis adds, "We both feel it's the right decision. We've become good friends with the only other apprentice in the company, Nathan Hayle, and several rangers have taken us under their wing. It's the first time for both of us that we feel like we have a family we can trust."

Dungaree Jeanne asks them, "Do you know where the rangers are headed to next?"

"There's been talk about a quest in Fort Detroit."

Johnny Appleseed strokes his beard and speculates. "Archbishop Bozo has long been accused of sympathizing with the Blackflame Cult. Rumor has it the Inquisition has ordered death to come for the Archbishop. If the baron of Amhirst is in league with the Inquisition, the rangers might have been tasked with fulfilling those orders.

"Still, it's a blessing. Chances are high that Zena's magica tree has locomutated itself somewhere along the shores of Lake Eerie. With your permission, Madame Dungaree, Zena and I can keep an eye on our two young friends here while we look for her tree."

"Permission granted," replies Dungaree Jeanne.

Zena is about to object but she realizes she has no objections. She tells her mother in Aenglish, "There is nothing for me here in Shentalpee City. My magica tree is gone. I lose elections and I not care what high elves think of me.

"My soul wants to believe in real God and my heart wants to learn magica trees. I not think of better guide for me than Reverend Appleseed."

Dungaree Jeanne gives her a hug. "You've been through a lot, dear, but I have to admit that my motherly instincts are telling me it was all worth it to finally see you come to your senses. Reverend Appleseed will be like a father to you, more so than Umpire Kibbler could ever have been."

Enganyon is the only one in the group who speaks no Aenglish but he suspect that last conversation did not go his way. As soon as her mother lets her go, Enganyon grabs Zena's hand and says to her in Eldric, "Mademoiselle Zena, I know my behavior has not made much sense to you, but with his dying words my father instructed me to tell the truth and the truth is—I love you. I love you and I've always loved you. I can explain everything if you just give me the chance."

Zena looks at him in disbelief. "Yeah, about that. My mother and I were just saying—"

"What ho!" shouts a commanding voice in Aenglish.

They all turn around and realize they are surrounded by the Crusader army.

ACT VII

WHAT HO!

Scene 1: All Together Now

Shentalpee City on Tuscoraura Mountain
Tiw's Day Vespers. Evening, 4th of July, 1284
Third of Saint Swithun

At that moment, the duke of Philadelphia rides forward on a large, sturdy warhorse, accompanied by his heralds, squires, champions, and his daughter, Lady Philippa, code-named Ariel. He calls down, "What ho! Are the elves capitulating?"

Dungaree Jeanne is standing right next to the duke's horse and, although her command of Aenglish is nearly flawless, she is shocked by the realization that she has no idea what the duke is trying to say.

She turns to Johnny Appleseed for a translation. "Capitulating . . . what ho? I don't get it."

"What ho!" replies Appleseed. He then turns to the duke and says to him, "The name's Johnny Appleseed. What ho, Duke!"

The duke politely replies, "What ho!"

Picking up Appleseed's cue, Louis and Clarke both start calling out, "What ho! What ho!"

The duke grunts and says, "It seems rather difficult to go on with the conversation under the current, adverse circumstances. May I propose a truce?"

Finally comprehending his words, Dungaree Jeanne replies in Aenglish, "There is no need, sir knight. The Crusade is over—the heresiarch is dead, and the high inquisitor burned all the riches of the elves to icicles."

"I am Duke William Pinne. As commander in chief of the crusading army, Madame Elve, I beg your pardon, but the war isn't over until I say it's over. A noble of my standing cannot depart empty-handed."

Dungaree Jeanne says in Aenglish, "Then all is well. Your Grace is seated on an excellent horse and you hold the bridle in your left hand. You are neither standing nor empty-handed. You may take your armies and leave Tuscoraura Mountain for good."

The duke of Philadelphia tries again. "Perhaps something got lost in the translation. Normally, a victorious army pillages the spoils of the battlefield to cover its payroll. We have done no pillaging and if you want to keep it that way, I expect payment. Unpaid soldiers do very nasty things, if you catch my drift."

Dungaree Jeanne stands up and says, "Let me translate this for you. Thanks to your high inquisitor's abuse of the blackflame, all our assets are frozen. As dungaree of Foreign Trade, I could work out a profitable trade pact between the fire elves of Tuscoraura Mountain and the wall humans of Philadelphia if you agree to a simple condition."

Bowing his head slightly, the duke says, "I am all ears, Madame Dungaree."

"You must tell the truth. Spread our story honestly. The world needs to know about what happened here. They need to be made aware of the dangers of the blackflame, the betrayal of the high inquisitor, and the futility of waging a Crusade against fire elves."

"Agreed. My court in Philadelphia is home to the finest bards and the most revered loremasters on this side of the Ocean of Atlantis. The clayborn of Vinland will know your story and we shall tell it true. As a token of goodwill, I invite you to come to Philadelphia as an honored guest of mine.

"At my court, we can iron out the nitty-gritty of a truly revolutionary free trade pact. Moreover, I shall give you final say in how the chronicles record the events that have transpired here today for the memory of the land of the free and the home of the brave."

Dungaree Jeanne eyes him and says, "Agreed. You may now leave in peace, and I shall find you in Philadelphia in one month's time."

"Begging your pardon, Madame Dungaree, but business is business. First, I must request a retainer for our trade agreement. The expenses of this Crusade have already emptied my coffers. I'd need two thousand dollars if I'm going to be able to keep my army under tight discipline on the march home. Unpaid troops are wont to riot and plunder the locals."

"I see." From a grimace to a twinkle in her eye, Dungaree Jeanne lights up and asks Johnny Appleseed, "Do you think you could work your magic for this noble lord and provide him with, say, two sacks of refined cocoa powder?"

With a wave of his magic wand, Johnny Appleseed intones, "Oh, fudge!"

A puff of brown smoke and delicious, brown powder floats in the air. Like a little boy trying to catch snowflakes on his tongue, the duke of Philadelphia arches his head back and tastes the chocolatey fog.

He nods and says, "Adieu, Madame Dungaree! My magicultors should be skilled enough to gather all this cocoa powder into gunnysacks. Your down payment on our future friendship will not be forgotten. For now, we depart in peace, and I look forward to your arrival in Philadelphia."

Dungaree Jeanne's face washes over with relief—and cocoa powder. "It will be a trip to remember."

The duke sighs, "I don't know if Philadelphia has much to offer compared to the wonders of this place."

Dungaree Jeanne assures him, "Oh, no worries, my lord. My heart tells me that this is just the start of many adventures grand and marvelous for both our peoples."

He waves his retinue to fall back and starts turning his horse around while he says, "You are obviously a lady who trusts her heart. I have no doubt that all will happen as you say."

After the duke departs, Dungaree Jeanne says in Aenglish, "Reverend Appleseed, do you see that fruit and vegetable stand at the base of that sequoia tree down that road? It's got a warehouse we can use as a make-shift hospital for all the wounded. May I ask you to go and start setting up inside? I'll gather elves to help." She turns to Louis and Clarke, asking, "Can you two get the rangers to put together a few stretchers for those that can't walk?"

Clarke bows his head as if taking orders from the Father Prior of his monastery, while Louis remains on the ground staring at the Sword of Layban.

At that moment, Ariel approaches and points to Louis. "Young man, you are carrying a sword that belongs to a princess of these people. I promised her she should have it, so I must insist you return it."

Louis replies, "She's inside the sword."

"What?"

Johnny Appleseed explains, "She sacrificed her life to stop the evil inquisitor by crossing the streams of the blackflame. It brought about the dark clouds above us and a strange fate for her. Her soul is now trapped inside the sword awaiting redemption."

Louis adds, "She has chosen me to fulfill her promise. I'm supposed to find some bronze plates."

Ariel is astonished. "You couldn't have known about her promise unless all you are telling me is true."

"Help! Help!" A young woman bursts into the scene. They all turn around. It's Sacagawea. She cries, "Monsignor Meyer! We need a miracle. Uncle Sam is dying. Come quickly!"

The Monsignor replies, "Calm down, dear. We are setting up a hospital now. Come we'll bring him there."

Sacagawea says, "No. We can't let any of the Aenglish here see him. They might arrest him and time is running out. We can't let him die!"

Johnny Appleseed sees her distress and says, "Jesus healed the centurion's servant from afar. If it's that urgent, we'll all pray together right here for your uncle to be healed no matter where he is." He points to Clarke and Monsignor Meyer, sensing that they are clerics as well. "Brothers, please join me in prayer."

Monsignor Meyer and Clarke kneel down to pray, folding their hands together but Johnny Appleseed remains standing and stretches his arms up to heaven. After they have all prayed for a while, Appleseed opens his eyes. "I'm sorry, daughter, but the answer is no."

"What?" Sacagawea turns to the Monsignor.

Monsignor Oscar Meyer nods his head. "I got the same answer to our prayers. God's saying no."

Sacagawea asks, "Is there a more powerful miracle worker around here who can save him?"

"No miracle workers have any power," replies Johnny Appleseed. "All miracles are gifts from God. He uses them to strengthen our faith and lead people to salvation, not to meddle with politics or make people rich. Viceroy Samuel de Champlain has had to carry a heavy cross over the past few months. He has sincerely repented of his sins and has prayed for a holy death. God has said it's his time to go home and nothing in this world or the next can change that."

Tears leak from her eyes.

Clarke adds, "Yes, God has plans for his salvation. He's going to a better place now."

Sacagawea rebels. "No! I worked too hard to save him; I'm not giving up on him now. If your God can't do it, then I'll find a more powerful god who can." With that, she runs off.

A heavy silence hangs in the chocolatey air for a short while as the cocoa powder settles and everyone sympathizes with Sacagawea's plight.

Duke William Pinne's magicultors interrupt the mood as they move in to collect the scattered cocoa powder into gunnysacks. They intone magic words and ply all their magic tricks but it's not working out too well for them.

The head magicultor whispers something into Ariel's ear and then she calls to Johnny Appleseed. "Reverend Appleseed, it seems gathering all this cocoa powder into gunnysacks is not as easy as you made it look. Could you please tell us the good word that makes it all possible?"

Johnny Appleseed swings his elbow upwards and hollers, "Oooooh, the Lord is good to me, and so I thank the Lord for giving me the things I need; the sun and the rain and the apple seed. The Lord is good to me. Amen! Amen! Amen! Amen! Amen!"

EPILOGUE

THEY LL CONTINUE

SINGING IT FOREVER

Scene 1: The Quest Giver

Shentalpee City on Tuscoraura Mountain
Frige's Day Compline. Night, 7th of July, 1284
Feast of the Translation of Saint Thomas à Becket's Bones

The governor-general's tent is well lit though it is past nightfall. The smell of linseed oil from the clay lamps and tallow from the candles makes the white smoke feel thick and heavy. For lack of a suitable goose, turkey, or even a crow feather, Amhirst is scratching out a flurry of missives and commands to his contacts, agents, and senior officers across Vinland with a chicken quill.

Sir Robert Roger has been standing in front of the governor-general's fold-up desk for quite some time now and decides it is better to risk his lord's displeasure by clearing his throat loudly than to stand there late into the night when fatigue and drowsiness might sour Amhirst's mood excessively.

Ahem . . .

The baron doesn't stir.

AHEM . . .

"Ah!" squeals the governor-general as he looks up from his scrolls in genuine fright. "Goodness gracious, man! How long have you been standing there? I didn't hear you come in."

Sir Robert Roger crumples up his round-brimmed ranger hat in his hands. "Pardon me, my lord. I was doing my best to make as much noise as possible so as to politely alert you to my arrival but, you know, a ranger lives in the bush. Moving silently is a matter of life and death. Some habits are hard to shake."

"Of course, of course. That's your specialty, isn't it?" Amhirst's eyes are red from overwork but he takes a moment to rub them so he can peer into Sir Robert Roger's eyes and pry into his inner thoughts. "Do you know why I summoned you here, Sir Robert Roger?"

"No, my lord." Sir Robert Roger begins to recite the line he's been rehearsing in his mind for the past half-hour or so. "But my hope would be that you have another quest to put my rangers at your service. Watching you rise up the ladder of success is the only reward we need. I can tell you that much."

Amhirst gazes at him intently for an uncomfortably long period, then stands up and starts to pace around the tent. His mood is pensive and his eyebrows are heavily furrowed. "Yes, yes, noble sentiments. Not just another quest, but a list of quests is what I need."

Sir Robert Roger says nothing.

Amhirst rubs his chin and cheeks, which are either long overdue for a shave or marking a conscientious effort to grow a beard. He asks again, "You know why I sent for you at this hour of the night, Sir Robert Roger?"

"I am all ears, my lord." Forasmuch as his father always told him to look a man straight in the eye when you talk to him, Sir Robert Roger avoids eye contact with the governor-general, instinctively staring at the lamp's yellow flame instead.

Although the battle is over, Sir Robert Roger is all too keenly aware that they are still on Crusade in enemy territory. He has allowed neither his troops nor himself a moment to relax. All the rangers start every day fully equipped and fully prepared for a fight.

"You are here because you know how to get the job done. I was arrested; you rescued me. I sent you to Tuscoraura Mountain when my life depended on it and you delivered the inquisitor at the right place and at the right time. You're not just a loyal soldier—you're a competent one."

"Thank you, my lord, I always—"

"Of course, of course." Amhirst cuts him off, and Sir Robert Roger reminds himself not to speak unless prompted to. "I'm sending you to Fort Detroit. My spies have gathered reliable intel suggesting that an Ottowa lord by the name of Sagamore Pontiak is fomenting a rebellion against the Aenglish Crown. He will probably strike at Fort Detroit first. Your primary quest is to thwart this rebellion either by diplomacy or force of arms.

"Furthermore, the newly appointed high inquisitor, Amerik Cardinal Vespuchi, wants me to arrest Fort Detroit's archbishop, named Bozo. Several high-level clerics have concerns that he's been clowning around with the occult, including dabbling with the Blackflame Cult. We know how dangerous they are."

"Yes indeed we do, my—"

Amherst doesn't wait for him to finish and just talks over him, "Cardinal Vespuchi told me to extend his personal guarantee of safe passage and a fair trial to Archbishop Bozo if he will come peaceably with you to Salim to clear himself of these allegations. If he refuses, then and only then are you authorized to take him to Salim by force. Understood?"

"Yes, my lord."

"There is one other issue I need you to look into. Upon the recommendation of my herald, Sir Sean Madigan, I rewarded a party of adventurers for completing a quest for which they produced no conclusive evidence. I didn't like the idea at the time but in hindsight, it seems like it was a good decision. They served us well in the Battle on Vandsee Estates, did they not?"

"Of whom do we speak, my lord?"

"Lady Philippa's party of adventurers. I believe her user name is Ariel while questing. As the duke of Philadelphia's daughter, I can only imagine what kind of shenanigans she pulled to make it seem like she fulfilled my quest while really serving her father's interests. What do you think?"

Finally feeling respected at having Amhirst consult him on an important matter, Sir Robert Roger replies, "As long as you are not requiring the Lady Philippa to betray her father, you would be well-served to have her as an ally."

"That's exactly what eats at me. That quest was to locate and eliminate the last surviving heir of the Marquis Ducaine. Other than this cryptic amulet, she has provided no evidence that the boy is dead. At first, I assumed it was simply the result of sloppy soldiering.

Now that I've seen them in action, I realize there is nothing sloppy about them.

"I have a terrible, sinking feeling that I just paid her party a small fortune to kidnap young Ducaine for him to be held in reserve as an ace in the hole until the duke is ready to make his move against Fort Pitt.

"Lord William Pinne does not need the title of viceroy to attain royal status in Vinland. According to some well-placed informants, he has already petitioned the pope for the royal title of grand duke. The pope denied the petition on the grounds that Philadelphia's territory is not extensive enough to merit the status of a grand duchy.

"King Eddard knows about this petition but he has to pretend as if he doesn't know, since the pope's affairs are supposed to be confidential. That is why the king gave Fort Pitt to me so readily—to keep it out of the duke's hands. Ever since Lord William Pinne received that response from the pope, he has been looking to expand.

"Nature prevents him from expanding east into the Ocean of Atlantis, and he cannot go north into the Seven Nations without provoking a war that he cannot win. To the south, the earl of Baltimoor's lands are already firmly set under Aenglish rule, so his only choice was to conquer the Frankish territories to his west—I beat him to it.

"As governor-general, my territories are twice as tempting to him since I am now the only noble left who could vie with him for supremacy in Vinland, and conquering Fort Pitt would not only take me down a notch but it would also give Lord Pinne sovereignty over vast swathes of territory that just might entitle him to renew his petition with the pope. In fact, one of my spies has recovered a discarded parchment detailing air-headed schemes to unite Philadelphia and Fort Pitt under a single banner called—get this—the Grand Duchy of Pinnesylvania.

"The man is a dreamer, to be sure, and I would happily ignore him if I did not recall my history lessons so vividly. The Merovingian Chronicles tell us how the pope granted Karl the Hammer, a mere steward, the royal title of king of Frankland to justify further conquests against his pagan neighbors.

"With all that in mind, I suspect he is doing everything possible to put Fort Pitt into enemy hands so he can legitimately conquer it for himself. Would I sound paranoid if I told you that I believe Lord William Pinne is behind Pontiak's rebellion?"

"Not at all, my lord."

"If I'm right, he is starting with Fort Detroit because he believes it will be an easy target. The Frankish population there is not happy with King Eddard's policy of canceling all their former treaties. They are looking for any excuse to reject Aenglish authority.

"Moreover, Sagamore Pontiak could easily win the Count de Cadillac's loyalty if he can prove himself a competent war leader—and display the political savvy necessary to keep his coalition together long enough to win over the Confederacy of Seven Nations to his side.

"So now the acting governor of Fort Pitt, Sir George Warshington, has just sent me a missive that a certain young man is being touted by some of the Frankish settlers there as Laurence Ducaine, the last surviving son and heir of the deceased Marquis Ducaine. Sir George Warshington insists that the boy's real name is actually Jack Robinson, but an impostor who stirs rebellion is just as dangerous as the real heir.

"If they rally around this boy in the name of the Frankish king or if the population of Fort Pitt declares itself for Sagamore Pontiak's rebellion, Lord William could then waltz right into Fort Pitt in the name of King Eddard, claiming to restore peace, and instead seize control of it for himself.

"I pulled the same trick myself—inciting the Vikings to rebel so my ally, Sir Samuel Maverick, could install himself as Duke of New Yourke.

"Sir Robert Roger, I am telling you all this because by now, your fortunes are tied to mine. If the House of Amhirst falls, your lucky stars fall with it. I care little for the fate of Fort Detroit, since King Eddard refused to appoint me its count in place of Cadillac, but you absolutely must find a way to crush Pontiak's rebellion before it gains enough momentum to threaten Fort Pitt.

"Furthermore, you must find a way to prevent young Laurence Ducaine—or anyone else claiming to be the heir to the Marquis Ducaine—from gaining enough of a following to foment a serious rebellion.

"The rebels wouldn't even need to win. Credible reports of a rebellion would be enough to furnish the duke of Philadelphia with an excuse to swoop in and claim the title of grand duke of Pinnesylvania before you can say Jack Robinson. You have to stop it before it even starts. Understood?"

"Understood, my lord."

"If Ariel has betrayed me and delivered the young Ducaine to her father instead of fulfilling the quest I so handsomely rewarded her for, then as a personal favor to me, I would kindly request that you assassinate her as well. Is that too much to ask?"

"Not at all, my lord."

"Splendid! Don't forget, Sir Robert Roger, that this scroll entitles you to stake your claim to any 10,000-acre homestead within my domains that is not already in the possession of another knight. I know I am asking a lot of you, but there are few men in Vinland I trust as wholeheartedly as I trust you. Can I count on you, Sir Robert Roger, to fulfill these quests for me?"

"All the way, my lord."

"Good! Dismissed."

Amhirst has already buried his head in his correspondence by the time it even occurs to Sir Robert Roger that he is supposed to leave. He turns around, then doubles back again and asks, "Why bother with this Bozo?"

Amhirst wrinkles his lip as he looks up. "What?"

"Excuse me, my lord, but you have so many extremely important matters to worry about. I'm supposed to crush rebellions and destroy some of the most powerful houses in Vinland. Why am I also the errand boy for the Inquisition?"

Amhirst puts his quill down, folds his hands and says gently, "If only I had the comfort of being so naive, I might get some more sleep. Right now, all the high inquisitors and cardinals have been wasting their lives away meddling in politics instead of praying and preaching the gospel. If those of us with real power stopped playing along with them, then they'd stop playing along with us."

"Oh." Sir Robert Roger wants to say more, but he can't remember what it is exactly.

The ranger captain starts walking out of the tent

when Amhirst suddenly lifts his head again and calls to him, "Ah! I almost forgot."

Barely does Sir Robert Roger glance back than the baron pitches a scrimshaw amulet at him. The ranger's reflexes are fast enough that he snatches it out of the air about an inch before crashing into his nose.

"What is this, my lord?"

"Ariel and her party of adventurers pawned it off as proof that they eliminated the last surviving son of the Marquis Ducaine. Supposedly, it belonged to the boy. You'll have to ask Brother Tuck what it means exactly, but it seems to suggest that the boy's mother buried a treasure for him under the church in Fort Detroit.

"Never mind any gems, silver, or gold you find there, but if she stashed away the Ducaine family ancestral sword or the Ducaine signet ring or some other token of authority, bring it to me at once. The last thing I need is an endless succession of morons using such baubles to claim to be the heir of Ducaine."

Sir Robert Roger rubs his nose and asks, "When you say never mind, you mean I can keep all the gems, silver, and gold that I find thanks to this amulet?"

"I consider you a friend. My friends never need to worry about silver or gold. Any more questions?"

"No, my lord."

"Good. Dismissed."

Scene 2: Betzy Rose Mansion

Betzy Rose Mansion, Red Giant's Base, Shentalpee City
Saturn's Day Prime. Dawn, 8th of July, 1284
Morrow of the Translation of Saint Thomas à Becket's Bones

By some miracle, Betzy Rose Mansion has suffered little from the blackflame storm that tore across Shentalpee City. Perhaps it was because Umpire Gandorf hacked down the bridge connecting Thor's Base to Red Giant's Base preventing its spread; perhaps offering hospitality to a holy man of God added some extra glow of protection. Whatever the reason a glorious morning dawns on Dungaree Jeanne's home.

Zena comes down the stairs to find her mother eating corn flakes with a spoon in her left hand and writing letters with an inked quill in her right. Zena sits down at the breakfast table with her favorite pigeon, Post, tucked under her arm and says, "You know, Mother, it's almost hard to believe that the sun is still shining so brightly and cheerfully after all the wanton death and destruction of the past few days."

Without looking up, Dungaree Jeanne replies, "If you must know, Zena dear, it's not hard for me to believe the sun is shining on glorious mornings like this. The sun always lights up the heavens, even when gloomy clouds cover it. It simply takes a noble spirit to believe it's still shining when you can't see it."

"You're so philosophical, Mom. Is that how you've made it through tough times . . . peering into the mysteries of the universe and deciphering the meaning of it all through the prism of an unflagging optimism?"

Dungaree Jeanne chomps on another spoonful of corn flakes and looks her daughter straight in the eye. "Not at all, Zena dear. The real secret is that I've turned to a bowl of the pigeon's corn flakes with heavy doses of maple syrup and doe milk in my darkest hours. Somehow, you stumbled upon the recipe for my secret comfort food, and my jealousy knows no bounds."

Zena feeds a few flakes to Post and bites into a few herself, saying, "Actually, this pigeon has taught me more than the secret to eating corn flakes. He has taught me that no matter how far away I fly, I'll always want to return home sooner or later."

"Thank you, Zena dear," she says, putting a hand on her daughter's arm. "That makes a mother feel good to hear it. When do you plan to leave with the Reverend Appleseed?"

"Tomorrow morning. He's giving me a day to say goodbye to the friends and family I love so much."

A knock at the door sends them both bounding to their feet. Madame Dungaree opens the door. She gives a knowing look to Zena and waves her into the parlor.

Dungaree Jeanne feigns surprise. "Oh, my fuzzy eyebrows! It's Monsieur Enganyon—or should I say—the monsieur Acting Major Leagues Umpire Enganyon! To what do we owe the great honor of such an avocation from your pressing duties?"

Enganyon replies in Runic, "Health and happiness to thee, Madame Dungaree and Dean. No trivial matter brings me to thy threshold this day. I must speak with Mademoiselle Zena urgently, if it is at all possible."

"It just so happens that she was saying her goodbyes in the parlor as you knocked. If you hurry, she might still be there."

"Thank you, Madame!" Enganyon rushes past her and walks into the parlor with a flourish. Getting down on one knee he says, "Oh, Mademoiselle Zena, thank the heavens thou art safe! My heart has been worried sick ever since I lost sight of thee when Thor's Base began to crumble."

"Then I am glad thou hast recovered from thy illness so easily!" Zena covers her mouth, pretending to be shy, but really hiding her snickering at his melodramatic show.

"Not at all, my beloved! I am not at all well. A fever still burns in my heart. The question I dare not ask . . . but must—" He bites his knuckle as if wrestling against his inner modesty. He then asks with ebullient ardor, "I must know if thou wilt still accept my love."

"Oh, that's very flattering, Monsieur Enganyon."

"No, no, no! What I mean to say is that thou hast discomfited me entirely. Before thee now kneels not merely another admirer of thine, but thy true love. Now that the evil umpire is no more and the threat to my family's good name and heritage is removed, I am free to be myself once again. And from the very depths of my being, I profess, Mademoiselle Zena, that I love thee and wish to make thee my lawfully wedded wife."

Zena looks up at the ceiling and taps her chin and says in Eldric, "Hmmm, that's all fine and dandy, but as I recall, there is a technicality by which, according to the books in the council chambers, I am still engaged to our dearly departed monsieur Captain Lynx."

Enganyon persists in speaking Runic. "If thou hast not heard, the Council of Perfects has confirmed my appointment as acting major leagues umpire in honor of my father's heroic sacrifice that saved Shentalpee

City—or at least spared it from a worse fate. In any event, I am acting head of state and can remove such an impediment with a simple command to my secretary."

Zena feigns to be very impressed but keeps speaking to him in Eldric to chip away at the dramatic effect he is going for. "Oh? You have a secretary now. You may also recall that our stewardess, Bartlebee, was falsely accused of betraying state secrets. That sleazy smear campaign still tarnishes my family's heritage."

Enganyon stands up. "As thou knowest, my dearest Zena, the perfidious Monsieur Kibbler plunged Shentalpee City into the most abject ruin it has faced in centuries. It will be the task of this generation, and possibly the next, to rebuild and recover from his evil deeds. No fire elf in his right mind would hold a false accusation concocted by the perfidious Monsieur Kibbler against thee. His piteous daughter only repeated those unworthy indictments against you because he used her as an unwitting pawn in one of his many foul schemes."

Zena thinks for a moment, then says, "As we have seen, my dear Monsieur Enganyon, not all fire elves are in their right mind. In the current turmoil, it would be all too easy for a political adversary to dig up false charges against my family to impede the momentum of my mother's League of Nations or her trade agreements, or even undermine my chances at getting elected umpire-in-chief in the rescheduled elections."

Enganyon strikes a noble pose. "Well then, if it distresses thee so, I shall challenge any such slanderer to a duel!"

Zena groans, "And win that duel the way your father won against my father? No thank you. Speaking of which, has anyone ever told you why they really fought that duel?"

"Naturally."

"Oh." Zena inspects the new doilies on the guest table and asks, "What was your understanding?"

Enganyon clasps her hand. "Why get fixated on the past when we have our whole future to plan?"

"Because the past just might dictate what is possible in the future and what is not."

"Thy intent befuddles me."

Zena sighs and says, "Reverend Appleseed claims that my father challenged your father to a duel over the putative paternity of my mother's pregnancy."

"So?"

"That means you could be my half-brother."

"Poppycock! Balderdash! Tommyrot! Hogwash and codswallop!"

"As long as it remains a possibility, our marriage could be invalidated by prying lawyers."

Enganyon snorts and whispers to her in Eldric with a conspiratorial tone, "My father knew this would come up one day. You weren't supposed to know because it's nothing but senseless trouble. You're not within any prohibited degree of consanguinity to me for the simple reason that my father is not related to me by blood."

"What?!?"

"Before the whole scandal between your mother and my father could reach the public, the erstwhile Umpire-in-Chief Drayton arranged my father's marriage to my mother with a very generous dowry because the umpire-in-chief himself had gotten her pregnant and didn't want his wife or the public to know about it.

"Yes, you are my father's daughter, but I am not my father's son. Still, my lineage comprises only the noblest and most illustrious families of Shentalpee City and should in no way cast a shadow over our happiness together."

Shocked at the revelation, Zena sits down and breathes deeply. Enganyon sits down next to her and puts an arm around her shoulders to show his support.

He resumes his discourse in Runic. "Think of the possibilities, Mademoiselle Zena. We were the only ones who stood up against the perfidious Monsieur Kibbler as he plotted to enslave Shentalpee City. Now all the high elves are saying they were on our side the whole time. The Council of Perfects has already promised to grant me a full term as Major Leagues Umpire. After the elections thou shalt surely be the next umpire-in-chief. Together, we can rule Shentalpee City as husband and wife."

"Yes," says Zena.

"Wait, what? Yes, what?" Enganyon is baffled.

"I will marry you as long as you sort out the betrothal paperwork and the false accusations against Bartlebee and publicize the family tree so no one has any more doubts about the legitimacy of my family's good name or our marriage."

"Consider it done!"

At that moment, Dungaree Jeanne comes barging into the room and rants, "Mademoiselle Zena! How could you ever accept such a lousy marriage proposal from a two-timing, yellow-bellied—"

Zena halts her mother's rant sternly. "Mother, Mother, Mother! After all those times you have scolded me for eavesdropping, you offend our privacy.

"The monsieur Acting Major Leagues Umpire here has some work to do before the betrothal is finalized. After he completes those tasks, if you still have any objections, we would be happy to entertain them in a civil manner before signing all the appropriate documents. Isn't that right, my dear Monsieur Enganyon?"

Enganyon stands slightly behind Zena to confront his future mother-in-law in Eldric. "Yeah! That's right. Don't worry, Madame Dean and Dungaree, you're not losing a daughter, you're gaining a son."

"But, Zena dear, do I need to remind you—"

Zena remains adamant. "No need to remind me of anything, Mother dearest! Please allow the monsieur Acting Major Leagues Umpire to prove himself to you and discuss the important reasons behind—"

Dungaree Jeanne interrupts her and persists, "But you're not seriously going to run for election as umpire-in-chief! I thought you learned your lesson after—"

"Mother!" shouts Zena. "Can we please discuss this as mature elves rather than standing here shouting at each other like a couple of teenagers?"

Dungaree Jeanne, red in the face, suddenly realizes that she has lost all control of her composure and takes a few nice, deep breaths to calm herself. "Very well then. Monsieur Enganyon, I warn you that if you break off this betrothal again, there will be dire consequences for you and your family. Duels are odious to me but there are other ways of dealing with enemies that can be just as gut-wrenching."

With a chipper smile, Enganyon bows and kisses their right hands. He then says, "And on that pleasant note, I shall take my leave of the two loveliest elves to inhabit Shentalpee City."

Zena shows him to the door and says, "Monsieur Umpire, when you have completed the quests that I have assigned to you, please find us in the abandoned Crusader camp. My mother has taken it upon herself to establish temporary shelters there for all the displaced elves who have lost their homes and livelihood on Black Tiw's Day."

"Is that what they are calling it now? Black Tiw's Day? I suppose the expression is apt. Very well then, I shall find thee there. Adieu, my fair lady! Adieu!"

After he leaves the threshold, Dungaree Jeanne cannot help but march up to the front door and slam it behind him. Waiting a short while to make sure he has gone out of earshot, she rails into Zena and says, "What on middle earth has possessed you to accept a marriage proposal from that faithless, cowardly, sniveling, good-for-nothing ex-boyfriend of yours after all he has put you through?"

With a calm and dignified demeanor, Zena says, "Mother dearest, please come into the parlor so we can discuss the reasons in a civil manner. Controlling one's temper is prerequisite to any leadership role."

Relishing the role reversal, Zena sits herself comfortably on the blue suede sofa and begins her explanation in Runic to give it an air of officiality. "First of all, Madame Dean of the League of Nations and Dungaree of Foreign Trade, if thou hast learned anything about me from our lifetime of familiarity, thou shouldst know that I am the kind of elve who always gets what she wants. For years, one of my primary goals has been to find myself engaged to

Monsieur Enganyon. He has talent, charm, achievements, good looks, athletic skill, and most importantly, he stems from one of the oldest and most respected families in Shentalpee City.

"That formerly undisclosed account about my being the scion of Clan Rashbold through my biological father, our dearly departed Major Leagues Umpire Gandorf, might have spared my teenage years some of the angst at trying to gain acceptance in high elf society. Still, the truth about Umpire Enganyon's lineage does nothing to diminish his standing in my eyes, since Umpire-in-Chief Drayton was in many respects one of the finest umpires Shentalpee City has known."

Dungaree Jeanne mutters loudly in Eldric, "He was kind of a jerk. He banished Umpire Kibbler's wife for no better reason than she was a dark elf who had gained power and prominence in fire elf society."

Zena responds in Runic, "They all have their flaws, Madame. They all have their flaws. Be that as it may, after endeavoring to win his hand in marriage for so many years, I would be loath to forswear it just at the moment of my victory. Have I mentioned that I am the kind of elve who always gets what she wants?"

"You have."

"Right, then. The second major reason I have for accepting Umpire Enganyon's proposal is one that thou shalt surely sympathize with."

"Try me."

"Those of us outside the governmental structures often scorn the expediencies of paperwork, but after having had my first engagement with Umpire Enganyon annulled so easily, even after the death of my first fiancé, for no reason superior than my failure to lodge the proper paperwork with the punctilious bureaucrats at the council chambers, I have pondered the situation at length and have arrived at an arrangement somewhat akin to revenge.

"Immediately after the monsieur Acting Major Leagues Umpire clears up the paperwork for our betrothal, my sojourn along the Great Lakes will begin. I must find my magica tree if I am ever to gain acceptance to Pinne Mage University, and I must hunt down this dwarf mercenary who calls himself Tom Thumb to rectify the harm done by Bartlebee's treason. Embarking upon both quests will take me away from Shentalpee City for several months, if not years.

"When I looked into abrogating my betrothal contract with our dearly departed monsieur Lynx at the council chambers, they told me that it is impossible under law to cancel a betrothal contract unilaterally without a death certificate for the absent party.

"Therefore, Monsieur Enganyon will not be able to cancel this betrothal contract with me while I am away dealing with the mercenary dwarves and pursuing my education in magiculture.

"In the meantime, all debt collectors will now have the right to demand any unpaid sums owed out of my coffers from him and his father's trust fund. That would rectify the huge debt that our dearly departed monsieur Major Leagues Umpire Gandorf strapped upon our backs when he betrayed your merchant convoy with the cocoa beans."

"Oh . . . so now he has to pay all our debts for us? I didn't even realize that was possible."

"High elves rarely speak about debts—shameful business. Now, here is the real beauty of it all: if the monsieur Acting Major Leagues Umpire continues his two-timing ways, an unbreakable betrothal contract with me will render his attempts to woo any other young elve behind my back a burdensome endeavor."

Dungaree Jeanne lightens up and says in Eldric, "So basically, you're forcing him to pay our debts and tying him up to keep him out of the dating scene."

Slipping into Eldric, Zena adds, "Who knows? I might even enjoy breaking his heart for a change."

Dungaree Jeanne announces in Runic, "In that case, o daughter of mine, thou hast my full maternal blessing for this betrothal." Then she switches back to Eldric and says, "Now, let's head down to the old Crusader camp and see if we can find a way to keep all those homeless elves' stomachs fed and their spirits high."

Scene 3: Home Run

Abandoned Crusader Camp on Tuscoraura Mountain
Thor's Day Vespers. Evening, 13th of July, 1284
Vigil of Saint Metheldred, Virgin and Martyr

The Crusader camp is slovenly but spacious. Although living behind walls is a foreign concept for elves, the hastily built wooden palisades and canvas awnings provide protection from sporadic rains and incursions from lingering undead ghouls and wendigos who hide during the day and prowl at night. With most of their workshops destroyed, the unemployed wood elves have little choice but to volunteer their time and talents for Dungaree Jeanne's reconstruction programs.

Much to Dungaree Jeanne's chagrin, the Tuscoraura elves' skill sets focus on designing fashionwear, cooking delicacies, and etching exquisite façades. They don't translate well into tasks such as digging trenches, transporting lumber, and laying foundations.

To her great delight hope comes in a different form—in the shape of the gnomish sense of compassion and neighborly goodwill. The Tuscoraura garden gnomes allow themselves to be easily persuaded to pitch in with their sharp shovels and calloused hands to handle some of the more laborious chores during the initial reconstruction phases.

Among elves, destroying a tree without a very clear and long-term purpose is not only shameful, but also criminal in nature. As such, Dungaree Jeanne spends long nights trying to figure out not only how to build sturdy, waterproof structures quickly, but also how to do so without cutting down any new trees—relying only on the timber and scraps from the Crusaders' palisade walls, siege towers, and assault ladders.

That kind of engineering prowess belongs only to dwarves, and thanks to the intercession of the lawspeaker, she manages to negotiate a contract with the Tuscoraura Mountain dwarves to lend their sturdy backs and their geometric genius to the project in exchange for vague promises of future compensation.

Thus, barely more than a week after Black Tiw's Day, there are no more homeless elves and the rangers, now members of the New World Order, find out that they have received their orders and it's time to depart. Madame Dungaree sends out the word that they all are invited to a farewell dinner.

Once they are all seated and the gnome caterers have brought out the food, she begins. "Mesdames, mesdemoiselles, and messieurs, it is a beautiful day in this neighborhood thanks to your hard work and dedication. So it is with great joy that I welcome you to your last dinner in this abandoned Crusader camp and to your first meal in Sylfralpee Vorsch, a name that translates into Aenglish as Silver Elf City.

"Now, I wish to offer a few parting gifts, the first of which is our thanks. If saving our city from certain and utter destruction has not racked up an enormous bond of gratitude on its own, then helping us rebuild what we lost without pay locks us into a debt we will never be able to pay off. Still, we shall try to repay you in every way possible.

"As an initial installment of that payment, we offer you our homes. You are my brothers and sisters, fathers and mothers, sons and daughters. You are my clan and my kith. You will always have a place to stay on Tuscoraura Mountain.

"The second gift should be proud medals, trophies, and engraved weapons to celebrate your victories. Due to the devastation we cannot produce them now. Instead, I offer you a special handshake.

"Whenever you offer this handshake with a thumb between the first two knuckles to any of the clayborn, it will be a debenture that you are to be treated as our brothers and sisters. You will always have a home in Sylfralpee City—free food, free clothes, and whatever services you need to protect your life, liberty, and the pursuit of happiness.

"I said that you owe us nothing more, but on second thought, one price I do set in exchange for all these benefits—you must be a neighbor for your peers in the New World Order from whatever race of the clayborn, no matter where they are living. If I hear that any of you refuses to be a kindness to a fellow silver elf or clayborn in need, then home base will not be your neighborhood any longer.

"Finally, my special thanks goes out to Mister Benjamin Frankelyn for negotiating the truce that allowed us fire elves to welcome so many humans into the order of silver elves—the New World Order!"

Scene 4: Paying it Forward

Silver Elf City on Tuscoraura Mountain
Frige's Day Nones. Noontide, 14th of July, 1284
Feast of Saint Metheldred, Virgin and Martyr

Missus Puma sneezes from the cloud of dust her feather duster has kicked up.

"Heilsa!" says her husband, Master Shoemaker Gulliber, walking in the door. "Or as those humans like to say, God bless you!" He tries to jam a half-empty wheelbarrow through the rickety door of their shelter in Silver Elf City. No one is homeless anymore, but at this point, few wood elves would call their hurriedly built shanties home quite yet.

The wheelbarrow's bed rattles with the few charred and broken bits of their old household belongings he was able to recover from among the ruins of Missus Cougar Highrune's house—some old stockings, a few dented pie plates and random fairings, like hardened gingerbread buttons.

From up on her improvised ladder she calls down, "Glad to see you made it back safe and sound, Gully! Were you able to find my bell-bottom? I really would love to be able to wear it to the Freyfest coming up at the end of July."

Master Gulliber's shoulders sag. "What a bust! The hot and cold flames clashed in weird patterns so nearly everything in the house got twisted or mangled. With all the room left in the wheelbarrow, I was going to bring home building materials and a few mementos from Missus Cougar, but I have no doubt those blighted gremlins were skulking around there last night because there were a whole slew of items that I saw untouched yesterday but are gone today. Maybe even some of those garden gnomes took a mind to looting, who knows?"

"So did you find my bell-bottom?"

"By my chattering teeth, Puma, I don't even know what a bell-bottom is. I could have been looking straight at it and walked right over it. The only thing I know is that I'm not going back there anytime soon. Both the dark wildfires and the Crusaders' bonfires took their toll scorching and crystalizing the support beams and architectural framework. It'd be a waste of half the afternoon trying to squeeze through that wreckage only to have it all fall on me. We've got work to do here if we are going to be opening up a respectable shoe shop."

Missus Puma climbs down the ladder and rummages through the wheelbarrow with a heavy sigh. "What am I going to wear to the Freyfest now?"

KNOCK, KNOCK!

"Who's there?" calls out Master Gulliber.

The muffled voice barely makes it past the heavy wooden door. "Dungeon."

"Dungeon who?"

"Dungeon know my voice by now?"

Missus Puma races to the door, screaming, "Oh my waxy ears, it's Dungaree Jean!" Immediately she opens it and bows. "Hale ant sail, Madame Dean of the League of Nations! So sorry we didn't recognize you! We're all going hard of hearing—"

Dungaree Jeanne walks in with a pleasant smile. "No worries, Missus Puma. Just because I have a few more responsibilities now doesn't mean I'm too busy to visit with friends."

As she says so, a dozen or so secretaries from her retinue follow her into the shelter, scribbling on wax tablets for dispatching messages through the twenty or more runners waiting outside to deliver her orders to the right people as soon as she issues them.

Master Gulliber's mouth hangs open as he repeats, "Not too busy to visit?"

Slightly embarrassed, Dungaree Jeanne tries to reassure them. "Pay no attention to all that. We threw the New World Order together so quickly that we skipped over a few details that needed to be ironed out. Now that most of its members will be leaving in the next few days, we are playing catch-up. Your shelter is about to get more crowded, but I'm sure you'll be glad to see these visitors."

Louis and Clarke walk in. Both Missus Puma and Master Gulliber throw their arms up high and rush to give them big hugs. Missus Puma says in her broken Aenglish, "Please, Mister Louis, you not go too? You are family! And we like Mister Clarke too. After Missus Cougar . . . it is so lonely. Please come live with us!"

Master Gulliber adds in smoother Aenglish, "My shoe business is really starting to take off, Louis. I could complete your training as an apprentice shoemaker and make you a rich man. Missus Puma here is thinking of starting her own restaurant, and Clarke could help her out with that.

"Now that you silver elves of the New World Order are allowed to live in elf society, you two could really show the fire elves of Tuscoraura Mountain that even humans have artistic potential—"

"Uh . . . excuse me, Master Gulliber," says Louis, raising a finger timidly. "But we're not silver elves."

Master Gulliber does not like interruptions and waves away the objection. "I know, I know, you prefer to be called silver humans, or new world orderlies, or something like that."

Clarke is always quick to correct an inaccuracy and reasserts, "No. You don't get it. Sir Robert Roger specifically told us that because we were apprentices, we don't get to join the New World Order."

Master Gulliber flags down Dungaree Jeanne's attention and says to her in Eldric, "Madame Dean of the League of Nations, I must protest. Louis and Clarke here fought with as much courage as any of the Major League elves and yet they have been excluded from the New World Order of Silver Elves."

Genuinely concerned, Dungaree Jeanne asks Louis and Clarke in Aenglish, "But how is that even possible? You joined Amhirst's company of rangers, didn't you? We inducted all the rangers, as far as I know."

"Not the apprentices," replies Clarke. "We were told to mind our own business."

"That's horrible!" cries Dungaree Jeanne. "We will have to remedy that immediately." Switching to Eldric she asks, "Mister Marstand, do I have anything on my schedule early tomorrow morning?"

"Madame Dean, your schedule is packed tight for the next two weeks."

"Well, how about dawn? I couldn't possibly have scheduled anything at the crack of dawn."

Marstand seems to be her chief secretary and genuinely concerned for her well-being. He replies, "But you need your sleep, Madame."

"I can catch up on my sleep in two weeks' time. Have the master of ceremonies prepare a little formality that I can officiate at dawn tomorrow. These two gentlemen deserve a place in the New World Order." Then, turning to Louis and Clarke, she says in Aenglish, "We'll meet you at the high inquisitors' old pavilion at dawn tomorrow. Bring your swords. You'll need them for the ceremony."

Louis huffs with a tinge of self-pity, "We don't have any swords. I've only got a lumber axe. Clarke's got the phoenix talon dagger and Hayle has nothing. You're going to induct Hayle too, aren't you?"

"Who's Hayle?"

"Nathan Hayle. He's the other apprentice in the company."

"No swords? Mister Marstand, make a note to speak with that tinker dwarf about whipping up some swords for tomorrow morning—wait! I just got a brilliant idea; but I'll still need that tinker dwarf."

"Yes, Madame," replies Marstand with a bow.

"Don't worry, we'll fix you up with swords. Just bring the phoenix talon dagger. That should work for Clarke. Now if you'll excuse me, I have to write a speech about—"

"There you are!" Speaking in Eldric, Enganyon flies in at them in the middle of her sentence.

Dungaree Jeanne exclaims, "Oh my swollen toes, Monsieur Enganyon! How does an educated high elf of aristocratic upbringing such as yourself so thoroughly forget his manners as to come barging into the home of another fire elf uninvited?"

Deeply embarrassed, Enganyon stumbles on his words. "But I never guessed . . . with all the crowds walking in and out . . . this awning . . . I just assumed this was a public pavilion."

Missus Puma holds up her hand to assure them all that no offense was taken and says in Eldric, "Monsieur Enganyon, you are always welcome in our home. If you came to pay your respects to the mother of Monsieur Lynx, I regret to inform you that the funeral was held last Saturn's Day. Her murk elf husband, Stallion, was so upset at her loss that he left Tuscoraura Mountain."

Enganyon's face grows sad. "Alas, I had not heard of her passing. My sincerest condolences. For my own rational mind, I am unable to see any sense in all the tragic loss of life in the past few weeks. By leaning on the preaching of Reverend Appleseed, I am led to believe that there are spiritual realities out there that would give hope that Monsieur Lynx and his mother are in a happier place and that the only real tragedy is the loss of their company among us until we see them again after our own departure from this world."

Dungaree Jeanne translates his words for Louis and Clarke, then comments, "That was well put. It warms my heart to see your growth in character. For a flicker of a moment, I see your father in you. His heroic death while defending our lives against those undead thralls brings both grief at his bereavement and admiration for the nobility of his spirit that drove him to defy all the pressures leading him toward evil and do what was right when it counted most."

Enganyon's eyes well with tears and he does not hesitate to capitalize on the emotional momentum. He says in Runic for full dramatic effect, "Thou seest, Madame Dean and Dungaree, that kind of person I am when, away from the assassin's blade, I do not have to pretend I am another. What further proof dost thou need that I shall become a most excellent husband to your lovely daughter? If only thou wouldst approve our union, it would be of immeasurable consolation to my tender soul."

Dungaree Jeanne does her best to suppress a chuckle at his theatrics while she says in Runic to maintain the charade, "Thou hast my thanks for showing such consideration in asking my consent to take my daughter's hand in marriage. Since it seems thou art firmly resolved to enter upon this union, my only condition is that you keep to it faithfully until death do you part."

Enganyon replies with tears of delight in Runic, "Oh, Madame Dean and Dungaree, thou hast made me the happiest elf ever to live on Tuscoraura Mountain. I shall hie away and carry the joyful tidings of thine approval to Mademoiselle Zena at once!"

As the youthful curmudgeon scampers off with glee, Dungaree Jeanne lets out her laughter and turns to Master Gulliber and Missus Puma and says in Eldric, "A part of me wishes I could stay here and enjoy your company but, to my deepest regret, the other part knows and urges that the survival of Silver Elf City is still not assured. Therefore, I must beg my leave."

Clasping both of Dungaree Jeanne's hands, Missus Puma replies in Eldric, "Dearest Madame Dean and Dungaree, my dizzy mind does not know whether to congratulate you or pity you on that flighty young elf you are about to call your son-in-law. My sincerest prayer is that he be a good and faithful husband to your daughter and that their years together be filled with happiness."

Dungaree Jeanne gives her a hug, saying, "May the heavenly powers grant all your prayers, Missus Puma. Before I go, I have a favor to ask."

Master Gulliber comes over and replies in Eldric, "Anything we can do to serve you is a joy, Madame Dean and Dungaree."

"There is a murk elf family that has been left homeless by the events of Black Tiw's Day. We have had to prioritize fire elves in the distribution of shelters, and now this family is without a home. Since you were so amiably received by Missus Cougar's murk elf husband when you came back and discovered you had no home, I was wondering if you'd pay the kindness forward and welcome this murk elf family under your own awning while we rebuild."

Missus Puma is thrilled to hear the news and says in Eldric, "Oh, we'd be so excited to have them! I was getting so lonely without Missus Cougar and Mister Stallion. Yes, thank you for arranging this!"

"Before you say yes, I must warn you that they already have two young girls and are expecting a third child any day now."

"Oh, I love children. Peace and quiet do not suit me at all. Bring them here as soon as you can, please!"

Dungaree Jeanne bows and says in Runic as she departs, "Adieu, then! It shall be done according to your word."

Scene 5: The Manchineel Candidate

Silver Elf City on Tuscoraura Mountain
Saturn's Day Prime. Dawn, 15th of July, 1284
Morrow of Saint Metheldred, Virgin and Martyr

Rosy-fingered dawn stretches out her arms with a yawn of gentle breezes. The three ranger apprentices—Louis of Joliette, David Clarke, and Nathan Hayle—gather together in the high inquisitors' pavilion. With no sign of Dungaree Jeanne or her retinue, the three apprentices make themselves at home sitting in the high inquisitors' chairs and trying out their beds. Hayle tries the biggest bed and finds it too hard. He then moves over to the next one and finds it too soft. But when he feels out the smallest bed he screams in terror, "Aaahhh!!!"

He pulls back the sheet and finds Sacagawea sleeping in the bed.

Just at that moment, Dungaree Jeanne walks into the pavilion with her retinue of secretaries and aids. Sacagawea opens her eyes wide in confusion as Dungaree Jeanne approaches her and asks in Aenglish, "Have you been overlooked for admission to the New World Order as well?"

Sacagawea replies, "Um . . . yes, ma'am."

"No worries, dear," replies Dungaree Jeanne with sensitivity. She can tell the young woman is upset about something but regrets the fact that she simply does not have time to go into it. "Please, just line up with the other apprentices along that wall. Did you bring a sword or a dagger?"

"Yes, ma'am."

"Perfect. Let's get started then."

Lining them up and surrounding them with a silver elf honor guard, Dungaree Jeanne improvises an induction ceremony. First, she walks up to Louis and pulls out the Sword of Layban. She taps him on the shoulders with it and says in Aenglish, "Louis of Joliette, for your heroic charge against the stay-puffed watermelon wight, I dub you a member of the New World Order of Silver Elves. Moreover, I bequeath unto you the Sword of Layban to serve, protect, and defend the innocent, the weak, and those who have no one to stand up for them. Do you accept this obligation that I place upon your shoulders?"

"I do."

Moving along, she unsheathes the ceremonial phoenix talon dagger and brings it toward Clarke's shoulders but he flinches and says, "Watch out, ma'am! It's soporific."

Dungaree Jeanne's face skews with puzzlement, not sure if he is refusing the honors or not. She asks, "Pardon me, Mister Clarke, but I don't understand. What does 'soporific' mean in Aenglish?"

"It means it makes you fall asleep. If you nick me with that blade, I'll fall asleep for hours."

Relieved, Dungaree Jeanne smiles and says, "Yes, naturally, I shall be careful. Now then, David Clarke, for your heroic attack against the heresiarch, I dub you a member of the New World Order of Silver Elves. Moreover, for wielding this phoenix talon dagger to bring succor to your neighbors at the goblin sacrificial altar and up in Shentalpee City, I bequeath it unto you to serve, protect, and defend the innocent, the weak, and those who have no one to stand up for them. Do you accept this obligation that I place upon your shoulders?"

"I do."

She pulls out a brilliant, dwarf-crafted silver dagger with an amber aether stone and a magnetite lodestone inlaid at the tips of the handguard. The pommel has affixed to it a pyrite fire stone. Nathan Hayle's keen memory tells him that those are the same source stones that once were on the archon stone amulet, which Vampire Kibbler had swallowed to make himself invincible. The origins of the other three source stones lead him to guess that where the handguard intersects the grip, the stone inlaid into the middle might actually be an archon stone.

Perceiving young Nathan Hayle's mind spinning over the stones, Dungaree Jeanne immediately explains, "Before we begin, I must explain. I had this dagger forged by the mountain dwarves from the amulet you helped dislodge from the chest of our evil, undead vampire-in-chief. They crafted this for me without payment and provided us with laborers on condition that I store my archon stone with them as collateral against future payments."

Nathan Hayle twitches his eyelids and skittishly asks, "But the other source stones are real, right? I was kind of thinking about getting into sorcery, and some working lodestones would be a great head start."

Dungaree Jeanne chuckles a little at his awkwardness but approves. "Absolutely! They say you are only fifteen years old and have already studied alchemy at the Collegiate School of Connettikit. You have great potential in the field of sorcery as well.

Smiling bashfully he says, "Yeah, that was kind of what I was hoping too."

"Well then, let's get on with it. Nathan Hayle, for your heroic charge against the traitorous former vampire-in-chief of Shentalpee City, I dub you a member of the New World Order of Silver Elves. Moreover, in recognition of your talents in sorcery and your courage against the undead, I bequeath unto you this silver dagger to serve, protect, and defend the innocent, the weak, and those who have no one to stand up for them. Do you accept this obligation that I place upon your shoulders?"

"I do."

Dungaree Jeanne steps sideward toward Sacagawea and asks kindly, "Your name, miss?"

"Sacagawea."

"Do you have a sword or a dagger I could use to dub you with?"

From her belt pouch Sacagawea draws a little bone blade and says, "I have a knife."

"That's not a knife," replies Dungaree Jeanne.

Sacagawea does not back off. "I used it to kill an alligator once."

Dungaree Jeanne pulls out her own sidearm, which is a least three times bigger than Sacagawea's and says, "Now this is a knife."

Seeing the bare blade, everyone backs off except Sacagawea. Dungaree Jeanne says, "Its blade is daubed with an elf concoction based on manchineel. I'll throw in a few vials of manchineel so you have a few to spare. Highly poisonous—incapacitates your opponent in a few breaths. Death follows shortly. Don't let kids play around with this."

Dungaree Jeanne re-sheathes it and then unbuckles her belt. She taps the sheathed knife on both of Sacagawea's shoulders and says, "Sacagawea, for coming to our aid, I dub you a member of the New World Order of Silver Elves. Moreover, for your courage in fighting off an alligator with that puny little nail filer, I bequeath this manchineel knife unto you to serve, protect, and defend the innocent, the weak, and those who have no one to stand up for them. Do you accept the obligation I place upon your shoulders?"

"I do."

She gives the group one last look, with motherly pride filling her eyes. "You may now consider yourselves full-fledged members of the New World Order of Silver Elves! Now, quickly, we must catch up with the rangers before they depart without you. Mister Marstand, did you remember to bring the ponies I requested?"

"As always, Madame Dean and Dungaree."

"Good! Begging your pardon, Miss Sacagawea, but—" Looking around, Dungaree Jeanne is surprised to see that Sacagawea has vanished completely. She shrugs her shoulders and says, "Let's mount up and ride out!"

Scene 6: A Monk's Mottos

Marchlands of Tuscoraura Mountain
Saturn's Day Terce. Morning, 15th of July, 1284
Morrow of Saint Metheldred, Virgin and Martyr

Galloping at full speed on her reindeer, Dungaree Jeanne catches sight of the rangers, pitching camp just beyond the marchlands. Although Enganyon is technically the acting head of state, he lacks the maturity or experience or empathy to provide any significant sense of safety or hope for the devastated community of Tuscoraura Elves. Dungaree Jeanne possesses all three qualities in measures packed down and overflowing. All look to her for guidance, expertise, and reassurance.

As is inevitable with her rise in status among the elves, her retinue keeps expanding. No less than thirty elves ride alongside her. The ranger scouts see her as well and draw their bows in nervous confusion at seeing so many riders coming at them with such speed. Dungaree Jeanne slows her cavalcade to a canter. The three apprentices wave their hands and shout, "Don't shoot! Don't shoot!"

Sir Kip Karlson is the first to recognize them and calls out, "Stand down! It's the Madame Dean of the New World Order!"

When she finally arrives at camp, Sir Robert Roger goes out with First Lieutenant Sir Jon Stark and Second Lieutenant Sir Benedict Arnald to greet her. Sir Robert Roger says, "Madame Dean, your haste makes us worry that some new danger has arisen."

"Thank the heavens, no, Monsieur Captain. We are all still safe. My haste is nothing more than the result of my anxiety at not giving you a proper farewell before you leave our borders."

Not even trying to hide his relief, Sir Robert Roger objects in a friendly tone, "But you have already given us a farewell feast."

Madame Dungaree shakes her head. "That was for all the silver elves together in general. I never got a chance to say personal goodbyes to our heroic rangers."

Sir Robert Roger bows his head slightly and says, "My apologies for not following all the silver elf customs, but we already have several urgent and important quests that call us away from Tuscoraura Mountain. With all due respect, please allow us to thank you once again for the honors you have bestowed upon us and the hospitality you have shown us, but we must be on our way."

Madame Dungaree dismounts and says, "Please, Monsieur Captain, permit me at least the privilege of shaking hands with each and every ranger."

"Of course, Madame Dean. Permission granted."

The rangers have already pitched their tents and are in the process of putting out campfires, a luxury they could afford ever since Dungaree Jeanne reinstated the Ivy League patrols and assured them that no trolls or goblins would give them any trouble.

The rangers' tents are arranged according to combat roles. At the edge of the camp are several squads of ranger scouts who act as lookouts and sharpshooters to foil any potential ambushes. To offer a proper farewell, Sir Kip Karlson gathers up his fellow ranger scouts—Dame Frances Marian, Sir Davy Crickett, Sir Ethen

Allan, Sir Rumpel Stilton, Sir Humbert of Denk, and Sir Jack Hancock. Once they are all together, Sir Kip says with a sad look, "Madame Dean, I am so sorry!"

Taken aback, she asks, "Why are you apologizing? You saved my people!"

Sir Kip replies, "You did nothing to deserve it, but it seems every sort of woe and misfortune imaginable has befallen you and your people. I guess I'm just sorry to see so many bad things happen to good people."

Dungaree Jeanne is visibly touched and says, "Aww, that's very kind of you to say. Your compassionate sentiments bespeak a noble heart within you. As for our misfortunes, it's just another adventure in a life for us to tackle. Our leaders brought these disasters upon us by reaching for powers they should not have. We are a democracy, so we must bear the responsibility when our elected leaders go wrong."

Sir Kip persists, "Why should you have to pay for the debts of those in power?"

Sir Rumpel Stilton, the dwarf magicultor and unofficial philosopher of the company, steps forward and adds his thoughts. "The great philosophers have a saying in Latin, *e pluribus unum*. Only by taking responsibility for others' actions can we be united, and only when we are united can we stand strong."

Dungaree Jeanne thinks for a moment and says, "Yes, that makes a lot of good sense." Turning around she says in Eldric, "Mister Marstand, make sure someone who knows Latin and Aenglish is writing this all down." Dungaree Jeanne switches back to Aenglish and reflects on Sir Rumpel Stilton's words with the ranger scouts, saying, "There will always be someone whose bad choices bring grief upon friends and kin.

But the nature of a hero is to be the one who rises up to the challenge, undertakes the adventure, and carries on the story. I hope the New World Order will be a union of such heroes."

"Aye! Aye!" cheer the ranger scouts. Sir Kip, about the same height as Dungaree Jeanne, steps forward to give her a big hug. The other rangers crouch down on one knee and give her hugs charged with sincere admiration and gratitude.

Dungaree Jeanne moves on to the next group of rangers, the huntsmen, who back up the scouts with their bows, knives, and fists when necessary. The veteran ranger Sir Cotrel Walker is their mentor. With him gather Sir Rip van Winkel, Sir Jim Bowey, Sir Daniel Morgon, Sir Daniel Boon, Sir Seth Werner, and the vivacious Irishman Sir Gilbert Sullivan.

Having overheard the other discussion, Sir Gilbert Sullivan, always one for drama, presses the issue. "It seems that everyone did what they did in God's name. How do we know whose side God is really on?"

Dungaree Jeanne replies, "Until recently, it was illegal for high elves to follow Christ, so I am only a baby Christian. But from what Reverend Appleseed has taught me, the Lord Jesus would say that the sign that God has approved our undertaking is that our labors have borne good fruit. Out of these dangers we walk forth with a new sense of kinship. The old world order was to destroy others because of their differences. The New World Order will be to build up the clayborn as our own brothers and sisters."

"*Annuit coeptis*!" echoes Sir Gilbert Sullivan. "God has approved our undertaking!"

"Aye! Aye!" cheer the ranger huntsmen.

With polite bows, handshakes, and hugs, they allow Dungaree Jeanne to move on to the last group of rangers, the heavies, whom Sir Robert Roger holds in reserve until the fighting gets intense. Although they get exposed to danger less often, the danger they do face is always clear, present, and intense. As such, they are all slashed up with scars and crooked noses and cracked jaws and foreheads.

The ranger giant, Sir Paul Bunyan, is their mentor. With him gather Sir Casey of Mudville, Sir John Henry of Big Bend, Sir Joe Magarac, Sir Joseph of Montferrand, whom they call Big Joe Mufferow, the ponderous Sir Febold Feboldson, and Sir Frankl Stein, whose love of literature surprises those who judge his huge frame and crude face as signs of a dim wit.

Having overheard the previous discussion, Sir Paul Bunyan says, "It's a pity we didn't kill that perfidious high inquisitor when we had the chance. Perhaps as members of the New World Order we will be more decisive when facing evil in the future."

Sir Frankl Stein has strong feelings about that and says, "Pity? If it were not for God's pity toward us, we'd all have perished for our sins long ago. We have to live and let live, and put our trust in God to rectify wrongs. If we are too eager to deal out death and punishment for the real or perceived grievances committed against us, sooner or later we will become the villains we were trying to fight."

Dungaree Jeanne agrees. "Yes, it is an easy pitfall to believe that right the wrongs by waging war against our enemies; but the fate of our adversaries is not for us to decide. We must trust the greater wisdom of the universe to settle scores on a large scale.

"Rather, we must decide to bring light and life to the people around us with the little time that is allotted to us in this world."

"In God we trust," reiterates Sir Frankl Stein.

Being the largest of all the rangers, the hugs they offer Dungaree Jeanne are the most awkward to execute—awkward but warm nonetheless.

She returns to Sir Robert Roger and says, "I treasure this opportunity to speak with your rangers personally. They have given me some great ideas for mottos that we could use for our New World Order."

Sir Benedict Arnald comments, "Overhearing these discussions has inspired me to gift you with a silver arrow and an olive branch that I have always kept with me as reminders of my mission as a soldier. The olive branch reminds me that as a Christian, I am always to seek peaceful resolutions to conflict. But the silver arrow asserts that as a warrior, I have to be ready to fight whenever my foes leave me no other option."

Sir Jon Stark adds, "Well said, Sir Benedict Arnald. As a company of rangers, we remind our men and women that our mission is to live free or die. Death is not the worst of evils."

Taking the gifts and advice, Dungaree Jeanne says, "Many thanks to you all, messieurs and mademoiselle Rangers! Our nation will treasure these tokens and wise advice." With that, she gives them each a warm handshake.

After seeing all the displays of affection, Sir Robert Roger goes down for a hug too and says, "Well met, Madame Dungaree, and fondest farewells to our friends and family on Tuscoraura Mountain."

Scene 7: The Next Generation

Shentalpee City on Tuscoraura Mountain
Moon Day Sext. Noontide, 17th of July, 1284
Feast of Saint Kenelm the King

Under the guidance of Lawspeaker Sturl Snorrison, the Tuscoraura Mountain dwarves have sponsored a hospital for any of the clayborn who were injured or left homeless or destitute by the events of Black Tiw's Day. When Dungaree Jeanne arrives at the hospital, little dwarf children run out to greet her, chanting, "Hey now! Jeanne's an all-star!"

After dismounting from her reindeer, Dungaree Jeanne greets the venerable old dwarf in Runic. "Health and happiness to thee, Monsieur Lawspeaker. This is absolutely marvelous! Howsoever thou hast convinced thy kin to pay for all this, it defies my comprehension."

"And my own, I assure thee, Madame Dungaree. Dwarves are ludicrous creatures like that. They go out of their way to prove to thee that they are so irritatingly stubborn. When thou seekest their aid they refuse it, and precisely when thou art jaded from asking for help and thou dost no longer seek it, they insist on lending succor and will not take no for an answer."

"I would rather choose to believe that it is the goodness at the foundations of their hearts."

"Yes, indeed, Madame Dean, and a lot of concrete."

Dungaree Jeanne lets herself laugh with such relish that the dwarf physicians and their patients peek to see where the jolly racket is coming from. "Speaking of stubbornness, hast thou seen my daughter?"

"Indeed I have! In fact, she asked me to deliver the message that Johnny Appleseed wishes to travel at least a half-day's journey before the heatwave we are experiencing should get any more oppressive. They depart from the Fonzi barbershop before midday, after taking their noontide meal."

"O my calloused heels! That's on the other side of Blue Hen's Base. I must hurry!"

"God's speed, Madame Dean. I wish that thou couldst hie there even faster than that, but the laws of nature are such that even the most hardened criminals cannot break them."

Dungaree Jeanne mounts her reindeer and gallops so fast that her flustered secretaries get strung out over half a mile. When she finally catches up to Zena she roars in Eldric, "Mademoiselle Zena, how could you even consider leaving Tuscoraura Mountain without saying goodbye?"

Still munching on a sliver of lamprey dipped in hot sauce, Zena replies, "As de facto head of state, you have so many pressing matters on your agenda that the reality is you simply cannot make time for every social call that polite society normally imposes on—"

"But, child of mine, I am your mother!"

"When I was home all day long, you never had time for me. Suddenly, now that I'm leaving, you have all the time in the world—"

"Mademoiselle Zena, don't start with me—"

"I'm not starting anything with you, Mother. I'm wrapping it all up—concluding our business."

"Zena dear, we're family. It's not business."

"You're right. It's not business; it's politics. Being head of state isn't good for me, but it suits you fine."

"Is THAT what this is all about? You're jealous because you think I want this responsibility for rebuilding Shentalpee City, finding shelter for refugees, sorting out so much petty nonsense—"

"I'll admit you're good at it, if you'll admit you've wanted it all along."

That last verbal blow staggers Dungaree Jeanne for a moment. She can't think of much to say so she falls back on an old baseline. "You're not walking away with the last word in this conversation."

"No; that wasn't my last word. I also feel compelled to mention that you are jealous of me."

"Me? Jealous of you? What on middle earth has possessed you with a thought like that, child?"

"I am about to marry the elf I always wanted to marry. You were never able to pull such a feat off."

"The elf you always wanted to marry—"

"And here he comes, running on foot with paperwork fluttering in the breeze. Oh, it's a dream come true."

"Your sarcasm troubles me deeply."

"Fret no longer, Madame Dean and Dungaree. Your political rival has arrived."

"My political rival?"

Enganyon, panting, asks, "Yes, it's wonderful how the elves have come together. No rivalries left, right?"

Zena says, "Excuse me, monsieur Acting Major Leagues Umpire, but are you the acting head of state or is my mother?"

Hoping it's a joke, Enganyon plays along. "Hah! That's funny. You've got a charming, clever wit, my dearest Zena. It's an essential component to success in a democratic system."

Zena does not let up. "Are you done lecturing us about the infrastructures of democracy?"

Enganyon catches the hint and steps back discreetly. He waves his fingers and says, "Oh uh, by all means. It looked like you and your mother were having an important discussion. Go right ahead and finish up and I'll wait right here."

Zena says, "My mother and I were just tending to some unfinished business."

Dungaree Jeanne pushes Zena aside and says, "I believe we have concluded our business, Monsieur Umpire. Please proceed with your exciting news."

Enganyon says, "Yes! I did it! I obtained all the proper paperwork, and now that I have your approval, I have a special question to ask of Mademoiselle Zena."

Obviously in a sour mood, Zena puts a hand on his chest and says, "Whoa, whoa, whoa! Hold up your reindeer, monsieur Acting Major Leagues Umpire! You will recall that the dying words of your father were to stop running from the truth, right?"

"Oh . . . er . . . right . . . about that—"

"I want the truth, the whole truth, and nothing but the truth. Got it?"

"The truth is . . . I love you, Mademoiselle Zena!"

Dungaree Jeanne jumps in. "Tell me honestly. Did your father orchestrate the ambush on my convoy?"

"No, no, no! Umpire Kibbler had planned that out as soon as it became clear that Mademoiselle Zena would be the last candidate standing against our dearly departed mademoiselle Umpire-in-Chief-elect Florenz.

"The entire Council of Perfects was in on it, and my father's position of authority as acting head of state was too tenuous to openly defy their orders. He had to carry through with it; but he left enough hints to tip you off so you could be prepared . . . and you were."

Dungaree Jeanne huffs, "I certainly guessed he was planning a trap. Whether or not he intentionally gave away his plans so I could be prepared, I highly doubt; but we will never know, will we?"

"Well, I suppose you're entitled to your doubts after all the deceptions, but what is certain, Madame Dean and Dungaree, is that I love your daughter. Do I have your permission now?"

"Oh all right."

Enganyon gets down on one knee and holds out a ring—the same ring he held last time he proposed—and says in Runic, "From the depths of my heart, Mademoiselle Zena, I love thee. Wilt thou marry me?"

Zena smiles facetiously and says in Eldric to break his momentum, "I don't know, monsieur acting Major Leagues Umpire. I kind of always knew I was attracted to you because you were the bad boy. Now that I'm finding out you were really a nice guy the whole time, I'm not so sure I'm in love with you anymore."

"What?" Enganyon's face drops. He flounders.

Enjoying his lost puppy look for a short while, she snatches the ring out of his hand and says, "Just kidding. Get over here and give me a big kiss."

As the kiss makes everyone around them feel awkward, Dungaree Jeanne slips the paperwork out of Enganyon's slack hands and calls two of her secretaries over. She then taps the lovebirds on the shoulder and says, "Excuse me. You wouldn't mind if I interrupt the moment to finalize the paperwork for your betrothal. Time is short. Just sign here first, please, and then I'll sign at the bottom that I witnessed the betrothal."

Enganyon takes a breath and mumbles, "Right."

Zena looks at the paperwork with a hint of suspicion. "Why are you so eager to get this paperwork signed, Mother?"

She shrugs. "You know, as de facto head of state, I've got so many pressing matters on my agenda that I sometimes have to abbreviate the formalities required by the social calls that polite society imposes on—"

Zena cuts her off. "You know what, Mom? I've said my piece. Let's move on. You only live once, right?"

"Absolutely, Mademoiselle Zena! That's exactly the attitude I raised you to have, so let's just get on with this and have you sign here. Mister Marstand, be a dear and dip this quill in some ink please?"

Zena takes the quill from Marstand with her eyes wide open but she fails to spot any clue of what her mother is up to. As soon as she hands the quill back, another secretary walks up with another stack of paperwork and hands it to Dungaree Jeanne.

She flips through the pages, inspects the last page carefully, and then holds it out to Enganyon and says, "Now that you are my future son-in-law—for good, this time—as well as my political ally, I was hoping we could address the housing and employment crisis afflicting our community in the wake of Black Tiw's Day. This is some paperwork to grant housing for a few immigrant families."

Enganyon purses his lips and says, "Let me assure you, Madame Dungaree, I trust you completely, but maybe you could briefly outline what you had in mind with this document here."

Dungaree Jeanne is only too happy to oblige. "Even though we have already put many construction projects into motion, Monsieur Acting Major Leagues Umpire, only high elves can walk freely from base to base without tedious permission slips. To expedite the process I admitted the dwarf, gnome, and human construction workers to the New World Order of Silver elves so that they can move through Shentalpee City unhindered. To speed up work, naturally."

"Naturally; but we don't want to water down the caliber of—"

Dungaree Jeanne cuts him off. "All excellent and thoroughly vetted clayborn, I assure you."

Enganyon starts to sweat. "I'm sure they are but they'll have to be prepared for civic responsibility."

"Absolutely, I agree. That is why I made sure we instill the ideals of democracy in all our new recruits. Who knows? Maybe someday, humans might aspire to their own version of democracy."

Enganyon snorts, "Boff! As long as their leader is tall, humans are happy. They don't trouble themselves to think through issues enough to make democracy flourish the way we do here."

Dungaree Jeanne eggs him on. "Yes, and Umpire Kibbler failed to establish himself as supreme ruler for life over us democratic elves thanks to your father's noble sacrifice, naturally."

Enganyon skims through some of the papers. "Naturally; but why does this piece of paper here use my authority to allow an immigrant murk elf family to stay in Silver Elf City after their visas are all expired?"

Her secretary hands Enganyon a freshly ink-dipped quill and holds up the scroll backed by a wooden tablet. Dungaree Jeanne only replies, "We need all the laborers we can get, naturally."

"Naturally," says Enganyon as he signs it. "But too many foreigners might be bad for—"

"Wait!" shouts Zena as she reviews the paperwork in her hands. "Why are you having us sign birthing permits?" She grabs the scroll and wooden tablet out of the secretary's hands to inspect it more closely.

Dungaree Jeanne shrugs. "Married couples need a birthing permit to live in Shentalpee City, naturally."

Zena winces. "We're not planning on having kids right away. Isn't it a little early to be thinking about all those minor details right now? I mean—"

"The gods are in the details, Zena."

Zena is more suspicious than ever. "My memory tells me the saying goes, 'The devils are in the details.'"

Dungaree Jeanne retorts, "Oh, Zena! Now is not the time to get all hung up on the particulars of these legal formalities. Our lawyers have reviewed these documents twice and have assured me that every word in there is entirely necessary."

Putting her hands on her hips, Zena says, "Okay, Mom. The game is up. You're trying to pull a fast one and I'm not signing on another dotted line until you give me the full scoop. What's this all about really?"

Dungaree Jeanne puts an arm around her daughter's shoulders and says, "You just said you're not planning on having kids anytime soon, and I have a murk elf family that just had a baby boy. Using all this destruction as an excuse, the Council of Perfects is refusing to grant birthing licenses to anyone except established Tuscoraura fire elf families. So they either have to leave or send their baby to the infantorium.

"This little piece of paper would allow you to adopt her baby and—problem solved. Everyone is happy."

"I can't take care of a child now."

"You don't have to. It's just a formality. You just subscribe to the legal status as adoptive parents and the birth mother will technically just be your wet nurse."

"We have to go through the adoption process too?"

"Don't worry, we're high elves. It's simple. I've got all the paperwork finished right here."

Zena barks at her mother, "Sorry, Mom, I'd love to help you out but I won't sign anything with thinking this through. Besides, we need to get going. Reverend Appleseed said we had to hit the road before this heatwave makes our journey any worse. I'll send you a letter with my decision."

Dungaree Jeanne tells Johnny Appleseed what they are arguing about and he says to Zena in Aenglish, "Every newborn life is precious. It's worth the inconvenience. Go ahead and do whatever you need to do, Mademoiselle Zena. I can wait."

Enganyon puts on a puzzled face and asks Dungaree Jeanne, "Wait! Did Mademoiselle Zena say she's going somewhere with the Reverend Appleseed?"

Zena waves her hands. "Oh, it's nothing. I've just gotta go find my magica tree. I'll be back in a jiffy."

"But that would take weeks, possibly months!"

"It could take years, but we can count on your faithfulness this time around, can't we?"

Enganyon puts a victimized look on his face. "But I never agreed to this trip!"

"That's because I never asked your permission."

"But, Mademoiselle Zena! I need you by my side to deal with all the stress and strife and conflicts."

"Don't worry, my mother's got it covered. She loves that kind of stuff."

Enganyon pulls Zena aside and says, "But that's exactly why I need you—so your mother doesn't roll me over."

She pats him on the cheek and says, "Oh, don't worry. She already has."

Seeing his distress, Dungaree Jeanne calls over to him, "Never fear, Monsieur Enganyon! I'll have it all settled before I leave for Philadelphia." Then she says to her daughter in Aenglish, "Are you going to be a good sport and run with me on this or do I need to start causing trouble?"

Zena gets nervous. "What kind of trouble?"

Dungaree Jeanne replies, "The Reverend Appleseed has agreed to cancel the trip entirely if I don't feel comfortable about you adventuring out on your own at such a tender age. You're only seventeen, you know."

With tears welling up in her eyes, Zena starts to whimper, "But, Mother, how could you do this to me?"

Seeing her about to cry, Johnny Appleseed reassures her with a kind smile and gentle words, "Don't be afraid, Mademoiselle Zena. You've found favor with God. This child will be a special gift to Vinland. All you have to do is decide on his name."

Zena pauses and thinks about it for a moment. All at once, her tears stop dripping and the wrinkle in her eyebrows loosens up and a smile glows on the corner of her lips. She straightens her shoulders and announces proudly, "His name will be Lynx."

GLOSSARY

Languages and Writing Systems

Aenglish – A dialect of the Toutonic languages spoken by humans in Aengland.

Algonkian – Exonym for Ashnabec languages and peoples.

Antinephiliac – A set of Semitic dialects spoken by those humans who trace their origins to Jershon, south of the land Bountiful.

Arabic – A set of Semitic dialects described by the ethnic Arab peoples as clearly understood.

Aramaic – A set of dialects that gained currency to form a universal trade language among ancient Semitic speaking peoples.

Ashnabec – Family of human languages spoken by those who describe themselves as good humans created by the divine breath of the Great Spirit.

Assyriac – A grouping of several languages using the Ashuri alphabet, including Gnomish and Human variants.

Athabask – Exonym for a family of languages spoken by those humans who trace their origins to Lake Athabaska in Saskatchewan.

Avrith – A set of Semitic dialects spoken by those who trace their origins to a common ancestor named Avram.

Brownish – A dialect of the Gaeldic languages spoken by Brownie gnomes from Albany.

Bunkum – Exonym for a set of trollic dialects.

Castellan – A dialect of the Latinic languages spoken by those who trace their origins to the castles on the Iberian Peninsula

Drivel – Exonym for a set of trollic dialects.

Drowish – A set of dark elf dialects spoken by those who trace their origins to the Drow River in Aphrica.

Dusternish – A light elf dialect spoken by those who trace their origins to Huldre Fen in Alfheim.

Dutch – A set of Nordlandic dialects described by the ethnic Viking peoples as clearly understood.

Dvarskal – Family of dwarvish languages spoken by those who trace their origins to the Pyrinoak Mountains.

Dwendish – Exonym for Iberian dwarvish dialects.

Eldralfar – Endonym for ethnic fire elves.

Eldric – A dialect of Elvish Runic spoken by fire elves who trace their origins to Mount Ragnarök.

Eldritch – Exonym for fire elf languages and peoples.

Endonym – A term that a particular people, culture, or language group uses to refer to themselves

Erinish – A set of Gaeldic dialects spoken by gnomes, trolls and humans from the Island of Erin.

Exonym – A term used by outsiders to refer to a particular people, culture, or language.

Folletto – A set of Italic dialects spoken by those limehill gnomes who trace their origins to a common ancestor, Fulmestus.

Frankish – A Toutonic-Latinic dialect spoken in Frankland that has become the *lingua franca* of diplomacy among Europans.

Fus·ha – A dialect of the Arabic languages that has become a *lingua sacra* among clerics of the Muslim Faith.

Gaeldic – A group of languages using the Ogham alphabet, with Gnomish, Trollic, and Human variants.

Gibberish – Exonym for a set of goblin dialects.

Gnorrachi – Endonym for the Pixish-Leprechaun dialect spoken by ethnic garden gnomes.

Gobbledygook – Exonym for a set of goblin dialects.

Graec – Family of human languages primarily spoken by those who trace their origins to a common ancestor named Graikos (also known as Hellen).

Hebrew – A dialect of the Avrith languages that has become the *lingua sacra* among leaders of the Jewish Faith.

Hellenic – A grouping of several languages using the Euclidean alphabet, including Gnomish, Trollic and Human variants.

Hobbish – A dialect of the Toutonic language spoken by gnomes in Aengland.

Hodensani – Endonym for longhouse human languages and peoples.

Irokian – Exonym for the Hodensani dialects spoken in the Confederacy of Seven Nations.

Italic – A set of dialects spoken by those tracing their origins to a common ancestor named Italus.

Jargan – Exonym for a set of trollic dialects.

Klipsk – A light elf dialect spoken by those cliff elves who trace their origins to Mount Kiragg in Alfheim.

Koinë – A dialect of the Hellenic languages that has become the *lingua sacra* among Christian clerics throughout Asia and the Holy Land.

Latin – A dialect of the Latinic languages that has become the *lingua sacra* among Christian clerics throughout Europa and Vinland.

Latinic – A grouping of several languages using the Roman alphabet, including Gnomish, Dwarvish, Trollic and Human variants.

Laymanite – A dialect of the Semitic languages primarily spoken by those who trace their origins to a common ancestor named Layman.

Leprechaun – Exonym for a set of dialects spoken by those gnomes who trace their origins to the area, around Lough Boderg and Lough Bofin in Erinland.

Luchporcpain – Endonym for the language spoken by ethnic Leprechaun gnomes.

Medifskar – Endonym for the language spoken by ethnic whaler dwarves.

Mumbo-Bantam– Exonym for a set of cave troll dialects.

Mumbo-Jumbo– Exonym for a set of large troll dialects.

Nabotean – A grouping of several Semitic languages using the Abjad alphabet, primarily Gnomish.

Narnese – A set of Italic dialects spoken by those shadow gnomes who trace their origins to Narnia in the Italic Peninsula.

Nawack – A set of dialects described by the ethnic Aztec peoples as clearly understood, some but not all are mutually intelligible.

Nissic – A light elf dialect spoken by those sea elves who trace their origins to Tomte Bay in Alfheim.

Nordic – A group of Toutonic languages spoken by humans, dwarves and elves in the Nordlandic regions of Europa.

Oxitan – A grouping of dialects spoken the region known as Oxitania including Gnomish, Elvish, Goblin, Troll, Dwarvish and Human variants.

Pixish – Exonym for a dialect of Gaeldic spoken by the Highland gnomes in Albany.

Puck – Exonym for a dialect of Gaeldic spoken by the Hebrides gnomes in Albany.

Rigmarole – Exonym for a set of goblin dialects.

Runic – A grouping of languages using the Futhark alphabet, including Elvish, Dwarvish, Trollic, and Human variants.

Scots – Exonym for set of Toutonic dialects spoken by the Lowland humans in Albany.

Syriac – A dialect of the Aramaic languages that has become the *lingua sacra* among Christian clerics throughout Asia and the Holy Land.

Tellurin – Family of light elf languages spoken by those who trace their origins to Alfheim in Nordland. (Tellurin refers to that same realm as Telluride.)

Toutonic – A family of languages spoken primarily by the humans, dwarves, gnomes and elves who dwell within or around the Holy Roman Empire

Trakota – A family of languages spoken primarily by the humans and gnomes of the Twelve Council Fires

Uto-Aztec – Exonym for a family of human languages spoken primarily by members of the Quadruple Alliance Empire.

Welch – A set of Gaeldic dialects spoken by those humans and gnomes who believe themselves to be favored by the ancient hawk deity named Gwalch.

Peoples and Places

Aegypt – Region in Aphrica ruled by a group of former slave warriors called the Marmelukes.

Aengland – An island kingdom that at the time of the events chronicled in this story (1284 AD) whose ruling elite spoke Frankish but the majority of its population spoke a set of Toutonic dialects known as Aenglish.

Albany – Exonym for the lands north of the Firth of Forth including Pixiland, Brownland, Scotsland, Puckland. At the time of the events chronicled in this story (1284 AD), the Shetland and Orcney Islands were Nordlandic settlements.

Albo-Erinish – An ethnic group of gnomes from mixed Gaeldic and Toutonic origins.

Alfheim – Region in Nordland that all light elf peoples consider their place of origin. Humans, dwarves and elves disagree as to its exact borders.

Amerika – Another name for Vinland or Turtle Island that gained currency after the famous expedition of Sacagawea, Louis and Clarke

Antinephilehies – Endonym for the Ammonite peoples.

Aphrica – The second largest continent in middle earth.

Aquatania – Western province in continental Europa under the authority of the Aenglish Crown.

Asgard – Region in Nordic mythology where the Aesir gods dwell, Tiw, Woden, Thor, and Frige.

Ashkuzi – Eponymous ancestor to whom a majority of Vinlander Jewish peoples trace their lineage.

Asia – A super continent in middle earth encompassing Asia major, Asia minor, Europa, and Hindia.

Aztec – Endonym for humans who trace their origins to the region of Aztlan.

Baltimoor – A city on the East Coast of Vinland.

Baskony – Western province in continental Europa under the authority of the Aenglish Crown. Dwarves are the ethnic majority in that region.

Baston – A city on the East Coast of Vinland.

Betzy Rose Mansion – Mansion on Red Giant's Base and home of Dungaree Jeanne Ranglursdottir.

Black Tar Base – One of the thirteen treetop bases that make up Shentalpee City on Tuscoraura Mountain.

Blue Hen's Base – One of the thirteen treetop bases that make up Shentalpee City on Tuscoraura Mountain.

Brookline – One of the Viking settlements recently conquered by Aenglish Crown troops.

Canoe Humans – Exonym for the humans who discovered Athabask fire.

Canuckia – The generic term for the northernmost provinces of Vinland.

Carlyle – Town that hosts the Carlyle Fair.

Cave Troll – A generic term for the small, mostly hairless trolls who generally live underground.

Child (*plural* Children) – A young human.

Citizens' Base – One of the thirteen treetop bases that make up Shentalpee City on Tuscoraura Mountain.

Clayborn – A term coined by the halfling monk Zedediah Springfield to describe the common origins of all gnomes, dwarves, humans, elves, trolls and goblins since most have an origin myth involving clay.

Colonial Base – One of the thirteen treetop bases that make up Shentalpee City on Tuscoraura Mountain.

Cottage Humans – Exonym for some Europan humans.

Deagle's Den – A Precinct in the garden gnome bailiwick on Tuscoraura Mountain.

Delawaerr – A confederacy of Ashnabec humans.

Dire Wolf Base – One of the thirteen treetop bases that make up Shentalpee City on Tuscoraura Mountain.

Drow (*plural* Drow) – Ethnic dark elves who trace their origins to the Drow River in Aphrica.

Dwarf (*feminine* Dwarve, *plural* Dwarves) – A generic term to describe clayborn with skin that tans brown in the sun, having round ears and small canine teeth. A heavily muscular race with long arms compared to other clayborn, they are generally broader than gnomes, humans or elves and their physical strength is not only a source of pride but also a significant factor in determining in social order.

Dwarfling – A young dwarf.

Eerie Glen – A colony of fire elves in Vinland.

Elf (*feminine* Elve, *plural* Elves) – A generic term to describe clayborn with skin that tans brown in the sun, having pointy ears and small canine teeth. A narrow-boned race with great skill in arts and crafts, their physical beauty is not only a source of pride but also a significant factor in determining social order.

Elfling – A young elf.

Erinland – An island west of Aengland. At the time of the events chronicled in this story (1284 AD), King Eddard was also Lord of Erinland.

Europa – A subcontinent of Asia.

Fennel Base – One of the thirteen treetop bases that make up Shentalpee City on Tuscoraura Mountain.

Fort Harris – A fort on the northwest border of Harris County to constructed by Count John Harris' father to defend against incursions from hostile neighbors.

Frankland – The most powerful successor state of the defunct Frankish Empire and the most powerful kingdom in Europa at the time of the events chronicled in this story (1284 AD).

Franks – An ethnic group of humans from mixed Gaeldic, Latinic, Nordic, and Toutonic origins. They emerged as the ruling ethnic group in Aengland, Frankland and Frankonia.

Freedrich – A town on the East Cost of Vinland that hosts the Great Freedrich Fair.

Garden Gnomes – The term used by humans, elves and dwarves to refer to gnomes who live in burrows and cultivate primarily subterranean crops such as carrots, potatoes, radishes, and mushrooms.

Gnome (*feminine* Gnomid) – A generic term to describe clayborn with skin that tans brown in the sun, having round ears and small canine teeth. They are generally smarter than humans, dwarves or elves and their cleverness is not only a source of pride but also a significant factor in determining social order.

Goblin (*feminine* Gobliness) – A generic term to describe clayborn with skin that tans green in the sun, pointy ears and a tusked overbite. Large goblins include those known as goblins proper, the Orcs, and the Bugbears. Gnome-sized goblins include those known as hobgoblins proper, the Cobalts, and the Kobolds.

Goyar – A light elf term used to describe those clayborn who are not light elves.

Greenskins – A derogatory term used by gnomes, humans, elves and dwarves to refer to goblins and trolls.

Halfling – A term for anyone with mixed ancestry but applied generically to gnomes born in Vinland who have mixed Europan ancestry.

Harris County – An Aenglish domain enfeoffed by the duke of Philadelphia to Count John Harris.

Harrisburgh – The principal city and feudal seat of Harris County.

Hellenes – Endonym for Graec-speaking peoples.

Heron Island – A colony of fire elves in Vinland.

Hill Dwarves – The term used by gnomes, humans, and elves to refer to dwarves who burrow into the soil to build their dwellings.

Hob – A tribe of Britannic gnomes.

Hoblet (*also misspelled* hobbit) – A young hob. This term is sometimes used to describe any young gnome since no proper term exists.

Holy Roman Empire – Political union of Europan territories centered around the Toutonic Kingdom whose Emperor was chosen by the nine Prince-electors, of which six were human, two gnome and one dwarf.

Human (*masculine* Man, *feminine* Woman, *plural* Humans) – A generic term to describe clayborn with skin that tans brown in the sun, having round ears and small canine teeth. The most populous race, they are generally taller than gnomes, dwarves or elves and their height is not only a source of pride but also a significant factor in determining social order.

Iberian Peninsula – The peninsula south of the Pyrinoak Mountains.

Illenoy Country – A region that was home to an alliance of a large number of unrelated nations who managed to set aside their ethnic and cultural differences for the sake of peace. The Frankish settlers there were accepted as just another tribe among many.

Island of Rhodes – An Aenglish colony on the East Coast of Vinland.

Italic Peninsula – The peninsula south of the Alpine Mountains.

Ithica – A town of Aenglish settlers on the border of Confederacy of Seven Nations and famous for its Silvermorn College of Sorcery.

Jerosolym – The Holy City targeted as the goal of the First Crusade. At the time of the events chronicled in this story (1284 AD), the Marmelukes of Aegypt controlled Jerosolym.

Joliette – A Frankish town in the Illenoy Country.

Kaybec – A County in northern Vinland conquered from the Franks by the Aenglish Earl, James Wolfe, just before the events chronicled in this story (1284 AD).

Kentikie County – An Aenglish domain enfeoffed by the duke of Virginia to Count James Harrod of Kent.

Lake Attawandaron – One of the Finger Lakes in the Confederacy of Seven Nations.

Lake Cayuga – One of the Finger Lakes in the Confederacy of Seven Nations whose southern tip touches Ithica.

Lathspell Mansion– Mansion on Mead Base and home of Major Leagues Umpire Gandorf Mithranderson.

Lexton – Town near Baston in the Duchy of Masswachoosut Bay later to become famous for the Battle of Lexton and Concord at the beginning of Vinland's War for Independence.

Longbardia– A province in the Italic Peninsula.

Longhouse Humans – The term used by gnomes, elves, and dwarves to refer to the Hodensani-speaking humans.

Lunden – The principal city in Aengland.

Lyósálfar – Endonym for the light elf peoples.

Manhatten – A city on the East Coast of Vinland recently conquered from the Vikings by the Aenglish Count, Richard Nicolas, at the time of the events chronicled in this story (1284 AD).

Marmelukes – Former slaves who had risen to become the ruling class of Aegypt.

Masswachoosut Bay – A duchy on the East Coast of Vinland.

Mead Base – One of the thirteen treetop bases that make up Shentalpee City on Tuscoraura Mountain.

Montroyal – A duchy in northern Vinland recently conquered from the Franks by the Aenglish Baron, Geoffrey Amhirst.

Mountain Dwarves – The term used by gnomes, humans and elves to refer to dwarves who tunnel into solid rock to build their dwellings.

Muskigee Creek – A colony of fire elves in Vinland.

Nemacolin's Trail – A thoroughfare through the Allegheny Mountains paved as a tollway by Lord Nybling Dankwart' mountain dwarves.

New Aengland – The official name for the Aenglish Crown lands in Vinland.

New Amsturldam – The official name for the Viking territories in Vinland.

New Frankland – The official name for the Frankish Crown lands in Vinland. Before the events chronicled in this story (1284 AD), New Frankland was ruled by a Frankish viceroy.

New Gersey – A county on the East Coast of Vinland.

New Yourke City – A city on the East Coast of Vinland. At the time of the events chronicled in this story (1284 AD), it was still called New Amsturldam City.

Nordland – A territory in the northern part of Europa ruled by a number of independent, petty nobles.

Ocean of Atlantis – The ocean separating Vinland from Europa and Aphrica.

Oregan – A territory on the West Coast of Vinland.

Orcs – New World goblins who are generally tall and thin, mistaken by Aenglish settlers as the Shetland and Orcney goblins, now called Old World Orcs, due to a superficial resemblance.

Ossernenon – A Mohawk village in the Confederacy of Seven Nations.

Ottowa Nation – An Ashnabec-speaking nation.

Oxitania – A region north of the Pyrinoak Mountains where Oxitan served as the trade language.

Perth Amboy – A city on the East Coast of Vinland where the Grand Mage of the Wald resides.

Philadelphia – A city on the East Coast of Vinland.

Pinkskins – A derogatory term used by goblins and trolls to refer to gnomes, humans, elves and dwarves.

Pinne Mage University – A university established by the noble Pinne family (the hereditary dukes of Philadelphia).

Pinnesylvania – At the time of the events chronicled in this story (1284 AD), the Grand Duchy of Pinnsylvania was just an ambition harbored by Lord William Pinne as a vehicle to accede to a royal throne.

Pixies – Exonym for gnomes living north of the Firth of Forth, depicting them as having a large number of blue tattoos.

Pope – The nominal overlord over Christendom.

Praga – A city in Europa where the Bohemian kings resided.

Pyrinoak Mountains – A range of mountains in southwest Europa that extends from the Bay of Biscay to the Mediterranean.

Quadruple Alliance Empire – Alliance of three human and one gnome city-states that led to the political dominance of the Nawak speaking peoples in the Southeast regions of Vinland.

Ragnarök – A volcano in Alfheim believed it to be extinct by the fire elves who settled inside. Its eruption in 1000 AD was said to herald the end of the world.

Red Giant's Base – One of the thirteen treetop bases that make up Shentalpee City on Tuscoraura Mountain.

Rock Pile Gnomes – The term used by humans, elves and dwarves to refer to gnomes who build homesteads by half digging into sod and half piling rocks on top.

Rofchester – An Aenglish trading port on the southern shore of Lake Onterio

Roma – The eternal city and seat of the pope, the highest ranking theocrat in Europa.

Salim – A small town near the city of Baston and the seat of the Holy Office of the Inquisition.

Senika Valley – A colony of fire elves in Vinland.

Shentalpee Vorsche – 'Fire Elf City' in Runic. A treetop settlement of fire elves constructed in 1197 AD.

Silvermorn College of Sorcery – A college of sorcery in the Aenglish town of Ithica.

Sun Base – One of the thirteen treetop bases that make up Shentalpee City on Tuscoraura Mountain.

Susquetoga – A Hodensani-speaking nation and tributary state to the Confederacy of Seven Nations.

Tartar – A exonym referring to Jangis Khan's hordes. Some scholars believe the word to mean that the hordes came straight out of hell (*Tartarus* in Graec) while others believe the word refers to the sauces they used to preserve food while traveling on horseback.

Thor's Base – One of the thirteen treetop bases that make up Shentalpee City on Tuscoraura Mountain.

Tomte Bay – A costal region in Alfheim settled by the ancestors of the sea elves.

Troll – A generic term to describe clayborn with skin that tans green in the sun, pointy ears and a tusked underbite. Large-bodied, hairy trolls are known as snow trolls and include the Sasquatch peoples in Canuckia, the Jotunn in Nordland, and the Ogars in Siberia. Small-bodied trolls are known as cave trolls and include the Gremlin peoples native to Vinland, the Troglodytes, the Boggarts, and the Gnolls.

Tunas – A city in northern Aphrica and the object of the Eighth Crusade.

Turtle Island – The most wide-spread name for Vinland used among its indigenous peoples.

Tuscoraura Mountain – A mountain within the Confederacy of Seven Nations.

Twelve Council Fires – Alliance of seven human and five gnome councils that constituted the Great Sioux Nation.

Vandsee Estates – The only sycamore treetop base on Tuscoraura Mountain and home to the Kibbler workshops. It is not counted as one of the thirteen bases that make up Shentalpee City.

Vikings – A generic term referring to seafaring Nordlanders and also a specific term referring to the descendants of the first Nordlanders who settled Vinland under Lief Erikson.

Vinland –Europan name for Turtle Island used by settlers before the journey of Sacagawea, Louis and Clarke.

Vlameers – A group of Nordlanders famous for the production of fabrics.

Wall Humans – The term used by gnomes, elves and dwarves to refer to humans who live behind walls, either in a fortified town or a castle.

Welchland – A principality to the west of Aengland. At the time of the events chronicled in this story (1284 AD), King Eddard Longshanks had recently promulgated the Statute of Rhuddlan, imposing Aenglish law upon Welchland.

Wigwam Humans – The term used by gnomes, elves and dwarves to refer to the Ashnabec-speaking humans.

Wildcat Base – One of the thirteen treetop bases that make up Shentalpee City on Tuscoraura Mountain.

Worship Base – One of the thirteen treetop bases that make up Shentalpee City on Tuscoraura Mountain.

Yulenisse – A tribe of sea elves, of which one branch traveled the Oregan Trail and became known as polar elves when they settled at a location that they calculated to be the magnetic polar north.

Time Terminology

Alfheim calendar – The old calendar used by light elves in Alfheim where the months are based on the phases of the moon but the seasons are based on observed equinoxes and solstices.

Annunciation – The feast day of the Angel Gabriel's apparition to Mary (Luke 1:26–38) designated in the Julian Calendar as New Year's Day.

Compline – A liturgical hour for prayers said before going to bed marking 9 p.m.

Crouchmas – The feast marking the day that Saint Helena discovered the True Cross.

Ember Woden's Day – The Wednesday after Pentecost.

Eve – The evening or day before a feast day.

Feast – A celebration of a saint or a holy mystery that marked the calendar for most people in the Middle Ages.

Feast of Corpus Christi – The Thursday after Trinity Sunday established as a solemnity by Pope Urban IV in 1264 AD to celebrate the Real Presence of Jesus in the Eucharist.

Good Frige's Day – The Friday before Easter.

Gregorian calendar – Our modern calendar named after Pope Gregory XIII which corrects the mathematical system of the Julian calendar to conform more precisely to the astronomical equinoxes and solstices.

Hock Moon Day – Monday of Hocktide, celebrated on the second week after Easter.

Holy Rood Day – The liturgical feast celebrating Saint Helena's discovery of the True Cross.

Julian calendar – The Roman calendar reformed by Julius Caesar, using a mathematical system used to reckon seasons. All dates in this text are given according to the Julian calendar which in the year 1284 AD was seven days earlier than the Gregorian calendar.

Lauds – A liturgical hour corresponding to 3 a.m.

Liturgical Hours – Before the invention of wristwatches, people in the Middle Ages relied on a community timepiece, usually the bell from a local monastery ringing more or less every three hours to call the monks to prayer. The time of day was then generally reckoned based on the name of the prayers that the monks were supposed to be reciting at that hour.

Matins – A liturgical hour corresponding to midnight.

Maundy Thor's Day – The Thursday before Easter.

Morrow – The day after a feast day.

Nativity of Saint John the Baptist – The Christian feast day (June 24th) designated on the Julian Calendar to celebrate the Midsummer Festival whether or not it coincided with the actual summer solstice.

Nocturns – A subdivision of the liturgical hour of Matins corresponding to the hours after midnight.

Nones – A liturgical hour corresponding to the ninth hour after sunrise or 3 p.m.

Prime – A liturgical hour corresponding to the first hour after sunrise or 6 a.m.

Sext – A liturgical hour corresponding to the sixth hour after sunrise or 12 p.m.

Solmanuther – Summer solstice or midsummer festival.

Spy Woden's Day – The Wednesday before Easter.

Terce – A liturgical hour corresponding to the third hour after sunrise or 9 a.m.

Third – The third day following a feast day.

Undern – Another name for the liturgical hour known as terce corresponding to 9 a.m.

Vespers – A liturgical hour corresponding to sunset or 6 p.m.

Vigil – The liturgical anticipation of a feast day.

Whit Moon Day – The Monday after Pentecost.

Military Terminology

Apgar – (*Eldric*) A hewing spear with a spearhead like a seax, or an elongated axe-head.

Atlatl – (*Nawak*) word for a stick balanced on the end of a throwing spear or javelin to propel it faster.

Bravo (*feminine* brava, *plural* bravi) – A fighter who specialized in the technique of fighting with a dueling sword in the right hand and a main-gauche in the left hand.

Buckler – A small shield designed to complement a dueling sword.

Catkin – A leather strap attached to the end of a hobgoblin war dart to propel it faster, also called an ankyle or an amentum.

Colonial marshals – A versatile company of adventurers who take oaths of loyalty to a liege lord and work to fight crime at home and defend the lord's interests abroad.

Fender – A special elf round shield especially for reindeer light cavalry.

Feudal knights – Land-owning heavy cavalry nobles who owe military service in exchange for their holdings.

Feudal levy – A military unit composed of serfs who owe military service as part of their feudal obligations to their lord.

Main-gauche – A long dagger specifically designed to be used in the left hand to compliment a sword in the right hand. A fighter who specialized in this technique was called a bravo.

Militia – A military unit composed of burghers and other free townsmen who owe military service as part of their taxes. The wealthy can often hire mercenaries in exchange for military service.

Pickets – Scouts that a military leader posts around an army or a camp to give early warning of enemy troops.

Sellsword – Another term for a mercenary.

Sergeant – Any professional soldier who is not a high elf or who does not belong to any form of nobility or aristocratic class. In Shentalpee City the term referred to wood elves who have been drafted into unpaid military service by any of the major military leagues.

Swashbuckler – A fighter who specialized in the technique of fighting with a dueling sword in the right hand and a buckler in the left hand.

Swordstaff – A spear whose blade is so long as to resemble a sword. It belongs to a large family of bladed polearms.

Targe – A round shield used by infantry.

Target – A smaller version of a targe shield.

Treeshadow – The hobgoblins who specialize in battle techniques fighting from up in trees.

War bill – A weapon based on a medieval pruning hook for tending orchards. The blade had a beak for yanking mounted soldiers off their horses and trapping lances, spears, and pikes.

War dart – A short, heavy javelin with a leather strap (catkin) attached to one.

Religious Terminology

Ammonite Christianity – A branch of Christianity in Vinland founded by the prophet Ammon.

Arian Christianity – A branch of Christianity named after the priest Arius who taught that Jesus is the Son of God, but not the eternal God.

Benedictine – An ancient and wealthy monastic order in Christianity, which focuses on stability and regular prayer according to Acts 1:14.

Blackflame Cult – A cult stemming from Cathar Christianity that promoted separation of body and soul as the answer to evil in this world.

Breviary – A shortened travel version of the full text of the Liturgy of the Hours, used by monks and nuns to pray the psalms, generally every three hours throughout the day and night.

Cardinal – A high-level title awarded to powerful clerics and a requirement for becoming pope.

Carmelites – A monastic order founded on Mount Carmel where the Prophet Elijah defeated four hundred fifty prophets of Baal as described in 1 Kings 18:16-45.

Cathar Christianity – A branch of Gnostic Christianity first preached by the prophet Albigeon who preached that the material world was fundamentally evil and goodness had to be exclusively spiritual.

Dominicans – A mendicant order that focuses on preaching according to Mark 16:15.

Franciscans – A mendicant order that focuses on simplicity of life according to Luke 9:58.

Frater (*Latin*) – A title of respect when addressing a male monk meaning brother in Latin.

Hospital – A military convent belonging to the Knights Hospitaller named after the Hospital of Saint John in Jerosolym where the order started.

Hospitallers – A group of warrior monks dedicated to caring for the sick and the poor. The Knights Hospitaller focus on healing and hospitality but also traditionally serve as the rear guard for any crusading army.

Inquisitor – A cleric tasked by Church authorities to seek out and uproot heresy.

Mendicant Order – A group of Christians who strive to follow the Gospels strictly by wandering around according to Matthew 4:23.

Monastic Order – A group of Christians who strive to follow the Gospels strictly by praying together and holding possessions in common according to Acts 2:44.

Nicene Christianity – A branch of Christianity named after the Council of Nicaea that defined Jesus as both the Son of God and coeternal with God the Father.

Palace – A military convent belonging to the Knights Paladin named after the ruins of the Palace of David in Jerosolym where the order started.

Paladins – A group of warrior monks dedicated to combatting praeternatural foes by exorcising demons and turning away curses and the undead. The Knights Paladin have a lifestyle of strict discipline in terms of prayer, fasting, and training for warfare.

Poodoo – The most powerful of the goblin gods, the god of night, sorcery, and destiny who requires bloody sacrifices to bestow good fortune.

Praeternatural – A term describing anything beyond physical realities found in nature, including witchcraft, ghosts, poltergeists, curses, hexes, undead and supernatural beings.

Psalms – Songs written by King David in praise of God. The Liturgy of the Hours focuses on chanting the psalms.

Serkas – A goblin god of war.

Soror (*Latin*) – A title of respect when addressing a female monk meaning sister in Latin.

Supernatural – A term describing God's acts beyond the limits of nature. Evil creatures perform praeternatural acts but not supernatural acts.

Templars – A group of warrior monks dedicated to defending pilgrims and assisting with the logistical difficulties of a pilgrimage. The Knights Templar came to see themselves as the overall guardians of Christians everywhere and got embroiled in politics and intrigues until their dissolution in 1312 A.D.

Temple – A military convent belonging to the Knights Templar named after the ruins of the Temple of Jerosolym where the order started.

Tironensians – A monastic order that focuses on prayer and silence according to Matthew 6:6.

Valhalla – A mythical feasting hall where Woden entertains the souls of chosen warriors who have fallen in battle.

Sorcery Terminology

Aerotheurgy (*Graec*) – The branch of sorcery specializing in the techniques of manipulating elemental air with an wind source stone (nacre).

Aethergy (*Graec*) – The branch of sorcery specializing in the techniques of manipulating elemental aether with an aether source stone (amber).

Amber – Though technically not a source stone, it is called the aether stone because it can channel and discharge aethereal energy. Amber is most effective when shaped into a dodecahedron (twelve-sided regular solid). It is also called the Jupiter stone.

Archon stone – A clump of *archea,* the physical element closest to prime matter. It is not found in nature and can only be extracted through alchemical processes.

Battlesage – A sorcerer who specializes in combat techniques. Battlesages can earn the title from an ennobled lord through battlefield merit, even without accreditation.

Halite – The water stone, also called salt crystal, used to influence water when polarized, heating it, cooling it, pushing it or pulling it. It is most powerful when crystallized in the shape of an icosahedron (twenty-sided regular solid). It is also called the Venus stone.

Hydrotheurgy (*Graec*) – The branch of sorcery specializing in the techniques of manipulating elemental water with an aquatic source stone (halite).

Ley lines – The geomagnetic lines that run deep in the earth and enhance metalleurgy. Their crossings determine the North and South Magnetic Poles.

Lodestone – The earth stone used to influence metals when polarized, heating them, cooling them, pushing them or pulling them. It is most powerful when crystallized in the shape of a cube (six-sided regular solid). It is also called the Saturn stone.

Master Sorcerer – A sorcerer who has successfully demonstrated and defended a masterpiece (*opus magnum*) before an accredited Sorcerers' Guild.

Metalleurgy (*Graec*) – The branch of sorcery specializing in the techniques of manipulating elemental metal with an earth source stone (lodestone).

Nacre – The wind stone, also mother-of-pearl, used to influence air when polarized, heating it, cooling it, pushing it or pulling it. It is most powerful when crystallized in the shape of an octahedron (eight-sided regular solid). Also called the Mercury stone.

Polarization – The process by which a living person directs the energies latent inside a source stone to charge the four basic elements along two axial poles—hot / cold and push / pull.

Pyrite – The fire stone, also called fool's gold, used to influence fire when polarized, quenching it, stoking it, pushing it or pulling it. It is most powerful when crystallized in the shape of a pyramid (four-sided regular solid). Also called the Mars stone.

Pyrotheurgy (*Graec*) – The branch of sorcery specializing in the techniques of manipulating elemental fire with a fire source stone (pyrite).

Sage – A sorcerer who is recognized by a regional council of sorcery guilds as having attained a master's proficiency in at least one branch of sorcery and at least a basic proficiency in all the other branches.

Sorcerer – A person who has completed an apprenticeship in any one of the branches of sorcery.

Sorcery – The branch of natural philosophy that studies techniques to use source stones to manipulate the elements.

Source stone – A physical object that a living being can polarize to attract, repel, heat, or cool one of the four primordial elements—earth, water, wind, fire. Amber channels aether but cannot polarize it.

Magical Terminology

Locomutation – A process similar to vaporization and condensation whereby a solid object transfers its position from one location to another by sublimation rather than by locomotion.

Mage – A master magicultor who has demonstrated the ability to reliably locomutate a living person.

Magic Word – A very specific utterance whose syllables and tonality provoke precisely the right vibrations to cause locomutation.

Magica Staff – A large, refined, and cultured trunk of a magica tree that enables a trained magicultor to bring about locomutation.

Magica Tree – A deciduous tree with a natural defense mechanism that allows it to locomutate when threatened.

Magica Wand – A small, refined, and cultured branch of a magica tree that enables a trained magicultor to bring about locomutation.

Magicultor – A person who has completed an apprenticeship in any one of the branches of magiculture.

Magiculture – The branch of natural philosophy that studies techniques to cultivate magica trees.

Pitch Pipe – A wind instrument that always produces precise tones. Pitch pipes suitable for magiculture are difficult and expensive to make and easily ruined but they allow those not endowed with perfect pitch to reliably bring about locomutation.

Pyromage – A mage who specializes in fire.

Wizard – A master magicultor who also completed an apprenticeship in any of the branches of sorcery or a master sorcerer who completed an apprenticeship in any of the branches of magiculture.

Necromancy Terminology

Archon stone – A clump of *archea,* the physical element closest to prime matter. It enables an undead wight to use sorcery and magiculture.

Blackflame – An unnatural version of fire that absorbs light, heat and vital energies.

Breastplate of Layban – A cuirass belonging to a rich but evil man from Jerosolym named Layban, who paid to have it enchanted.

Exorcism – A prayer of blessing aimed at expelling a praeternatural evil spirit from the body of the person or animal that it possesses.

Ghost – An undead rational person whose spirit is permanently dissociated from its mortal coil and inhabits some other element. Most ghosts can only inhabit the lightest elements such as air or fire but strong-willed spirits can inhabit water or even solids.

Ghoul – An undead wight who retains free will.

Golem – A ghost that inhabits a pure solid such as refined metal or ice. In the case of an extremely powerful ghost, the golem may inhabit an impure solid such as stone or clay.

Jinn – A ghost that inhabits fire. A benevolent jinn is called a genie; a malevolent jinn is called a jinx.

Lich – A dead person or animal whose body is controlled by a praeternatural evil spirit. The lich has no relation to the deceased person or animal except that sometimes the praeternatural evil spirit will imitate the deceased in order to deceive and manipulate the living.

Monster – An undead animal whose spirit inhabits the same mortal coil as when alive. Becoming undead normally causes the animal to panic.

Poltergeist – An undead malevolent animal whose spirit is permanently dissociated from its mortal coil and inhabits some element, such as air, fire, water or even metal. (*Also see Serendib.*)

Possessed – A living person or animal whose mind and body are controlled by a praeternatural evil spirit. The person or animal possessed has no recollection of their acts during the possession.

Reanimate – Performing a necromantic ritual on a corpse that is mostly or completely dead.

Revenant – An undead animal or person who was returned to its mortal coil after being mostly or completely dead.

Serendib – A benevolent poltergeist causing good luck.

Sprite – A ghost that inhabits fog, mist, vapor, steam or, in the case of a more powerful sprite, water.

Stormcrow – A role in a blackflame ceremony involving the Sword of Layban. Its precise functions and purposes have been lost over the centuries but from the chronicles of Tuscoraura Mountain it seems that proper stormcrows can reanimate a dead animal with blackflame at will.

Sword of Layban – A sword belonging to a rich but evil man from Jerosolym named Layban. Its workmanship was exceedingly fine with a hilt of pure gold and a blade of the most precious steel. Layban had been dabbling in necromancy and hired the best necromancers of the day to enchant the weapon.

Sylph – A ghost that inhabits air. Most sylphs are only capable of stirring up gentle breezes but a strong-willed sylph can whisper in the wind.

Thrall – An undead wight whose free will is constrained by the will of a powerful necromancer by means of evil rituals or cursed artefacts.

Transmogrify – To force the spirit of a person or animal into an undead state while still alive.

Undead – When the spirit of a mortal person or animal can no longer experiences this world as a participant it is considered dead. If that spirit can still interact with the world by controlling its body from the outside as a puppeteer controls a puppet it is said to be undead. The undead cannot influence any natural element or material object other than its former body without an archon stone acting as a bridge between the spirit and material worlds.

Wendigo – An undead wight whose experience in the netherworld has so terrified or blighted its spirit that it reacts to every living creature with crazed violence.

Wight – An undead rational person whose spirit inhabits the same mortal coil as when alive. A wight no longer has gender and is properly referred to as 'it'.

Zombie – A person who has been transmogrified into the undead state while still alive. Necromancers generally find this easier to accomplish and safer than attempting to reanimate the dead.

Political and Economic Terminology

Base Umpire – An elected official with jurisdiction over one of the thirteen bases of Shentalpee City who casts the deciding vote in the Council of the Esteemed for that base.

Black Tuesday – The day black wildfires destroyed much of Shentalpee City. Most of the elves survived the attack but the economic damage ruined their economy for nearly a decade.

Copper Coins – Copper coins would not be invented in Aengland until 1787 AD.

Council of Perfects – The highest governing body in Shentalpee City.

Council of the Esteemed – A locally elected council with legislative and judicial powers over one of the thirteen bases in Shentalpee City. Each Council of the Esteemed also governs all the wood elf villages leading off of it.

Dime – The smallest denomination of coinage in the Aenglish economy worth one-tenth of a penny. The coin was minted with debased silver and was worth approximately one dollar today.

Dollar – The Vinlander money of account worth four-fifths of a shilling. Silver pennies minted in Philadelphia were not as pure as the sterling silver coins minted in Lunden: the Vinlander pound was worth only twelve Troy ounces while the Aenglish pound sterling was worth fifteen Troy ounces. Vinlanders named their money of account after an ancient Viking coin—the lion dollar.

Double Eagle – A gold coin minted in Shentalpee City worth twenty dollars or one Vinlander pound.

Dungaree of Foreign Trade – An official at Shentalpee City appointed to advise on Foreign Trade.

Eighth Crusade – A Crusade led by King Louis IX in 1270 against Tunas, in the Islamic province of Ifriqiya. A disastrous and expensive defeat, thereafter no Europan monarch dared waste any significant time or effort to support the Crusader States.

Farthing – A silver coin worth a quarter of a penny. The Aenglish also sometimes cut a regular silver penny into quarters to pay small bills.

First Crusade – Constantinian Emperor Alexios asked Pope Urban to send military aid to Asia Minor after a series of crushing defeats at the hands of the Turcs. The Pope's soldiers ended up causing much havoc for both Alexios and the Turcs before founding the Crusader States in the Holy Land.

Florin – A gold coin minted in the city of Florenz worth one-third of a pound sterling.

Founding Mothers and Fathers – The fire elves who drafted a charter for the Tuscoraura elves in 1066 AD. The term includes those who drafted the Magnificent Charter of 1197 AD when work on Shentalpee City was finally completed.

Gentelves – 'Ladies and gentelves' is the proper way to address wood elves in an audience.

Groat – In 1279 AD, King Eddard introduced the groat, a larger silver coin worth four pence.

Halfpenny – (*also ha'penny*) A silver coin worth half a penny. The Aenglish also sometimes cut a regular silver penny in half.

Illuminati – A fairly irrelevant group of power brokers hyped up by conspiracy theorists.

Kallistocracy (*Graec*) – Rule by the most good-looking.

Livre Parisis – (*also Paris Pound*) A money of account used in Frankland. At the time of the events chronicled in this story (1284 AD), one pound sterling was worth four and a half Paris pounds.

Madame (pronounced *ma-dam*) / *plural* Mesdames (pronounced *may-dam*) – A Frankish loan word used as a title of respect to address a high elve who has declared social majority.

Mademoiselle (pronounced *mad-mwa-zell*) / *plural* Mesdemoiselles (pronounced *maid-mwa-zell*) – A Frankish loan word used as a title of respect to address a high elve before social majority.

Marchlands – The borderlands of Shentalpee City on Tuscoraura Mountain.

Mark – An international money of account worth two-thirds of a pound sterling. Also a measure of silver by weight. It enabled people to pay off debts in silverware, candlesticks, and other silver items without having to sell off those items for coins.

Money of Account – A currency, like the mark, that does not necessarily have a coin associated with it.

Monroe Doctrine – The declared policy of the United States after gaining independence from Aengland stating that the government is opposed to Europan attempts to control territories in the new world.

Monsieur (pronounced *ma-sya*) / *plural* Messieurs (pronounced *may-sya*) – A Frankish loan word used as a title of respect to address a high elf.

Ninth Crusade – Before becoming king, Eddard Longshanks promised to go on the Eighth Crusade but arrived too late. He decided to go instead to the Holy Land where he carried out a series of raids and brokered a few treaties.

Noocracy (*Graec*) – Rule by the most intelligent.

Nomocratic Prefect – A person who oversees the laws.

Penny (*plural* pence) – The most common coin in the Kingdom of Aengland. At the time of the events chronicled in this story (1284 AD), the sterling silver penny from Aengland had about the same buying power as ten U.S. dollars in 2020 A.D.

Pound Sterling – A money of account for reckoning the Aenglish sterling silver penny. Sterling silver was ninety-two and a half percent pure, making it the purest silver coin in Europa at the time of the events described in this chronicle (1284 AD).

Quarter – Another name for a farthing.

Sagamore – A title of authority among Ashnabec-speaking peoples.

Seventh Crusade – A Crusade led by King Louis IX in 1248 against al-Qahira, the capital city of Aegypt. It ended in disaster due to bad tactics and the rampant spread of dysentery.

Thor's Hammer Pendant – In Shentalpee City, wood elves and visitors were only allowed to visit Thor's Base and the use of suspension bridges leading to other bases was restricted to high elves only. Visitors had to wear a state-approved Thor's Hammer Pendant in order to cross the bridges alone.

Umpirage – The office or authority of an umpire.

Umpire-in-Chief – An elected official with jurisdiction over all thirteen bases of Shentalpee City who casts the deciding vote on the Council of Perfects.

Foreign Language Expressions

Adagio a Piacere (*Italic*) – Artwork moving at a pace that is as easy as you like.

Agigo Rekweh (*Ashnabec*) – Beloved man. Title of leadership among some Ashnabec peoples.

Alufvodar (*Elvish Runic*) – A divinity also known as the All-Elf-Father among some light elf peoples.

Andrea Nanoa (*Dwarvish Runic*) – Brave dwarf. The proper way to address a dwarf.

Ant thou? (*Eldric*) – And you?

Beannach (*Gnorrachi*) – Greetings.

Bergfleet Flag (*Eldric*) – Ivy League.

Breska (Medifskar) – Charge!

Bríatharogam – A two word kenning or poem which explains the meanings of the names of the letters in the Ogham alphabet.

Drassil – A dwarvish scatological expletive.

Egg fur ham, Hare Gipper. Wilt thou coma mitt mere? (*Eldric*) – I am going home, Mister Lynx. Do you want to come with me?

Egg hair guess (*Eldric*) – I hear a goose.

Egg heat (*Eldric*) – My name is…

Eldralfar (*Elvish Runic*) – Fire elf.

Far on egg? (*Eldric*) – Where am I?

Fate heater thou (*Eldric*) – What is your name?

Fate thither that (*Eldric*) – What does that mean?

Fifth saga hen? (*Eldric*) – What is he saying?

Fro Otter Harrun (*Eldric*) – From Clan Highrune.

Frown (*Eldric*) – Missus.

Game at keenest thither (*Eldric*) – Happy to meet you.

Gezondhide (*Eldric*) – Gesundheit or 'to your health' as in 'bless you' when someone sneezes.

Goyar (*Eldric*) – A light elf term used to describe any and all clayborn who are not light elves.

Hale ant Sail (*Eldric*) – (*greeting*) Health and happiness!
Hare (*Eldric*) – Mister.
Harelfur (*plural* Harelfar) (*Eldric*) – A high elf.
Kaishu (*Dwarvish Runic*) – Greetings.
Kamputer (*Eldric*) – A hobgoblin.
Key-sha-la-mi-lang-up – A Divinity also known as the Master of Life among some Ashnabec peoples.
Kum an (*Eldric*) – Come on!
Lakunto Tesaged (*Dwarvish Runic*) – (*greeting*) Daytime blessings.
Landomere (*Eldric*) – The marchlands or outermost border of the Tuscoraura Mountain communities.
Lyósálfur (*plural* Lyósálfar) (*Elvish Runic*) – A light elf.
Salve, patres conscripti cardinales (*Latin*) – Greetings, cardinals conscript fathers. (This is the proper greeting for a Roman senator, not a cardinal, but the confusion is easy to make.)
Shentalpee Vorsche (*Elvish Runic*) – Fire Elf City.
Shentalphur (*Elvish Runic*) – Elf Fire.
Ska-no hunwey (*Ashnabec*) – Greetings!
Statmalalthi (*Medifskar*) – City mercenaries.
Tame till at ran outer henny (*Eldric*) – Time to run out of here
These heilaugur matter as if logger glue ease. Hen moot guest thine hand take. (*Eldric*) – These holy men are like police. They intend to arrest your guest.
Thou oak saga (*Eldric*) – You also speak.
Tighern gnormach (Gnorrachi) – Noble gnome. The proper way to address a gnome.
Wur (*Medifskar*) – Water

Less Common Aenglish Expressions

Ambulant – Walking.
Amorous – Inclined towards romantic love.
Aspergillum – A sprig used to sprinkle holy water.
Balustrade – A low parapet or barrier with a row of balusters topped by a rail.
Blackflame – An unnatural version of fire that absorbs light, heat and vital energies.
Book-kin – All those who are or ought to be your friends because they love books as much as you.
Caterwauling – A harsh cry.
Clepsydra – A water clock.
Conurbity – A collection of urban centers. Shentalpee City is technically a conurbity, not a city.
Corundum – The crystalline mineral from which rubies and sapphires are derived.
Debenture – A bond or pledge bond that relies on the good faith of the person who issues it.
Diffident – Lacking confidence in oneself or in the person asking a favor.
Discomfit – To undo or defeat someone; to unsettle.
Dizzies – Makes one dizzy.
Dragon – A mythical creature that has wings and arms. A fantasy variation of a real-life wyvern.
Dwarfin – Relating to the physical, spiritual, mental or personal characteristics of dwarves.
Dwarfling – A young dwarf.
Dwarfy – Improper adjective relating to dwarves, which should be replaced with words such as dwarf, dwarfin, dwarven, dwarvish.
Dwarven – Relating to objects, activities, or ideas produced by dwarves.
Dwarvish – Relating to the ethnicities or languages of the dwarves.

Eccentric – Not quite centered, strange.

Elfin – Relating to the physical, spiritual, mental or personal characteristics of elves.

Elfling – A young elf.

Elfy – Improper adjective relating to elves, which should be replaced with words such as elf, elfin, elven, elvish.

Elven – Relating to objects, activities, or ideas produced by elves.

Elvish – Relating to the ethnicities or languages of the elves.

Exactitude – Exactness, accuracy; being exact.

Façade – The front view of a building. (*Figuratively*) A false or deceptive outward appearance.

Fidel – A medieval version of the fiddle.

Firewall – A wall of fire, especially a wall of elf fire.

Flagellum – A whip that monks use to inflict pain on themselves in reparation for sins.

Frugality – The virtue of not wasting money.

Gaffe – A social mistake, especially one that is embarrassing.

Garrulous – Prone to speak too much, chatty.

Gentelf – Proper way to address a wood elf.

Giddify – To make someone giddy or happy.

Harbinger – An omen; person, or event that foretells a more momentous person or event.

Hue – An alarm. In Aenglish common law, a citizen who witnesses a crime must try to stop it or at least alert others by shouting as loud as possible to help stop it.

Idiosyncrasy – A weird personality trait.

Irksome – Annoying.

Leading off of – Within the jurisdiction of. In Shentalpee City wood elf villages were all under the jurisdiction of a particular treelofted base and were said to lead off of that base.

Machinations – Schemes, plots.

Numismatics – The study of coins. In historical research, the inscriptions and images on coins can give a lot of information about what was going on in the past.

O (*Graec*) – A vocative particle used to call the attention of the person you wish to talk to.

Oh – An interjection used to express strong emotion.

Opulent – Visibly wealthy, obviously rich.

Orthography – The science of spelling words correctly.

Ostentation – A fancy word for showing off.

Phoenix – A very large bird of prey.

Phreatic Eruption – A type of volcanic eruption that primarily releases toxic gases into the air.

Poise – Composure; having a bearing or attitude that displays confidence and skill.

Potable – Drinkable; water that is safe to drink.

Quease – To make one's stomach queasy.

Sarcophagus (*plural* sarcophagi) – A stone coffin, usually one that stays above ground.

Scrod – Any cod, pollock, haddock, or other whitefish.

Skein – A specific length of yarn or a bunch of yarn that is all tangled up.

Smogulous – Having fumes that choke or make a person sick.

Status quo (*Latin*) – The state of the way things are now.

Thee / thou / thy / thine – (*Archaic—singular second person pronouns*) You / you / your / your.

Thew – Attractive physical musculature.

Thrawl – (*Archaic*) A stone slab for keeping food cool.

Treeloft – Any building or structure that is suspended up in the trees.

Trice – A short period of time. The concepts of minutes and seconds had not yet gained currency in 1284 AD.

Viol – A medieval version of the violin.

Wainwright – Someone who builds or repairs wagons.

Warp and woof – The weaving pattern in a fabric. Warp refers to the threads running lengthwise and the woof refers to the threads running crosswise.

Wyvern – A very large, flying agamid lizard.

Ye – (*Archaic—plural second person pronoun*) You.

DRAMATIS PERSONAE

Elves

Bucklead Yallson of Clan Bonesalp – A captain in the Ivy Leagues who takes his elite status very seriously.

Bunzi Kiquerson of Clan Landive – A Justiciar League Officer who likes to bully weaker elves around.

Buttercup Dolsdottir of Clan Chamara – A successful wood elve fruit and vegetable vendor.

Cougar Arminsdottir of Clan Highrune – A former adventurer and mother of Lynx.

Dean Norwall Dotasdottir of Clan Tryndaryze – The dean of the League of Licornes.

Drayton Harperson of Clan Kaputy – The former umpire-in-chief of Shentalpee City who exiled Florenz's mother for being a powerful dark elve.

Elmer Chouinard – A Fadet cliff elf from Vaucluse in Oxitania who lost everything to the Cathar Crusade and then became a deacon in the Blackflame Cult.

Elvmore Easleson of Clan Gygax – A senior officer in the Rough Riders.

Enganyon Gandorfson of Clan Rashbold – A rebellious teenage high elf.

Florenz Kibblersdottir of Clan Ithelion – A candidate for Umpire-in-Chief of Shentalpee City.

Freya Pavonsdottir of Clan Lumpkin – A junior officer in the Ivy Leagues.

Gandorf Mithranderson of Clan Rashbold – The Major Leagues Umpire of Shentalpee City.

Gulliber Swiffson of Clan Adidazar – A wood elf master shoemaker from Tuscoraura Mountain.

Gunnar Sveltson of Clan Theodoric – The captain of a company of mercenaries called the Rough Riders.

Halvard Prinson of Clan Sandford – The dean of the Ivy League.

Jeanne Ranglursdottir of Clan Manganime – The Dungaree of Foreign Trade for Shentalpee City.

Jormungand Rucchison of Clan Firearrow – A junior officer in the Ivy Leagues

Kallel Cribdson of Clan Kentigern – The dean of the Justiciar League.

Kellock Kashison of Clan Ferrer – A wealthy high elf investor.

Kordon Bleuson of Clan Kozeen – The High Commissioner for the Council of Perfects.

Kris Kringleson of Clan Thirforth – The noocratic prefect of the polar elves.

Lynx Cougarson of Clan Highrune – A wood elf who is one of the protagonists in this story.

Manzone Renson of Clan Borromee – A high elf and the captain of a company of mercenary bravos.

Marstand Wodrowson of Clan Kentigern – Secretary to the dean of the League of Nations.

Onashelf Aebersdottir of Clan Elkbell – A senior officer in the Ivy Leagues.

Puma Imelsdottir of Clan Highrune –A wood elf from Tuscoraura Mountain taken into slavery.

Stallion Rambson of Clan Morroblitz – A murk elf adventurer and stepfather to Lynx.

Trelany – An elve brava working for Captain Manzone.

Umpire Kibbler Earnestson of Clan Ithelion – The current Umpire-in-Chief of Shentalpee City.

Whoopee – A dark elf magicultor in Benjamin Frankelyn's party of adventurers, properly called Prospero.

Zena Jeansdottir of Clan Manganime – A candidate for Umpire-in-Chief of Shentalpee City.

Dwarves

Blainn – A *statmalalth* or city mercenary fighter. The brother of Bremmer.

Bremmer – A *statmalalth* or city mercenary fighter. The brother of Blainn.

Etzel of the White Mountains – The father of Lord Nybling Dankwart.

Felker Sinbolt – The ancient noble of the Ramapough Trench dwarves.

Grumpy – The codename for a mounted crossbow dwarf hired by the elve brava, Trelany.

Gunthar Ortwin – The landseer of the Pocono Mountain dwarves.

Kremhild – The second wife of Lord Etzel of the White Mountains.

Merdoc – The fenrik or lieutenant of the mercenary company of crossbow dwarves called the Magnificent Eight.

Nybling Dankwart – The great dainn of Allegheny Mountain dwarves.

Balrock – The last of the Jintel, a race of giant dwarves.

Oscar Meyer – The codename for a half-goblin, half-dwarf cleric belonging to Benjamin Frankelyn's party of adventurers.

Peter Sheen – A Dominican priest and special inquisitor for the Blackflame Heresy in Vinland.

Schneevitchen – The oberst or leader of the mercenary company of crossbow dwarves called the Magnificent Eight.

Sturl Snorrison – The Lawspeaker for the mountain dwarves of Tuscoraura.

Rumpel Stilton – The only dwarf ranger in the company of the Queen's Rangers and a skilled magicultor. He later became infamous as an extortionist.

Goblins

Gog – The war chief of Magog goblins.
Samba – The son of Gog.
Zilla – The second wife of Gog and mother of Skaar by King Ctong.
Skaar – The stepson of Gog and eldest son of Zilla.
Ctong – The king of the Weemaway goblins.

Gnomes

Armigan – The nahod or leader of a company of gnome slingers called the Warband.
Atlas – The codename for a gnome con artist hired by the elve brava, Trelany.
Bartlebee Nerchmell – The stewardess for Betzy Rose Mansion.
Blunderbore Penwith – The head steward for the Vandsee Estates.
Bodo Fraggins – The high sheriff of the Wilming Halflings of Wilmington.
Bumbledor Grayer – The chief warden for the Deagle's Den precinct of the Gnomish Bailiwick of the Tuscoraura halflings.
Daym Skorr – The father of Lord Heathe Skorr.
Flobbin – A halfling mercenary sorcerer.
Gansforth Stoor – A deputy warden for the Deagle's Den precinct of the Gnomish Bailiwick of the Tuscoraura halflings.
Gustavus Thornbury – The provost of the Trent Knockers of Trenton.
Harfud Fellowhide – The high bailiff over the Tuscoraura garden gnomes.
Heathe Skorr – The count of the Korrigan Gnomes of Barres.

Hugo Aramingo – The burgraff of the Kabouter Gnomes of Northern Liberties.

Jack Spriggins – A master gardener and impoverished member of the gnomish gentry.

Kip Karlson – The only gnome ranger in Sir Robert Roger's company, the Queen's Rangers.

Luempa-Wuempas – A group of Hungarian gnomes who immigrated to Vinland after the Cuman Rebellion stirred up fears of a second Tartar invasion.

Metro Gnomes – A mercenary company of sharpshooting gnome slingers.

Nittany O'Martix – The famous halfling—half-leprechaun and half-hob—serving as dean of Pinne Mage University.

Patufet Stromfis – The peerless grand schwurf of the Payo Schwurfs.

Richwell Kensing – The bailiff of the Warwick Hobs of Southwark.

Sander Brandson – The prince of the Korrigan Gnomes of Scarsdale.

Humans

Aelfreda Harris – An accomplished battlemage and leader of a company of colonial marshals.

Al Carbone – A brutish brigand hired by the elve brava, Trelany.

Amerik Cardinal Vespuchi – The papal nuncio to Vinland, eventually appointed high inquisitor.

Aramis – A dashing swashbuckler hired by Captain Manzone's bravos.

Ariel – The codename for Philippa Pinne of Lincoln, daughter of the duke of Philadelphia.

Athos – A dashing swashbuckler hired by Captain Manzone's bravos.

Babyface Nelson – An itinerant jester hired by the elve brava, Trelany.

Banastre Tarleton – A ruthless knight who fought for Aengland during the War of Independence.

Benedict Arnald – The second lieutenant in the company of the Queen's Rangers.

Benjamin Chandler of Baston – An escaped apprentice Chandler taking refuge in Silvermorn College.

Buckeyed Woodchuck – A seer and spiritual guide for the Punxsutawney nation.

Casey of Mudville – A husky Erinish ranger armed with a large, two-handed oaken bat. It is said he never misses whenever he swings his bat.

Cornwell Ezra – The Grand Sage of Silvermorn College of Sorcery

Cotrel Walker – A ranger famed for his combat skills both with and without weapons from the Principality of Texico.

Crazy Bull – A Trakota Shaman hired by the elve brava, Trelany.

Custaloga – A sagamore among the Delawaerr nation.

Daniel Boon – A famous ranger, frontiersman, and politician from Virginia who promoted Kentikie statehood after the War of Independence.

Daniel Morgon – A ranger and the cousin of Daniel Boon who later formed Morgon's Rangers to help in the War of Independence.

David Clarke – A novice Carmelite cleric who survived an assassination attempt by a mermaid.

Davy Crickett – A ranger and frontiersman who later became a successful politician known as the "King of the Wild Frontier." Opposed to the United States' role in the Trail of Tears, he left the U.S. in protest and became a leader in the Texico War of Independence, eventually dying in the Battle of the Alamo along with his fellow ranger, Sir Jim Bowey.

Doctor Estrange – The baron of Amhirst's personal physician.

Dolon of Meadville – A herald famous for winning many foot races in tournaments and fairs.

Donatello Marquette – The former Frankish count of Milwaukie.

Dutch – A desperado fleeing the law hired by the elve brava, Trelany.

Eddard Longshanks – The king of Aengland.

Erik the Red – Leif Erikson's pagan father, whose persecution of Christianity forced the recently converted Leif to flee from Greenland with a group of Christian Vikings to Vinland.

Ethen Allan – A ranger who later helped form a ranging company called the Green Mountain Boys along with Sir Seth Werner in the War of Independence.

Febold Feboldson – A heavy-set ranger who makes his weight felt.

Frances Marian – The only female ranger among the Queen's Rangers who later formed a ranging company called the Green Berets in the War of Independence.

Frankl Stein – A tall and strong ranger who reads voraciously.

Gad Kolfack of Brookline – The captain of a mercenary company called the Glorious Dastards.

Geoffrey Amhirst of Sevenoaks – The baron of Amhirst and commander-general of His Highness King Eddard's expeditionary forces to Montroyal.

George Warshington of Mount Vernon – The acting Governor of Fort Pitt.

Gilbert Sullivan – A ranger-bard skilled with a shillelagh, a harp, and an Erinish whistle.

Glover Marmaduke – The chief inspector of the docks for the city of Marblehead.

Grand Mage of the Wald – The title for the highest authority on magiculture in Vinland.

Healaman – A prophet and the leader of two thousand young warriors.

Henry Fordham – A former monk who joined the Queen's Rangers after leaving his monastery.

Henry Garland – A valiant knight who lead the troops in the victorious Seige of Fort Ducaine. He was appointed captain of the Fort Pitt militia.

Humbert of Denk – A ranger-bard who later gained fame for composing the "Ballad of Hansel and Gretel".

Jack de Molay – The preceptor of the Rofchester Temple (Knights Templar).

Jack Hancock – A nimble and quick ranger who is always eager to be the first and the best.

James Wolf – A victorious Aenglish war leader who was killed by a stray crossbow bolt moments after conquering the City of Kaybec.

Jangis Khan – A famous Tartar warlord who spread fear all across Eurasia with his conquests.

Jim Bowey – A skilled knife fighter who amassed a great fortune after retiring from the Queen's Rangers through manufacturing and selling silver war knives.

Joagbert Castor – The heresiarch of the Blackflame Cult.

Joe Magarac – A prisoner of war who won a place in the Queen's Rangers through his hard work and astounding battlefield feats.

John Elder – The Bishop of the Paxton Diocese and the leader of a vigilante group, the Paxton Boys.

John Fourbes – The baronet of Fourbes who organized the conquest of Fort Ducaine with the help of Sir George Warshington but fell ill before leading it.

John Harris – The Aenglish count of Harrisburgh.

John Harris II – The son of Lord John Harris and acting castellan of Fort Harris.

John Hathorne – The captain of the Salim militia and chief magistrate of the Masswachoosut Bay Superior Court of Judicature.

John Henry of Big Bend – A former Aphrican slave among the Queen's Rangers who hammered out his freedom with the strokes of his war mallet.

John Nesley – The Aenglish baron of Hershel.

Johnny Appleseed – Also known as John Chapman of Leominster. A Christian missionary who sought to combat hunger in Vinland.

Jon Stark – The first lieutenant in the company of the Queen's Rangers.

Joseph of Montferrand – A French-Canuck ranger also known as Big Joe Mufferow.

Karaoke – Mispronunciation of Kahnawroke, an exiled Fox chieftain, hired by the elve brava, Trelany.

Katechna – Leader of the longhouse humans of Tuscoraura Mountain and known to the Aenglish as King Hancock.

King Louis the Pious – The former king of Frankland who died on the Eighth Crusade in 1270 AD.

Lazarillo de Tormes – A javelin-throwing picaro hired by the elve brava, Trelany.

Leevai Strauss of Butterheim – A wealthy fabric merchant and Merchants' Guild Master.

Leonard Joliette – The former Frankish ruler of Fort Michilimackinac and founder of Joliette City.

Louis Shoemaker of Joliette – An orphan who was treated miserably as a shoemaker's apprentice.

Maderno Orsini – One of three high inquisitors.

Mallow Club – A War Chief of the Altoona nation.

Mearl – An uncivilized tavern brawler hired by the elve brava, Trelany.

Michelangelo Ducaine of Menneville – The deceased Marquis of Fort Ducaine (now Fort Pitt).

Mickey Oswald – The captain of a company of graduates from Silvermorn College of Sorcery serving under the baron of Amhirst.

Moses Rambam of Cordova – The head rabbi of a mercenary company called the *Bikur Holim*.

Nate Bumpo – An ethnic Aenglish frontiersman raised among the Delawaerr as Straight-Tongue hired by the elve brava, Trelany.

Nathaniel Green – A wealthy merchant and the father of Nathaniel Green Jr. who became a famous war leader in the War of Independence.

Nathaniel Hayle of Coventry – An apprentice ranger and boy genius.

Oconostota – The red war chief of the Punxsutawney.

Oliver Roland – The commander of the Masswachoosut Bay Palace (Knights Paladin).

Paterno Orsini – One of three high inquisitors.

Paul Bunyan – A French-Canuck woodcutter who stands seven feet tall brandishing a double-edged lumberjack axe and serves as the mentor for the heavy rangers.

Petur Styvesant – The former Viking governor of Manhatten.

Piccolo Orsini – One of three high inquisitors.

Pierre Radisson – The commander-elect of Saratoga Springs Hospital (Knights Hospitaller).

Pontiak – An Ottowa sagamore and long-time ally of the Frankish settlers in Vinland.

Pope Martin IV – The Bishop of Roma and the highest-level cleric in the Church.

Porthos – A dashing swashbuckler hired by Captain Manzone's bravos.

Raphael de la Moto Cadillac – The count of Fort Detroit who surrendered to the Aenglish on condition that he retain his title and role as count.

Richard Bentley – A former monk who joined the Queen's Rangers after his parents' marriage of thirty years was annulled against their wishes.

Richard Nicolas – The Aenglish count who conquered New Amsturldam, intending to rename it New Lancaster. He died in battle after victory over the Vikings had been assured.

Rip van Winkel – A veteran soldier who joined the rangers with his dog, Wolf, to get away from his nagging wife.

Robert Roger of Methuen – The captain and founder of the company of the Queen's Rangers.

Sacagawea – An Shoshoni prisoner of war from the Snake peoples who was raised among Trakota captors and sold as a slave to a French trader who married her.

Samuel de Champlane – The former Frankish viceroy of Vinland affectionately known among his subjects and allies as Uncle Sam.

Samuel Maverick – A follower of the baron of Amhirst, eventually appointed the viscount of New Yourke.

Sean Madigan – The chief herald and advisor to the baron of Amhirst.

Seth Werner – A ranger who later formed the Green Mountain Boys along with Sir Ethen Allan during the War of Independence.

Shabtai Zephathai of Delooth – A battlemage and poet and the leader of the mercenary company of Magicultors and Sorcerers called the Skybrim.

Tearlach Mitty – The Grand Mage of the Wald.

Terry – The codename for Terence Bolero of San Luis, a fighter.

Thomas Habalhob – A former monk who joined the Queen's Rangers after getting excommunicated over a debt owed to a bishop's nephew.

Tsheetz – A sagamore and beloved man of the Altoona.

Tuck Curtal – A Benedictine Brother acting as the baron of Amhirst's Clerk (Clarke).

Walter Rally – The newly appointed coroner for Ithica.

William McIntosh – A Scots ranger who likes apples.

William Pinne of Tower Hill – The duke of Philadelphia and father of Lady Philippa Pinne and Sir William Pinne the Younger.

Zedediah Springfield – A monk who coined the term 'clayborn' to express solidarity among the different races of middle earth.

Trolls

Big Foot – A Sasquatch troll fighter hired by the elve brava, Trelany.

Hugo – A Sasquatch troll who became a deacon in the Blackflame Cult.

Gilchrist Keyes Revel Lindenberg was a twentieth-century scholar of Medieval Dwarvish and Elvish languages and culture. After lengthy schooling, he traveled the world as a young gnome, seeking not wisdom but proficiency in foreign languages. Realizing that wisdom would have been the better choice, he tucked himself away in an idyllic mansion overlooking Lake Winnipesaukee to accomplish for the New World what Eddard Gibbons had achieved for the old but with less bias against Christianity and with more dramatic flair and adventuresome verve.

Johnny Appleseed and the Tuscoraura Elves

Ask any of the residents on Tuscoraura Mountain—high elves, wood elves, garden gnomes, mountain dwarves, or longhouse humans—and they will tell you that in the upcoming election seventeen-year-old Mademoiselle Zena Jeannesdottir is a sure candidate for the next umpire-in-chief of Fire Elf City, one hundred fifty feet up in the treetops.

Over and above her good-looks and her knack for politics, Zena has the magic touch…that unique ability to tame a magica tree at the stroke of her fingertips.

In one day, her mother upsets it all when she invites the famous Christian druid Johnny Appleseed to preach at the elves' extravagant New Year's Eve party. On a mission to end the hunger and bloodshed plaguing Vinland, he freely offers the Tuscoraura elves the good spell of the Lord Jesus, the apple seed, and the secret to blackflame.

But something is rotten in Vinland! Fearing the blackflame's potential as a weapon of mass destruction the Inquisition has launched a manhunt to haul in this ragamuffin preacher before his gifts fall into the wrong hands. Moreover, the high elves are appalled at his crude manners, shabby overalls, and unfashionable tin pot hat. Despite his good intentions, Johnny Appleseed sends Zena's campaign into a tailspin.

With the elections just weeks away, Zena is convinced that only the debonair rascal, Enganyon, holds the key to restoring the voters' confidence…and finding true love. All the while her hapless admirer, Lynx, tries to convince her that Enganyon only has eyes for Mademoiselle Florenz Kibblersdottir, her best friend and chief rival on the ballot.

When Lynx enlists the help of two rangers' apprentices, Louis and Clarke, they set out on adventures in this humorous and epic alternate history of how medieval Vinland came to be modern Amerika.

www.ingramcontent.com/pod-product-compliance
Lightning Source LLC
Chambersburg PA
CBHW030556310726
48979CB00003B/464

* 9 7 8 1 7 3 4 8 3 4 6 7 3 *